T… f J.R.R. Tolkien's ep…

… of the Ring have become involved in separate adventures as the quest continues. Aragorn, revealed as the hidden heir of the ancient Kings of the West, joined with the Riders of Rohan against the forces of Isengard, and took part in the desperate victory of the Hornburg. Merry and Pippin, captured by the orcs, escaped to Fangorn Forest and there encountered the Ents.

Gandalf returned, miraculously, and defeated the evil wizard, Saruman. Meanwhile, Sam and Frodo progressed towards Mordor to destroy the Ring, accompanied by Sméagol – Gollum, still obsessed by his 'preciouss'. After a battle with the giant spider, Shelob, Sam left his master for dead; but Frodo is still alive – in the hands of the orcs. And all the time the armies of the Dark Lord are amassing.

This is the third part of a new three-book edition in B-format paperback which reproduces the complete unabridged text of the three books, *The Fellowship of the Ring*, *The Two Towers* and *The Return of the King*, that together make up *The Lord of the Rings*. This reset edition contains newly drawn maps by Stephen Raw, based on Christopher Tolkien's original maps.

WORKS BY J.R.R. TOLKIEN

The Hobbit
Leaf by Niggle
On Fairy Stories
Farmer Giles of Ham
The Homecoming of Beorhtnoth
The Lord of the Rings
The Adventures of Tom Bombadil
The Road Goes Ever On (with Donald Swann)
Smith of Wootton Major

WORKS PUBLISHED POSTHUMOUSLY

Sir Gawain, Pearl and Sir Orfeo
The Father Christmas Letters
The Silmarillion
Pictures by JRR Tolkien
Unfinished Tales
The Letters of JRR Tolkien
Mr Bliss
Finn and Hengest
The Monsters and the Critics and Other Essays
Roverandom

THE HISTORY OF MIDDLE-EARTH
BY CHRISTOPHER TOLKIEN

I The Book of Lost Tales Part 1
II The Book of Lost Tales Part 2
III The Lays of Beleriand
IV The Shaping of Middle-earth
V The Lost Road and Other Writings
VI The Return of the Shadow
VII The Treason of Isengard
VIII The War of the Ring
IX Sauron Defeated
X Morgoth's Ring
XI The War of the Jewels
XII The Peoples of Middle-earth

TOLKIEN

The Return of the King

Being the third part of
The Lord of the Rings

BY

J.R.R. TOLKIEN

TED SMART

This edition produced for The Book People Ltd,
Hall Wood Avenue, Haydock, St Helens WA11 9UL

HarperCollins*Publishers*
77–85 Fulham Palace Road,
Hammersmith, London W6 8JB

This paperback edition 1997
5 7 9 8

This edition has been reset and the maps
have been redrawn by Stephen Raw

Previously published in paperback by
HarperCollins*Publishers* 1993
Reprinted six times
and by Grafton 1991
Reprinted three times

First published by HarperCollins*Publishers* 1991

First published in Great Britain by
George Allen & Unwin 1955
Second edition 1966
First published in Unwin paperback in 1974

ISBN 0 007 63768 3

Set in Plantin Light

Printed and bound in Great Britain by
Omnia Books Limited, Glasgow

Three Rings for the Elven-kings under the sky,
Seven for the Dwarf-lords in their halls of stone,
Nine for Mortal Men doomed to die,
One for the Dark Lord on his dark throne
In the Land of Mordor where the Shadows lie.
One Ring to rule them all, One Ring to find them,
One Ring to bring them all and in the darkness bind them
In the Land of Mordor where the Shadows lie.

CONTENTS

SYNOPSIS

This is the third part of THE LORD OF THE RINGS.

The first part, *The Fellowship of the Ring*, told how Gandalf the Grey discovered that the ring possessed by Frodo and the Hobbit was in fact the One Ring, ruler of all the Rings of Power. It recounted the flight of Frodo and his companions from the quiet Shire of their home, pursued by the terror of the Black Riders of Mordor, until at last, with the aid of Aragorn the Ranger of Eriador, they came through desperate perils to the House of Elrond in Rivendell.

There was held the great Council of Elrond, at which it was decided to attempt the destruction of the Ring, and Frodo was appointed the Ring-bearer. The Companions of the Ring were then chosen, who were to aid him in his quest: to come if he could to the Mountain of Fire in Mordor, the land of the Enemy himself, where alone the Ring could be unmade. In this fellowship were Aragorn, and Boromir son of the Lord of Gondor, representing Men; Legolas son of the Elven-king of Mirkwood, for the Elves; Gimli son of Glóin of the Lonely Mountain, for the Dwarves; Frodo with his servant Samwise, and his two young kinsmen Meriadoc and Peregrin, for the Hobbits; and Gandalf the Grey.

The Companions journeyed in secret far from Rivendell in the North, until baffled in their attempt to cross the high pass of Caradhras in winter, they were led by Gandalf through the hidden gate and entered the vast Mines of Moria, seeking a way beneath the mountains. There Gandalf, in battle with a dreadful spirit of the underworld, fell into a dark abyss. But Aragorn, now revealed as the hidden heir of the ancient Kings of the West, led the company on from the East Gate of Moria, through the Elvish land of Lórien, and down the great River Anduin, until they came to the Falls of Rauros. Already they had become aware that their journey was watched by spies, and that the creature Gollum, who once had possessed the Ring and still lusted for it, was following their trail.

It now became necessary for them to decide whether they should turn east to Mordor; or go on with Boromir to the aid of Minas Tirith, chief city of Gondor, in the coming war; or should divide. When it became clear that the Ring-bearer was resolved to continue his hopeless journey to the land of the Enemy, Boromir attempted to seize the Ring by force. The first part ended with the fall of Boromir to the lure of the Ring; with the escape and disappearance of Frodo and his servant Samwise; and the scattering of the remainder of the Fellowship by a sudden attack of orc-soldiers, some in the service of the Dark Lord of Mordor, some of the traitor Saruman of Isengard. The Quest of the Ring-bearer seemed already overtaken by disaster.

The second part, (Books Three and Four), *The Two Towers*, recounted the deeds of all the company after the breaking of the Fellowship of the Ring. Book Three told of the repentance and death of Boromir, and of his funeral in a boat committed to the Falls of Rauros; of the capture of Meriadoc and Peregrin by orc-solders, who bore them towards Isengard over the eastern plains of Rohan; and of their pursuit by Aragorn, Legolas and Gimli.

The Riders of Rohan then appeared. A troop of horsemen, led by Éomer the Marshal, surrounded the orcs on the borders of the Forest of Fangorn, and destroyed them; but the hobbits escaped into the wood and there met Treebeard the Ent, secret master of Fangorn. In his company they witnessed the rousing of the wrath of the Tree-folk and their march on Isengard.

In the meanwhile Aragorn and his companions met Éomer returning from the battle. He provided them with horses, and they rode on to the forest. There while searching in vain for the hobbits, they met Gandalf again, returned from death, now the White Rider, yet veiled still in grey. With him they rode over Rohan to the halls of King Théoden of the Mark, where Gandalf healed the aged king and rescued him from the spells of Wormtongue, his evil counsellor, secret ally of Saruman. They rode then with the king and his host against the forces of Isengard, and took part in the desperate victory of the Hornburg. Gandalf then led them to Isengard, and they found the great fortress laid in ruins by the Tree-folk, and Saruman and Wormtongue besieged in the indomitable tower of Orthanc.

In the parley before the door Saruman refused to repent, and Gandalf deposed him and broke his staff, leaving him to the vigilance of the Ents. From a high window Wormtongue hurled a stone at Gandalf; but it missed him, and was picked up by Peregrin. This proved to be one of the three surviving *palantíri*, the Seeing Stones of Númenor. Later at night Peregrin succumbed to the lure of the

Stone; he stole it and looked in it, and so was revealed to Sauron. The book ended with the coming of a Nazgûl over the plains of Rohan, a Ringwraith mounted on a flying steed, presage of imminent war. Gandalf delivered the *palantír* to Aragorn, and taking Peregrin rode away to Minas Tirith.

Book Four turned to Frodo and Samwise, now lost in the bleak hills of Emyn Muil. It told how they escaped from the hills, and were overtaken by Sméagol-Gollum; and how Frodo tamed Gollum and almost overcame his malice, so that Gollum led them through the Dead Marshes and ruined lands to the Morannon, the Black Gate of the Land of Mordor in the North.

There it was impossible to enter and Frodo accepted Gollum's advice: to seek a 'secret entrance' that he knew of, away south in the Mountains of Shadow, the western walls of Mordor. As they journeyed thither they were taken by a scouting-force of the Men of Gondor led by Faramir brother of Boromir. Faramir discovered the nature of their quest, but resisted the temptation to which Boromir had succumbed, and sent them forward on the last stage of their journey to Cirith Ungol, the Spider's Pass; though he warned them that it was a place of mortal peril, of which Gollum had told them less than he knew. Even as they reached the Cross-roads and took the path to the ghastly city of Minas Morgul, a great darkness issued from Mordor, covering all the lands. Then Sauron sent forth his first army, led by the black King of the Ringwraiths: the War of the Ring had begun.

Gollum guided the hobbits to a secret way that avoided Minas Morgul, and in the darkness they came at last to Cirith Ungol. There Gollum fell back into evil, and attempted to betray them to the monstrous guardian of the pass, Shelob. He was frustrated by the heroism of Samwise, who beat off his attack, and wounded Shelob.

The second part ends with the choices of Samwise. Frodo, stung by Shelob, lies dead, as it seems: the quest must end in disaster, or Samwise must abandon his master. At length he takes the Ring and attempts to carry on the hopeless quest alone. But just as he is about to cross into the land of Mordor, orcs come up from Minas Morgul and down from the tower of Cirith Ungol that guards the crown of the pass. Hidden by the Ring Samwise learns from the bickering of the orcs that Frodo is not dead but drugged. Too late he pursues them; but the orcs carry off the body of Frodo down a tunnel leading to the rear gate of their tower. Samwise falls in a swoon before it as it closes with a clang.

This, the third and last part, will tell of the opposing strategies of Gandalf and Sauron, until the final catastrophe and the end of the great darkness. We return first to the fortunes of battle in the West.

THE RETURN OF THE KING

BEING THE THIRD PART

OF

The Lord of the Rings

BOOK FIVE

CHAPTER I

MINAS TIRITH

Pippin looked out from the shelter of Gandalf's cloak. He wondered if he was awake or still sleeping, still in the swift-moving dream in which he had been wrapped so long since the great ride began. The dark world was rushing by and the wind sang loudly in his ears. He could see nothing but the wheeling stars, and away to his right vast shadows against the sky where the mountains of the South marched past. Sleepily he tried to reckon the times and stages of their journey, but his memory was drowsy and uncertain.

There had been the first ride at terrible speed without a halt, and then in the dawn he had seen a pale gleam of gold, and they had come to the silent town and the great empty house on the hill. And hardly had they reached its shelter when the winged shadow had passed over once again, and men wilted with fear. But Gandalf had spoken soft words to him, and he had slept in a corner, tired but uneasy, dimly aware of comings and goings and of men talking and Gandalf giving orders. And then again riding, riding in the night. This was the second, no, the third night since he had looked in the Stone. And with that hideous memory he woke fully, and shivered, and the noise of the wind became filled with menacing voices.

A light kindled in the sky, a blaze of yellow fire behind dark barriers. Pippin cowered back, afraid for a moment, wondering into what dreadful country Gandalf was bearing him. He rubbed his eyes, and then he saw that it was the moon rising above the eastern shadows, now almost at the full. So the night was not yet old and for hours the dark journey would go on. He stirred and spoke.

'Where are we, Gandalf?' he asked.

'In the realm of Gondor,' the wizard answered. 'The land of Anórien is still passing by.'

There was a silence again for a while. Then, 'What is that?' cried Pippin suddenly, clutching at Gandalf's cloak. 'Look! Fire, red fire! Are there dragons in this land? Look, there is another!'

For answer Gandalf cried aloud to his horse. 'On, Shadowfax! We must hasten. Time is short. See! The beacons of Gondor are alight, calling for aid. War is kindled. See, there is the fire on Amon Dîn, and flame on Eilenach; and there they go speeding west: Nardol, Erelas, Min-Rimmon, Calenhad, and the Halifirien on the borders of Rohan.'

But Shadowfax paused in his stride, slowing to a walk, and then he lifted up his head and neighed. And out of the darkness the answering neigh of other horses came; and presently the thudding of hoofs was heard, and three riders swept up and passed like flying ghosts in the moon and vanished into the West. Then Shadowfax gathered himself together and sprang away, and the night flowed over him like a roaring wind.

Pippin became drowsy again and paid little attention to Gandalf telling him of the customs of Gondor, and how the Lord of the City had beacons built on the tops of outlying hills along both borders of the great range, and maintained posts at these points where fresh horses were always in readiness to bear his errand-riders to Rohan in the North, or to Belfalas in the South. 'It is long since the beacons of the North were lit,' he said; 'and in the ancient days of Gondor they were not needed, for they had the Seven Stones.' Pippin stirred uneasily.

'Sleep again, and do not be afraid!' said Gandalf. 'For you are not going like Frodo to Mordor, but to Minas Tirith, and there you will be as safe as you can be anywhere in these days. If Gondor falls, or the Ring is taken, then the Shire will be no refuge.'

'You do not comfort me,' said Pippin, but nonetheless sleep crept over him. The last thing that he remembered before he fell into deep dream was a glimpse of high white peaks, glimmering like floating isles above the clouds as they caught the light of the westering moon. He wondered where Frodo was, and if he was already in Mordor, or if he was dead; and he did not know that Frodo from far away looked on that same moon as it set beyond Gondor ere the coming of the day.

Pippin woke to the sound of voices. Another day of hiding and a night of journey had fleeted by. It was twilight: the cold dawn was at hand again, and chill grey mists were about them. Shadowfax stood steaming with sweat, but he held his neck proudly and showed no sign of weariness. Many tall men heavily cloaked stood beside him, and behind them in the mist loomed a wall of stone. Partly ruinous it seemed, but already before the night was passed the sound of hurried labour could be heard: beat of hammers, clink of trowels, and the creak of wheels. Torches and flares glowed dully here and there in the fog. Gandalf was speaking to the men that barred his way, and as he listened Pippin became aware that he himself was being discussed.

'Yea truly, we know you, Mithrandir,' said the leader of the men, 'and you know the pass-words of the Seven Gates and are free to go forward. But we do not know your companion. What is he? A dwarf out of the mountains in the North? We wish for no strangers in the land at this time, unless they be mighty men of arms in whose faith and help we can trust.'

'I will vouch for him before the seat of Denethor,' said Gandalf. 'And as for valour, that cannot be computed by stature. He has passed through more battles and perils than you have, Ingold, though you be twice his height; and he comes now from the storming of Isengard, of which we bear tidings, and great weariness is on him, or I would wake him. His name is Peregrin, a very valiant man.'

'Man?' said Ingold dubiously, and the others laughed.

'Man!' cried Pippin, now thoroughly roused. 'Man! Indeed not! I am a hobbit and no more valiant than I am a man, save perhaps now and again by necessity. Do not let Gandalf deceive you!'

'Many a doer of great deeds might say no more,' said Ingold. 'But what is a hobbit?'

'A Halfling,' answered Gandalf. 'Nay, not the one that was spoken of,' he added seeing the wonder in the men's faces. 'Not he, yet one of his kindred.'

'Yes, and one who journeyed with him,' said Pippin. 'And Boromir of your City was with us, and he saved me in the snows of the North, and at the last he was slain defending me from many foes.'

'Peace!' said Gandalf. 'The news of that grief should have been told first to the father.'

'It has been guessed already,' said Ingold; 'for there have been strange portents here of late. But pass on now quickly! For the Lord of Minas Tirith will be eager to see any that bear the latest tidings of his son, be he man or——'

'Hobbit,' said Pippin. 'Little service can I offer to your lord, but what I can do, I would do, remembering Boromir the brave.'

'Fare you well!' said Ingold; and the men made way for Shadowfax, and he passed through a narrow gate in the wall. 'May you bring good counsel to Denethor in his need, and to us all, Mithrandir!' Ingold cried. 'But you come with tidings of grief and danger, as is your wont, they say.'

'Because I come seldom but when my help is needed,' answered Gandalf. 'And as for counsel, to you I would say that you are over-late in repairing the wall of the Pelennor. Courage will now be your best defence against the storm that is at hand – that and such hope as I bring. For not all the tidings that I bring are evil. But leave your trowels and sharpen your swords!'

'The work will be finished ere evening,' said Ingold. 'This is the last portion of the wall to be put in defence: the least open to attack, for it looks towards our friends of Rohan. Do you know aught of them? Will they answer the summons, think you?'

'Yes, they will come. But they have fought many battles at your back. This road and no road looks towards safety any longer. Be vigilant! But for Gandalf Stormcrow you would have seen a host of foes coming out of Anórien and no Riders of Rohan. And you may yet. Fare you well, and sleep not!'

Gandalf passed now into the wide land beyond the Rammas Echor. So the men of Gondor called the out-wall that they had built with great labour, after Ithilien fell under the shadow of their Enemy. For ten leagues or more it ran from the mountains' feet and so back again, enclosing in its fence the fields of the Pelennor: fair and fertile townlands on the long slopes and terraces falling to the deep levels of the Anduin. At its furthest point from the Great Gate of the City, north-eastward, the wall was four leagues distant, and there from a frowning bank it overlooked the long flats beside the river, and men had made it high and strong; for at that point, upon a walled causeway, the road came in from the fords and bridges of Osgiliath and passed through a guarded gate between embattled towers. At its nearest point the wall was little more than one league from the City, and that was south-eastward. There Anduin, going in a wide knee about the hills of Emyn Arnen in South Ithilien, bent sharply west, and the out-wall rose upon its very brink; and beneath it lay the quays and landings of the Harlond for craft that came upstream from the southern fiefs.

The townlands were rich, with wide tilth and many orchards, and homesteads there were with oast and garner, fold and byre, and many rills rippling through the green from the highlands down to Anduin. Yet the herdsmen and husbandmen that dwelt there were not many, and the most part of the people of Gondor lived in the seven circles of the City, or in the high vales of the mountain-borders, in Lossarnach, or further south in fair Lebennin with its five swift streams. There dwelt a hardy folk between the mountains and the sea. They were reckoned men of Gondor, yet their blood was mingled, and there were short and swarthy folk among them whose sires came more from the forgotten men who housed in the shadow of the hills in the Dark Years ere the coming of the kings. But beyond, in the great fief of Belfalas, dwelt Prince Imrahil in his castle of Dol Amroth by the sea, and he was of high blood, and his folk also, tall men and proud with sea-grey eyes.

Now after Gandalf had ridden for some time the light of day grew in the sky, and Pippin roused himself and looked up. To his left lay a sea of mist, rising to a bleak shadow in the East; but to his right great mountains reared their heads, ranging from the West to a steep and sudden end, as if in the making of the land the River had burst through a great barrier, carving out a mighty valley to be a land of battle and debate in times to come. And there where the White Mountains of Ered Nimrais came to their end he saw, as Gandalf had promised, the dark mass of Mount Mindolluin, the deep purple shadows of its high glens, and its tall face whitening in the rising day. And upon its out-thrust knee was the Guarded City, with its seven walls of stone so strong and old that it seemed to have been not builded but carven by giants out of the bones of the earth.

Even as Pippin gazed in wonder the walls passed from looming grey to white, blushing faintly in the dawn; and suddenly the sun climbed over the eastern shadow and sent forth a shaft that smote the face of the City. Then Pippin cried aloud, for the Tower of Ecthelion, standing high within the topmost wall, shone out against the sky, glimmering like a spike of pearl and silver, tall and fair and shapely, and its pinnacle glittered as if it were wrought of crystals; and white banners broke and fluttered from the battlements in the morning breeze, and high and far he heard a clear ringing as of silver trumpets.

So Gandalf and Peregrin rode to the Great Gate of the Men of Gondor at the rising of the sun, and its iron doors rolled back before them.

'Mithrandir! Mithrandir!' men cried. 'Now we know that the storm is indeed nigh!'

'It is upon you,' said Gandalf. 'I have ridden on its wings. Let me pass! I must come to your Lord Denethor, while his stewardship lasts. Whatever betide, you have come to the end of the Gondor that you have known. Let me pass!'

Then men fell back before the command of his voice and questioned him no further, though they gazed in wonder at the hobbit that sat before him and at the horse that bore him. For the people of the City used horses very little and they were seldom seen in their streets, save only those ridden by the errand-riders of their lord. And they said: 'Surely that is one of the great steeds of the King of Rohan? Maybe the Rohirrim will come soon to strengthen us.' But Shadowfax walked proudly up the long winding road.

For the fashion of Minas Tirith was such that it was built on seven levels, each delved into the hill, and about each was set a wall, and in each wall was a gate. But the gates were not set in a line: the Great Gate in the City Wall was at the east point of the circuit, but the next faced half south, and the third half north, and so to and fro upwards; so that the paved way that climbed towards the Citadel turned first this way and then that across the face of the hill. And each time that it passed the line of the Great Gate it went through an arched tunnel, piercing a vast pier of rock whose huge out-thrust bulk divided in two all the circles of the City save the first. For partly in the primeval shaping of the hill, partly by the mighty craft and labour of old, there stood up from the rear of the wide court behind the Gate a towering bastion of stone, its edge sharp as a ship-keel facing east. Up it rose, even to the level of the topmost circle, and there was crowned by a battlement; so that those in the Citadel might, like mariners in a mountainous ship, look from its peak sheer down upon the Gate seven hundred feet below. The entrance to the Citadel also looked eastward, but was delved in the heart of the rock; thence a long lamp-lit slope ran up to the seventh gate. Thus men reached at last the High Court, and the Place of the Fountain before the feet of the White Tower: tall and shapely, fifty fathoms from its base to the pinnacle, where the banner of the Stewards floated a thousand feet above the plain.

A strong citadel it was indeed, and not to be taken by a host of enemies, if there were any within that could hold weapons; unless some foe could come behind and scale the lower skirts of Mindolluin, and so come upon the narrow shoulder that joined the Hill of Guard to the mountain mass. But that shoulder, which rose to the height of the fifth wall, was hedged with great ramparts right up to the precipice that overhung its western end; and in that space stood the houses and domed tombs of bygone kings and lords, for ever silent between the mountain and the tower.

Pippin gazed in growing wonder at the great stone city, vaster and more splendid than anything that he had dreamed of; greater and stronger than Isengard, and far more beautiful. Yet it was in truth falling year by year into decay; and already it lacked half the men that could have dwelt at ease there. In every street they passed some great house or court over whose doors and arched gates were carved many fair letters of strange and ancient shapes: names Pippin guessed of great men and kindreds that had once dwelt there; and yet now they were silent, and no footsteps rang on their wide pavements, nor voice was heard in their halls, nor any face looked out from door or empty window.

At last they came out of shadow to the seventh gate, and the warm sun that shone down beyond the river, as Frodo walked in the glades of Ithilien, glowed here on the smooth walls and rooted pillars, and the great arch with keystone carven in the likeness of a crowned and kingly head. Gandalf dismounted, for no horse was allowed in the Citadel, and Shadowfax suffered himself to be led away at the soft word of his master.

The Guards of the gate were robed in black, and their helms were of strange shape, high-crowned, with long cheek-guards close-fitting to the face, and above the cheek-guards were set the white wings of sea-birds; but the helms gleamed with a flame of silver, for they were indeed wrought of *mithril*, heirlooms from the glory of old days. Upon the black surcoats were embroidered in white a tree blossoming like snow beneath a silver crown and many-pointed stars. This was the livery of the heirs of Elendil, and none wore it now in all Gondor, save the Guards of the Citadel before the Court of the Fountain where the White Tree once had grown.

Already it seemed that word of their coming had gone before them; and at once they were admitted, silently, and without question. Quickly Gandalf strode across the white-paved court. A sweet fountain played there in the morning sun, and a sward of bright green lay about it; but in the midst, drooping over the pool, stood a dead tree, and the falling drops dripped sadly from its barren and broken branches back into the clear water.

Pippin glanced at it as he hurried after Gandalf. It looked mournful, he thought, and he wondered why the dead tree was left in this place where everything else was well tended.

Seven stars and seven stones and one white tree.

The words that Gandalf had murmured came back into his mind. And then he found himself at the doors of the great hall beneath the gleaming tower; and behind the wizard he passed the tall silent door-wardens and entered the cool echoing shadows of the house of stone.

They walked down a paved passage, long and empty, and as they went Gandalf spoke softly to Pippin. 'Be careful of your words, Master Peregrin! This is no time for hobbit pertness. Théoden is a kindly old man. Denethor is of another sort, proud and subtle, a man of far greater lineage and power, though he is not called a king. But he will speak most to you, and question you much, since you can tell him of his son Boromir. He loved him greatly: too much perhaps; and the more so because they were unlike. But under cover of this love he will think it easier to learn what he wishes from you rather than from me. Do not tell him more than you need, and leave quiet the matter of Frodo's errand. I will deal with that in due time. And say nothing about Aragorn either, unless you must.'

'Why not? What is wrong with Strider?' Pippin whispered. 'He meant to come here, didn't he? And he'll be arriving soon himself, anyway.'

'Maybe, maybe,' said Gandalf. 'Though if he comes, it is likely to be in some way that no one expects, not even Denethor. It will be better so. At least he should come unheralded by us.'

Gandalf halted before a tall door of polished metal. 'See, Master Pippin, there is no time to instruct you now in the history of Gondor; though it might have been better, if you had learned something of it, when you were still birds-nesting and playing truant in the woods of the Shire. Do as I bid! It is scarcely wise when bringing the news of the death of his heir to a mighty lord to speak over much of the coming of one who will, if he comes, claim the kingship. Is that enough?'

'Kingship?' said Pippin amazed.

'Yes,' said Gandalf. 'If you have walked all these days with closed ears and mind asleep, wake up now!' He knocked on the door.

The door opened, but no one could be seen to open it. Pippin looked into a great hall. It was lit by deep windows in the wide aisles at either side, beyond the rows of tall pillars that upheld the roof. Monoliths of black marble, they rose to great capitals carved in many strange figures of beasts and leaves; and far above in shadow the wide vaulting gleamed with dull gold, inset with flowing traceries of many colours. No hangings nor storied webs, nor any things of woven stuff or of wood, were to be seen in that long solemn hall;

but between the pillars there stood a silent company of tall images graven in cold stone.

Suddenly Pippin was reminded of the hewn rocks of Argonath, and awe fell on him, as he looked down that avenue of kings long dead. At the far end upon a dais of many steps was set a high throne under a canopy of marble shaped like a crowned helm; behind it was carved upon the wall and set with gems an image of a tree in flower. But the throne was empty. At the foot of the dais, upon the lowest step which was broad and deep, there was a stone chair, black and unadorned, and on it sat an old man gazing at his lap. In his hand was a white rod with a golden knob. He did not look up. Solemnly they paced the long floor towards him, until they stood three paces from his footstool. Then Gandalf spoke.

'Hail, Lord and Steward of Minas Tirith, Denethor son of Ecthelion! I am come with counsel and tidings in this dark hour.'

Then the old man looked up. Pippin saw his carven face with its proud bones and skin like ivory, and the long curved nose between the dark deep eyes; and he was reminded not so much of Boromir as of Aragorn. 'Dark indeed is the hour,' said the old man, 'and at such times you are wont to come, Mithrandir. But though all the signs forebode that the doom of Gondor is drawing nigh, less now to me is that darkness than my own darkness. It has been told to me that you bring with you one who saw my son die. Is this he?'

'It is,' said Gandalf. 'One of the twain. The other is with Théoden of Rohan and may come hereafter. Halflings they are, as you see, yet this is not he of whom the omens spoke.'

'Yet a Halfling still,' said Denethor grimly, 'and little love do I bear the name, since those accursed words came to trouble our counsels and drew away my son on the wild errand to his death. My Boromir! Now we have need of you. Faramir should have gone in his stead.'

'He would have gone,' said Gandalf. 'Be not unjust in your grief! Boromir claimed the errand and would not suffer any other to have it. He was a masterful man, and one to take what he desired. I journeyed far with him and learned much of his mood. But you speak of his death. You have had news of that ere we came?'

'I have received this,' said Denethor, and laying down his rod he lifted from his lap the thing that he had been gazing at. In each hand he held up one half of a great horn cloven through the middle: a wild-ox horn bound with silver.

'That is the horn that Boromir always wore!' cried Pippin.

'Verily,' said Denethor. 'And in my turn I bore it, and so did each eldest son of our house, far back into the vanished years before the failing of the kings, since Vorondil father of Mardil hunted the wild kine of Araw in the far fields of Rhûn. I heard it blowing dim upon the northern marches thirteen days ago, and the River brought it to me, broken: it will wind no more.' He paused and there was a heavy silence. Suddenly he turned his black glance upon Pippin. 'What say you to that, Halfling?'

'Thirteen, thirteen days,' faltered Pippin. 'Yes, I think that would be so. Yes, I stood beside him, as he blew the horn. But no help came. Only more orcs.'

'So,' said Denethor, looking keenly at Pippin's face. 'You were there? Tell me more! Why did no help come? And how did you escape, and yet he did not, so mighty a man as he was, and only orcs to withstand him?'

Pippin flushed and forgot his fear. 'The mightiest man may be slain by one arrow,' he said; 'and Boromir was pierced by many. When last I saw him he sank beside a tree and plucked a black-feathered shaft from his side. Then I swooned and was made captive. I saw him no more, and know no more. But I honour his memory, for he was very valiant. He died to save us, my kinsman Meriadoc and myself, waylaid in the woods by the soldiery of the Dark Lord; and though he fell and failed, my gratitude is none the less.'

Then Pippin looked the old man in the eye, for pride stirred strangely within him, still stung by the scorn and suspicion in that cold voice. 'Little service, no doubt, will so great a lord of Men think to find in a hobbit, a halfling from the northern Shire; yet such as it is, I will offer it, in payment of my debt.' Twitching aside his grey cloak, Pippin drew forth his small sword and laid it at Denethor's feet.

A pale smile, like a gleam of cold sun on a winter's evening, passed over the old man's face; but he bent his head and held out his hand, laying the shards of the horn aside. 'Give me the weapon!' he said.

Pippin lifted it and presented the hilt to him. 'Whence came this?' said Denethor. 'Many, many years lie on it. Surely this is a blade wrought by our own kindred in the North in the deep past?'

'It came out of the mounds that lie on the borders of my country,' said Pippin. 'But only evil wights dwell there now, and I will not willingly tell more of them.'

'I see that strange tales are woven about you,' said Denethor, 'and once again it is shown that looks may belie the man – or the halfling. I accept your service. For you are not daunted by words; and you have courteous speech, strange though the sound of it may be to us in the South. And we shall have need of all folk of courtesy, be they great or small, in the days to come. Swear to me now!'

'Take the hilt,' said Gandalf, 'and speak after the Lord, if you are resolved on this.'

'I am,' said Pippin.

The old man laid the sword along his lap, and Pippin put his hand to the hilt, and said slowly after Denethor:

'Here do I swear fealty and service to Gondor, and to the Lord and Steward of the realm, to speak and to be silent, to do and to let be, to come and to go, in need or plenty, in peace or war, in living or dying, from this hour henceforth, until my lord release me, or death take me, or the world end. So say I, Peregrin son of Paladin of the Shire of the Halflings.'

'And this do I hear, Denethor son of Ecthelion, Lord of Gondor, Steward of the High King, and I will not forget it, nor fail to reward that which is given: fealty with love, valour with honour, oath-breaking with vengeance.' Then Pippin received back his sword and put it in its sheath.

'And now,' said Denethor, 'my first command to you: speak and be not silent! Tell me your full tale, and see that you recall all that you can of Boromir, my son. Sit now and begin!' As he spoke he struck a small silver gong that stood near his footstool, and at once servants came forward. Pippin saw then that they had been standing in alcoves on either side of the door, unseen as he and Gandalf entered.

'Bring wine and food and seats for the guests,' said Denethor, 'and see that none trouble us for one hour.'

'It is all that I have to spare, for there is much else to heed,' he said to Gandalf. 'Much of more import, it may seem, and yet to me less pressing. But maybe we can speak again at the end of the day.'

'And earlier, it is to be hoped,' said Gandalf. 'For I have not ridden hither from Isengard, one hundred and fifty leagues, with the speed of wind, only to bring you one small warrior, however courteous. Is it naught to you that Théoden has fought a great battle, and that Isengard is overthrown, and that I have broken the staff of Saruman?'

'It is much to me. But I know already sufficient of these deeds for my own counsel against the menace of the East.' He turned his dark eyes on Gandalf, and now Pippin saw a likeness between the two, and he felt the strain between them, almost as if he saw a line of smouldering fire, drawn from eye to eye, that might suddenly burst into flame.

Denethor looked indeed much more like a great wizard than Gandalf did, more kingly, beautiful, and powerful; and older. Yet by a sense other than sight Pippin perceived that Gandalf had the greater power and the deeper wisdom, and a majesty that was veiled. And he was older, far older. 'How much older?' he wondered, and then he thought how odd it was that he had never thought about it before. Treebeard had said something about wizards, but even then he had not thought of Gandalf as one of them. What was Gandalf? In what far time and place did he come into the world, and when would he leave it? And then his musings broke off, and he saw that Denethor and Gandalf still looked each other in the eye, as if reading the other's mind. But it was Denethor who first withdrew his gaze.

'Yea,' he said; 'for though the Stones be lost, they say, still the lords of

Gondor have keener sight than lesser men, and many messages come to them. But sit now!'

Then men came bearing a chair and a low stool, and one brought a salver with a silver flagon and cups, and white cakes. Pippin sat down, but he could not take his eyes from the old lord. Was it so, or had he only imagined it, that as he spoke of the Stones a sudden gleam of his eye had glanced upon Pippin's face?

'Now tell me your tale, my liege,' said Denethor, half kindly, half mockingly. 'For the words of one whom my son so befriended will be welcome indeed.'

Pippin never forgot that hour in the great hall under the piercing eye of the Lord of Gondor, stabbed ever and anon by his shrewd questions, and all the while conscious of Gandalf at his side, watching and listening, and (so Pippin felt) holding in check a rising wrath and impatience. When the hour was over and Denethor again rang the gong, Pippin felt worn out. 'It cannot be more than nine o'clock,' he thought. 'I could now eat three breakfasts on end.'

'Lead the Lord Mithrandir to the housing prepared for him,' said Denethor, 'and his companion may lodge with him for the present, if he will. But be it known that I have now sworn him to my service, and he shall be known as Peregrin son of Paladin and taught the lesser pass-words. Send word to the Captains that they shall wait on me here, as soon as may be after the third hour has rung.

'And you, my Lord Mithrandir, shall come too, as and when you will. None shall hinder your coming to me at any time, save only in my brief hours of sleep. Let your wrath at an old man's folly run off, and then return to my comfort!'

'Folly?' said Gandalf. 'Nay, my lord, when you are a dotard you will die. You can use even your grief as a cloak. Do you think that I do not understand your purpose in questioning for an hour one who knows the least, while I sit by?'

'If you understand it, then be content,' returned Denethor. 'Pride would be folly that disdained help and counsel at need; but you deal out such gifts according to your own designs. Yet the Lord of Gondor is not to be made the tool of other men's purposes, however worthy. And to him there is no purpose higher in the world as it now stands than the good of Gondor; and the rule of Gondor, my lord, is mine and no other man's, unless the king should come again.'

'Unless the king should come again?' said Gandalf. 'Well, my lord Steward, it is your task to keep some kingdom still against that event, which few now look to see. In that task you shall have all the aid that you are pleased to ask for. But I will say this: the rule of no realm is mine, neither of Gondor nor any other, great or small. But all worthy things that are in peril as the world now stands, those are my care. And for my part, I shall not wholly fail of my task, though Gondor should perish, if anything passes through this night that can still grow fair or bear fruit and flower again in days to come. For I also am a steward. Did you not know?' And with that he turned and strode from the hall with Pippin running at his side.

Gandalf did not look at Pippin or speak a word to him as they went. Their guide brought them from the doors of the hall, and then led them across the Court of the Fountain into a lane between tall buildings of stone. After several turns they came to a house close to the wall of the citadel upon the north side, not far from the shoulder that linked the hill with the mountain. Within, upon the first floor above the street, up a wide carven stair, he showed them to a fair room, light and airy, with goodly hangings of dull gold sheen unfigured. It was sparely furnished, having but a small table, two chairs and a bench; but at either side there were curtained alcoves and well-clad beds within with vessels and basins for washing. There were three high narrow windows that looked northward over the great curve of Anduin, still shrouded in mists, towards the Emyn Muil and Rauros far away. Pippin had to climb on the bench to look out over the deep stone sill.

'Are you angry with me, Gandalf?' he said, as their guide went out and closed the door. 'I did the best I could.'

'You did indeed!' said Gandalf, laughing suddenly; and he came and stood beside Pippin, putting his arm about the hobbit's shoulders, and gazing out of the window. Pippin glanced in some wonder at the face now close beside his own, for the sound of that laugh had been gay and merry. Yet in the wizard's face he saw at first only lines of care and sorrow; though as he looked more intently he perceived that under all there was a great joy: a fountain of mirth enough to set a kingdom laughing, were it to gush forth.

'Indeed you did your best,' said the wizard; 'and I hope that it may be long before you find yourself in such a tight corner again between two such terrible old men. Still the Lord of Gondor learned more from you than you may have guessed, Pippin. You could not hide the fact that Boromir did not lead the Company from Moria, and that there was one among you of high honour who was coming to Minas Tirith; and that he had a famous sword. Men think much about the stories of old days in Gondor; and Denethor has given long thought to the rhyme and to the words *Isildur's Bane*, since Boromir went away.

'He is not as other men of this time, Pippin, and whatever be his descent from father to son, by some chance the blood of Westernesse runs nearly true in him; as it does in his other son, Faramir, and yet did not in Boromir whom he loved best. He has long sight. He can perceive, if he bends his will thither, much of what is passing in the minds of men, even of those that dwell far off. It is difficult to deceive him, and dangerous to try.

'Remember that! For you are now sworn to his service. I do not know what put it into your head, or your heart, to do that. But it was well done. I did not hinder it, for generous deed should not be checked by cold counsel. It touched his heart, as well (may I say it) as pleasing his humour. And at least you are free now to move about as you will in Minas Tirith – when you are not on duty. For there is another side to it. You are at his command; and he will not forget. Be wary still!'

He fell silent and sighed. 'Well, no need to brood on what tomorrow may bring. For one thing, tomorrow will be certain to bring worse than today, for many days to come. And there is nothing more that I can do to help it. The board is set, and the pieces are moving. One piece that I greatly desire to find is Faramir, now the heir of Denethor. I do not think that he is in the City; but I have had no time to gather news. I must go, Pippin. I must go to this lords' council and learn what I can. But the Enemy has the move, and he is about to open his full game. And pawns are likely to see as much of it as any, Peregrin son of Paladin, soldier of Gondor. Sharpen your blade!'

Gandalf went to the door, and there he turned. 'I am in haste, Pippin,' he said. 'Do me a favour when you go out. Even before you rest, if you are not too weary. Go and find Shadowfax and see how he is housed. These people are kindly to beasts, for they are a good and wise folk, but they have less skill with horses than some.'

With that Gandalf went out; and as he did so, there came the note of a clear sweet bell ringing in a tower of the citadel. Three strokes it rang, like silver in the air, and ceased: the third hour from the rising of the sun.

After a minute Pippin went to the door and down the stair and looked about the street. The sun was now shining warm and bright, and the towers and tall houses cast long clear-cut shadows westward. High in the blue air Mount Mindolluin lifted its white helm and snowy cloak. Armed men went to and fro in the ways of the City, as if going at the striking of the hour to changes of post and duty.

'Nine o'clock we'd call it in the Shire,' said Pippin aloud to himself. 'Just the time for a nice breakfast by the open window in spring sunshine. And how I should like breakfast! Do these people ever have it, or is it over? And when do they have dinner, and where?'

Presently he noticed a man, clad in black and white, coming along the narrow street from the centre of the citadel towards him. Pippin felt lonely and made up his mind to speak as the man passed; but he had no need. The man came straight up to him.

'You are Peregrin the Halfling?' he said. 'I am told that you have been sworn to the service of the Lord and of the City. Welcome!' He held out his hand and Pippin took it.

'I am named Beregond son of Baranor. I have no duty this morning, and I have been sent to you to teach you the pass-words, and to tell you some of the many things that no doubt you will wish to know. And for my part, I would learn of you also. For never before have we seen a halfling in this land and though we have heard rumour of them, little is said of them in any tale that we know. Moreover you are a friend of Mithrandir. Do you know him well?'

'Well,' said Pippin. 'I have known *of* him all my short life, as you might say; and lately I have travelled far with him. But there is much to read in that book, and I cannot claim to have seen more than a page or two. Yet perhaps I know him as well as any but a few. Aragorn was the only one of our Company, I think, who really knew him.'

'Aragorn?' said Beregond. 'Who is he?'

'Oh,' stammered Pippin, 'he was a man who went about with us. I think he is in Rohan now.'

'You have been in Rohan, I hear. There is much that I would ask you of that land also; for we put much of what little hope we have in its people. But I am forgetting my errand, which was first to answer what you would ask. What would you know, Master Peregrin?'

'Er well,' said Pippin, 'if I may venture to say so, rather a burning question in my mind at present is, well, what about breakfast and all that? I mean, what are the meal-times, if you understand me, and where is the dining-room, if there is one? And the inns? I looked, but never a one could I see as we rode up, though I had been borne up by the hope of a draught of ale as soon as we came to the homes of wise and courtly men.'

Beregond looked at him gravely. 'An old campaigner, I see,' he said. 'They say that men who go warring afield look ever to the next hope of food and of drink; though I am not a travelled man myself. Then you have not yet eaten today?'

'Well, yes, to speak in courtesy, yes,' said Pippin. 'But no more than a cup of wine and a white cake or two by the kindness of your lord; but he racked me for it with an hour of questions, and that is hungry work.'

Beregond laughed. 'At the table small men may do the greater deeds, we say. But you have broken your fast as well as any man in the Citadel, and with greater honour. This is a fortress and a tower of guard and is now in posture of war. We rise ere the Sun, and take a morsel in the grey light, and go to our duties at the opening hour. But do not despair!' He laughed again, seeing the dismay in Pippin's face. 'Those who have had *heavy* duty take somewhat to refresh their strength in the mid-morning. Then there is the nuncheon, at noon or after as duties allow; and men gather for the daymeal, and such mirth as there still may be, about the hour of sunset.

'Come! We will walk a little and then go find us some refreshment, and eat and drink on the battlement, and survey the fair morning.'

'One moment!' said Pippin blushing. 'Greed, or hunger by your courtesy, put it out of my mind. But Gandalf, Mithrandir as you call him, asked me to see to his horse – Shadowfax, a great steed of Rohan, and the apple of the king's eye, I am told, though he has given him to Mithrandir for his services. I think his new master loves the beast better than he loves many men, and if his good will is of any value to this city, you will treat Shadowfax with all honour: with greater kindness than you have treated this hobbit, if it is possible.'

'Hobbit?' said Beregond.

'That is what we call ourselves,' said Pippin.

'I am glad to learn it,' said Beregond, 'for now I may say that strange accents do not mar fair speech, and hobbits are a fair-spoken folk. But come! You shall make me acquainted with this good horse. I love beasts, and we see them seldom in this stony city; for my people came from the mountain-vales, and before that from Ithilien. But fear not! The visit shall be short, a mere call of courtesy, and we will go thence to the butteries.'

Pippin found that Shadowfax had been well housed and tended. For in the sixth circle, outside the walls of the citadel, there were some fair stables where a few swift horses were kept, hard by the lodgings of the errand-riders of the Lord: messengers always ready to go at the urgent command of Denethor or his chief captains. But now all the horses and the riders were out and away.

Shadowfax whinnied as Pippin entered the stable and turned his head. 'Good morning!' said Pippin. 'Gandalf will come as soon as he may. He is busy, but he sends greetings, and I am to see that all is well with you; and you resting, I hope, after your long labours.'

Shadowfax tossed his head and stamped. But he allowed Beregond to handle his head gently and stroke his great flanks.

'He looks as if he were spoiling for a race, and not newly come from a great journey,' said Beregond. 'How strong and proud he is! Where is his harness? It should be rich and fair.'

'None is rich and fair enough for him,' said Pippin. 'He will have none. If he will consent to bear you, bear you he does; and if not, well, no bit, bridle, whip, or thong will tame him. Farewell, Shadowfax! Have patience. Battle is coming.'

Shadowfax lifted up his head and neighed, so that the stable shook, and they covered their ears. Then they took their leave, seeing that the manger was well filled.

'And now for our manger,' said Beregond, and he led Pippin back to the citadel, and so to a door in the north side of the great tower. There they went down a long cool stair into a wide alley lit with lamps. There were hatches in the walls at the side, and one of these was open.

'This is the storehouse and buttery of my company of the Guard,' said Beregond. 'Greetings, Targon!' he called through the hatch. 'It is early yet, but here is a newcomer that the Lord has taken into his service. He has ridden long and far with a tight belt, and has had sore labour this morning, and he is hungry. Give us what you have!'

They got there bread, and butter, and cheese and apples: the last of the winter store, wrinkled but sound and sweet; and a leather flagon of new-drawn ale, and wooden platters and cups. They put all into a wicker basket and climbed back into the sun; and Beregond brought Pippin to a place at the east end of the great out-thrust battlement where there was an embrasure in the walls with a stone seat beneath the sill. From there they could look out on the morning over the world.

They ate and drank; and they talked now of Gondor and its ways and customs, now of the Shire and the strange countries that Pippin had seen. And ever as they talked Beregond was more amazed, and looked with greater wonder at the hobbit, swinging his short legs as he sat on the seat, or standing tiptoe upon it to peer over the sill at the lands below.

'I will not hide from you, Master Peregrin,' said Beregond, 'that to us you look almost as one of our children, a lad of nine summers or so; and yet you have endured perils and seen marvels that few of our greybeards could boast of. I thought it was the whim of our Lord to take him a noble page, after the manner of the kings of old, they say. But I see that it is not so, and you must pardon my foolishness.'

'I do,' said Pippin. 'Though you are not far wrong. I am still little more than a boy in the reckoning of my own people, and it will be four years yet before I "come of age", as we say in the Shire. But do not bother about me. Come and look and tell me what I can see.'

The sun was now climbing, and the mists in the vale below had been drawn up. The last of them were floating away, just overhead, as wisps of white cloud borne on the stiffening breeze from the East, that was now flapping and tugging the flags and white standards of the citadel. Away down in the valley-bottom, five leagues or so as the eye leaps, the Great River could now be seen grey and glittering, coming out of the north-west, and bending in a mighty sweep south and west again, till it was lost to view in a haze and shimmer, far beyond which lay the Sea fifty leagues away.

Pippin could see all the Pelennor laid out before him, dotted into the distance with farmsteads and little walls, barns and byres, but nowhere could he see any kine or other beasts. Many roads and tracks crossed the green fields, and there was much coming and going: wains moving in lines towards the Great Gate, and others passing out. Now and again a horseman would ride up, and leap from the saddle and hasten into the City. But most of the traffic went out along the chief highway, and that turned south, and then bending swifter than the River skirted the hills and passed soon from sight. It was wide and well-paved, and along its eastern edge ran a broad green riding-track, and beyond that a wall. On the ride horsemen galloped to and fro, but all the street seemed to be choked with great covered wains going south. But soon Pippin saw that all was in fact well-ordered: the wains were moving in three lines, one swifter drawn by horses; another slower, great waggons with fair housings of many colours, drawn by oxen; and along the west rim of the road many smaller carts hauled by trudging men.

'That is the road to the vales of Tumladen and Lossarnach, and the mountain-villages, and then on to Lebennin,' said Beregond. 'There go the last of the wains that bear away to refuge the aged, the children, and the women that must go with them. They must all be gone from the Gate and the road clear for a league before noon: that was the order. It is a sad necessity.' He sighed. 'Few, maybe, of those now sundered will meet again. And there were always too few children in this city; but now there are none – save some young lads that will not depart, and may find some task to do: my own son is one of them.'

They fell silent for a while. Pippin gazed anxiously eastward, as if at any moment he might see thousands of orcs pouring over the fields. 'What can I see there?' he asked, pointing down to the middle of the great curve of the Anduin. 'Is that another city, or what is it?'

'It was a city,' said Beregond, 'the chief city of Gondor, of which this was only a fortress. For that is the ruin of Osgiliath on either side of Anduin, which our enemies took and burned long ago. Yet we won it back in the days of the youth of Denethor: not to dwell in, but to hold as an outpost, and to rebuild the bridge for the passage of our arms. And then came the Fell Riders out of Minas Morgul.'

'The Black Riders?' said Pippin, opening his eyes, and they were wide and dark with an old fear re-awakened.

'Yes, they were black,' said Beregond, 'and I see that you know something of them, though you have not spoken of them in any of your tales.'

'I know of them,' said Pippin softly, 'but I will not speak of them now, so near, so near.' He broke off and lifted his eyes above the River, and it seemed to him that all he could see was a vast and threatening shadow. Perhaps it was mountains looming on the verge of sight, their jagged edges softened by wellnigh twenty leagues of misty air; perhaps it was but a cloud-wall, and beyond that again a yet deeper gloom. But even as he looked it seemed to his eyes that the gloom was growing and gathering, very slowly, slowly rising to smother the regions of the sun.

'So near to Mordor?' said Beregond quietly. 'Yes, there it lies. We seldom name it; but we have dwelt ever in sight of that shadow: sometimes it seems fainter and more distant; sometimes nearer and darker. It is growing and darkening now; and therefore our fear and disquiet grow too. And the Fell Riders, less than a year ago they won back the crossings, and many of our best men were slain. Boromir it was that drove the enemy at last back from this western shore, and we hold still the near half of Osgiliath. For a little while. But we await now a new onslaught there. Maybe the chief onslaught of the war that comes.'

'When?' said Pippin. 'Have you a guess? For I saw the beacons last night and the errand-riders; and Gandalf said that it was a sign that war had begun. He seemed in a desperate hurry. But now everything seems to have slowed up again.'

'Only because everything is now ready,' said Beregond. 'It is but the deep breath before the plunge.'

'But why were the beacons lit last night?'

'It is over-late to send for aid when you are already besieged,' answered Beregond. 'But I do not know the counsel of the Lord and his captains. They have many ways of gathering news. And the Lord Denethor is unlike other men: he sees far. Some say that as he sits alone in his high chamber in the Tower at night, and bends his thought this way and that, he can read somewhat of the future; and that he will at times search even the mind of the Enemy, wrestling with him. And so it is that he is old, worn before his time. But however that may be, my lord Faramir is abroad, beyond the River on some perilous errand, and he may have sent tidings.

'But if you would know what I think set the beacons ablaze, it was the news that came yestereve out of Lebennin. There is a great fleet drawing near to the mouths of Anduin, manned by the corsairs of Umbar in the South. They have long ceased to fear the might of Gondor, and they have allied them with the Enemy, and now make a heavy stroke in his cause. For this attack will draw off much of the help that we looked to have from Lebennin and Belfalas, where folk are hardy and numerous. All the more do our thoughts go north to Rohan; and the more glad are we for these tidings of victory that you bring.

'And yet' – he paused and stood up, and looked round, north, east, and south – 'the doings at Isengard should warn us that we are caught now in a great net and strategy. This is no longer a bickering at the fords, raiding from Ithilien and from Anórien, ambushing and pillaging. This is a great war long-planned, and we are but one piece in it, whatever pride may say. Things move in the far East beyond the Inland Sea, it is reported; and north in Mirkwood and beyond; and south in Harad. And now all realms shall be put to the test, to stand, or fall – under the Shadow.

'Yet, Master Peregrin, we have this honour: ever we bear the brunt of the chief hatred of the Dark Lord, for that hatred comes down out of the depths of time and over the deeps of the Sea. Here will the hammer-stroke fall hardest. And for that reason Mithrandir came hither in such haste. For if we fall, who shall stand? And, Master Peregrin, do you see any hope that we shall stand?'

Pippin did not answer. He looked at the great walls, and the towers and brave banners, and the sun in the high sky, and then at the gathering gloom in the East; and he thought of the long fingers of that Shadow: of the orcs in the woods and the mountains, the treason of Isengard, the birds of evil eye, and the Black Riders even in the lanes of the Shire – and of the winged terror, the Nazgûl. He shuddered, and hope seemed to wither. And even at that moment the sun for a second faltered and was obscured, as though a dark wing had passed across it. Almost beyond hearing he thought he caught, high and far up in the heavens, a cry: faint, but heart-quelling, cruel and cold. He blanched and cowered against the wall.

'What was that?' asked Beregond. 'You also felt something?'

'Yes,' muttered Pippin. 'It is the sign of our fall, and the shadow of doom, a Fell Rider of the air.'

'Yes, the shadow of doom,' said Beregond. 'I fear that Minas Tirith shall fall. Night comes. The very warmth of my blood seems stolen away.'

For a time they sat together with bowed heads and did not speak. Then suddenly Pippin looked up and saw that the sun was still shining and the banners still streaming in the breeze. He shook himself. 'It is passed,' he said. 'No, my heart will not yet despair. Gandalf fell and has returned and is with us. We may stand, if only on one leg, or at least be left still upon our knees.'

'Rightly said!' cried Beregond, rising and striding to and fro. 'Nay, though all things must come utterly to an end in time, Gondor shall not perish yet. Not though the walls be taken by a reckless foe that will build a hill of carrion before them. There are still other fastnesses, and secret ways of escape into the mountains. Hope and memory shall live still in some hidden valley where the grass is green.'

'All the same, I wish it was over for good or ill,' said Pippin. 'I am no warrior at all and dislike any thought of battle; but waiting on the edge of one that I can't escape is worst of all. What a long day it seems already! I should be happier, if we were not obliged to stand and watch, making no move, striking nowhere first. No stroke would have been struck in Rohan, I think, but for Gandalf.'

'Ah, there you lay your finger on the sore that many feel!' said Beregond.

'But things may change when Faramir returns. He is bold, more bold than many deem; for in these days men are slow to believe that a captain can be wise and learned in the scrolls of lore and song, as he is, and yet a man of hardihood and swift judgement in the field. But such is Faramir. Less reckless and eager than Boromir, but not less resolute. Yet what indeed can he do? We cannot assault the mountains of – of yonder realm. Our reach is shortened, and we cannot strike till some foe comes within it. Then our hand must be heavy!' He smote the hilt of his sword.

Pippin looked at him: tall and proud and noble, as all the men that he had yet seen in that land; and with a glitter in his eye as he thought of the battle. 'Alas! my own hand feels as light as a feather,' he thought, but he said nothing. 'A pawn did Gandalf say? Perhaps; but on the wrong chessboard.'

So they talked until the sun reached its height, and suddenly the noon-bells were rung, and there was a stir in the citadel; for all save the watchmen were going to their meal.

'Will you come with me?' said Beregond. 'You may join my mess for this day. I do not know to what company you will be assigned; or the Lord may hold you at his own command. But you will be welcome. And it will be well to meet as many men as you may, while there is yet time.'

'I shall be glad to come,' said Pippin. 'I am lonely, to tell you the truth. I left my best friend behind in Rohan, and I have had no one to talk to or jest with. Perhaps I could really join your company? Are you the captain? If so, you could take me on, or speak for me?'

'Nay, nay,' Beregond laughed, 'I am no captain. Neither office nor rank nor lordship have I, being but a plain man of arms of the Third Company of the Citadel. Yet, Master Peregrin, to be only a man of arms of the Guard of the Tower of Gondor is held worthy in the City, and such men have honour in the land.'

'Then it is far beyond me,' said Pippin. 'Take me back to our room, and if Gandalf is not there, I will go where you like – as your guest.'

Gandalf was not in the lodging and had sent no message; so Pippin went with Beregond and was made known to the men of the Third Company. And it seemed that Beregond got as much honour from it as his guest, for Pippin was very welcome. There had already been much talk in the citadel about Mithrandir's companion and his long closeting with the Lord; and rumour declared that a Prince of the Halflings had come out of the North to offer allegiance to Gondor and five thousand swords. And some said that when the Riders came from Rohan each would bring behind him a halfling warrior, small maybe, but doughty.

Though Pippin had regretfully to destroy this hopeful tale, he could not be rid of his new rank, only fitting, men thought, to one befriended by Boromir and honoured by the Lord Denethor; and they thanked him for coming among them, and hung on his words and stories of the outlands, and gave him as much food and ale as he could wish. Indeed his only trouble was to be 'wary' according to the counsel of Gandalf, and not to let his tongue wag freely after the manner of a hobbit among friends.

At length Beregond rose. 'Farewell for this time!' he said. 'I have duty now till sundown, as have all the others here, I think. But if you are lonely, as you say, maybe you would like a merry guide about the City. My son would go with you gladly. A good lad, I may say. If that pleases you, go down to the lowest circle and ask for the Old Guesthouse in the Rath Celerdain, the Lampwrights' Street. You will find him there with other lads that are remaining in the City. There may be things worth seeing down at the Great Gate ere the closing.'

He went out, and soon after all the others followed. The day was still fine, though it was growing hazy, and it was hot for March, even so far southwards. Pippin felt sleepy, but the lodging seemed cheerless, and he decided to go down and explore the City. He took a few morsels that he had saved to Shadowfax, and they were graciously accepted, though the horse seemed to have no lack. Then he walked on down many winding ways.

People stared much as he passed. To his face men were gravely courteous, saluting him after the manner of Gondor with bowed head and hands upon the breast; but behind him he heard many calls, as those out of doors cried to others within to come and see the Prince of the Halflings, the companion of Mithrandir. Many used some other tongue than the Common Speech, but it was not long before he learned at least what was meant by *Ernil i Pheriannath* and knew that his title had gone down before him into the City.

He came at last by arched streets and many fair alleys and pavements to the lowest and widest circle, and there he was directed to the Lampwrights' Street, a broad way running towards the Great Gate. In it he found the Old Guesthouse, a large building of grey weathered stone with two wings running back from the street, and between them a narrow greensward, behind which was the many-windowed house, fronted along its whole width by a pillared porch and a flight of steps down on to the grass. Boys were playing among the pillars, the only children that Pippin had seen in Minas Tirith, and he stopped to look at them. Presently one of them caught sight of him, and with a shout he sprang across the grass and came into the street, followed by several others. There he stood in front of Pippin, looking him up and down.

'Greetings!' said the lad. 'Where do you come from? You are a stranger in the City.'

'I was,' said Pippin; 'but they say I have become a man of Gondor.'

'Oh come!' said the lad. 'Then we are all men here. But how old are you, and what is your name? I am ten years already, and shall soon be five feet. I am taller than you. But then my father is a Guard, one of the tallest. What is your father?'

'Which question shall I answer first?' said Pippin. 'My father farms the lands round Whitwell near Tuckborough in the Shire. I am nearly twenty-nine, so I pass you there; though I am but four feet, and not likely to grow any more, save sideways.'

'Twenty-nine!' said the lad and whistled. 'Why, you are quite old! As old as my uncle Iorlas. Still,' he added hopefully, 'I wager I could stand you on your head or lay you on your back.'

'Maybe you could, if I let you,' said Pippin with a laugh. 'And maybe I could do the same to you: we know some wrestling tricks in my little country. Where, let me tell you, I am considered uncommonly large and strong; and I have never allowed anyone to stand me on my head. So if it came to a trial and nothing else would serve, I might have to kill you. For when you are older, you will learn that folk are not always what they seem; and though you may have taken me for a soft stranger-lad and easy prey, let me warn you: I am not, I am a halfling, hard, bold, and wicked!' Pippin pulled such a grim face that the boy stepped back a pace, but at once he returned with clenched fists and the light of battle in his eye.

'No!' Pippin laughed. 'Don't believe what strangers say of themselves either! I am not a fighter. But it would be politer in any case for the challenger to say who he is.'

The boy drew himself up proudly. 'I am Bergil son of Beregond of the Guards,' he said.

'So I thought,' said Pippin, 'for you look like your father. I know him and he sent me to find you.'

'Then why did you not say so at once?' said Bergil, and suddenly a look of dismay came over his face. 'Do not tell me that he has changed his mind, and will send me away with the maidens! But no, the last wains have gone.'

'His message is less bad than that, if not good,' said Pippin. 'He says that if you would prefer it to standing me on my head, you might show me round the City for a while and cheer my loneliness. I can tell you some tales of far countries in return.'

Bergil clapped his hands, and laughed with relief. 'All is well,' he cried. 'Come then! We were soon going to the Gate to look on. We will go now.'

'What is happening there?'

'The Captains of the Outlands are expected up the South Road ere sundown. Come with us and you will see.'

Bergil proved a good comrade, the best company Pippin had had since he parted from Merry, and soon they were laughing and talking gaily as they went about the streets, heedless of the many glances that men gave them. Before long they found themselves in a throng going towards the Great Gate. There Pippin went up much in the esteem of Bergil, for when he spoke his name and the pass-word the guard saluted him and let him pass through; and what was more, he allowed him to take his companion with him.

'That is good!' said Bergil. 'We boys are no longer allowed to pass the Gate without an elder. Now we shall see better.'

Beyond the Gate there was a crowd of men along the verge of the road and of the great paved space into which all the ways to Minas Tirith ran. All eyes were turned southwards, and soon a murmur rose: 'There is dust away there! They are coming!'

Pippin and Bergil edged their way forward to the front of the crowd, and waited. Horns sounded at some distance, and the noise of cheering rolled towards them like a gathering wind. Then there was a loud trumpet-blast, and all about them people were shouting.

'Forlong! Forlong!' Pippin heard men calling. 'What do they say?' he asked.

'Forlong has come,' Bergil answered; 'old Forlong the Fat, the Lord of Lossarnach. That is where my grandsire lives. Hurrah! Here he is. Good old Forlong!'

Leading the line there came walking a big thick-limbed horse, and on it sat a man of wide shoulders and huge girth, but old and grey-bearded, yet mail-clad and black-helmed and bearing a long heavy spear. Behind him marched proudly a dusty line of men, well-armed and bearing great battle-axes; grim-faced they were, and shorter and somewhat swarthier than any men that Pippin had yet seen in Gondor.

'Forlong!' men shouted. 'True heart, true friend! Forlong!' But when the men of Lossarnach had passed they muttered: 'So few! Two hundreds, what are they? We hoped for ten times the number. That will be the new tidings of the black fleet. They are sparing only a tithe of their strength. Still every little is a gain.'

And so the companies came and were hailed and cheered and passed through the Gate, men of the Outlands marching to defend the City of Gondor in a dark hour; but always too few, always less than hope looked for or need asked. The men of Ringló Vale behind the son of their lord, Dervorin striding on foot: three hundreds. From the uplands of Morthond, the great Blackroot Vale, tall Duinhir with his sons, Duilin and Derufin, and five hundred bowmen. From the Anfalas, the Langstrand far away, a long line of men of many sorts, hunters and herdsmen and men of little villages, scantily equipped save for the household of Golasgil their lord. From Lamedon, a few grim hillmen without a captain. Fisher-folk of the Ethir, some hundred or more spared from the ships. Hirluin the Fair of the Green Hills from Pinnath Gelin with three hundreds of gallant green-clad men. And last and proudest, Imrahil, Prince of Dol Amroth, kinsman of the Lord, with gilded banners bearing his token of the Ship and the Silver Swan, and a company of knights in full harness riding grey horses; and behind them seven hundreds of men at arms, tall as lords, grey-eyed, dark-haired, singing as they came.

And that was all, less than three thousands full told. No more would come. Their cries and the tramp of their feet passed into the City and died away. The onlookers stood silent for a while. Dust hung in the air, for the wind had died and the evening was heavy. Already the closing hour was drawing nigh, and the red sun had gone behind Mindolluin. Shadow came down on the City.

Pippin looked up, and it seemed to him that the sky had grown ashen-grey, as if a vast dust and smoke hung above them, and light came dully through it. But in the West the dying sun had set all the fume on fire, and now Mindolluin stood black against a burning smoulder flecked with embers. 'So ends a fair day in wrath!' he said, forgetful of the lad at his side.

'So it will, if I have not returned before the sundown-bells,' said Bergil. 'Come! There goes the trumpet for the closing of the Gate.'

Hand in hand they went back into the City, the last to pass the Gate before it was shut; and as they reached the Lampwrights' Street all the bells in the towers tolled solemnly. Lights sprang in many windows, and from the houses and wards of the men at arms along the walls there came the sound of song.

'Farewell for this time,' said Bergil. 'Take my greetings to my father, and thank him for the company that he sent. Come again soon, I beg. Almost I wish now that there was no war, for we might have had some merry times. We might have journeyed to Lossarnach, to my grandsire's house; it is good to be there in Spring, the woods and fields are full of flowers. But maybe we will go thither together yet. They will never overcome our Lord, and my father is very valiant. Farewell and return!'

They parted and Pippin hurried back towards the citadel. It seemed a long way, and he grew hot and very hungry; and night closed down swift and dark. Not a star pricked the sky. He was late for the daymeal in the mess, and Beregond greeted him gladly, and sat him at his side to hear news of his son. After the meal Pippin stayed a while, and then took his leave, for a strange gloom was on him, and now he desired very much to see Gandalf again.

'Can you find your way?' said Beregond at the door of the small hall, on the north side of the citadel, where they had sat. 'It is a black night, and all the blacker since orders came that lights are to be dimmed within the City, and none are to shine out from the walls. And I can give you news of another order: you will be summoned to the Lord Denethor early tomorrow. I fear you will not be for the Third Company. Still we may hope to meet again. Farewell and sleep in peace!'

The lodging was dark, save for a little lantern set on the table. Gandalf was not there. Gloom settled still more heavily on Pippin. He climbed on the bench and tried to peer out of a window, but it was like looking into a pool of ink. He got down and closed the shutter and went to bed. For a while he lay and listened for sounds of Gandalf's return, and then he fell into an uneasy sleep.

In the night he was wakened by a light, and he saw that Gandalf had come and was pacing to and fro in the room beyond the curtain of the alcove. There were candles on the table and rolls of parchment. He heard the wizard sigh, and mutter: 'When will Faramir return?'

'Hullo!' said Pippin, poking his head round the curtain. 'I thought you had forgotten all about me. I am glad to see you back. It has been a long day.'

'But the night will be too short,' said Gandalf. 'I have come back here, for I must have a little peace, alone. You should sleep, in a bed while you still may. At the sunrise I shall take you to the Lord Denethor again. No, when the summons comes, not at sunrise. The Darkness has begun. There will be no dawn.'

CHAPTER II

THE PASSING OF THE GREY COMPANY

Gandalf was gone, and the thudding hoofs of Shadowfax were lost in the night, when Merry came back to Aragorn. He had only a light bundle, for he had lost his pack at Parth Galen, and all he had was a few useful things he had picked up among the wreckage of Isengard. Hasufel was already saddled. Legolas and Gimli with their horse stood close by.

'So four of the Company still remain,' said Aragorn. 'We will ride on together. But we shall not go alone, as I thought. The king is now determined to set out at once. Since the coming of the winged shadow, he desires to return to the hills under cover of night.'

'And then whither?' said Legolas.

'I cannot say yet,' Aragorn answered. 'As for the king, he will go to the muster that he commanded at Edoras, four nights from now. And there, I think, he will hear tidings of war, and the Riders of Rohan will go down to Minas Tirith. But for myself, and any that will go with me . . .'

'I for one!' cried Legolas. 'And Gimli with him!' said the Dwarf.

'Well, for myself,' said Aragorn, 'it is dark before me. I must go down also to Minas Tirith, but I do not yet see the road. An hour long prepared approaches.'

'Don't leave me behind!' said Merry. 'I have not been of much use yet; but I don't want to be laid aside, like baggage to be called for when all is over. I don't think the Riders will want to be bothered with me now. Though, of course, the king did say that I was to sit by him when he came to his house and tell him all about the Shire.'

'Yes,' said Aragorn, 'and your road lies with him, I think, Merry. But do not look for mirth at the ending. It will be long, I fear, ere Théoden sits at ease again in Meduseld. Many hopes will wither in this bitter Spring.'

Soon all were ready to depart: twenty-four horses, with Gimli behind Legolas, and Merry in front of Aragorn. Presently they were riding swiftly through the night. They had not long passed the mounds at the Fords of Isen, when a Rider galloped up from the rear of their line.

'My lord,' he said to the king, 'there are horsemen behind us. As we crossed the fords I thought that I heard them. Now we are sure. They are overtaking us, riding hard.'

Théoden at once called a halt. The Riders turned about and seized their spears. Aragorn dismounted and set Merry on the ground, and drawing his sword he stood by the king's stirrup. Éomer and his esquire rode back to the rear. Merry felt more like unneeded baggage than ever, and he wondered, if there was a fight, what he should do. Supposing the king's small escort was trapped and overcome, but he escaped into the darkness – alone in the wild fields of Rohan with no idea of where he was in all the endless miles? 'No good!' he thought. He drew his sword and tightened his belt.

The sinking moon was obscured by a great sailing cloud, but suddenly it rode out clear again. Then they all heard the sound of hoofs, and at the same moment they saw dark shapes coming swiftly on the path from the fords. The moonlight glinted here and there on the points of spears. The number of the pursuers could not be told, but they seemed no fewer than the king's escort, at the least.

When they were some fifty paces off, Éomer cried in a loud voice: 'Halt! Halt! Who rides in Rohan?'

The pursuers brought their steeds to a sudden stand. A silence followed; and then in the moonlight, a horseman could be seen dismounting and walking slowly forward. His hand showed white as he held it up, palm outward, in token of peace; but the king's men gripped their weapons. At ten paces the man stopped. He was tall, a dark standing shadow. Then his clear voice rang out.

'Rohan? Rohan did you say? That is a glad word. We seek that land in haste from long afar.'

'You have found it,' said Éomer. 'When you crossed the fords yonder you entered it. But it is the realm of Théoden the King. None ride here save by his leave. Who are you? And what is your haste?'

'Halbarad Dúnadan, Ranger of the North I am,' cried the man. 'We seek one Aragorn son of Arathorn, and we heard that he was in Rohan.'

'And you have found him also!' cried Aragorn. Giving his reins to Merry, he ran forward and embraced the newcomer. 'Halbarad!' he said. 'Of all joys this is the least expected!'

Merry breathed a sigh of relief. He had thought that this was some last trick of Saruman's, to waylay the king while he had only a few men about him; but it seemed that there would be no need to die in Théoden's defence, not yet at any rate. He sheathed his sword.

'All is well,' said Aragorn, turning back. 'Here are some of my own kin from the far land where I dwelt. But why they come, and how many they be, Halbarad shall tell us.'

'I have thirty with me,' said Halbarad. 'That is all of our kindred that could be gathered in haste; but the brethren Elladan and Elrohir have ridden with us, desiring to go to the war. We rode as swiftly as we might when your summons came.'

'But I did not summon you,' said Aragorn, 'save only in wish. My thoughts have often turned to you, and seldom more than tonight; yet I have sent no word. But come! All such matters must wait. You find us riding in haste and danger. Ride with us now, if the king will give his leave.'

Théoden was indeed glad of the news. 'It is well!' he said. 'If these kinsmen be in any way like to yourself, my lord Aragorn, thirty such knights will be a strength that cannot be counted by heads.'

Then the Riders set out again, and Aragorn for a while rode with the Dúnedain; and when they had spoken of tidings in the North and in the South, Elrohir said to him:

'I bring word to you from my father: *The days are short. If thou art in haste, remember the Paths of the Dead.*'

'Always my days have seemed to me too short to achieve my desire,' answered Aragorn. 'But great indeed will be my haste ere I take that road.'

'That will soon be seen,' said Elrohir. 'But let us speak no more of these things upon the open road!'

And Aragorn said to Halbarad: 'What is that that you bear, kinsman?' For he saw that instead of a spear he bore a tall staff, as it were a standard, but it was close-furled in a black cloth bound about with many thongs.

'It is a gift that I bring you from the Lady of Rivendell,' answered Halbarad. 'She wrought it in secret, and long was the making. But she also sends word to you: *The days now are short. Either our hope cometh, or all hopes end. Therefore I send thee what I have made for thee. Fare well, Elfstone!*'

And Aragorn said: 'Now I know what you bear. Bear it still for me a while!' And he turned and looked away to the North under the great stars, and then he fell silent and spoke no more while the night's journey lasted.

The night was old and the East grey when they rode up at last from Deeping-coomb and came back to the Hornburg. There they were to lie and rest for a brief while and take counsel.

Merry slept until he was roused by Legolas and Gimli. 'The Sun is high,' said Legolas. 'All others are up and doing. Come, Master Sluggard, and look at this place while you may!'

'There was a battle here three nights ago,' said Gimli, 'and here Legolas and I played a game that I won only by a single orc. Come and see how it was! And there are caves, Merry, caves of wonder! Shall we visit them, Legolas, do you think?'

'Nay! There is no time,' said the Elf. 'Do not spoil the wonder with haste! I have given you my word to return hither with you, if a day of peace and freedom comes again. But it is now near to noon, and at that hour we eat, and then set out again, I hear.'

Merry got up and yawned. His few hours' sleep had not been nearly enough; he was tired and rather dismal. He missed Pippin, and felt that he was only a burden, while everybody was making plans for speed in a business that he did not fully understand. 'Where is Aragorn?' he asked.

'In a high chamber of the Burg,' said Legolas. 'He has neither rested nor slept, I think. He went thither some hours ago, saying that he must take thought, and only his kinsman, Halbarad, went with him; but some dark doubt or care sits on him.'

'They are a strange company, these newcomers,' said Gimli. 'Stout men and lordly they are, and the Riders of Rohan look almost as boys beside them; for they are grim men of face, worn like weathered rocks for the most part, even as Aragorn himself; and they are silent.'

'But even as Aragorn they are courteous, if they break their silence,' said Legolas. 'And have you marked the brethren Elladan and Elrohir? Less sombre is their gear than the others', and they are fair and gallant as Elven-lords; and that is not to be wondered at in the sons of Elrond of Rivendell.'

'Why have they come? Have you heard?' asked Merry. He had now dressed, and he flung his grey cloak about his shoulders; and the three passed out together towards the ruined gate of the Burg.

'They answered a summons, as you heard,' said Gimli. 'Word came to Rivendell, they say: *Aragorn has need of his kindred. Let the Dúnedain ride to him in Rohan!* But whence this message came they are now in doubt. Gandalf sent it, I would guess.'

'Nay, Galadriel,' said Legolas. 'Did she not speak through Gandalf of the ride of the Grey Company from the North?'

'Yes, you have it,' said Gimli. 'The Lady of the Wood! She read many hearts and desires. Now why did not we wish for some of our own kinsfolk, Legolas?'

Legolas stood before the gate and turned his bright eyes away north and east, and his fair face was troubled. 'I do not think that any would come,' he answered. 'They have no need to ride to war; war already marches on their own lands.'

For a while the three companions walked together, speaking of this and that turn of the battle, and they went down from the broken gate, and passed the mounds of the fallen on the greensward beside the road, until they stood on Helm's Dike and looked into the Coomb. The Death Down already stood there, black and tall and stony, and the great trampling and scoring of the grass by the Huorns could be plainly seen. The Dunlendings and many men of the garrison of the Burg were at work on the Dike or in the fields and about the battered walls behind; yet all seemed strangely quiet: a weary valley resting after a great storm. Soon they turned back and went to the midday meal in the hall of the Burg.

The king was already there, and as soon as they entered he called for Merry and had a seat set for him at his side. 'It is not as I would have it,' said Théoden; 'for this is little like my fair house in Edoras. And your friend is gone, who should also be here. But it may be long ere we sit, you and I, at the high table in Meduseld; there will be no time for feasting when I return thither. But come now! Eat and drink, and let us speak together while we may. And then you shall ride with me.'

'May I?' said Merry, surprised and delighted. 'That would be splendid!' He had never felt more grateful for any kindness in words. 'I am afraid I am only in everybody's way,' he stammered; 'but I should like to do anything I could, you know.'

'I doubt it not,' said the king. 'I have had a good hill-pony made ready for you. He will bear you as swift as any horse by the roads that we shall take. For I will ride from the Burg by mountain paths, not by the plain, and so come to Edoras by way of Dunharrow where the Lady Éowyn awaits me. You shall be my esquire, if you will. Is there gear of war in this place, Éomer, that my sword-thain could use?'

'There are no great weapon-hoards here, lord,' answered Éomer. 'Maybe a light helm might be found to fit him; but we have no mail or sword for one of his stature.'

'I have a sword,' said Merry, climbing from his seat, and drawing from its black sheath his small bright blade. Filled suddenly with love for this old man, he knelt on one knee, and took his hand and kissed it. 'May I lay the sword of Meriadoc of the Shire on your lap, Théoden King?' he cried. 'Receive my service, if you will!'

'Gladly will I take it,' said the king; and laying his long old hands upon the brown hair of the hobbit, he blessed him. 'Rise now, Meriadoc, esquire of Rohan of the household of Meduseld!' he said. 'Take your sword and bear it unto good fortune!'

'As a father you shall be to me,' said Merry.

'For a little while,' said Théoden.

They talked then together as they ate, until presently Éomer spoke. 'It is near the hour that we set for our going, lord,' he said. 'Shall I bid men sound the horns? But where is Aragorn? His place is empty and he has not eaten.'

'We will make ready to ride,' said Théoden; 'but let word be sent to the Lord Aragorn that the hour is nigh.'

The king with his guard and Merry at his side passed down from the gate of the Burg to where the Riders were assembling on the green. Many were already mounted. It would be a great company; for the king was leaving only a small garrison in the Burg, and all who could be spared were riding to the weapontake at Edoras. A thousand spears had indeed already ridden away at night; but still there would be some five hundred more to go with the king, for the most part men from the fields and dales of Westfold.

A little apart the Rangers sat, silent, in an ordered company, armed with spear and bow and sword. They were clad in cloaks of dark grey, and their hoods were cast now over helm and head. Their horses were strong and of proud bearing, but rough-haired; and one stood there without a rider, Aragorn's own horse that they had brought from the North; Roheryn was his name. There was no gleam of stone or gold, nor any fair thing in all their gear and harness; nor did their riders bear any badge or token, save only that each cloak was pinned upon the left shoulder by a brooch of silver shaped like a rayed star.

The king mounted his horse, Snowmane, and Merry sat beside him on his pony: Stybba was his name. Presently Éomer came out from the gate, and with him was Aragorn, and Halbarad bearing the great staff close-furled in black, and two tall men, neither young nor old. So much alike were they, the sons of Elrond, that few could tell them apart: dark-haired, grey-eyed, and their faces elven-fair, clad alike in bright mail beneath cloaks of silver-grey. Behind them walked Legolas and Gimli. But Merry had eyes only for Aragorn, so startling was the change that he saw in him, as if in one night many years had fallen on his head. Grim was his face, grey-hued and weary.

'I am troubled in mind, lord,' he said, standing by the king's horse. 'I have heard strange words, and I see new perils far off. I have laboured long in thought, and now I fear that I must change my purpose. Tell me, Théoden, you ride now to Dunharrow, how long will it be ere you come there?'

'It is now a full hour past noon,' said Éomer. 'Before the night of the third day from now we should come to the Hold. The Moon will then be one night past his full, and the muster that the king commanded will be held the day after. More speed we cannot make, if the strength of Rohan is to be gathered.'

Aragorn was silent for a moment. 'Three days,' he murmured, 'and the muster of Rohan will only be begun. But I see that it cannot now be hastened.' He looked up, and it seemed that he had made some decision; his face was less troubled. 'Then, by your leave, lord, I must take new counsel for myself and my kindred. We must ride our own road, and no longer in secret. For me the time of stealth has passed. I will ride east by the swiftest way, and I will take the Paths of the Dead.'

'The Paths of the Dead!' said Théoden, and trembled. 'Why do you speak of them?' Éomer turned and gazed at Aragorn, and it seemed to Merry that the faces of the Riders that sat within hearing turned pale at the words. 'If there be in truth such paths,' said Théoden, 'their gate is in Dunharrow; but no living man may pass it.'

'Alas! Aragorn my friend!' said Éomer. 'I had hoped that we should ride to war together; but if you seek the Paths of the Dead, then our parting is come, and it is little likely that we shall ever meet again under the Sun.'

'That road I will take, nonetheless,' said Aragorn. 'But I say to you, Éomer, that in battle we may yet meet again, though all the hosts of Mordor should stand between.'

'You will do as you will, my lord Aragorn,' said Théoden. 'It is your doom, maybe, to tread strange paths that others dare not. This parting grieves me, and my strength is lessened by it; but now I must take the mountain-roads and delay no longer. Farewell!'

'Farewell, lord!' said Aragorn. 'Ride unto great renown! Farewell, Merry! I leave you in good hands, better than we hoped when we hunted the orcs to Fangorn. Legolas and Gimli will still hunt with me, I hope; but we shall not forget you.'

'Good-bye!' said Merry. He could find no more to say. He felt very small, and he was puzzled and depressed by all these gloomy words. More than ever he missed the unquenchable cheerfulness of Pippin. The Riders were ready, and their horses were fidgeting; he wished they would start and get it over.

Now Théoden spoke to Éomer, and he lifted up his hand and cried aloud, and with that word the Riders set forth. They rode over the Dike and down the Coomb, and then, turning swiftly eastwards, they took a path that skirted the foothills for a mile or so, until bending south it passed back among the hills and disappeared from view. Aragorn rode to the Dike and watched till the king's men were far down the Coomb. Then he turned to Halbarad.

'There go three that I love, and the smallest not the least,' he said. 'He knows not to what end he rides; yet if he knew, he still would go on.'

'A little people, but of great worth are the Shire-folk,' said Halbarad. 'Little do they know of our long labour for the safekeeping of their borders, and yet I grudge it not.'

'And now our fates are woven together,' said Aragorn. 'And yet, alas! here we must part. Well, I must eat a little, and then we also must hasten away. Come, Legolas and Gimli! I must speak with you as I eat.'

Together they went back into the Burg; yet for some time Aragorn sat silent at the table in the hall, and the others waited for him to speak. 'Come!' said Legolas at last. 'Speak and be comforted, and shake off the shadow! What has happened since we came back to this grim place in the grey morning?'

'A struggle somewhat grimmer for my part than the battle of the Hornburg,' answered Aragorn. 'I have looked in the Stone of Orthanc, my friends.'

'You have looked in that accursed stone of wizardry!' exclaimed Gimli with fear and astonishment in his face. 'Did you say aught to – him? Even Gandalf feared that encounter.'

'You forget to whom you speak,' said Aragorn sternly, and his eyes glinted. 'What do you fear that I should say to him? Did I not openly proclaim my title before the doors of Edoras? Nay, Gimli,' he said in a softer voice, and the grimness left his face, and he looked like one who has laboured in sleepless pain for many nights. 'Nay, my friends, I am the lawful master of the Stone, and I had both the right and the strength to use it, or so I judged. The right cannot be doubted. The strength was enough – barely.'

He drew a deep breath. 'It was a bitter struggle, and the weariness is slow to pass. I spoke no word to him, and in the end I wrenched the Stone to my own will. That alone he will find hard to endure. And he beheld me. Yes, Master Gimli, he saw me, but in other guise than you see me here. If that will aid him, then I have done ill. But I do not think so. To know that I lived and walked the earth was a blow to his heart, I deem; for he knew it not till now. The eyes in Orthanc did not see through the armour of Théoden; but Sauron has not forgotten Isildur and the sword of Elendil. Now in the very hour of his great designs the heir of Isildur and the Sword are revealed; for I showed the blade re-forged to him. He is not so mighty yet that he is above fear; nay, doubt ever gnaws him.'

'But he wields great dominion, nonetheless,' said Gimli; 'and now he will strike more swiftly.'

'The hasty stroke goes oft astray,' said Aragorn. 'We must press our Enemy, and no longer wait upon him for the move. See my friends, when I had mastered the Stone, I learned many things. A grave peril I saw coming unlooked-for upon Gondor from the South that will draw off great strength from the defence of Minas Tirith. If it is not countered swiftly, I deem that the City will be lost ere ten days be gone.'

'Then lost it must be,' said Gimli. 'For what help is there to send thither, and how could it come there in time?'

'I have no help to send, therefore I must go myself,' said Aragorn. 'But there is only one way through the mountains that will bring me to the coastlands before all is lost. That is the Paths of the Dead.'

'The Paths of the Dead!' said Gimli. 'It is a fell name; and little to the liking to the Men of Rohan, as I saw. Can the living use such a road and not perish? And even if you pass that way, what will so few avail to counter the strokes of Mordor?'

'The living have never used that road since the coming of the Rohirrim,' said Aragorn, 'for it is closed to them. But in this dark hour the heir of Isildur may use it, if he dare. Listen! This is the word that the sons of Elrond bring to me from their father in Rivendell, wisest in lore: *Bid Aragorn remember the words of the seer, and the Paths of the Dead.*'

'And what may be the words of the seer?' said Legolas.

'Thus spoke Malbeth the Seer, in the days of Arvedui, last king at Fornost,' said Aragorn:

Over the land there lies a long shadow,
westward reaching wings of darkness.
The Tower trembles; to the tombs of kings
doom approaches. The Dead awaken;
for the hour is come for the oathbreakers:
at the Stone of Erech they shall stand again
and hear there a horn in the hills ringing.
Whose shall the horn be? Who shall call them
from the grey twilight, the forgotten people?
The heir of him to whom the oath they swore.
From the North shall he come, need shall drive him:
he shall pass the Door to the Paths of the Dead.

'Dark ways, doubtless,' said Gimli, 'but no darker than these staves are to me.'

'If you would understand them better, then I bid you come with me,' said Aragorn; 'for that way I now shall take. But I do not go gladly; only need drives me. Therefore, only of your free will would I have you come, for you will find both toil and great fear, and maybe worse.'

'I will go with you even on the Paths of the Dead, and to whatever end they may lead,' said Gimli.

'I also will come,' said Legolas, 'for I do not fear the Dead.'

'I hope that the forgotten people will not have forgotten how to fight,' said Gimli; 'for otherwise I see not why we should trouble them.'

'That we shall know if ever we come to Erech,' said Aragorn. 'But the oath that they broke was to fight against Sauron, and they must fight therefore, if they are to fulfil it. For at Erech there stands yet a black stone that was brought, it was said, from Númenor by Isildur; and it was set upon a hill, and upon it the King of the Mountains swore allegiance to him in the beginning of the realm of Gondor. But when Sauron returned and grew in might again, Isildur summoned the Men of the Mountains to fulfil their oath, and they would not: for they had worshipped Sauron in the Dark Years.

'Then Isildur said to their king: "Thou shalt be the last king. And if the West prove mightier than thy Black Master, this curse I lay upon thee and thy folk: to rest never until your oath is fulfilled. For this war will last through years uncounted, and you shall be summoned once again ere the end." And they fled before the wrath of Isildur, and did not dare to go forth to war on Sauron's part; and they hid themselves in secret places in the mountains and had no dealings with other men, but slowly dwindled in the barren hills. And the terror of the Sleepless Dead lies about the Hill of Erech and all places where that people lingered. But that way I must go, since there are none living to help me.'

He stood up. 'Come!' he cried, and drew his sword, and it flashed in the twilit hall of the Burg. 'To the Stone of Erech! I seek the Paths of the Dead. Come with me who will!'

Legolas and Gimli made no answer, but they rose and followed Aragorn from the hall. On the green there waited, still and silent, the hooded Rangers. Legolas and Gimli mounted. Aragorn sprang upon Roheryn. Then Halbarad lifted a great horn, and the blast of it echoed in Helm's Deep: and with that they leapt away, riding down the Coomb like thunder, while all the men that were left on Dike or Burg stared in amaze.

And while Théoden went by slow paths in the hills, the Grey Company passed swiftly over the plain, and on the next day in the afternoon they came to Edoras; and there they halted only briefly, ere they passed up the valley, and so came to Dunharrow as darkness fell.

The Lady Éowyn greeted them and was glad of their coming; for no mightier men had she seen than the Dúnedain and the fair sons of Elrond; but on Aragorn most of all her eyes rested. And when they sat at supper with her, they talked together, and she heard of all that had passed since Théoden rode away, concerning which only hasty tidings had yet reached her; and when she heard of the battle in Helm's Deep and the great slaughter of their foes, and of the charge of Théoden and his knights, then her eyes shone.

But at last she said: 'Lords, you are weary and shall now go to your beds with such ease as can be contrived in haste. But tomorrow fairer housing shall be found for you.'

But Aragorn said: 'Nay, lady, be not troubled for us! If we may lie here tonight and break our fast tomorrow, it will be enough. For I ride on an errand most urgent, and with the first light of morning we must go.'

She smiled on him and said: 'Then it was kindly done, lord, to ride so many miles out of your way to bring tidings to Éowyn, and to speak with her in her exile.'

'Indeed no man would count such a journey wasted,' said Aragorn; 'and yet, lady, I could not have come hither, if it were not that the road which I must take leads me to Dunharrow.'

And she answered as one that likes not what is said: 'Then, lord, you are astray; for out of Harrowdale no road runs east or south; and you had best return as you came.'

'Nay, lady,' said he, 'I am not astray; for I walked in this land ere you were born to grace it. There is a road out of this valley, and that road I shall take. Tomorrow I shall ride by the Paths of the Dead.'

Then she stared at him as one that is stricken, and her face blanched, and for long she spoke no more, while all sat silent. 'But, Aragorn,' she said at last, 'is it then your errand to seek death? For that is all that you will find on that road. They do not suffer the living to pass.'

'They may suffer me to pass,' said Aragorn; 'but at the least I will adventure it. No other road will serve.'

'But this is madness,' she said. 'For here are men of renown and prowess, whom you should not take into the shadows, but should lead to war, where men are needed. I beg you to remain and ride with my brother; for then all our hearts will be gladdened, and our hope be the brighter.'

'It is not madness, lady,' he answered; 'for I go on a path appointed. But those who follow me do so of their free will; and if they wish now to remain and ride with the Rohirrim, they may do so. But I shall take the Paths of the Dead, alone, if needs be.'

Then they said no more, and they ate in silence; but her eyes were ever upon Aragorn, and the others saw that she was in great torment of mind. At length they arose, and took their leave of the Lady, and thanked her for her care, and went to their rest.

But as Aragorn came to the booth where he was to lodge with Legolas and Gimli, and his companions had gone in, there came the Lady Éowyn after him and called to him. He turned and saw her as a glimmer in the night, for she was clad in white; but her eyes were on fire.

'Aragorn,' she said, 'why will you go on this deadly road?'

'Because I must,' he said. 'Only so can I see any hope of doing my part in the war against Sauron. I do not choose paths of peril, Éowyn. Were I to go where my heart dwells, far in the North I would now be wandering in the fair valley of Rivendell.'

For a while she was silent, as if pondering what this might mean. Then suddenly she laid her hand on his arm. 'You are a stern lord and resolute,' she said; 'and thus do men win renown.' She paused. 'Lord,' she said, 'if you must go, then let me ride in your following. For I am weary of skulking in the hills, and wish to face peril and battle.'

'Your duty is with your people,' he answered.

'Too often have I heard of duty,' she cried. 'But am I not of the House of Eorl, a shieldmaiden and not a dry-nurse? I have waited on faltering feet long enough. Since they falter no longer, it seems, may I not now spend my life as I will?'

'Few may do that with honour,' he answered. 'But as for you, lady: did you not accept the charge to govern the people until their lord's return? If you had not been chosen, then some marshal or captain would have been set in the same place, and he could not ride away from his charge, were he weary of it or no.'

'Shall I always be chosen?' she said bitterly. 'Shall I always be left behind when the Riders depart, to mind the house while they win renown, and find food and beds when they return?'

'A time may come soon,' said he, 'when none will return. Then there will be need of valour without renown, for none shall remember the deeds that are done in the last defence of your homes. Yet the deeds will not be less valiant because they are unpraised.'

And she answered: 'All your words are but to say: you are a woman, and your part is in the house. But when the men have died in battle and honour, you have leave to be burned in the house, for the men will need it no more. But I am of the House of Eorl and not a serving-woman. I can ride and wield blade, and I do not fear either pain or death.'

'What do you fear, lady?' he asked.

'A cage,' she said. 'To stay behind bars, until use and old age accept them, and all chance of doing great deeds is gone beyond recall or desire.'

'And yet you counselled me not to adventure on the road that I had chosen, because it is perilous?'

'So may one counsel another,' she said. 'Yet I do not bid you flee from peril, but to ride to battle where your sword may win renown and victory. I would not see a thing that is high and excellent cast away needlessly.'

'Nor would I,' he said. 'Therefore I say to you, lady: Stay! For you have no errand to the South.'

'Neither have those others who go with thee. They go only because they would not be parted from thee – because they love thee.' Then she turned and vanished into the night.

When the light of day was come into the sky but the sun was not yet risen above the high ridges in the East, Aragorn made ready to depart. His company was all mounted, and he was about to leap into the saddle, when the Lady Éowyn came to bid them farewell. She was clad as a Rider and girt with a sword. In her hand she bore a cup, and she set it to her lips and drank a little, wishing them good speed; and then she gave the cup to Aragorn, and he drank, and he said: 'Farewell, Lady of Rohan! I drink to the fortunes of your House, and of you, and of all your people. Say to your brother: beyond the shadows we may meet again!'

Then it seemed to Gimli and Legolas who were nearby that she wept, and in one so stern and proud that seemed the more grievous. But she said: 'Aragorn, wilt thou go?'

'I will,' he said.

'Then wilt thou not let me ride with this company, as I have asked?'

'I will not, lady,' he said. 'For that I could not grant without leave of the king and of your brother; and they will not return until tomorrow. But I count now every hour, indeed every minute. Farewell!'

Then she fell on her knees, saying: 'I beg thee!'

'Nay, lady,' he said, and taking her by the hand he raised her. Then he kissed her hand, and sprang into the saddle, and rode away, and did not look back; and only those who knew him well and were near to him saw the pain that he bore.

But Éowyn stood still as a figure carven in stone, her hands clenched at her sides, and she watched them until they passed into the shadows under the black Dwimorberg, the Haunted Mountain, in which was the Door of the Dead. When they were lost to view, she turned, stumbling as one that is blind, and went back to her lodging. But none of her folk saw this parting, for they hid themselves in fear and would not come forth until the day was up, and the reckless strangers were gone.

And some said: 'They are Elvish wights. Let them go where they belong, into the dark places, and never return. The times are evil enough.'

The light was still grey as they rode, for the sun had not yet climbed over the black ridges of the Haunted Mountain before them. A dread fell on them, even as they passed between the lines of ancient stones and so came to the Dimholt. There under the gloom of black trees that not even Legolas could long endure they found a hollow place opening at the mountain's root, and right in their path stood a single mighty stone like a finger of doom.

'My blood runs chill,' said Gimli, but the others were silent, and his voice fell dead on the dank fir-needles at his feet. The horses would not pass the threatening stone, until the riders dismounted and led them about. And so they came at last deep into the glen; and there stood a sheer wall of rock, and in the wall the Dark Door gaped before them like the mouth of night. Signs and figures were carved above its wide arch too dim to read, and fear flowed from it like a grey vapour.

The company halted, and there was not a heart among them that did not quail, unless it were the heart of Legolas of the Elves, for whom the ghosts of Men have no terror.

'This is an evil door,' said Halbarad, 'and my death lies beyond it. I will dare to pass it nonetheless; but no horse will enter.'

'But we must go in, and therefore the horses must go too,' said Aragorn. 'For if ever we come through this darkness, many leagues lie beyond, and every hour that is lost there will bring the triumph of Sauron nearer. Follow me!'

Then Aragorn led the way, and such was the strength of his will in that hour that all the Dúnedain and their horses followed him. And indeed the love that the horses of the Rangers bore for their riders was so great that they were willing to face even the terror of the Door, if their masters' hearts were steady as they walked beside them. But Arod, the horse of Rohan, refused the way, and he stood sweating and trembling in a fear that was grievous to see. Then Legolas laid his hands on his eyes and sang some words that went soft in the gloom, until he suffered himself to be led, and Legolas passed in. And there stood Gimli the Dwarf left all alone.

His knees shook, and he was wroth with himself. 'Here is a thing unheard of!' he said. 'An Elf will go underground and a Dwarf dare not!' With that he plunged in. But it seemed to him that he dragged his feet like lead over the threshold; and at once a blindness came upon him, even upon Gimli Glóin's son who had walked unafraid in many deep places of the world.

Aragorn had brought torches from Dunharrow, and now he went ahead bearing one aloft; and Elladan with another went at the rear, and Gimli, stumbling behind, strove to overtake him. He could see nothing but the dim flame of the torches; but if the company halted, there seemed an endless whisper of voices all about him, a murmur of words in no tongue that he had ever heard before.

Nothing assailed the company nor withstood their passage, and yet steadily fear grew on the Dwarf as he went on: most of all because he knew now that there could be no turning back; all the paths behind were thronged by an unseen host that followed in the dark.

So time unreckoned passed, until Gimli saw a sight that he was ever afterwards loth to recall. The road was wide, as far as he could judge, but now the company came suddenly into a great empty space, and there were no longer any walls upon either side. The dread was so heavy on him that he could hardly walk. Away to the left something glittered in the gloom as Aragorn's torch drew near. Then Aragorn halted and went to look what it might be.

'Does he feel no fear?' muttered the Dwarf. 'In any other cave Gimli

Glóin's son would have been the first to run to the gleam of gold. But not here! Let it lie!'

Nonetheless he drew near, and saw Aragorn kneeling, while Elladan held aloft both torches. Before him were the bones of a mighty man. He had been clad in mail, and still his harness lay there whole; for the cavern's air was as dry as dust, and his hauberk was gilded. His belt was of gold and garnets, and rich with gold was the helm upon his bony head face downward on the floor. He had fallen near the far wall of the cave, as now could be seen, and before him stood a stony door closed fast: his finger-bones were still clawing at the cracks. A notched and broken sword lay by him, as if he had hewn at the rock in his last despair.

Aragorn did not touch him, but after gazing silently for a while he rose and sighed. 'Hither shall the flowers of *simbelmynë* come never unto world's end,' he murmured. 'Nine mounds and seven there are now green with grass, and through all the long years he has lain at the door that he could not unlock. Whither does it lead? Why would he pass? None shall ever know!

'For that is not my errand!' he cried, turning back and speaking to the whispering darkness behind. 'Keep your hoards and your secrets hidden in the Accursed Years! Speed only we ask. Let us pass, and then come! I summon you to the Stone of Erech!'

There was no answer, unless it were an utter silence more dreadful than the whispers before; and then a chill blast came in which the torches flickered and went out, and could not be rekindled. Of the time that followed, one hour or many, Gimli remembered little. The others pressed on, but he was ever hindmost, pursued by a groping horror that seemed always just about to seize him; and a rumour came after him like the shadow-sound of many feet. He stumbled on until he was crawling like a beast on the ground and felt that he could endure no more: he must either find an ending and escape or run back in madness to meet the following fear.

Suddenly he heard the tinkle of water, a sound hard and clear as a stone falling into a dream of dark shadow. Light grew, and lo! the company passed through another gateway, high-arched and broad, and a rill ran out beside them; and beyond, going steeply down, was a road between sheer cliffs, knife-edged against the sky far above. So deep and narrow was that chasm that the sky was dark, and in it small stars glinted. Yet as Gimli after learned it was still two hours ere sunset of the day on which they had set out from Dunharrow; though for all that he could then tell it might have been twilight in some later year, or in some other world.

The Company now mounted again, and Gimli returned to Legolas. They rode in file, and evening came on and a deep blue dusk; and still fear pursued them. Legolas turning to speak to Gimli looked back and the Dwarf saw before his face the glitter in the Elf's bright eyes. Behind them rode Elladan, last of the Company, but not the iast of those that took the downward road.

'The Dead are following,' said Legolas. 'I see shapes of Men and of horses, and pale banners like shreds of cloud, and spears like winter-thickets on a misty night. The Dead are following.'

'Yes, the Dead ride behind. They have been summoned,' said Elladan.

The Company came at last out of the ravine, as suddenly as if they had issued from a crack in a wall; and there lay the uplands of a great vale before them, and the stream beside them went down with a cold voice over many falls.

'Where in Middle-earth are we?' said Gimli; and Elladan answered: 'We have descended from the uprising of the Morthond, the long chill river that flows at last to the sea that washes the walls of Dol Amroth. You will not need to ask hereafter how comes its name: Blackroot men call it.'

The Morthond Vale made a great bay that beat up against the sheer southern faces of the mountains. Its steep slopes were grass-grown; but all was grey in that hour, for the sun had gone, and far below lights twinkled in the homes of Men. The vale was rich and many folk dwelt there.

Then without turning Aragorn cried aloud so that all could hear: 'Friends, forget your weariness! Ride now, ride! We must come to the Stone of Erech ere this day passes, and long still is the way.' So without looking back they rode the mountain-fields, until they came to a bridge over the growing torrent and found a road that went down into the land.

Lights went out in house and hamlet as they came, and doors were shut, and folk that were afield cried in terror and ran wild like hunted deer. Ever there rose the same cry in the gathering night: 'The King of the Dead ! The King of the Dead is come upon us!'

Bells were ringing far below, and all men fled before the face of Aragorn; but the Grey Company in their haste rode like hunters, until their horses were stumbling with weariness. And thus, just ere midnight, and in a darkness as black as the caverns in the mountains, they came at last to the Hill of Erech.

Long had the terror of the Dead lain upon that hill and upon the empty fields about it. For upon the top stood a black stone, round as a great globe, the height of a man, though its half was buried in the ground. Unearthly it looked, as though it had fallen from the sky, as some believed; but those who remembered still the lore of Westernesse told that it had been brought out of the ruin of Númenor and there set by Isildur at his landing. None of the people of the valley dared to approach it, nor would they dwell near; for they said that it was a trysting-place of the Shadow-men and there they would gather in times of fear, thronging round the Stone and whispering.

To that Stone the Company came and halted in the dead of night. Then Elrohir gave to Aragorn a silver horn, and he blew upon it; and it seemed to those that stood near that they heard a sound of answering horns, as if it was an echo in deep caves far away. No other sound they heard, and yet they were aware of a great host gathered all about the hill on which they stood; and a chill wind like the breath of ghosts came down from the mountains. But Aragorn dismounted, and standing by the Stone he cried in a great voice:

'Oathbreakers, why have ye come?'

And a voice was heard out of the night that answered him, as if from far away:

'To fulfil our oath and have peace.'

Then Aragorn said: 'The hour is come at last. Now I go to Pelargir upon Anduin, and ye shall come after me. And when all this land is clean of the servants of Sauron, I will hold the oath fulfilled, and ye shall have peace and depart for ever. For I am Elessar, Isildur's heir of Gondor.'

And with that he bade Halbarad unfurl the great standard which he had brought; and behold! it was black, and if there was any device upon it, it was hidden in the darkness. Then there was silence, and not a whisper nor a sigh was heard again all the long night. The Company camped beside the Stone, but they slept little, because of the dread of the Shadows that hedged them round.

But when the dawn came, cold and pale, Aragorn rose at once, and he led the Company forth upon the journey of greatest haste and weariness that any among them had known, save he alone, and only his will held them to go on. No other mortal Men could have endured it, none but the Dúnedain of the North, and with them Gimli the Dwarf and Legolas of the Elves.

They passed Tarlang's Neck and came into Lamedon; and the Shadow Host pressed behind and fear went on before them, until they came to Calembel upon Ciril, and the sun went down like blood behind Pinnath Gelin away in the West behind them. The township and the fords of Ciril they found deserted, for many men had gone away to war, and all that were left fled to the hills at the rumour of the coming of the King of the

Dead. But the next day there came no dawn, and the Grey Company passed on into the darkness of the Storm of Mordor and were lost to mortal sight; but the Dead followed them.

CHAPTER III

THE MUSTER OF ROHAN

Now all roads were running together to the East to meet the coming of war and the onset of the Shadow. And even as Pippin stood at the Great Gate of the City and saw the Prince of Dol Amroth ride in with his banners, the King of Rohan came down out of the hills.

Day was waning. In the last rays of the sun the Riders cast long pointed shadows that went on before them. Darkness had already crept beneath the murmuring fir-woods that clothed the steep mountain-sides. The king rode now slowly at the end of the day. Presently the path turned round a huge bare shoulder of rock and plunged into the gloom of soft-sighing trees. Down, down they went in a long winding file. When at last they came to the bottom of the gorge they found that evening had fallen in the deep places. The sun was gone. Twilight lay upon the waterfalls.

All day far below them a leaping stream had run down from the high pass behind, cleaving its narrow way between pine-clad walls; and now through a stony gate it flowed out and passed into a wider vale. The Riders followed it, and suddenly Harrowdale lay before them, loud with the noise of waters in the evening. There the white Snowbourn, joined by the lesser stream, went rushing, fuming on the stones, down to Edoras and the green hills and the plains. Away to the right at the head of the great dale the mighty Starkhorn loomed up above its vast buttresses swathed in cloud; but its jagged peak, clothed in everlasting snow, gleamed far above the world, blue-shadowed upon the East, red-stained by the sunset in the West.

Merry looked out in wonder upon this strange country, of which he had heard many tales upon their long road. It was a skyless world, in which his eye, through dim gulfs of shadowy air, saw only ever-mounting slopes, great walls of stone behind great walls, and frowning precipices wreathed with mist. He sat for a moment half dreaming, listening to the noise of water, the whisper of dark trees, the crack of stone, and the vast waiting silence that brooded behind all sound. He loved mountains, or he had loved the thought of them marching on the edge of stories brought from far away; but now he was borne down by the insupportable weight of Middle-earth. He longed to shut out the immensity in a quiet room by a fire.

He was very tired, for though they had ridden slowly, they had ridden with very little rest. Hour after hour for nearly three weary days he had jogged up and down, over passes, and through long dales, and across many streams. Sometimes where the way was broader he had ridden at the king's side, not noticing that many of the Riders smiled to see the two together: the hobbit on his little shaggy grey pony, and the Lord of Rohan on his great white horse. Then he had talked to Théoden, telling him about his home and the doings of the Shire-folk, or listening in turn to tales of the Mark and its mighty men of old. But most of the time, especially on this last day, Merry had ridden by himself just behind the king, saying nothing, and trying to understand the slow sonorous speech of Rohan that he heard the men behind him using. It was a language in which there seemed to be many words that he knew, though spoken more richly and strongly than in the Shire, yet he could not piece the words together. At times some Rider would lift up his clear voice in stirring song, and Merry felt his heart leap, though he did not know what it was about.

All the same he had been lonely, and never more so than now at the day's end. He wondered where in all this strange world Pippin had got to; and what would become of Aragorn and Legolas and Gimli. Then suddenly like a cold touch on his heart he thought of Frodo and Sam. 'I am forgetting them!' he said to himself reproachfully. 'And yet they are more important than all the rest of us. And I came to help them; but now they must be hundreds of miles away, if they are still alive.' He shivered.

'Harrowdale at last!' said Éomer. 'Our journey is almost at an end.' They halted. The paths out of the narrow gorge fell steeply. Only a glimpse, as through a tall window, could be seen of the great valley in the gloaming below. A single small light could be seen twinkling by the river.

'This journey is over, maybe,' said Théoden, 'but I have far yet to go. Last night the moon was full, and in the morning I shall ride to Edoras to the gathering of the Mark.'

'But if you would take my counsel,' said Éomer in a low voice, 'you would then return hither, until the war is over, lost or won.'

Théoden smiled. 'Nay, my son, for so I will call you, speak not the soft words of Wormtongue in my old ears!' He drew himself up and looked back at the long line of his men fading into the dusk behind. 'Long years in the space of days it seems since I rode west; but never will I lean on a staff again. If the war is lost, what good will be my hiding in the hills? And if it is won, what grief will it be, even if I fall, spending my last strength? But we will leave this now. Tonight I will lie in the Hold of Dunharrow. One evening of peace at least is left us. Let us ride on!'

In the deepening dusk they came down into the valley. Here the Snowbourn flowed near to the western walls of the dale, and soon the path led them to a ford where the shallow waters murmured loudly on the stones.

The ford was guarded. As the king approached many men sprang up out of the shadow of the rocks; and when they saw the king they cried with glad voices: 'Théoden King! Théoden King! The King of the Mark returns!'

Then one blew a long call on a horn. It echoed in the valley. Other horns answered it, and lights shone out across the river.

And suddenly there rose a great chorus of trumpets from high above, sounding from some hollow place, as it seemed, that gathered their notes into one voice and sent it rolling and beating on the walls of stone.

So the King of the Mark came back victorious out of the West to Dunharrow beneath the feet of the White Mountains. There he found the remaining strength of his people already assembled; for as soon as his coming was known captains rode to meet him at the ford, bearing messages from Gandalf. Dúnhere, chieftain of the folk of Harrowdale, was at their head.

'At dawn three days ago, lord,' he said, 'Shadowfax came like a wind out of the West to Edoras, and Gandalf brought tidings of your victory to gladden our hearts. But he brought also word from you to hasten the gathering of the Riders. And then came the winged Shadow.'

'The winged Shadow?' said Théoden. 'We saw it also, but that was in the dead of night before Gandalf left us.'

'Maybe, lord,' said Dúnhere. 'Yet the same, or another like to it, a flying darkness in the shape of a monstrous bird, passed over Edoras that morning, and all men were shaken with fear. For it stooped upon Meduseld, and as it came low, almost to the gable, there came a cry that stopped our hearts. Then it was that Gandalf counselled us not to assemble in the fields, but to meet you here in the valley under the mountains. And he bade us to kindle no more lights or fires than barest need asked. So it has been done. Gandalf spoke with great authority. We trust that it is as you would wish. Naught has been seen in Harrowdale of these evil things.'

'It is well,' said Théoden. 'I will ride now to the Hold, and there before I go to rest I will meet the marshals and captains. Let them come to me as soon as may be!'

The road now led eastward straight across the valley, which was at that point little more than half a mile in width. Flats and meads of rough grass, grey now in the falling night, lay all about, but in front on the far side of the dale Merry saw a frowning wall, a last outlier of the great roots of the Starkhorn, cloven by the river in ages past.

On all the level spaces there was great concourse of men. Some thronged to the roadside, hailing the king and the riders from the West with glad cries; but stretching away into the distance behind there were ordered rows of tents and booths, and lines of picketed horses, and great store of arms, and piled spears bristling like thickets of new-planted trees. Now all the great assembly was falling into shadow, and yet, though the night-chill blew cold from the heights, no lanterns glowed, no fires were lit. Watchmen heavily cloaked paced to and fro.

Merry wondered how many Riders there were. He could not guess their number in the gathering gloom, but it looked to him like a great army, many thousands strong. While he was peering from side to side the king's party came up under the looming cliff on the eastern side of the valley; and there suddenly the path began to climb, and Merry looked up in amazement. He was on a road the like of which he had never seen before, a great work of men's hands in years beyond the reach of song. Upwards it wound, coiling like a snake, boring its way across the sheer slope of rock. Steep as a stair, it looped backwards and forwards as it climbed. Up it horses could walk, and wains could be slowly hauled; but no enemy could come that way, except out of the air, if it was defended from above. At each turn of the road there were great standing stones that had been carved in the likeness of men, huge and clumsy-limbed, squatting cross-legged with their stumpy arms folded on fat bellies. Some in the wearing of the years had lost all features save the dark holes of their eyes that still stared sadly at the passers-by. The Riders hardly glanced at them. The Púkel-men they called them, and heeded them little: no power or terror was left in them; but Merry gazed at them with wonder and a feeling almost of pity, as they loomed up mournfully in the dusk.

After a while he looked back and found that he had already climbed some hundreds of feet above the valley, but still far below he could dimly see a winding line of Riders crossing the ford and filing along the road towards the camp prepared for them. Only the king and his guard were going up into the Hold.

At last the king's company came to a sharp brink, and the climbing road passed into a cutting between walls of rock, and so went up a short slope and out on to a wide upland. The Firienfeld men called it, a green mountain-field of grass and heath, high above the deep-delved courses of the Snowbourn, laid upon the lap of the great mountains behind: the Starkhorn southwards, and northwards the saw-toothed mass of Írensaga, between which there faced the riders, the grim black wall of the Dwimorberg, the Haunted Mountain rising out of steep slopes of sombre pines. Dividing the upland into two there marched a double line of unshaped standing stones that dwindled into the dusk and vanished in the trees. Those who dared to follow that road came soon to the black Dimholt under Dwimorberg, and the menace of the pillar of stone, and the yawning shadow of the forbidden door.

Such was the dark Dunharrow, the work of long-forgotten men. Their name was lost and no song or legend remembered it. For what purpose they had made this place, as a town or secret temple or a tomb of kings, none in Rohan could say. Here they laboured in the Dark Years, before ever a ship came to the western shores, or Gondor of the Dúnedain was built; and now they had vanished, and only the old Púkel-men were left, still sitting at the turnings of the road.

Merry stared at the lines of marching stones: they were worn and black; some were leaning, some were fallen, some cracked or broken; they looked like rows of old and hungry teeth. He wondered what they could be, and he hoped that the king was not going to follow them into the darkness beyond. Then he saw that there were clusters of tents and booths on either side of the stony way; but these were not set near the trees, and seemed rather to huddle away from them towards the brink of the cliff. The greater number were on the right, where the Firienfeld was wider; and on the left there was a smaller camp, in the midst of which stood a tall pavilion. From this side a rider now came out to meet them, and they turned from the road.

As they drew near Merry saw that the rider was a woman with long braided hair gleaming in the twilight, yet she wore a helm and was clad to the waist like a warrior and girded with a sword.

'Hail, Lord of the Mark!' she cried. 'My heart is glad at your returning.'

'And you, Éowyn,' said Théoden, 'is all well with you?'

'All is well,' she answered; yet it seemed to Merry that her voice belied her, and he would have thought that she had been weeping, if that could be believed of one so stern of face. 'All is well. It was a weary road for the people to take, torn suddenly from their homes. There were hard words, for it is long since war has driven us from the green fields; but there have been no evil deeds. All is now ordered, as you see. And your lodging is prepared for you; for I have had full tidings of you and knew the hour of your coming.'

'So Aragorn has come then,' said Éomer. 'Is he still here?'

'No, he is gone,' said Éowyn turning away and looking at the mountains dark against the East and South.

'Whither did he go?' asked Éomer.

'I do not know,' she answered. 'He came at night, and rode away yestermorn, ere the Sun had climbed over the mountain-tops. He is gone.'

'You are grieved, daughter,' said Théoden. 'What has happened? Tell me, did he speak of that road?' He pointed away along the darkening lines of stones towards the Dwimorberg. 'Of the Paths of the Dead?'

'Yes, lord,' said Éowyn. 'And he has passed into the shadow from which none have returned. I could not dissuade him. He is gone.'

'Then our paths are sundered,' said Éomer. 'He is lost. We must ride without him, and our hope dwindles.'

Slowly they passed through the short heath and upland grass, speaking no more, until they came to the king's pavilion. There Merry found that everything was made ready, and that he himself was not forgotten. A little tent had been pitched for him beside the king's lodging; and there he sat alone, while men passed to and fro, going in to the king and taking counsel with him. Night came on and the half-seen heads of the mountains westward were crowned with stars, but the East was dark and blank. The marching stones faded slowly from sight, but still beyond them, blacker than the gloom, brooded the vast crouching shadow of the Dwimorberg.

'The Paths of the Dead,' he muttered to himself. 'The Paths of the Dead? What does all this mean? They have all left me now. They have all gone to some doom: Gandalf and Pippin to war in the East; and Sam and Frodo to Mordor; and Strider and Legolas and Gimli to the Paths of the Dead. But my turn will come soon enough, I suppose. I wonder what they are all talking about, and what the king means to do. For I must go where he goes now.'

In the midst of these gloomy thoughts he suddenly remembered that he was very hungry, and he got up to go and see if anyone else in this strange camp felt the same. But at that very moment a trumpet sounded, and a man came summoning him, the king's esquire, to wait at the king's board.

In the inner part of the pavilion was a small space, curtained off with broidered hangings, and strewn with skins; and there at a small table sat Théoden with Éomer and Éowyn, and Dúnhere, lord of Harrowdale. Merry stood beside the king's stool and waited on him, till presently the old man, coming out of deep thought, turned to him and smiled.

'Come, Master Meriadoc!' he said. 'You shall not stand. You shall sit beside me, as long as I remain in my own lands, and lighten my heart with tales.'

Room was made for the hobbit at the king's left hand, but no one called for any tale. There was indeed little speech, and they ate and drank for the most part in silence, until at last, plucking up courage, Merry asked the question that was tormenting him.

'Twice now, lord, I have heard of the Paths of the Dead,' he said. 'What are they? And where has Strider, I mean the Lord Aragorn, where has he gone?'

The king sighed, but no one answered, until at last Éomer spoke. 'We do not know, and our hearts are heavy,' he said. 'But as for the Paths of the Dead, you have yourself walked on their first steps. Nay, I speak no words of ill omen! The road that we have climbed is the approach to the Door, yonder in the Dimholt. But what lies beyond no man knows.'

'No man knows,' said Théoden: 'yet ancient legend, now seldom spoken, has somewhat to report. If these old tales speak true that have come down from father to son in the House of Eorl, then the Door under Dwimorberg leads to a secret way that goes beneath the mountain to some forgotten end. But none have ever ventured in to search its secrets, since Baldor, son of Brego, passed the Door and was never seen among men again. A rash vow he spoke, as he drained the horn at that feast which Brego made to hallow new-built Meduseld, and he came never to the high seat of which he was the heir.

'Folk say that Dead Men out of the Dark Years guard the way and will suffer no living man to come to their hidden halls; but at whiles they may themselves be seen passing out of the door like shadows and down the stony road. Then the people of Harrowdale shut fast their doors and shroud their windows and are afraid. But the Dead come seldom forth and only at times of great unquiet and coming death.'

'Yet it is said in Harrowdale,' said Éowyn in a low voice, 'that in the moonless nights but little while ago a great host in strange array passed by. Whence they came none knew, but they went up the stony road and vanished into the hill, as if they went to keep a tryst.'

'Then why has Aragorn gone that way?' asked Merry. 'Don't you know anything that would explain it?'

'Unless he has spoken words to you as his friend that we have not heard,' said Éomer, 'none now in the land of the living can tell his purpose.'

'Greatly changed he seemed to me since I saw him first in the king's house,' said Éowyn: 'grimmer, older. Fey I thought him, and like one whom the Dead call.'

'Maybe he was called,' said Théoden; 'and my heart tells me that I shall not see him again. Yet he is a kingly man of high destiny. And take comfort in this, daughter, since comfort you seem to need in your grief for this guest. It is said that when the Eorlingas came out of the North and passed at length up the Snowbourn, seeking strong places of refuge in time of need, Brego and his son Baldor climbed the Stair of the Hold and so came before the Door. On the threshold sat an old man, aged beyond guess of years; tall and kingly he had been, but now he was withered as an old stone. Indeed for stone they took him, for he moved not, and he said no word, until they sought to pass him by and enter. And then a voice came out of him, as it were out of the ground, and to their amaze it spoke in the western tongue: *The way is shut.*

'Then they halted and looked at him and saw that he lived still; but he did not look at them. *The way is shut*, his voice said again. *It was made by those who are Dead, and the Dead keep it, until the time comes. The way is shut.*

'*And when will that time be?*' said Baldor. But no answer did he ever get. For the old man died in that hour and fell upon his face; and no other tidings of the ancient dwellers in the mountains have our folk ever learned. Yet maybe at last the time foretold has come, and Aragorn may pass.'

'But how shall a man discover whether that time be come or no, save by daring the Door?' said Éomer. 'And that way I would not go though all the hosts of Mordor stood before me, and I were alone and had no other refuge. Alas that a fey mood should fall on a man so greathearted in this hour of need! Are there not evil things enough abroad without seeking them under the earth? War is at hand.'

He paused, for at that moment there was a noise outside, a man's voice crying the name of Théoden, and the challenge of the guard.

Presently the captain of the Guard thrust aside the curtain. 'A man is here, lord,' he said, 'an errand-rider of Gondor. He wishes to come before you at once.'

'Let him come!' said Théoden.

A tall man entered, and Merry choked back a cry; for a moment it seemed to him that Boromir was alive again and had returned. Then he saw that it was not so; the man was a stranger, though as like to Boromir as if he were one of his kin, tall and grey-eyed and proud. He was clad as a rider with a cloak of dark green over a coat of fine mail; on the front of his helm was wrought a small silver star. In his hand he bore a single arrow, black-feathered and barbed with steel, but the point was painted red.

He sank on one knee and presented the arrow to Théoden. 'Hail, Lord of the Rohirrim, friend of Gondor!' he said. 'Hirgon I am, errand-rider of Denethor, who bring you this token of war. Gondor is in great need. Often the Rohirrim have aided us, but now the Lord Denethor asks for all your strength and all your speed, lest Gondor fall at last.'

'The Red Arrow!' said Théoden, holding it, as one who receives a summons long expected and yet dreadful when it comes. His hand trembled. 'The Red Arrow has not been seen in the Mark in all my years! Has it indeed come to that? And what does the Lord Denethor reckon that all my strength and all my speed may be?'

'That is best known to yourself, lord,' said Hirgon. 'But ere long it may well come to pass that Minas Tirith is surrounded, and unless you have the strength to break a siege of many powers, the Lord Denethor bids me say that he judges that the strong arms of the Rohirrim would be better within his walls than without.'

'But he knows that we are a people who fight rather upon horseback and in the open, and that we are also a scattered people and time is needed for the gathering of our Riders. Is it not true, Hirgon, that the Lord of Minas Tirith knows more than he sets in his message? For we are already at war, as you may have seen, and you do not find us all unprepared. Gandalf the Grey has been among us, and even now we are mustering for battle in the East.'

'What the Lord Denethor may know or guess of all these things I cannot say,' answered Hirgon. 'But indeed our case is desperate. My lord does not issue any command to you, he begs you only to remember old friendship and oaths long spoken, and for your own good to do all that you may. It is reported to us that many kings have ridden in from the East to the service of Mordor. From the North to the field of Dagorlad there is skirmish and rumour of war. In the South the Haradrim are moving, and fear has fallen on all our coastlands, so that little help will come to us thence. Make haste! For it is before the walls of Minas Tirith that the doom of our time will be decided, and if the tide be not stemmed there, then it will flow over all the fair fields of Rohan, and even in this Hold among the hills there shall be no refuge.'

'Dark tidings,' said Théoden, 'yet not all unguessed. But say to Denethor that even if Rohan itself felt no peril, still we would come to his aid. But we have suffered much loss in our battles with Saruman the traitor, and we must still think of our frontier to the north and east, as his own tidings make clear. So great a power as the Dark Lord seems now to wield might well contain us in battle before the City and yet strike with great force across the River away beyond the Gate of Kings.

'But we will speak no longer counsels of prudence. We will come. The weapontake was set for the morrow. When all is ordered we will set out. Ten thousand spears I might have sent riding over the plain to the dismay of your foes. It will be less now, I fear; for I will not leave my strongholds all unguarded. Yet six thousands at the least shall ride behind me. For say to Denethor that in this hour the King of the Mark himself will come down to the land of Gondor, though maybe he will not ride back. But it is a long road, and man and beast must reach the end with strength to fight. A week it may be from tomorrow's morn ere you hear the cry of the Sons of Eorl coming from the North.'

'A week!' said Hirgon. 'If it must be so, it must. But you are like to find only ruined walls in seven days from now, unless other help unlooked-for comes. Still, you may at the least disturb the Orcs and Swarthy Men from their feasting in the White Tower.'

'At the least we will do that,' said Théoden. 'But I myself am new-come from battle and long journey, and I will now go to rest. Tarry here this night. Then you shall look on the muster of Rohan and ride away the gladder for the sight, and the swifter for the rest. In the morning counsels are best, and night changes many thoughts.'

With that the king stood up, and they all rose. 'Go now each to your rest,' he said, 'and sleep well. And you, Master Meriadoc, I need no more tonight. But be ready to my call as soon as the Sun is risen.'

'I will be ready,' said Merry, 'even if you bid me ride with you on the Paths of the Dead.'

'Speak not words of omen!' said the king. 'For there may be more roads than one that could bear that name. But I did not say that I would bid you ride with me on any road. Good night!'

'I won't be left behind, to be called for on return!' said Merry. 'I won't be left, I won't.' And repeating this over and over again to himself he fell asleep at last in his tent.

He was wakened by a man shaking him. 'Wake up, wake up, Master Holbytla!' he cried; and at length Merry came out of deep dreams and sat up with a start. It still seemed very dark, he thought.

'What is the matter?' he asked.

'The king calls for you.'

'But the Sun has not risen, yet,' said Merry.

'No, and will not rise today, Master Holbytla. Nor ever again, one would think under this cloud. But time does not stand still, though the Sun be lost. Make haste!'

Flinging on some clothes, Merry looked outside. The world was darkling. The very air seemed brown, and all things about were black and grey and shadowless; there was a great stillness. No shape of cloud could be seen, unless it were far away westward, where the furthest groping fingers of the great gloom still crawled onwards and a little light leaked through them. Overhead there hung a heavy roof, sombre and featureless, and light seemed rather to be failing than growing.

Merry saw many folk standing, looking up and muttering; all their faces were grey and sad, and some were afraid. With a sinking heart he made his way to the king. Hirgon the rider of Gondor was there before him, and beside him stood now another man, like him and dressed alike, but shorter and broader. As Merry entered he was speaking to the king.

'It comes from Mordor, lord,' he said. 'It began last night at sunset. From the hills in the Eastfold of your realm I saw it rise and creep across the sky, and all night as I rode it came behind eating up the stars. Now the great cloud hangs over all the land between here and the Mountains of Shadow; and it is deepening. War has already begun.'

For a while the king sat silent. At last he spoke. 'So we come to it in the end,' he said: 'the great battle of our time, in which many things shall pass away. But at least there is no longer need for hiding. We will ride the straight way and the open road and with all our speed. The muster shall begin at once, and wait for none that tarry. Have you good store in Minas Tirith? For if we must ride now in all haste, then we must ride light, with but meal and water enough to last us into battle.'

'We have very great store long prepared,' answered Hirgon. 'Ride now as light and as swift as you may!'

'Then call the heralds, Éomer,' said Théoden. 'Let the Riders be marshalled!'

Éomer went out, and presently the trumpets rang in the Hold and were answered by many others from below; but their voices no longer sounded clear and brave as they had seemed to Merry the night before. Dull they seemed and harsh in the heavy air, braying ominously.

The king turned to Merry. 'I am going to war, Master Meriadoc,' he said. 'In a little while I shall take the road. I release you from my service, but not from my friendship. You shall abide here, and if you will, you shall serve the Lady Éowyn, who will govern the folk in my stead.'

'But, but, lord,' Merry stammered, 'I offered you my sword. I do not want to be parted from you like this, Théoden King. And as all my friends have gone to the battle, I should be ashamed to stay behind.'

'But we ride on horses tall and swift,' said Théoden; 'and great though your heart be, you cannot ride on such beasts.'

'Then tie me on to the back of one, or let me hang on a stirrup, or something,' said Merry. 'It is a long way to run; but run I shall, if I cannot ride, even if I wear my feet off and arrive weeks too late.'

Théoden smiled. 'Rather than that I would bear you with me on Snowmane,' he said. 'But at the least you shall ride with me to Edoras and look on Meduseld; for that way I shall go. So far Stybba can bear you: the great race will not begin till we reach the plains.'

Then Éowyn rose up. 'Come now, Meriadoc!' she said. 'I will show you the gear that I have prepared for you.' They went out together. 'This request only did Aragorn make to me,' said Éowyn, as they passed among the tents, 'that you should be armed for battle. I have granted it, as I could. For my heart tells me that you will need such gear ere the end.'

Now she led Merry to a booth among the lodges of the king's guard; and there an armourer brought out to her a small helm, and a round shield, and other gear.

'No mail have we to fit you,' said Éowyn, 'nor any time for the forging of such a hauberk; but here is also a stout jerkin of leather, a belt, and a knife. A sword you have.'

Merry bowed, and the lady showed him the shield, which was like the shield that had been given to Gimli, and it bore on it the device of the white horse. 'Take all these things,' she said, 'and bear them to good fortune! Farewell now, Master Meriadoc! Yet maybe we shall meet again, you and I.'

So it was that amid a gathering gloom the King of the Mark made ready to lead all his Riders on the eastward road. Hearts were heavy and many quailed in the shadow. But they were a stern people, loyal to their lord, and little weeping or murmuring was heard, even in the camp in the Hold where the exiles from Edoras were housed, women and children and old men. Doom hung over them, but they faced it silently.

Two swift hours passed, and now the king sat upon his white horse, glimmering in the half-light. Proud and tall he seemed, though the hair that flowed beneath his high helm was like snow; and many marvelled at him and took heart to see him unbent and unafraid.

There on the wide flats beside the noisy river were marshalled in many companies well nigh five and fifty hundreds of Riders fully armed, and many hundreds of other men with spare horses lightly burdened. A single trumpet sounded. The king raised his hand, and then silently the host of the Mark began to move. Foremost went twelve of the king's household-men, Riders of renown. Then the king followed with Éomer on his right. He had said farewell to Éowyn above in the Hold, and the memory was grievous; but now he turned his mind to the road that lay ahead. Behind him Merry rode on Stybba with the errand riders of Gondor, and behind them again twelve more of the king's household. They passed down the long ranks of waiting men with stern and unmoved faces. But when they had come almost to the end of the line one looked up glancing keenly at the hobbit. A young man, Merry thought as he returned the glance, less in height and girth than most. He caught the glint of clear grey eyes; and then he shivered, for it came suddenly to him that it was the face of one without hope who goes in search of death.

On down the grey road they went beside the Snowbourn rushing on its stones; through the hamlets of Underharrow and Upbourn, where many sad faces of women looked out from dark doors; and so without horn or harp or music of men's voices the great ride into the East began with which the songs of Rohan were busy for many long lives of men thereafter.

From dark Dunharrow in the dim morning
with thane and captain rode Thengel's son:
to Edoras he came, the ancient halls
of the Mark-wardens mist-enshrouded;
golden timbers were in gloom mantled.
Farewell he bade to his free people,
hearth and high-seat, and the hallowed places,
where long he had feasted ere the light faded.
Forth rode the king, fear behind him,
fate before him. Fealty kept he;
oaths he had taken, all fulfilled them.
Forth rode Théoden. Five nights and days
east and onward rode the Eorlingas
through Folde and Fenmarch and the Firienwood,
six thousand spears to Sunlending,
Mundburg the mighty under Mindolluin,
Sea-kings' city in the South-kingdom
foe-beleaguered, fire-encircled.
Doom drove them on. Darkness took them,
horse and horseman; hoofbeats afar
sank into silence: so the songs tell us.

It was indeed in deepening gloom that the king came to Edoras, although it was then but noon by the hour. There he halted only a short while and strengthened his host by some three score of Riders that came late to the weapontake. Now having eaten he made ready to set out again, and he wished his esquire a kindly farewell. But Merry begged for the last time not to be parted from him.

'This is no journey for such steeds as Stybba, as I have told you,' said Théoden. 'And in such a battle as we think to make on the fields of Gondor what would you do, Master Meriadoc, swordthain though you be, and greater of heart than of stature?'

'As for that, who can tell?' answered Merry. 'But why, lord, did you receive me as swordthain, if not to stay by your side? And I would not have it said of me in song only that I was always left behind!'

'I received you for your safe-keeping,' answered Théoden; 'and also to do as I might bid. None of my Riders can bear you as burden. If the battle were before my gates, maybe your deeds would be remembered by the minstrels; but it is a hundred leagues and two to Mundburg where Denethor is lord. I will say no more.'

Merry bowed and went away unhappily, and stared at the lines of horsemen. Already the companies were preparing to start: men were tightening girths, looking to saddles, caressing their horses; some gazed uneasily at the lowering sky. Unnoticed a Rider came up and spoke softly in the hobbit's ear.

'*Where will wants not, a way opens*, so we say,' he whispered; 'and so I have found myself.' Merry looked up and saw that it was the young Rider whom he had noticed in the morning. 'You wish to go whither the Lord of the Mark goes: I see it in your face.'

'I do,' said Merry.

'Then you shall go with me,' said the Rider. 'I will bear you before me, under my cloak until we are far afield, and this darkness is yet darker. Such good will should not be denied. Say no more to any man, but come!'

'Thank you indeed!' said Merry. 'Thank you, sir, though I do not know your name.'

'Do you not?' said the Rider softly. 'Then call me Dernhelm.'

Thus it came to pass that when the king set out, before Dernhelm sat Meriadoc the hobbit, and the great grey steed Windfola made little of the burden; for Dernhelm was less in weight than many men, though lithe and well-knit in frame.

On into the shadow they rode. In the willow-thickets where Snowbourn flowed into Entwash, twelve leagues east of Edoras, they camped that night. And then on again through the Folde; and through the Fenmarch, where to their right great oakwoods climbed on the skirts of the hills under the shades of dark Halifirien by the borders of Gondor; but away to their left the mists lay on the marshes fed by the mouths of Entwash. And as they rode rumour came of war in the North. Lone men, riding wild, brought word of foes assailing their east-borders, of orc-hosts marching in the Wold of Rohan.

'Ride on! Ride on!' cried Éomer. 'Too late now to turn aside. The fens of Entwash must guard our flank. Haste now we need. Ride on!'

And so King Théoden departed from his own realm, and mile by mile the long road wound away, and the beacon hills marched past: Calenhad, Min-Rimmon, Erelas, Nardol. But their fires were quenched. All the lands were grey and still; and ever the shadow deepened before them, and hope waned in every heart.

CHAPTER IV

THE SIEGE OF GONDOR

Pippin was roused by Gandalf. Candles were lit in their chamber, for only a dim twilight came through the windows; the air was heavy as with approaching thunder.

'What is the time?' said Pippin yawning.

'Past the second hour,' said Gandalf. 'Time to get up and make yourself presentable. You are summoned to the Lord of the City to learn your new duties.'

'And will he provide breakfast?'

'No! I have provided it: all that you will get till noon. Food is now doled out by order.'

Pippin looked ruefully at the small loaf and (he thought) very inadequate pat of butter which was set out for him, beside a cup of thin milk. 'Why did you bring me here?' he said.

'You know quite well,' said Gandalf. 'To keep you out of mischief; and if you do not like being here, you can remember that you brought it on yourself.' Pippin said no more.

Before long he was walking with Gandalf once more down the cold corridor to the door of the Tower Hall. There Denethor sat in a grey gloom, like an old patient spider, Pippin thought; he did not seem to have moved since the day before. He beckoned Gandalf to a seat, but Pippin was left for a while standing unheeded. Presently the old man turned to him:

'Well, Master Peregrin, I hope that you used yesterday to your profit, and to your liking? Though I fear that the board is barer in this city than you could wish.'

Pippin had an uncomfortable feeling that most of what he had said or done was somehow known to the Lord of the City, and much was guessed of what he thought as well. He did not answer.

'What would you do in my service?'

'I thought, sir, that you would tell me my duties.'

'I will, when I learn what you are fit for,' said Denethor. 'But that I shall learn soonest, maybe, if I keep you beside me. The esquire of my chamber has begged leave to go to the out-garrison, so you shall take his place for a while. You shall wait on me, bear errands, and talk to me, if war and council leave me any leisure. Can you sing?'

'Yes,' said Pippin. 'Well, yes, well enough for my own people. But we have no songs fit for great halls and evil times, lord. We seldom sing of anything more terrible than wind or rain. And most of my songs are about things that make us laugh; or about food and drink, of course.'

'And why should such songs be unfit for my halls, or for such hours as these? We who have lived long under the Shadow may surely listen to echoes from a land untroubled by it? Then we may feel that our vigil was not fruitless, though it may have been thankless.'

Pippin's heart sank. He did not relish the idea of singing any song of the Shire to the Lord of Minas Tirith, certainly not the comic ones that he knew best; they were too, well, rustic for such an occasion. He was however spared the ordeal for the present. He was not commanded to sing. Denethor turned to Gandalf, asking questions about the Rohirrim and their policies, and the position of Éomer, the king's nephew. Pippin marvelled at the amount that the Lord seemed to know about a people that lived far away, though it must, he thought, be many years since Denethor himself had ridden abroad.

Presently Denethor waved to Pippin and dismissed him again for a while. 'Go to the armouries of the Citadel,' he said, 'and get you there the livery and gear of the Tower. It will be ready. It was commanded yesterday. Return when you are clad!'

It was as he said; and Pippin soon found himself arrayed in strange garments, all of black and silver. He had a small hauberk, its rings forged of steel, maybe, yet black as jet; and a high-crowned helm with small raven-wings on either side, set with a silver star in the centre of the circlet. Above the mail was a short surcoat of black, but broidered on the breast in silver with the token of the Tree. His old clothes were folded and put away, but he was permitted to keep the grey cloak of Lórien, though not to wear it when on duty. He looked now, had he known it, verily *Ernil i Pheriannath*, the Prince of the Halflings, that folk had called him; but he felt uncomfortable. And the gloom began to weigh on his spirits.

It was dark and dim all day. From the sunless dawn until evening the heavy shadow had deepened, and all hearts in the City were oppressed. Far above a great cloud streamed slowly westward from the Black Land, devouring light, borne upon a wind of war; but below the air was still and breathless, as if all the Vale of Anduin waited for the onset of a ruinous storm.

About the eleventh hour, released at last for a while from service, Pippin came out and went in search of food and drink to cheer his heavy heart and make his task of waiting more supportable. In the messes he met Beregond again, who had just come from an errand over the Pelennor out to the Guard-towers upon the Causeway. Together they strolled out to the walls; for Pippin felt imprisoned indoors, and stifled even in the lofty citadel. Now they sat side by side again in the embrasure looking eastward, where they had eaten and talked the day before.

It was the sunset-hour, but the great pall had now stretched far into the West, and only as it sank at last into the Sea did the Sun escape to send out a brief farewell gleam before the night, even as Frodo saw it at the Cross-roads touching the head of the fallen king. But to the fields of the Pelennor, under the shadow of Mindolluin, there came no gleam: they were brown and drear.

Already it seemed years to Pippin since he had sat there before, in some half-forgotten time when he had still been a hobbit, a light-hearted wanderer touched little by the perils he had passed through. Now he was one small soldier in a city preparing for a great assault, clad in the proud but sombre manner of the Tower of Guard.

In some other time and place Pippin might have been pleased with his new array, but he knew now that he was taking part in no play; he was in deadly earnest the servant of a grim master in the greatest peril. The hauberk was burdensome, and the helm weighed upon his head. His cloak he had cast aside upon the seat. He turned his tired gaze away from the darkling fields below and yawned, and then he sighed.

'You are weary of this day?' said Beregond.

'Yes,' said Pippin, 'very: tired out with idleness and waiting. I have kicked my heels at the door of my master's chamber for many slow hours, while he has debated with Gandalf and the Prince and other great persons. And I'm not used, Master Beregond, to waiting hungry on others while they eat. It is a sore trial for a hobbit, that. No doubt you will think I should feel the honour more deeply. But what is the good of such honour? Indeed what is the good even of food and drink under this creeping shadow? What does it mean? The very air seems thick and brown! Do you often have such glooms when the wind is in the East?'

'Nay,' said Beregond, 'this is no weather of the world. This is some device of his malice; some broil of fume from the Mountain of Fire that he sends to darken hearts and counsel. And so it doth indeed. I wish the Lord Faramir would return. He would not be dismayed. But now, who knows if he will ever come back across the River out of the Darkness?'

'Yes,' said Pippin, 'Gandalf, too, is anxious. He was disappointed, I think, not to find Faramir here. And where has he got to himself? He left the Lord's council before the noon-meal, and in no good mood either, I thought. Perhaps he has some foreboding of bad news.'

Suddenly as they talked they were stricken dumb, frozen as it were to listening stones. Pippin cowered down with his hands pressed to his ears;

but Beregond, who had been looking out from the battlement as he spoke of Faramir, remained there, stiffened, staring out with starting eyes. Pippin knew the shuddering cry that he had heard: it was the same that he had heard long ago in the Marish of the Shire, but now it was grown in power and hatred, piercing the heart with a poisonous despair.

At last Beregond spoke with an effort. 'They have come!' he said. 'Take courage and look! There are fell things below.'

Reluctantly Pippin climbed on to the seat and looked out over the wall. The Pelennor lay dim beneath him, fading away to the scarce guessed line of the Great River. But now wheeling swiftly across it, like shadows of untimely night, he saw in the middle airs below him five birdlike forms, horrible as carrion-fowl yet greater than eagles, cruel as death. Now they swooped near, venturing almost within bowshot of the walls, now they circled away.

'Black Riders!' muttered Pippin. 'Black Riders of the air! But see, Beregond!' he cried. 'They are looking for something, surely? See how they wheel and swoop, always down to that point over there! And can you see something moving on the ground? Dark little things. Yes, men on horses: four or five. Ah! I cannot stand it! Gandalf! Gandalf save us!'

Another long screech rose and fell, and he threw himself back again from the wall, panting like a hunted animal. Faint and seemingly remote through that shuddering cry he heard winding up from below the sound of a trumpet ending on a long high note.

'Faramir! The Lord Faramir! It is his call!' cried Beregond. 'Brave heart! But how can he win to the Gate, if these foul hell-hawks have other weapons than fear? But look! They hold on. They will make the Gate. No! the horses are running mad. Look! the men are thrown; they are running on foot. No, one is still up, but he rides back to the others. That will be the Captain: he can master both beasts and men. Ah! there one of the foul things is stooping on him. Help! help! Will no one go out to him? Faramir!'

With that Beregond sprang away and ran off into the gloom. Ashamed of his terror, while Beregond of the Guard thought first of the captain whom he loved, Pippin got up and peered out. At that moment he caught a flash of white and silver coming from the North, like a small star down on the dusky fields. It moved with the speed of an arrow and grew as it came, converging swiftly with the flight of the four men towards the Gate. It seemed to Pippin that a pale light was spread about it and the heavy shadows gave way before it; and then as it drew near he thought that he heard, like an echo in the walls, a great voice calling.

'Gandalf!' he cried. 'Gandalf! He always turns up when things are darkest. Go on! Go on, White Rider! Gandalf, Gandalf!' he shouted wildly, like an onlooker at a great race urging on a runner who is far beyond encouragement.

But now the dark swooping shadows were aware of the newcomer. One wheeled towards him; but it seemed to Pippin that he raised his hand, and from it a shaft of white light stabbed upwards. The Nazgûl gave a long wailing cry and swerved away; and with that the four others wavered, and then rising in swift spirals they passed away eastward vanishing into the lowering cloud above; and down on the Pelennor it seemed for a while less dark.

Pippin watched, and he saw the horseman and the White Rider meet and halt, waiting for those on foot. Men now hurried out to them from the City; and soon they all passed from sight under the outer walls, and he knew that they were entering the Gate. Guessing that they would come at once to the Tower and the Steward, he hurried to the entrance of the citadel. There he was joined by many others who had watched the race and the rescue from the high walls.

It was not long before a clamour was heard in the streets leading up from the outer circles, and there was much cheering and crying of the names of Faramir and Mithrandir. Presently Pippin saw torches, and followed by a press of people two horsemen riding slowly: one was in white but shining no longer, pale in the twilight as if his fire was spent or veiled; the other was dark and his head was bowed. They dismounted, and as grooms took Shadowfax and the other horse, they walked forward to the sentinel at the gate: Gandalf steadily, his grey cloak flung back, and a fire still smouldering in his eyes; the other, clad all in green, slowly, swaying a little as a weary or a wounded man.

Pippin pressed forward as they passed under the lamp beneath the gate-arch, and when he saw the pale face of Faramir he caught his breath. It was the face of one who has been assailed by a great fear or anguish, but has mastered it and now is quiet. Proud and grave he stood for a moment as he spoke to the guard, and Pippin gazing at him saw how closely he resembled his brother Boromir – whom Pippin had liked from the first, admiring the great man's lordly but kindly manner. Yet suddenly for Faramir his heart was strangely moved with a feeling that he had not known before. Here was one with an air of high nobility such as Aragorn at times revealed, less high perhaps, yet also less incalculable and remote: one of the Kings of Men born into a later time, but touched with the wisdom and sadness of the Elder Race. He knew now why Beregond spoke his name with love. He was a captain that men would follow, that he would follow, even under the shadow of the black wings.

'Faramir!' he cried aloud with the others. 'Faramir!' And Faramir, catching his strange voice among the clamour of the men of the City, turned and looked down at him and was amazed.

'Whence come you?' he said. 'A halfling, and in the livery of the Tower! Whence . . . ?'

But with that Gandalf stepped to his side and spoke. 'He came with me from the land of the Halflings,' he said. 'He came with me. But let us not tarry here. There is much to say and to do, and you are weary. He shall come with us. Indeed he must, for if he does not forget his new duties more easily than I do, he must attend on his lord again within this hour. Come, Pippin, follow us!'

So at length they came to the private chamber of the Lord of the City. There deep seats were set about a brazier of charcoal; and wine was brought; and there Pippin, hardly noticed, stood behind the chair of Denethor and felt his weariness little, so eagerly did he listen to all that was said.

When Faramir had taken white bread and drunk a draught of wine, he sat upon a low chair at his father's left hand. Removed a little upon the other side sat Gandalf in a chair of carven wood; and he seemed at first to be asleep. For at the beginning Faramir spoke only of the errand upon which he had been sent out ten days before, and he brought tidings of Ithilien and of movements of the Enemy and his allies; and he told of the fight on the road when the men of Harad and their great beast were overthrown: a captain reporting to his master such matters as had often been heard before, small things of border-war that now seemed useless and petty, shorn of their renown.

Then suddenly Faramir looked at Pippin. 'But now we come to strange matters,' he said. 'For this is not the first halfling that I have seen walking out of northern legends into the Southlands.'

At that Gandalf sat up and gripped the arms of his chair; but he said nothing, and with a look stopped the exclamation on Pippin's lips. Denethor looked at their faces and nodded his head, as though in sign that he had read much there before it was spoken. Slowly, while the others sat silent and still, Faramir told his tale, with his eyes for the most part on Gandalf, though now and again his glance strayed to Pippin, as if to refresh his memory of others that he had seen.

As his story was unfolded of his meeting with Frodo and his servant and of the events at Henneth Annûn, Pippin became aware that Gandalf's hands were trembling as they clutched the carven wood. White they seemed now and very old, and as he looked at them, suddenly with a thrill of fear Pippin knew that Gandalf, Gandalf himself, was troubled, even afraid. The air of the room was close and still. At last when Faramir spoke of his parting with the travellers, and of their resolve to go to Cirith Ungol, his voice fell, and he shook his head and sighed. Then Gandalf sprang up.

'Cirith Ungol? Morgul Vale?' he said. 'The time, Faramir, the time? When did you part with them? When would they reach that accursed valley?'

'I parted with them in the morning two days ago,' said Faramir. 'It is fifteen leagues thence to the vale of the Morgulduin, if they went straight south; and then they would be still five leagues westward of the accursed Tower. At swiftest they could not come there before today, and maybe they have not come there yet. Indeed I see what you fear. But the darkness is not due to their venture. It began yestereve, and all Ithilien was under shadow last night. It is clear to me that the Enemy has long planned an assault on us, and its hour had already been determined before ever the travellers left my keeping.'

Gandalf paced the floor. 'The morning of two days ago, nigh on three days of journey! How far is the place where you parted?'

'Some twenty-five leagues as a bird flies,' answered Faramir. 'But I could not come more swiftly. Yestereve I lay at Cair Andros, the long isle in the River northward which we hold in defence; and horses are kept on the hither bank. As the dark drew on I knew that haste was needed, so I rode thence with three others that could also be horsed. The rest of my company I sent south to strengthen the garrison at the fords of Osgiliath. I hope that I have not done ill?' He looked at his father.

'Ill?' cried Denethor, and his eyes flashed suddenly. 'Why do you ask? The men were under your command. Or do you ask for my judgement on all your deeds? Your bearing is lowly in my presence, yet it is long now since you turned from your own way at my counsel. See, you have spoken skilfully, as ever; but I, have I not seen your eye fixed on Mithrandir, seeking whether you said well or too much? He has long had your heart in his keeping.

'My son, your father is old but not yet dotard. I can see and hear, as was my wont; and little of what you have half said or left unsaid is now hidden from me. I know the answer to many riddles. Alas, alas for Boromir!'

'If what I have done displeases you, my father,' said Faramir quietly, 'I wish I had known your counsel before the burden of so weighty a judgement was thrust on me.'

'Would that have availed to change your judgement?' said Denethor. 'You would still have done just so, I deem. I know you well. Ever your desire is to appear lordly and generous as a king of old, gracious, gentle. That may well befit one of high race, if he sits in power and peace. But in desperate hours gentleness may be repaid with death.'

'So be it,' said Faramir.

'So be it!' cried Denethor. 'But not with your death only, Lord Faramir: with the death also of your father, and of all your people, whom it is your part to protect now that Boromir is gone.'

'Do you wish then,' said Faramir, 'that our places had been exchanged?'

'Yes, I wish that indeed,' said Denethor. 'For Boromir was loyal to me and no wizard's pupil. He would have remembered his father's need, and would not have squandered what fortune gave. He would have brought me a mighty gift.'

For a moment Faramir's restraint gave way. 'I would ask you, my father, to remember why it was that I, not he, was in Ithilien. On one occasion at least your counsel has prevailed, not long ago. It was the Lord of the City that gave the errand to him.'

'Stir not the bitterness in the cup that I mixed for myself,' said Denethor. 'Have I not tasted it now many nights upon my tongue, foreboding that worse yet lay in the dregs? As now indeed I find. Would it were not so! Would that this thing had come to me!'

'Comfort yourself!' said Gandalf. 'In no case would Boromir have brought it to you. He is dead, and died well; may he sleep in peace! Yet you deceive yourself. He would have stretched out his hand to this thing, and taking it he would have fallen. He would have kept it for his own, and when he returned you would not have known your son.'

The face of Denethor set hard and cold. 'You found Boromir less apt to your hand, did you not?' he said softly. 'But I who was his father say that he would have brought it to me. You are wise, maybe, Mithrandir, yet with all your subtleties you have not all wisdom. Counsels may be found that are neither the webs of wizards nor the haste of fools. I have in this matter more lore and wisdom than you deem.'

'What then is your wisdom?' said Gandalf.

'Enough to perceive that there are two follies to avoid. To use this thing is perilous. At this hour, to send it in the hands of a witless halfling into the land of the Enemy himself, as you have done, and this son of mine, that is madness.'

'And the Lord Denethor what would he have done?'

'Neither. But most surely not for any argument would he have set this thing at a hazard beyond all but a fool's hope, risking our utter ruin, if the Enemy should recover what he lost. Nay, it should have been kept, hidden, hidden dark and deep. Not used, I say, unless at the uttermost end of need, but set beyond his grasp, save by a victory so final that what then befell would not trouble us, being dead.'

'You think, as is your wont, my lord, of Gondor only,' said Gandalf. 'Yet there are other men and other lives, and time still to be. And for me, I pity even his slaves.'

'And where will other men look for help, if Gondor falls?' answered Denethor. 'If I had this thing now in the deep vaults of this citadel, we should not then shake with dread under this gloom, fearing the worst, and our counsels would be undisturbed. If you do not trust me to endure the test, you do not know me yet.'

'Nonetheless I do not trust you,' said Gandalf. 'Had I done so, I could have sent this thing hither to your keeping and spared myself and others much anguish. And now hearing you speak I trust you less, no more than Boromir. Nay, stay your wrath! I do not trust myself in this, and I refused this thing, even as a freely given gift. You are strong and can still in some matters govern yourself, Denethor; yet if you had received this thing, it would have overthrown you. Were it buried beneath the roots of Mindolluin, still it would burn your mind away, as the darkness grows, and the yet worse things follow that soon shall come upon us.'

For a moment the eyes of Denethor glowed again as he faced Gandalf, and Pippin felt once more the strain between their wills; but now almost it seemed as if their glances were like blades from eye to eye, flickering as they fenced. Pippin trembled fearing some dreadful stroke. But suddenly Denethor relaxed and grew cold again. He shrugged his shoulders.

'If I had! If you had!' he said. 'Such words and ifs are vain. It has gone into the Shadow, and only time will show what doom awaits it, and us. The time will not be long. In what is left, let all who fight the Enemy in their fashion be at one, and keep hope while they may, and after hope still the hardihood to die free.' He turned to Faramir. 'What think you of the garrison at Osgiliath?'

'It is not strong,' said Faramir. 'I have sent the company of Ithilien to strengthen it, as I have said.'

'Not enough, I deem,' said Denethor. 'It is there that the first blow will fall. They will have need of some stout captain there.'

'There and elsewhere in many places,' said Faramir, and sighed. 'Alas for my brother, whom I too loved!' He rose. 'May I have your leave, father?' And then he swayed and leaned upon his father's chair.

'You are weary, I see,' said Denethor. 'You have ridden fast and far, and under shadows of evil in the air, I am told.'

'Let us not speak of that!' said Faramir.

'Then we will not,' said Denethor. 'Go now and rest as you may. Tomorrow's need will be sterner.'

All now took leave of the Lord of the City and went to rest while they still could. Outside there was a starless blackness as Gandalf, with Pippin beside him bearing a small torch, made his way to their lodging. They did not speak until they were behind closed doors. Then at last Pippin took Gandalf's hand.

'Tell me,' he said, 'is there any hope? For Frodo, I mean; or at least mostly for Frodo.'

Gandalf put his hand on Pippin's head. 'There never was much hope,' he answered. 'Just a fool's hope, as I have been told. And when I heard of Cirith Ungol——' He broke off and strode to the window, as if his eyes could pierce the night in the East. 'Cirith Ungol!' he muttered. 'Why that way, I wonder?' He turned. 'Just now, Pippin, my heart almost failed me, hearing that name. And yet in truth I believe that the news that Faramir brings has some hope in it. For it seems clear that our Enemy has opened his war at last and made the first move while Frodo was still free. So now for many days he will have his eye turned this way and that, away from his own land. And yet, Pippin, I feel from afar his haste and fear. He has begun sooner than he would. Something has happened to stir him.'

Gandalf stood for a moment in thought. 'Maybe,' he muttered. 'Maybe even your foolishness helped, my lad. Let me see: some five days ago now he would discover that we had thrown down Saruman, and had taken the Stone. Still what of that? We could not use it to much purpose, or without his knowing. Ah! I wonder. Aragorn? His time draws near. And he is strong and stern underneath, Pippin; bold, determined, able to take his own counsel and dare great risks at need. That may be it. He may have used the Stone and shown himself to the Enemy, challenging him, for this very purpose. I wonder. Well, we shall not know the answer till the Riders of Rohan come, if they do not come too late. There are evil days ahead. To sleep while we may!'

'But,' said Pippin.

'But what?' said Gandalf. 'Only one *but* will I allow tonight.'

'Gollum,' said Pippin. 'How on earth could they be going about *with* him, even following him? And I could see that Faramir did not like the place he was taking them to any more than you do. What is wrong?'

'I cannot answer that now,' said Gandalf. 'Yet my heart guessed that Frodo and Gollum would meet before the end. For good, or for evil. But of Cirith Ungol I will not speak tonight. Treachery, treachery I fear; treachery of that miserable creature. But so it must be. Let us remember that a traitor may betray himself and do good that he does not intend. It can be so, sometimes. Good night!'

The next day came with a morning like a brown dusk, and the hearts of men, lifted for a while by the return of Faramir, sank low again. The winged Shadows were not seen again that day, yet ever and anon, high above the city, a faint cry would come, and many who heard it would stand stricken with a passing dread, while the less stout-hearted quailed and wept.

And now Faramir was gone again. 'They give him no rest,' some murmured. 'The Lord drives his son too hard, and now he must do the duty of two, for himself and for the one that will not return.' And ever men looked northward, asking: 'Where are the Riders of Rohan?'

In truth Faramir did not go by his own choosing. But the Lord of the City was master of his Council, and he was in no mood that day to bow to others. Early in the morning the Council had been summoned. There all the captains judged that because of the threat in the South their force was too weak to make any stroke of war on their own part, unless perchance the Riders of Rohan yet should come. Meanwhile they must man the walls and wait.

'Yet,' said Denethor, 'we should not lightly abandon the outer defences, the Rammas made with so great a labour. And the Enemy must pay dearly for the crossing of the River. That he cannot do, in force to assail the City, either north of Cair Andros because of the marshes, or southwards towards Lebennin because of the breadth of the River, that needs many boats. It is at Osgiliath that he will put his weight, as before when Boromir denied him the passage.'

'That was but a trial,' said Faramir. 'Today we may make the Enemy pay ten times our loss at the passage and yet rue the exchange. For he can afford to lose a host better than we to lose a company. And the retreat of those that we put out far afield will be perilous, if he wins across in force.'

'And what of Cair Andros?' said the Prince. 'That, too, must be held, if Osgiliath is defended. Let us not forget the danger on our left. The Rohirrim may come, and they may not. But Faramir has told us of great strength drawing ever to the Black Gate. More than one host may issue from it, and strike for more than one passage.'

'Much must be risked in war,' said Denethor. 'Cair Andros is manned, and no more can be sent so far. But I will not yield the River and the Pelennor unfought – not if there is a captain here who has still the courage to do his lord's will.'

Then all were silent. But at length Faramir said: 'I do not oppose your will, sire. Since you are robbed of Boromir, I will go and do what I can in his stead – if you command it.'

'I do so,' said Denethor.

'Then farewell!' said Faramir. 'But if I should return, think better of me!'

'That depends on the manner of your return,' said Denethor.

Gandalf it was that last spoke to Faramir ere he rode east. 'Do not throw your life away rashly or in bitterness,' he said. 'You will be needed here, for other things than war. Your father loves you, Faramir, and will remember it ere the end. Farewell!'

So now the Lord Faramir had gone forth again, and had taken with him such strength of men as were willing to go or could be spared. On the walls some gazed through the gloom towards the ruined city, and they wondered what chanced there, for nothing could be seen. And others, as ever, looked north and counted the leagues to Théoden in Rohan. 'Will he come? Will he remember our old alliance?' they said.

'Yes, he will come,' said Gandalf, 'even if he comes too late. But think! At best the Red Arrow cannot have reached him more than two days ago, and the miles are long from Edoras.'

It was night again ere news came. A man rode in haste from the fords, saying that a host had issued from Minas Morgul and was already drawing nigh to Osgiliath; and it had been joined by regiments from the South, Haradrim, cruel and tall. 'And we have learned,' said the messenger, 'that the Black Captain leads them once again, and the fear of him has passed before him over the River.'

With those ill-boding words the third day closed since Pippin came to Minas Tirith. Few went to rest, for small hope had any now that even Faramir could hold the fords for long.

The next day, though the darkness had reached its full and grew no deeper, it weighed heavier on men's hearts, and a great dread was on them. Ill news came soon again. The passage of Anduin was won by the Enemy. Faramir was retreating to the wall of the Pelennor, rallying his men to the Causeway Forts; but he was ten times outnumbered.

'If he wins back at all across the Pelennor, his enemies will be on his heels,' said the messenger. 'They have paid dear for the crossing, but less dearly than we hoped. The plan has been well laid. It is now seen that in secret they have long been building floats and barges in great number in East Osgiliath. They swarmed across like beetles. But it is the Black Captain that defeats us. Few will stand and abide even the rumour of his coming. His own folk quail at him, and they would slay themselves at his bidding.'

'Then I am needed there more than here,' said Gandalf, and rode off at once, and the glimmer of him faded soon from sight. And all that night Pippin alone and sleepless stood upon the wall and gazed eastward.

The bells of day had scarcely rung out again, a mockery in the unlightened dark, when far away he saw fires spring up, across in the dim spaces where the walls of the Pelennor stood. The watchmen cried aloud, and all men in the City stood to arms. Now ever and anon there was a red flash, and slowly through the heavy air dull rumbles could be heard.

'They have taken the wall!' men cried. 'They are blasting breaches in it. They are coming!'

'Where is Faramir?' cried Beregond in dismay. 'Say not that he has fallen!'

It was Gandalf that brought the first tidings. With a handful of horsemen he came in the middle morning, riding as escort to a line of wains. They were filled with wounded men, all that could be saved from the wreck of the Causeway Forts. At once he went to Denethor. The Lord of the City sat now in a high chamber above the Hall of the White Tower with Pippin at his side; and through the dim windows, north and south and east, he bent his dark eyes, as if to pierce the shadows of doom that ringed him round. Most to the North he looked, and would pause at whiles to listen as if by some ancient art his ears might hear the thunder of hoofs on the plains far away.

'Is Faramir come?' he asked.

'No,' said Gandalf. 'But he still lived when I left him. Yet he is resolved to stay with the rearguard, lest the retreat over the Pelennor become a rout. He may, perhaps, hold his men together long enough, but I doubt it. He is pitted against a foe too great. For one has come that I feared.'

'Not – the Dark Lord?' cried Pippin, forgetting his place in his terror.

Denethor laughed bitterly. 'Nay, not yet, Master Peregrin! He will not come save only to triumph over me when all is won. He uses others as his weapons. So do all great lords, if they are wise, Master Halfling. Or why should I sit here in my tower and think, and watch, and wait, spending even my sons? For I can still wield a brand.'

He stood up and cast open his long black cloak, and behold! he was clad in mail beneath, and girt with a long sword, great-hilted in a sheath of black and silver. 'Thus have I walked, and thus now for many years have I slept,' he said, 'lest with age the body should grow soft and timid.'

'Yet now under the Lord of Barad-dûr the most fell of all his captains is already master of your outer walls,' said Gandalf. 'King of Angmar long ago, Sorcerer, Ringwraith, Lord of the Nazgûl, a spear of terror in the hand of Sauron, shadow of despair.'

'Then, Mithrandir, you had a foe to match you,' said Denethor. 'For myself, I have long known who is the chief captain of the hosts of the Dark Tower. Is this all that you have returned to say? Or can it be that you have withdrawn because you are overmatched?'

Pippin trembled, fearing that Gandalf would be stung to sudden wrath, but his fear was needless. 'It might be so,' Gandalf answered softly. 'But our trial of strength is not yet come. And if words spoken of old be true, not by the hand of man shall he fall, and hidden from the Wise is the doom that awaits him. However that may be, the Captain of Despair does not press forward, yet. He rules rather according to the wisdom that you have just spoken, from the rear, driving his slaves in madness on before.

'Nay, I came rather to guard the hurt men that can yet be healed; for the Rammas is breached far and wide, and soon the host of Morgul will enter in at many points. And I came chiefly to say this. Soon there will be battle on the fields. A sortie must be made ready. Let it be of mounted men. In them lies our brief hope, for in one thing only is the enemy still poorly provided: he has few horsemen.'

'And we also have few. Now would the coming of Rohan be in the nick of time,' said Denethor.

'We are likely to see other newcomers first,' said Gandalf. 'Fugitives from Cair Andros have already reached us. The isle has fallen. Another army is come from the Black Gate, crossing from the north-east.'

'Some have accused you, Mithrandir, of delighting to bear ill news,' said Denethor, 'but to me this is no longer news: it was known to me ere nightfall yesterday. As for the sortie, I had already given thought to it. Let us go down.'

Time passed. At length watchers on the walls could see the retreat of the out-companies. Small bands of weary and often wounded men came first with little order; some were running wildly as if pursued. Away to the eastward the distant fires flickered, and now it seemed that here and there they crept across the plain. Houses and barns were burning. Then from many points little rivers of red flame came hurrying on, winding through the gloom, converging towards the line of the broad road that led from the City-gate to Osgiliath.

'The enemy,' men murmured. 'The dike is down. Here they come pouring through the breaches! And they carry torches, it seems. Where are our own folk?'

It drew now to evening by the hour, and the light was so dim that even far-sighted men upon the Citadel could discern little clearly out upon the fields, save only the burnings that ever multiplied, and the lines of fire that grew in length and speed. At last, less than a mile from the City, a more ordered mass of men came into view, marching not running, still holding together.

The watchers held their breath. 'Faramir must be there,' they said. 'He can govern man and beast. He will make it yet.'

Now the main retreat was scarcely two furlongs distant. Out of the gloom behind a small company of horsemen galloped, all that was left of the rearguard. Once again they turned at bay, facing the oncoming lines of fire. Then suddenly there was a tumult of fierce cries. Horsemen of the enemy swept up. The lines of fire became flowing torrents, file upon file of Orcs bearing flames, and wild Southron men with red banners, shouting with harsh tongues, surging up, overtaking the retreat. And with a piercing cry out of the dim sky fell the winged shadows, the Nazgûl stooping to the kill.

The retreat became a rout. Already men were breaking away, flying wild and witless here and there, flinging away their weapons, crying out in fear, falling to the ground.

And then a trumpet rang from the Citadel, and Denethor at last released the sortie. Drawn up within the shadow of the Gate and under the looming walls outside they had waited for his signal: all the mounted men that were left in the City. Now they sprang forward, formed, quickened to a gallop, and charged with a great shout. And from the walls an answering shout went up; for foremost on the field rode the swan-knights of Dol Amroth with their Prince and his blue banner at their head.

'Amroth for Gondor!' they cried. 'Amroth to Faramir!'

Like thunder they broke upon the enemy on either flank of the retreat; but one rider outran them all, swift as the wind in the grass: Shadowfax bore him, shining, unveiled once more, a light starting from his upraised hand.

The Nazgûl screeched and swept away, for their Captain was not yet come to challenge the white fire of his foe. The hosts of Morgul intent on their prey, taken at unawares in wild career, broke, scattering like sparks in a gale. The out-companies with a great cheer turned and smote their pursuers. Hunters became the hunted. The retreat became an onslaught. The field was strewn with stricken orcs and men, and a reek arose of torches cast away, sputtering out in swirling smoke. The cavalry rode on.

But Denethor did not permit them to go far. Though the enemy was checked, and for the moment driven back, great forces were flowing in from the East. Again the trumpet rang, sounding the retreat. The cavalry of Gondor halted. Behind their screen the out-companies re-formed. Now steadily they came marching back. They reached the Gate of the City and entered, stepping proudly; and proudly the people of the City looked on them and cried their praise, and yet they were troubled in heart. For the companies were grievously reduced. Faramir had lost a third of his men. And where was he?

Last of all he came. His men passed in. The mounted knights returned, and at their rear the banner of Dol Amroth, and the Prince. And in his arms before him on his horse he bore the body of his kinsman, Faramir son of Denethor, found upon the stricken field.

'Faramir! Faramir!' men cried, weeping in the streets. But he did not answer, and they bore him away up the winding road to the Citadel and his father. Even as the Nazgûl had swerved aside from the onset of the White Rider, there came flying a deadly dart, and Faramir, as he held at bay a mounted champion of Harad, had fallen to the earth. Only the charge of Dol Amroth had saved him from the red southland swords that would have hewed him as he lay.

The Prince Imrahil brought Faramir to the White Tower, and he said: 'Your son has returned, lord, after great deeds,' and he told all that he had seen. But Denethor rose and looked on the face of his son and was silent. Then he bade them make a bed in the chamber and lay Faramir upon it and depart. But he himself went up alone into the secret room under the summit of the Tower; and many who looked up thither at that time saw a pale light that gleamed and flickered from the narrow windows for a while, and then flashed and went out. And when Denethor descended again he went to Faramir and sat beside him without speaking, but the face of the Lord was grey, more deathlike than his son's.

So now at last the City was besieged, enclosed in a ring of foes. The Rammas was broken, and all the Pelennor abandoned to the Enemy. The last word to come from outside the walls was brought by men flying down the northward road ere the Gate was shut. They were the remnant of the guard that was kept at that point where the way from Anórien and Rohan ran into the townlands. Ingold led them, the same who had admitted Gandalf and Pippin less than five days before, while the sun still rose and there was hope in the morning.

'There is no news of the Rohirrim,' he said. 'Rohan will not come now. Or if they come, it will not avail us. The new host that we had tidings of has come first, from over the River by way of Andros, it is said. They are strong: battalions of Orcs of the Eye, and countless companies of Men of a new sort that we have not met before. Not tall, but broad and grim, bearded like dwarves, wielding great axes. Out of some savage land in the wide East they come, we deem. They hold the northward road; and many have passed on into Anórien. The Rohirrim cannot come.'

The Gate was shut. All night watchmen on the walls heard the rumour of the enemy that roamed outside, burning field and tree, and hewing any man that they found abroad, living or dead. The numbers that had already passed over the River could not be guessed in the darkness, but when morning, or its dim shadow, stole over the plain, it was seen that even fear by night had scarcely over-counted them. The plain was dark with their marching companies, and as far as eyes could strain in the mirk there sprouted, like a foul fungus-growth, all about the beleaguered city great camps of tents, black or sombre red.

Busy as ants hurrying orcs were digging, digging lines of deep trenches in a huge ring, just out of bowshot from the walls; and as the trenches were made each was filled with fire, though how it was kindled or fed, by art or devilry, none could see. All day the labour went forward, while the men of Minas Tirith looked on, unable to hinder it. And as each length of trench was completed, they could see great wains approaching; and soon yet more companies of the enemy were swiftly setting up, each behind the cover of a trench, great engines for the casting of missiles. There were none upon the City walls large enough to reach so far or to stay the work.

At first men laughed and did not greatly fear such devices. For the main wall of the City was of great height and marvellous thickness, built ere the power and craft of Númenor waned in exile; and its outward face was like to the Tower of Orthanc, hard and dark and smooth, unconquerable by steel or fire, unbreakable except by some convulsion that would rend the very earth on which it stood.

'Nay,' they said, 'not if the Nameless One himself should come, not even he could enter here while we yet live.' But some answered: 'While we yet live? How long? He has a weapon that has brought low many strong places since the world began. Hunger. The roads are cut. Rohan will not come.'

But the engines did not waste shot upon the indomitable wall. It was no brigand or orc-chieftain that ordered the assault upon the Lord of Mordor's greatest foe. A power and mind of malice guided it. As soon as the great catapults were set, with many yells and the creaking of rope and winch, they began to throw missiles marvellously high, so that they passed right above the battlement and fell thudding within the first circle of the City; and many of them by some secret art burst into flame as they came toppling down.

Soon there was great peril of fire behind the wall, and all who could be spared were busy quelling the flames that sprang up in many places. Then among the greater casts there fell another hail, less ruinous but more horrible. All about the streets and lanes behind the Gate it tumbled down, small round shot that did not burn. But when men ran to learn what it might be, they cried aloud or wept. For the enemy was flinging into the City all the heads of those who had fallen fighting at Osgiliath, or on the Rammas, or in the fields. They were grim to look on; for though some were crushed and shapeless, and some had been cruelly hewn, yet many had features that could be told, and it seemed that they had died in pain; and all were branded with the foul token of the Lidless Eye. But marred and dishonoured as they were, it often chanced that thus a man would see again the face of someone that he had known, who had walked proudly once in arms, or tilled the fields, or ridden in upon a holiday from the green vales in the hills.

In vain men shook their fists at the pitiless foes that swarmed before the Gate. Curses they heeded not, nor understood the tongues of western men, crying with harsh voices like beasts and carrion-birds. But soon there were few left in Minas Tirith who had the heart to stand up and defy the hosts of Mordor. For yet another weapon, swifter than hunger, the Lord of the Dark Tower had: dread and despair.

The Nazgûl came again, and as their Dark Lord now grew and put forth his strength, so their voices, which uttered only his will and his malice, were filled with evil and horror. Ever they circled above the City, like vultures that expect their fill of doomed men's flesh. Out of sight and shot they flew, and yet were ever present, and their deadly voices rent the air. More unbearable they became, not less, at each new cry. At length even the stout-hearted would fling themselves to the ground as the hidden menace passed over them, or they would stand, letting their weapons fall from nerveless hands while into their minds a blackness came, and they thought no more of war; but only of hiding and of crawling, and of death.

During all this black day Faramir lay upon his bed in the chamber of the White Tower, wandering in a desperate fever; dying someone said, and soon 'dying' all men were saying upon the walls and in the streets. And by him his father sat, and said nothing, but watched, and gave no longer any heed to the defence.

No hours so dark had Pippin known, not even in the clutches of the Uruk-hai. It was his duty to wait upon the Lord, and wait he did, forgotten it seemed, standing by the door of the unlit chamber, mastering his own fears as best he could. And as he watched, it seemed to him that Denethor grew old before his eyes, as if something had snapped in his proud will, and his stern mind was overthrown. Grief maybe had wrought it, and remorse. He saw tears on that once tearless face, more unbearable than wrath.

'Do not weep, lord,' he stammered. 'Perhaps he will get well. Have you asked Gandalf?'

'Comfort me not with wizards!' said Denethor. 'The fool's hope has failed. The Enemy has found it, and now his power waxes; he sees our very thoughts, and all we do is ruinous.

'I sent my son forth, unthanked, unblessed, out into needless peril, and here he lies with poison in his veins. Nay, nay, whatever may now betide in war, my line too is ending, even the House of the Stewards has failed.

Mean folk shall rule the last remnant of the Kings of Men, lurking in the hills until all are hounded out.'

Men came to the door crying for the Lord of the City. 'Nay, I will not come down,' he said. 'I must stay beside my son. He might still speak before the end. But that is near. Follow whom you will, even the Grey Fool, though his hope has failed. Here I stay.'

So it was that Gandalf took command of the last defence of the City of Gondor. Wherever he came men's hearts would lift again, and the winged shadows pass from memory. Tirelessly he strode from Citadel to Gate, from north to south about the wall; and with him went the Prince of Dol Amroth in his shining mail. For he and his knights still held themselves like lords in whom the race of Númenor ran true. Men that saw them whispered saying: 'Belike the old tales speak well; there is Elvish blood in the veins of that folk, for the people of Nimrodel dwelt in that land once long ago.' And then one would sing amid the gloom some staves of the Lay of Nimrodel, or other songs of the Vale of Anduin out of vanished years.

And yet – when they had gone, the shadows closed on men again, and their hearts went cold, and the valour of Gondor withered into ash. And so slowly they passed out of a dim day of fears into the darkness of a desperate night. Fires now raged unchecked in the first circle of the City, and the garrison upon the outer wall was already in many places cut off from retreat. But the faithful who remained there at their posts were few; most had fled beyond the second gate.

Far behind the battle the River had been swiftly bridged, and all day more force and gear of war had poured across. Now at last in the middle night the assault was loosed. The vanguard passed through the trenches of fire by many devious paths that had been left between them. On they came, reckless of their loss as they approached, still bunched and herded, within the range of bowmen on the wall. But indeed there were too few now left there to do them great damage, though the light of the fires showed up many a mark for archers of such skill as Gondor once had boasted. Then perceiving that the valour of the City was already beaten down, the hidden Captain put forth his strength. Slowly the great siege-towers built in Osgiliath rolled forward through the dark.

Messengers came again to the chamber in the White Tower, and Pippin let them enter, for they were urgent. Denethor turned his head slowly from Faramir's face, and looked at them silently.

'The first circle of the City is burning, lord,' they said. 'What are your commands? You are still the Lord and Steward. Not all will follow Mithrandir. Men are flying from the walls and leaving them unmanned.'

'Why? Why do the fools fly?' said Denethor. 'Better to burn sooner than late, for burn we must. Go back to your bonfire! And I? I will go now to my pyre. To my pyre! No tomb for Denethor and Faramir. No tomb! No long slow sleep of death embalmed. We will burn like heathen kings before ever a ship sailed hither from the West. The West has failed. Go back and burn!'

The messengers without bow or answer turned and fled.

Now Denethor stood up and released the fevered hand of Faramir that he had held. 'He is burning, already burning,' he said sadly. 'The house of his spirit crumbles.' Then stepping softly towards Pippin he looked down at him.

'Farewell!' he said. 'Farewell, Peregrin son of Paladin! Your service has been short, and now it is drawing to an end. I release you from the little that remains. Go now, and die in what way seems best to you. And with whom you will, even that friend whose folly brought you to this death. Send for my servants and then go. Farewell!'

'I will not say farewell, my lord,' said Pippin kneeling. And then suddenly hobbit-like once more, he stood up and looked the old man in the eyes. 'I will take your leave, sir,' he said; 'for I want to see Gandalf very much indeed. But he is no fool; and I will not think of dying until he despairs of life. But from my word and your service I do not wish to be released while you live. And if they come at last to the Citadel, I hope to be here and stand beside you and earn perhaps the arms that you have given me.'

'Do as you will, Master Halfling,' said Denethor. 'But my life is broken. Send for my servants!' He turned back to Faramir.

Pippin left him and called for the servants, and they came: six men of the household, strong and fair; yet they trembled at the summons. But in a quiet voice Denethor bade them lay warm coverlets on Faramir's bed and take it up. And they did so, and lifting up the bed they bore it from the chamber. Slowly they paced to trouble the fevered man as little as might be, and Denethor, now bending on a staff, followed them; and last came Pippin.

Out from the White Tower they walked, as if to a funeral, out into the darkness, where the overhanging cloud was lit beneath with flickers of dull red. Softly they paced the great courtyard, and at a word from Denethor halted beside the Withered Tree.

All was silent, save for the rumour of war in the City down below, and they heard the water dripping sadly from the dead branches into the dark pool. Then they went on through the Citadel gate, where the sentinel stared at them in wonder and dismay as they passed by. Turning westward they came at length to a door in the rearward wall of the sixth circle. Fen Hollen it was called, for it was kept ever shut save at times of funeral, and only the Lord of the City might use that way, or those who bore the token of the tombs and tended the houses of the dead. Beyond it went a winding road that descended in many curves down to the narrow land under the shadow of Mindolluin's precipice where stood the mansions of the dead Kings and of their Stewards.

A porter sat in a little house beside the way, and with fear in his eyes he came forth bearing a lantern in his hand. At the Lord's command he unlocked the door, and silently it swung back; and they passed through, taking the lantern from his hand. It was dark on the climbing road between ancient walls and many-pillared balusters looming in the swaying lantern-beam. Their slow feet echoed as they walked down, down, until at last they came to the Silent Street, Rath Dínen, between pale domes and empty halls and images of men long dead; and they entered into the House of the Stewards and set down their burden.

There Pippin, staring uneasily about him, saw that he was in a wide vaulted chamber, draped as it were with the great shadows that the little lantern threw upon its shrouded walls. And dimly to be seen were many rows of tables, carved of marble; and upon each table lay a sleeping form, hands folded, head pillowed upon stone. But one table near at hand stood broad and bare. Upon it at a sign from Denethor they laid Faramir and his father side by side, and covered them with one covering, and stood then with bowed heads as mourners beside a bed of death. Then Denethor spoke in a low voice.

'Here we will wait,' he said. 'But send not for the embalmers. Bring us wood quick to burn, and lay it all about us, and beneath; and pour oil upon it. And when I bid you thrust in a torch. Do this and speak no more to me. Farewell!'

'By your leave, lord!' said Pippin and turned and fled in terror from the deathly house. 'Poor Faramir!' he thought. 'I must find Gandalf. Poor Faramir! Quite likely he needs medicine more than tears. Oh, where can I find Gandalf? In the thick of things, I suppose; and he will have no time to spare for dying men or madmen.'

At the door he turned to one of the servants who had remained on guard there. 'Your master is not himself,' he said. 'Go slow! Bring no fire to this place while Faramir lives! Do nothing until Gandalf comes!'

'Who is the master of Minas Tirith?' the man answered. 'The Lord Denethor or the Grey Wanderer?'

'The Grey Wanderer or no one, it would seem,' said Pippin, and he sped back and up the winding way as swiftly as his feet would carry him, past the astonished porter, out through the door, and on, till he came near the gate of the Citadel. The sentinel hailed him as he went by, and he recognized the voice of Beregond.

'Whither do you run, Master Peregrin?' he cried.

'To find Mithrandir,' Pippin answered.

'The Lord's errands are urgent and should not be hindered by me,' said Beregond; 'but tell me quickly, if you may: what goes forward? Whither has my Lord gone? I have just come on duty, but I heard that he passed towards the Closed Door, and men were bearing Faramir before him.'

'Yes,' said Pippin, 'to the Silent Street.'

Beregond bowed his head to hide his tears. 'They said that he was dying,' he sighed, 'and now he is dead.'

'No,' said Pippin, 'not yet. And even now his death might be prevented, I think. But the Lord of the City, Beregond, has fallen before his city is taken. He is fey and dangerous.' Quickly he told of Denethor's strange words and deeds. 'I must find Gandalf at once.'

'Then you must go down to the battle.'

'I know. The Lord has given me leave. But, Beregond, if you can, do something to stop any dreadful thing happening.'

'The Lord does not permit those who wear the black and silver to leave their post for any cause, save at his own command.'

'Well, you must choose between orders and the life of Faramir,' said Pippin. 'And as for orders, I think you have a madman to deal with, not a lord. I must run. I will return if I can.'

He ran on, down, down towards the outer city. Men flying back from the burning passed him, and some seeing his livery turned and shouted, but he paid no heed. At last he was through the Second Gate, beyond which great fires leaped up between the walls. Yet it seemed strangely silent. No noise or shouts of battle or din of arms could be heard. Then suddenly there was a dreadful cry and a great shock, and a deep echoing boom. Forcing himself on against a gust of fear and horror that shook him almost to his knees, Pippin turned a corner opening on the wide place behind the City Gate. He stopped dead. He had found Gandalf; but he shrank back, cowering into a shadow.

Ever since the middle night the great assault had gone on. The drums rolled. To the north and to the south company upon company of the enemy pressed to the walls. There came great beasts, like moving houses in the red and fitful light, the *mûmakil* of the Harad dragging through the lanes amid the fires huge towers and engines. Yet their Captain cared not greatly what they did or how many might be slain: their purpose was only to test the strength of the defence and to keep the men of Gondor busy in many places. It was against the Gate that he would throw his heaviest weight. Very strong it might be, wrought of steel and iron, and guarded with towers and bastions of indomitable stone, yet it was the key, the weakest point in all that high and impenetrable wall.

The drums rolled louder. Fires leaped up. Great engines crawled across the field; and in the midst was a huge ram, great as a forest-tree a hundred feet in length, swinging on mighty chains. Long had it been forging in the dark smithies of Mordor, and its hideous head, founded of black steel, was shaped in the likeness of a ravening wolf; on it spells of ruin lay. Grond they named it, in memory of the Hammer of the Underworld of old. Great beasts drew it, orcs surrounded it, and behind walked mountain-trolls to wield it.

But about the Gate resistance still was stout, and there the knights of Dol Amroth and the hardiest of the garrison stood at bay. Shot and dart fell thick; siege-towers crashed or blazed suddenly like torches. All before the walls on either side of the Gate the ground was choked with wreck and with bodies of the slain; yet still driven as by a madness more and more came up.

Grond crawled on. Upon its housing no fire would catch; and though now and again some great beast that hauled it would go mad and spread stamping ruin among the orcs innumerable that guarded it, their bodies were cast aside from its path and others took their place.

Grond crawled on. The drums rolled wildly. Over the hills of slain a hideous shape appeared: a horseman, tall, hooded, cloaked in black. Slowly, trampling the fallen, he rode forth, heeding no longer any dart. He halted and held up a long pale sword. And as he did so a great fear fell on all, defender and foe alike; and the hands of men drooped to their sides, and no bow sang. For a moment all was still.

The drums rolled and rattled. With a vast rush Grond was hurled forward by huge hands. It reached the Gate. It swung. A deep boom rumbled through the City like thunder running in the clouds. But the doors of iron and posts of steel withstood the stroke.

Then the Black Captain rose in his stirrups and cried aloud in a dreadful voice, speaking in some forgotten tongue words of power and terror to rend both heart and stone.

Thrice he cried. Thrice the great ram boomed. And suddenly upon the last stroke the Gate of Gondor broke. As if stricken by some blasting spell it burst asunder: there was a flash of searing lightning, and the doors tumbled in riven fragments to the ground.

In rode the Lord of the Nazgûl. A great black shape against the fires beyond he loomed up, grown to a vast menace of despair. In rode the Lord of the Nazgûl, under the archway that no enemy ever yet had passed, and all fled before his face.

All save one. There waiting, silent and still in the space before the Gate, sat Gandalf upon Shadowfax: Shadowfax who alone among the free horses of the earth endured the terror, unmoving, steadfast as a graven image in Rath Dínen.

'You cannot enter here,' said Gandalf, and the huge shadow halted. 'Go back to the abyss prepared for you! Go back! Fall into the nothingness that awaits you and your Master. Go!'

The Black Rider flung back his hood, and behold! he had a kingly crown; and yet upon no head visible was it set. The red fires shone between it and the mantled shoulders vast and dark. From a mouth unseen there came a deadly laughter.

'Old fool!' he said. 'Old fool! This is my hour. Do you not know Death when you see it? Die now and curse in vain!' And with that he lifted high his sword and flames ran down the blade.

Gandalf did not move. And in that very moment, away behind in some courtyard of the City, a cock crowed. Shrill and clear he crowed, recking nothing of wizardry or war, welcoming only the morning that in the sky far above the shadows of death was coming with the dawn.

And as if in answer there came from far away another note. Horns, horns, horns. In dark Mindolluin's sides they dimly echoed. Great horns of the North wildly blowing. Rohan had come at last.

CHAPTER V

THE RIDE OF THE ROHIRRIM

It was dark and Merry could see nothing as he lay on the ground rolled in a blanket; yet though the night was airless and windless, all about him hidden trees were sighing softly. He lifted his head. Then he heard it again: a sound like faint drums in the wooded hills and mountain-steps. The throb would cease suddenly and then be taken up again at some other point, now nearer, now further off. He wondered if the watchmen had heard it.

He could not see them, but he knew that all round him were the companies of the Rohirrim. He could smell the horses in the dark, and could hear their shiftings and their soft stamping on the needle-covered ground. The host was bivouacked in the pine-woods that clustered about Eilenach Beacon, a tall hill standing up from the long ridges of the Druadan Forest that lay beside the great road in East Anórien.

Tired as he was Merry could not sleep. He had ridden now for four days on end, and the ever-deepening gloom had slowly weighed down his heart. He began to wonder why he had been so eager to come, when he had been given every excuse, even his lord's command, to stay behind. He wondered, too, if the old King knew that he had been disobeyed and was angry. Perhaps not. There seemed to be some understanding between Dernhelm and Elfhelm, the Marshal who commanded the *éored* in which they were riding. He and all his men ignored Merry and pretended not to hear if he spoke. He might have been just another bag that Dernhelm was carrying. Dernhelm was no comfort: he never spoke to anyone. Merry felt small, unwanted, and lonely. Now the time was anxious, and the host was in peril. They were less than a day's ride from the out-walls of Minas Tirith that encircled the townlands. Scouts had been sent ahead. Some had not returned. Others hastening back had reported that the road was held in force against them. A host of the enemy was encamped upon it, three miles west of Amon Dîn, and some strength of men was already thrusting along the road and was no more than three leagues away. Orcs were roving in the hills and woods along the roadside. The king and Éomer held council in the watches of the night.

Merry wanted somebody to talk to, and he thought of Pippin. But that only increased his restlessness. Poor Pippin, shut up in the great city of stone, lonely and afraid. Merry wished he was a tall Rider like Éomer and could blow a horn or something and go galloping to his rescue. He sat up, listening to the drums that were beating again, now nearer at hand. Presently he heard voices speaking low, and he saw dim half-shrouded lanterns passing through the trees. Men nearby began to move uncertainly in the dark.

A tall figure loomed up and stumbled over him, cursing the tree-roots. He recognized the voice of Elfhelm the Marshal.

'I am not a tree-root, Sir,' he said, 'nor a bag, but a bruised hobbit. The least you can do in amends is to tell me what is afoot.'

'Anything that can keep so in this devil's mirk,' answered Elfhelm. 'But my lord sends word that we must set ourselves in readiness: orders may come for a sudden move.'

'Is the enemy coming then?' asked Merry anxiously. 'Are those their drums? I began to think I was imagining them, as no one else seemed to take any notice of them.'

'Nay, nay,' said Elfhelm, 'the enemy is on the road not in the hills. You hear the Woses, the Wild Men of the Woods: thus they talk together from afar. They still haunt Druadan Forest, it is said. Remnants of an older time they be, living few and secretly, wild and wary as the beasts. They go not to war with Gondor or the Mark; but now they are troubled by the darkness and the coming of the orcs: they fear lest the Dark Years be returning, as seems likely enough. Let us be thankful that they are not hunting us: for they use poisoned arrows, it is said, and they are woodcrafty beyond compare. But they have offered their services to Théoden. Even now one of their headmen is being taken to the king. Yonder go the lights. So much I have heard but no more. And now I must busy myself with my lord's commands. Pack yourself up, Master Bag!' He vanished into the shadows.

Merry did not like this talk of wild men and poisoned darts, but quite apart from that a great weight of dread was on him. Waiting was unbearable. He longed to know what was going to happen. He got up and soon was walking warily in pursuit of the last lantern before it disappeared among the trees.

Presently he came to an open space where a small tent had been set up for the king under a great tree. A large lantern, covered above, was hanging from a bough and cast a pale circle of light below. There sat Théoden and Éomer, and before them on the ground sat a strange squat shape of a man, gnarled as an old stone, and the hairs of his scanty beard straggled on his lumpy chin like dry moss. He was short-legged and fat-armed, thick and stumpy, and clad only with grass about his waist. Merry felt that he had seen him before somewhere, and suddenly he remembered the Púkel-men of Dunharrow. Here was one of those old images brought to life, or maybe a creature descended in true line through endless years from the models used by the forgotten craftsmen long ago.

There was a silence as Merry crept nearer, and then the Wild Man began to speak, in answer to some question, it seemed. His voice was deep and guttural, yet to Merry's surprise he spoke the Common Speech, though in a halting fashion, and uncouth words were mingled with it.

'No, father of Horse-men,' he said, 'we fight not. Hunt only. Kill *gorgûn* in woods, hate orc-folk. You hate *gorgûn* too. We help as we can. Wild Men have long ears and long eyes; know all paths. Wild Men live here before Stone-houses; before Tall Men come up out of Water.'

'But our need is for aid in battle,' said Éomer. 'How will you and your folk help us?'

'Bring news,' said the Wild Man. 'We look out from hills. We climb big mountain and look down. Stone-city is shut. Fire burns there outside; now inside too. You wish to come there? Then you must be quick. But *gorgûn* and men out of far-away,' he waved a short gnarled arm eastward, 'sit on horse-road. Very many, more than Horse-men.'

'How do you know that?' said Éomer.

The old man's flat face and dark eyes showed nothing, but his voice was sullen with displeasure. 'Wild Men are wild, free, but not children,' he answered. 'I am great headman, Ghân-buri-Ghân. I count many things: stars in sky, leaves on trees, men in the dark. You have a score of scores counted ten times and five. They have more. Big fight, and who will win? And many more walk round walls of Stone-houses.'

'Alas! he speaks all too shrewdly,' said Théoden. 'And our scouts say that they have cast trenches and stakes across the road. We cannot sweep them away in sudden onset.'

'And yet we need great haste,' said Éomer. 'Mundburg is on fire!'

'Let Ghân-buri-Ghân finish!' said the Wild Man. 'More than one road he knows. He will lead you by road where no pits are, no *gorgûn* walk, only Wild Men and beasts. Many paths were made when Stonehouse-folk were stronger. They carved hills as hunters carve beast-flesh. Wild Men think they ate stone for food. They went through Drúadan to Rimmon with great wains. They go no longer. Road is forgotten, but not by Wild Men. Over hill and behind hill it lies still under grass and tree, there behind Rimmon and down to Dîn, and back at the end to Horse-men's road. Wild Men will show you that road. Then you will kill *gorgûn* and drive away bad dark with bright iron, and Wild Men can go back to sleep in the wild woods.'

Éomer and the king spoke together in their own tongue. At length Théoden turned to the Wild Man. 'We will receive your offer,' he said. 'For though we leave a host of foes behind, what matter? If the Stone-city falls, then we shall have no returning. If it is saved, then the orc-host itself will be cut off. If you are faithful, Ghân-buri-Ghân, then we will give you rich reward, and you shall have the friendship of the Mark for ever.'

'Dead men are not friends to living men, and give them no gifts,' said the Wild Man. 'But if you live after the Darkness, then leave Wild Men alone in the woods and do not hunt them like beasts any more. Ghân-buri-Ghân will not lead you into trap. He will go himself with father of Horsemen, and if he leads you wrong, you will kill him.'

'So be it!' said Théoden.

'How long will it take to pass by the enemy and come back to the road?' asked Éomer. 'We must go at foot-pace, if you guide us; and I doubt not the way is narrow.'

'Wild Men go quick on feet,' said Ghân. 'Way is wide for four horses in Stonewain Valley yonder,' he waved his hand southwards; 'but narrow at beginning and at end. Wild Man could walk from here to Dîn between sunrise and noon.'

'Then we must allow at least seven hours for the leaders,' said Éomer; 'but we must reckon rather on some ten hours for all. Things unforeseen may hinder us, and if our host is all strung out, it will be long ere it can be set in order when we issue from the hills. What is the hour now?'

'Who knows?' said Théoden. 'All is night now.'

'It is all dark, but it is not all night,' said Ghân. 'When Sun comes we feel her, even when she is hidden. Already she climbs over East-mountains. It is the opening of day in the sky-fields.'

'Then we must set out as soon as may be,' said Éomer. 'Even so we cannot hope to come to Gondor's aid today.'

Merry waited to hear no more, but slipped away to get ready for the summons to the march. This was the last stage before the battle. It did not seem likely to him that many of them would survive it. But he thought of Pippin and the flames in Minas Tirith and thrust down his own dread.

All went well that day, and no sight or sound had they of the enemy waiting to waylay them. The Wild Men had put out a screen of wary hunters, so that no orc or roving spy should learn of the movements in the hills. The light was more dim than ever as they drew nearer to the beleaguered city, and the Riders passed in long files like dark shadows of men and horses. Each company was guided by a wild woodman; but old Ghân walked beside the king. The start had been slower than was hoped, for it had taken time for the Riders, walking and leading their horses, to find paths over the thickly wooded ridges behind their camp and down into the hidden Stonewain Valley. It was late in the afternoon when the leaders came to wide grey thickets stretching beyond the eastward side of Amon Dîn, and masking a great gap in the line of hills that from Nardol to Dîn ran east and west. Through the gap the forgotten wain-road long ago had run down, back into the main horse-way from the City through Anórien; but now for many lives of men trees had had their way with it, and it had vanished, broken and buried under the leaves of uncounted years. But the thickets offered to the Riders their last hope of cover before they went into open battle; for beyond them lay the road and the plains of Anduin, while east and southwards the slopes were bare and rocky, as the writhen hills gathered themselves together and climbed up, bastion upon bastion, into the great mass and shoulders of Mindolluin.

The leading company was halted, and as those behind filed up out of the trough of the Stonewain Valley they spread out and passed to camping-places under the grey trees. The king summoned the captains to council. Éomer sent out scouts to spy upon the road; but old Ghân shook his head.

'No good to send Horse-men,' he said. 'Wild Men have already seen all that can be seen in the bad air. They will come soon and speak to me here.'

The captains came; and then out of the trees crept warily other púkel-shapes so like old Ghân that Merry could hardly tell them apart. They spoke to Ghân in a strange throaty language.

Presently Ghân turned to the king. 'Wild Men say many things,' he said. 'First, be wary! Still many men in camp beyond Dîn, an hour's walk yonder,' he waved his arm west towards the black beacon. 'But none to see between here and Stone-folk's new walls. Many busy there. Walls stand up no longer: *gorgûn* knock them down with earth-thunder and with clubs of black iron. They are unwary and do not look about them. They think their friends watch all roads!' At that old Ghân made a curious gurgling noise, and it seemed that he was laughing.

'Good tidings!' cried Éomer. 'Even in this gloom hope gleams again. Our Enemy's devices oft serve us in his despite. The accursed darkness itself has been a cloak to us. And now, lusting to destroy Gondor and throw it down stone from stone, his orcs have taken away my greatest fear. The out-wall could have been held long against us. Now we can sweep through – if once we win so far.'

'Once again I thank you, Ghân-buri-Ghân of the woods,' said Théoden. 'Good fortune go with you for tidings and for guidance!'

'Kill *gorgûn*! Kill orc-folk! No other words please Wild Men,' answered Ghân. 'Drive away bad air and darkness with bright iron!'

'To do these things we have ridden far,' said the king, 'and we shall attempt them. But what we shall achieve only tomorrow will show.'

Ghân-buri-Ghân squatted down and touched the earth with his horny brow in token of farewell. Then he got up as if to depart. But suddenly he stood looking up like some startled woodland animal snuffling a strange air. A light came in his eyes.

'Wind is changing!' he cried, and with that, in a twinkling as it seemed, he and his fellows had vanished into the glooms, never to be seen by any Rider of Rohan again. Not long after far away eastward the faint drums throbbed again. Yet to no heart in all the host came any fear that the Wild Men were unfaithful, strange and unlovely though they might appear.

'We need no further guidance,' said Elfhelm; 'for there are riders in the host who have ridden down to Mundburg in days of peace. I for one. When we come to the road it will veer south, and there will lie before us still seven leagues ere we reach the wall of the townlands. Along most of that way there is much grass on either side of the road. On that stretch the errand-riders of Gondor reckoned to make their greatest speed. We may ride it swiftly and without great rumour.'

'Then since we must look for fell deeds and the need of all our strength,' said Éomer, 'I counsel that we rest now, and set out hence by night, and so time our going that we come upon the fields when tomorrow is as light as it will be, or when our lord give the signal.'

To this the king assented, and the captains departed. But soon Elfhelm returned. 'The scouts have found naught to report beyond the grey wood, lord,' he said, 'save two men only: two dead men and two dead horses.'

'Well?' said Éomer. 'What of it?'

'This, lord: they were errand-riders of Gondor; Hirgon was one maybe. At least his hand still clasped the Red Arrow, but his head was hewn off. And this also: it would seem by the signs that they were fleeing *westward* when they fell. As I read it, they found the enemy already on the out-wall, or assailing it, when they returned – and that would be two nights ago, if they used fresh horses from the posts, as is their wont. They could not reach the City and turned back.'

'Alas!' said Théoden. 'Then Denethor has heard no news of our riding and will despair of our coming.'

'*Need brooks no delay, yet late is better than never*,' said Éomer. 'And mayhap in this time shall the old saw be proved truer than ever before since men spoke with mouth.'

It was night. On either side of the road the host of Rohan was moving silently. Now the road passing about the skirts of Mindolluin turned southward. Far away and almost straight ahead there was a red glow under the black sky and the sides of the great mountain loomed dark against it. They were drawing near the Rammas of the Pelennor; but the day was not yet come.

The king rode in the midst of the leading company, his household-men about him. Elfhelm's *éored* came next; and now Merry noticed that Dernhelm had left his place and in the darkness was moving steadily forward, until at last he was riding just in rear of the king's guard. There came a check. Merry heard voices in front speaking softly. Out-riders had come back who had ventured forward almost to the wall. They came to the king.

'There are great fires, lord,' said one. 'The City is all set about with flame, and the field is full of foes. But all seem drawn off to the assault. As well as we could guess, there are few left upon the out-wall, and they are heedless, busy in destruction.'

'Do you remember the Wild Man's words, lord?' said another. 'I live upon the open Wold in days of peace; Wídfara is my name, and to me also the air brings messages. Already the wind is turning. There comes a breath out of the South; there is a sea-tang in it, faint though it be. The morning will bring new things. Above the reek it will be dawn when you pass the wall.'

'If you speak truly, Wídfara, then may you live beyond this day in years of blessedness!' said Théoden. He turned to the men of his household who were near, and he spoke now in a clear voice so that many also of the riders of the first *éored* heard him:

'Now is the hour come, Riders of the Mark, sons of Eorl! Foes and fire are before you, and your homes far behind. Yet, though you fight upon an alien field, the glory that you reap there shall be your own for ever. Oaths ye have taken: now fulfil them all, to lord and land and league of friendship!'

Men clashed spear upon shield.

'Éomer, my son! You lead the first *éored*,' said Théoden; 'and it shall go behind the king's banner in the centre. Elfhelm, lead your company to the right when we pass the wall. And Grimbold shall lead his towards the left. Let the other companies behind follow these three that lead, as they have chance. Strike wherever the enemy gathers. Other plans we cannot make, for we know not yet how things stand upon the field. Forth now, and fear no darkness!'

The leading company rode off as swiftly as they could, for it was still deep dark, whatever change Wídfara might forebode. Merry was riding behind Dernhelm, clutching with the left hand while with the other he tried to loosen his sword in its sheath. He felt now bitterly the truth of the old king's words: *in such a battle what would you do, Meriadoc?* Just this,' he thought: 'encumber a rider, and hope at best to stay in my seat and not be pounded to death by galloping hoofs!'

It was no more than a league to where the out-walls had stood. They soon reached them; too soon for Merry. Wild cries broke out, and there was some clash of arms, but it was brief. The orcs busy about the walls were few and amazed, and they were quickly slain or driven off. Before the ruin of the north-gate in the Rammas the king halted again. The first *éored* drew up behind him and about him on either side. Dernhelm kept close to the king, though Elfhelm's company was away on the right. Grimbold's men turned aside and passed round to a great gap in the wall further eastward.

Merry peered from behind Dernhelm's back. Far away, maybe ten miles or more, there was a great burning, but between it and the Riders lines of fire blazed in a vast crescent, at the nearest point less than a league distant. He could make out little more on the dark plain, and as yet he neither saw any hope of morning, nor felt any wind, changed or unchanged.

Now silently the host of Rohan moved forward into the field of Gondor, pouring in slowly but steadily, like the rising tide through breaches in a dike that men have thought secure. But the mind and will of the Black Captain were bent wholly on the falling city, and as yet no tidings came to him warning that his designs held any flaw.

After a while the king led his men away somewhat eastward, to come between the fires of the siege and the outer fields. Still they were unchallenged, and still Théoden gave no signal. At last he halted once again. The City was now nearer. A smell of burning was in the air and a very shadow of death. The horses were uneasy. But the king sat upon Snowmane, motionless, gazing upon the agony of Minas Tirith, as if stricken suddenly by anguish, or by dread. He seemed to shrink down, cowed by age. Merry himself felt as if a great weight of horror and doubt had settled on him. His heart beat slowly. Time seemed poised in uncertainty. They were too late! Too late was worse than never! Perhaps Théoden would quail, bow his old head, turn, slink away to hide in the hills.

Then suddenly Merry felt it at last, beyond doubt: a change. Wind was in his face! Light was glimmering. Far, far away, in the South the clouds could be dimly seen as remote grey shapes, rolling up, drifting: morning lay beyond them.

But at that same moment there was a flash, as if lightning had sprung from the earth beneath the City. For a searing second it stood dazzling far off in black and white, its topmost tower like a glittering needle; and then as the darkness closed again there came rolling over the fields a great *boom*.

At that sound the bent shape of the king sprang suddenly erect. Tall and proud he seemed again; and rising in his stirrups he cried in a loud voice, more clear than any there had ever heard a mortal man achieve before:

Arise, arise, Riders of Théoden!
Fell deeds awake: fire and slaughter!
spear shall be shaken, shield be splintered,
a sword-day, a red day, ere the sun rises!
Ride now, ride now! Ride to Gondor!

With that he seized a great horn from Guthláf his banner-bearer, and he blew such a blast upon it that it burst asunder. And straightway all the horns in the host were lifted up in music, and the blowing of the horns of Rohan in that hour was like a storm upon the plain and a thunder in the mountains.

Ride now, ride now! Ride to Gondor!

Suddenly the king cried to Snowmane and the horse sprang away. Behind him his banner blew in the wind, white horse upon a field of green, but he outpaced it. After him thundered the knights of his house, but he was ever before them. Éomer rode there, the white horsetail on his helm floating in his speed, and the front of the first *éored* roared like a breaker foaming to the shore, but Théoden could not be overtaken. Fey he seemed, or the battle-fury of his fathers ran like new fire in his veins, and he was borne up on Snowmane like a god of old, even as Oromë the Great in the battle of the Valar when the world was young. His golden shield was uncovered, and lo! it shone like an image of the Sun, and the grass flamed into green about the white feet of his steed. For morning came, morning and a wind from the sea; and darkness was removed, and the hosts of Mordor wailed, and terror took them, and they fled, and died, and the hoofs of wrath rode over them. And then all the host of Rohan burst into song, and they sang as they slew, for the joy of battle was on them, and the sound of their singing that was fair and terrible came even to the City.

CHAPTER VI

THE BATTLE OF THE PELENNOR FIELDS

But it was no orc-chieftain or brigand that led the assault upon Gondor. The darkness was breaking too soon, before the date that his Master had set for it: fortune had betrayed him for the moment, and the world had turned against him; victory was slipping from his grasp even as he stretched out his hand to seize it. But his arm was long. He was still in command, wielding great powers. King, Ringwraith, Lord of the Nazgûl, he had many weapons. He left the Gate and vanished.

Théoden King of the Mark had reached the road from the Gate to the River, and he turned towards the City that was now less than a mile distant. He slackened his speed a little, seeking new foes, and his knights came about him, and Dernhelm was with them. Ahead nearer the walls Elfhelm's men were among the siege-engines, hewing, slaying, driving their foes into the fire-pits. Well nigh all the northern half of the Pelennor was overrun, and there camps were blazing, orcs were flying towards the River like herds before the hunters; and the Rohirrim went hither and thither at their will. But they had not yet overthrown the siege, nor won the Gate. Many foes stood before it, and on the further half of the plain were other hosts still unfought. Southward beyond the road lay the main force of the Haradrim, and there their horsemen were gathered about the standard of their chieftain. And he looked out, and in the growing light he saw the banner of the king, and that it was far ahead of the battle with few men about it. Then he was filled with a red wrath and shouted aloud, and displaying his standard, black serpent upon scarlet, he came against the white horse and the green with great press of men; and the drawing of the scimitars of the Southrons was like a glitter of stars.

Then Théoden was aware of him, and would not wait for his onset, but crying to Snowmane he charged headlong to greet him. Great was the clash of their meeting. But the white fury of the Northmen burned the hotter, and more skilled was their knighthood with long spears and bitter. Fewer were they but they clove through the Southrons like a fire-bolt in a forest. Right through the press drove Théoden Thengel's son, and his spear was shivered as he threw down their chieftain. Out swept his sword, and he spurred to the standard, hewed staff and bearer; and the black serpent foundered. Then all that was left unslain of their cavalry turned and fled far away.

But lo! suddenly in the midst of the glory of the king his golden shield was dimmed. The new morning was blotted from the sky. Dark fell about him. Horses reared and screamed. Men cast from the saddle lay grovelling on the ground.

'To me! To me!' cried Théoden. 'Up Eorlingas! Fear no darkness!' But Snowmane wild with terror stood up on high, fighting with the air, and then with a great scream he crashed upon his side: a black dart had pierced him. The king fell beneath him.

The great shadow descended like a falling cloud. And behold! it was a winged creature: if bird, then greater than all other birds, and it was naked, and neither quill nor feather did it bear, and its vast pinions were as webs of hide between horned fingers; and it stank. A creature of an older world maybe it was, whose kind, lingering in forgotten mountains cold beneath the Moon, outstayed their day, and in hideous eyrie bred this last untimely brood, apt to evil. And the Dark Lord took it, and nursed it with fell meats, until it grew beyond the measure of all other things that fly; and he gave it to his servant to be his steed. Down, down it came, and then, folding its fingered webs, it gave a croaking cry, and settled upon the body of Snowmane, digging in its claws, stooping its long naked neck.

Upon it sat a shape, black-mantled, huge and threatening. A crown of steel he bore, but between rim and robe naught was there to see, save only a deadly gleam of eyes: the Lord of the Nazgûl. To the air he had returned, summoning his steed ere the darkness failed, and now he was come again, bringing ruin, turning hope to despair, and victory to death. A great black mace he wielded.

But Théoden was not utterly forsaken. The knights of his house lay slain about him, or else mastered by the madness of their steeds were borne far away. Yet one stood there still: Dernhelm the young, faithful beyond fear; and he wept, for he had loved his lord as a father. Right through the charge Merry had been borne unharmed behind him, until the Shadow came; and then Windfola had thrown them in his terror, and now ran wild upon the plain. Merry crawled on all fours like a dazed beast, and such a horror was on him that he was blind and sick.

'King's man! King's man!' his heart cried within him. 'You must stay by him. As a father you shall be to me, you said.' But his will made no answer, and his body shook. He dared not open his eyes or look up.

Then out of the blackness in his mind he thought that he heard Dernhelm speaking; yet now the voice seemed strange, recalling some other voice that he had known.

'Begone, foul dwimmerlaik, lord of carrion! Leave the dead in peace!'

A cold voice answered: 'Come not between the Nazgûl and his prey! Or he will not slay thee in thy turn. He will bear thee away to the houses of lamentation, beyond all darkness, where thy flesh shall be devoured, and thy shrivelled mind be left naked to the Lidless Eye.'

A sword rang as it was drawn. 'Do what you will; but I will hinder it, if I may.'

'Hinder me? Thou fool. No living man may hinder me!'

Then Merry heard of all sounds in that hour the strangest. It seemed that Dernhelm laughed, and the clear voice was like the ring of steel. 'But no living man am I! You look upon a woman. Éowyn I am, Éomund's daughter. You stand between me and my lord and kin. Begone, if you be not deathless! For living or dark undead, I will smite you, if you touch him.'

The winged creature screamed at her, but the Ringwraith made no answer, and was silent, as if in sudden doubt. Very amazement for a moment conquered Merry's fear. He opened his eyes and the blackness was lifted from them. There some paces from him sat the great beast, and all seemed dark about it, and above it loomed the Nazgûl Lord like a shadow of despair. A little to the left facing them stood she whom he had called Dernhelm. But the helm of her secrecy had fallen from her, and her bright hair, released from its bonds, gleamed with pale gold upon her shoulders. Her eyes grey as the sea were hard and fell, and yet tears were on her cheek. A sword was in her hand, and she raised her shield against the horror of her enemy's eyes.

Éowyn it was, and Dernhelm also. For into Merry's mind flashed the memory of the face that he saw at the riding from Dunharrow: the face of one that goes seeking death, having no hope. Pity filled his heart and great wonder, and suddenly the slow-kindled courage of his race awoke. He clenched his hand. She should not die, so fair, so desperate! At least she should not die alone, unaided.

The face of their enemy was not turned towards him, but still he hardly dared to move, dreading lest the deadly eyes should fall on him. Slowly, slowly he began to crawl aside; but the Black Captain, in doubt and malice intent upon the woman before him, heeded him no more than a worm in the mud.

Suddenly the great beast beat its hideous wings, and the wind of them was foul. Again it leaped into the air, and then swiftly fell down upon Éowyn, shrieking, striking with beak and claw.

Still she did not blench: maiden of the Rohirrim, child of kings, slender but as a steel-blade, fair yet terrible. A swift stroke she dealt, skilled and deadly. The outstretched neck she clove asunder, and the hewn head fell like a stone. Backward she sprang as the huge shape crashed to ruin, vast wings outspread, crumpled on the earth; and with its fall the shadow passed away. A light fell about her, and her hair shone in the sunrise.

Out of the wreck rose the Black Rider, tall and threatening, towering above her. With a cry of hatred that stung the very ears like venom he let fall his mace. Her shield was shivered in many pieces, and her arm was broken; she stumbled to her knees. He bent over her like a cloud, and his eyes glittered; he raised his mace to kill.

But suddenly he too stumbled forward with a cry of bitter pain, and his stroke went wide, driving into the ground. Merry's sword had stabbed him from behind, shearing through the black mantle, and passing up beneath the hauberk had pierced the sinew behind his mighty knee.

'Éowyn! Éowyn!' cried Merry. Then tottering, struggling up, with her last strength she drove her sword between crown and mantle, as the great shoulders bowed before her. The sword broke sparkling into many shards. The crown rolled away with a clang. Éowyn fell forward upon her fallen foe. But lo! the mantle and hauberk were empty. Shapeless they lay now on the ground, torn and tumbled; and a cry went up into the shuddering air, and faded to a shrill wailing, passing with the wind, a voice bodiless and thin that died, and was swallowed up, and was never heard again in that age of this world.

And there stood Meriadoc the hobbit in the midst of the slain, blinking like an owl in the daylight, for tears blinded him; and through a mist he looked on Éowyn's fair head, as she lay and did not move; and he looked on the face of the king, fallen in the midst of his glory. For Snowmane in his agony had rolled away from him again; yet he was the bane of his master.

Then Merry stooped and lifted his hand to kiss it, and lo! Théoden opened his eyes, and they were clear, and he spoke in a quiet voice though laboured.

'Farewell, Master Holbytla!' he said. 'My body is broken. I go to my fathers. And even in their mighty company I shall not now be ashamed. I felled the black serpent. A grim morn, and a glad day, and a golden sunset!'

Merry could not speak, but wept anew. 'Forgive me, lord,' he said at last, 'if I broke your command, and yet have done no more in your service than to weep at our parting.'

The old king smiled. 'Grieve not! It is forgiven. Great heart will not be denied. Live now in blessedness; and when you sit in peace with your pipe, think of me! For never now shall I sit with you in Meduseld, as I promised, or listen to your herb-lore.' He closed his eyes, and Merry bowed beside him. Presently he spoke again. 'Where is Éomer? For my eyes darken, and I would see him ere I go. He must be king after me. And I would send word to Éowyn. She, she would not have me leave her, and now I shall not see her again, dearer than daughter.'

'Lord, lord,' began Merry brokenly, 'she is——'; but at that moment there was a great clamour, and all about them horns and trumpets were blowing. Merry looked round: he had forgotten the war, and all the world beside, and many hours it seemed since the king rode to his fall, though in truth it was only a little while. But now he saw that they were in danger of being caught in the very midst of the great battle that would soon be joined.

New forces of the enemy were hastening up the road from the River; and from under the walls came the legions of Morgul; and from the southward fields came footmen of Harad with horsemen before them, and behind them rose the huge backs of the *mûmakil* with war-towers upon them. But northward the white crest of Éomer led the great front of the Rohirrim which he had again gathered and marshalled; and out of the City came all the strength of men that was in it, and the silver swan of Dol Amroth was borne in the van, driving the enemy from the Gate.

For a moment the thought flitted through Merry's mind: 'Where is Gandalf? Is he not here? Could he not have saved the king and Éowyn?' But thereupon Éomer rode up in haste, and with him came the knights of the household that still lived and had now mastered their horses. They looked in wonder at the carcase of the fell beast that lay there; and their steeds would not go near. But Éomer leaped from the saddle, and grief and dismay fell upon him as he came to the king's side and stood there in silence.

Then one of the knights took the king's banner from the hand of Guthláf the banner-bearer who lay dead, and he lifted it up. Slowly Théoden opened his eyes. Seeing the banner he made a sign that it should be given to Éomer.

'Hail, King of the Mark!' he said. 'Ride now to victory! Bid Éowyn farewell!' And so he died, and knew not that Éowyn lay near him. And those who stood by wept, crying: 'Théoden King! Théoden King!'

But Éomer said to them:

> *Mourn not overmuch! Mighty was the fallen,*
> *meet was his ending. When his mound is raised,*
> *women then shall weep. War now calls us!*

Yet he himself wept as he spoke. 'Let his knights remain here,' he said, 'and bear his body in honour from the field, lest the battle ride over it! Yea, and all these other of the king's men that lie here.' And he looked at the slain, recalling their names. Then suddenly he beheld his sister Éowyn as she lay, and he knew her. He stood a moment as a man who is pierced in the midst of a cry by an arrow through the heart; and then his face went deathly white, and a cold fury rose in him, so that all speech failed him for a while. A fey mood took him.

'Éowyn, Éowyn!' he cried at last. 'Éowyn, how come you here? What madness or devilry is this? Death, death, death! Death take us all!'

Then without taking counsel or waiting for the approach of the men of the City, he spurred headlong back to the front of the great host, and blew a horn, and cried aloud for the onset. Over the field rang his clear voice calling: 'Death! Ride, ride to ruin and the world's ending!'

And with that the host began to move. But the Rohirrim sang no more. *Death* they cried with one voice loud and terrible, and gathering speed like a great tide their battle swept about their fallen king and passed, roaring away southwards.

And still Meriadoc the hobbit stood there blinking through his tears, and no one spoke to him, indeed none seemed to heed him. He brushed away the tears, and stooped to pick up the green shield that Éowyn had given him, and he slung it at his back. Then he looked for his sword that he had let fall; for even as he struck his blow his arm was numbed, and now he could only use his left hand. And behold! there lay his weapon, but the blade was smoking like a dry branch that has been thrust in a fire; and as he watched it, it writhed and withered and was consumed.

So passed the sword of the Barrow-downs, work of Westernesse. But glad would he have been to know its fate who wrought it slowly long ago in the North-kingdom when the Dúnedain were young, and chief among their foes was the dread realm of Angmar and its sorcerer king. No other blade, not though mightier hands had wielded it, would have dealt that foe a wound so bitter, cleaving the undead flesh, breaking the spell that knit his unseen sinews to his will.

Men now raised the king, and laying cloaks upon spear-truncheons they made shift to bear him away towards the City; and others lifted Éowyn gently up and bore her after him. But the men of the king's household they could not yet bring from the field; for seven of the king's knights had fallen there, and Déorwine their chief was among them. So they laid them apart from their foes and the fell beast and set spears about them. And afterwards when all was over men returned and made a fire there and burned the carcase of the beast; but for Snowmane they dug a grave and set up a stone upon which was carved in the tongues of Gondor and the Mark:

Faithful servant yet master's bane,
Lightfoot's foal, swift Snowmane.

Green and long grew the grass on Snowmane's Howe, but ever black and bare was the ground where the beast was burned.

Now slowly and sadly Merry walked beside the bearers, and he gave no more heed to the battle. He was weary and full of pain, and his limbs trembled as with a chill. A great rain came out of the Sea, and it seemed that all things wept for Théoden and Éowyn, quenching the fires in the City with grey tears. It was through a mist that presently he saw the van of the men of Gondor approaching. Imrahil, Prince of Dol Amroth, rode up and drew rein before them.

'What burden do you bear, Men of Rohan?' he cried.

'Théoden King,' they answered. 'He is dead. But Éomer King now rides in the battle: he with the white crest in the wind.'

Then the prince went from his horse, and knelt by the bier in honour of the king and his great onset; and he wept. And rising he looked then on Éowyn and was amazed. 'Surely, here is a woman?' he said. 'Have even the women of the Rohirrim come to war in our need?'

'Nay! One only,' they answered. 'The Lady Éowyn is she, sister of Éomer; and we knew naught of her riding until this hour, and greatly we rue it.'

Then the prince seeing her beauty, though her face was pale and cold, touched her hand as he bent to look more closely on her. 'Men of Rohan!' he cried. 'Are there no leeches among you? She is hurt, to the death maybe, but I deem that she yet lives.' And he held the bright-burnished vambrace that was upon his arm before her cold lips, and behold! a little mist was laid on it hardly to be seen.

'Haste now is needed,' he said, and he sent one riding back swiftly to the City to bring aid. But he bowing low to the fallen, bade them farewell, and mounting rode away into battle.

And now the fighting waxed furious on the fields of the Pelennor; and the din of arms rose upon high, with the crying of men and the neighing of horses. Horns were blown and trumpets were braying, and the *mûmakil* were bellowing as they were goaded to war. Under the south walls of the City the footmen of Gondor now drove against the legions of Morgul that were still gathered there in strength. But the horsemen rode eastward to the succour of Éomer: Húrin the Tall, Warden of the Keys, and the Lord of Lossarnach, and Hirluin of the Green Hills, and Prince Imrahil the fair with his knights all about him.

Not too soon came their aid to the Rohirrim; for fortune had turned against Éomer, and his fury had betrayed him. The great wrath of his onset had utterly overthrown the front of his enemies, and great wedges of his Riders had passed clear through the ranks of the Southrons, discomfiting their horsemen and riding their footmen to ruin. But wherever the *mûmakil* came there the horses would not go, but blenched and swerved away; and the great monsters were unfought, and stood like towers of defence, and the Haradrim rallied about them. And if the Rohirrim at their onset were thrice outnumbered by the Haradrim alone, soon their case became worse; for new strength came now streaming to the field out of Osgiliath. There they had been mustered for the sack of the City and the rape of Gondor, waiting on the call of their Captain. He now was destroyed; but Gothmog the lieutenant of Morgul had flung them into the fray; Easterlings with axes, and Variags of Khand, Southrons in scarlet, and out of Far Harad black men like half-trolls with white eyes and red tongues. Some now hastened up behind the Rohirrim, others held westward to hold off the forces of Gondor and prevent their joining with Rohan.

It was even as the day thus began to turn against Gondor and their hope wavered that a new cry went up in the City, it being then mid-morning, and a great wind blowing, and the rain flying north, and the sun shining. In that clear air watchmen on the walls saw afar a new sight of fear, and their last hope left them.

For Anduin, from the bend at the Harlond, so flowed that from the City men could look down it lengthwise for some leagues, and the far-sighted could see any ships that approached. And looking thither they cried in dismay; for black against the glittering stream they beheld a fleet borne up on the wind: dromunds, and ships of great draught with many oars, and with black sails bellying in the breeze.

'The Corsairs of Umbar!' men shouted. 'The Corsairs of Umbar! Look! The Corsairs of Umbar are coming! So Belfalas is taken, and the Ethir, and Lebennin is gone. The Corsairs are upon us! It is the last stroke of doom!'

And some without order, for none could be found to command them in the City, ran to the bells and tolled the alarm; and some blew the trumpets sounding the retreat. 'Back to the walls!' they cried. 'Back to the walls! Come back to the City before all are overwhelmed!' But the wind that sped the ships blew all their clamour away.

The Rohirrim indeed had no need of news or alarm. All too well they could see for themselves the black sails. For Éomer was now scarcely a mile from the Harlond, and a great press of his first foes was between him and the haven there, while new foes came swirling behind, cutting him off from the Prince. Now he looked to the River, and hope died in his heart, and the wind that he had blessed he now called accursed. But the hosts of

Mordor were enheartened, and filled with a new lust and fury they came yelling to the onset.

Stern now was Éomer's mood, and his mind clear again. He let blow the horns to rally all men to his banner that could come thither; for he thought to make a great shield-wall at the last, and stand, and fight there on foot till all fell, and do deeds of song on the fields of Pelennor, though no man should be left in the West to remember the last King of the Mark. So he rode to a green hillock and there set his banner, and the White Horse ran rippling in the wind.

Out of doubt, out of dark to the day's rising
I came singing in the sun, sword unsheathing.
To hope's end I rode and to heart's breaking:
Now for wrath, now for ruin and a red nightfall!

These staves he spoke, yet he laughed as he said them. For once more lust of battle was on him; and he was still unscathed, and he was young, and he was king: the lord of a fell people. And lo! even as he laughed at despair he looked out again on the black ships, and he lifted up his sword to defy them.

And then wonder took him, and a great joy; and he cast his sword up in the sunlight and sang as he caught it. And all eyes followed his gaze, and behold! upon the foremost ship a great standard broke, and the wind displayed it as she turned towards the Harlond. There flowered a White Tree, and that was for Gondor; but Seven Stars were about it, and a high crown above it, the signs of Elendil that no lord had borne for years beyond count. And the stars flamed in the sunlight, for they were wrought of gems by Arwen daughter of Elrond; and the crown was bright in the morning, for it was wrought of mithril and gold.

Thus came Aragorn son of Arathorn, Elessar, Isildur's heir, out of the Paths of the Dead, borne upon a wind from the Sea to the kingdom of Gondor; and the mirth of the Rohirrim was a torrent of laughter and a flashing of swords, and the joy and wonder of the City was a music of trumpets and a ringing of bells. But the hosts of Mordor were seized with bewilderment, and a great wizardry it seemed to them that their own ships should be filled with their foes; and a black dread fell on them, knowing that the tides of fate had turned against them and their doom was at hand.

East rode the knights of Dol Amroth driving the enemy before them: troll-men and Variags and orcs that hated the sunlight. South strode Éomer and men fled before his face, and they were caught between the hammer and the anvil. For now men leaped from the ships to the quays of the Harlond and swept north like a storm. There came Legolas, and Gimli wielding his axe, and Halbarad with the standard, and Elladan and Elrohir with stars on their brow, and the dour-handed Dúnedain, Rangers of the North, leading a great valour of the folk of Lebennin and Lamedon and the fiefs of the South. But before all went Aragorn with the Flame of the West, Andúril like a new fire kindled, Narsil re-forged as deadly as of old; and upon his brow was the Star of Elendil.

And so at length Éomer and Aragorn met in the midst of the battle, and they leaned on their swords and looked on one another and were glad.

'Thus we meet again, though all the hosts of Mordor lay between us,' said Aragorn. 'Did I not say so at the Hornburg?'

'So you spoke,' said Éomer, 'but hope oft deceives, and I knew not then that you were a man foresighted. Yet twice blessed is help unlooked for, and never was a meeting of friends more joyful.' And they clasped hand in hand. 'Nor indeed more timely,' said Éomer. 'You come none too soon, my friend. Much loss and sorrow has befallen us.'

'Then let us avenge it, ere we speak of it!' said Aragorn, and they rode back to battle together.

Hard fighting and long labour they had still; for the Southrons were bold men and grim, and fierce in despair; and the Easterlings were strong and war-hardened and asked for no quarter. And so in this place and that, by burned homestead or barn, upon hillock or mound, under wall or on field, still they gathered and rallied and fought until the day wore away.

Then the Sun went at last behind Mindolluin and filled all the sky with a great burning, so that the hills and the mountains were dyed as with blood; fire glowed in the River, and the grass of the Pelennor lay red in the nightfall. And in that hour the great Battle of the field of Gondor was over; and not one living foe was left within the circuit of the Rammas. All were slain save those who fled to die, or to drown in the red foam of the River. Few ever came eastward to Morgul or Mordor; and to the land of the Haradrim came only a tale from far off: a rumour of the wrath and terror of Gondor.

Aragorn and Éomer and Imrahil rode back towards the Gate of the City, and they were now weary beyond joy or sorrow. These three were unscathed, for such was their fortune and the skill and might of their arms, and few indeed had dared to abide them or look on their faces in the hour of their wrath. But many others were hurt or maimed or dead upon the field. The axes hewed Forlong as he fought alone and unhorsed; and both Duilin of Morthond and his brother were trampled to death when they assailed the *mûmakil*, leading their bowmen close to shoot at the eyes of the monsters. Neither Hirluin the fair would return to Pinnath Gelin, nor

Grimbold to Grimslade, nor Halbarad to the Northlands, dour-handed Ranger. No few had fallen, renowned or nameless, captain or soldier; for it was a great battle and the full count of it no tale has told. So long afterward a maker in Rohan said in his song of the Mounds of Mundburg:

We heard of the horns in the hills ringing,
the swords shining in the South-kingdom.
Steeds went striding to the Stoningland
as wind in the morning. War was kindled.
There Théoden fell, Thengling mighty,
to his golden halls and green pastures
in the Northern fields never returning,
high lord of the host. Harding and Guthláf,
Dúnhere and Déorwine, doughty Grimbold,
Herefara and Herubrand, Horn and Fastred,
fought and fell there in a far country:
in the Mounds of Mundburg under mould they lie
with their league-fellows, lords of Gondor.
Neither Hirluin the Fair to the hills by the sea,
nor Forlong the old to the flowering vales
ever, to Arnach, to his own country
returned in triumph; nor the tall bowmen,
Derufin and Duilin, to their dark waters,
meres of Morthond under mountain-shadows.
Death in the morning and at day's ending
lords took and lowly. Long now they sleep
under grass in Gondor by the Great River.
Grey now as tears, gleaming silver,
red then it rolled, roaring water:
foam dyed with blood flamed at sunset;
as beacons mountains burned at evening;
red fell the dew in Rammas Echor.

CHAPTER VII

THE PYRE OF DENETHOR

When the dark shadow at the Gate withdrew Gandalf still sat motionless. But Pippin rose to his feet, as if a great weight had been lifted from him; and he stood listening to the horns, and it seemed to him that they would break his heart with joy. And never in after years could he hear a horn blown in the distance without tears starting in his eyes. But now suddenly his errand returned to his memory, and he ran forward. At that moment Gandalf stirred and spoke to Shadowfax, and was about to ride through the Gate.

'Gandalf, Gandalf!' cried Pippin, and Shadowfax halted.

'What are you doing here?' said Gandalf. 'Is it not a law in the City that those who wear the black and silver must stay in the Citadel, unless their lord gives them leave?'

'He has,' said Pippin. 'He sent me away. But I am frightened. Something terrible may happen up there. The Lord is out of his mind, I think. I am afraid he will kill himself, and kill Faramir too. Can't you do something?'

Gandalf looked through the gaping Gate, and already on the fields he heard the gathering sound of battle. He clenched his hand. 'I must go,' he said. 'The Black Rider is abroad, and he will yet bring ruin on us. I have no time.'

'But Faramir!' cried Pippin. 'He is not dead, and they will burn him alive, if someone does not stop them.'

'Burn him alive?' said Gandalf. 'What is this tale? Be quick!'

'Denethor has gone to the Tombs,' said Pippin, 'and he has taken Faramir, and he says we are all to burn, and he will not wait, and they are to make a pyre and burn him on it, and Faramir as well. And he has sent men to fetch wood and oil. And I have told Beregond, but I'm afraid he won't dare to leave his post: he is on guard. And what can he do anyway?' So Pippin poured out his tale, reaching up and touching Gandalf's knee with trembling hands. 'Can't you save Faramir?'

'Maybe I can,' said Gandalf; 'but if I do, then others will die, I fear. Well, I must come, since no other help can reach him. But evil and sorrow will come of this. Even in the heart of our stronghold the Enemy has power to strike us: for his will it is that is at work.'

Then having made up his mind he acted swiftly; and catching up Pippin and setting him before him, he turned Shadowfax with a word. Up the climbing streets of Minas Tirith they clattered, while the noise of war rose behind them. Everywhere men were rising from their despair and dread, seizing their weapons, crying one to another: 'Rohan has come!' Captains were shouting, companies were mustering; many already were marching down to the Gate.

They met the Prince Imrahil, and he called to them: 'Whither now, Mithrandir? The Rohirrim are fighting on the fields of Gondor! We must gather all the strength that we can find.'

'You will need every man and more,' said Gandalf. 'Make all haste. I will come when I can. But I have an errand to the Lord Denethor that will not wait. Take command in the Lord's absence!'

They passed on; and as they climbed and drew near to the Citadel they felt the wind blowing in their faces, and they caught the glimmer of morning far away, a light growing in the southern sky. But it brought little hope to them, not knowing what evil lay before them, fearing to come too late.

'Darkness is passing,' said Gandalf, 'but it still lies heavy on this City.'

At the gate of the Citadel they found no guard. 'Then Beregond has gone,' said Pippin more hopefully. They turned away and hastened along the road to the Closed Door. It stood wide open, and the porter lay before it. He was slain and his key had been taken.

'Work of the Enemy!' said Gandalf. 'Such deeds he loves: friend at war with friend; loyalty divided in confusion of hearts.' Now he dismounted and bade Shadowfax return to his stable. 'For, my friend,' he said, 'you and I should have ridden to the fields long ago, but other matters delay me. Yet come swiftly if I call!'

They passed the Door and walked on down the steep winding road. Light was growing, and the tall columns and carven figures beside the way went slowly by like grey ghosts.

Suddenly the silence was broken, and they heard below them cries and the ringing of swords: such sounds as had not been heard in the hallowed places since the building of the City. At last they came to Rath Dínen and hastened towards the House of the Stewards, looming in the twilight under its great dome.

'Stay! Stay!' cried Gandalf, springing forward to the stone stair before the door. 'Stay this madness!'

For there were the servants of Denethor with swords and torches in their hands; but alone in the porch upon the topmost step stood Beregond, clad in the black and silver of the Guard; and he held the door against them. Two of them had already fallen to his sword, staining the hallows with their blood; and the others cursed him, calling him outlaw and traitor to his master.

Even as Gandalf and Pippin ran forward, they heard from within the house of the dead the voice of Denethor crying: 'Haste, haste! Do as I have bidden! Slay me this renegade! Or must I do so myself?' Thereupon the door which Beregond held shut with his left hand was wrenched open, and there behind him stood the Lord of the City, tall and fell; a light like flame was in his eyes, and he held a drawn sword.

But Gandalf sprang up the steps, and the men fell back from him and covered their eyes; for his coming was like the incoming of a white light into a dark place, and he came with great anger. He lifted up his hand, and in the very stroke, the sword of Denethor flew up and left his grasp and fell behind him in the shadows of the house; and Denethor stepped backward before Gandalf as one amazed.

'What is this, my lord?' said the wizard. 'The houses of the dead are no places for the living. And why do men fight here in the Hallows when there is war enough before the Gate? Or has our Enemy come even to Rath Dínen?'

'Since when has the Lord of Gondor been answerable to thee?' said Denethor. 'Or may I not command my own servants?'

'You may,' said Gandalf. 'But others may contest your will, when it is turned to madness and evil. Where is your son, Faramir?'

'He lies within,' said Denethor, 'burning, already burning. They have set a fire in his flesh. But soon all shall be burned. The West has failed. It shall all go up in a great fire, and all shall be ended. Ash! Ash and smoke blown away on the wind!'

Then Gandalf seeing the madness that was on him feared that he had already done some evil deed, and he thrust forward, with Beregond and Pippin behind him, while Denethor gave back until he stood beside the table within. But there they found Faramir, still dreaming in his fever, lying upon the table. Wood was piled under it, and high all about it, and all was drenched with oil, even the garments of Faramir and the coverlets; but as yet no fire had been set to the fuel. Then Gandalf revealed the strength that lay hid in him, even as the light of his power was hidden under his grey mantle. He leaped up on to the faggots, and raising the sick man lightly he sprang down again, and bore him towards the door. But as he did so Faramir moaned and called on his father in his dream.

Denethor started as one waking from a trance, and the flame died in his eyes, and he wept; and he said: 'Do not take my son from me! He calls for me.'

'He calls,' said Gandalf, 'but you cannot come to him yet. For he must seek healing on the threshold of death, and maybe find it not. Whereas your part is to go out to the battle of your City, where maybe death awaits you. This you know in your heart.'

'He will not wake again,' said Denethor. 'Battle is vain. Why should we wish to live longer? Why should we not go to death side by side?'

'Authority is not given to you, Steward of Gondor, to order the hour of your death,' answered Gandalf. 'And only the heathen kings, under the domination of the Dark Power, did thus, slaying themselves in pride and despair, murdering their kin to ease their own death.' Then passing through the door he took Faramir from the deadly house and laid him on the bier on which he had been brought, and which had now been set in the porch. Denethor followed him, and stood trembling, looking with longing on the face of his son. And for a moment, while all were silent and still, watching the Lord in his throes, he wavered.

'Come!' said Gandalf. 'We are needed. There is much that you can yet do.'

Then suddenly Denethor laughed. He stood up tall and proud again, and stepping swiftly back to the table he lifted from it the pillow on which his head had lain. Then coming to the doorway he drew aside the covering, and lo! he had between his hands a *palantír*. And as he held it up, it seemed to those that looked on that the globe began to glow with an inner flame, so that the lean face of the Lord was lit as with a red fire, and it seemed cut out of hard stone, sharp with black shadows, noble, proud, and terrible. His eyes glittered.

'Pride and despair!' he cried. 'Didst thou think that the eyes of the White Tower were blind? Nay, I have seen more than thou knowest, Grey Fool. For thy hope is but ignorance. Go then and labour in healing! Go forth and fight! Vanity. For a little space you may triumph on the field, for a day. But against the Power that now arises there is no victory. To this City only the first finger of its hand has yet been stretched. All the East is moving. And even now the wind of thy hope cheats thee and wafts up Anduin a fleet with black sails. The West has failed. It is time for all to depart who would not be slaves.'

'Such counsels will make the Enemy's victory certain indeed,' said Gandalf.

'Hope on then!' laughed Denethor. 'Do I not know thee, Mithrandir? Thy hope is to rule in my stead, to stand behind every throne, north, south, or west. I have read thy mind and its policies. Do I not know that you commanded this halfling here to keep silence? That you brought him hither to be a spy within my very chamber? And yet in our speech together I have learned the names and purpose of all thy companions. So! With the left hand thou wouldst use me for a little while as a shield against Mordor, and with the right bring up this Ranger of the North to supplant me.

'But I say to thee, Gandalf Mithrandir, I will not be thy tool! I am Steward of the House of Anárion. I will not step down to be the dotard chamberlain of an upstart. Even were his claim proved to me, still he comes but of the line of Isildur. I will not bow to such a one, last of a ragged house long bereft of lordship and dignity.'

'What then would you have,' said Gandalf, 'if your will could have its way?'

'I would have things as they were in all the days of my life,' answered Denethor, 'and in the days of my longfathers before me: to be the Lord of this City in peace, and leave my chair to a son after me, who would be his own master and no wizard's pupil. But if doom denies this to me, then I will have *naught*: neither life diminished, nor love halved, nor honour abated.'

'To me it would not seem that a Steward who faithfully surrenders his charge is diminished in love or in honour,' said Gandalf. 'And at the least you shall not rob your son of his choice while his death is still in doubt.'

At those words Denethor's eyes flamed again, and taking the Stone under his arm he drew a knife and strode towards the bier. But Beregond sprang forward and set himself before Faramir.

'So!' cried Denethor. 'Thou hadst already stolen half my son's love. Now thou stealest the hearts of my knights also, so that they rob me wholly of my son at the last. But in this at least thou shalt not defy my will: to rule my own end.'

'Come hither!' he cried to his servants. 'Come, if you are not all recreant!' Then two of them ran up the steps to him. Swiftly he snatched a torch from the hand of one and sprang back into the house. Before Gandalf could hinder him he thrust the brand amid the fuel, and at once it crackled and roared into flame.

Then Denethor leaped upon the table, and standing there wreathed in fire and smoke he took up the staff of his stewardship that lay at his feet and broke it on his knee. Casting the pieces into the blaze he bowed and laid himself on the table, clasping the *palantír* with both hands upon his breast. And it was said that ever after, if any man looked in that Stone, unless he had a great strength of will to turn it to other purpose, he saw only two aged hands withering in flame.

Gandalf in grief and horror turned his face away and closed the door. For a while he stood in thought, silent upon the threshold, while those outside heard the greedy roaring of the fire within. And then Denethor gave a great cry, and afterwards spoke no more, nor was ever again seen by mortal men.

'So passes Denethor, son of Ecthelion,' said Gandalf. Then he turned to Beregond and the Lord's servants that stood there aghast. 'And so pass also the days of Gondor that you have known; for good or evil they are ended. Ill deeds have been done here; but let now all enmity that lies between you be put away, for it was contrived by the Enemy and works his will. You have been caught in a net of warring duties that you did not weave. But think, you servants of the Lord, blind in your obedience, that but for the treason of Beregond Faramir, Captain of the White Tower, would now also be burned.

'Bear away from this unhappy place your comrades who have fallen. And we will bear Faramir, Steward of Gondor, to a place where he can sleep in peace, or die if that be his doom.'

Then Gandalf and Beregond taking up the bier bore it away towards the Houses of Healing, while behind them walked Pippin with downcast head. But the servants of the Lord stood gazing as stricken men at the house of the dead; and even as Gandalf came to the end of Rath Dínen there was a great noise. Looking back they saw the dome of the house crack and smokes issue forth; and then with a rush and rumble of stone it fell in a flurry of fire; but still unabated the flames danced and flickered among the ruins. Then in terror the servants fled and followed Gandalf.

At length they came back to the Steward's Door, and Beregond looked with grief at the porter. 'This deed I shall ever rue,' he said; 'but a madness of haste was on me, and he would not listen, but drew sword against me.' Then taking the key that he had wrested from the slain man he closed the door and locked it. 'This should now be given to the Lord Faramir,' he said.

'The Prince of Dol Amroth is in command in the absence of the Lord,' said Gandalf; 'but since he is not here, I must take this on myself. I bid you keep the key and guard it, until the City is set in order again.'

Now at last they passed into the high circles of the City, and in the light of morning they went their way towards the Houses of Healing; and these were fair houses set apart for the care of those who were grievously sick, but now they were prepared for the tending of men hurt in battle or dying. They stood not far from the Citadel-gate, in the sixth circle, nigh to its southward wall, and about them was a garden and a greensward with trees, the only such place in the City. There dwelt the few women that had been permitted to remain in Minas Tirith, since they were skilled in healing or in the service of the healers.

But even as Gandalf and his companions came carrying the bier to the main door of the Houses, they heard a great cry that went up from the field before the Gate and rising shrill and piercing into the sky passed, and died away on the wind. So terrible was the cry that for a moment all stood still, and yet when it had passed, suddenly their hearts were lifted up in such a hope as they had not known since the darkness came out of the

East; and it seemed to them that the light grew clear and the sun broke through the clouds.

But Gandalf's face was grave and sad, and bidding Beregond and Pippin to take Faramir into the Houses of Healing, he went up on to the walls nearby; and there like a figure carven in white he stood in the new sun and looked out. And he beheld with the sight that was given to him all that had befallen; and when Éomer rode out from the forefront of his battle and stood beside those who lay upon the field, he sighed, and he cast his cloak about him again, and went from the walls. And Beregond and Pippin found him standing in thought before the door of the Houses when they came out.

They looked at him, and for a while he was silent. At last he spoke. 'My friends,' he said, 'and all you people of this city and of the Western lands! Things of great sorrow and renown have come to pass. Shall we weep or be glad? Beyond hope the Captain of our foes has been destroyed, and you have heard the echo of his last despair. But he has not gone without woe and bitter loss. And that I might have averted but for the madness of Denethor. So long has the reach of our Enemy become! Alas! but now I perceive how his will was able to enter into the very heart of the City.

'Though the Stewards deemed that it was a secret kept only by themselves, long ago I guessed that here in the White Tower, one at least of the Seven Seeing Stones was preserved. In the days of his wisdom Denethor would not presume to use it to challenge Sauron, knowing the limits of his own strength. But his wisdom failed; and I fear that as the peril of his realm grew he looked in the Stone and was deceived: far too often, I guess, since Boromir departed. He was too great to be subdued to the will of the Dark Power, he saw nonetheless only those things which that Power permitted him to see. The knowledge which he obtained was, doubtless, often of service to him; yet the vision of the great might of Mordor that was shown to him fed the despair of his heart until it overthrew his mind.'

'Now I understand what seemed so strange to me!' said Pippin, shuddering at his memories as he spoke. 'The Lord went away from the room where Faramir lay; and it was only when he returned that I first thought he was changed, old and broken.'

'It was in the very hour that Faramir was brought to the Tower that many of us saw a strange light in the topmost chamber,' said Beregond. 'But we have seen that light before, and it has long been rumoured in the City that the Lord would at times wrestle in thought with his Enemy.'

'Alas! then I have guessed rightly,' said Gandalf. 'Thus the will of Sauron entered into Minas Tirith; and thus I have been delayed here. And here I shall still be forced to remain, for I shall soon have other charges, not Faramir only.

'Now I must go down to meet those who come. I have seen a sight upon the field that is very grievous to my heart, and greater sorrow may yet come to pass. Come with me, Pippin! But you, Beregond, should return to the Citadel and tell the chief of the Guard there what has befallen. It will be his duty, I fear, to withdraw you from the Guard; but say to him that, if I may give him counsel, you should be sent to the Houses of Healing, to be the guard and servant of your captain, and to be at his side when he awakes – if that shall ever be again. For by you he was saved from the fire. Go now! I shall return soon.'

With that he turned away and went with Pippin down towards the lower city. And even as they hastened on their way the wind brought a grey rain, and all the fires sank, and there arose a great smoke before them.

CHAPTER VIII

THE HOUSES OF HEALING

A mist was in Merry's eyes of tears and weariness when they drew near the ruined Gate of Minas Tirith. He gave little heed to the wreck and slaughter that lay about all. Fire and smoke and stench was in the air; for many engines had been burned or cast into the fire-pits, and many of the slain also, while here and there lay many carcases of the great Southron monsters, half-burned, or broken by stone-cast, or shot through the eyes by the valiant archers of Morthond. The flying rain had ceased for a time, and the sun gleamed up above; but all the lower city was still wrapped in a smouldering reek.

Already men were labouring to clear a way through the jetsam of battle; and now out from the Gate came some bearing litters. Gently they laid Éowyn upon soft pillows; but the king's body they covered with a great cloth of gold, and they bore torches about him, and their flames, pale in the sunlight, were fluttered by the wind.

So Théoden and Éowyn came to the City of Gondor, and all who saw them bared their heads and bowed; and they passed through the ash and fume of the burned circle, and went on and up along the streets of stone. To Merry the ascent seemed agelong, a meaningless journey in a hateful dream, going on and on to some dim ending that memory cannot seize.

Slowly the lights of the torches in front of him flickered and went out, and he was walking in a darkness; and he thought: 'This is a tunnel leading to a tomb; there we shall stay forever.' But suddenly into his dream there fell a living voice.

'Well, Merry! Thank goodness I have found you!'

He looked up and the mist before his eyes cleared a little. There was Pippin! They were face to face in a narrow lane, and but for themselves it was empty. He rubbed his eyes.

'Where is the king?' he said. 'And Éowyn?' Then he stumbled and sat down on a doorstep and began to weep again.

'They have gone up into the Citadel,' said Pippin. 'I think you must have fallen asleep on your feet and taken the wrong turning. When we found that you were not with them, Gandalf sent me to look for you. Poor old Merry! How glad I am to see you again! But you are worn out, and I won't bother you with any talk. But tell me, are you hurt, or wounded?'

'No,' said Merry. 'Well, no, I don't think so. But I can't use my right arm, Pippin, not since I stabbed him. And my sword burned all away like a piece of wood.'

Pippin's face was anxious. 'Well, you had better come with me as quick as you can,' he said. 'I wish I could carry you. You aren't fit to walk any further. They shouldn't have let you walk at all; but you must forgive them. So many dreadful things have happened in the City, Merry, that one poor hobbit coming in from the battle is easily overlooked.'

'It's not always a misfortune being overlooked,' said Merry. 'I was overlooked just now by – no, no, I can't speak of it. Help me, Pippin! It's all going dark again, and my arm is so cold.'

'Lean on me, Merry lad!' said Pippin. 'Come now! Foot by foot. It's not far.'

'Are you going to bury me?' said Merry.

'No, indeed!' said Pippin, trying to sound cheerful, though his heart was wrung with fear and pity. 'No, we are going to the Houses of Healing.'

They turned out of the lane that ran between tall houses and the outer wall of the fourth circle, and they regained the main street climbing up to the Citadel. Step by step they went, while Merry swayed and murmured as one in sleep.

'I'll never get him there,' thought Pippin. 'Is there no one to help me? I can't leave him here.' Just then to his surprise a boy came running up behind, and as he passed he recognized Bergil Beregond's son.

'Hullo, Bergil!' he called. 'Where are you going? Glad to see you again, and still alive!'

'I am running errands for the Healers,' said Bergil. 'I cannot stay.'

'Don't!' said Pippin. 'But tell them up there that I have a sick hobbit, a *perian* mind you, come from the battle-field. I don't think he can walk so far. If Mithrandir is there, he will be glad of the message.' Bergil ran on.

'I'd better wait here,' thought Pippin. So he let Merry sink gently down on to the pavement in a patch of sunlight, and then he sat down beside him, laying Merry's head in his lap. He felt his body and limbs gently, and took his friend's hands in his own. The right hand felt icy to the touch.

It was not long before Gandalf himself came in search of them. He stooped over Merry and caressed his brow; then he lifted him carefully. 'He should have been borne in honour into this city,' he said. 'He has well repaid my trust; for if Elrond had not yielded to me, neither of you would have set out; and then far more grievous would the evils of this day have been.' He sighed. 'And yet here is another charge on my hands, while all the time the battle hangs in the balance.'

So at last Faramir and Éowyn and Meriadoc were laid in beds in the Houses of Healing; and there they were tended well. For though all lore was in these latter days fallen from its fullness of old, the leechcraft of Gondor was still wise, and skilled in the healing of wound and hurt, and all such sickness as east of the Sea mortal men were subject to. Save old age only. For that they had found no cure; and indeed the span of their lives had now waned to little more than that of other men, and those among them who passed the tale of five score years with vigour were grown few, save in some houses of purer blood. But now their art and knowledge were baffled; for there were many sick of a malady that would not be healed; and they called it the Black Shadow, for it came from the Nazgûl. And those who were stricken with it fell slowly into an ever deeper dream, and then passed to silence and a deadly cold, and so died. And it seemed to the tenders of the sick that on the Halfling and on the Lady of Rohan this malady lay heavily. Still at whiles as the morning wore away they would speak, murmuring in their dreams; and the watchers listened to all that they said, hoping perhaps to learn something that would help them to understand their hurts. But soon they began to fall down into the darkness, and as the sun turned west a grey shadow crept over their faces. But Faramir burned with a fever that would not abate.

Gandalf went from one to the other full of care, and he was told all that the watchers could hear. And so the day passed, while the great battle outside went on with shifting hopes and strange tidings; and still Gandalf waited and watched and did not go forth; till at last the red sunset filled all the sky, and the light through the windows fell on the grey faces of the sick. Then it seemed to those who stood by that in the glow the faces flushed softly as with health returning, but it was only a mockery of hope.

Then an old wife, Ioreth, the eldest of the women who served in that house, looking on the fair face of Faramir, wept, for all the people loved him. And she said: 'Alas! if he should die. Would that there were kings in Gondor, as there were once upon a time, they say! For it is said in old lore: *The hands of the king are the hands of a healer.* And so the rightful king could ever be known.'

And Gandalf, who stood by, said: 'Men may long remember your words, Ioreth! For there is hope in them. Maybe a king has indeed returned to Gondor; or have you not heard the strange tidings that have come to the City?'

'I have been too busy with this and that to heed all the crying and shouting,' she answered. 'All I hope is that those murdering devils do not come to this House and trouble the sick.'

Then Gandalf went out in haste, and already the fire in the sky was burning out, and the smouldering hills were fading, while ash-grey evening crept over the fields.

Now as the sun went down Aragorn and Éomer and Imrahil drew near the City with their captains and knights; and when they came before the Gate Aragorn said:

'Behold the Sun setting in a great fire! It is a sign of the end and fall of many things, and a change in the tides of the world. But this City and realm has rested in the charge of the Stewards for many long years, and I fear that if I enter it unbidden, then doubt and debate may arise, which should not be while this war is fought. I will not enter in, nor make any claim, until it be seen whether we or Mordor shall prevail. Men shall pitch my tents upon the field, and here I will await the welcome of the Lord of the City.'

But Éomer said: 'Already you have raised the banner of the Kings and displayed the tokens of Elendil's House. Will you suffer these to be challenged?'

'No,' said Aragorn. 'But I deem the time unripe; and I have no mind for strife except with our Enemy and his servants.'

And the Prince Imrahil said: 'Your words, lord, are wise, if one who is a kinsman of the Lord Denethor may counsel you in this matter. He is strong-willed and proud, but old; and his mood has been strange since his son was stricken down. Yet I would not have you remain like a beggar at the door.'

'Not a beggar,' said Aragorn. 'Say a captain of the Rangers, who are unused to cities and houses of stone.' And he commanded that his banner should be furled; and he did off the Star of the North Kingdom and gave it to the keeping of the sons of Elrond.

Then the Prince Imrahil and Éomer of Rohan left him and passed through the City and the tumult of the people, and mounted to the Citadel; and they came to the Hall of the Tower, seeking the Steward. But they found his chair empty, and before the dais lay Théoden King of the Mark upon a bed of state; and twelve torches stood about it, and twelve guards, knights both of Rohan and Gondor. And the hangings of the bed were of green and white, but upon the king was laid the great cloth of gold up to his breast, and upon that his unsheathed sword, and at his feet his shield. The light of the torches shimmered in his white hair like sun in the spray of a fountain, but his face was fair and young, save that a peace lay on it beyond the reach of youth; and it seemed that he slept.

When they had stood silent for a time beside the king, Imrahil said: 'Where is the Steward? And where also is Mithrandir?'

And one of the guards answered: 'The Steward of Gondor is in the Houses of Healing.'

But Éomer said: 'Where is the Lady Éowyn, my sister; for surely she should be lying beside the king, and in no less honour? Where have they bestowed her?'

And Imrahil said: 'But the Lady Éowyn was yet living when they bore her hither. Did you not know?'

Then hope unlooked-for came so suddenly to Éomer's heart, and with it the bite of care and fear renewed, that he said no more, but turned and went swiftly from the hall; and the Prince followed him. And when they came forth evening had fallen and many stars were in the sky. And there came Gandalf on foot and with him one cloaked in grey; and they met before the doors of the Houses of Healing. And they greeted Gandalf and said: 'We seek the Steward, and men say that he is in this House. Has any hurt befallen him? And the Lady Éowyn, where is she?'

And Gandalf answered: 'She lies within and is not dead, but is near death. But the Lord Faramir was wounded by an evil dart, as you have heard, and he is now the Steward; for Denethor has departed, and his house is in ashes.' And they were filled with grief and wonder at the tale that he told.

But Imrahil said: 'So victory is shorn of gladness, and it is bitter bought, if both Gondor and Rohan are in one day bereft of their lords. Éomer rules the Rohirrim. Who shall rule the City meanwhile? Shall we not send now for the Lord Aragorn?'

And the cloaked man spoke and said: 'He is come.' And they saw as he stepped into the light of the lantern by the door that it was Aragorn, wrapped in the grey cloak of Lórien above his mail, and bearing no other token than the green stone of Galadriel. 'I have come because Gandalf begs me to do so,' he said. 'But for the present I am but the Captain of the Dúnedain of Arnor; and the Lord of Dol Amroth shall rule the City until Faramir awakes. But it is my counsel that Gandalf should rule us all in the days that follow and in our dealings with the Enemy.' And they agreed upon that.

Then Gandalf said: 'Let us not stay at the door, for the time is urgent. Let us enter! For it is only in the coming of Aragorn that any hope remains for the sick that lie in the House. Thus spake Ioreth, wise-woman of Gondor: *The hands of the king are the hands of a healer, and so shall the rightful king be known*.'

Then Aragorn entered first and the others followed. And there at the door were two guards in the livery of the Citadel: one tall, but the other scarce the height of a boy; and when he saw them he cried aloud in surprise and joy.

'Strider! How splendid! Do you know, I guessed it was you in the black ships. But they were all shouting *corsairs* and wouldn't listen to me. How did you do it?'

Aragorn laughed, and took the hobbit by the hand. 'Well met indeed!' he said. 'But there is not time yet for travellers' tales.'

But Imrahil said to Éomer: 'Is it thus that we speak to our kings? Yet maybe he will wear his crown in some other name!'

And Aragorn hearing him, turned and said: 'Verily, for in the high tongue of old I am *Elessar*, the Elfstone, and *Envinyatar*, the Renewer': and he lifted from his breast the green stone that lay there. 'But Strider shall be the name of my house, if that be ever established. In the high tongue it will not sound so ill, and *Telcontar* I will be and all the heirs of my body.'

And with that they passed into the House; and as they went towards the rooms where the sick were tended Gandalf told of the deeds of Éowyn and Meriadoc. 'For,' he said, 'long have I stood by them, and at first they spoke much in their dreaming, before they sank into the deadly darkness. Also it is given to me to see many things far off.'

Aragorn went first to Faramir, and then to the Lady Éowyn, and last to Merry. When he had looked on the faces of the sick and seen their hurts he sighed. 'Here I must put forth all such power and skill as is given to me,' he said. 'Would that Elrond were here, for he is the eldest of all our race, and has the greater power.'

And Éomer seeing that he was both sorrowful and weary said: 'First you must rest, surely, and at the least eat a little?'

But Aragorn answered: 'Nay, for these three, and most soon for Faramir, time is running out. All speed is needed.'

Then he called to Ioreth and he said: 'You have store in this House of the herbs of healing?'

'Yes, lord,' she answered; 'but not enough, I reckon, for all that will need them. But I am sure I do not know where we shall find more; for all things are amiss in these dreadful days, what with fires and burnings, and the lads that run errands so few, and all the roads blocked. Why, it is days out of count since ever a carrier came in from Lossarnach to the market! But we do our best in this House with what we have, as I am sure your lordship will know.'

'I will judge that when I see,' said Aragorn. 'One thing also is short, time for speech. Have you *athelas*?'

'I do not know, I am sure, lord,' she answered, 'at least not by that name. I will go and ask of the herb-master; he knows all the old names.'

'It is also called *kingsfoil*,' said Aragorn; 'and maybe you know it by that name, for so the country-folk call it in these latter days.'

'Oh that!' said Ioreth. 'Well, if your lordship had named it at first I could have told you. No, we have none of it, I am sure. Why, I have never heard that it had any great virtue; and indeed I have often said to my sisters when we came upon it growing in the woods: "kingsfoil", I said, "'tis a strange name, and I wonder why 'tis called so; for if I were a king, I would have plants more bright in my garden". Still it smells sweet when bruised, does it not? If sweet is the right word: wholesome, maybe, is nearer.'

'Wholesome verily,' said Aragorn. 'And now, dame, if you love the Lord Faramir, run as quick as your tongue and get me kingsfoil, if there is a leaf in the City.'

'And if not,' said Gandalf, 'I will ride to Lossarnach with Ioreth behind me, and she shall take me to the woods, but not to her sisters. And Shadowfax shall show her the meaning of haste.'

When Ioreth was gone, Aragorn bade the other women to make water hot. Then he took Faramir's hand in his, and laid the other hand upon the sick man's brow. It was drenched with sweat; but Faramir did not move or make any sign, and seemed hardly to breathe.

'He is nearly spent,' said Aragorn turning to Gandalf. 'But this comes not from the wound. See! that is healing. Had he been smitten by some dart of the Nazgûl, as you thought, he would have died that night. This hurt was given by some Southron arrow, I would guess. Who drew it forth? Was it kept?'

'I drew it forth,' said Imrahil, 'and staunched the wound. But I did not keep the arrow, for we had much to do. It was, as I remember, just such a dart as the Southrons use. Yet I believed that it came from the Shadows above, for else his fever and sickness were not to be understood; since the wound was not deep or vital. How then do you read the matter?'

'Weariness, grief for his father's mood, a wound, and over all the Black Breath,' said Aragorn. 'He is a man of staunch will, for already he had come close under the Shadow before ever he rode to battle on the out-walls. Slowly the dark must have crept on him, even as he fought and strove to hold his outpost. Would that I could have been here sooner!'

Thereupon the herb-master entered. 'Your lordship asked for *kingsfoil*, as the rustics name it,' he said; 'or *athelas* in the noble tongue, or to those who know somewhat of the Valinorean . . .'

'I do so,' said Aragorn, 'and I care not whether you say now *asëa aranion* or *kingsfoil*, so long as you have some.'

'Your pardon lord!' said the man. 'I see you are a lore-master, not merely a captain of war. But alas! sir, we do not keep this thing in the Houses of Healing, where only the gravely hurt or sick are tended. For it has no virtue that we know of, save perhaps to sweeten a fouled air, or to drive away some passing heaviness. Unless, of course, you give heed to rhymes of old days which women such as our good Ioreth still repeat without understanding.

When the black breath blows
and death's shadow grows
and all lights pass,
come athelas! come athelas!
Life to the dying
In the king's hand lying!

It is but a doggrel, I fear, garbled in the memory of old wives. Its meaning I leave to your judgement, if indeed it has any. But old folk still use an infusion of the herb for headaches.'

'Then in the name of the king, go and find some old man of less lore and more wisdom who keeps some in his house!' cried Gandalf.

Now Aragorn knelt beside Faramir, and held a hand upon his brow. And those that watched felt that some great struggle was going on. For Aragorn's face grew grey with weariness; and ever and anon he called the name of Faramir, but each time more faintly to their hearing, as if Aragorn himself was removed from them, and walked afar in some dark vale, calling for one that was lost.

And at last Bergil came running in, and he bore six leaves in a cloth. 'It is kingsfoil, Sir,' he said; 'but not fresh, I fear. It must have been culled two weeks ago at the least. I hope it will serve, Sir?' Then looking at Faramir he burst into tears.

But Aragorn smiled. 'It will serve,' he said. 'The worst is now over. Stay and be comforted!' Then taking two leaves, he laid them on his hands and breathed on them, and then he crushed them, and straightway a living freshness filled the room, as if the air itself awoke and tingled, sparkling with joy. And then he cast the leaves into the bowls of steaming water that were brought to him, and at once all hearts were lightened. For the fragrance that came to each was like a memory of dewy mornings of unshadowed sun in some land of which the fair world in Spring is itself but a fleeting memory. But Aragorn stood up as one refreshed, and his eyes smiled as he held a bowl before Faramir's dreaming face.

'Well now! Who would have believed it?' said Ioreth to a woman that stood beside her. 'The weed is better than I thought. It reminds me of the roses of Imloth Melui when I was a lass, and no king could ask for better.'

Suddenly Faramir stirred, and he opened his eyes, and he looked on Aragorn who bent over him; and a light of knowledge and love was kindled in his eyes, and he spoke softly. 'My lord, you called me. I come. What does the king command?'

'Walk no more in the shadows, but awake!' said Aragorn. 'You are weary. Rest a while, and take food, and be ready when I return.'

'I will, lord,' said Faramir. 'For who would lie idle when the king has returned?'

'Farewell then for a while!' said Aragorn. 'I must go to others who need me.' And he left the chamber with Gandalf and Imrahil; but Beregond and his son remained behind, unable to contain their joy. As he followed Gandalf and shut the door Pippin heard Ioreth exclaim:

'King! Did you hear that? What did I say? The hands of a healer, I said.' And soon the word had gone out from the House that the king was indeed come among them, and after war he brought healing; and the news ran through the City.

But Aragorn came to Éowyn, and he said: 'Here there is a grievous hurt and a heavy blow. The arm that was broken has been tended with due skill, and it will mend in time, if she has the strength to live. It is the shield-arm that is maimed; but the chief evil comes through the sword-arm. In that there now seems no life, although it is unbroken.

'Alas! For she was pitted against a foe beyond the strength of her mind or body. And those who will take a weapon to such an enemy must be sterner than steel, if the very shock shall not destroy them. It was an evil doom that set her in his path. For she is a fair maiden, fairest lady of a house of queens. And yet I know not how I should speak of her. When I first looked on her and perceived her unhappiness, it seemed to me that I saw a white flower standing straight and proud, shapely as a lily, and yet knew that it was hard, as if wrought by elf-wrights out of steel. Or was it, maybe, a frost that had turned its sap to ice, and so it stood, bitter-sweet, still fair to see, but stricken, soon to fall and die? Her malady begins far back before this day, does it not, Éomer?'

'I marvel that you should ask me, lord,' he answered. 'For I hold you blameless in this matter, as in all else; yet I knew not that Éowyn, my sister, was touched by any frost, until she first looked on you. Care and dread she had, and shared with me, in the days of Wormtongue and the king's bewitchment; and she tended the king in growing fear. But that did not bring her to this pass!'

'My friend,' said Gandalf, 'you had horses, and deeds of arms, and the free fields; but she, born in the body of a maid, had a spirit and courage at least the match of yours. Yet she was doomed to wait upon an old man, whom she loved as a father, and watch him falling into a mean dishonoured dotage; and her part seemed to her more ignoble than that of the staff he leaned on.

'Think you that Wormtongue had poison only for Théoden's ears? *Dotard! What is the house of Eorl but a thatched barn where brigands drink in the reek, and their brats roll on the floor among their dogs?* Have you not heard those words before? Saruman spoke them, the teacher of Wormtongue. Though I do not doubt that Wormtongue at home wrapped their meaning in terms more cunning. My lord, if your sister's love for you, and her will still bent to her duty, had not restrained her lips, you might have heard even such things as these escape them. But who knows what she spoke to the darkness, alone, in the bitter watches of the night, when all her life seemed shrinking, and the walls of her bower closing in about her, a hutch to trammel some wild thing in?'

Then Éomer was silent, and looked on his sister, as if pondering anew all the days of their past life together. But Aragorn said: 'I saw also what you saw, Éomer. Few other griefs amid the ill chances of this world have more bitterness and shame for a man's heart than to behold the love of a lady so fair and brave that cannot be returned. Sorrow and pity have followed me ever since I left her desperate in Dunharrow and rode to the Paths of the Dead; and no fear upon that way was so present as the fear for what might befall her. And yet, Éomer, I say to you that she loves you more truly than me; for you she loves and knows; but in me she loves only a shadow and a thought: a hope of glory and great deeds, and lands far from the fields of Rohan.

'I have, maybe, the power to heal her body, and to recall her from the dark valley. But to what she will awake: hope, or forgetfulness, or despair, I do not know. And if to despair, then she will die, unless other healing comes which I cannot bring. Alas! for her deeds have set her among the queens of great renown.'

Then Aragorn stooped and looked in her face, and it was indeed white as a lily, cold as frost, and hard as graven stone. But he bent and kissed her on the brow, and called her softly, saying:

'Éowyn Éomund's daughter, awake! For your enemy has passed away!'

She did not stir, but now she began again to breathe deeply, so that her breast rose and fell beneath the white linen of the sheet. Once more Aragorn bruised two leaves of *athelas* and cast them into steaming water; and he laved her brow with it, and her right arm lying cold and nerveless on the coverlet.

Then, whether Aragorn had indeed some forgotten power of Westernesse, or whether it was but his words of the Lady Éowyn that wrought on them, as the sweet influence of the herb stole about the chamber it seemed to those who stood by that a keen wind blew through the window, and it bore no scent, but was an air wholly fresh and clean and young, as if it had not before been breathed by any living thing and came new-made from snowy mountains high beneath a dome of stars, or from shores of silver far away washed by seas of foam.

'Awake, Éowyn, Lady of Rohan!' said Aragorn again, and he took her right hand in his and felt it warm with life returning. 'Awake! The shadow is gone and all darkness is washed clean!' Then he laid her hand in Éomer's and stepped away. 'Call her!' he said, and he passed silently from the chamber.

'Éowyn, Éowyn!' cried Éomer amid his tears. But she opened her eyes and said: 'Éomer! What joy is this? For they said that you were slain. Nay, but that was only the dark voices in my dream. How long have I been dreaming?'

'Not long, my sister,' said Éomer. 'But think no more on it!'

'I am strangely weary,' she said. 'I must rest a little. But tell me, what of the Lord of the Mark? Alas! Do not tell me that that was a dream; for I know that it was not. He is dead as he foresaw.'

'He is dead,' said Éomer, 'but he bade me say farewell to Éowyn, dearer than daughter. He lies now in great honour in the Citadel of Gondor.'

'That is grievous,' she said. 'And yet it is good beyond all that I dared hope in the dark days, when it seemed that the House of Eorl was sunk in honour less than any shepherd's cot. And what of the king's esquire, the Halfling? Éomer, you shall make him a knight of the Riddermark, for he is valiant!'

'He lies nearby in this House, and I will go to him,' said Gandalf. 'Éomer shall stay here for a while. But do not speak yet of war or woe, until you are made whole again. Great gladness it is to see you wake again to health and hope, so valiant a lady!'

'To health?' said Éowyn. 'It may be so. At least while there is an empty saddle of some fallen Rider that I can fill, and there are deeds to do. But to hope? I do not know.'

Gandalf and Pippin came to Merry's room, and there they found Aragorn standing by the bed. 'Poor old Merry!' cried Pippin, and he ran to the bedside, for it seemed to him that his friend looked worse and a greyness was in his face, as if a weight of years of sorrow lay on him; and suddenly a fear seized Pippin that Merry would die.

'Do not be afraid,' said Aragorn. 'I came in time, and I have called him back. He is weary now, and grieved, and he has taken a hurt like the Lady Éowyn, daring to smite that deadly thing. But these evils can be amended, so strong and gay a spirit is in him. His grief he will not forget; but it will not darken his heart, it will teach him wisdom.'

Then Aragorn laid his hand on Merry's head, and passing his hand gently through the brown curls, he touched the eyelids, and called him by name. And when the fragrance of *athelas* stole through the room, like the scent of orchards, and of heather in the sunshine full of bees, suddenly Merry awoke, and he said:

'I am hungry. What is the time?'

'Past supper-time now,' said Pippin; 'though I daresay I could bring you something, if they will let me.'

'They will indeed,' said Gandalf. 'And anything else that this Rider of Rohan may desire, if it can be found in Minas Tirith, where his name is in honour.'

'Good!' said Merry. 'Then I would like supper first, and after that a pipe.' At that his face clouded. 'No, not a pipe. I don't think I'll smoke again.'

'Why not?' said Pippin.

'Well,' answered Merry slowly. 'He is dead. It has brought it all back to me. He said he was sorry he had never had a chance of talking herb-lore with me. Almost the last thing he ever said. I shan't ever be able to smoke again without thinking of him, and that day, Pippin, when he rode up to Isengard and was so polite.'

'Smoke then, and think of him!' said Aragorn. 'For he was a gentle heart and a great king and kept his oaths; and he rose out of the shadows to a last fair morning. Though your service to him was brief, it should be a memory glad and honourable to the end of your days.'

Merry smiled. 'Well then,' he said, 'if Strider will provide what is needed, I will smoke and think. I had some of Saruman's best in my pack, but what became of it in the battle, I am sure I don't know.'

'Master Meriadoc,' said Aragorn, 'if you think that I have passed through the mountains and the realm of Gondor with fire and sword to bring herbs to a careless soldier who throws away his gear, you are mistaken. If your pack has not been found, then you must send for the herb-master of this House. And he will tell you that he did not know that the herb you desire had any virtues, but that it is called *westmansweed* by the vulgar, and *galenas* by the noble, and other names in other tongues more learned, and after adding a few half-forgotten rhymes that he does not understand, he will regretfully inform you that there is none in the House, and he will leave you to reflect on the history of tongues. And so now must I. For I have not slept in such a bed as this, since I rode from Dunharrow, nor eaten since the dark before dawn.'

Merry seized his hand and kissed it. 'I am frightfully sorry,' he said.

'Go at once! Ever since that night at Bree we have been a nuisance to you. But it is the way of my people to use light words at such times and say less than they mean. We fear to say too much. It robs us of the right words when a jest is out of place.'

'I know that well, or I would not deal with you in the same way,' said Aragorn. 'May the Shire live for ever unwithered!' And kissing Merry he went out, and Gandalf went with him.

Pippin remained behind. 'Was there ever any one like him?' he said. 'Except Gandalf, of course. I think they must be related. My dear ass, your pack is lying by your bed, and you had it on your back when I met you. He saw it all the time, of course. And anyway I have some stuff of my own. Come on now! Longbottom Leaf it is. Fill up while I run and see about some food. And then let's be easy for a bit. Dear me! We Tooks and Brandybucks, we can't live long on the heights.'

'No,' said Merry. 'I can't. Not yet, at any rate. But at least, Pippin, we can now see them, and honour them. It is best to love first what you are fitted to love, I suppose: you must start somewhere and have some roots, and the soil of the Shire is deep. Still there are things deeper and higher; and not a gaffer could tend his garden in what he calls peace but for them, whether he knows about them or not. I am glad that I know about them, a little. But I don't know why I am talking like this. Where is that leaf? And get my pipe out of my pack, if it isn't broken.'

Aragorn and Gandalf went now to the Warden of the Houses of Healing, and they counselled him that Faramir and Éowyn should remain there and still be tended with care for many days.

'The Lady Éowyn,' said Aragorn, 'will wish soon to rise and depart; but she should not be permitted to do so, if you can in any way restrain her, until at least ten days be passed.'

'As for Faramir,' said Gandalf, 'he must soon learn that his father is dead. But the full tale of the madness of Denethor should not be told to him, until he is quite healed and has duties to do. See that Beregond and the *perian* who were present do not speak to him of these things yet!'

'And the other *perian*, Meriadoc, who is under my care, what of him?' said the Warden.

'It is likely that he will be fit to arise tomorrow, for a short while,' said Aragorn. 'Let him do so, if he wishes. He may walk a little in the care of his friends.'

'They are a remarkable race,' said the Warden, nodding his head. 'Very tough in the fibre, I deem.'

At the doors of the Houses many were already gathered to see Aragorn, and they followed after him; and when at last he had supped, men came and prayed that he would heal their kinsmen or their friends whose lives were in peril through hurt or wound, or who lay under the Black Shadow. And Aragorn arose and went out, and he sent for the sons of Elrond, and together they laboured far into the night. And word went through the City: 'The King is come again indeed.' And they named him Elfstone, because of the green stone that he wore, and so the name which it was foretold at his birth that he should bear was chosen for him by his own people.

And when he could labour no more, he cast his cloak about him, and slipped out of the City, and went to his tent just ere dawn and slept for a little. And in the morning the banner of Dol Amroth, a white ship like a swan upon blue water, floated from the Tower, and men looked up and wondered if the coming of the King had been but a dream.

CHAPTER IX

THE LAST DEBATE

The morning came after the day of battle, and it was fair with light clouds and the wind turning westward. Legolas and Gimli were early abroad, and they begged leave to go up into the City; for they were eager to see Merry and Pippin.

'It is good to learn that they are still alive,' said Gimli; 'for they cost us great pains in our march over Rohan, and I would not have such pains all wasted.'

Together the Elf and the Dwarf entered Minas Tirith, and folk that saw them pass marvelled to see such companions; for Legolas was fair of face beyond the measure of Men, and he sang an elven-song in a clear voice as he walked in the morning; but Gimli stalked beside him, stroking his beard and staring about him.

'There is some good stone-work here,' he said as he looked at the walls; 'but also some that is less good, and the streets could be better contrived. When Aragorn comes into his own, I shall offer him the service of stonewrights of the Mountain, and we will make this a town to be proud of.'

'They need more gardens,' said Legolas. 'The houses are dead, and there is too little here that grows and is glad. If Aragorn comes into his own, the people of the Wood shall bring him birds that sing and trees that do not die.'

At length they came to the Prince Imrahil, and Legolas looked at him and bowed low; for he saw that here indeed was one who had elven-blood in his veins. 'Hail, lord!' he said. 'It is long since the people of Nimrodel left the woodlands of Lórien, and yet still one may see that not all sailed from Amroth's haven west over water.'

'So it is said in the lore of my land,' said the Prince; 'yet never has one of the fair folk been seen there for years beyond count. And I marvel to see one here now in the midst of sorrow and war. What do you seek?'

'I am one of the Nine Companions who set out with Mithrandir from Imladris,' said Legolas; 'and with this Dwarf, my friend, I came with the Lord Aragorn. But now we wish to see our friends, Meriadoc and Peregrin, who are in your keeping, we are told.'

'You will find them in the Houses of Healing, and I will lead you thither,' said Imrahil.

'It will be enough if you send one to guide us, lord,' said Legolas. 'For Aragorn sends this message to you. He does not wish to enter the City again at this time. Yet there is need for the captains to hold council at once, and he prays that you and Éomer of Rohan will come down to his tents, as soon as may be. Mithrandir is already there.'

'We will come,' said Imrahil; and they parted with courteous words.

'That is a fair lord and a great captain of men,' said Legolas. 'If Gondor has such men still in these days of fading, great must have been its glory in the days of its rising.'

'And doubtless the good stone-work is the older and was wrought in the first building,' said Gimli. 'It is ever so with the things that Men begin: there is a frost in Spring, or a blight in Summer, and they fail of their promise.'

'Yet seldom do they fail of their seed,' said Legolas. 'And that will lie in the dust and rot to spring up again in times and places unlooked-for. The deeds of Men will outlast us, Gimli.'

'And yet come to naught in the end but might-have-beens, I guess,' said the Dwarf.

'To that the Elves know not the answer,' said Legolas.

With that the servant of the Prince came and led them to the Houses of Healing; and there they found their friends in the garden, and their meeting was a merry one. For a while they walked and talked, rejoicing for a brief space in peace and rest under the morning high up in the windy circles of the City. Then when Merry became weary, they went and sat upon the wall with the greensward of the Houses of Healing behind them; and away southward before them was the Anduin glittering in the sun, as it flowed away, out of the sight even of Legolas, into the wide flats and green haze of Lebennin and South Ithilien.

And now Legolas fell silent, while the others talked, and he looked out against the sun, and as he gazed he saw white sea-birds beating up the River.

'Look!' he cried. 'Gulls! They are flying far inland. A wonder they are to me and a trouble to my heart. Never in all my life had I met them, until we came to Pelargir, and there I heard them crying in the air as we rode to the battle of the ships. Then I stood still, forgetting war in Middle-earth; for their wailing voices spoke to me of the Sea. The Sea! Alas! I have not yet beheld it. But deep in the hearts of all my kindred lies the sea-longing, which it is perilous to stir. Alas! for the gulls. No peace shall I have again under beech or under elm.'

'Say not so!' said Gimli. 'There are countless things still to see in

Middle-earth, and great works to do. But if all the fair folk take to the Havens, it will be a duller world for those who are doomed to stay.'

'Dull and dreary indeed!' said Merry. 'You must not go to the Havens, Legolas. There will always be some folk, big or little, and even a few wise dwarves like Gimli, who need you. At least I hope so. Though I feel somehow that the worst of this war is still to come. How I wish it was all over, and well over!'

'Don't be so gloomy!' cried Pippin. 'The Sun is shining, and here we are together for a day or two at least. I want to hear more about you all. Come, Gimli! You and Legolas have mentioned your strange journey with Strider about a dozen times already this morning. But you haven't told me anything about it.'

'The Sun may shine here,' said Gimli, 'but there are memories of that road that I do not wish to recall out of the darkness. Had I known what was before me, I think that not for any friendship would I have taken the Paths of the Dead.'

'The Paths of the Dead?' said Pippin. 'I heard Aragorn say that, and I wondered what he could mean. Won't you tell us some more?'

'Not willingly,' said Gimli. 'For upon that road I was put to shame: Gimli Glóin's son, who had deemed himself more tough than Men, and hardier under earth than any Elf. But neither did I prove; and I was held to the road only by the will of Aragorn.'

'And by the love of him also,' said Legolas. 'For all those who come to know him come to love him after his own fashion, even the cold maiden of the Rohirrim. It was at early morn of the day ere you came there, Merry, that we left Dunharrow, and such a fear was on all the folk that none would look on our going, save the Lady Éowyn, who lies now hurt in the House below. There was grief at that parting, and I was grieved to behold it.'

'Alas! I had heart only for myself,' said Gimli. 'Nay! I will not speak of that journey.'

He fell silent; but Pippin and Merry were so eager for news that at last Legolas said: 'I will tell you enough for your peace; for I felt not the horror, and I feared not the shadows of Men, powerless and frail as I deemed them.'

Swiftly then he told of the haunted road under the mountains, and the dark tryst at Erech, and the great ride thence, ninety leagues and three, to Pelargir on Anduin. 'Four days and nights, and on into a fifth, we rode from the Black Stone,' he said. 'And lo! in the darkness of Mordor my hope rose; for in that gloom the Shadow Host seemed to grow stronger and more terrible to look upon. Some I saw riding, some striding, yet all moving with the same great speed. Silent they were, but there was a gleam in their eyes. In the uplands of Lamedon they overtook our horses, and swept round us, and would have passed us by, if Aragorn had not forbidden them.

'At his command they fell back. "Even the shades of Men are obedient to his will," I thought. "They may serve his needs yet!"

'One day of light we rode, and then came the day without dawn, and still we rode on, and Ciril and Ringló we crossed; and on the third day we came to Linhir above the mouth of Gilrain. And there men of Lamedon contested the fords with fell folk of Umbar and Harad who had sailed up the river. But defenders and foes alike gave up the battle and fled when we came, crying out that the King of the Dead was upon them. Only Angbor, Lord of Lamedon, had the heart to abide us; and Aragorn bade him gather his folk and come behind, if they dared, when the Grey Host had passed.

'"At Pelargir the Heir of Isildur will have need of you," he said.

'Thus we crossed over Gilrain, driving the allies of Mordor in rout before us; and then we rested a while. But soon Aragorn arose, saying: "Lo! already Minas Tirith is assailed. I fear that it will fall ere we come to its aid." So we mounted again before night had passed and went on with all the speed that our horses could endure over the plains of Lebennin.'

Legolas paused and sighed, and turning his eyes southward softly he sang:

Silver flow the streams from Celos to Erui
In the green fields of Lebennin!
Tall grows the grass there. In the wind from the Sea
The white lilies sway,
And the golden bells are shaken of mallos and alfirin
In the green fields of Lebennin,
In the wind from the Sea!

'Green are those fields in the songs of my people; but they were dark then, grey wastes in the blackness before us. And over the wide land, trampling unheeded the grass and the flowers, we hunted our foes through a day and a night, until we came at the bitter end to the Great River at last.

'Then I thought in my heart that we drew near to the Sea; for wide was the water in the darkness, and sea-birds innumerable cried on its shores. Alas for the wailing of the gulls! Did not the Lady tell me to beware of them? And now I cannot forget them.'

'For my part I heeded them not,' said Gimli; 'for we came then at last upon battle in earnest. There at Pelargir lay the main fleet of Umbar, fifty great ships and smaller vessels beyond count. Many of those that we pursued had reached the havens before us, and brought their fear with them; and some of the ships had put off, seeking to escape down the River or to reach the far shore; and many of the smaller craft were ablaze. But the Haradrim, being now driven to the brink, turned at bay, and they were fierce in despair; and they laughed when they looked on us, for they were a great army still.

'But Aragorn halted and cried with a great voice: "Now come! By the Black Stone I call you!" And suddenly the Shadow Host that had hung back at the last came up like a grey tide, sweeping all away before it. Faint cries I heard, and dim horns blowing, and a murmur as of countless far voices: it was like the echo of some forgotten battle in the Dark Years long ago. Pale swords were drawn; but I know not whether their blades would still bite, for the Dead needed no longer any weapon but fear. None would withstand them.

'To every ship they came that was drawn up, and then they passed over the water to those that were anchored; and all the mariners were filled with a madness of terror and leaped overboard, save the slaves chained to the oars. Reckless we rode among our fleeing foes, driving them like leaves, until we came to the shore. And then to each of the great ships that remained Aragorn sent one of the Dúnedain, and they comforted the captives that were aboard, and bade them put aside fear and be free.

'Ere that dark day ended none of the enemy were left to resist us; all were drowned, or were flying south in the hope to find their own lands upon foot. Strange and wonderful I thought it that the designs of Mordor should be overthrown by such wraiths of fear and darkness. With its own weapons was it worsted!'

'Strange indeed,' said Legolas. 'In that hour I looked on Aragorn and thought how great and terrible a Lord he might have become in the strength of his will, had he taken the Ring to himself. Not for naught does Mordor fear him. But nobler is his spirit than the understanding of Sauron; for is he not of the children of Lúthien? Never shall that line fail, though the years may lengthen beyond count.'

'Beyond the eyes of the Dwarves are such foretellings,' said Gimli. 'But mighty indeed was Aragorn that day. Lo! all the black fleet was in his hands; and he chose the greatest ship to be his own, and he went up into it. Then he let sound a great concourse of trumpets taken from the enemy; and the Shadow Host withdrew to the shore. There they stood silent, hardly to be seen, save for a red gleam in their eyes that caught the glare of the ships that were burning. And Aragorn spoke in a loud voice to the Dead Men, crying:

'"Hear now the words of the Heir of Isildur! Your oath is fulfilled. Go back and trouble not the valleys ever again! Depart and be at rest!"

'And thereupon the King of the Dead stood out before the host and broke his spear and cast it down. Then he bowed low and turned away; and swiftly the whole grey host drew on and vanished like a mist that is driven back by a sudden wind; and it seemed to me that I awoke from a dream.

'That night we rested while others laboured. For there were many captives set free, and many slaves released who had been folk of Gondor taken in raids; and soon also there was a great gathering of men out of Lebennin and the Ethir, and Angbor of Lamedon came up with all the horsemen that he could muster. Now that the fear of the Dead was removed they came to aid us and to look on the Heir of Isildur; for the rumour of that name had run like fire in the dark.

'And that is near the end of our tale. For during that evening and night many ships were made ready and manned; and in the morning the fleet set forth. Long past it now seems, yet it was but the morn of the day ere yesterday, the sixth since we rode from Dunharrow. But still Aragorn was driven by fear that time was too short.

' "It is forty leagues and two from Pelargir to the landings at the Harlond," he said. "Yet to the Harlond we must come tomorrow or fail utterly."

'The oars were now wielded by free men, and manfully they laboured; yet slowly we passed up the Great River, for we strove against its stream, and though that is not swift down in the South, we had no help of wind. Heavy would my heart have been, for all our victory at the havens, if Legolas had not laughed suddenly.

' "Up with your beard, Durin's son!" he said. "For thus is it spoken: *Oft hope is born, when all is forlorn.*" But what hope he saw from afar he would not tell. When night came it did but deepen the darkness, and our hearts were hot, for away in the North we saw a red glow under the cloud, and Aragorn said: "Minas Tirith is burning."

'But at midnight hope was indeed born anew. Sea-crafty men of the Ethir gazing southward spoke of a change coming with a fresh wind from the Sea. Long ere day the masted ships hoisted sail, and our speed grew, until dawn whitened the foam at our prows. And so it was, as you know, that we came in the third hour of the morning with a fair wind and the Sun unveiled, and we unfurled the great standard in battle. It was a great day and a great hour, whatever may come after.'

'Follow what may, great deeds are not lessened in worth,' said Legolas. 'Great deed was the riding of the Paths of the Dead, and great it shall remain, though none be left in Gondor to sing of it in the days that are to come.'

'And that may well befall,' said Gimli. 'For the faces of Aragorn and

Gandalf are grave. Much I wonder what counsels they are taking in the tents there below. For my part, like Merry, I wish that with our victory the war was now over. Yet whatever is still to do, I hope to have a part in it, for the honour of the folk of the Lonely Mountain.'

'And I for the folk of the Great Wood,' said Legolas, 'and for the love of the Lord of the White Tree.'

Then the companions fell silent, but a while they sat there in the high place, each busy with his own thoughts, while the Captains debated.

When the Prince Imrahil had parted from Legolas and Gimli, at once he sent for Éomer; and he went down with him from the City, and they came to the tents of Aragorn that were set up on the field not far from the place where King Théoden had fallen. And there they took counsel together with Gandalf and Aragorn and the sons of Elrond.

'My lords,' said Gandalf, 'listen to the words of the Steward of Gondor before he died: *You may triumph on the fields of the Pelennor for a day, but against the Power that has now arisen there is no victory*. I do not bid you despair, as he did, but to ponder the truth in these words.

'The Stones of Seeing do not lie, and not even the Lord of Barad-dûr can make them do so. He can, maybe, by his will choose what things shall be seen by weaker minds, or cause them to mistake the meaning of what they see. Nonetheless it cannot be doubted that when Denethor saw great forces arrayed against him in Mordor, and more still being gathered, he saw that which truly is.

'Hardly has our strength sufficed to beat off the first great assault. The next will be greater. This war then is without final hope, as Denethor perceived. Victory cannot be achieved by arms, whether you sit here to endure siege after siege, or march out to be overwhelmed beyond the River. You have only a choice of evils; and prudence would counsel you to strengthen such strong places as you have, and there await the onset; for so shall the time before your end be made a little longer.'

'Then you would have us retreat to Minas Tirith, or Dol Amroth, or to Dunharrow, and there sit like children on sand-castles when the tide is flowing?' said Imrahil.

'That would be no new counsel,' said Gandalf. 'Have you not done this and little more in all the days of Denethor? But no! I said this would be prudent. I do not counsel prudence. I said victory could not be achieved by arms. I still hope for victory, but not by arms. For into the midst of all these policies comes the Ring of Power, the foundation of Barad-dûr, and the hope of Sauron.

'Concerning this thing, my lords, you now all know enough for the understanding of our plight, and of Sauron's. If he regains it, your valour is vain, and his victory will be swift and complete: so complete that none can foresee the end of it while this world lasts. If it is destroyed, then he will fall; and his fall will be so low that none can foresee his arising ever again. For he will lose the best part of the strength that was native to him in his beginning, and all that was made or begun with that power will crumble, and he will be maimed for ever, becoming a mere spirit of malice that gnaws itself in the shadows, but cannot again grow or take shape. And so a great evil of this world will be removed.

'Other evils there are that may come; for Sauron is himself but a servant or emissary. Yet it is not our part to master all the tides of the world, but to do what is in us for the succour of those years wherein we are set, uprooting the evil in the fields that we know, so that those who live after may have clean earth to till. What weather they shall have is not ours to rule.

'Now Sauron knows all this, and he knows that this precious thing which he lost has been found again; but he does not yet know where it is, or so we hope. And therefore he is now in great doubt. For if we have found this thing, there are some among us with strength enough to wield it. That too he knows. For do I not guess rightly, Aragorn, that you have shown yourself to him in the Stone of Orthanc?'

'I did so ere I rode from the Hornburg,' answered Aragorn. 'I deemed that the time was ripe, and that the Stone had come to me for just such a purpose. It was then ten days since the Ring-bearer went east from Rauros, and the Eye of Sauron, I thought, should be drawn out from his own land. Too seldom has he been challenged since he returned to his Tower. Though if I had foreseen how swift would be his onset in answer, maybe I should not have dared to show myself. Bare time was given me to come to your aid.'

'But how is this?' asked Éomer. 'All is vain, you say, if he has the Ring. Why should he think it not vain to assail us, if we have it?'

'He is not yet sure,' said Gandalf, 'and he has not built up his power by waiting until his enemies are secure, as we have done. Also we could not learn how to wield the full power all in a day. Indeed it can be used only by one master alone, not by many; and he will look for a time of strife, ere one of the great among us makes himself master and puts down the others. In that time the Ring might aid him, if he were sudden.

'He is watching. He sees much and hears much. His Nazgûl are still abroad. They passed over this field ere the sunrise, though few of the weary and sleeping were aware of them. He studies the signs: the Sword that robbed him of his treasure re-made; the winds of fortune turning in our favour, and the defeat unlooked-for of his first assault; the fall of his great Captain.

'His doubt will be growing, even as we speak here. His Eye is now straining towards us, blind almost to all else that is moving. So we must keep it. Therein lies all our hope. This, then, is my counsel. We have not the Ring. In wisdom or great folly it has been sent away to be destroyed, lest it destroy us. Without it we cannot by force defeat his force. But we must at all costs keep his Eye from his true peril. We cannot achieve victory by arms, but by arms we can give the Ring-bearer his only chance, frail though it be.

'As Aragorn has begun, so we must go on. We must push Sauron to his last throw. We must call out his hidden strength, so that he shall empty his land. We must march out to meet him at once. We must make ourselves the bait, though his jaws should close on us. He will take that bait, in hope and in greed, for he will think that in such rashness he sees the pride of the new Ringlord: and he will say: "So! he pushes out his neck too soon and too far. Let him come on, and behold I will have him in a trap from which he cannot escape. There I will crush him, and what he has taken in his insolence shall be mine again for ever."

'We must walk open-eyed into that trap, with courage, but small hope for ourselves. For, my lords, it may well prove that we ourselves shall perish utterly in a black battle far from the living lands; so that even if Barad-dûr be thrown down, we shall not live to see a new age. But this, I deem, is our duty. And better so than to perish nonetheless – as we surely shall, if we sit here – and know as we die that no new age shall be.'

They were silent for a while. At length Aragorn spoke. 'As I have begun, so I will go on. We come now to the very brink, where hope and despair are akin. To waver is to fall. Let none now reject the counsels of Gandalf, whose long labours against Sauron come at last to their test. But for him all would long ago have been lost. Nonetheless I do not yet claim to command any man. Let others choose as they will.'

Then said Elrohir: 'From the North we came with this purpose, and from Elrond our father we brought this very counsel. We will not turn back.'

'As for myself,' said Éomer, 'I have little knowledge of these deep matters; but I need it not. This I know, and it is enough, that as my friend Aragorn succoured me and my people, so I will aid him when he calls. I will go.'

'As for me,' said Imrahil, 'the Lord Aragorn I hold to be my liege-lord, whether he claim it or no. His wish is to me a command. I will go also. Yet for a while I stand in the place of the Steward of Gondor, and it is mine to think first of its people. To prudence some heed must still be given. For we must prepare against all chances, good as well as evil. Now, it may be that we shall triumph, and while there is any hope of this, Gondor must be protected. I would not have us return with victory to a City in ruins and a land ravaged behind us. And yet we learn from the Rohirrim that there is an army still unfought upon our northern flank.'

'That is true,' said Gandalf. 'I do not counsel you to leave the City all unmanned. Indeed the force that we lead east need not be great enough for any assault in earnest upon Mordor, so long as it be great enough to challenge battle. And it must move soon. Therefore I ask the Captains: what force could we muster and lead out in two days' time at the latest? And they must be hardy men that go willingly, knowing their peril.'

'All are weary, and very many have wounds light or grievous,' said Éomer, 'and we have suffered much loss of our horses, and that is ill to bear. If we must ride soon, then I cannot hope to lead even two thousands, and yet leave as many for the defence of the City.'

'We have not only to reckon with those who fought on this field,' said Aragorn. 'New strength is on the way from the southern fiefs, now that the coasts have been rid. Four thousands I sent marching from Pelargir through Lossarnach two days ago; and Angbor the fearless rides before them. If we set out in two days more, they will draw nigh ere we depart. Moreover many were bidden to follow me up the River in any craft they could gather; and with this wind they will soon be at hand, indeed several ships have already come to the Harlond. I judge that we could lead out seven thousands of horse and foot, and yet leave the City in better defence than it was when the assault began.'

'The Gate is destroyed,' said Imrahil, 'and where now is the skill to rebuild it and set it up anew?'

'In Erebor in the Kingdom of Dáin there is such skill,' said Aragorn; 'and if all our hopes do not perish, then in time I will send Gimli Glóin's son to ask for wrights of the Mountain. But men are better than gates, and no gate will endure against our Enemy if men desert it.'

This then was the end of the debate of the lords: that they should set forth on the second morning from that day with seven thousands, if these might be found; and the great part of this force should be on foot, because of the evil lands into which they would go. Aragorn should find some two thousands of those that he had gathered to him in the South; but Imrahil should find three and a half thousands; and Éomer five hundreds of the Rohirrim who were unhorsed but themselves warworthy, and he himself should lead five hundreds of his best Riders on horse; and another company of five hundred horse there should be, among which should ride the sons of Elrond with the Dúnedain and the knights of Dol Amroth: all told six thousand foot and a thousand horse. But the main strength of the Rohirrim that remained horsed and able to fight, some three thousand under the command of Elfhelm, should waylay the West Road against the enemy that was in Anórien. And at once swift riders were sent out to gather what news they could northwards; and eastwards from Osgiliath and the road to Minas Morgul.

And when they had reckoned up all their strength and taken thought for the journeys they should make and the roads they should choose, Imrahil suddenly laughed aloud.

'Surely,' he cried, 'this is the greatest jest in all the history of Gondor: that we should ride with seven thousands, scarce as many as the vanguard of its army in the days of its power, to assail the mountains and the impenetrable gate of the Black Land! So might a child threaten a mail-clad knight with a bow of string and green willow! If the Dark Lord knows so much as you say, Mithrandir, will he not rather smile than fear, and with his little finger crush us like a fly that tries to sting him?'

'No, he will try to trap the fly and take the sting,' said Gandalf. 'And there are names among us that are worth more than a thousand mail-clad knights apiece. No, he will not smile.'

'Neither shall we,' said Aragorn. 'If this be jest, then it is too bitter for laughter. Nay, it is the last move in a great jeopardy, and for one side or the other it will bring the end of the game.' Then he drew Andúril and held it up glittering in the sun. 'You shall not be sheathed again until the last battle is fought,' he said.

CHAPTER X

THE BLACK GATE OPENS

Two days later the army of the West was all assembled on the Pelennor. The host of Orcs and Easterlings had turned back out of Anórien, but harried and scattered by the Rohirrim they had broken and fled with little fighting towards Cair Andros; and with that threat destroyed and new strength arriving out of the South the City was as well manned as might be. Scouts reported that no enemies remained upon the roads east as far as the Cross-roads of the Fallen King. All now was ready for the last throw.

Legolas and Gimli were to ride again together in the company of Aragorn and Gandalf, who went in the van with the Dúnedain and the sons of Elrond. But Merry to his shame was not to go with them.

'You are not fit for such a journey,' said Aragorn. 'But do not be ashamed. If you do no more in this war, you have already earned great honour. Peregrin shall go and represent the Shirefolk; and do not grudge him his chance of peril, for though he has done as well as his fortune allowed him, he has yet to match your deed. But in truth all now are in like danger. Though it may be our part to find a bitter end before the Gate of Mordor, if we do so, then you will come also to a last stand, either here or wherever the black tide overtakes you. Farewell!'

And so despondently Merry now stood and watched the mustering of the army. Bergil was with him, and he also was downcast; for his father was to march leading a company of the Men of the City: he could not rejoin the Guard until his case was judged. In that same company Pippin was also to go, as a soldier of Gondor. Merry could see him not far off, a small but upright figure among the tall men of Minas Tirith.

At last the trumpets rang and the army began to move. Troop by troop, and company by company, they wheeled and went off eastward. And long after they had passed away out of sight down the great road to the Causeway, Merry stood there. The last glint of the morning sun on spear and helm twinkled and was lost, and still he remained with bowed head and heavy heart, feeling friendless and alone. Everyone that he cared for had gone away into the gloom that hung over the distant eastern sky; and little hope at all was left in his heart that he would ever see any of them again.

As if recalled by his mood of despair, the pain in his arm returned, and he felt weak and old, and the sunlight seemed thin. He was roused by the touch of Bergil's hand.

'Come, Master Perian!' said the lad. 'You are still in pain, I see. I will help you back to the Healers. But do not fear! They will come back. The Men of Minas Tirith will never be overcome. And now they have the Lord Elfstone, and Beregond of the Guard too.'

Ere noon the army came to Osgiliath. There all the workers and craftsmen that could be spared were busy. Some were strengthening the ferries and boat-bridges that the enemy had made and in part destroyed when they fled; some gathered stores and booty; and others on the eastern side across the River were throwing up hasty works of defence.

The vanguard passed on through the ruins of Old Gondor, and over the wide River, and on up the long straight road that in the high days had been made to run from the fair Tower of the Sun to the tall Tower of the Moon, which now was Minas Morgul in its accursed vale. Five miles beyond Osgiliath they halted, ending their first day's march.

But the horsemen pressed on and ere evening they came to the Cross-roads and the great ring of trees, and all was silent. No sign of any enemy had they seen, no cry or call had been heard, no shaft had sped from rock or thicket by the way, yet ever as they went forward they felt the watchfulness of the land increase. Tree and stone, blade and leaf were listening. The darkness had been dispelled, and far away westward sunset was on the Vale of Anduin, and the white peaks of the mountains blushed in the blue air; but a shadow and a gloom brooded upon the Ephel Dúath.

Then Aragorn set trumpeters at each of the four roads that ran into the ring of trees, and they blew a great fanfare, and the heralds cried aloud: 'The Lords of Gondor have returned and all this land that is theirs they take back.' The hideous orc-head that was set upon the carven figure was cast down and broken in pieces, and the old king's head was raised and set in its place once more, still crowned with white and golden flowers; and men laboured to wash and pare away all the foul scrawls that orcs had put upon the stone.

Now in their debate some had counselled that Minas Morgul should first be assailed, and if they might take it, it should be utterly destroyed. 'And, maybe,' said Imrahil, 'the road that leads thence to the pass above will prove an easier way of assault upon the Dark Lord than his northern gate.'

But against this Gandalf had spoken urgently, because of the evil that dwelt in the valley, where the minds of living men would turn to madness and horror, and because also of the news that Faramir had brought. For if the Ring-bearer had indeed attempted that way, then above all they should not draw the Eye of Mordor thither. So the next day when the main host came up, they set a strong guard upon the Cross-roads to make some defence, if Mordor should send a force over the Morgul Pass, or should bring more men up from the South. For that guard they chose mostly archers who knew the ways of Ithilien and would lie hid in the woods and slopes about the meeting of the ways. But Gandalf and Aragorn rode with the vanguard to the entrance of Morgul Vale and looked on the evil city.

It was dark and lifeless; for the Orcs and lesser creatures of Mordor that had dwelt there had been destroyed in battle, and the Nazgûl were abroad. Yet the air of the valley was heavy with fear and enmity. Then they broke the evil bridge and set red flames in the noisome fields and departed.

The day after, being the third day since they set out from Minas Tirith, the army began its northward march along the road. It was some hundred miles by that way from the Cross-roads to the Morannon, and what might befall them before they came so far none knew. They went openly but heedfully, with mounted scouts before them on the road, and others on foot upon either side, especially on the eastward flank; for there lay dark thickets, and a tumbled land of rocky ghylls and crags, behind which the long grim slopes of the Ephel Dúath clambered up. The weather of the world remained fair, and the wind held in the west, but nothing could waft away the glooms and the sad mists that clung about the Mountains of Shadow; and behind them at whiles great smokes would arise and hover in the upper winds.

Ever and anon Gandalf let blow the trumpets, and the heralds would cry: 'The Lords of Gondor are come! Let all leave this land or yield them up!' But Imrahil said: 'Say not *The Lords of Gondor*. Say *The King Elessar*. For that is true, even though he has not yet sat upon the throne; and it will give the Enemy more thought, if the heralds use that name.' And thereafter thrice a day the heralds proclaimed the coming of the King Elessar. But none answered the challenge.

Nonetheless, though they marched in seeming peace, the hearts of all the army, from the highest to the lowest, were downcast, and with every mile that they went north foreboding of evil grew heavier on them. It was near the end of the second day of their march from the Cross-roads that they first met any offer of battle. For a strong force of Orcs and Easterlings attempted to take their leading companies in an ambush; and that was in the very place where Faramir had waylaid the men of Harad, and the road went in a deep cutting through an out-thrust of the eastward hills. But the Captains of the West were well warned by their scouts, skilled men from Henneth Annûn led by Mablung; and so the ambush was itself trapped. For horsemen went wide about westward and came up on the flank of the enemy and from behind, and they were destroyed or driven east into the hills.

But the victory did little to enhearten the captains. 'It is but a feint,' said Aragorn; 'and its chief purpose, I deem, was rather to draw us on by a false guess of our Enemy's weakness than to do us much hurt, yet.' And from that evening onward the Nazgûl came and followed every move of the army. They still flew high and out of sight of all save Legolas, and yet their presence could be felt, as a deepening of shadow and a dimming of the sun; and though the Ringwraiths did not yet stoop low upon their foes and were silent, uttering no cry, the dread of them could not be shaken off.

So time and the hopeless journey wore away. Upon the fourth day from the Cross-roads and the sixth from Minas Tirith they came at last to the end of the living lands, and began to pass into the desolation that lay before the gates of the Pass of Cirith Gorgor; and they could descry the marshes and the desert that stretched north and west to the Emyn Muil. So desolate were those places and so deep the horror that lay on them that some of the host were unmanned, and they could neither walk nor ride further north.

Aragorn looked at them, and there was pity in his eyes rather than wrath; for these were young men from Rohan, from Westfold far away, or husbandmen from Lossarnach, and to them Mordor had been from childhood a name of evil, and yet unreal, a legend that had no part in their simple life; and now they walked like men in a hideous dream made true, and they understood not this war nor why fate should lead them to such a pass.

'Go!' said Aragorn. 'But keep what honour you may, and do not run! And there is a task which you may attempt and so be not wholly shamed. Take your way south-west till you come to Cair Andros, and if that is still held by enemies, as I think, then re-take it, if you can; and hold it to the last in defence of Gondor and Rohan!'

Then some being shamed by his mercy overcame their fear and went on, and the others took new hope, hearing of a manful deed within their measure that they could turn to, and they departed. And so, since many men had already been left at the Cross-roads, it was with less than six thousands that the Captains of the West came at last to challenge the Black Gate and the might of Mordor.

They advanced now slowly, expecting at every hour some answer to their challenge, and they drew together, since it was but waste of men to send out scouts or small parties from the main host. At nightfall of the fifth day of the march from Morgul Vale they made their last camp, and set fires about it of such dead wood and heath as they could find. They passed the hours of night in wakefulness and they were aware of many things half-seen that walked and prowled all about them, and they heard the howling of wolves. The wind had died and all the air seemed still. They could see little, for though it was cloudless and the waxing moon was four nights old, there were smokes and fumes that rose out of the earth and the white crescent was shrouded in the mists of Mordor.

It grew cold. As morning came the wind began to stir again, but now it came from the North, and soon it freshened to a rising breeze. All the night-walkers were gone, and the land seemed empty. North amid their noisome pits lay the first of the great heaps and hills of slag and broken rock and blasted earth, the vomit of the maggot-folk of Mordor; but south and now near loomed the great rampart of Cirith Gorgor, and the Black Gate amidmost, and the two Towers of the Teeth tall and dark upon either side. For in their last march the Captains had turned away from the old road as it bent east, and avoided the peril of the lurking hills, and so now they were approaching the Morannon from the north-west, even as Frodo had done.

The two vast iron doors of the Black Gate under its frowning arch were fast closed. Upon the battlement nothing could be seen. All was silent but watchful. They were come to the last end of their folly, and stood forlorn and chill in the grey light of early day before towers and walls which their army could not assault with hope, not even if it had brought thither engines of great power, and the Enemy had no more force than would suffice for the manning of the gate and wall alone. Yet they knew that all the hills and rocks about the Morannon were filled with hidden foes, and the shadowy defile beyond was bored and tunnelled by teeming broods of evil things. And as they stood they saw all the Nazgûl gathered together, hovering above the Towers of the Teeth like vultures; and they knew that they were watched. But still the Enemy made no sign.

No choice was left them but to play their part to its end. Therefore Aragorn now set the host in such array as could best be contrived; and they were drawn up on two great hills of blasted stone and earth that orcs had piled in years of labour. Before them towards Mordor lay like a moat a great mire of reeking mud and foul-smelling pools. When all was ordered, the Captains rode forth towards the Black Gate with a great guard of horsemen and the banner and heralds and trumpeters. There was Gandalf as chief herald, and Aragorn with the sons of Elrond, and Éomer of Rohan, and Imrahil; and Legolas and Gimli and Peregrin were bidden to go also, so that all the enemies of Mordor should have a witness.

They came within cry of the Morannon, and unfurled the banner, and blew upon their trumpets; and the heralds stood out and sent their voices up over the battlement of Mordor.

'Come forth!' they cried. 'Let the Lord of the Black Land come forth!

Justice shall be done upon him. For wrongfully he has made war upon Gondor and wrested its lands. Therefore the King of Gondor demands that he should atone for his evils, and depart then for ever. Come forth!'

There was a long silence, and from wall and gate no cry or sound was heard in answer. But Sauron had already laid his plans, and he had a mind first to play these mice cruelly before he struck to kill. So it was that, even as the Captains were about to turn away, the silence was broken suddenly. There came a long rolling of great drums like thunder in the mountains, and then a braying of horns that shook the very stones and stunned men's ears. And thereupon the door of the Black Gate was thrown open with a great clang, and out of it there came an embassy from the Dark Tower.

At its head there rode a tall and evil shape, mounted upon a black horse, if horse it was; for it was huge and hideous, and its face was a frightful mask, more like a skull than a living head, and in the sockets of its eyes and in its nostrils there burned a flame. The rider was robed all in black, and black was his lofty helm; yet this was no Ringwraith but a living man. The Lieutenant of the Tower of Barad-dûr he was, and his name is remembered in no tale; for he himself had forgotten it, and he said: 'I am the Mouth of Sauron.' But it is told that he was a renegade, who came of the race of those that are named the Black Númenoreans; for they established their dwellings in Middle-earth during the years of Sauron's domination, and they worshipped him, being enamoured of evil knowledge. And he entered the service of the Dark Tower when it first rose again, and because of his cunning he grew ever higher in the Lord's favour; and he learned great sorcery, and knew much of the mind of Sauron; and he was more cruel than any orc.

He it was that now rode out, and with him came only a small company of black-harnessed soldiery, and a single banner, black but bearing on it in red the Evil Eye. Now halting a few paces before the Captains of the West he looked them up and down and laughed.

'Is there anyone in this rout with authority to treat with me?' he asked. 'Or indeed with wit to understand me? Not thou at least!' he mocked, turning to Aragorn with scorn. 'It needs more to make a king than a piece of elvish glass, or a rabble such as this. Why, any brigand of the hills can show as good a following!'

Aragorn said naught in answer, but he took the other's eye and held it, and for a moment they strove thus; but soon, though Aragorn did not stir nor move hand to weapon, the other quailed and gave back as if menaced with a blow. 'I am a herald and ambassador, and may not be assailed!' he cried.

'Where such laws hold,' said Gandalf, 'it is also the custom for ambassadors to use less insolence. But no one has threatened you. You have naught to fear from us, until your errand is done. But unless your master has come to new wisdom, then with all his servants you will be in great peril.'

'So!' said the Messenger. 'Then thou art the spokesman, old greybeard? Have we not heard of thee at whiles, and of thy wanderings, ever hatching plots and mischief at a safe distance? But this time thou hast stuck out thy nose too far, Master Gandalf; and thou shalt see what comes to him who sets his foolish webs before the feet of Sauron the Great. I have tokens that I was bidden to show to thee – to thee in especial, if thou shouldst dare to come.' He signed to one of his guards, and he came forward bearing a bundle swathed in black cloths.

The Messenger put these aside, and there to the wonder and dismay of all the Captains he held up first the short sword that Sam had carried, and next a grey cloak with an elven-brooch, and last the coat of mithril-mail that Frodo had worn wrapped in his tattered garments. A blackness came before their eyes, and it seemed to them in a moment of silence that the world stood still, but their hearts were dead and their last hope gone. Pippin who stood behind Prince Imrahil sprang forward with a cry of grief.

'Silence!' said Gandalf sternly, thrusting him back; but the Messenger laughed aloud.

'So you have yet another of these imps with you!' he cried. 'What use you find in them I cannot guess; but to send them as spies into Mordor is beyond even your accustomed folly. Still, I thank him, for it is plain that this brat at least has seen these tokens before, and it would be vain for you to deny them now.'

'I do not wish to deny them,' said Gandalf. 'Indeed, I know them all and all their history, and despite your scorn, foul Mouth of Sauron, you cannot say as much. But why do you bring them here?'

'Dwarf-coat, elf-cloak, blade of the downfallen West, and spy from the little rat-land of the Shire – nay, do not start! We know it well – here are the marks of a conspiracy. Now, maybe he that bore these things was a creature that you would not grieve to lose, and maybe otherwise: one dear to you, perhaps? If so, take swift counsel with what little wit is left to you. For Sauron does not love spies, and what his fate shall be depends now on your choice.'

No one answered him; but he saw their faces grey with fear and the horror in their eyes, and he laughed again, for it seemed to him that his sport went well. 'Good, good!' he said. 'He was dear to you, I see. Or else his errand was one that you did not wish to fail? It has. And now he shall endure the slow torment of years, as long and slow as our arts in the Great Tower can contrive, and never be released, unless maybe when he is changed and broken, so that he may come to you, and you shall see what you have done. This shall surely be unless you accept my Lord's terms.'

'Name the terms,' said Gandalf steadily, but those nearby saw the anguish in his face, and now he seemed an old and wizened man, crushed, defeated at last. They did not doubt that he would accept.

'These are the terms,' said the Messenger, and smiled as he eyed them one by one. 'The rabble of Gondor and its deluded allies shall withdraw at once beyond the Anduin, first taking oaths never again to assail Sauron the Great in arms, open or secret. All lands east of the Anduin shall be Sauron's for ever, solely. West of the Anduin as far as the Misty Mountains and the Gap of Rohan shall be tributary to Mordor, and men there shall bear no weapons, but shall have leave to govern their own affairs. But they shall help to rebuild Isengard which they have wantonly destroyed, and that shall be Sauron's, and there his lieutenant shall dwell: not Saruman, but one more worthy of trust.'

Looking in the Messenger's eyes they read his thought. He was to be that lieutenant, and gather all that remained of the West under his sway; he would be their tyrant and they his slaves.

But Gandalf said: 'This is much to demand for the delivery of one servant: that your Master should receive in exchange what he must else fight many a war to gain! Or has the field of Gondor destroyed his hope in war, so that he falls to haggling? And if indeed we rated this prisoner so high, what surety have we that Sauron, the Base Master of Treachery, will keep his part? Where is this prisoner? Let him be brought forth and yielded to us, and then we will consider these demands.'

It seemed then to Gandalf, intent, watching him as a man engaged in fencing with a deadly foe, that for the taking of a breath the Messenger was at a loss; yet swiftly he laughed again.

'Do not bandy words in your insolence with the Mouth of Sauron!' he cried. 'Surety you crave! Sauron gives none. If you sue for his clemency you must first do his bidding. These are his terms. Take them or leave them!'

'These we will take!' said Gandalf suddenly. He cast aside his cloak and a white light shone forth like a sword in that black place. Before his upraised hand the foul Messenger recoiled, and Gandalf coming seized and took from him the tokens: coat, cloak, and sword. 'These we will take in memory of our friend,' he cried. 'But as for your terms, we reject them utterly. Get you gone, for your embassy is over and death is near to you. We did not come here to waste words in treating with Sauron, faithless and accursed; still less with one of his slaves. Begone!'

Then the Messenger of Mordor laughed no more. His face was twisted with amazement and anger to the likeness of some wild beast that, as it crouches on its prey, is smitten on the muzzle with a stinging rod. Rage filled him and his mouth slavered, and shapeless sounds of fury came strangling from his throat. But he looked at the fell faces of the Captains and their deadly eyes, and fear overcame his wrath. He gave a great cry, and turned, leaped upon his steed, and with his company galloped madly back to Cirith Gorgor. But as they went his soldiers blew their horns in signal long arranged; and even before they came to the gate Sauron sprang his trap.

Drums rolled and fires leaped up. The great doors of the Black Gate swung back wide. Out of it streamed a great host as swiftly as swirling waters when a sluice is lifted.

The Captains mounted again and rode back, and from the host of Mordor there went up a jeering yell. Dust rose smothering the air, as from nearby there marched up an army of Easterlings that had waited for the signal in the shadows of Ered Lithui beyond the further Tower. Down from the hills on either side of the Morannon poured Orcs innumerable. The men of the West were trapped, and soon, all about the grey mounds where they stood, forces ten times and more than ten times their match would ring them in a sea of enemies. Sauron had taken the proffered bait in jaws of steel.

Little time was left to Aragorn for the ordering of his battle. Upon the one hill he stood with Gandalf, and there fair and desperate was raised the banner of the Tree and Stars. Upon the other hill hard by stood the banners of Rohan and Dol Amroth, White Horse and Silver Swan. And about each hill a ring was made facing all ways, bristling with spear and sword. But in the front towards Mordor where the first bitter assault would come there stood the sons of Elrond on the left with the Dúnedain about them, and on the right the Prince Imrahil with the men of Dol Amroth tall and fair, and picked men of the Tower of Guard.

The wind blew, and the trumpets sang, and arrows whined; but the sun now climbing towards the South was veiled in the reeks of Mordor, and through a threatening haze it gleamed, remote, a sullen red, as if it were the ending of the day, or the end maybe of all the world of light. And out of the gathering mirk the Nazgûl came with their cold voices crying words of death; and then all hope was quenched.

Pippin had bowed crushed with horror when he heard Gandalf reject the terms and doom Frodo to the torment of the Tower; but he had mastered himself, and now he stood beside Beregond in the front rank of Gondor with Imrahil's men. For it seemed best to him to die soon and leave the bitter story of his life, since all was in ruin.

'I wish Merry was here,' he heard himself saying, and quick thoughts raced through his mind, even as he watched the enemy come charging to the assault. 'Well, well, now at any rate I understand poor Denethor a little better. We might die together, Merry and I, and since die we must, why not? Well, as he is not here, I hope he'll find an easier end. But now I must do my best.'

He drew his sword and looked at it, and the intertwining shapes of red and gold; and the flowing characters of Númenor glinted like fire upon the blade. 'This was made for just such an hour,' he thought. 'If only I could smite that foul Messenger with it, then almost I should draw level with old Merry. Well, I'll smite some of this beastly brood before the end. I wish I could see cool sunlight and green grass again!'

Then even as he thought these things the first assault crashed into them. The orcs hindered by the mires that lay before the hills halted and poured their arrows into the defending ranks. But through them there came striding up, roaring like beasts, a great company of hill-trolls out of Gorgoroth. Taller and broader than Men they were, and they were clad only in close-fitting mesh of horny scales, or maybe that was their hideous hide; but they bore round bucklers huge and black and wielded heavy hammers in their knotted hands. Reckless they sprang into the pools and waded across, bellowing as they came. Like a storm they broke upon the line of the men of Gondor, and beat upon helm and head, and arm and shield, as smiths hewing the hot bending iron. At Pippin's side Beregond was stunned and overborne, and he fell; and the great troll-chief that smote him down bent over him, reaching out a clutching claw; for these fell creatures would bite the throats of those that they threw down.

Then Pippin stabbed upwards, and the written blade of Westernesse pierced through the hide and went deep into the vitals of the troll, and his black blood came gushing out. He toppled forward and came crashing down like a falling rock, burying those beneath him. Blackness and stench and crushing pain came upon Pippin, and his mind fell away into a great darkness.

'So it ends as I guessed it would,' his thought said, even as it fluttered away; and it laughed a little within him ere it fled, almost gay it seemed to be casting off at last all doubt and care and fear. And then even as it winged away into forgetfulness it heard voices, and they seemed to be crying in some forgotten world far above:

'The Eagles are coming! The Eagles are coming!'

For one moment more Pippin's thought hovered. 'Bilbo!' it said. 'But no! That came in his tale, long long ago. This is my tale, and it is ended now. Good-bye!' And his thought fled far away and his eyes saw no more.

BOOK SIX

CHAPTER I

THE TOWER OF CIRITH UNGOL

Sam roused himself painfully from the ground. For a moment he wondered where he was, and then all the misery and despair returned to him. He was in the deep dark outside the under-gate of the orcs' stronghold; its brazen doors were shut. He must have fallen stunned when he hurled himself against them; but how long he had lain there he did not know. Then he had been on fire, desperate and furious; now he was shivering and cold. He crept to the doors and pressed his ears against them.

Far within he could hear faintly the voices of orcs clamouring, but soon they stopped or passed out of hearing, and all was still. His head ached and his eyes saw phantom lights in the darkness, but he struggled to steady himself and think. It was clear at any rate that he had no hope of getting into the orc-hold by that gate; he might wait there for days before it was opened, and he could not wait: time was desperately precious. He no longer had any doubt about his duty: he must rescue his master or perish in the attempt.

'The perishing is more likely, and will be a lot easier anyway,' he said grimly to himself, as he sheathed Sting and turned from the brazen doors. Slowly he groped his way back in the dark along the tunnel, not daring to use the elven-light; and as he went he tried to fit together the events since Frodo and he had left the Cross-roads. He wondered what the time was. Somewhere between one day and the next, he supposed; but even of the days he had quite lost count. He was in a land of darkness where the days of the world seemed forgotten, and where all who entered were forgotten too.

'I wonder if they think of us at all,' he said, 'and what is happening to them all away there.' He waved his hand vaguely in the air before him; but he was in fact now facing southwards, as he came back to Shelob's tunnel, not west. Out westward in the world it was drawing to noon upon the fourteenth day of March in the Shire-reckoning, and even now Aragorn was leading the black fleet from Pelargir, and Merry was riding with the Rohirrim down the Stonewain Valley, while in Minas Tirith flames were rising and Pippin watched the madness growing in the eyes of Denethor. Yet amid all their cares and fear the thoughts of their friends turned constantly to Frodo and Sam. They were not forgotten. But they were far beyond aid, and no thought could yet bring any help to Samwise Hamfast's son; he was utterly alone.

He came back at last to the stone door of the orc-passage, and still unable to discover the catch or bolt that held it, he scrambled over as before and dropped softly to the ground. Then he made his way stealthily to the outlet of Shelob's tunnel, where the rags of her great web were still blowing and swaying in the cold airs. For cold they seemed to Sam after the noisome darkness behind; but the breath of them revived him. He crept cautiously out.

All was ominously quiet. The light was no more than that of dusk at a dark day's end. The vast vapours that arose in Mordor and went streaming westward passed low overhead, a great welter of cloud and smoke now lit again beneath with a sullen glow of red.

Sam looked up towards the orc-tower, and suddenly from its narrow windows lights stared out like small red eyes. He wondered if they were some signal. His fear of the orcs, forgotten for a while in his wrath and desperation, now returned. As far as he could see, there was only one possible course for him to take: he must go on and try to find the main entrance to the dreadful tower; but his knees felt weak, and he found that he was trembling. Drawing his eyes down from the tower and the horns of the Cleft before him, he forced his unwilling feet to obey him, and slowly, listening with all his ears, peering into the dense shadows of the rocks beside the way, he retraced his steps, past the place where Frodo fell, and still the stench of Shelob lingered, and then on and up, until he stood again in the very cleft where he had put on the Ring and seen Shagrat's company go by.

There he halted and sat down. For the moment he could drive himself no further. He felt that if once he went beyond the crown of the pass and took one step veritably down into the land of Mordor, that step would be irrevocable. He could never come back. Without any clear purpose he drew out the Ring and put it on again. Immediately he felt the great burden of its weight, and felt afresh, but now more strong and urgent than ever, the malice of the Eye of Mordor, searching, trying to pierce the shadows that it had made for its own defence, but which now hindered it in its unquiet and doubt.

As before, Sam found that his hearing was sharpened, but that to his sight the things of this world seemed thin and vague. The rocky walls of the path were pale, as if seen through a mist, but still at a distance he heard the bubbling of Shelob in her misery; and harsh and clear, and very close it seemed, he heard cries and the clash of metal. He sprang to his feet, and pressed himself against the wall beside the road. He was glad of the Ring, for here was yet another company of orcs on the march. Or so at first he thought. Then suddenly he realized that it was not so, his hearing had deceived him: the orc-cries came from the tower, whose topmost horn was now right above him, on the left hand of the Cleft.

Sam shuddered and tried to force himself to move. There was plainly some devilry going on. Perhaps in spite of all orders the cruelty of the orcs had mastered them, and they were tormenting Frodo, or even savagely hacking him to pieces. He listened; and as he did a gleam of hope came to him. There could not be much doubt: there was fighting in the tower, the orcs must be at war among themselves, Shagrat and Gorbag had come to blows. Faint as was the hope that his guess brought him, it was enough to rouse him. There might be just a chance. His love for Frodo rose above all other thoughts, and forgetting his peril he cried aloud: 'I'm coming Mr. Frodo!'

He ran forward to the climbing path, and over it. At once the road turned left and plunged steeply down. Sam had crossed into Mordor.

He took off the Ring, moved it may be by some deep premonition of danger, though to himself he thought only that he wished to see more clearly. 'Better have a look at the worst,' he muttered. 'No good blundering about in a fog!'

Hard and cruel and bitter was the land that met his gaze. Before his feet the highest ridge of the Ephel Dúath fell steeply in great cliffs down into a dark trough, on the further side of which there rose another ridge, much lower, its edge notched and jagged with crags like fangs that stood out black against the red light behind them: it was the grim Morgai, the inner ring of the fences of the land. Far beyond it, but almost straight ahead, across a wide lake of darkness dotted with tiny fires, there was a great burning glow; and from it rose in huge columns a swirling smoke, dusty red at the roots, black above where it merged into the billowing canopy that roofed in all the accursed land.

Sam was looking at Orodruin, the Mountain of Fire. Ever and anon the furnaces far below its ashen cone would grow hot and with a great surging and throbbing pour forth rivers of molten rock from chasms in its sides. Some would flow blazing towards Barad-dûr down great channels; some would wind their way into the stony plain, until they cooled and lay like twisted dragon-shapes vomited from the tormented earth. In such an hour of labour Sam beheld Mount Doom, and the light of it, cut off by the high screen of the Ephel Dúath from those who climbed up the path from the West, now glared against the stark rock faces, so that they seemed to be drenched with blood.

In that dreadful light Sam stood aghast, for now, looking to his left, he could see the Tower of Cirith Ungol in all its strength. The horn that he had seen from the other side was only its topmost turret. Its eastern face stood up in three great tiers from a shelf in the mountain-wall far below; its back was to a great cliff behind, from which it jutted out in pointed bastions, one above the other, diminishing as they rose, with sheer sides of cunning masonry that looked north-east and south-east. About the lowest tier, two hundred feet below where Sam now stood, there was a battlemented wall enclosing a narrow court. Its gate, upon the near south-eastern side, opened on a broad road, the outer parapet of which ran upon the brink of a precipice, until it turned southward and went winding down into the darkness to join the road that came over the Morgul Pass. Then on it went through a jagged rift in the Morgai out into the valley of Gorgoroth and away to Barad-dûr. The narrow upper way on which Sam stood leapt swiftly down by stair and steep path to meet the main road under the frowning walls close to the Tower-gate.

As he gazed at it suddenly Sam understood, almost with a shock, that this stronghold had been built not to keep enemies out of Mordor, but to keep them in. It was indeed one of the works of Gondor long ago, an eastern outpost of the defences of Ithilien, made when, after the Last Alliance, Men of Westernesse kept watch on the evil land of Sauron where his creatures still lurked. But as with Narchost and Carchost, the Towers of the Teeth, so here too the vigilance had failed, and treachery had yielded up the Tower to the Lord of the Ringwraiths, and now for long years it had been held by evil things. Since his return to Mordor, Sauron had found it useful; for he had few servants but many slaves of fear, and still its chief purpose as of old was to prevent escape from Mordor. Though if an enemy were so rash as to try to enter that land secretly, then it was also a last unsleeping guard against any that might pass the vigilance of Morgul and of Shelob.

Only too clearly Sam saw how hopeless it would be for him to creep down under those many-eyed walls and pass the watchful gate. And even if he did so, he could not go far on the guarded road beyond: not even the black shadows, lying deep where the red glow could not reach, would shield him long from the night-eyed orcs. But desperate as that road might be, his task was now far worse: not to avoid the gate and escape, but to enter it, alone.

His thought turned to the Ring, but there was no comfort there, only dread and danger. No sooner had he come in sight of Mount Doom, burning far away, than he was aware of a change in his burden. As it drew near the great furnaces where, in the deeps of time, it had been shaped and forged, the Ring's power grew, and it became more fell, untameable save by some mighty will. As Sam stood there, even though the Ring was not on him but hanging by its chain about his neck, he felt himself enlarged, as if he were robed in a huge distorted shadow of himself, a vast and ominous threat halted upon the walls of Mordor. He felt that he had from now on only two choices: to forbear the Ring, though it would torment him; or to claim it, and challenge the Power that sat in its dark hold beyond the valley of shadows. Already the Ring tempted him, gnawing at his will and reason. Wild fantasies arose in his mind; and he saw Samwise the Strong, Hero of the Age, striding with a flaming sword across the darkened land, and armies flocking to his call as he marched to the overthrow of Barad-dûr. And then all the clouds rolled away, and the white sun shone, and at his command the vale of Gorgoroth became a garden of flowers and trees and brought forth fruit. He had only to put on the Ring and claim it for his own, and all this could be.

In that hour of trial it was the love of his master that helped most to hold him firm; but also deep down in him lived still unconquered his plain hobbit-sense: he knew in the core of his heart that he was not large enough to bear such a burden, even if such visions were not a mere cheat to betray him. The one small garden of a free gardener was all his need and due, not a garden swollen to a realm; his own hands to use, not the hands of others to command.

'And anyway all these notions are only a trick,' he said to himself. 'He'd spot me and cow me, before I could so much as shout out. He'd spot me, pretty quick, if I put the Ring on now, in Mordor. Well, all I can say is: things look as hopeless as a frost in spring. Just when being invisible would be really useful, I can't use the Ring! And if ever I get any further, it's going to be nothing but a drag and a burden every step. So what's to be done?'

He was not really in any doubt. He knew that he must go down to the gate and not linger any more. With a shrug of his shoulders, as if to shake off the shadow and dismiss the phantoms, he began slowly to descend. With each step he seemed to diminish. He had not gone far before he had shrunk again to a very small and frightened hobbit. He was now passing under the very walls of the Tower, and the cries and sounds of fighting could be heard with his unaided ears. At the moment the noise seemed to be coming from the court behind the outer wall.

Sam was about half way down the path when out of the dark gateway into the red glow there came two orcs running. They did not turn towards him. They were making for the main road; but even as they ran they stumbled and fell to the ground and lay still. Sam had seen no arrows, but he guessed that the orcs had been shot down by others on the battlements or hidden in the shadow of the gate. He went on, hugging the wall on his left. One look upward had shown him that there was no hope of climbing it. The stone-work rose thirty feet, without a crack or ledge, to overhanging courses like inverted steps. The gate was the only way.

He crept on; and as he went he wondered how many orcs lived in the Tower with Shagrat, and how many Gorbag had, and what they were quarrelling about, if that was what was happening. Shagrat's company had seemed to be about forty, and Gorbag's more than twice as large; but of course Shagrat's patrol had only been a part of his garrison. Almost certainly they were quarrelling about Frodo, and the spoil. For a second Sam halted, for suddenly things seemed clear to him, almost as if he had seen them with his eyes. The mithril coat! Of course, Frodo was wearing it, and they would find it. And from what Sam had heard Gorbag would covet it. But the orders of the Dark

Tower were at present Frodo's only protection, and if they were set aside, Frodo might be killed out of hand at any moment.

'Come on, you miserable sluggard!' Sam cried to himself. 'Now for it!' He drew Sting and ran towards the open gate. But just as he was about to pass under its great arch he felt a shock: as if he had run into some web like Shelob's, only invisible. He could see no obstacle, but something too strong for his will to overcome barred the way. He looked about, and then within the shadow of the gate he saw the Two Watchers.

They were like great figures seated upon thrones. Each had three joined bodies, and three heads facing outward, and inward, and across the gateway. The heads had vulture-faces, and on their great knees were laid clawlike hands. They seemed to be carved out of huge blocks of stone, immovable, and yet they were aware: some dreadful spirit of evil vigilance abode in them. They knew an enemy. Visible or invisible none could pass unheeded. They would forbid his entry, or his escape.

Hardening his will Sam thrust forward once again, and halted with a jerk, staggering as if from a blow upon his breast and head. Then greatly daring, because he could think of nothing else to do, answering a sudden thought that came to him, he drew slowly out the phial of Galadriel and held it up. Its white light quickened swiftly, and the shadows under the dark arch fled. The monstrous Watchers sat there cold and still, revealed in all their hideous shape. For a moment Sam caught a glitter in the black stones of their eyes, the very malice of which made him quail; but slowly he felt their will waver and crumble into fear.

He sprang past them; but even as he did so, thrusting the phial back into his bosom, he was aware, as plainly as if a bar of steel had snapped to behind him, that their vigilance was renewed. And from those evil heads there came a high shrill cry that echoed in the towering walls before him. Far up above, like an answering signal, a harsh bell clanged a single stroke.

'That's done it!' said Sam. 'Now I've rung the front-door bell! Well, come on somebody!' he cried. 'Tell Captain Shagrat that the great Elf-warrior has called, with his elf-sword too!'

There was no answer. Sam strode forward. Sting glittered blue in his hand. The courtyard lay in deep shadow, but he could see that the pavement was strewn with bodies. Right at his feet were two orc-archers with knives sticking in their backs. Beyond lay many more shapes; some singly as they had been hewn down or shot; others in pairs, still grappling one another, dead in the very throes of stabbing, throttling, biting. The stones were slippery with dark blood.

Two liveries Sam noticed, one marked by the Red Eye, the other by a Moon disfigured with a ghastly face of death; but he did not stop to look more closely. Across the court a great door at the foot of the Tower stood half open, and a red light came through; a large orc lay dead upon the threshold. Sam sprang over the body and went in; and then he peered about at a loss.

A wide and echoing passage led back from the door towards the mountain-side. It was dimly lit with torches flaring in brackets on the walls but its distant end was lost in gloom. Many doors and openings could be seen on this side and that; but it was empty save for two or three more bodies sprawling on the floor. From what he had heard of the captains' talk Sam knew that, dead or alive, Frodo would most likely be found in a chamber high up in the turret far above; but he might search for a day before he found the way.

'It'll be near the back, I guess,' Sam muttered. 'The whole Tower climbs backwards-like. And anyway I'd better follow these lights.'

He advanced down the passage, but slowly now, each step more reluctant. Terror was beginning to grip him again. There was no sound save the rap of his feet, which seemed to grow to an echoing noise, like the slapping of great hands upon the stones. The dead bodies; the emptiness; the dank black walls that in the torchlight seemed to drip with blood; the fear of sudden death lurking in doorway or shadow; and behind all his mind the waiting watchful malice at the gate: it was almost more than he could screw himself to face. He would have welcomed a fight – with not too many enemies at a time – rather than this hideous brooding uncertainty. He forced himself to think of Frodo, lying bound or in pain or dead somewhere in this dreadful place. He went on.

He had passed beyond the torchlight, almost to a great arched door at the end of the passage, the inner side of the under-gate, as he rightly guessed, when there came from high above a dreadful choking shriek. He stopped short. Then he heard feet coming. Someone was running in great haste down an echoing stairway overhead.

His will was too weak and slow to restrain his hand. It dragged at the chain and clutched the Ring. But Sam did not put it on; for even as he clasped it to his breast, an orc came clattering down. Leaping out of a dark opening at the right, it ran towards him. It was no more than six paces from him when, lifting its head, it saw him; and Sam could hear its gasping breath and see the glare in its bloodshot eyes. It stopped short aghast. For what it saw was not a small frightened hobbit trying to hold a steady sword: it saw a great silent shape, cloaked in a grey shadow, looming against the wavering light behind; in one hand it held a sword, the very light of which was a bitter pain, the other was clutched at its breast, but held concealed some nameless menace of power and doom.

For a moment the orc crouched, and then with a hideous yelp of fear it turned and fled back as it had come. Never was any dog more heartened when its enemy turned tail than Sam at this unexpected flight. With a shout he gave chase.

'Yes! The Elf-warrior is loose!' he cried. 'I'm coming. Just you show me the way up, or I'll skin you!'

But the orc was in its own haunts, nimble and well-fed. Sam was a stranger, hungry and weary. The stairs were high and steep and winding. Sam's breath began to come in gasps. The orc had soon passed out of sight, and now only faintly could be heard the slapping of its feet as it went on and up. Every now and again it gave a yell, and the echo ran along the walls. But slowly all sound of it died away.

Sam plodded on. He felt that he was on the right road, and his spirits had risen a good deal. He thrust the Ring away and tightened his belt. 'Well, well!' he said. 'If only they all take such a dislike to me and my Sting, this may turn out better than I hoped. And anyway it looks as if Shagrat, Gorbag, and company have done nearly all my job for me. Except for that little frightened rat, I do believe there's nobody left alive in the place!'

And with that he stopped, brought up hard, as if he had hit his head against the stone wall. The full meaning of what he had said struck him like a blow. Nobody left alive! Whose had been that horrible dying shriek? 'Frodo, Frodo! Master!' he cried half sobbing. 'If they've killed you, what shall I do? Well, I'm coming at last, right to the top, to see what I must.'

Up, up he went. It was dark save for an occasional torch flaring at a turn, or beside some opening that led into the higher levels of the Tower. Sam tried to count the steps, but after two hundred he lost his reckoning. He was moving quietly now; for he thought that he could hear the sound of voices talking, still some way above. More than one rat remained alive it seemed.

All at once, when he felt that he could pump out no more breath, nor force his knees to bend again, the stair ended. He stood still. The voices were now loud and near. Sam peered about. He had climbed right to the flat roof of the third and highest tier of the Tower: an open space, about twenty yards across, with a low parapet. There the stair was covered by a small domed chamber in the midst of the roof, with low doors facing east and west. Eastward Sam could see the plain of Mordor vast and dark below, and the burning mountain far away. A fresh turmoil was surging in its deep wells, and the rivers of fire blazed so fiercely that even at this distance of many miles the light of them lit the tower-top with a red glare. Westward the view was blocked by the base of the great turret that stood at the back of this upper court and reared its horn high above the crest of the encircling hills. Light gleamed in a window-slit. Its door was not ten yards from where Sam stood. It was open but dark, and from just within its shadow the voices came.

At first Sam did not listen; he took a pace out of the eastward door and looked about. At once he saw that up here the fighting had been fiercest. All the court was choked with dead orcs, or their severed and scattered heads and limbs. The place stank of death. A snarl followed by a blow and a cry sent him darting back into hiding. An orc-voice rose in anger, and he knew it again at once, harsh, brutal, cold. It was Shagrat speaking, Captain of the Tower.

'You won't go again, you say? Curse you, Snaga, you little maggot! If you think I'm so damaged that it's safe to flout me, you're mistaken. Come here, and I'll squeeze your eyes out, like I did to Radbug just now. And when some new lads come, I'll deal with you: I'll send you to Shelob.'

'They won't come, not before you're dead anyway,' answered Snaga surlily. 'I've told you twice that Gorbag's swine got to the gate first, and none of ours got out. Lagduf and Muzgash ran through, but they were shot. I saw it from a window, I tell you. And they were the last.'

'Then you must go. I must stay here anyway. But I'm hurt. The Black Pits take that filthy rebel Gorbag!' Shagrat's voice trailed off into a string of foul names and curses. 'I gave him better than I got, but he knifed me, the dung, before I throttled him. You must go, or I'll eat you. News must get through to Lugbúrz, or we'll both be for the Black Pits. Yes, you too. You won't escape by skulking here.'

'I'm not going down those stairs again,' growled Snaga, 'be you captain or no. Nar! Keep your hands off your knife, or I'll put an arrow in your guts. You won't be a captain long when They hear about all these goings-on. I've fought for the Tower against those stinking Morgul-rats, but a nice mess you two precious captains have made of things, fighting over the swag.'

'That's enough from you,' snarled Shagrat. 'I had my orders. It was Gorbag started it, trying to pinch that pretty shirt.'

'Well, you put his back up, being so high and mighty. And he had more sense than you anyway. He told you more than once that the most dangerous of these spies was still loose, and you wouldn't listen. And you won't listen now. Gorbag was right, I tell you. There's a great fighter about, one of those bloody-handed Elves, or one of the filthy *tarks*.* He's coming here, I tell you. You heard the bell. He's got past the Watchers, and that's *tark's* work. He's on the stairs. And until he's off them, I'm not going down. Not if you were a Nazgûl, I wouldn't.'

'So that's it, is it?' yelled Shagrat. 'You'll do this, and you'll not do that? And when he does come, you'll bolt and leave me? No, you won't! I'll put red maggot-holes in your belly first.'

Out of the turret-door the smaller orc came flying. Behind him came Shagrat, a large orc with long arms that, as he ran crouching, reached to the

* See Appendix F, p. 1105.

ground. But one arm hung limp and seemed to be bleeding; the other hugged a large black bundle. In the red glare Sam, cowering behind the stair-door, caught a glimpse of his evil face as it passed: it was scored as if by rending claws and smeared with blood; slaver dripped from its protruding fangs; the mouth snarled like an animal.

As far as Sam could see, Shagrat hunted Snaga round the roof, until ducking and eluding him the smaller orc with a yelp darted back into the turret and disappeared. Then Shagrat halted. Out of the eastward door Sam could see him now by the parapet, panting, his left claw clenching and unclenching feebly. He put the bundle on the floor and with his right claw drew out a long red knife and spat on it. Going to the parapet he leaned over, looking down into the outer court far below. Twice he shouted but no answer came.

Suddenly, as Shagrat was stooped over the battlement, his back to the rooftop, Sam to his amazement saw that one of the sprawling bodies was moving. It was crawling. It put out a claw and clutched the bundle. It staggered up. In its other hand it held a broad-headed spear with a short broken haft. It was poised for a stabbing thrust. But at that very moment a hiss escaped its teeth, a gasp of pain or hate. Quick as a snake Shagrat slipped aside, twisted round, and drove his knife into his enemy's throat.

'Got you, Gorbag!' he cried. 'Not quite dead, eh? Well, I'll finish my job now.' He sprang on to the fallen body, and stamped and trampled it in his fury, stooping now and again to stab and slash it with his knife. Satisfied at last, he threw back his head and let out a horrible gurgling yell of triumph. Then he licked his knife, and put it between his teeth, and catching up the bundle he came loping towards the near door of the stairs.

Sam had no time to think. He might have slipped out of the other door, but hardly without being seen; and he could not have played hide-and-seek with this hideous orc for long. He did what was probably the best thing he could have done. He sprang out to meet Shagrat with a shout. He was no longer holding the Ring, but it was there, a hidden power, a cowing menace to the slaves of Mordor; and in his hand was Sting, and its light smote the eyes of the orc like the glitter of cruel stars in the terrible elf-countries, the dream of which was a cold fear to all his kind. And Shagrat could not both fight and keep hold of his treasure. He stopped, growling, baring his fangs. Then once more, orc-fashion, he leapt aside, and as Sam sprang at him, using the heavy bundle as both shield and weapon, he thrust it hard into his enemy's face. Sam staggered, and before he could recover, Shagrat darted past and down the stairs.

Sam ran after him, cursing, but he did not go far. Soon the thought of Frodo returned to him, and he remembered that the other orc had gone back into the turret. Here was another dreadful choice, and he had no time to ponder it. If Shagrat got away, he would soon get help and come back. But if

Sam pursued him, the other orc might do some horrible deed up there. And anyway Sam might miss Shagrat or be killed by him. He turned quickly and ran back up the stairs. 'Wrong again, I expect,' he sighed. 'But it's my job to go right up to the top first, whatever happens afterwards.'

Away below Shagrat went leaping down the stairs and out over the court and through the gate, bearing his precious burden. If Sam could have seen him and known the grief that his escape would bring, he might have quailed. But now his mind was set on the last stage of his search. He came cautiously to the turret-door and stepped inside. It opened into darkness. But soon his staring eyes were aware of a dim light at his right hand. It came from an opening that led to another stairway, dark and narrow: it appeared to go winding up the turret along the inside of its round outer wall. A torch was glimmering from somewhere up above.

Softly Sam began to climb. He came to the guttering torch, fixed above a door on his left that faced a window-slit looking out westward: one of the red eyes that he and Frodo had seen from down below by the tunnel's mouth. Quickly Sam passed the door and hurried on to the second storey, dreading at any moment to be attacked and to feel throttling fingers seize his throat from behind. He came next to a window looking east and another torch above the door to a passage through the middle of the turret. The door was open, the passage dark save for the glimmer of the torch and the red glare from outside filtering through the window-slit. But here the stair stopped and climbed no further. Sam crept into the passage. On either side there was a low door; both were closed and locked. There was no sound at all.

'A dead end,' muttered Sam; 'and after all my climb! This can't be the top of the tower. But what can I do now?'

He ran back to the lower storey and tried the door. It would not move. He ran up again, and sweat began to trickle down his face. He felt that even minutes were precious, but one by one they escaped; and he could do nothing. He cared no longer for Shagrat or Snaga or any other orc that was ever spawned. He longed only for his master, for one sight of his face or one touch of his hand.

At last, weary and feeling finally defeated, he sat on a step below the level of the passage-floor and bowed his head into his hands. It was quiet, horribly quiet. The torch, that was already burning low when he arrived, sputtered and went out; and he felt the darkness cover him like a tide. And then softly, to his own surprise, there at the vain end of his long journey and his grief, moved by what thought in his heart he could not tell, Sam began to sing.

His voice sounded thin and quavering in the cold dark tower: the voice of a forlorn and weary hobbit that no listening orc could possibly mistake for the clear song of an Elven-lord. He murmured old childish tunes out of the Shire, and snatches of Mr. Bilbo's rhymes that came into his mind like fleeting glimpses of the country of his home. And then suddenly new strength rose in him, and his voice rang out, while words of his own came unbidden to fit the simple tune.

In western lands beneath the Sun
the flowers may rise in Spring,
the trees may bud, the waters run,
the merry finches sing.
Or there maybe 'tis cloudless night
and swaying beeches bear
the Elven-stars as jewels white
amid their branching hair.

Though here at journey's end I lie
in darkness buried deep,
beyond all towers strong and high,
beyond all mountains steep,
above all shadows rides the Sun
and Stars for ever dwell:
I will not say the Day is done,
nor bid the Stars farewell.

'Beyond all towers strong and high,' he began again, and then he stopped short. He thought that he had heard a faint voice answering him. But now he could hear nothing. Yes, he could hear something, but not a voice. Footsteps were approaching. Now a door was being opened quietly in the passage above; the hinges creaked. Sam crouched down listening. The door closed with a dull thud; and then a snarling orc-voice rang out.

'Ho la! You up there, you dunghill rat! Stop your squeaking, or I'll come and deal with you. D'you hear?'

There was no answer.

'All right,' growled Snaga. 'But I'll come and have a look at you all the same, and see what you're up to.'

The hinges creaked again, and Sam, now peering over the corner of the passage-threshold, saw a flicker of light in an open doorway, and the dim shape of an orc coming out. He seemed to be carrying a ladder. Suddenly the answer dawned on Sam: the topmost chamber was reached by a trap-door in the roof of the passage. Snaga thrust the ladder upwards, steadied it, and then clambered out of sight. Sam heard a bolt drawn back. Then he heard the hideous voice speaking again.

'You lie quiet, or you'll pay for it! You've not got long to live in peace, I guess; but if you don't want the fun to begin right now, keep your trap shut, see? There's a reminder for you!' There was a sound like the crack of a whip.

At that rage blazed in Sam's heart to a sudden fury. He sprang up, ran, and went up the ladder like a cat. His head came out in the middle of the floor of a large round chamber. A red lamp hung from its roof; the westward window-slit was high and dark. Something was lying on the floor by the wall under the window, but over it a black orc-shape was straddled. It raised a whip a second time, but the blow never fell.

With a cry Sam leapt across the floor, Sting in hand. The orc wheeled round, but before it could make a move Sam slashed its whip-hand from its arm. Howling with pain and fear but desperate the orc charged head-down at him. Sam's next blow went wide, and thrown off his balance he fell backwards, clutching at the orc as it stumbled over him. Before he could scramble up he heard a cry and a thud. The orc in its wild haste had tripped on the ladder-head and fallen through the open trap-door. Sam gave no more thought to it. He ran to the figure huddled on the floor. It was Frodo.

He was naked, lying as if in a swoon on a heap of filthy rags: his arm was flung up, shielding his head, and across his side there ran an ugly whip-weal.

'Frodo! Mr. Frodo, my dear!' cried Sam, tears almost blinding him. 'It's Sam, I've come!' He half lifted his master and hugged him to his breast. Frodo opened his eyes.

'Am I still dreaming?' he muttered. 'But the other dreams were horrible.'

'You're not dreaming at all, Master,' said Sam. 'It's real. It's me. I've come.'

'I can hardly believe it,' said Frodo, clutching him. 'There was an orc with a whip, and then it turns into Sam! Then I wasn't dreaming after all when I heard that singing down below, and I tried to answer? Was it you?'

'It was indeed, Mr. Frodo. I'd given up hope, almost. I couldn't find you.'

'Well, you have now, Sam, dear Sam,' said Frodo, and he lay back in Sam's gentle arms, closing his eyes, like a child at rest when night-fears are driven away by some loved voice or hand.

Sam felt that he could sit like that in endless happiness; but it was not allowed. It was not enough for him to find his master, he had still to try and save him. He kissed Frodo's forehead. 'Come! Wake up, Mr. Frodo!' he said, trying to sound as cheerful as he had when he drew back the curtains at Bag End on a summer's morning.

Frodo sighed and sat up. 'Where are we? How did I get here?' he asked.

'There's no time for tales till we get somewhere else, Mr. Frodo,' said Sam. 'But you're in the top of that tower you and me saw from away down by the tunnel before the orcs got you. How long ago that was I don't know. More than a day, I guess.'

'Only that?' said Frodo. 'It seems weeks. You must tell me all about it, if we get a chance. Something hit me, didn't it? And I fell into darkness and foul dreams, and woke and found that waking was worse. Orcs were all round me. I think they had just been pouring some horrible burning drink down my throat. My head grew clear, but I was aching and weary. They stripped me of everything; and then two great brutes came and questioned me, questioned me until I thought I should go mad, standing over me, gloating, fingering their knives. I'll never forget their claws and eyes.'

'You won't, if you talk about them, Mr. Frodo,' said Sam. 'And if we don't want to see them again, the sooner we get going the better. Can you walk?'

'Yes, I can walk,' said Frodo, getting up slowly. 'I am not hurt, Sam. Only I feel very tired, and I've a pain here.' He put his hand to the back of his neck above his left shoulder. He stood up, and it looked to Sam as if he was clothed in flame: his naked skin was scarlet in the light of the lamp above. Twice he paced across the floor.

'That's better!' he said, his spirits rising a little. 'I didn't dare to move when I was left alone, or one of the guards came. Until the yelling and fighting began. The two big brutes: they quarrelled, I think. Over me and my things. I lay here terrified. And then all went deadly quiet, and that was worse.'

'Yes, they quarrelled, seemingly,' said Sam. 'There must have been a couple of hundred of the dirty creatures in this place. A bit of a tall order for Sam Gamgee, as you might say. But they've done all the killing of themselves. That's lucky, but it's too long to make a song about, till we're out of here. Now what's to be done? You can't go walking in the Black Land in naught but your skin, Mr. Frodo.'

'They've taken everything, Sam,' said Frodo. 'Everything I had. Do you understand? *Everything!*' He cowered on the floor again with bowed head, as his own words brought home to him the fullness of the disaster, and despair overwhelmed him. 'The quest has failed, Sam. Even if we get out of here, we can't escape. Only Elves can escape. Away, away out of Middle-earth, far away over the Sea. If even that is wide enough to keep the Shadow out.'

'No, *not* everything, Mr. Frodo. And it hasn't failed, not yet. I took it, Mr. Frodo, begging your pardon. And I've kept it safe. It's round my neck now, and a terrible burden it is, too.' Sam fumbled for the Ring and its chain. 'But I suppose you must take it back.' Now it had come to it, Sam felt reluctant to give up the Ring and burden his master with it again.

'You've got it?' gasped Frodo. 'You've got it here? Sam, you're a marvel!' Then quickly and strangely his tone changed. 'Give it to me!' he cried, standing up, holding out a trembling hand. 'Give it me at once! You can't have it!'

'All right, Mr. Frodo,' said Sam, rather startled. 'Here it is!' Slowly he drew the Ring out and passed the chain over his head. 'But you're in the land of Mordor now, sir; and when you get out, you'll see the Fiery Mountain and all. You'll find the Ring very dangerous now, and very hard to bear. If it's too hard a job, I could share it with you, maybe?'

'No, no!' cried Frodo, snatching the Ring and chain from Sam's hands. 'No you won't, you thief!' He panted, staring at Sam with eyes wide with fear and enmity. Then suddenly, clasping the Ring in one clenched fist, he stood aghast. A mist seemed to clear from his eyes, and he passed a hand over his aching brow. The hideous vision had seemed so real to him, half bemused as he was still with wound and fear. Sam had changed before his very eyes into an orc again, leering and pawing at his treasure, a foul little creature with greedy eyes and slobbering mouth. But now the vision had passed. There was Sam kneeling before him, his face wrung with pain, as if he had been stabbed in the heart; tears welled from his eyes.

'O Sam!' cried Frodo. 'What have I said? What have I done? Forgive me! After all you have done. It is the horrible power of the Ring. I wish it had never, never, been found. But don't mind me, Sam. I must carry the burden to the end. It can't be altered. You can't come between me and this doom.'

'That's all right, Mr. Frodo,' said Sam, rubbing his sleeve across his eyes. 'I understand. But I can still help, can't I? I've got to get you out of here. At once, see! But first you want some clothes and gear, and then some food. The clothes will be the easiest part. As we're in Mordor, we'd best dress up Mordor-fashion; and anyway there isn't no choice. It'll have to be orc-stuff for you, Mr. Frodo, I'm afraid. And for me too. If we go together, we'd best match. Now put this round you!'

Sam unclasped his grey cloak and cast it about Frodo's shoulders. Then unslinging his pack he laid it on the floor. He drew Sting from its sheath. Hardly a flicker was to be seen upon its blade. 'I was forgetting this, Mr. Frodo,' he said. 'No, they didn't get everything! You lent me Sting, if you remember, and the Lady's glass. I've got them both still. But lend them to me a little longer, Mr. Frodo. I must go and see what I can find. You stay here. Walk about a bit and ease your legs. I shan't be long. I shan't have to go far.'

'Take care, Sam!' said Frodo. 'And be quick! There may be orcs still alive, lurking in wait.'

'I've got to chance it,' said Sam. He stepped to the trap-door and slipped down the ladder. In a minute his head reappeared. He threw a long knife on the floor.

'There's something that might be useful,' he said. 'He's dead: the one that whipped you. Broke his neck, it seems, in his hurry. Now you draw up the ladder, if you can, Mr. Frodo; and don't you let it down till you hear me call the pass-word. *Elbereth* I'll call. What the Elves say. No orc would say that.'

Frodo sat for a while and shivered, dreadful fears chasing one another through his mind. Then he got up, drew the grey elven-cloak about him, and to keep his mind occupied, began to walk to and fro, prying and peering into every corner of his prison.

It was not very long, though fear made it seem an hour at least, before he heard Sam's voice calling softly from below: *Elbereth*, *Elbereth*. Frodo let down the light ladder. Up came Sam, puffing, heaving a great bundle on his head. He let it fall with a thud.

'Quick now, Mr. Frodo!' he said. 'I've had a bit of a search to find anything small enough for the likes of us. We'll have to make do. But we must hurry. I've met nothing alive, and I've seen nothing, but I'm not easy. I think this place is being watched. I can't explain it, but well: it feels to me as if one of those foul flying Riders was about, up in the blackness where he can't be seen.'

He opened the bundle. Frodo looked in disgust at the contents, but there was nothing for it: he had to put the things on, or go naked. There were long hairy breeches of some unclean beast-fell, and a tunic of dirty leather. He drew them on. Over the tunic went a coat of stout ring-mail, short for a full-sized orc, too long for Frodo and heavy. About it he clasped a belt, at which there hung a short sheath holding a broad-bladed stabbing-sword. Sam had brought several orc-helmets. One of them fitted Frodo well enough, a black cap with iron rim, and iron hoops covered with leather upon which the Evil Eye was painted in red above the beaklike nose-guard.

'The Morgul-stuff, Gorbag's gear, was a better fit and better made,' said Sam; 'but it wouldn't do, I guess, to go carrying his tokens into Mordor, not after this business here. Well, there you are, Mr. Frodo. A perfect little orc, if I may make so bold – at least you would be, if we could cover your face with a mask, give you longer arms, and make you bow-legged. This will hide some of the tell-tales.' He put a large black cloak round Frodo's shoulders. 'Now you're ready! You can pick up a shield as we go.'

'What about you, Sam?' said Frodo. 'Aren't we going to match?'

'Well, Mr. Frodo, I've been thinking,' said Sam. 'I'd best not leave any of my stuff behind, and we can't destroy it. And I can't wear orc-mail over all my clothes, can I? I'll just have to cover up.'

He knelt down and carefully folded his elven-cloak. It went into a surprisingly small roll. This he put into his pack that lay on the floor. Standing up, he slung it behind his back, put an orc-helm on his head, and cast another black cloak about his shoulders. 'There!' he said. 'Now we match, near enough. And now we must be off!'

'I can't go all the way at a run, Sam,' said Frodo with a wry smile. 'I hope you've made inquiries about inns along the road? Or have you forgotten about food and drink?'

'Save me, but so I had!' said Sam. He whistled in dismay. 'Bless me, Mr.

Frodo, but you've gone and made me that hungry and thirsty! I don't know when drop or morsel last passed my lips. I'd forgotten it, trying to find you. But let me think! Last time I looked I'd got about enough of that waybread, and of what Captain Faramir gave us, to keep me on my legs for a couple of weeks at a pinch. But if there's a drop left in my bottle, there's no more. That's not going to be enough for two, nohow. Don't orcs eat, and don't they drink? Or do they just live on foul air and poison?'

'No, they eat and drink, Sam. The Shadow that bred them can only mock, it cannot make: not real new things of its own. I don't think it gave life to the orcs, it only ruined them and twisted them; and if they are to live at all, they have to live like other living creatures. Foul waters and foul meats they'll take, if they can get no better, but not poison. They've fed me, and so I'm better off than you. There must be food and water somewhere in this place.'

'But there's no time to look for them,' said Sam.

'Well, things are a bit better than you think,' said Frodo. 'I have had a bit of luck while you were away. Indeed they did not take everything. I've found my food-bag among some rags on the floor. They've rummaged it, of course. But I guess they disliked the very look and smell of the *lembas*, worse than Gollum did. It's scattered about and some of it is trampled and broken, but I've gathered it together. It's not far short of what you've got. But they've taken Faramir's food, and they've slashed up my water-bottle.'

'Well, there's no more to be said,' said Sam. 'We've got enough to start on. But the water's going to be a bad business. But come, Mr. Frodo! Off we go, or a whole lake of it won't do us any good!'

'Not till you've had a mouthful, Sam,' said Frodo. 'I won't budge. Here, take this elven-cake, and drink that last drop in your bottle! The whole thing is quite hopeless, so it's no good worrying about tomorrow. It probably won't come.'

At last they started. Down the ladder they climbed, and then Sam took it and laid it in the passage beside the huddled body of the fallen orc. The stair was dark, but on the roof-top the glare of the Mountain could still be seen, though it was dying down now to a sullen red. They picked up two shields to complete their disguise and then went on.

Down the great stairway they plodded. The high chamber of the turret behind, where they had met again, seemed almost homely: they were out in the open again now, and terror ran along the walls. All might be dead in the Tower of Cirith Ungol, but it was steeped in fear and evil still.

At length they came to the door upon the outer court, and they halted. Even from where they stood they felt the malice of the Watchers beating on them, black silent shapes on either side of the gate through which the glare of Mordor dimly showed. As they threaded their way among the hideous bodies of the orcs each step became more difficult. Before they even reached the archway they were brought to a stand. To move an inch further was a pain and weariness to will and limb.

Frodo had no strength for such a battle. He sank to the ground. 'I can't go on, Sam,' he murmured. 'I'm going to faint. I don't know what's come over me.'

'I do, Mr. Frodo. Hold up now! It's the gate. There's some devilry there. But I got through, and I'm going to get out. It can't be more dangerous than before. Now for it!'

Sam drew out the elven-glass of Galadriel again. As if to do honour to his hardihood, and to grace with splendour his faithful brown hobbit-hand that had done such deeds, the phial blazed forth suddenly, so that all the shadowy court was lit with a dazzling radiance like lightning; but it remained steady and did not pass.

'*Gilthoniel, A Elbereth!*' Sam cried. For, why he did not know, his thought sprang back suddenly to the Elves in the Shire, and the song that drove away the Black Rider in the trees.

'*Aiya elenion ancalima!*' cried Frodo once again behind him.

The will of the Watchers was broken with a suddenness like the snapping of a cord, and Frodo and Sam stumbled forward. Then they ran. Through the gate and past the great seated figures with their glittering eyes. There was a crack. The keystone of the arch crashed almost on their heels, and the wall above crumbled, and fell in ruin. Only by a hair did they escape. A bell clanged; and from the Watchers there went up a high and dreadful wail. Far up above in the darkness it was answered. Out of the black sky there came dropping like a bolt a winged shape, rending the clouds with a ghastly shriek.

CHAPTER II

THE LAND OF SHADOW

Sam had just wits enough left to thrust the phial back into his breast. 'Run, Mr. Frodo!' he cried. 'No, not that way! There's a sheer drop over the wall. Follow me!'

Down the road from the gate they fled. In fifty paces, with a swift bend round a jutting bastion of the cliff, it took them out of sight from the Tower. They had escaped for the moment. Cowering back against the rock they drew breath, and then they clutched at their hearts. Perching now on the wall beside the ruined gate the Nazgûl sent out its deadly cries. All the cliffs echoed.

In terror they stumbled on. Soon the road bent sharply eastward again and exposed them for a dreadful moment to view from the Tower. As they flitted across they glanced back and saw the great black shape upon the battlement; then they plunged down between high rock-walls in a cutting that fell steeply to join the Morgul-road. They came to the way-meeting. There was still no sign of orcs, nor of an answer to the cry of the Nazgûl; but they knew that the silence would not last long. At any moment now the hunt would begin.

'This won't do, Sam,' said Frodo. 'If we were real orcs, we ought to be dashing back to the Tower, not running away. The first enemy we meet will know us. We must get off this road somehow.'

'But we can't,' said Sam, 'not without wings.'

The eastern faces of the Ephel Dúath were sheer, falling in cliff and precipice to the black trough that lay between them and the inner ridge. A short way beyond the way-meeting, after another steep incline, a flying bridge of stone leapt over the chasm and bore the road across into the tumbled slopes and glens of the Morgai. With a desperate spurt Frodo and Sam dashed along the bridge; but they had hardly reached its further end when they heard the hue and cry begin. Away behind them, now high above on the mountain-side, loomed the Tower of Cirith Ungol, its stones glowing dully. Suddenly its harsh bell clanged again, and then broke into a shattering peal. Horns sounded. And now from beyond the bridge-end came answering cries. Down in the dark trough, cut off from the dying glare of Orodruin, Frodo and Sam could not see ahead, but already they heard the tramp of iron-shod feet, and upon the road there rang the swift clatter of hoofs.

'Quick, Sam! Over we go!' cried Frodo. They scrambled on to the low parapet of the bridge. Fortunately there was no longer any dreadful drop into the gulf, for the slopes of the Morgai had already risen almost to the level of the road; but it was too dark for them to guess the depth of the fall.

'Well, here goes, Mr. Frodo,' said Sam. 'Good-bye!'

He let go. Frodo followed. And even as they fell they heard the rush of horsemen sweeping over the bridge and the rattle of orc-feet running up behind. But Sam would have laughed, if he had dared. Half fearing a breaking plunge down on to unseen rocks the hobbits landed, in a drop of no more than a dozen feet, with a thud and a crunch into the last thing that they had expected: a tangle of thorny bushes. There Sam lay still, softly sucking a scratched hand.

When the sound of hoof and foot had passed he ventured a whisper. 'Bless me, Mr. Frodo, but I didn't know as anything grew in Mordor! But if I had a'known, this is just what I'd have looked for. These thorns must be a foot long by the feel of them; they've stuck through everything I've got on. Wish I'd a'put that mailshirt on!'

'Orc-mail doesn't keep these thorns out,' said Frodo. 'Not even a leather jerkin is any good.'

They had a struggle to get out of the thicket. The thorns and briars were as tough as wire and as clinging as claws. Their cloaks were rent and tattered before they broke free at last.

'Now down we go, Sam,' Frodo whispered. 'Down into the valley quick, and then turn northward, as soon as ever we can.'

Day was coming again in the world outside, and far beyond the glooms of Mordor the Sun was climbing over the eastern rim of Middle-earth; but here all was still dark as night. The Mountain smouldered and its fires went out. The glare faded from the cliffs. The easterly wind that had been blowing ever since they left Ithilien now seemed dead. Slowly and painfully they clambered down, groping, stumbling, scrambling among rock and briar and dead wood in the blind shadows, down and down until they could go no further.

At length they stopped, and sat side by side, their backs against a boulder. Both were sweating. 'If Shagrat himself was to offer me a glass of water, I'd shake his hand,' said Sam.

'Don't say such things!' said Frodo. 'It only makes it worse.' Then he stretched himself out, dizzy and weary, and he spoke no more for a while. At last with a struggle he got up again. To his amazement he found that Sam was asleep. 'Wake up, Saml' he said. 'Come on! It's time we made another effort.'

Sam scrambled to his feet. 'Well I never!' he said. 'I must have dropped off. It's a long time, Mr. Frodo, since I had a proper sleep, and my eyes just closed down on their own.'

Frodo now led the way, northward as near as he could guess, among the stones and boulders lying thick at the bottom of the great ravine. But presently he stopped again.

'It's no good, Sam,' he said. 'I can't manage it. This mail-shirt, I mean. Not in my present state. Even my mithril-coat seemed heavy when I was tired. This is far heavier. And what's the use of it? We shan't win through by fighting.'

'But we may have some to do,' said Sam. 'And there's knives and stray arrows. That Gollum isn't dead, for one thing. I don't like to think of you with naught but a bit of leather between you and a stab in the dark.'

'Look here, Sam dear lad,' said Frodo: 'I am tired, weary, I haven't a hope left. But I have to go on trying to get to the Mountain, as long as I can move. The Ring is enough. This extra weight is killing me. It must go. But don't think I'm ungrateful. I hate to think of the foul work you must have had among the bodies to find it for me.'

'Don't talk about it, Mr. Frodo. Bless you! I'd carry you on my back, if I could. Let it go then!'

Frodo laid aside his cloak and took off the orc-mail and flung it away. He shivered a little. 'What I really need is something warm,' he said. 'It's gone cold, or else I've caught a chill.'

'You can have my cloak, Mr. Frodo,' said Sam. He unslung his pack and took out the elven-cloak. 'How's this, Mr. Frodo?' he said. 'You wrap that orc-rag close round you, and put the belt outside it. Then this can go over all. It don't look quite orc-fashion, but it'll keep you warmer; and I daresay it'll keep you from harm better than any other gear. It was made by the Lady.'

Frodo took the cloak and fastened the brooch. 'That's better!' he said. 'I feel much lighter. I can go on now. But this blind dark seems to be getting into my heart. As I lay in prison, Sam, I tried to remember the Brandywine, and Woody End, and The Water running through the mill at Hobbiton. But I can't see them now.'

'There now, Mr. Frodo, it's you that's talking of water this time!' said Sam. 'If only the Lady could see us or hear us, I'd say to her: "Your Ladyship, all we want is light and water: just clean water and plain daylight, better than any jewels, begging your pardon." But it's a long way to Lórien.' Sam sighed and waved his hand towards the heights of the Ephel Dúath, now only to be guessed as a deeper blackness against the black sky.

They started off again. They had not gone far when Frodo paused. 'There's a Black Rider over us,' he said. 'I can feel it. We had better keep still for a while.'

Crouched under a great boulder they sat facing back westward and did not speak for some time. Then Frodo breathed a sigh of relief. 'It's passed,' he said. They stood up, and then they both stared in wonder. Away to their left, southward, against a sky that was turning grey, the peaks and high ridges of the great range began to appear dark and black, visible shapes. Light was growing behind them. Slowly it crept towards the North. There was battle far above in the high spaces of the air. The billowing clouds of Mordor were being driven back, their edges tattering as a wind out of the living world came up and swept the fumes and smokes towards the dark land of their home. Under the lifting skirts of the dreary canopy dim light leaked into Mordor like pale morning through the grimed window of a prison.

'Look at it, Mr. Frodo!' said Sam. 'Look at it! The wind's changed. Something's happening. He's not having it all his own way. His darkness is breaking up out in the world there. I wish I could see what is going on!'

It was the morning of the fifteenth of March, and over the Vale of Anduin the Sun was rising above the eastern shadow, and the south-west wind was blowing. Théoden lay dying on the Pelennor Fields.

As Frodo and Sam stood and gazed, the rim of light spread all along the line of the Ephel Dúath, and then they saw a shape, moving at a great speed out of the West, at first only a black speck against the glimmering strip above the mountain-tops, but growing, until it plunged like a bolt into the dark canopy and passed high above them. As it went it sent out a long shrill cry, the voice of a Nazgûl; but this cry no longer held any terror for them: it was a cry of woe and dismay, ill tidings for the Dark Tower. The Lord of the Ringwraiths had met his doom.

'What did I tell you? Something's happening!' cried Sam. '"The war's going well," said Shagrat; but Gorbag he wasn't so sure. And he was right there too. Things are looking up, Mr. Frodo. Haven't you got some hope now?'

'Well no, not much, Sam,' Frodo sighed. 'That's away beyond the mountains. We're going east not west. And I'm so tired. And the Ring is so heavy, Sam. And I begin to see it in my mind all the time, like a great wheel of fire.'

Sam's quick spirits sank again at once. He looked at his master anxiously, and he took his hand. 'Come, Mr. Frodo!' he said. 'I've got one thing I wanted: a bit of light. Enough to help us, and yet I guess it's dangerous too. Try a bit further, and then we'll lie close and have a rest. But take a morsel to eat now, a bit of the Elves' food; it may hearten you.'

Sharing a wafer of *lembas*, and munching it as best they could with their parched mouths, Frodo and Sam plodded on. The light, though no more than a grey dusk, was now enough for them to see that they were deep in the valley between the mountains. It sloped up gently northward, and at its bottom went the bed of a now dry and withered stream. Beyond its stony course they saw a beaten path that wound its way under the feet of the westward cliffs. Had they known, they could have reached it quicker, for it was a track that left the main Morgul-road at the western bridge-end and went down by a long stair cut in the rock to the valley's bottom. It was used by patrols or by messengers going swiftly to lesser posts and strongholds north-away, between Cirith Ungol and the narrows of Isenmouthe, the iron jaws of Carach Angren.

It was perilous for the hobbits to use such a path, but they needed speed, and Frodo felt that he could not face the toil of scrambling among the boulders or in the trackless glens of the Morgai. And he judged that northward was, maybe, the way that their hunters would least expect them to take. The road east to the plain, or the pass back westward, those they would first search most thoroughly. Only when he was well north of the Tower did he mean to turn and seek for some way to take him east, east on the last desperate stage of his journey. So now they crossed the stony bed and took to the orc-path, and for some time they marched along it. The cliffs at their left were overhung, and they could not be seen from above; but the path made many bends, and at each bend they gripped their sword-hilts and went forward cautiously.

The light grew no stronger, for Orodruin was still belching forth a great fume that, beaten upwards by the opposing airs, mounted higher and higher, until it reached a region above the wind and spread in an immeasurable roof, whose central pillar rose out of the shadows beyond their view. They had trudged for more than an hour when they heard a sound that brought them to a halt. Unbelievable, but unmistakable. Water trickling. Out of a gully on the left, so sharp and narrow that it looked as if the black cliff had been cloven by some huge axe, water came dripping down: the last remains, maybe, of some sweet rain gathered from sunlit seas, but ill-fated to fall at last upon the walls of the Black Land and wander fruitless down into the dust. Here it came out of the rock in a little falling streamlet, and flowed across the path, and turning south ran away swiftly to be lost among the dead stones.

Sam sprang towards it. 'If ever I see the Lady again, I will tell her!' he cried. 'Light and now water!' Then he stopped. 'Let me drink first, Mr. Frodo,' he said.

'All right, but there's room enough for two.'

'I didn't mean that,' said Sam. 'I mean: if it's poisonous, or something that will show its badness quick, well, better me than you, master, if you understand me.'

'I do. But I think we'll trust our luck together, Sam; or our blessing. Still, be careful now, if it's very cold!'

The water was cool but not icy, and it had an unpleasant taste, at once bitter and oily, or so they would have said at home. Here it seemed beyond all praise, and beyond fear or prudence. They drank their fill, and Sam replenished his water-bottle. After that Frodo felt easier, and they went on for several miles, until the broadening of the road and the beginnings of a rough wall along its edge warned them that they were drawing near to another orc-hold.

'This is where we turn aside, Sam,' said Frodo. 'And we must turn east.' He sighed as he looked at the gloomy ridges across the valley. 'I have just about enough strength left to find some hole away up there. And then I must rest a little.'

The river-bed was now some way below the path. They scrambled down to it, and began to cross it. To their surprise they came upon dark pools fed by threads of water trickling down from some source higher up the valley. Upon its outer marges under the westward mountains Mordor was a dying land, but it was not yet dead. And here things still grew, harsh, twisted, bitter, struggling for life. In the glens of the Morgai on the other side of the valley low scrubby trees lurked and clung, coarse grey grass-tussocks fought with the stones, and withered mosses crawled on them; and everywhere great writhing, tangled brambles sprawled. Some had long stabbing thorns, some hooked barbs that rent like knives. The sullen shrivelled leaves of a past year hung on them, grating and rattling in the sad airs, but their maggot-ridden buds were only just opening. Flies, dun or grey, or black, marked like orcs with a red eye-shaped blotch, buzzed and stung; and above the briar-thickets clouds of hungry midges danced and reeled.

'Orc-gear's no good,' said Sam waving his arms. 'I wish I'd got an orc's hide!'

At last Frodo could go no further. They had climbed up a narrow shelving ravine, but they still had a long way to go before they could even come in sight of the last craggy ridge. 'I must rest now, Sam, and sleep if I can,' said Frodo. He looked about, but there seemed nowhere even for an animal to crawl into in this dismal country. At length, tired out, they slunk under a curtain of brambles that hung down like a mat over a low rock-face.

There they sat and made such a meal as they could. Keeping back the precious *lembas* for the evil days ahead, they ate the half of what remained in Sam's bag of Faramir's provision: some dried fruit, and a small slip of cured meat; and they sipped some water. They had drunk again from the pools in the valley, but they were very thirsty again. There was a bitter tang in the air of Mordor that dried the mouth. When Sam thought of water even his hopeful spirit quailed. Beyond the Morgai there was the dreadful plain of Gorgoroth to cross.

'Now you go to sleep first, Mr. Frodo,' he said. 'It's getting dark again. I reckon this day is nearly over.'

Frodo sighed and was asleep almost before the words were spoken. Sam struggled with his own weariness, and he took Frodo's hand; and there he sat silent till deep night fell. Then at last, to keep himself awake, he crawled from the hiding-place and looked out. The land seemed full of creaking and cracking and sly noises, but there was no sound of voice or of foot. Far above the Ephel Dúath in the West the night-sky was still dim and pale. There, peeping among the cloud-wrack above a dark tor high up in the mountains, Sam saw a white star twinkle for a while. The beauty of it smote his heart, as he looked up out of the forsaken land, and hope returned to him. For like a shaft, clear and cold, the thought pierced him that in the end the Shadow was only a small and passing thing: there was light and high beauty for ever beyond its reach. His song in the Tower had been defiance rather than hope; for then he was thinking of himself. Now, for a moment, his own fate, and even his master's, ceased to trouble him. He crawled back into the brambles and laid himself by Frodo's side, and putting away all fear he cast himself into a deep untroubled sleep.

They woke together, hand in hand. Sam was almost fresh, ready for another day; but Frodo sighed. His sleep had been uneasy, full of dreams of fire, and waking brought him no comfort. Still his sleep had not been without all healing virtue: he was stronger, more able to bear his burden one stage further. They did not know the time, nor how long they had slept; but after a morsel of food and a sip of water they went on up the ravine, until it ended in a sharp slope of screes and sliding stones. There the last living things gave up their struggle; the tops of the Morgai were grassless, bare, jagged, barren as a slate.

After much wandering and search they found a way that they could climb, and with a last hundred feet of clawing scramble they were up. They came to a cleft between two dark crags, and passing through found themselves on the very edge of the last fence of Mordor. Below them, at the bottom of a fall of some fifteen hundred feet, lay the inner plain stretching away into a formless gloom beyond their sight. The wind of the world blew now from the West, and the great clouds were lifted high, floating away eastward; but still only a grey light came to the dreary fields of

Gorgoroth. There smokes trailed on the ground and lurked in hollows, and fumes leaked from fissures in the earth.

Still far away, forty miles at least, they saw Mount Doom, its feet founded in ashen ruin, its huge cone rising to a great height, where its reeking head was swathed in cloud. Its fires were now dimmed, and it stood in smouldering slumber, as threatening and dangerous as a sleeping beast. Behind it there hung a vast shadow, ominous as a thunder-cloud, the veils of Barad-dûr that was reared far away upon a long spur of the Ashen Mountains thrust down from the North. The Dark Power was deep in thought, and the Eye turned inward, pondering tidings of doubt and danger: a bright sword, and a stern and kingly face it saw, and for a while it gave little thought to other things; and all its great stronghold, gate on gate, and tower on tower, was wrapped in a brooding gloom.

Frodo and Sam gazed out in mingled loathing and wonder on this hateful land. Between them and the smoking mountain, and about it north and south, all seemed ruinous and dead, a desert burned and choked. They wondered how the Lord of this realm maintained and fed his slaves and his armies. Yet armies he had. As far as their eyes could reach, along the skirts of the Morgai and away southward, there were camps, some of tents, some ordered like small towns. One of the largest of these was right below them. Barely a mile out into the plain it clustered like some huge nest of insects, with straight dreary streets of huts and long low drab buildings. About it the ground was busy with folk going to and fro; a wide road ran from it south-east to join the Morgul-way, and along it many lines of small black shapes were hurrying.

'I don't like the look of things at all,' said Sam. 'Pretty hopeless, I call it – saving that where there's such a lot of folk there must be wells or water, not to mention food. And these are Men not Orcs, or my eyes are all wrong.'

Neither he nor Frodo knew anything of the great slave-worked fields away south in this wide realm, beyond the fumes of the Mountain by the dark sad waters of Lake Núrnen; nor of the great roads that ran away east and south to tributary lands, from which the soldiers of the Tower brought long waggon-trains of goods and booty and fresh slaves. Here in the northward regions were the mines and forges, and the musterings of long-planned war; and here the Dark Power, moving its armies like pieces on the board, was gathering them together. Its first moves, the first feelers of its strength, had been checked upon its western line, southward and northward. For the moment it withdrew them, and brought up new forces, massing them about Cirith Gorgor for an avenging stroke. And if it had also been its purpose to defend the Mountain against all approach, it could scarcely have done more.

'Well!' Sam went on. 'Whatever they have to eat and drink, we can't get it. There's no way down that I can see. And we couldn't cross all that open country crawling with enemies, even if we did get down.'

'Still we shall have to try,' said Frodo. 'It's no worse than I expected. I never hoped to get across. I can't see any hope of it now. But I've still got to do the best I can. At present that is to avoid being captured as long as possible. So we must still go northwards, I think, and see what it is like where the open plain is narrower.'

'I guess what it'll be like,' said Sam. 'Where it's narrower the Orcs and Men will just be packed closer. You'll see, Mr. Frodo.'

'I dare say I shall, if we ever get so far,' said Frodo and turned away.

They soon found that it was impossible to make their way along the crest of the Morgai, or anywhere along its higher levels, pathless as they were and scored with deep ghylls. In the end they were forced to go back down the ravine that they had climbed and seek for a way along the valley. It was rough going, for they dared not cross over to the path on the westward side. After a mile or more they saw, huddled in a hollow at the cliff's foot, the orc-hold that they had guessed was near at hand: a wall and a cluster of stone huts set about the dark mouth of a cave. There was no movement to be seen, but the hobbits crept by cautiously, keeping as much as they could to the thorn-brakes that grew thickly at this point along both sides of the old water-course.

They went two or three miles further, and the orc-hold was hidden from sight behind them; but they had hardly begun to breathe more freely again when harsh and loud they heard orc-voices. Quickly they slunk out of sight behind a brown and stunted bush. The voices drew nearer. Presently two orcs came into view. One was clad in ragged brown and was armed with a bow of horn; it was of a small breed, black-skinned, with wide and snuffling nostrils: evidently a tracker of some kind. The other was a big fighting-orc, like those of Shagrat's company, bearing the token of the Eye. He also had a bow at his back and carried a short broad-headed spear. As usual they were quarrelling, and being of different breeds they used the Common Speech after their fashion.

Hardly twenty paces from where the hobbits lurked the small orc stopped. 'Nar!' it snarled. 'I'm going home.' It pointed across the valley to the orc-hold. 'No good wearing my nose out on stones any more. There's not a trace left, I say. I've lost the scent through giving way to you. It went up into the hills, not along the valley, I tell you.'

'Not much use are you, you little snufflers?' said the big orc. 'I reckon eyes are better than your snotty noses.'

'Then what have you seen with them?' snarled the other. 'Garn! You don't even know what you're looking for.'

'Whose blame's that?' said the soldier. 'Not mine. That comes from Higher Up. First they say it's a great Elf in bright armour, then it's a sort of small dwarf-man, then it must be a pack of rebel Uruk-hai; or maybe it's all the lot together.'

'Ar!' said the tracker. 'They've lost their heads, that's what it is. And some of the bosses are going to lose their skins too, I guess, if what I hear is true: Tower raided and all, and hundreds of your lads done in, and prisoner got away. If that's the way you fighters go on, small wonder there's bad news from the battles.'

'Who says there's bad news?' shouted the soldier.

'Ar! Who says there isn't?'

'That's cursed rebel-talk, and I'll stick you, if you don't shut it down, see?'

'All right, all right!' said the tracker. 'I'll say no more and go on thinking. But what's the black sneak got to do with it all? That gobbler with the flapping hands?'

'I don't know. Nothing, maybe. But he's up to no good, nosing around, I'll wager. Curse him! No sooner had he slipped us and run off than word came he's wanted alive, wanted quick.'

'Well, I hope they get him and put him through it,' growled the tracker. 'He messed up the scent back there, pinching that cast-off mail-shirt that he found, and paddling all round the place before I could get there.'

'It saved his life anyhow,' said the soldier. 'Why, before I knew he was wanted I shot him, as neat as neat, at fifty paces right in the back; but he ran on.'

'Garn! You missed him,' said the tracker. 'First you shoot wild, then you run too slow, and then you send for the poor trackers. I've had enough of you.' He loped off.

'You come back,' shouted the soldier, 'or I'll report you!'

'Who to? Not to your precious Shagrat. He won't be captain any more.'

'I'll give your name and number to the Nazgûl,' said the soldier lowering his voice to a hiss. 'One of *them*'s in charge at the Tower now.'

The other halted, and his voice was full of fear and rage. 'You cursed peaching sneakthief!' he yelled. 'You can't do your job, and you can't even stick by your own folk. Go to your filthy Shriekers, and may they freeze the flesh off you! If the enemy doesn't get them first. They've done in Number One, I've heard, and I hope it's true!'

The big orc, spear in hand, leapt after him. But the tracker, springing behind a stone, put an arrow in his eye as he ran up, and he fell with a crash. The other ran off across the valley and disappeared.

For a while the hobbits sat in silence. At length Sam stirred. 'Well, I call that neat as neat,' he said. 'If this nice friendliness would spread about in Mordor, half our trouble would be over.'

'Quietly, Sam,' Frodo whispered. 'There may be others about. We have evidently had a very narrow escape, and the hunt was hotter on our tracks than we guessed. But that *is* the spirit of Mordor, Sam; and it has spread to every corner of it. Orcs have always behaved like that, or so all tales say, when they are on their own. But you can't get much hope out of it. They hate us far more, altogether and all the time. If those two had seen us, they would have dropped all their quarrel until we were dead.'

There was another long silence. Sam broke it again, but with a whisper this time. 'Did you hear what they said about *that gobbler*, Mr. Frodo? I told you Gollum wasn't dead yet, didn't I?'

'Yes, I remember. And I wondered how you knew,' said Frodo. 'Well, come now! I think we had better not move out from here again, until it has gone quite dark. So you shall tell me how you know, and all about what happened. If you can do it quietly.'

'I'll try,' said Sam, 'but when I think of that Stinker I get so hot I could shout.'

There the hobbits sat under the cover of the thorny bush, while the drear light of Mordor faded slowly into a deep and starless night; and Sam spoke into Frodo's ear all that he could find words for of Gollum's treacherous attack, the horror of Shelob, and his own adventures with the orcs. When he had finished, Frodo said nothing but took Sam's hand and pressed it. At length he stirred.

'Well, I suppose we must be going on again,' he said. 'I wonder how long it will be before we really are caught and all the toiling and the slinking will be over, and in vain.' He stood up. 'It's dark, and we cannot use the Lady's glass. Keep it safe for me, Sam. I have nowhere to keep it now, except in my hand, and I shall need both hands in the blind night. But Sting I give to you. I have got an orc-blade, but I do not think it will be my part to strike any blow again.'

It was difficult and dangerous moving in the night in the pathless land; but slowly and with much stumbling the two hobbits toiled on hour by hour northward along the eastern edge of the stony valley. When a grey light crept back over the western heights, long after day had opened in the lands beyond, they went into hiding again and slept a little, turn by turn. In his times of waking Sam was busy with thoughts of food. At last when Frodo roused himself and spoke of eating and making ready for yet another effort, he asked the question that was troubling him most.

'Begging your pardon, Mr. Frodo,' he said, 'but have you any notion how far there is still to go?'

'No, not any clear notion, Sam,' Frodo answered. 'In Rivendell before I set out I was shown a map of Mordor that was made before the Enemy came back here; but I only remember it vaguely. I remember clearest that there was a place in the north where the western range and the northern range send out spurs that nearly meet. That must be twenty leagues at least from the bridge back by the Tower. It might be a good point at which to cross. But of course, if we get there, we shall be further than we were from the Mountain, sixty miles from it, I should think. I guess that we have gone about twelve leagues north from the bridge now. Even if all goes well, I could hardly reach the Mountain in a week. I am afraid, Sam, that the burden will get very heavy, and I shall go still slower as we get nearer.'

Sam sighed. 'That's just as I feared,' he said. 'Well, to say nothing of water, we've got to eat less, Mr. Frodo, or else move a bit quicker, at any rate while we're still in this valley. One more bite and all the food's ended, save the Elves' waybread.'

'I'll try and be a bit quicker, Sam,' said Frodo, drawing a deep breath. 'Come on then! Let's start another march!'

It was not yet quite dark again. They plodded along, on into the night. The hours passed in a weary stumbling trudge with a few brief halts. At the first hint of grey light under the skirts of the canopy of shadow they hid themselves again in a dark hollow under an overhanging stone.

Slowly the light grew, until it was clearer than it yet had been. A strong wind from the West was now driving the fumes of Mordor from the upper airs. Before long the hobbits could make out the shape of the land for some miles about them. The trough between the mountains and the Morgai had steadily dwindled as it climbed upwards, and the inner ridge was now no more than a shelf in the steep faces of the Ephel Dúath; but to the east it fell as sheerly as ever down into Gorgoroth. Ahead the water-course came to an end in broken steps of rock; for out from the main range there sprang a high barren spur, thrusting eastward like a wall. To meet it there stretched out from the grey and misty northern range of Ered Lithui a long jutting arm; and between the ends there was a narrow gap: Carach Angren, the Isenmouthe, beyond which lay the deep dale of Udûn. In that dale behind the Morannon were the tunnels and deep armouries that the servants of Mordor had made for the defence of the Black Gate of their land; and there now their Lord was gathering in haste great forces to meet the onslaught of the Captains of the West. Upon the out-thrust spurs forts and towers were built, and watch-fires burned; and all across the gap an earth-wall had been raised, and a deep trench delved that could be crossed only by a single bridge.

A few miles north, high up in the angle where the western spur branched away from the main range, stood the old castle of Durthang, now one of the many orc-holds that clustered about the dale of Udûn. A road, already visible in the growing light, came winding down from it, until only a mile or two from where the hobbits lay it turned east and ran along a shelf cut in the side of the spur, and so went down into the plain, and on to the Isenmouthe.

To the hobbits as they looked out it seemed that all their journey north had been useless. The plain to their right was dim and smoky, and they could see there neither camps nor troops moving; but all that region was under the vigilance of the forts of Carach Angren.

'We have come to a dead end, Sam,' said Frodo. 'If we go on, we shall only come up to that orc-tower, but the only road to take is that road that comes down from it – unless we go back. We can't climb up westward, or climb down eastward.'

'Then we must take the road, Mr. Frodo,' said Sam. 'We must take it and chance our luck, if there is any luck in Mordor. We might as well give ourselves up as wander about any more, or try to go back. Our food won't last. We've got to make a dash for it!'

'All right, Sam,' said Frodo. 'Lead me! As long as you've got any hope left. Mine is gone. But I can't dash, Sam. I'll just plod along after you.'

'Before you start any more plodding, you need sleep and food, Mr. Frodo. Come and take what you can get of them!'

He gave Frodo water and an additional wafer of the waybread, and he made a pillow of his cloak for his master's head. Frodo was too weary to debate the matter, and Sam did not tell him that he had drunk the last drop of their water, and eaten Sam's share of the food as well as his own. When Frodo was asleep Sam bent over him and listened to his breathing and scanned his face. It was lined and thin, and yet in sleep it looked content and unafraid. 'Well, here goes, Master!' Sam muttered to himself. 'I'll have to leave you for a bit and trust to luck. Water we must have, or we'll get no further.'

Sam crept out, and flitting from stone to stone with more than hobbit-care, he went down to the water-course, and then followed it for some way as it climbed north, until he came to the rock-steps where long ago, no doubt, its spring had come gushing down in a little waterfall. All now seemed dry and silent; but refusing to despair Sam stooped and listened, and to his delight he caught the sound of trickling. Clambering a few steps up he found a tiny stream of dark water that came out from the hill-side and filled a little bare pool, from which again it spilled, and vanished then under the barren stones.

Sam tasted the water, and it seemed good enough. Then he drank deeply, refilled the bottle, and turned to go back. At that moment he caught a glimpse of a black form or shadow flitting among the rocks away near Frodo's hiding-place. Biting back a cry, he leapt down from the spring and ran, jumping from stone to stone. It was a wary creature, difficult to see, but Sam had little doubt about it: he longed to get his hands on its neck. But it heard him coming and slipped quickly away. Sam thought he saw a last fleeting glimpse of it, peering back over the edge of the eastward precipice, before it ducked and disappeared.

'Well, luck did not let me down,' muttered Sam, 'but that was a near thing! Isn't it enough to have orcs by the thousand without that stinking villain coming nosing round? I wish he had been shot!' He sat down by Frodo and did not rouse him; but he did not dare to go to sleep himself. At last when he felt his eyes closing and knew that his struggle to keep awake could not go on much longer, he wakened Frodo gently.

'That Gollum's about again, I'm afraid, Mr. Frodo,' he said. 'Leastways, if it wasn't him, then there's two of him. I went away to find some water and spied him nosing round just as I turned back. I reckon it isn't safe for us both to sleep together, and begging your pardon, but I can't hold up my lids much longer.'

'Bless you, Sam!' said Frodo. 'Lie down and take your proper turn! But I'd rather have Gollum than orcs. At any rate he won't give us away to them – not unless he's caught himself.'

'But he might do a bit of robbery and murder on his own,' growled Sam. 'Keep your eyes open, Mr. Frodo! There's a bottle full of water. Drink up. We can fill it again when we go on.' With that Sam plunged into sleep.

Light was fading again when he woke. Frodo sat propped against the rock behind, but he had fallen asleep. The water-bottle was empty. There was no sign of Gollum.

Mordor-dark had returned, and the watch-fires on the heights burned fierce and red, when the hobbits set out again on the most dangerous stage of all their journey. They went first to the little spring, and then climbing warily up they came to the road at the point where it swung east towards the Isenmouthe twenty miles away. It was not a broad road, and it had no wall or parapet along the edge, and as it ran on the sheer drop from its brink became deeper and deeper. The hobbits could hear no movements, and after listening for a while they set off eastward at a steady pace.

After doing some twelve miles, they halted. A short way back the road had bent a little northward and the stretch that they had passed over was now screened from sight. This proved disastrous. They rested for some minutes and then went on; but they had not taken many steps when suddenly in the stillness of the night they heard the sound that all along they had secretly dreaded: the noise of marching feet. It was still some way behind them, but looking back they could see the twinkle of torches coming round the bend less than a mile away, and they were moving fast: too fast for Frodo to escape by flight along the road ahead.

'I feared it, Sam,' said Frodo. 'We've trusted to luck, and it has failed us. We're trapped.' He looked wildly up at the frowning wall, where the road-builders of old had cut the rock sheer for many fathoms above their heads. He ran to the other side and looked over the brink into a dark pit of gloom. 'We're trapped at last!' he said. He sank to the ground beneath the wall of rock and bowed his head.

'Seems so,' said Sam. 'Well, we can but wait and see.' And with that he sat down beside Frodo under the shadow of the cliff.

They did not have to wait long. The orcs were going at a great pace. Those in the foremost files bore torches. On they came, red flames in the dark, swiftly growing. Now Sam too bowed his head, hoping that it would hide his face when the torches reached them; and he set their shields before their knees to hide their feet.

'If only they are in a hurry and will let a couple of tired soldiers alone and pass on!' he thought.

And so it seemed that they would. The leading orcs came loping along, panting, holding their heads down. They were a gang of the smaller breeds being driven unwilling to their Dark Lord's wars; all they cared for was to get the march over and escape the whip. Beside them, running up and down the line, went two of the large fierce *uruks*, cracking lashes and shouting. File after file passed, and the tell-tale torchlight was already some way ahead. Sam held his breath. Now more than half the line had gone by. Then suddenly one of the slave-drivers spied the two figures by the road-side. He flicked a whip at them and yelled: 'Hi, you! Get up!' They did not answer, and with a shout he halted the whole company.

'Come on, you slugs!' he cried. 'This is no time for slouching.' He took a step towards them, and even in the gloom he recognized the devices on their shields. 'Deserting, eh?' he snarled. 'Or thinking of it? All your folk should have been inside Udûn before yesterday evening. You know that. Up you get and fall in, or I'll have your numbers and report you.'

They struggled to their feet, and keeping bent, limping like footsore soldiers, they shuffled back towards the rear of the line. 'No, not at the rear!' the slave-driver shouted. 'Three files up. And stay there, or you'll know it, when I come down the line!' He sent his long whip-lash cracking over their heads; then with another crack and a yell he started the company off again at a brisk trot.

It was hard enough for poor Sam, tired as he was; but for Frodo it was a torment, and soon a nightmare. He set his teeth and tried to stop his mind from thinking, and he struggled on. The stench of the sweating orcs about him was stifling, and he began to gasp with thirst. On, on they went, and he bent all his will to draw his breath and to make his legs keep going; and yet to what evil end he toiled and endured he did not dare to think. There was no hope of falling out unseen. Now and again the orc-driver fell back and jeered at them.

'There now!' he laughed, flicking at their legs. 'Where there's a whip there's a will, my slugs. Hold up! I'd give you a nice freshener now, only you'll get as much lash as your skins will carry when you come in late to your camp. Do you good. Don't you know we're at war?'

They had gone some miles, and the road was at last running down a long slope into the plain, when Frodo's strength began to give out and his will wavered. He lurched and stumbled. Desperately Sam tried to help him and hold him up, though he felt that he could himself hardly stay the pace much longer. At any moment now he knew that the end would come: his master would faint or fall, and all would be discovered, and their bitter efforts be in vain. 'I'll have that big slave-driving devil anyway,' he thought.

Then just as he was putting his hand to the hilt of his sword, there came an unexpected relief. They were out on the plain now and drawing near the entrance to Udûn. Some way in front of it, before the gate at the bridge-end, the road from the west converged with others coming from the south, and from Barad-dûr. Along all the roads troops were moving; for the Captains of the West were advancing and the Dark Lord was speeding his forces north. So it chanced that several companies came together at the road-meeting, in the dark beyond the light of the watch-fires on the wall. At once there was great jostling and cursing as each troop tried to get first to the gate and the ending of their march. Though the drivers yelled and plied their whips, scuffles broke out and some blades were drawn. A troop of heavy-armed *uruks* from Barad-dûr charged into the Durthang line and threw them into confusion.

Dazed as he was with pain and weariness, Sam woke up, grasped quickly at his chance, and threw himself to the ground, dragging Frodo down with him. Orcs fell over them, snarling and cursing. Slowly on hand and knee the hobbits crawled away out of the turmoil, until at last unnoticed they dropped over the further edge of the road. It had a high kerb by which troop-leaders could guide themselves in black night or fog, and it was banked up some feet above the level of the open land.

They lay still for a while. It was too dark to seek for cover, if indeed there was any to find; but Sam felt that they ought at least to get further away from the highways and out of the range of torchlight.

'Come on, Mr. Frodo!' he whispered. 'One more crawl, and then you can lie still.'

With a last despairing effort Frodo raised himself on his hands, and struggled on for maybe twenty yards. Then he pitched down into a shallow pit that opened unexpectedly before them, and there he lay like a dead thing.

CHAPTER III

MOUNT DOOM

Sam put his ragged orc-cloak under his master's head, and covered them both with the grey robe of Lórien; and as he did so his thoughts went out to that fair land, and to the Elves, and he hoped that the cloth woven by their hands might have some virtue to keep them hidden beyond all hope in this wilderness of fear. He heard the scuffling and cries die down as the troops passed on through the Isenmouthe. It seemed that in the confusion and the mingling of many companies of various kinds they had not been missed, not yet at any rate.

Sam took a sip of water, but pressed Frodo to drink, and when his master had recovered a little he gave him a whole wafer of their precious waybread and made him eat it. Then, too worn out even to feel much fear, they stretched themselves out. They slept a little in uneasy fits; for their sweat grew chill on them, and the hard stones bit them, and they shivered. Out of the north from the Black Gate through Cirith Gorgor there flowed whispering along the ground a thin cold air.

In the morning a grey light came again, for in the high regions the West Wind still blew, but down on the stones behind the fences of the Black Land the air seemed almost dead, chill and yet stifling. Sam looked up out of the hollow. The land all about was dreary, flat and drab-hued. On the roads nearby nothing was moving now; but Sam feared the watchful eyes on the wall of the Isenmouthe, no more than a furlong away northward. South-eastward, far off like a dark standing shadow, loomed the Mountain. Smokes were pouring from it, and while those that rose into the upper air trailed away eastward, great rolling clouds floated down its sides and spread over the land. A few miles to the north-east the foothills of the Ashen Mountains stood like sombre grey ghosts, behind which the misty northern heights rose like a line of distant cloud hardly darker than the lowering sky.

Sam tried to guess the distances and to decide what way they ought to take. 'It looks every step of fifty miles,' he muttered gloomily, staring at the threatening mountain, 'and that'll take a week, if it takes a day, with Mr. Frodo as he is.' He shook his head, and as he worked things out, slowly a new dark thought grew in his mind. Never for long had hope died in his staunch heart, and always until now he had taken some thought for their return. But the bitter truth came home to him at last: at best their provision would take them to their goal; and when the task was done, there they would come to an end, alone, houseless, foodless in the midst of a terrible desert. There could be no return.

'So that was the job I felt I had to do when I started,' thought Sam: 'to help Mr. Frodo to the last step and then die with him? Well, if that is the job then I must do it. But I would dearly like to see Bywater again, and Rosie Cotton and her brothers, and the Gaffer and Marigold and all. I can't think somehow that Gandalf would have sent Mr. Frodo on this errand, if there hadn't a' been any hope of his ever coming back at all. Things all went wrong when he went down in Moria. I wish he hadn't. He would have done something.'

But even as hope died in Sam, or seemed to die, it was turned to a new strength. Sam's plain hobbit-face grew stern, almost grim, as the will hardened in him, and he felt through all his limbs a thrill, as if he was turning into some creature of stone and steel that neither despair nor weariness nor endless barren miles could subdue.

With a new sense of responsibility he brought his eyes back to the ground near at hand, studying the next move. As the light grew a little he saw to his surprise that what from a distance had seemed wide and featureless flats were in fact all broken and tumbled. Indeed the whole surface of the plains of Gorgoroth was pocked with great holes, as if, while it was still a waste of soft mud, it had been smitten with a shower of bolts and huge slingstones. The largest of these holes were rimmed with ridges of broken rock, and broad fissures ran out from them in all directions. It was a land in which it would be possible to creep from hiding to hiding, unseen by all but the most watchful eyes: possible at least for one who was strong and had no need for speed. For the hungry and worn, who had far to go before life failed, it had an evil look.

Thinking of all these things Sam went back to his master. He had no need to rouse him. Frodo was lying on his back with eyes open, staring at the cloudy sky. 'Well, Mr. Frodo,' said Sam, 'I've been having a look round and thinking a bit. There's nothing on the roads, and we'd best be getting away while there's a chance. Can you manage it?'

'I can manage it,' said Frodo. 'I must.'

Once more they started, crawling from hollow to hollow, flitting behind such cover as they could find, but moving always in a slant towards the foothills of the northern range. But as they went the most easterly of the roads followed them, until it ran off, hugging the skirts of the mountains, away into a wall of black shadow far ahead. Neither man nor orc now moved along its flat grey stretches; for the Dark Lord had almost completed the movement of his forces, and even in the fastness of his own realm he sought the secrecy of night, fearing the winds of the world that had turned against him, tearing aside his veils, and troubled with tidings of bold spies that had passed through his fences.

The hobbits had gone a few weary miles when they halted. Frodo seemed nearly spent. Sam saw that he could not go much further in this fashion, crawling, stooping, now picking a doubtful way very slowly, now hurrying at a stumbling run.

'I'm going back on to the road while the light lasts, Mr. Frodo,' he said. 'Trust to luck again! It nearly failed us last time, but it didn't quite. A steady pace for a few more miles, and then a rest.'

He was taking a far greater risk than he knew; but Frodo was too much occupied with his burden and with the struggle in his mind to debate, and almost too hopeless to care. They climbed on to the causeway and trudged along, down the hard cruel road that led to the Dark Tower itself. But their luck held, and for the rest of that day they met no living or moving thing; and when night fell they vanished into the darkness of Mordor. All the land now brooded as at the coming of a great storm: for the Captains of the West had passed the Cross-roads and set flames in the deadly fields of Imlad Morgul.

So the desperate journey went on, as the Ring went south and the banners of the kings rode north. For the hobbits each day, each mile, was more bitter than the one before, as their strength lessened and the land became more evil. They met no enemies by day. At times by night, as they cowered or drowsed uneasily in some hiding beside the road, they heard cries and the noise of many feet or the swift passing of some cruelly ridden steed. But far worse than all such perils was the ever-approaching threat that beat upon them as they went: the dreadful menace of the Power that waited, brooding in deep thought and sleepless malice behind the dark veil about its Throne. Nearer and nearer it drew, looming blacker, like the oncoming of a wall of night at the last end of the world.

There came at last a dreadful nightfall; and even as the Captains of the West drew near to the end of the living lands, the two wanderers came to an hour of blank despair. Four days had passed since they had escaped from the orcs, but the time lay behind them like an ever-darkening dream. All this last day Frodo had not spoken, but had walked half-bowed, often stumbling, as if his eyes no longer saw the way before his feet. Sam guessed that among all their pains he bore the worst, the growing weight of the Ring, a burden on the body and a torment to his mind. Anxiously Sam had noted how his master's left hand would often be raised as if to ward off a blow, or to screen his shrinking eyes from a dreadful Eye that sought to look in them. And sometimes his right hand would creep to his breast, clutching, and then slowly, as the will recovered mastery, it would be withdrawn.

Now as the blackness of night returned Frodo sat, his head between his knees, his arms hanging wearily to the ground where his hands lay feebly twitching. Sam watched him, till night covered them both and hid them from one another. He could no longer find any words to say; and he turned to his own dark thoughts. As for himself, though weary and under a shadow of fear, he still had some strength left. The *lembas* had a virtue without which they would long ago have lain down to die. It did not satisfy desire, and at times Sam's mind was filled with the memories of food, and the longing for simple bread and meats. And yet this waybread of the Elves had a potency that increased as travellers relied on it alone and did not mingle it with other foods. It fed the will, and it gave strength to endure, and to master sinew and limb beyond the measure of mortal kind. But now a new decision must be made. They could not follow this road any longer; for it went on eastward into the great Shadow, but the Mountain now loomed upon their right, almost due south, and they must turn towards it. Yet still before it there stretched a wide region of fuming, barren, ash-ridden land.

'Water, water!' muttered Sam. He had stinted himself, and in his parched mouth his tongue seemed thick and swollen; but for all his care they now had very little left, perhaps half his bottle, and maybe there were still days to go. All would long ago have been spent, if they had not dared to follow the orc-road. For at long intervals on that highway cisterns had been built for the use of troops sent in haste through the waterless regions. In one Sam had found some water left, stale, muddied by the orcs, but still sufficient for their desperate case. Yet that was now a day ago. There was no hope of any more.

At last wearied with his cares Sam drowsed, leaving the morrow till it came; he could do no more. Dream and waking mingled uneasily. He saw lights like gloating eyes, and dark creeping shapes, and he heard noises as of wild beasts or the dreadful cries of tortured things; and he would start up to find the world all dark and only empty blackness all about him. Once only, as he stood and stared wildly round, did it seem that, though now awake, he could still see pale lights like eyes; but soon they flickered and vanished.

The hateful night passed slowly and reluctantly. Such daylight as followed was dim; for here as the Mountain drew near the air was ever mirky, while out from the Dark Tower there crept the veils of Shadow that Sauron wove about himself. Frodo was lying on his back not moving. Sam stood beside him, reluctant to speak, and yet knowing that the word now lay with him: he must set his master's will to work for another effort. At length, stooping and caressing Frodo's brow, he spoke in his ear.

'Wake up, Master!' he said. 'Time for another start.'

As if roused by a sudden bell, Frodo rose quickly, and stood up and looked away southwards; but when his eyes beheld the Mountain and the desert he quailed again.

'I can't manage it, Sam,' he said. 'It is such a weight to carry, such a weight.'

Sam knew before he spoke, that it was vain, and that such words might do more harm than good, but in his pity he could not keep silent. 'Then let me carry it a bit for you, Master,' he said. 'You know I would, and gladly, as long as I have any strength.'

A wild light came into Frodo's eyes. 'Stand away! Don't touch me!' he cried. 'It is mine, I say. Be off!' His hand strayed to his sword-hilt. But then quickly his voice changed. 'No, no, Sam,' he said sadly. 'But you must understand. It is my burden, and no one else can bear it. It is too late now, Sam dear. You can't help me in that way again. I am almost in its power now. I could not give it up, and if you tried to take it I should go mad.'

Sam nodded. 'I understand,' he said. 'But I've been thinking, Mr. Frodo, there's other things we might do without. Why not lighten the load a bit? We're going that way now, as straight as we can make it.' He pointed to the Mountain. 'It's no good taking anything we're not sure to need.'

Frodo looked again towards the Mountain. 'No,' he said, 'we shan't need much on that road. And at its end nothing.' Picking up his orc-shield he flung it away and threw his helmet after it. Then pulling off the grey cloak he undid the heavy belt and let it fall to the ground, and the sheathed sword with it. The shreds of the black cloak he tore off and scattered.

'There, I'll be an orc no more,' he cried, 'and I'll bear no weapon, fair or foul. Let them take me, if they will!'

Sam did likewise, and put aside his orc-gear; and he took out all the things in his pack. Somehow each of them had become dear to him, if only because he had borne them so far with so much toil. Hardest of all it was to part with his cooking-gear. Tears welled in his eyes at the thought of casting it away.

'Do you remember that bit of rabbit, Mr. Frodo?' he said. 'And our place under the warm bank in Captain Faramir's country, the day I saw an oliphaunt?'

'No, I am afraid not, Sam,' said Frodo. 'At least, I know that such things happened, but I cannot see them. No taste of food, no feel of water, no sound of wind, no memory of tree or grass or flower, no image of moon or star are left to me. I am naked in the dark, Sam, and there is no veil between me and the wheel of fire. I begin to see it even with my waking eyes, and all else fades.'

Sam went to him and kissed his hand. 'Then the sooner we're rid of it, the sooner to rest,' he said haltingly, finding no better words to say. 'Talking won't mend nothing,' he muttered to himself, as he gathered up all the things that they had chosen to cast away. He was not willing to leave them lying open in the wilderness for any eyes to see. 'Stinker picked up that orc-shirt, seemingly, and he isn't going to add a sword to it. His hands are bad enough when empty. And he isn't going to mess with my pans!' With that he carried all the gear away to one of the many gaping fissures that scored the land and threw them in. The clatter of his precious pans as they fell down into the dark was like a death-knell to his heart.

He came back to Frodo, and then of his elven-rope he cut a short piece to serve his master as a girdle and bind the grey cloak close about his waist. The rest he carefully coiled and put back in his pack. Beside that he kept only the remnants of their waybread and the water-bottle, and Sting still hanging by his belt; and hidden away in a pocket of his tunic next his breast the phial of Galadriel and the little box that she gave him for his own.

Now at last they turned their faces to the Mountain and set out, thinking no more of concealment, bending their weariness and failing wills only to the one task of going on. In the dimness of its dreary day few things even in that land of vigilance could have espied them, save from close at hand. Of all the slaves of the Dark Lord, only the Nazgûl could have warned him of the peril that crept, small but indomitable, into the very heart of his guarded realm. But the Nazgûl and their black wings were abroad on other errand: they were gathered far away, shadowing the march of the Captains of the West, and thither the thought of the Dark Tower was turned.

That day it seemed to Sam that his master had found some new strength, more than could be explained by the small lightening of the load that he had to carry. In the first marches they went further and faster than he had hoped. The land was rough and hostile, and yet they made much progress, and ever the Mountain drew nearer. But as the day wore on and all too soon the dim light began to fail, Frodo stooped again, and began to stagger, as if the renewed effort had squandered his remaining strength.

At their last halt he sank down and said: 'I'm thirsty, Sam,' and did not speak again. Sam gave him a mouthful of water; only one more mouthful remained. He went without himself; and now as once more the night of Mordor closed over them, through all his thoughts there came the memory of water; and every brook or stream or fount that he had ever seen, under green willow-shades or twinkling in the sun, danced and rippled for his torment behind the blindness of his eyes. He felt the cool mud about his toes as he paddled in the Pool at Bywater with Jolly Cotton and Tom and Nibs, and their sister Rosie. 'But that was years ago,' he sighed, 'and far away. The way back, if there is one, goes past the Mountain.'

He could not sleep and he held a debate with himself. 'Well, come now, we've done better than you hoped,' he said sturdily. 'Began well anyway. I reckon we crossed half the distance before we stopped. One more day will do it.' And then he paused.

'Don't be a fool, Sam Gamgee,' came an answer in his own voice. 'He won't go another day like that, if he moves at all. And you can't go on much longer giving him all the water and most of the food.'

'I can go on a good way though, and I will.'

'Where to?'

'To the Mountain, of course.'

'But what then, Sam Gamgee, what then? When you get there, what are you going to do? He won't be able to do anything for himself.'

To his dismay Sam realized that he had not got an answer to this. He had no clear idea at all. Frodo had not spoken much to him of his errand, and Sam only knew vaguely that the Ring had somehow to be put into the fire. 'The Cracks of Doom,' he muttered, the old name rising to his mind. 'Well, if Master knows how to find them, I don't.'

'There you are!' came the answer. 'It's all quite useless. He said so himself. You are the fool, going on hoping and toiling. You could have lain down and gone to sleep together days ago, if you hadn't been so dogged. But you'll die just the same, or worse. You might just as well lie down now and give it up. You'll never get to the top anyway.'

'I'll get there, if I leave everything but my bones behind,' said Sam. 'And I'll carry Mr. Frodo up myself, if it breaks my back and heart. So stop arguing!'

At that moment Sam felt a tremor in the ground beneath him, and he heard or sensed a deep remote rumble as of thunder imprisoned under the earth. There was a brief red flame that flickered under the clouds and died away. The Mountain too slept uneasily.

The last stage of their journey to Orodruin came, and it was a torment greater than Sam had ever thought that he could bear. He was in pain, and so parched that he could no longer swallow even a mouthful of food. It remained dark, not only because of the smokes of the Mountain: there seemed to be a storm coming up, and away to the south-east there was a shimmer of lightnings under the black skies. Worst of all, the air was full of fumes; breathing was painful and difficult, and a dizziness came on them, so that they staggered and often fell. And yet their wills did not yield, and they struggled on.

The Mountain crept up ever nearer, until, if they lifted their heavy heads, it filled all their sight, looming vast before them: a huge mass of ash and slag and burned stone, out of which a sheer-sided cone was raised into the clouds. Before the daylong dusk ended and true night came again they had crawled and stumbled to its very feet.

With a gasp Frodo cast himself on the ground. Sam sat by him. To his surprise he felt tired but lighter, and his head seemed clear again. No more debates disturbed his mind. He knew all the arguments of despair and would not listen to them. His will was set, and only death would break it. He felt no longer either desire or need of sleep, but rather of watchfulness. He knew that all the hazards and perils were now drawing together to a point: the next day would be a day of doom, the day of final effort or disaster, the last gasp.

But when would it come? The night seemed endless and timeless, minute after minute falling dead and adding up to no passing hour, bringing no change. Sam began to wonder if a second darkness had begun and no day would ever reappear. At last he groped for Frodo's hand. It was cold and trembling. His master was shivering.

'I didn't ought to have left my blanket behind,' muttered Sam; and lying down he tried to comfort Frodo with his arms and body. Then sleep took him, and the dim light of the last day of their quest found them side by side. The wind had fallen the day before as it shifted from the West, and now it came from the North and began to rise; and slowly the light of the unseen Sun filtered down into the shadows where the hobbits lay.

'Now for it! Now for the last gasp!' said Sam as he struggled to his feet. He bent over Frodo, rousing him gently. Frodo groaned; but with a great effort of will he staggered up; and then he fell upon his knees again. He raised his eyes with difficulty to the dark slopes of Mount Doom towering above him, and then pitifully he began to crawl forward on his hands.

Sam looked at him and wept in his heart, but no tears came to his dry and stinging eyes. 'I said I'd carry him, if it broke my back,' he muttered, 'and I will!'

'Come, Mr. Frodo!' he cried. 'I can't carry it for you, but I can carry you and it as well. So up you get! Come on, Mr. Frodo dear! Sam will give you a ride. Just tell him where to go, and he'll go.'

As Frodo clung upon his back, arms loosely about his neck, legs clasped firmly under his arms, Sam staggered to his feet; and then to his amazement he felt the burden light. He had feared that he would have barely strength to lift his master alone, and beyond that he had expected to share in the dreadful dragging weight of the accursed Ring. But it was not so. Whether because Frodo was so worn by his long pains, wound of knife, and venomous sting, and sorrow, fear, and homeless wandering, or because some gift of final strength was given to him, Sam lifted Frodo with no more difficulty than if he were carrying a hobbit-child pig-a-back in some romp on the lawns or hayfields of the Shire. He took a deep breath and started off.

They had reached the Mountain's foot on its northern side, and a little to the westward; there its long grey slopes, though broken, were not sheer. Frodo did not speak, and so Sam struggled on as best he could, having no guidance but the will to climb as high as might be before his strength gave out and his will broke. On he toiled, up and up, turning this way and that to lessen the slope, often stumbling forward, and at the last crawling like a snail with a heavy burden on its back. When his will could drive him no further, and his limbs gave way, he stopped and laid his master gently down.

Frodo opened his eyes and drew a breath. It was easier to breathe up here above the reeks that coiled and drifted down below. 'Thank you, Sam,' he said in a cracked whisper. 'How far is there to go?'

'I don't know,' said Sam, 'because I don't know where we're going.'

He looked back, and then he looked up; and he was amazed to see how far his last effort had brought him. The Mountain standing ominous and alone had looked taller than it was. Sam saw now that it was less lofty than the high passes of the Ephel Dúath which he and Frodo had scaled. The confused and tumbled shoulders of its great base rose for maybe three thousand feet above the plain, and above them was reared half as high again its tall central cone, like a vast oast or chimney capped with a jagged crater. But already Sam was more than half way up the base, and the plain of Gorgoroth was dim below him, wrapped in fume and shadow. As he looked up he would have given a shout, if his parched throat had allowed him; for amid the rugged humps and shoulders above him he saw plainly a path or road. It climbed like a rising girdle from the west and wound snakelike about the Mountain, until before it went round out of view it reached the foot of the cone upon its eastern side.

Sam could not see the course immediately above him, where it was lowest, for a steep slope went up from where he stood; but he guessed that if he could only struggle on just a little way further up, they would strike this path. A gleam of hope returned to him. They might conquer the Mountain yet. 'Why, it might have been put there a-purpose!' he said to himself. 'If it wasn't there, I'd have to say I was beaten in the end.'

The path was not put there for the purposes of Sam. He did not know it, but he was looking at Sauron's Road from Barad-dûr to the Sammath Naur, the Chambers of Fire. Out from the Dark Tower's huge western gate it came over a deep abyss by a vast bridge of iron, and then passing into the plain it ran for a league between two smoking chasms, and so reached a long sloping causeway that led up on to the Mountain's eastern side. Thence, turning and encircling all its wide girth from south to north, it climbed at last, high in the upper cone, but still far from the reeking summit, to a dark entrance that gazed back east straight to the Window of the Eye in Sauron's shadow-mantled fortress. Often blocked or destroyed by the tumults of the Mountain's furnaces, always that road was repaired and cleared again by the labours of countless orcs.

Sam drew a deep breath. There was a path, but how he was to get up the slope to it he did not know. First he must ease his aching back. He lay flat beside Frodo for a while. Neither spoke. Slowly the light grew. Suddenly a sense of urgency which he did not understand came to Sam. It was almost as if he had been called: 'Now, now, or it will be too late!' He braced himself and got up. Frodo also seemed to have felt the call. He struggled to his knees.

'I'll crawl, Sam,' he gasped.

So foot by foot, like small grey insects, they crept up the slope. They came to the path and found that it was broad, paved with broken rubble and beaten ash. Frodo clambered on to it, and then moved as if by some compulsion he turned slowly to face the East. Far off the shadows of Sauron hung; but torn by some gust of wind out of the world, or else moved by some great disquiet within, the mantling clouds swirled, and for a moment drew aside; and then he saw, rising black, blacker and darker than the vast shades amid which it stood, the cruel pinnacles and iron crown of the topmost tower of Barad-dûr. One moment only it stared out, but as from some great window immeasurably high there stabbed northward a flame of red, the flicker of a piercing Eye; and then the shadows were furled again and the terrible vision was removed. The Eye was not turned to them: it was gazing north to where the Captains of the West stood at bay, and thither all its malice was now bent, as the Power moved to strike its deadly blow; but Frodo at that dreadful glimpse fell as one stricken mortally. His hand sought the chain about his neck.

Sam knelt by him. Faint, almost inaudibly, he heard Frodo whispering: 'Help me, Sam! Help me, Sam! Hold my hand! I can't stop it.' Sam took his master's hands and laid them together, palm to palm, and kissed them; and then he held them gently between his own. The thought came suddenly to him: 'He's spotted us! It's all up, or it soon will be. Now, Sam Gamgee, this is the end of ends.'

Again he lifted Frodo and drew his hands down to his own breast, letting his master's legs dangle. Then he bowed his head and struggled off along the climbing road. It was not as easy a way to take as it had looked at first. By fortune the fires that had poured forth in the great turmoils when Sam stood upon Cirith Ungol had flowed down mainly on the southern and western slopes, and the road on this side was not blocked. Yet in many places it had crumbled away or was crossed by gaping rents. After climbing eastward for some time it bent back upon itself at a sharp angle and went westward for a space. There at the bend it was cut deep through a crag of old weathered stone once long ago vomited from the Mountain's furnaces. Panting under his load Sam turned the bend; and even as he did so, out of the corner of his eye, he had a glimpse of something falling from the crag, like a small piece of black stone that had toppled off as he passed.

A sudden weight smote him and he crashed forward, tearing the backs of his hands that still clasped his master's. Then he knew what had happened, for above him as he lay he heard a hated voice.

'Wicked masster!' it hissed. 'Wicked masster cheats us; cheats Sméagol, *gollum*. He musstn't go that way. He musstn't hurt Preciouss. Give it to Sméagol, yess, give it to us! Give it to uss!'

With a violent heave Sam rose up. At once he drew his sword; but he could do nothing. Gollum and Frodo were locked together. Gollum was tearing at his master, trying to get at the chain and the Ring. This was probably the only thing that could have roused the dying embers of Frodo's heart and will: an attack, an attempt to wrest his treasure from him by force. He fought back with a sudden fury that amazed Sam, and Gollum also. Even so things might have gone far otherwise, if Gollum himself had remained unchanged; but whatever dreadful paths, lonely and hungry and waterless, he had trodden, driven by a devouring desire and a terrible fear, they had left grievous marks on him. He was a lean, starved, haggard thing, all bones and tight-drawn sallow skin. A wild light flamed in his eyes, but his malice was no longer matched by his old griping strength. Frodo flung him off and rose up quivering.

'Down, down!' he gasped, clutching his hand to his breast, so that beneath the cover of his leather shirt he clasped the Ring. 'Down, you creeping thing, and out of my path! Your time is at an end. You cannot betray me or slay me now.'

Then suddenly, as before under the eaves of the Emyn Muil, Sam saw these two rivals with other vision. A crouching shape, scarcely more than the shadow of a living thing, a creature now wholly ruined and defeated, yet filled with a hideous lust and rage; and before it stood stern, untouchable now by pity, a figure robed in white, but at its breast it held a wheel of fire. Out of the fire there spoke a commanding voice.

'Begone, and trouble me no more! If you touch me ever again, you shall be cast yourself into the Fire of Doom.'

The crouching shape backed away, terror in its blinking eyes, and yet at the same time insatiable desire.

Then the vision passed and Sam saw Frodo standing, hand on breast, his breath coming in great gasps, and Gollum at his feet, resting on his knees with his wide-splayed hands upon the ground.

'Look out!' cried Sam. 'He'll spring!' He stepped forward, brandishing his sword. 'Quick, Master!' he gasped. 'Go on! Go on! No time to lose. I'll deal with him. Go on!'

Frodo looked at him as if at one now far away. 'Yes, I must go on,' he said. 'Farewell, Sam! This is the end at last. On Mount Doom doom shall fall. Farewell!' He turned and went on, walking slowly but erect, up the climbing path.

'Now!' said Sam. 'At last I can deal with you!' He leaped forward with drawn blade ready for battle. But Gollum did not spring. He fell flat upon the ground and whimpered.

'Don't kill us,' he wept. 'Don't hurt us with nassty cruel steel! Let us live, yes, live just a little longer. Lost lost! We're lost. And when Precious goes we'll die, yes, die into the dust.' He clawed up the ashes of the path with his long fleshless fingers. 'Dusst!' he hissed.

Sam's hand wavered. His mind was hot with wrath and the memory of evil. It would be just to slay this treacherous, murderous creature, just and many times deserved; and also it seemed the only safe thing to do. But deep in his heart there was something that restrained him: he could not strike this thing lying in the dust, forlorn, ruinous, utterly wretched. He himself, though only for a little while, had borne the Ring, and now dimly he guessed the agony of Gollum's shrivelled mind and body, enslaved to that Ring, unable to find peace or relief ever in life again. But Sam had no words to express what he felt.

'Oh, curse you, you stinking thing!' he said. 'Go away! Be off! I don't trust you, not as far as I could kick you; but be off. Or I *shall* hurt you, yes, with nasty cruel steel.'

Gollum got up on all fours, and backed away for several paces, and then he turned, and as Sam aimed a kick at him he fled away down the path. Sam gave no more heed to him. He suddenly remembered his master. He looked up the path and could not see him. As fast as he could he trudged up the road. If he had looked back, he might have seen not far below Gollum turn again, and then with a wild light of madness glaring in his eyes come, swiftly but warily, creeping on behind, a slinking shadow among the stones.

The path climbed on. Soon it bent again and with a last eastward course passed in a cutting along the face of the cone and came to the dark door in the Mountain's side, the door of the Sammath Naur. Far away now rising towards the South the sun, piercing the smokes and haze, burned ominous, a dull bleared disc of red; but all Mordor lay about the Mountain like a dead land, silent, shadow-folded, waiting for some dreadful stroke.

Sam came to the gaping mouth and peered in. It was dark and hot, and a deep rumbling shook the air. 'Frodo! Master!' he called. There was no answer. For a moment he stood, his heart beating with wild fears, and then he plunged in. A shadow followed him.

At first he could see nothing. In his great need he drew out once more the phial of Galadriel, but it was pale and cold in his trembling hand and threw no light into that stifling dark. He was come to the heart of the realm of Sauron and the forges of his ancient might, greatest in Middle-earth; all other powers were here subdued. Fearfully he took a few uncertain steps in the dark, and then all at once there came a flash of red that leaped upward, and smote the high black roof. Then Sam saw that he was in a long cave or tunnel that bored into the Mountain's smoking cone. But only a short way ahead its floor and the walls on either side were cloven by a great fissure, out of which the red glare came, now leaping up, now dying down into darkness; and all the while far below there was a rumour and a trouble as of great engines throbbing and labouring.

The light sprang up again, and there on the brink of the chasm, at the very Crack of Doom, stood Frodo, black against the glare, tense, erect, but still as if he had been turned to stone.

'Master!' cried Sam.

Then Frodo stirred and spoke with a clear voice, indeed with a voice clearer and more powerful than Sam had ever heard him use, and it rose above the throb and turmoil of Mount Doom, ringing in the roof and walls.

'I have come,' he said. 'But I do not choose now to do what I came to do. I will not do this deed. The Ring is mine!' And suddenly, as he set it on his finger, he vanished from Sam's sight. Sam gasped, but he had no chance to cry out, for at that moment many things happened.

Something struck Sam violently in the back, his legs were knocked from under him and he was flung aside, striking his head against the stony floor, as a dark shape sprang over him. He lay still and for a moment all went black.

And far away, as Frodo put on the Ring and claimed it for his own, even in Sammath Naur the very heart of his realm, the Power in Barad-dûr was shaken, and the Tower trembled from its foundations to its proud and bitter crown. The Dark Lord was suddenly aware of him, and his Eye piercing all shadows looked across the plain to the door that he had made; and the magnitude of his own folly was revealed to him in a blinding flash, and all the devices of his enemies were at last laid bare. Then his wrath blazed in consuming flame, but his fear rose like a vast black smoke to choke him. For he knew his deadly peril and the thread upon which his doom now hung.

From all his policies and webs of fear and treachery, from all his stratagems and wars his mind shook free; and throughout his realm a tremor ran, his slaves quailed, and his armies halted, and his captains suddenly steerless, bereft of will, wavered and despaired. For they were forgotten. The whole mind and purpose of the Power that wielded them was now bent with overwhelming force upon the Mountain. At his summons, wheeling with a rending cry, in a last desperate race there flew, faster than the winds, the Nazgûl, the Ringwraiths, and with a storm of wings they hurtled southwards to Mount Doom.

Sam got up. He was dazed, and blood streaming from his head dripped in his eyes. He groped forward, and then he saw a strange and terrible thing. Gollum on the edge of the abyss was fighting like a mad thing with an unseen foe. To and fro he swayed, now so near the brink that almost he tumbled in, now dragging back, falling to the ground, rising, and falling again. And all the while he hissed but spoke no words.

The fires below awoke in anger, the red light blazed, and all the cavern was filled with a great glare and heat. Suddenly Sam saw Gollum's long hands draw upwards to his mouth; his white fangs gleamed, and then snapped as they bit. Frodo gave a cry, and there he was, fallen upon his knees at the chasm's edge. But Gollum, dancing like a mad thing, held aloft the ring, a finger still thrust within its circle. It shone now as if verily it was wrought of living fire.

'Precious, precious, precious!' Gollum cried. 'My Precious! O my Precious!' And with that, even as his eyes were lifted up to gloat on his prize, he stepped too far, toppled, wavered for a moment on the brink, and then with a shriek he fell. Out of the depths came his last wail *Precious*, and he was gone.

There was a roar and a great confusion of noise. Fires leaped up and licked the roof. The throbbing grew to a great tumult, and the Mountain shook. Sam ran to Frodo and picked him up and carried him out to the door. And there upon the dark threshold of the Sammath Naur, high above the plains of Mordor, such wonder and terror came on him that he stood still forgetting all else, and gazed as one turned to stone.

A brief vision he had of swirling cloud, and in the midst of it towers and battlements, tall as hills, founded upon a mighty mountain-throne above immeasurable pits; great courts and dungeons, eyeless prisons sheer as cliffs, and gaping gates of steel and adamant: and then all passed. Towers fell and mountains slid; walls crumbled and melted, crashing down; vast spires of smoke and spouting steams went billowing up, up, until they toppled like an overwhelming wave, and its wild crest curled and came foaming down upon the land. And then at last over the miles between there came a rumble, rising to a deafening crash and roar; the earth shook, the plain heaved and cracked, and Orodruin reeled. Fire belched from its riven summit. The skies burst into thunder seared with lightning. Down like lashing whips fell a torrent of black rain. And into the heart of the storm, with a cry that pierced all other sounds, tearing the clouds asunder, the Nazgûl came, shooting like flaming bolts, as caught in the fiery ruin of hill and sky they crackled, withered, and went out.

'Well, this is the end, Sam Gamgee,' said a voice by his side. And there was Frodo, pale and worn, and yet himself again; and in his eyes there was peace now, neither strain of will, nor madness, nor any fear. His burden was taken away. There was the dear master of the sweet days in the Shire.

'Master!' cried Sam, and fell upon his knees. In all that ruin of the world for the moment he felt only joy, great joy. The burden was gone. His master had been saved; he was himself again, he was free. And then Sam caught sight of the maimed and bleeding hand.

'Your poor hand!' he said. 'And I have nothing to bind it with, or comfort it. I would have spared him a whole hand of mine rather. But he's gone now beyond recall, gone for ever.'

'Yes,' said Frodo. 'But do you remember Gandalf's words: *Even Gollum may have something yet to do*? But for him, Sam, I could not have destroyed the Ring. The Quest would have been in vain, even at the bitter end. So let us forgive him! For the Quest is achieved, and now all is over. I am glad you are here with me. Here at the end of all things, Sam.'

CHAPTER IV

THE FIELD OF CORMALLEN

All about the hills the hosts of Mordor raged. The Captains of the West were foundering in a gathering sea. The sun gleamed red, and under the wings of the Nazgûl the shadows of death fell dark upon the earth. Aragorn stood beneath his banner, silent and stern, as one lost in thought of things long past or far away; but his eyes gleamed like stars that shine the brighter as the night deepens. Upon the hill-top stood Gandalf, and he was white and cold and no shadow fell on him. The onslaught of Mordor broke like a wave on the beleaguered hills, voices roaring like a tide amid the wreck and crash of arms.

As if to his eyes some sudden vision had been given, Gandalf stirred; and he turned, looking back north where the skies were pale and clear. Then he lifted up his hands and cried in a loud voice ringing above the din: *The Eagles are coming!* And many voices answered crying: *The Eagles are coming! The Eagles are coming!* The hosts of Mordor looked up and wondered what this sign might mean.

There came Gwaihir the Windlord, and Landroval his brother, greatest of all the Eagles of the North, mightiest of the descendants of old Thorondor, who built his eyries in the inaccessible peaks of the Encircling Mountains when Middle-earth was young. Behind them in long swift lines came all their vassals from the northern mountains, speeding on a gathering wind. Straight down upon the Nazgûl they bore, stooping suddenly out of the high airs, and the rush of their wide wings as they passed over was like a gale.

But the Nazgûl turned and fled, and vanished into Mordor's shadows, hearing a sudden terrible call out of the Dark Tower; and even at that moment all the hosts of Mordor trembled, doubt clutched their hearts, their laughter failed, their hands shook and their limbs were loosed. The Power that drove them on and filled them with hate and fury was wavering, its will was removed from them; and now looking in the eyes of their enemies they saw a deadly light and were afraid.

Then all the Captains of the West cried aloud, for their hearts were filled with a new hope in the midst of darkness. Out from the beleaguered hills knights of Gondor, Riders of Rohan, Dúnedain of the North, close-serried companies, drove against their wavering foes, piercing the press with the thrust of bitter spears. But Gandalf lifted up his arms and called once more in a clear voice:

'Stand, Men of the West! Stand and wait! This is the hour of doom.'

And even as he spoke the earth rocked beneath their feet. Then rising swiftly up, far above the Towers of the Black Gate, high above the mountains, a vast soaring darkness sprang into the sky, flickering with fire. The earth groaned and quaked. The Towers of the Teeth swayed, tottered, and fell down; the mighty rampart crumbled; the Black Gate was hurled in ruin; and from far away, now dim, now growing, now mounting to the clouds, there came a drumming rumble, a roar, a long echoing roll of ruinous noise.

'The realm of Sauron is ended!' said Gandalf. 'The Ring-bearer has fulfilled his Quest.' And as the Captains gazed south to the Land of Mordor, it seemed to them that, black against the pall of cloud, there rose a huge shape of shadow, impenetrable, lightning-crowned, filling all the sky. Enormous it reared above the world, and stretched out towards them a vast threatening hand, terrible but impotent: for even as it leaned over them, a great wind took it, and it was all blown away, and passed; and then a hush fell.

The Captains bowed their heads; and when they looked up again, behold! their enemies were flying and the power of Mordor was scattering like dust in the wind. As when death smites the swollen brooding thing that inhabits their crawling hill and holds them all in sway, ants will wander witless and purposeless and then feebly die, so the creatures of Sauron, orc or troll or beast spell-enslaved, ran hither and thither mindless; and some slew themselves, or cast themselves in pits, or fled wailing back to hide in holes and dark lightless places far from hope. But the Men of Rhûn and of Harad, Easterling and Southron, saw the ruin of their war and the great majesty and glory of the Captains of the West. And those that were deepest and longest in evil servitude, hating the West, and yet were men proud and bold, in their turn now gathered themselves for a last stand of desperate battle. But the most part fled eastward as they could; and some cast their weapons down and sued for mercy.

Then Gandalf, leaving all such matters of battle and command to Aragorn and the other lords, stood upon the hill-top and called; and down to him came the great eagle, Gwaihir the Windlord, and stood before him.

'Twice you have borne me, Gwaihir my friend,' said Gandalf. 'Thrice shall pay for all, if you are willing. You will not find me a burden much greater than when you bore me from Zirakzigil, where my old life burned away.'

'I would bear you,' answered Gwaihir, 'whither you will, even were you made of stone.'

'Then come, and let your brother go with us, and some other of your folk who is most swift! For we have need of speed greater than any wind, outmatching the wings of the Nazgûl.'

'The North Wind blows, but we shall outfly it,' said Gwaihir. And he lifted up Gandalf and sped away south, and with him went Landroval, and Meneldor young and swift. And they passed over Udûn and Gorgoroth and saw all the land in ruin and tumult beneath them, and before them Mount Doom blazing, pouring out its fire.

'I am glad that you are here with me,' said Frodo. 'Here at the end of all things, Sam.'

'Yes, I am with you, Master,' said Sam, laying Frodo's wounded hand gently to his breast. 'And you're with me. And the journey's finished. But after coming all that way I don't want to give up yet. It's not like me, somehow, if you understand.'

'Maybe not, Sam,' said Frodo; 'but it's like things are in the world. Hopes fail. An end comes. We have only a little time to wait now. We are lost in ruin and downfall, and there is no escape.'

'Well, Master, we could at least go further from this dangerous place here, from this Crack of Doom, if that's its name. Now couldn't we? Come, Mr. Frodo, let's go down the path at any rate!'

'Very well, Sam. If you wish to go, I'll come,' said Frodo; and they rose and went slowly down the winding road; and even as they passed towards the Mountain's quaking feet, a great smoke and steam belched from the Sammath Naur, and the side of the cone was riven open, and a huge fiery vomit rolled in slow thunderous cascade down the eastern mountain-side.

Frodo and Sam could go no further. Their last strength of mind and body was swiftly ebbing. They had reached a low ashen hill piled at the Mountain's foot; but from it there was no more escape. It was an island now, not long to endure, amid the torment of Orodruin. All about it the earth gaped, and from deep rifts and pits smoke and fumes leaped up. Behind them the Mountain was convulsed. Great rents opened in its side. Slow rivers of fire came down the long slopes towards them. Soon they would be engulfed. A rain of hot ash was falling.

They stood now; and Sam still holding his master's hand caressed it. He sighed. 'What a tale we have been in, Mr. Frodo, haven't we?' he said. 'I wish I could hear it told! Do you think they'll say: *Now comes the story of Nine-fingered Frodo and the Ring of Doom*? And then everyone will hush, like we did, when in Rivendell they told us the tale of Beren One-hand and the Great Jewel. I wish I could hear it! And I wonder how it will go on after our part.'

But even while he spoke so, to keep fear away until the very last, his eyes still strayed north, north into the eye of the wind, to where the sky far off was clear, as the cold blast, rising to a gale, drove back the darkness and the ruin of the clouds.

And so it was that Gwaihir saw them with his keen far-seeing eyes, as down the wild wind he came, and daring the great peril of the skies he circled in the air: two small dark figures, forlorn, hand in hand upon a little hill, while the world shook under them, and gasped, and rivers of fire drew near. And even as he espied them and came swooping down, he saw them fall, worn out, or choked with fumes and heat, or stricken down by despair at last, hiding their eyes from death.

Side by side they lay; and down swept Gwaihir, and down came Landroval and Meneldor the swift; and in a dream, not knowing what fate had befallen them, the wanderers were lifted up and borne far away out of the darkness and the fire.

When Sam awoke, he found that he was lying on some soft bed, but over him gently swayed wide beechen boughs, and through their young leaves sunlight glimmered, green and gold. All the air was full of a sweet mingled scent.

He remembered that smell: the fragrance of Ithilien. 'Bless me!' he mused. 'How long have I been asleep?' For the scent had borne him back to the day when he had lit his little fire under the sunny bank; and for the moment all else between was out of waking memory. He stretched and drew a deep breath. 'Why, what a dream I've had!' he muttered. 'I am glad to wake!' He sat up and then he saw that Frodo was lying beside him, and slept peacefully, one hand behind his head, and the other resting upon the coverlet. It was the right hand, and the third finger was missing.

Full memory flooded back, and Sam cried aloud: 'It wasn't a dream! Then where are we?'

And a voice spoke softly behind him: 'In the land of Ithilien, and in the keeping of the King; and he awaits you.' With that Gandalf stood before him, robed in white, his beard now gleaming like pure snow in the twinkling of the leafy sunlight. 'Well, Master Samwise, how do you feel?' he said.

But Sam lay back, and stared with open mouth, and for a moment, between bewilderment and great joy, he could not answer. At last he gasped: 'Gandalf! I thought you were dead! But then I thought I was dead myself. Is everything sad going to come untrue? What's happened to the world?'

'A great Shadow has departed,' said Gandalf, and then he laughed, and the sound was like music, or like water in a parched land; and as he listened the thought came to Sam that he had not heard laughter, the pure sound of merriment, for days upon days without count. It fell upon his ears like the echo of all the joys he had ever known. But he himself burst into tears. Then, as a sweet rain will pass down a wind of spring and the sun will shine out the clearer, his tears ceased, and his laughter welled up, and laughing he sprang from his bed.

'How do I feel?' he cried. 'Well, I don't know how to say it. I feel, I feel' – he waved his arms in the air – 'I feel like spring after winter, and sun on the leaves; and like trumpets and harps and all the songs I have ever heard!' He stopped and he turned towards his master. 'But how's Mr. Frodo?' he said. 'Isn't it a shame about his poor hand? But I hope he's all right otherwise. He's had a cruel time.'

'Yes, I am all right otherwise,' said Frodo, sitting up and laughing in his turn. 'I fell asleep again waiting for you, Sam, you sleepyhead. I was awake early this morning, and now it must be nearly noon.'

'Noon?' said Sam, trying to calculate. 'Noon of what day?'

'The fourteenth of the New Year,' said Gandalf; 'or if you like, the eighth day of April in the Shire reckoning.* But in Gondor the New Year will always now begin upon the twenty-fifth of March when Sauron fell, and when you were brought out of the fire to the King. He has tended you, and now he awaits you. You shall eat and drink with him. When you are ready I will lead you to him.'

'The King?' said Sam. 'What king, and who is he?'

'The King of Gondor and Lord of the Western Lands,' said Gandalf; 'and he has taken back all his ancient realm. He will ride soon to his crowning, but he waits for you.'

'What shall we wear?' said Sam; for all he could see was the old and tattered clothes that they had journeyed in, lying folded on the ground beside their beds.

'The clothes that you wore on your way to Mordor,' said Gandalf. 'Even the orc-rags that you bore in the black land, Frodo, shall be preserved. No silks and linens, nor any armour or heraldry could be more honourable. But later I will find some other clothes, perhaps.'

Then he held out his hands to them, and they saw that one shone with light. 'What have you got there?' Frodo cried. 'Can it be – ?'

'Yes, I have brought your two treasures. They were found on Sam when you were rescued; the Lady Galadriel's gifts: your glass, Frodo; and your box, Sam. You will be glad to have these safe again.'

When they were washed and clad, and had eaten a light meal, the Hobbits followed Gandalf. They stepped out of the beech-grove in which they had

* There were thirty days in March (or Rethe) in the Shire calendar.

lain, and passed on to a long green lawn, glowing in sunshine, bordered by stately dark-leaved trees laden with scarlet blossom. Behind them they could hear the sound of falling water, and a stream ran down before them between flowering banks, until it came to a greenwood at the lawn's foot and passed then on under an archway of trees, through which they saw the shimmer of water far away.

As they came to the opening in the wood, they were surprised to see knights in bright mail and tall guards in silver and black standing there, who greeted them with honour and bowed before them. And then one blew a long trumpet, and they went on through the aisle of trees beside the singing stream. So they came to a wide green land, and beyond it was a broad river in a silver haze, out of which rose a long wooded isle, and many ships lay by its shores. But on the field where they now stood a great host was drawn up, in ranks and companies glittering in the sun. And as the Hobbits approached swords were unsheathed, and spears were shaken, and horns and trumpets sang, and men cried with many voices and in many tongues:

'Long live the Halflings! Praise them with great praise!
Cuio i Pheriain anann! Aglar'ni Pheriannath!
Praise them with great praise, Frodo and Samwise!
Daur a Berhael, Conin en Annûn! Eglerio!
Praise them!
Eglerio!
A laita te, laita te! Andave laituvalmet!
Praise them!
Cormacolindor, a laita tárienna!
Praise them! The Ring-bearers, praise them with great praise!'

And so the red blood blushing in their faces and their eyes shining with wonder, Frodo and Sam went forward and saw that amidst the clamorous host were set three high-seats built of green turves. Behind the seat upon the right floated, white on green, a great horse running free; upon the left was a banner, silver upon blue, a ship swan-prowed faring on the sea; but behind the highest throne in the midst of all a great standard was spread in the breeze, and there a white tree flowered upon a sable field beneath a shining crown and seven glittering stars. On the throne sat a mail-clad man, a great sword was laid across his knees, but he wore no helm. As they drew near he rose. And then they knew him, changed as he was, so high and glad of face, kingly, lord of Men, dark-haired with eyes of grey.

Frodo ran to meet him, and Sam followed close behind. 'Well, if this isn't the crown of all!' he said. 'Strider, or I'm still asleep!'

'Yes, Sam, Strider,' said Aragorn. 'It is a long way, is it not, from Bree, where you did not like the look of me? A long way for us all, but yours has been the darkest road.'

And then to Sam's surprise and utter confusion he bowed his knee before them; and taking them by the hand, Frodo upon his right and Sam upon his left, he led them to the throne, and setting them upon it, he turned to the men and captains who stood by and spoke, so that his voice rang over all the host, crying:

'Praise them with great praise!'

And when the glad shout had swelled up and died away again, to Sam's final and complete satisfaction and pure joy, a minstrel of Gondor stood forth, and knelt, and begged leave to sing. And behold! he said:

'Lo! lords and knights and men of valour unashamed, kings and princes, and fair people of Gondor, and Riders of Rohan, and ye sons of Elrond, and Dúnedain of the North, and Elf and Dwarf, and greathearts of the Shire, and all free folk of the West, now listen to my lay. For I will sing to you of Frodo of the Nine Fingers and the Ring of Doom.'

And when Sam heard that he laughed aloud for sheer delight, and he stood up and cried: 'O great glory and splendour! And all my wishes have come true!' And then he wept.

And all the host laughed and wept, and in the midst of their merriment and tears the clear voice of the minstrel rose like silver and gold, and all men were hushed. And he sang to them, now in the Elven-tongue, now in the speech of the West, until their hearts, wounded with sweet words, overflowed, and their joy was like swords, and they passed in thought out to regions where pain and delight flow together and tears are the very wine of blessedness.

And at the last, as the Sun fell from the noon and the shadows of the trees lengthened, he ended. 'Praise them with great praise!' he said and knelt. And then Aragorn stood up, and all the host arose, and they passed to pavilions made ready, to eat and drink and make merry while the day lasted.

Frodo and Sam were led apart and brought to a tent, and there their old raiment was taken off, but folded and set aside with honour; and clean linen was given to them. Then Gandalf came and in his arms, to the wonder of Frodo, he bore the sword and the elven-cloak and the mithril-coat that had been taken from him in Mordor. For Sam he brought a coat of gilded mail, and his elven-cloak all healed of the soils and hurts that it had suffered; and then he laid before them two swords.

'I do not wish for any sword,' said Frodo.

'Tonight at least you should wear one,' said Gandalf.

Then Frodo took the small sword that had belonged to Sam, and had been laid at his side in Cirith Ungol. 'Sting I gave to you Sam,' he said.

'No, master! Mr. Bilbo gave it to you, and it goes with his silver coat; he would not wish anyone else to wear it now.'

Frodo gave way; and Gandalf, as if he were their esquire, knelt and girt the sword-belts about them, and then rising he set circlets of silver upon their heads. And when they were arrayed they went to the great feast; and they sat at the King's table with Gandalf, and King Éomer of Rohan, and the Prince Imrahil and all the chief captains; and there also were Gimli and Legolas.

But when, after the Standing Silence, wine was brought there came in two esquires to serve the kings; or so they seemed to be: one was clad in the silver and sable of the Guards of Minas Tirith, and the other in white and green. But Sam wondered what such young boys were doing in an army of mighty men. Then suddenly as they drew near and he could see them plainly, he exclaimed:

'Why, look Mr. Frodo! Look here! Well, if it isn't Pippin. Mr. Peregrin Took I should say, and Mr. Merry! How they have grown! Bless me! But I can see there's more tales to tell than ours.'

'There are indeed,' said Pippin turning towards him. 'And we'll begin telling them, as soon as this feast is ended. In the meantime you can try Gandalf. He's not so close as he used to be, though he laughs now more than he talks. For the present Merry and I are busy. We are knights of the City and of the Mark, as I hope you observe.'

At last the glad day ended; and when the Sun was gone and the round Moon rode slowly above the mists of Anduin and flickered through the fluttering leaves, Frodo and Sam sat under the whispering trees amid the fragrance of fair Ithilien; and they talked deep into the night with Merry and Pippin and Gandalf, and after a while Legolas and Gimli joined them. There Frodo and Sam learned much of all that had happened to the Company after their fellowship was broken on the evil day at Parth Galen by Rauros Falls; and still there was always more to ask and more to tell.

Orcs, and talking trees, and leagues of grass, and galloping riders, and glittering caves, and white towers and golden halls, and battles, and tall ships sailing, all these passed before Sam's mind until he felt bewildered. But amidst all these wonders he returned always to his astonishment at the size of Merry and Pippin; and he made them stand back to back with Frodo and himself. He scratched his head. 'Can't understand it at your age!' he said. 'But there it is: you're three inches taller than you ought to be, or I'm a dwarf.'

'That you certainly are not,' said Gimli. 'But what did I say? Mortals cannot go drinking ent-draughts and expect no more to come of them than of a pot of beer.'

'Ent-draughts?' said Sam. 'There you go about Ents again; but what they are beats me. Why, it will take weeks before we get all these things sized up!'

'Weeks indeed,' said Pippin. 'And then Frodo will have to be locked up in a tower in Minas Tirith and write it all down. Otherwise he will forget half of it, and poor old Bilbo will be dreadfully disappointed.'

At length Gandalf rose. 'The hands of the King are hands of healing, dear friends,' he said. 'But you went to the very brink of death ere he recalled you, putting forth all his power, and sent you into the sweet forgetfulness of sleep. And though you have indeed slept long and blessedly, still it is now time to sleep again.'

'And not only Sam and Frodo here,' said Gimli, 'but you too, Pippin. I love you, if only because of the pains you have cost me, which I shall never forget. Nor shall I forget finding you on the hill of the last battle. But for Gimli the Dwarf you would have been lost then. But at least I know now the look of a hobbit's foot, though it be all that can be seen under a heap of bodies. And when I heaved that great carcase off you, I made sure you were dead. I could have torn out my beard. And it is only a day yet since you were first up and abroad again. To bed now you go. And so shall I.'

'And I,' said Legolas, 'shall walk in the woods of this fair land, which is rest enough. In days to come, if my Elven-lord allows, some of our folk shall remove hither; and when we come it shall be blessed, for a while. For a while: a month, a life, a hundred years of Men. But Anduin is near, and Anduin leads down to the Sea. To the Sea!

To the Sea, to the Sea! The white gulls are crying,
The wind is blowing, and the white foam is flying.
West, west away, the round sun is falling.
Grey ship, grey ship, do you hear them calling,
The voices of my people that have gone before me?
I will leave, I will leave the woods that bore me;
For our days are ending and our years failing.
I will pass the wide waters lonely sailing.
Long are the waves on the Last Shore falling,
Sweet are the voices in the Lost Isle calling,
In Eressëa, in Elvenhome that no man can discover,
Where the leaves fall not: land of my people for ever!'

And so singing Legolas went away down the hill.

Then the others also departed, and Frodo and Sam went to their beds and slept. And in the morning they rose again in hope and peace; and they spent many days in Ithilien. For the Field of Cormallen, where the host was now encamped, was near to Henneth Annûn, and the stream that flowed from its falls could be heard in the night as it rushed down through its rocky gate, and passed through the flowery meads into the tides of Anduin by the Isle of Cair Andros. The hobbits wandered here and there visiting again the places that they had passed before; and Sam hoped always in some shadow of the woods or secret glade to catch, maybe, a glimpse of the great Oliphaunt. And when he learned that at the siege of Gondor there had been a great number of these beasts but that they were all destroyed, he thought it a sad loss.

'Well, one can't be everywhere at once, I suppose,' he said. 'But I missed a lot, seemingly.'

In the meanwhile the host made ready for the return to Minas Tirith. The weary rested and the hurt were healed. For some had laboured and fought much with the remnants of the Easterlings and Southrons, until all were subdued. And, latest of all, those returned who had passed into Mordor and destroyed the fortresses in the north of the land.

But at the last when the month of May was drawing near the Captains of the West set out again; and they went aboard ship with all their men, and they sailed from Cair Andros down Anduin to Osgiliath; and there they remained for one day; and the day after they came to the green fields of the Pelennor and saw again the white towers under tall Mindolluin, the City of the Men of Gondor, last memory of Westernesse, that had passed through the darkness and fire to a new day.

And there in the midst of the fields they set up their pavilions and awaited the morning; for it was the Eve of May, and the King would enter his gates with the rising of the Sun.

CHAPTER V

THE STEWARD AND THE KING

Over the city of Gondor doubt and great dread had hung. Fair weather and clear sun had seemed but a mockery to men whose days held little hope, and who looked each morning for news of doom. Their lord was dead and burned, dead lay the King of Rohan in their citadel, and the new king that had come to them in the night was gone again to a war with powers too dark and terrible for any might or valour to conquer. And no news came. After the host left Morgul Vale and took the northward road beneath the shadow of the mountains no messenger had returned nor any rumour of what was passing in the brooding East.

When the Captains were but two days gone, the Lady Éowyn bade the women who tended her to bring her raiment, and she would not be gainsaid, but rose; and when they had clothed her and set her arm in a sling of linen, she went to the Warden of the Houses of Healing.

'Sir,' she said, 'I am in great unrest, and I cannot lie longer in sloth.'

'Lady,' he answered, 'you are not yet healed, and I was commanded to tend you with especial care. You should not have risen from your bed for seven days yet, or so I was bidden. I beg you to go back.'

'I am healed,' she said, 'healed at least in body, save my left arm only, and that is at ease. But I shall sicken anew, if there is naught that I can do. Are there no tidings of war? The women can tell me nothing.'

'There are no tidings,' said the Warden, 'save that the Lords have ridden to Morgul Vale; and men say that the new captain out of the North is their chief. A great lord is that, and a healer; and it is a thing passing strange to me that the healing hand should also wield the sword. It is not thus in Gondor now, though once it was so, if old tales be true. But for long years we healers have only sought to patch the rents made by the men of swords. Though we should still have enough to do without them: the world is full enough of hurts and mischances without wars to multiply them.'

'It needs but one foe to breed a war, not two, Master Warden,' answered Éowyn. 'And those who have not swords can still die upon them. Would you have the folk of Gondor gather you herbs only, when the Dark Lord gathers armies? And it is not always good to be healed in body. Nor is it always evil to die in battle, even in bitter pain. Were I permitted, in this dark hour I would choose the latter.'

The Warden looked at her. Tall she stood there, her eyes bright in her white face, her hand clenched as she turned and gazed out of his window that opened to the East. He sighed and shook his head. After a pause she turned to him again.

'Is there no deed to do?' she said. 'Who commands in this City?'

'I do not rightly know,' he answered. 'Such things are not my care. There is a marshal over the Riders of Rohan; and the Lord Húrin, I am told, commands the men of Gondor. But the Lord Faramir is by right the Steward of the City.'

'Where can I find him?'

'In this house, lady. He was sorely hurt, but is now set again on the way to health. But I do not know——'

'Will you not bring me to him? Then you will know.'

The Lord Faramir was walking alone in the garden of the Houses of Healing, and the sunlight warmed him, and he felt life run new in his veins; but his heart was heavy, and he looked out over the walls eastward. And coming, the Warden spoke his name, and he turned and saw the Lady Éowyn of Rohan; and he was moved with pity, for he saw that she was hurt, and his clear sight perceived her sorrow and unrest.

'My lord,' said the Warden, 'here is the Lady Éowyn of Rohan. She rode with the king and was sorely hurt, and dwells now in my keeping. But she is not content, and she wishes to speak to the Steward of the City.'

'Do not misunderstand him, lord,' said Éowyn. 'It is not lack of care that grieves me. No houses could be fairer, for those who desire to be healed. But I cannot lie in sloth, idle, caged. I looked for death in battle. But I have not died, and battle still goes on.'

At a sign from Faramir, the Warden bowed and departed. 'What would you have me do, lady?' said Faramir. 'I also am a prisoner of the healers.' He looked at her, and being a man whom pity deeply stirred, it seemed to him that her loveliness amid her grief would pierce his heart. And she looked at him and saw the grave tenderness in his eyes, and yet knew, for she was bred among men of war, that here was one whom no Rider of the Mark would outmatch in battle.

'What do you wish?' he said again. 'If it lies in my power, I will do it.'

'I would have you command this Warden, and bid him let me go,' she said; but though her words were still proud, her heart faltered, and for the first time she doubted herself. She guessed that this tall man, both stern and gentle, might think her merely wayward, like a child that has not the firmness of mind to go on with a dull task to the end.

'I myself am in the Warden's keeping,' answered Faramir. 'Nor have I yet taken up my authority in the City. But had I done so, I should still listen to his counsel, and should not cross his will in matters of his craft, unless in some great need.'

'But I do not desire healing,' she said. 'I wish to ride to war like my brother Éomer, or better like Théoden the king, for he died and has both honour and peace.'

'It is too late, lady, to follow the Captains, even if you had the strength,' said Faramir. 'But death in battle may come to us all yet, willing or unwilling. You will be better prepared to face it in your own manner, if while there is still time you do as the Healer commanded. You and I, we must endure with patience the hours of waiting.'

She did not answer, but as he looked at her it seemed to him that something in her softened, as though a bitter frost were yielding at the first faint presage of Spring. A tear sprang in her eye and fell down her cheek, like a glistening rain-drop. Her proud head drooped a little. Then quietly, more as if speaking to herself than to him: 'But the healers would have me lie abed seven days yet,' she said. 'And my window does not look eastward.' Her voice was now that of a maiden young and sad.

Faramir smiled, though his heart was filled with pity. 'Your window does not look eastward?' he said. 'That can be amended. In this I will command the Warden. If you will stay in this house in our care, lady, and take your rest, then you shall walk in this garden in the sun, as you will; and you shall look east, whither all our hopes have gone. And here you will find me, walking and waiting, and also looking east. It would ease my care, if you would speak to me, or walk at whiles with me.'

Then she raised her head and looked him in the eyes again; and a colour came in her pale face. 'How should I ease your care, my lord?' she said. 'And I do not desire the speech of living men.'

'Would you have my plain answer?' he said.

'I would.'

'Then, Éowyn of Rohan, I say to you that you are beautiful. In the valleys of our hills there are flowers fair and bright, and maidens fairer still; but neither flower nor lady have I seen till now in Gondor so lovely, and so sorrowful. It may be that only a few days are left ere darkness falls upon our world, and when it comes I hope to face it steadily; but it would ease my heart, if while the Sun yet shines, I could see you still. For you and I have both passed under the wings of the Shadow, and the same hand drew us back.'

'Alas, not me, lord!' she said. 'Shadow lies on me still. Look not to me for healing! I am a shieldmaiden and my hand is ungentle. But I thank you for this at least, that I need not keep to my chamber. I will walk abroad by the grace of the Steward of the City.' And she did him a courtesy and walked back to the house. But Faramir for a long while walked alone in the garden, and his glance now strayed rather to the house than to the eastward walls.

When he returned to his chamber he called for the Warden, and heard all that he could tell of the Lady of Rohan.

'But I doubt not, lord,' said the Warden, 'that you would learn more from the Halfling that is with us; for he was in the riding of the king, and with the Lady at the end, they say.'

And so Merry was sent to Faramir, and while that day lasted they talked long together, and Faramir learned much, more even than Merry put into words; and he thought that he understood now something of the grief and unrest of Éowyn of Rohan. And in the fair evening Faramir and Merry walked in the garden, but she did not come.

But in the morning, as Faramir came from the Houses, he saw her, as she stood upon the walls; and she was clad all in white, and gleamed in the sun. And he called to her, and she came down, and they walked on the grass or sat under a green tree together, now in silence, now in speech. And each day after they did likewise. And the Warden looking from his window was glad in heart, for he was a healer, and his care was lightened; and certain it was that, heavy as was the dread and foreboding of those days upon the hearts of men, still these two of his charges prospered and grew daily in strength.

And so the fifth day came since the Lady Éowyn went first to Faramir; and they stood now together once more upon the walls of the City and looked out. No tidings had yet come, and all hearts were darkened. The weather, too, was bright no longer. It was cold. A wind that had sprung up in the night was blowing now keenly from the North, and it was rising; but the lands about looked grey and drear.

They were clad in warm raiment and heavy cloaks, and over all the Lady Éowyn wore a great blue mantle of the colour of deep summer-night, and it was set with silver stars about hem and throat. Faramir had sent for this robe and had wrapped it about her; and he thought that she looked fair and queenly indeed as she stood there at his side. The mantle was wrought for his mother, Finduilas of Amroth, who died untimely, and was to him but a memory of loveliness in far days and of his first grief; and her robe seemed to him raiment fitting for the beauty and sadness of Éowyn.

But she now shivered beneath the starry mantle, and she looked northward, above the grey hither lands, into the eye of the cold wind where far away the sky was hard and clear.

'What do you look for, Éowyn?' said Faramir.

'Does not the Black Gate lie yonder?' said she. 'And must he not now be come thither? It is seven days since he rode away.'

'Seven days,' said Faramir. 'But think not ill of me, if I say to you: they have brought me both a joy and a pain that I never thought to know. Joy to see you; but pain, because now the fear and doubt of this evil time are grown dark indeed. Éowyn, I would not have this world end now, or lose so soon what I have found.'

'Lose what you have found, lord?' she answered; but she looked at him gravely and her eyes were kind. 'I know not what in these days you have found that you could lose. But come, my friend, let us not speak of it! Let us not speak at all! I stand upon some dreadful brink, and it is utterly dark in the abyss before my feet, but whether there is any light behind me I cannot tell. For I cannot turn yet. I wait for some stroke of doom.'

'Yes, we wait for the stroke of doom,' said Faramir. And they said no more; and it seemed to them as they stood upon the wall that the wind died, and the light failed, and the Sun was bleared, and all sounds in the City or in the lands about were hushed: neither wind, nor voice, nor bird-call, nor rustle of leaf, nor their own breath could be heard; the very beating of their hearts was stilled. Time halted.

And as they stood so, their hands met and clasped, though they did not know it. And still they waited for they knew not what. Then presently it seemed to them that above the ridges of the distant mountains another vast mountain of darkness rose, towering up like a wave that should engulf the world, and about it lightnings flickered; and then a tremor ran through the earth, and they felt the walls of the City quiver. A sound like a sigh went up from all the lands about them; and their hearts beat suddenly again.

'It reminds me of Númenor,' said Faramir, and wondered to hear himself speak.

'Of Númenor?' said Éowyn.

'Yes,' said Faramir, 'of the land of Westernesse that foundered, and of the great dark wave climbing over the green lands and above the hills, and coming on, darkness unescapable. I often dream of it.'

'Then you think that the Darkness is coming?' said Éowyn. 'Darkness Unescapable?' And suddenly she drew close to him.

'No,' said Faramir, looking into her face. 'It was but a picture in the mind. I do not know what is happening. The reason of my waking mind tells me that great evil has befallen and we stand at the end of days. But my heart says nay; and all my limbs are light, and a hope and joy are come to me that no reason can deny. Éowyn, Éowyn, White Lady of Rohan, in this hour I do not believe that any darkness will endure!' And he stooped and kissed her brow.

And so they stood on the walls of the City of Gondor, and a great wind rose and blew, and their hair, raven and golden, streamed out mingling in the air. And the Shadow departed, and the Sun was unveiled, and light leaped forth; and the waters of Anduin shone like silver, and in all the houses of the City men sang for the joy that welled up in their hearts from what source they could not tell.

And before the Sun had fallen far from the noon out of the East there came a great Eagle flying, and he bore tidings beyond hope from the Lords of the West, crying:

Sing now, ye people of the Tower of Anor,
for the Realm of Sauron is ended for ever,
and the Dark Tower is thrown down.

Sing and rejoice, ye people of the Tower of Guard,
for your watch hath not been in vain,
and the Black Gate is broken,
and your King hath passed through,
and he is victorious.

Sing and be glad, all ye children of the West,
for your King shall come again,
and he shall dwell among you
all the days of your life.

And the Tree that was withered shall be renewed,
and he shall plant it in the high places,
and the City shall be blessed.

Sing all ye people!

And the people sang in all the ways of the City.

The days that followed were golden, and Spring and Summer joined and made revel together in the fields of Gondor. And tidings now came by swift riders from Cair Andros of all that was done, and the City made ready for the coming of the King. Merry was summoned and rode away with the wains that took store of goods to Osgiliath and thence by ship to Cair Andros; but Faramir did not go, for now being healed he took upon him his authority and the Stewardship, although it was only for a little while, and his duty was to prepare for one who should replace him.

And Éowyn did not go, though her brother sent word begging her to come to the field of Cormallen. And Faramir wondered at this, but he saw her seldom, being busy with many matters; and she dwelt still in the Houses of Healing and walked alone in the garden, and her face grew pale again, and it seemed that in all the City she only was ailing and sorrowful.

And the Warden of the Houses was troubled, and he spoke to Faramir.

Then Faramir came and sought her, and once more they stood on the walls together; and he said to her: 'Éowyn, why do you tarry here, and do not go to the rejoicing in Cormallen beyond Cair Andros, where your brother awaits you?'

And she said: 'Do you not know?'

But he answered: 'Two reasons there may be, but which is true, I do not know.'

And she said: 'I do not wish to play at riddles. Speak plainer!'

'Then if you will have it so, lady,' he said: 'you do not go, because only your brother called for you, and to look on the Lord Aragorn, Elendil's heir, in his triumph would now bring you no joy. Or because I do not go, and you desire still to be near me. And maybe for both these reasons, and you yourself cannot choose between them. Éowyn, do you not love me, or will you not?'

'I wished to be loved by another,' she answered. 'But I desire no man's pity.'

'That I know,' he said. 'You desired to have the love of the Lord Aragorn. Because he was high and puissant, and you wished to have renown and glory and to be lifted far above the mean things that crawl on the earth. And as a great captain may to a young soldier he seemed to you admirable. For so he is, a lord among men, the greatest that now is. But when he gave you only understanding and pity, then you desired to have nothing, unless a brave death in battle. Look at me, Éowyn!'

And Éowyn looked at Faramir long and steadily; and Faramir said: 'Do not scorn pity that is the gift of a gentle heart, Éowyn! But I do not offer you my pity. For you are a lady high and valiant and have yourself won renown that shall not be forgotten; and you are a lady beautiful, I deem, beyond even the words of the Elven-tongue to tell. And I love you. Once I pitied your sorrow. But now, were you sorrowless, without fear or any lack, were you the blissful Queen of Gondor, still I would love you. Éowyn, do you not love me?'

Then the heart of Éowyn changed, or else at last she understood it. And suddenly her winter passed, and the sun shone on her.

'I stand in Minas Anor, the Tower of the Sun,' she said; 'and behold! the Shadow has departed! I will be a shieldmaiden no longer, nor vie with the great Riders, nor take joy only in the songs of slaying. I will be a healer, and love all things that grow and are not barren.' And again she looked at Faramir. 'No longer do I desire to be a queen,' she said.

Then Faramir laughed merrily. 'That is well,' he said; 'for I am not a king. Yet I will wed with the White Lady of Rohan, if it be her will. And if she will, then let us cross the River and in happier days let us dwell in fair Ithilien and there make a garden. All things will grow with joy there, if the White Lady comes.'

'Then must I leave my own people, man of Gondor?' she said. 'And would you have your proud folk say of you: "There goes a lord who tamed a wild shieldmaiden of the North! Was there no woman of the race of Númenor to choose?"'

'I would,' said Faramir. And he took her in his arms and kissed her under the sunlit sky, and he cared not that they stood high upon the walls in the sight of many. And many indeed saw them and the light that shone about them as they came down from the walls and went hand in hand to the Houses of Healing.

And to the Warden of the Houses Faramir said: 'Here is the Lady Éowyn of Rohan, and now she is healed.'

And the Warden said: 'Then I release her from my charge and bid her farewell, and may she suffer never hurt nor sickness again. I commend her to the care of the Steward of the City, until her brother returns.'

But Éowyn said: 'Yet now that I have leave to depart, I would remain. For this House has become to me of all dwellings the most blessed.' And she remained there until King Éomer came.

All things were now made ready in the City; and there was great concourse of people, for the tidings had gone out into all parts of Gondor, from Min-Rimmon even to Pinnath Gelin and the far coasts of the sea; and all that could come to the City made haste to come. And the City was filled again with women and fair children that returned to their homes laden with flowers; and from Dol Amroth came the harpers that harped most skilfully in all the land; and there were players upon viols and upon flutes and upon horns of silver, and clear-voiced singers from the vales of Lebennin.

At last an evening came when from the walls the pavilions could be seen upon the field, and all night lights were burning as men watched for the dawn. And when the sun rose in the clear morning above the mountains in the East, upon which shadows lay no more, then all the bells rang, and all the banners broke and flowed in the wind; and upon the White Tower of the citadel the standard of the Stewards, bright argent like snow in the sun, bearing no charge nor device, was raised over Gondor for the last time.

Now the Captains of the West led their host towards the City, and folk saw them advance in line upon line, flashing and glinting in the sunrise and rippling like silver. And so they came before the Gateway and halted a furlong from the walls. As yet no gates had been set up again, but a barrier was laid across the entrance to the City, and there stood men at arms in silver and black with long swords drawn. Before the barrier stood

Faramir the Steward, and Húrin Warden of the Keys, and other captains of Gondor, and the Lady Éowyn of Rohan with Elfhelm the Marshal and many knights of the Mark; and upon either side of the Gate was a great press of fair people in raiment of many colours and garlands of flowers.

So now there was a wide space before the walls of Minas Tirith, and it was hemmed in upon all sides by the knights and the soldiers of Gondor and of Rohan, and by the people of the City and of all parts of the land. A hush fell upon all as out from the host stepped the Dúnedain in silver and grey; and before them came walking slow the Lord Aragorn. He was clad in black mail girt with silver, and he wore a long mantle of pure white clasped at the throat with a great jewel of green that shone from afar; but his head was bare save for a star upon his forehead bound by a slender fillet of silver. With him were Éomer of Rohan, and the Prince Imrahil, and Gandalf robed all in white, and four small figures that many men marvelled to see.

'Nay, cousin! they are not boys,' said Ioreth to her kinswoman from Imloth Melui, who stood beside her. 'Those are *Periain*, out of the far country of the Halflings, where they are princes of great fame, it is said. I should know, for I had one to tend in the Houses. They are small, but they are valiant. Why, cousin, one of them went with only his esquire into the Black Country and fought with the Dark Lord all by himself, and set fire to his Tower, if you can believe it. At least that is the tale in the City. That will be the one that walks with our Elfstone. They are dear friends, I hear. Now he is a marvel, the Lord Elfstone: not too soft in his speech, mind you, but he has a golden heart, as the saying is; and he has the healing hands. "The hands of the king are the hands of a healer", I said; and that was how it was all discovered. And Mithrandir, he said to me: "Ioreth, men will long remember your words", and——'

But Ioreth was not permitted to continue the instruction of her kinswoman from the country, for a single trumpet rang, and a dead silence followed. Then forth from the Gate went Faramir with Húrin of the Keys, and no others, save that behind them walked four men in the high helms and armour of the Citadel, and they bore a great casket of black *lebethron* bound with silver.

Faramir met Aragorn in the midst of those there assembled, and he knelt, and said: 'The last Steward of Gondor begs leave to surrender his office.' And he held out a white rod; but Aragorn took the rod and gave it back, saying: 'That office is not ended, and it shall be thine and thy heirs' as long as my line shall last. Do now thy office!'

Then Faramir stood up and spoke in a clear voice: 'Men of Gondor, hear now the Steward of this Realm! Behold! one has come to claim the kingship again at last. Here is Aragorn son of Arathorn, chieftain of the

Dúnedain of Arnor, Captain of the Host of the West, bearer of the Star of the North, wielder of the Sword Reforged, victorious in battle, whose hands bring healing, the Elfstone, Elessar of the line of Valandil, Isildur's son, Elendil's son of Númenor. Shall he be king and enter into the City and dwell there?'

And all the host and all the people cried *yea* with one voice.

And Ioreth said to her kinswoman: 'This is just a ceremony such as we have in the City, cousin; for he has already entered, as I was telling you; and he said to me——' And then again she was obliged to silence, for Faramir spoke again.

'Men of Gondor, the loremasters tell that it was the custom of old that the king should receive the crown from his father ere he died; or if that might not be, that he should go alone and take it from the hands of his father in the tomb where he was laid. But since things must now be done otherwise, using the authority of the Steward, I have today brought hither from Rath Dínen the crown of Eärnur the last king, whose days passed in the time of our longfathers of old.'

Then the guards stepped forward, and Faramir opened the casket, and he held up an ancient crown. It was shaped like the helms of the Guards of the Citadel, save that it was loftier, and it was all white, and the wings at either side were wrought of pearl and silver in the likeness of the wings of a sea-bird, for it was the emblem of kings who came over the Sea; and seven gems of adamant were set in the circlet, and upon its summit was set a single jewel the light of which went up like a flame.

Then Aragorn took the crown and held it up and said:

Et Eärello Endorenna utúlien. Sinome maruvan ar Hildinyar tenn' Ambar-metta!

And those were the words that Elendil spoke when he came up out of the Sea on the wings of the wind: 'Out of the Great Sea to Middle-earth I am come. In this place will I abide, and my heirs, unto the ending of the world.'

Then to the wonder of many Aragorn did not put the crown upon his head, but gave it back to Faramir, and said: 'By the labour and valour of many I have come into my inheritance. In token of this I would have the Ring-bearer bring the crown to me, and let Mithrandir set it upon my head, if he will; for he has been the mover of all that has been accomplished, and this is his victory.'

Then Frodo came forward and took the crown from Faramir and bore it to Gandalf; and Aragorn knelt, and Gandalf set the White Crown upon his head, and said:

'Now come the days of the King, and may they be blessed while the thrones of the Valar endure!'

But when Aragorn arose all that beheld him gazed in silence, for it seemed to them that he was revealed to them now for the first time. Tall as the sea-kings of old, he stood above all that were near; ancient of days he seemed and yet in the flower of manhood; and wisdom sat upon his brow, and strength and healing were in his hands, and a light was about him. And then Faramir cried:

'Behold the King!'

And in that moment all the trumpets were blown, and the King Elessar went forth and came to the barrier, and Húrin of the Keys thrust it back; and amid the music of harp and of viol and of flute and the singing of clear voices the King passed through the flower-laden streets, and came to the Citadel, and entered in; and the banner of the Tree and the Stars was unfurled upon the topmost tower, and the reign of King Elessar began, of which many songs have told.

In his time the City was made more fair than it had ever been, even in the days of its first glory; and it was filled with trees and with fountains, and its gates were wrought of mithril and steel, and its streets were paved with white marble; and the Folk of the Mountain laboured in it, and the Folk of the Wood rejoiced to come there; and all was healed and made good, and the houses were filled with men and women and the laughter of children, and no window was blind nor any courtyard empty; and after the ending of the Third Age of the world into the new age it preserved the memory and the glory of the years that were gone.

In the days that followed his crowning the King sat on his throne in the Hall of the Kings and pronounced his judgements. And embassies came from many lands and peoples, from the East and the South, and from the borders of Mirkwood, and from Dunland in the west. And the King pardoned the Easterlings that had given themselves up, and sent them away free, and he made peace with the peoples of Harad; and the slaves of Mordor he released and gave to them all the lands about Lake Núrnen to be their own. And there were brought before him many to receive his praise and reward for their valour; and last the captain of the Guard brought to him Beregond to be judged.

And the King said to Beregond: 'Beregond, by your sword blood was spilled in the Hallows, where that is forbidden. Also you left your post without leave of Lord or of Captain. For these things, of old, death was the penalty. Now therefore I must pronounce your doom.

'All penalty is remitted for your valour in battle, and still more because all that you did was for the love of the Lord Faramir. Nonetheless you must leave the Guard of the Citadel, and you must go forth from the City of Minas Tirith.'

Then the blood left Beregond's face, and he was stricken to the heart and bowed his head. But the King said:

'So it must be, for you are appointed to the White Company, the Guard of Faramir, Prince of Ithilien, and you shall be its captain and dwell in Emyn Arnen in honour and peace, and in the service of him for whom you risked all, to save him from death.'

And then Beregond, perceiving the mercy and justice of the King, was glad, and kneeling kissed his hand, and departed in joy and content. And Aragorn gave to Faramir Ithilien to be his princedom, and bade him dwell in the hills of Emyn Arnen within sight of the City.

'For,' said he, 'Minas Ithil in Morgul Vale shall be utterly destroyed, and though it may in time to come be made clean, no man may dwell there for many long years.'

And last of all Aragorn greeted Éomer of Rohan, and they embraced, and Aragorn said: 'Between us there can be no word of giving or taking, nor of reward; for we are brethren. In happy hour did Eorl ride from the North, and never has any league of peoples been more blessed, so that neither has ever failed the other, nor shall fail. Now, as you know, we have laid Théoden the Renowned in a tomb in the Hallows, and there he shall lie for ever among the Kings of Gondor, if you will. Or if you desire it, we will come to Rohan and bring him back to rest with his own people.'

And Éomer answered: 'Since the day when you rose before me out of the green grass of the downs I have loved you, and that love shall not fail. But now I must depart for a while to my own realm, where there is much to heal and set in order. But as for the Fallen, when all is made ready we will return for him; but here let him sleep a while.'

And Éowyn said to Faramir: 'Now I must go back to my own land and look on it once again, and help my brother in his labour; but when one whom I long loved as father is laid at last to rest, I will return.'

So the glad days passed; and on the eighth day of May the Riders of Rohan made ready, and rode off by the North-way, and with them went the sons of Elrond. All the road was lined with people to do them honour and praise them, from the Gate of the City to the walls of the Pelennor. Then all others that dwelt afar went back to their homes rejoicing; but in the City there was labour of many willing hands to rebuild and renew and to remove all the scars of war and the memory of the darkness.

The hobbits still remained in Minas Tirith, with Legolas and Gimli; for Aragorn was loth for the fellowship to be dissolved. 'At last all such things must end,' he said, 'but I would have you wait a little while longer: for the end of the deeds that you have shared in has not yet come. A day draws near that I have looked for in all the years of my manhood, and when it comes I would have my friends beside me.' But of that day he would say no more.

In those days the Companions of the Ring dwelt together in a fair house with Gandalf, and they went to and fro as they wished. And Frodo said to Gandalf: 'Do you know what this day is that Aragorn speaks of? For we are happy here, and I don't wish to go; but the days are running away, and Bilbo is waiting; and the Shire is my home.'

'As for Bilbo,' said Gandalf, 'he is waiting for the same day, and he knows what keeps you. And as for the passing of the days, it is now only May and high summer is not yet in; and though all things may seem changed, as if an age of the world had gone by, yet to the trees and the grass it is less than a year since you set out.'

'Pippin,' said Frodo, 'didn't you say that Gandalf was less close than of old? He was weary of his labours then, I think. Now he is recovering.'

And Gandalf said: 'Many folk like to know beforehand what is to be set on the table; but those who have laboured to prepare the feast like to keep their secret; for wonder makes the words of praise louder. And Aragorn himself waits for a sign.'

There came a day when Gandalf could not be found, and the Companions wondered what was going forward. But Gandalf took Aragorn out from the City by night, and he brought him to the southern feet of Mount Mindolluin; and there they found a path made in ages past that few now dared to tread. For it led up on to the mountain to a high hallow where only the kings had been wont to go. And they went up by steep ways, until they came to a high field below the snows that clad the lofty peaks, and it looked down over the precipice that stood behind the City. And standing there they surveyed the lands, for the morning was come; and they saw the towers of the City far below them like white pencils touched by the sunlight, and all the Vale of Anduin was like a garden, and the Mountains of Shadow were veiled in a golden mist. Upon the one side their sight reached to the grey Emyn Muil, and the glint of Rauros was like a star twinkling far off; and upon the other side they saw the River like a ribbon laid down to Pelargir, and beyond that was a light on the hem of the sky that spoke of the Sea.

And Gandalf said: 'This is your realm, and the heart of the greater realm that shall be. The Third Age of the world is ended, and the new age is begun; and it is your task to order its beginning and to preserve what may be preserved. For though much has been saved, much must now pass away; and the power of the Three Rings also is ended. And all the lands that you see, and those that lie round about them, shall be dwellings of

Men. For the time comes of the Dominion of Men, and the Elder Kindred shall fade or depart.'

'I know it well, dear friend,' said Aragorn; 'but I would still have your counsel.'

'Not for long now,' said Gandalf. 'The Third Age was my age. I was the Enemy of Sauron; and my work is finished. I shall go soon. The burden must lie now upon you and your kindred.'

'But I shall die,' said Aragorn. 'For I am a mortal man, and though being what I am and of the race of the West unmingled, I shall have life far longer than other men, yet that is but a little while; and when those who are now in the wombs of women are born and have grown old, I too shall grow old. And who then shall govern Gondor and those who look to this City as to their queen, if my desire be not granted? The Tree in the Court of the Fountain is still withered and barren. When shall I see a sign that it will ever be otherwise?'

'Turn your face from the green world, and look where all seems barren and cold!' said Gandalf.

Then Aragorn turned, and there was a stony slope behind him running down from the skirts of the snow; and as he looked he was aware that alone there in the waste a growing thing stood. And he climbed to it, and saw that out of the very edge of the snow there sprang a sapling tree no more than three foot high. Already it had put forth young leaves long and shapely, dark above and silver beneath, and upon its slender crown it bore one small cluster of flowers whose white petals shone like the sunlit snow.

Then Aragorn cried: '*Yé! utúvienyes!* I have found it! Lo! here is a scion of the Eldest of Trees! But how comes it here? For it is not itself yet seven years old.'

And Gandalf coming looked at it, and said: 'Verily this is a sapling of the line of Nimloth the fair; and that was a seedling of Galathilion, and that a fruit of Telperion of many names, Eldest of Trees. Who shall say how it comes here in the appointed hour? But this is an ancient hallow, and ere the kings failed or the Tree withered in the court, a fruit must have been set here. For it is said that, though the fruit of the Tree comes seldom to ripeness, yet the life within may then lie sleeping through many long years, and none can foretell the time in which it will awake. Remember this. For if ever a fruit ripens, it should be planted, lest the line die out of the world. Here it has lain hidden on the mountain, even as the race of Elendil lay hidden in the wastes of the North. Yet the line of Nimloth is older far than your line, King Elessar.'

Then Aragorn laid his hand gently to the sapling, and lo! it seemed to hold only lightly to the earth, and it was removed without hurt; and Aragorn bore it back to the Citadel. Then the withered tree was uprooted, but with reverence; and they did not burn it, but laid it to rest in the silence of Rath Dínen. And Aragorn planted the new tree in the court by the fountain, and swiftly and gladly it began to grow; and when the month of June entered in it was laden with blossom.

'The sign has been given,' said Aragorn, 'and the day is not far off.' And he set watchmen upon the walls.

It was the day before Midsummer when messengers came from Amon Dîn to the City, and they said that there was a riding of fair folk out of the North, and they drew near now to the walls of the Pelennor. And the King said: 'At last they have come. Let all the City be made ready!'

Upon the very Eve of Midsummer, when the sky was blue as sapphire and white stars opened in the East, but the West was still golden, and the air was cool and fragrant, the riders came down the North-way to the gates of Minas Tirith. First rode Elrohir and Elladan with a banner of silver, and then came Glorfindel and Erestor and all the household of Rivendell, and after them came the Lady Galadriel and Celeborn, Lord of Lothlórien, riding upon white steeds and with them many fair folk of their land, grey-cloaked with white gems in their hair; and last came Master Elrond, mighty among Elves and Men, bearing the sceptre of Annúminas, and beside him upon a grey palfrey rode Arwen his daughter, Evenstar of her people.

And Frodo when he saw her come glimmering in the evening, with stars on her brow and a sweet fragrance about her, was moved with great wonder, and he said to Gandalf: 'At last I understand why we have waited! This is the ending. Now not day only shall be beloved, but night too shall be beautiful and blessed and all its fear pass away!'

Then the King welcomed his guests, and they alighted; and Elrond surrendered the sceptre, and laid the hand of his daughter in the hand of the King, and together they went up into the High City, and all the stars flowered in the sky. And Aragorn the King Elessar wedded Arwen Undómiel in the City of the Kings upon the day of Midsummer, and the tale of their long waiting and labours was come to fulfilment.

CHAPTER VI

MANY PARTINGS

When the days of rejoicing were over at last the Companions thought of returning to their own homes. And Frodo went to the King as he was sitting with the Queen Arwen by the fountain, and she sang a song of Valinor, while the Tree grew and blossomed. They welcomed Frodo and rose to greet him; and Aragorn said:

'I know what you have come to say, Frodo: you wish to return to your own home. Well, dearest friend, the tree grows best in the land of its sires; but for you in all the lands of the West there will ever be a welcome. And though your people have had little fame in the legends of the great, they will now have more renown than any wide realms that are no more.'

'It is true that I wish to go back to the Shire,' said Frodo. 'But first I must go to Rivendell. For if there could be anything wanting in a time so blessed, I missed Bilbo; and I was grieved when among all the household of Elrond I saw that he was not come.'

'Do you wonder at that, Ring-bearer?' said Arwen. 'For you know the power of that thing which is now destroyed; and all that was done by that power is now passing away. But your kinsman possessed this thing longer than you. He is ancient in years now, according to his kind; and he awaits you, for he will not again make any long journey save one.'

'Then I beg leave to depart soon,' said Frodo.

'In seven days we will go,' said Aragorn. 'For we shall ride with you far on the road, even as far as the country of Rohan. In three days now Éomer will return hither to bear Théoden back to rest in the Mark, and we shall ride with him to honour the fallen. But now before you go I will confirm the words that Faramir spoke to you, and you are made free for ever of the realm of Gondor; and all your companions likewise. And if there were any gifts that I could give to match with your deeds you should have them; but whatever you desire you shall take with you, and you shall ride in honour and arrayed as princes of the land.'

But the Queen Arwen said: 'A gift I will give you. For I am the daughter of Elrond. I shall not go with him now when he departs to the Havens; for mine is the choice of Lúthien, and as she so have I chosen, both the sweet and the bitter. But in my stead you shall go, Ring-bearer, when the time comes, and if you then desire it. If your hurts grieve you still and the memory of your burden is heavy, then you may pass into the West, until all your wounds and weariness are healed. But wear this now in memory of Elfstone and Evenstar with whom your life has been woven!'

And she took a white gem like a star that lay upon her breast hanging upon a silver chain, and she set the chain about Frodo's neck. 'When the memory of the fear and the darkness troubles you,' she said, 'this will bring you aid.'

In three days, as the King had said, Éomer of Rohan came riding to the City, and with him came an *éored* of the fairest knights of the Mark. He was welcomed; and when they sat all at table in Merethrond, the Great Hall of Feasts, he beheld the beauty of the ladies that he saw and was filled with great wonder. And before he went to his rest he sent for Gimli the Dwarf, and he said to him: 'Gimli Glóin's son, have you your axe ready?'

'Nay, lord,' said Gimli, 'but I can speedily fetch it, if there be need.'

'You shall judge,' said Éomer. 'For there are certain rash words concerning the Lady in the Golden Wood that lie still between us. And now I have seen her with my eyes.'

'Well, lord,' said Gimli, 'and what say you now?'

'Alas!' said Éomer. 'I will not say that she is the fairest lady that lives.'

'Then I must go for my axe,' said Gimli.

'But first I will plead this excuse,' said Éomer. 'Had I seen her in other company, I would have said all that you could wish. But now I will put Queen Arwen Evenstar first, and I am ready to do battle on my own part with any who deny me. Shall I call for my sword?'

Then Gimli bowed low. 'Nay, you are excused for my part, lord,' he said. 'You have chosen the Evening; but my love is given to the Morning. And my heart forebodes that soon it will pass away for ever.'

At last the day of departure came, and a great and fair company made ready to ride north from the City. Then the kings of Gondor and Rohan went to the Hallows and they came to the tombs in Rath Dínen, and they bore away King Théoden upon a golden bier, and passed through the City in silence. Then they laid the bier upon a great wain with Riders of Rohan all about it and his banner borne before; and Merry being Théoden's esquire rode upon the wain and kept the arms of the king.

For the other Companions steeds were furnished according to their stature; and Frodo and Samwise rode at Aragorn's side, and Gandalf rode upon Shadowfax, and Pippin rode with the knights of Gondor; and Legolas and Gimli as ever rode together upon Arod.

In that riding went also Queen Arwen, and Celeborn and Galadriel with their folk, and Elrond and his sons; and the princes of Dol Amroth and of Ithilien, and many captains and knights. Never had any king of the Mark such company upon the road as went with Théoden Thengel's son to the land of his home.

Without haste and at peace they passed into Anórien, and they came to the Grey Wood under Amon Dîn; and there they heard a sound as of drums beating in the hills, though no living thing could be seen. Then Aragorn let the trumpets be blown; and heralds cried:

'Behold, the King Elessar is come! The Forest of Drúadan he gives to Ghân-buri-ghân and to his folk, to be their own for ever; and hereafter let no man enter it without their leave!'

Then the drums rolled loudly, and were silent.

At length after fifteen days of journey the wain of King Théoden passed through the green fields of Rohan and came to Edoras; and there they all rested. The Golden Hall was arrayed with fair hangings and it was filled with light, and there was held the highest feast that it had known since the days of its building. For after three days the Men of the Mark prepared the funeral of Théoden; and he was laid in a house of stone with his arms and many other fair things that he had possessed, and over him was raised a great mound, covered with green turves of grass and of white evermind. And now there were eight mounds on the east-side of the Barrowfield.

Then the Riders of the King's House upon white horses rode round about the barrow and sang together a song of Théoden Thengel's son that Gléowine his minstrel made, and he made no other song after. The slow voices of the Riders stirred the hearts even of those who did not know the speech of that people; but the words of the song brought a light to the eyes of the folk of the Mark as they heard again afar the thunder of the hooves of the North and the voice of Eorl crying above the battle upon the Field of Celebrant; and the tale of the kings rolled on, and the horn of Helm was loud in the mountains, until the Darkness came and King Théoden arose and rode through the Shadow to the fire, and died in splendour, even as the Sun, returning beyond hope, gleamed upon Mindolluin in the morning.

Out of doubt, out of dark, to the day's rising
he rode singing in the sun, sword unsheathing.
Hope he rekindled, and in hope ended;
over death, over dread, over doom lifted
out of loss, out of life, unto long glory.

But Merry stood at the foot of the green mound, and he wept, and when the song was ended he arose and cried:

'Théoden King, Théoden King! Farewell! As a father you were to me, for a little while. Farewell!'

When the burial was over and the weeping of women was stilled, and Théoden was left at last alone in his barrow, then folk gathered to the Golden Hall for the great feast and put away sorrow; for Théoden had lived to full years and ended in honour no less than the greatest of his sires. And when the time came that in the custom of the Mark they should drink to the memory of the kings, Éowyn Lady of Rohan came forth, golden as the sun and white as snow, and she bore a filled cup to Éomer.

Then a minstrel and loremaster stood up and named all the names of the Lords of the Mark in their order: Eorl the Young; and Brego builder of the Hall; and Aldor brother of Baldor the hapless; and Fréa, and Fréawine, and Goldwine, and Déor, and Gram; and Helm who lay hid in Helm's Deep when the Mark was overrun; and so ended the nine mounds of the west-side, for in that time the line was broken, and after came the mounds of the east-side: Fréalaf, Helm's sister-son, and Léofa, and Walda, and Folca, and Folcwine, and Fengel, and Thengel, and Théoden the latest. And when Théoden was named Éomer drained the cup. Then Éowyn bade those that served to fill the cups, and all there assembled rose and drank to the new king, crying: 'Hail, Éomer, King of the Mark!'

At the last when the feast drew to an end Éomer arose and said: 'Now this is the funeral feast of Théoden the King; but I will speak ere we go of tidings of joy, for he would not grudge that I should do so, since he was ever a father to Éowyn my sister. Hear then all my guests, fair folk of many realms, such as have never before been gathered in this hall! Faramir, Steward of Gondor, and Prince of Ithilien, asks that Éowyn Lady of Rohan should be his wife, and she grants it full willing. Therefore they shall be trothplighted before you all.'

And Faramir and Éowyn stood forth and set hand in hand; and all there drank to them and were glad. 'Thus,' said Éomer, 'is the friendship of the Mark and of Gondor bound with a new bond, and the more do I rejoice.'

'No niggard are you, Éomer,' said Aragorn, 'to give thus to Gondor the fairest thing in your realm!'

Then Éowyn looked in the eyes of Aragorn, and she said: 'Wish me joy, my liege-lord and healer!'

And he answered: 'I have wished thee joy ever since first I saw thee. It heals my heart to see thee now in bliss.'

When the feast was over, those who were to go took leave of King Éomer. Aragorn and his knights, and the people of Lórien and of Rivendell, made ready to ride; but Faramir and Imrahil remained at Edoras; and Arwen

Evenstar remained also, and she said farewell to her brethren. None saw her last meeting with Elrond her father, for they went up into the hills and there spoke long together, and bitter was their parting that should endure beyond the ends of the world.

At the last before the guests set out Éomer and Éowyn came to Merry, and they said: 'Farewell now, Meriadoc of the Shire and Holdwine of the Mark! Ride to good fortune, and ride back soon to our welcome!'

And Éomer said: 'Kings of old would have laden you with gifts that a wain could not bear for your deeds upon the fields of Mundburg; and yet you will take naught, you say, but the arms that were given to you. This I suffer, for indeed I have no gift that is worthy; but my sister begs you to receive this small thing, as a memorial of Dernhelm and of the horns of the Mark at the coming of the morning.'

Then Éowyn gave to Merry an ancient horn, small but cunningly wrought all of fair silver with a baldric of green; and wrights had engraven upon it swift horsemen riding in a line that wound about it from the tip to the mouth; and there were set runes of great virtue.

'This is an heirloom of our house,' said Éowyn. 'It was made by the Dwarves, and came from the hoard of Scatha the Worm. Eorl the Young brought it from the North. He that blows it at need shall set fear in the hearts of his enemies and joy in the hearts of his friends, and they shall hear him and come to him.'

Then Merry took the horn, for it could not be refused, and he kissed Éowyn's hand; and they embraced him, and so they parted for that time.

Now the guests were ready, and they drank the stirrup-cup, and with great praise and friendship they departed, and came at length to Helm's Deep, and there they rested two days. Then Legolas repaid his promise to Gimli and went with him to the Glittering Caves; and when they returned he was silent, and would say only that Gimli alone could find fit words to speak of them. 'And never before has a Dwarf claimed a victory over an Elf in a contest of words,' said he. 'Now therefore let us go to Fangorn and set the score right!'

From Deeping-coomb they rode to Isengard, and saw how the Ents had busied themselves. All the stone-circle had been thrown down and removed, and the land within was made into a garden filled with orchards and trees, and a stream ran through it; but in the midst of all there was a lake of clear water, and out of it the Tower of Orthanc rose still, tall and impregnable, and its black rock was mirrored in the pool.

For a while the travellers sat where once the old gates of Isengard had stood, and there were now two tall trees like sentinels at the beginning of a green-bordered path that ran towards Orthanc; and they looked in wonder at the work that had been done, but no living thing could they see far or near. But presently they heard a voice calling *hoom-hom*, *hoom-hom*; and there came Tree-beard striding down the path to greet them with Quickbeam at his side.

'Welcome to the Treegarth of Orthanc!' he said. 'I knew that you were coming, but I was at work up the valley; there is much still to be done. But you have not been idle either away in the south and the east, I hear; and all that I hear is good, very good.' Then Treebeard praised all their deeds, of which he seemed to have full knowledge; and at last he stopped and looked long at Gandalf.

'Well, come now!' he said. 'You have proved mightiest, and all your labours have gone well. Where now would you be going? And why do you come here?'

'To see how your work goes, my friend,' said Gandalf, 'and to thank you for your aid in all that has been achieved.'

'*Hoom*, well, that is fair enough,' said Treebeard; 'for to be sure Ents have played their part. And not only in dealing with that, *hoom*, that accursed tree-slayer that dwelt here. For there was a great inrush of those, *burárum*, those evileyed-blackhanded-bowlegged-flinthearted-clawfingered-foulbellied-bloodthirsty, *morimaitesincahonda*, *hoom*, well, since you are hasty folk and their full name is as long as years of torment, those vermin of orcs; and they came over the River and down from the North and all round the wood of Laurelindórenan, which they could not get into, thanks to the Great ones who are here.' He bowed to the Lord and Lady of Lórien.

'And these same foul creatures were more than surprised to meet us out on the Wold, for they had not heard of us before; though that might be said also of better folk. And not many will remember us, for not many escaped us alive, and the River had most of those. But it was well for you, for if they had not met us, then the king of the grassland would not have ridden far, and if he had there would have been no home to return to.'

'We know it well,' said Aragorn, 'and never shall it be forgotten in Minas Tirith or in Edoras.'

'*Never* is too long a word even for me,' said Treebeard. 'Not while your kingdoms last, you mean; but they will have to last long indeed to seem long to Ents.'

'The New Age begins,' said Gandalf, 'and in this age it may well prove that the kingdoms of Men shall outlast you, Fangorn my friend. But now come tell me: what of the task that I set you? How is Saruman? Is he not weary of Orthanc yet? For I do not suppose that he will think you have improved the view from his windows.'

Treebeard gave Gandalf a long look, almost a cunning look, Merry thought. 'Ah!' he said. 'I thought you would come to that. Weary of Orthanc? Very weary at last; but not so weary of his tower as he was weary of my voice. *Hoom!* I gave him some long tales, or at least what might be thought long in your speech.'

'Then why did he stay to listen? Did you go into Orthanc?' asked Gandalf.

'*Hoom*, no, not into Orthanc!' said Treebeard. 'But he came to his window and listened, because he could not get news in any other way, and though he hated the news, he was greedy to have it; and I saw that he heard it all. But I added a great many things to the news that it was good for him to think of. He grew very weary. He always was hasty. That was his ruin.'

'I observe, my good Fangorn,' said Gandalf, 'that with great care you say *dwelt*, *was*, *grew*. What about *is*? Is he dead?'

'No, not dead, so far as I know,' said Treebeard. 'But he is gone. Yes, he is gone seven days. I let him go. There was little left of him when he crawled out, and as for that worm-creature of his, he was like a pale shadow. Now do not tell me, Gandalf, that I promised to keep him safe; for I know it. But things have changed since then. And I kept him until he was safe, safe from doing any more harm. You should know that above all I hate the caging of live things, and I will not keep even such creatures as these caged beyond great need. A snake without fangs may crawl where he will.'

'You may be right,' said Gandalf; 'but this snake had still one tooth left, I think. He had the poison of his voice, and I guess that he persuaded you, even you Treebeard, knowing the soft spot in your heart. Well, he is gone, and there is no more to be said. But the Tower of Orthanc now goes back to the King, to whom it belongs. Though maybe he will not need it.'

'That will be seen later,' said Aragorn. 'But I will give to Ents all this valley to do with as they will, so long as they keep a watch upon Orthanc and see that none enter it without my leave.'

'It is locked,' said Treebeard. 'I made Saruman lock it and give me the keys. Quickbeam has them.'

Quickbeam bowed like a tree bending in the wind and handed to Aragorn two great black keys of intricate shape, joined by a ring of steel. 'Now I thank you once more,' said Aragorn, 'and I bid you farewell. May your forest grow again in peace. When this valley is filled there is room and to spare west of the mountains, where once you walked long ago.'

Treebeard's face became sad. 'Forests may grow,' he said. 'Woods may spread. But not Ents. There are no Entings.'

'Yet maybe there is now more hope in your search,' said Aragorn. 'Lands will lie open to you eastward that have long been closed.'

But Treebeard shook his head and said: 'It is far to go. And there are too many Men there in these days. But I am forgetting my manners! Will you stay here and rest a while? And maybe there are some that would be pleased to pass through Fangorn Forest and so shorten their road home?' He looked at Celeborn and Galadriel.

But all save Legolas said that they must now take their leave and depart either south or west. 'Come, Gimli!' said Legolas. 'Now by Fangorn's leave I will visit the deep places of the Entwood and see such trees as are nowhere else to be found in Middle-earth. You shall come with me and keep your word; and thus we will journey on together to our own lands in Mirkwood and beyond.' To this Gimli agreed, though with no great delight, it seemed.

'Here then at last comes the ending of the Fellowship of the Ring,' said Aragorn. 'Yet I hope that ere long you will return to my land with the help that you promised.'

'We will come, if our own lords allow it,' said Gimli. 'Well, farewell, my hobbits! You should come safe to your own homes now, and I shall not be kept awake for fear of your peril. We will send word when we may, and some of us may yet meet at times; but I fear that we shall not all be gathered together ever again.'

Then Treebeard said farewell to each of them in turn, and he bowed three times slowly and with great reverence to Celeborn and Galadriel. 'It is long, long since we met by stock or by stone, *A vanimar, vanimálion nostari!*' he said. 'It is sad that we should meet only thus at the ending. For the world is changing: I feel it in the water, I feel it in the earth, and I smell it in the air. I do not think we shall meet again.'

And Celeborn said: 'I do not know, Eldest.' But Galadriel said: 'Not in Middle-earth, nor until the lands that lie under the wave are lifted up again. Then in the willow-meads of Tasarinan we may meet in the Spring. Farewell!'

Last of all Merry and Pippin said good-bye to the old Ent, and he grew gayer as he looked at them. 'Well, my merry folk,' he said, 'will you drink another draught with me before you go?'

'Indeed we will,' they said, and he took them aside into the shade of one of the trees, and there they saw that a great stone jar had been set. And Treebeard filled three bowls, and they drank; and they saw his strange eyes looking at them over the rim of his bowl. 'Take care, take care!' he said. 'For you have already grown since I saw you last.' And they laughed and drained their bowls.

'Well, good-bye!' he said. 'And don't forget that if you hear any news of the Entwives in your land, you will send word to me.' Then he waved his great hands to all the company and went off into the trees.

The travellers now rode with more speed, and they made their way towards the Gap of Rohan; and Aragorn took leave of them at last close to that very place where Pippin had looked into the Stone of Orthanc. The Hobbits were grieved at this parting; for Aragorn had never failed them and he had been their guide through many perils.

'I wish we could have a Stone that we could see all our friends in,' said Pippin, 'and that we could speak to them from far away!'

'Only one now remains that you could use,' answered Aragorn; 'for you would not wish to see what the Stone of Minas Tirith would show you. But the Palantír of Orthanc the King will keep, to see what is passing in his realm, and what his servants are doing. For do not forget, Peregrin Took, that you are a knight of Gondor, and I do not release you from your service. You are going now on leave, but I may recall you. And remember, dear friends of the Shire, that my realm lies also in the North, and I shall come there one day.'

Then Aragorn took leave of Celeborn and Galadriel; and the Lady said to him: 'Elfstone, through darkness you have come to your hope, and have now all your desire. Use well the days!'

But Celeborn said: 'Kinsman, farewell! May your doom be other than mine, and your treasure remain with you to the end!'

With that they parted, and it was then the time of sunset; and when after a while they turned and looked back, they saw the King of the West sitting upon his horse with his knights about him; and the falling Sun shone upon them and made all their harness to gleam like red gold, and the white mantle of Aragorn was turned to a flame. Then Aragorn took the green stone and held it up, and there came a green fire from his hand.

Soon the dwindling company, following the Isen, turned west and rode through the Gap into the waste lands beyond, and then they turned northwards, and passed over the borders of Dunland. The Dunlendings fled and hid themselves, for they were afraid of Elvish folk, though few indeed ever came to their country; but the travellers did not heed them, for they were still a great company and were well provided with all that they needed; and they went on their way at their leisure, setting up their tents when they would.

On the sixth day since their parting from the King they journeyed through a wood climbing down from the hills at the feet of the Misty Mountains that now marched on their right hand. As they came out again into the open country at sundown they overtook an old man leaning on a staff, and he was clothed in rags of grey or dirty white, and at his heels went another beggar, slouching and whining.

'Well Saruman!' said Gandalf. 'Where are you going?'

'What is that to you?' he answered. 'Will you still order my goings, and are you not content with my ruin?'

'You know the answers,' said Gandalf: 'no and no. But in any case the time of my labours now draws to an end. The King has taken on the burden. If you had waited at Orthanc, you would have seen him, and he would have shown you wisdom and mercy.'

'Then all the more reason to have left sooner,' said Saruman; 'for I desire neither of him. Indeed if you wish for an answer to your first question, I am seeking a way out of his realm.'

'Then once more you are going the wrong way,' said Gandalf, 'and I see no hope in your journey. But will you scorn our help? For we offer it to you.'

'To me?' said Saruman. 'Nay, pray do not smile at me! I prefer your frowns. And as for the Lady here, I do not trust her: she always hated me, and schemed for your part. I do not doubt that she has brought you this way to have the pleasure of gloating over my poverty. Had I been warned of your pursuit, I would have denied you the pleasure.'

'Saruman,' said Galadriel, 'we have other errands and other cares that seem to us more urgent than hunting for you. Say rather that you are overtaken by good fortune; for now you have a last chance.'

'If it be truly the last, I am glad,' said Saruman; 'for I shall be spared the trouble of refusing it again. All my hopes are ruined, but I would not share yours. If you have any.'

For a moment his eyes kindled. 'Go!' he said. 'I did not spend long study on these matters for naught. You have doomed yourselves, and you know it. And it will afford me some comfort as I wander to think that you pulled down your own house when you destroyed mine. And now, what ship will bear you back across so wide a sea?' he mocked. 'It will be a grey ship, and full of ghosts.' He laughed, but his voice was cracked and hideous.

'Get up, you idiot!' he shouted to the other beggar, who had sat down on the ground; and he struck him with his staff. 'Turn about! If these fine folk are going our way, then we will take another. Get on, or I'll give you no crust for your supper!'

The beggar turned and slouched past whimpering: 'Poor old Gríma! Poor old Gríma! Always beaten and cursed. How I hate him! I wish I could leave him!'

'Then leave him!' said Gandalf.

But Wormtongue only shot a glance of his bleared eyes full of terror at Gandalf, and then shuffled quickly past behind Saruman. As the wretched pair passed by the company they came to the hobbits, and Saruman stopped and stared at them; but they looked at him with pity.

'So you have come to gloat too, have you, my urchins?' he said. 'You don't care what a beggar lacks, do you? For you have all you want, food and fine clothes, and the best weed for your pipes. Oh yes, I know! I know where it comes from. You would not give a pipeful to a beggar, would you?'

'I would, if I had any,' said Frodo.

'You can have what I have got left,' said Merry, 'if you will wait a moment.' He got down and searched in the bag at his saddle. Then he handed to Saruman a leather pouch. 'Take what there is,' he said. 'You are welcome to it; it came from the flotsam of Isengard.'

'Mine, mine, yes and dearly bought!' cried Saruman, clutching at the pouch. 'This is only a repayment in token; for you took more, I'll be bound. Still, a beggar must be grateful, if a thief returns him even a morsel of his own. Well, it will serve you right when you come home, if you find things less good in the Southfarthing than you would like. Long may your land be short of leaf!'

'Thank you!' said Merry. 'In that case I will have my pouch back, which is not yours and has journeyed far with me. Wrap the weed in a rag of your own.'

'One thief deserves another,' said Saruman, and turned his back on Merry, and kicked Wormtongue, and went away towards the wood.

'Well, I like that!' said Pippin. 'Thief indeed! What of our claim for waylaying, wounding, and orc-dragging us through Rohan?'

'Ah!' said Sam. 'And *bought* he said. How, I wonder? And I didn't like the sound of what he said about the Southfarthing. It's time we got back.'

'I'm sure it is,' said Frodo. 'But we can't go any quicker, if we are to see Bilbo. I am going to Rivendell first, whatever happens.'

'Yes, I think you had better do that,' said Gandalf. 'But alas for Saruman! I fear nothing more can be made of him. He has withered altogether. All the same, I am not sure that Treebeard is right: I fancy he could do some mischief still in a small mean way.'

Next day they went on into northern Dunland, where no men now dwelt, though it was a green and pleasant country. September came in with golden days and silver nights, and they rode at ease until they reached the Swanfleet river, and found the old ford, east of the falls where it went down suddenly into the lowlands. Far to the west in a haze lay the meres and eyots through which it wound its way to the Greyflood: there countless swans housed in a land of reeds.

So they passed into Eregion, and at last a fair morning dawned, shimmering above gleaming mists; and looking from their camp on a low hill the travellers saw away in the east the Sun catching three peaks that thrust up into the sky through floating clouds: Caradhras, Celebdil, and Fanuidhol. They were near to the Gates of Moria.

Here now for seven days they tarried, for the time was at hand for another parting which they were loth to make. Soon Celeborn and Galadriel and their folk would turn eastward, and so pass by the Redhorn Gate and down the Dimrill Stair to the Silverlode and to their own country. They had journeyed thus far by the west-ways, for they had much to speak of with Elrond and with Gandalf, and here they lingered still in converse with their friends. Often long after the hobbits were wrapped in sleep they would sit together under the stars, recalling the ages that were gone and all their joys and labours in the world, or holding council, concerning the days to come. If any wanderer had chanced to pass, little would he have seen or heard, and it would have seemed to him only that he saw grey figures, carved in stone, memorials of forgotten things now lost in unpeopled lands. For they did not move or speak with mouth, looking from mind to mind; and only their shining eyes stirred and kindled as their thoughts went to and fro.

But at length all was said, and they parted again for a while, until it was time for the Three Rings to pass away. Quickly fading into the stones and the shadows the grey-cloaked people of Lórien rode towards the mountains; and those who were going to Rivendell sat on the hill and watched, until there came out of the gathering mist a flash; and then they saw no more. Frodo knew that Galadriel had held aloft her ring in token of farewell.

Sam turned away and sighed: 'I wish I was going back to Lórien!'

At last one evening they came over the high moors, suddenly as to travellers it always seemed, to the brink of the deep valley of Rivendell and saw far below the lamps shining in Elrond's house. And they went down and crossed the bridge and came to the doors, and all the house was filled with light and song for joy at Elrond's homecoming.

First of all, before they had eaten or washed or even shed their cloaks, the hobbits went in search of Bilbo. They found him all alone in his little room. It was littered with papers and pens and pencils; but Bilbo was sitting in a chair before a small bright fire. He looked very old, but peaceful, and sleepy.

He opened his eyes and looked up as they came in. 'Hullo, hullo!' he said. 'So you've come back? And tomorrow's my birthday, too. How clever of you! Do you know, I shall be one hundred and twenty-nine? And in one year more, if I am spared, I shall equal the Old Took. I should like to beat him; but we shall see.'

After the celebration of Bilbo's birthday the four hobbits stayed in Rivendell for some days, and they sat much with their old friend, who spent most of his time now in his room, except at meals. For these he was still very punctual as a rule, and he seldom failed to wake up in time for them. Sitting round the fire they told him in turn all that they could remember of their journeys and adventures. At first he pretended to take some notes; but he often fell asleep; and when he woke he would say: 'How splendid! How wonderful! But where were we?' Then they went on with the story from the point where he had begun to nod.

The only part that seemed really to rouse him and hold his attention was the account of the crowning and marriage of Aragorn. 'I was invited to the wedding, of course,' he said. 'And I have waited for it long enough. But somehow, when it came to it, I found I had so much to do here; and packing is such a bother.'

When nearly a fortnight had passed Frodo looked out of his window and saw that there had been a frost in the night, and the cobwebs were like white nets. Then suddenly he knew that he must go, and say good-bye to Bilbo. The weather was still calm and fair, after one of the most lovely summers that people could remember; but October had come, and it must break soon and begin to rain and blow again. And there was still a very long way to go. Yet it was not really the thought of the weather that stirred him. He had a feeling that it was time he went back to the Shire. Sam shared it. Only the night before he had said:

'Well, Mr. Frodo, we've been far and seen a deal, and yet I don't think we've found a better place than this. There's something of everything here, if you understand me: the Shire and the Golden Wood and Gondor and kings' houses and inns and meadows and mountains all mixed. And yet, somehow, I feel we ought to be going soon. I'm worried about my gaffer, to tell you the truth.'

'Yes, something of everything, Sam, except the Sea,' Frodo had answered; and he repeated it now to himself: 'Except the Sea.'

That day Frodo spoke to Elrond, and it was agreed that they should leave the next morning. To their delight Gandalf said: 'I think I shall come too. At least as far as Bree. I want to see Butterbur.'

In the evening they went to say good-bye to Bilbo. 'Well, if you must go, you must,' he said. 'I am sorry. I shall miss you. It is nice just to know that you are about the place. But I am getting very sleepy.' Then he gave Frodo his mithril-coat and Sting, forgetting that he had already done so; and he gave him also three books of lore that he had made at various times, written in his spidery hand, and labelled on their red backs: *Translations from the Elvish, by B.B.*

To Sam he gave a little bag of gold. 'Almost the last drop of the Smaug vintage,' he said. 'May come in useful, if you think of getting married, Sam.' Sam blushed.

'I have nothing much to give to you young fellows,' he said to Merry and Pippin, 'except good advice.' And when he had given them a fair sample of this, he added a last item in Shire-fashion: 'Don't let your heads get too big for your hats! But if you don't finish growing up soon, you are going to find hats and clothes expensive.'

'But if you want to beat the Old Took,' said Pippin, 'I don't see why we shouldn't try and beat the Bullroarer.'

Bilbo laughed, and he produced out of a pocket two beautiful pipes with pearl mouth-pieces and bound with fine-wrought silver. 'Think of me when you smoke them!' he said. 'The Elves made them for me, but I don't smoke now.' And then suddenly he nodded and went to sleep for a little; and when he woke up again he said: 'Now where were we? Yes, of course, giving presents. Which reminds me: what's become of my ring, Frodo, that you took away?'

'I have lost it, Bilbo dear,' said Frodo. 'I got rid of it, you know.'

'What a pity!' said Bilbo. 'I should have liked to see it again. But no, how silly of me! That's what you went for, wasn't it: to get rid of it? But it is all so confusing, for such a lot of other things seem to have got mixed up with it: Aragorn's affairs, and the White Council, and Gondor, and the Horsemen, and Southrons, and oliphaunts – did you really see one, Sam? – and caves and towers and golden trees, and goodness knows what besides.

'I evidently came back by much too straight a road from my trip. I think Gandalf might have shown me round a bit. But then the auction would have been over before I got back, and I should have had even more trouble than I did. Anyway it's too late now; and really I think it's much more comfortable to sit here and hear about it all. The fire's very cosy here, and the food's *very* good, and there are Elves when you want them. What more could one want?

The Road goes ever on and on
Out from the door where it began.
Now far ahead the Road has gone,
Let others follow it who can!
Let them a journey new begin,
But I at last with weary feet
Will turn towards the lighted inn,
My evening-rest and sleep to meet.'

And as Bilbo murmured the last words his head dropped on his chest and he slept soundly.

The evening deepened in the room, and the firelight burned brighter; and they looked at Bilbo as he slept and saw that his face was smiling. For some time they sat in silence; and then Sam looking round at the room and the shadows flickering on the walls, said softly:

'I don't think, Mr. Frodo, that he's done much writing while we've been away. He won't ever write our story now.'

At that Bilbo opened an eye, almost as if he had heard. Then he roused himself. 'You see, I am getting so sleepy,' he said. 'And when I have time to write, I only really like writing poetry. I wonder, Frodo my dear fellow, if you would very much mind tidying things up a bit before you go? Collect all my notes and papers, and my diary too, and take them with you, if you will. You see, I haven't much time for the selection and the arrangement and all that. Get Sam to help, and when you've knocked things into shape, come back, and I'll run over it. I won't be too critical.'

'Of course I'll do it!' said Frodo. 'And of course I'll come back soon: it won't be dangerous any more. There is a real king now, and he will soon put the roads in order.'

'Thank you, my dear fellow!' said Bilbo. 'That really is a very great relief to my mind.' And with that he fell asleep again.

The next day Gandalf and the hobbits took leave of Bilbo in his room, for it was cold out of doors; and then they said farewell to Elrond and all his household.

As Frodo stood upon the threshold, Elrond wished him a fair journey, and blessed him, and he said:

'I think, Frodo, that maybe you will not need to come back, unless you come very soon. For about this time of the year, when the leaves are gold before they fall, look for Bilbo in the woods of the Shire. I shall be with him.'

These words no one else heard, and Frodo kept them to himself.

CHAPTER VII

HOMEWARD BOUND

At last the hobbits had their faces turned towards home. They were eager now to see the Shire again; but at first they rode only slowly, for Frodo had been ill at ease. When they came to the Ford of Bruinen, he had halted, and seemed loth to ride into the stream; and they noted that for a while his eyes appeared not to see them or things about him. All that day he was silent. It was the sixth of October.

'Are you in pain, Frodo?' said Gandalf quietly as he rode by Frodo's side.

'Well, yes I am,' said Frodo. 'It is my shoulder. The wound aches, and the memory of darkness is heavy on me. It was a year ago today.'

'Alas! there are some wounds that cannot be wholly cured,' said Gandalf.

'I fear it may be so with mine,' said Frodo. 'There is no real going back. Though I may come to the Shire, it will not seem the same; for I shall not be the same. I am wounded with knife, sting, and tooth, and a long burden. Where shall I find rest?'

Gandalf did not answer.

By the end of the next day the pain and unease had passed, and Frodo was merry again, as merry as if he did not remember the blackness of the day before. After that the journey went well, and the days went quickly by; for they rode at leisure, and often they lingered in the fair woodlands where the leaves were red and yellow in the autumn sun. At length they came to Weathertop; and it was then drawing towards evening and the shadow of the hill lay dark on the road. Then Frodo begged them to hasten, and he would not look towards the hill, but rode through its shadow with head bowed and cloak drawn close about him. That night the weather changed, and a wind came from the West laden with rain, and it blew loud and chill, and the yellow leaves whirled like birds in the air. When they came to the Chetwood already the boughs were almost bare, and a great curtain of rain veiled Bree Hill from their sight.

So it was that near the end of a wild and wet evening in the last days of October the five travellers rode up the climbing road and came to the South-gate of Bree. It was locked fast; and the rain blew in their faces, and in the darkening sky low clouds went hurrying by, and their hearts sank a little, for they had expected more welcome.

When they had called many times, at last the Gate-keeper came out, and they saw that he carried a great cudgel. He looked at them with fear and suspicion; but when he saw that Gandalf was there, and that his companions were hobbits, in spite of their strange gear, then he brightened and wished them welcome.

'Come in!' he said, unlocking the gate. 'We won't stay for news out here in the cold and the wet, a ruffianly evening. But old Barley will no doubt give you a welcome at *The Pony*, and there you'll hear all there is to hear.'

'And there you'll hear later all that we say, and more,' laughed Gandalf. 'How is Harry?'

The Gate-keeper scowled. 'Gone,' he said. 'But you'd best ask Barliman. Good evening!'

'Good evening to you!' they said, and passed through; and then they noticed that behind the hedge at the road-side a long low hut had been built, and a number of men had come out and were staring at them over the fence. When they came to Bill Ferny's house they saw that the hedge there was tattered and unkempt, and the windows were all boarded up.

'Do you think you killed him with that apple, Sam?' said Pippin.

'I'm not so hopeful, Mr. Pippin,' said Sam. 'But I'd like to know what became of that poor pony. He's been on my mind many a time, and the wolves howling and all.'

At last they came to *The Prancing Pony*, and that at least looked outwardly unchanged; and there were lights behind the red curtains in the lower windows. They rang the bell, and Nob came to the door, and opened it a crack and peeped through; and when he saw them standing under the lamp he gave a cry of surprise.

'Mr. Butterbur! Master!' he shouted. 'They've come back!'

'Oh have they? I'll learn them,' came Butterbur's voice, and out he came with a rush, and he had a club in his hand. But when he saw who they were he stopped short, and the black scowl on his face changed to wonder and delight.

'Nob, you woolly-pated ninny!' he cried. 'Can't you give old friends their names? You shouldn't go scaring me like that, with times as they are. Well, well! And where have you come from? I never expected to see any of you folk again, and that's a fact: going off into the Wild with that Strider, and all those Black Men about. But I'm right glad to see you, and none more than Gandalf. Come in! Come in! The same rooms as before? They're free. Indeed most rooms are empty these days, as I'll not hide from you, for you'll find it out soon enough. And I'll see what can be done about supper, as soon as may be; but I'm short-handed at present. Hey, Nob you slowcoach! Tell Bob! Ah, but there I'm forgetting, Bob's gone: goes home to his folk at nightfall now. Well, take the guests' ponies to the stables, Nob! And you'll be taking your horse to his stable yourself, Gandalf, I don't doubt. A fine beast, as I said when I first set eyes on him. Well, come in! Make yourselves at home!'

Mr. Butterbur had at any rate not changed his manner of talking, and still seemed to live in his old breathless bustle. And yet there was hardly anybody about, and all was quiet; from the Common Room there came a low murmur of no more than two or three voices. And seen closer in the light of two candles that he lit and carried before them the landlord's face looked rather wrinkled and careworn.

He led them down the passage to the parlour that they had used on that strange night more than a year ago; and they followed him, a little disquieted, for it seemed plain to them that old Barliman was putting a brave face on some trouble. Things were not what they had been. But they said nothing, and waited.

As they expected Mr. Butterbur came to the parlour after supper to see if all had been to their liking. As indeed it had: no change for the worse had yet come upon the beer or the victuals at *The Pony*, at any rate. 'Now I won't make so bold as to suggest you should come to the Common Room tonight,' said Butterbur. 'You'll be tired; and there isn't many folk there this evening, anyway. But if you could spare me half an hour before you go to your beds, I would dearly like to have some talk with you, quiet-like by ourselves.'

'That is just what we should like, too,' said Gandalf. 'We are not tired. We have been taking things easy. We were wet, cold and hungry, but all that you have cured. Come, sit down! And if you have any pipe-weed, we'll bless you.'

'Well, if you'd called for anything else, I'd have been happier,' said Butterbur. 'That's just a thing that we're short of, seeing how we've only got what we grow ourselves, and that's not enough. There's none to be had from the Shire these days. But I'll do what I can.'

When he came back he brought them enough to last them for a day or two, a wad of uncut leaf. 'Southlinch,' he said, 'and the best we have; but not the match of Southfarthing, as I've always said, though I'm all for Bree in most matters, begging your pardon.'

They put him in a large chair by the wood-fire, and Gandalf sat on the other side of the hearth, and the hobbits in low chairs between them; and then they talked for many times half an hour, and exchanged all such news as Mr. Butterbur wished to hear or give. Most of the things which they had to tell were a mere wonder and bewilderment to their host, and far beyond his vision; and they brought forth few comments other than: 'You don't say,' often repeated in defiance of the evidence of Mr. Butterbur's own ears. 'You don't say, Mr. Baggins, or is it Mr. Underhill? I'm getting so mixed up. You don't say, Master Gandalf! Well I never! Who'd have thought it in our times!'

But he did say much on his own account. Things were far from well, he would say. Business was not even fair, it was downright bad. 'No one comes nigh Bree now from Outside,' he said. 'And the inside folks, they stay at home mostly and keep their doors barred. It all comes of those newcomers and gangrels that began coming up the Greenway last year, as you may remember; but more came later. Some were just poor bodies running away from trouble; but most were bad men, full o' thievery and mischief. And there was trouble right here in Bree, bad trouble. Why, we had a real set-to, and there were some folk killed, killed dead! If you'll believe me.'

'I will indeed,' said Gandalf. 'How many?'

'Three and two,' said Butterbur, referring to the big folk and the little. 'There was poor Mat Heathertoes, and Rowlie Appledore, and little Tom Pickthorn from over the Hill; and Willie Banks from up-away, and one of the Underhills from Staddle: all good fellows, and they're missed. And Harry Goatleaf that used to be on the West-gate, and that Bill Ferny, they came in on the strangers' side, and they've gone off with them; and it's my belief they let them in. On the night of the fight, I mean. And that was after we showed them the gates and pushed them out: before the year's end, that was; and the fight was early in the New Year, after the heavy snow we had.

'And now they're gone for robbers and live outside, hiding in the woods beyond Archet, and out in the wilds north-away. It's like a bit of the bad old times tales tell of, I say. It isn't safe on the road and nobody goes far, and folk lock up early. We have to keep watchers all round the fence and put a lot of men on the gates at nights.'

'Well, no one troubled us,' said Pippin, 'and we came along slowly, and kept no watch. We thought we'd left all trouble behind us.'

'Ah, that you haven't, Master, more's the pity,' said Butterbur. 'But it's no wonder they left you alone. They wouldn't go for armed folk, with swords and helmets and shields and all. Make them think twice, that would. And I must say it put me aback a bit when I saw you.'

Then the hobbits suddenly realized that people had looked at them with amazement not out of surprise at their return so much as in wonder at their gear. They themselves had become so used to warfare and to riding in well-arrayed companies that they had quite forgotten that the bright mail peeping from under their cloaks, and the helms of Gondor and the Mark, and the fair devices on their shields, would seem outlandish in their own country. And Gandalf, too, was now riding on his tall grey horse, all clad in white with a great mantle of blue and silver over all, and the long sword Glamdring at his side.

Gandalf laughed. 'Well, well,' he said, 'if they are afraid of just five of us, then we have met worse enemies on our travels. But at any rate they will give you peace at night while we stay.'

'How long will that be?' said Butterbur. 'I'll not deny we should be glad to have you about for a bit. You see, we're not used to such troubles; and the Rangers have all gone away, folk tell me. I don't think we've rightly understood till now what they did for us. For there's been worse than robbers about. Wolves were howling round the fences last winter. And there's dark shapes in the woods, dreadful things that it makes the blood run cold to think of. It's been very disturbing, if you understand me.'

'I expect it has,' said Gandalf. 'Nearly all lands have been disturbed these days, very disturbed. But cheer up, Barliman! You have been on the edge of very great troubles, and I am only glad to hear that you have not been deeper in. But better times are coming. Maybe, better than any you remember. The Rangers have returned. We came back with them. And there is a king again, Barliman. He will soon be turning his mind this way.

'Then the Greenway will be opened again, and his messengers will come north, and there will be comings and goings, and the evil things will be driven out of the waste-lands. Indeed the waste in time will be waste no longer, and there will be people and fields where once there was wilderness.'

Mr. Butterbur shook his head. 'If there's a few decent respectable folk on the roads, that won't do no harm,' he said. 'But we don't want no more rabble and ruffians. And we don't want no outsiders at Bree, nor near Bree at all. We want to be let alone. I don't want a whole crowd o' strangers camping here and settling there and tearing up the wild country.'

'You will be let alone, Barliman,' said Gandalf. 'There is room enough for realms between Isen and Greyflood, or along the shore-lands south of the Brandywine, without any one living within many days' ride of Bree. And many folk used to dwell away north, a hundred miles or more from here, at the far end of the Greenway: on the North Downs or by Lake Evendim.'

'Up away by Deadmen's Dike?' said Butterbur, looking even more dubious. 'That's haunted land, they say. None but a robber would go there.'

'The Rangers go there,' said Gandalf. 'Deadmen's Dike, you say. So it has been called for long years; but its right name, Barliman, is Fornost Erain, Norbury of the Kings. And the King will come there again one day; and then you'll have some fair folk riding through.'

'Well, that sounds more hopeful, I'll allow,' said Butterbur. 'And it will be good for business, no doubt. So long as he lets Bree alone.'

'He will,' said Gandalf. 'He knows it and loves it.'

'Does he now?' said Butterbur looking puzzled. 'Though I'm sure I don't know why he should, sitting in his big chair up in his great castle, hundreds of miles away. And drinking wine out of a golden cup, I shouldn't wonder. What's *The Pony* to him, or mugs o' beer? Not but what my beer's good, Gandalf. It's been uncommon good, since you came in the autumn of last year and put a good word on it. And that's been a comfort in trouble, I will say.'

'Ah!' said Sam. 'But he says your beer is always good.'

'He says?'

'Of course he does. He's Strider. The chief of the Rangers. Haven't you got that into your head yet?'

It went in at last, and Butterbur's face was a study in wonder. The eyes in his broad face grew round, and his mouth opened wide, and he gasped. 'Strider!' he exclaimed when he got back his breath. 'Him with a crown and all and a golden cup! Well, what are we coming to?'

'Better times, for Bree at any rate,' said Gandalf.

'I hope so, I'm sure,' said Butterbur. 'Well, this has been the nicest chat I've had in a month of Mondays. And I'll not deny that I'll sleep easier tonight and with a lighter heart. You've given me a powerful lot to think over, but I'll put that off until tomorrow. I'm for bed, and I've no doubt you'll be glad of your beds too. Hey, Nob!' he called, going to the door. 'Nob, you slowcoach!'

'Nob!' he said to himself, slapping his forehead. 'Now what does that remind me of?'

'Not another letter you've forgotten, I hope, Mr. Butterbur?' said Merry.

'Now, now, Mr. Brandybuck, don't go reminding me of that! But there, you've broken my thought. Now where was I? Nob, stables, ah! that was it. I've something that belongs to you. If you recollect Bill Ferny and the horsethieving: his pony as you bought, well, it's here. Come back all of itself, it did. But where it had been to you know better than me. It was as shaggy as an old dog and as lean as a clothes-rail, but it was alive. Nob's looked after it.'

'What! My Bill?' cried Sam. 'Well, I was born lucky, whatever my gaffer may say. There's another wish come true! Where is he?' Sam would not go to bed until he had visited Bill in his stable.

The travellers stayed in Bree all the next day, and Mr. Butterbur could not complain of his business next evening at any rate. Curiosity overcame all fears, and his house was crowded. For a while out of politeness the hobbits visited the Common Room in the evening and answered a good many questions. Bree memories being retentive, Frodo was asked many times if he had written his book.

'Not yet,' he answered. 'I am going home now to put my notes in order.' He promised to deal with the amazing events at Bree, and so give a bit of interest to a book that appeared likely to treat mostly of the remote and less important affairs 'away south'.

Then one of the younger folk called for a song. But at that a hush fell, and he was frowned down, and the call was not repeated. Evidently there was no wish for any uncanny events in the Common Room again.

No trouble by day, nor any sound by night, disturbed the peace of Bree while the travellers remained there; but the next morning they got up early, for as the weather was still rainy they wished to reach the Shire before night, and it was a long ride. The Bree folk were all out to see them off, and were in merrier mood than they had been for a year; and those who had not seen the strangers in all their gear before gaped with wonder at them: at Gandalf with his white beard, and the light that seemed to gleam from him, as if his blue mantle was only a cloud over sunshine; and at the four hobbits like riders upon errantry out of almost forgotten tales. Even those who had laughed at all the talk about the King began to think there might be some truth in it.

'Well, good luck on your road, and good luck to your homecoming!' said Mr. Butterbur. 'I should have warned you before that all's not well in the Shire neither, if what we hear is true. Funny goings on, they say. But one thing drives out another, and I was full of my own troubles. But if I may be so bold, you've come back changed from your travels, and you look now like folk as can deal with troubles out of hand. I don't doubt you'll soon set all to rights. Good luck to you! And the oftener you come back the better I'll be pleased.'

They wished him farewell and rode away, and passed through the West-gate and on towards the Shire. Bill the pony was with them, and as before he had a good deal of baggage, but he trotted along beside Sam and seemed well content.

'I wonder what old Barliman was hinting at,' said Frodo.

'I can guess some of it,' said Sam gloomily. 'What I saw in the Mirror: trees cut down and all, and my old gaffer turned out of the Row. I ought to have hurried back quicker.'

'And something's wrong with the Southfarthing evidently,' said Merry. 'There's a general shortage of pipe-weed.'

'Whatever it is,' said Pippin, 'Lotho will be at the bottom of it: you can be sure of that.'

'Deep in, but not at the bottom,' said Gandalf. 'You have forgotten Saruman. He began to take an interest in the Shire before Mordor did.'

'Well, we've got you with us,' said Merry, 'so things will soon be cleared up.'

'I am with you at present,' said Gandalf, 'but soon I shall not be. I am not coming to the Shire. You must settle its affairs yourselves; that is what you have been trained for. Do you not yet understand? My time is over: it is no longer my task to set things to rights, nor to help folk to do so. And as for you, my dear friends, you will need no help. You are grown up now. Grown indeed very high; among the great you are, and I have no longer any fear at all for any of you.

'But if you would know, I am turning aside soon. I am going to have a long talk with Bombadil: such a talk as I have not had in all my time. He is a moss-gatherer, and I have been a stone doomed to rolling. But my rolling days are ending, and now we shall have much to say to one another.'

In a little while they came to the point on the East Road where they had taken leave of Bombadil; and they hoped and half expected to see him standing there to greet them as they went by. But there was no sign of him; and there was a grey mist on the Barrow-downs southwards, and a deep veil over the Old Forest far away.

They halted and Frodo looked south wistfully. 'I should dearly like to see the old fellow again,' he said. 'I wonder how he is getting on?'

'As well as ever, you may be sure,' said Gandalf. 'Quite untroubled; and I should guess, not much interested in anything that we have done or seen, unless perhaps in our visits to the Ents. There may be a time later for you to go and see him. But if I were you, I should press on now for home, or you will not come to the Brandywine Bridge before the gates are locked.'

'But there aren't any gates,' said Merry, 'not on the Road; you know that quite well. There's the Buckland Gate, of course; but they'll let me through that at any time.'

'There weren't any gates, you mean,' said Gandalf. 'I think you will find some now. And you might have more trouble even at the Buckland Gate than you think. But you'll manage all right. Good-bye, dear friends! Not for the last time, not yet. Good-bye!'

He turned Shadowfax off the Road, and the great horse leaped the green dike that here ran beside it; and then at a cry from Gandalf he was gone, racing towards the Barrow-downs like a wind from the North.

'Well here we are, just the four of us that started out together,' said Merry. 'We have left all the rest behind, one after another. It seems almost like a dream that has slowly faded.'

'Not to me,' said Frodo. 'To me it feels more like falling asleep again.'

CHAPTER VIII

THE SCOURING OF THE SHIRE

It was after nightfall when, wet and tired, the travellers came at last to the Brandywine, and they found the way barred. At either end of the Bridge there was a great spiked gate; and on the further side of the river they could see that some new houses had been built: two-storeyed with narrow straight-sided windows, bare and dimly lit, all very gloomy and un-Shirelike.

They hammered on the outer gate and called, but there was at first no answer; and then to their surprise someone blew a horn, and the lights in the windows went out. A voice shouted in the dark:

'Who's that? Be off! You can't come in. Can't you read the notice: *No admittance between sundown and sunrise*?'

'Of course we can't read the notice in the dark,' Sam shouted back. 'And if hobbits of the Shire are to be kept out in the wet on a night like this, I'll tear down your notice when I find it.'

At that a window slammed, and a crowd of hobbits with lanterns poured out of the house on the left. They opened the further gate, and some came over the bridge. When they saw the travellers they seemed frightened.

'Come along!' said Merry, recognizing one of the hobbits. 'If you don't know me, Hob Hayward, you ought to. I am Merry Brandybuck, and I should like to know what all this is about, and what a Bucklander like you is doing here. You used to be on the Hay Gate.'

'Bless me! It's Master Merry, to be sure, and all dressed up for fighting!' said old Hob. 'Why, they said you was dead! Lost in the Old Forest by all accounts. I'm pleased to see you alive after all!'

'Then stop gaping at me through the bars, and open the gate!' said Merry.

'I'm sorry, Master Merry, but we have orders.'

'Whose orders?'

'The Chief's up at Bag End.'

'Chief? Chief? Do you mean Mr. Lotho?' said Frodo.

'I suppose so, Mr. Baggins; but we have to say just "the Chief" nowadays.'

'Do you indeed!' said Frodo. 'Well, I am glad he has dropped the Baggins at any rate. But it is evidently high time that the family dealt with him and put him in his place.'

A hush fell on the hobbits beyond the gate. 'It won't do no good talking that way,' said one. 'He'll get to hear of it. And if you make so much noise, you'll wake the Chief's Big Man.'

'We shall wake him up in a way that will surprise him,' said Merry. 'If you mean that your precious Chief has been hiring ruffians out of the wild, then we've not come back too soon.' He sprang from his pony, and seeing the notice in the light of the lanterns, he tore it down and threw it over the gate. The hobbits backed away and made no move to open it. 'Come on, Pippin!' said Merry. 'Two is enough.'

Merry and Pippin climbed the gate, and the hobbits fled. Another horn sounded. Out of the bigger house on the right a large heavy figure appeared against a light in the doorway.

'What's all this,' he snarled as he came forward. 'Gate-breaking? You clear out, or I'll break your filthy little necks!' Then he stopped, for he had caught the gleam of swords.

'Bill Ferny,' said Merry, 'if you don't open that gate in ten seconds, you'll regret it. I shall set steel to you, if you don't obey. And when you have opened the gates you will go through them and never return. You are a ruffian and a highway-robber.'

Bill Ferny flinched and shuffled to the gate and unlocked it. 'Give me the key!' said Merry. But the ruffian flung it at his head and then darted out into the darkness. As he passed the ponies one of them let fly with his heels and just caught him as he ran. He went off with a yelp into the night and was never heard of again.

'Neat work, Bill,' said Sam, meaning the pony.

'So much for your Big Man,' said Merry. 'We'll see the Chief later. In the meantime we want a lodging for the night, and as you seem to have pulled down the Bridge Inn and built this dismal place instead, you'll have to put us up.'

'I am sorry, Mr. Merry,' said Hob, 'but it isn't allowed.'

'What isn't allowed?'

'Taking in folk off-hand like, and eating extra food, and all that,' said Hob.

'What's the matter with the place?' said Merry. 'Has it been a bad year, or what? I thought it had been a fine summer and harvest.'

'Well no, the year's been good enough,' said Hob. 'We grows a lot of food, but we don't rightly know what becomes of it. It's all these "gatherers" and "sharers", I reckon, going round counting and measuring and taking off to storage. They do more gathering than sharing, and we never see most of the stuff again.'

'Oh come!' said Pippin yawning. 'This is all too tiresome for me tonight. We've got food in our bags. Just give us a room to lie down in. It'll be better than many places I have seen.'

The hobbits at the gate still seemed ill at ease, evidently some rule or other was being broken; but there was no gainsaying four such masterful travellers, all armed, and two of them uncommonly large and strong-looking. Frodo ordered the gates to be locked again. There was some sense at any rate in keeping a guard, while ruffians were still about. Then the four companions went into the hobbit guard-house and made themselves as comfortable as they could. It was a bare and ugly place, with a mean little grate that would not allow a good fire. In the upper rooms were little rows of hard beds, and on every wall there was a notice and a list of Rules. Pippin tore them down. There was no beer and very little food, but with what the travellers brought and shared out they all made a fair meal; and Pippin broke Rule 4 by putting most of next day's allowance of wood on the fire.

'Well now, what about a smoke, while you tell us what has been happening in the Shire?' he said.

'There isn't no pipe-weed now,' said Hob; 'at least only for the Chief's men. All the stocks seem to have gone. We do hear that waggon-loads of it went away down the old road out of the Southfarthing, over Sarn Ford way. That would be the end o' last year, after you left. But it had been going away quietly before that, in a small way. That Lotho——'

'Now you shut up, Hob Hayward!' cried several of the others. 'You know talk o' that sort isn't allowed. The Chief will hear of it, and we'll all be in trouble.'

'He wouldn't hear naught, if some of you here weren't sneaks,' rejoined Hob hotly.

'All right, all right!' said Sam. 'That's quite enough. I don't want to hear no more. No welcome, no beer, no smoke, and a lot of rules and orc-talk instead. I hoped to have a rest, but I can see there's work and trouble ahead. Let's sleep and forget it till morning!'

The new 'Chief' evidently had means of getting news. It was a good forty miles from the Bridge to Bag End, but someone made the journey in a hurry. So Frodo and his friends soon discovered.

They had not made any definite plans, but had vaguely thought of going down to Crickhollow together first, and resting there a bit. But now, seeing what things were like, they decided to go straight to Hobbiton. So the next day they set out along the Road and jogged along steadily. The wind had dropped but the sky was grey. The land looked rather sad and forlorn; but it was after all the first of November and the fag-end of Autumn. Still there seemed an unusual amount of burning going on, and smoke rose from many points round about. A great cloud of it was going up far away in the direction of the Woody End.

As evening fell they were drawing near to Frogmorton, a village right on the Road, about twenty-two miles from the Bridge. There they meant to stay the night; *The Floating Log* at Frogmorton was a good inn. But as they came to the east end of the village they met a barrier with a large board saying NO ROAD; and behind it stood a large band of Shirriffs with staves in their hands and feathers in their caps, looking both important and rather scared.

'What's all this?' said Frodo, feeling inclined to laugh.

'This is what it is, Mr. Baggins,' said the leader of the Shirriffs, a two-feather hobbit: 'You're arrested for Gate-breaking, and Tearing up of Rules, and Assaulting Gate-keepers, and Trespassing, and Sleeping in Shire-buildings without Leave, and Bribing Guards with Food.'

'And what else?' said Frodo.

'That'll do to go on with,' said the Shirriff-leader.

'I can add some more, if you'd like it,' said Sam. 'Calling your Chief Names, Wishing to punch his Pimply Face, and Thinking you Shirriffs look a lot of Tom-fools.'

'There now, Mister, that'll do. It's the Chief's orders that you're to come along quiet. We're going to take you to Bywater and hand you over to the Chief's Men; and when he deals with your case you can have your say. But if you don't want to stay in the Lockholes any longer than you need, I should cut the say short, if I was you.'

To the discomfiture of the Shirriffs Frodo and his companions all roared with laughter. 'Don't be absurd!' said Frodo. 'I am going where I please, and in my own time. I happen to be going to Bag End on business, but if you insist on going too, well that is your affair.'

'Very well, Mr. Baggins,' said the leader, pushing the barrier aside. 'But don't forget I've arrested you.'

'I won't,' said Frodo. 'Never. But I may forgive you. Now I am not going any further today, so if you'll kindly escort me to *The Floating Log*, I'll be obliged.'

'I can't do that, Mr. Baggins. The inn's closed. There's a Shirriff-house at the far end of the village. I'll take you there.'

'All right,' said Frodo. 'Go on and we'll follow.'

Sam had been looking the Shirriffs up and down and had spotted one that he knew. 'Hey, come here Robin Smallburrow!' he called. 'I want a word with you.'

With a sheepish glance at his leader, who looked wrathful but did not dare to interfere, Shirriff Smallburrow fell back and walked beside Sam, who got down off his pony.

'Look here, Cock-robin!' said Sam. 'You're Hobbiton-bred and ought to have more sense, coming a-waylaying Mr. Frodo and all. And what's all this about the inn being closed?'

'They're all closed,' said Robin. 'The Chief doesn't hold with beer. Leastways that is how it started. But now I reckon it's his Men that has it all. And he doesn't hold with folk moving about; so if they will or they must, then they has to go to the Shirriff-house and explain their business.'

'You ought to be ashamed of yourself having anything to do with such nonsense,' said Sam. 'You used to like the inside of an inn better than the outside yourself. You were always popping in, on duty or off.'

'And so I would be still, Sam, if I could. But don't be hard on me. What can I do? You know how I went for a Shirriff seven years ago, before any of this began. Gave me a chance of walking round the country and seeing folk, and hearing the news, and knowing where the good beer was. But now it's different.'

'But you can give it up, stop Shirriffing, if it has stopped being a respectable job,' said Sam.

'We're not allowed to,' said Robin.

'If I hear *not allowed* much oftener,' said Sam, 'I'm going to get angry.'

'Can't say as I'd be sorry to see it,' said Robin lowering his voice. 'If we all got angry together something might be done. But it's these Men, Sam, the Chief's Men. He sends them round everywhere, and if any of us small folk stand up for our rights, they drag him off to the Lockholes. They took old Flourdumpling, old Will Whitfoot the Mayor, first, and they've taken a lot more. Lately it's been getting worse. Often they beat 'em now.'

'Then why do you do their work for them?' said Sam angrily. 'Who sent you to Frogmorton?'

'No one did. We stay here in the big Shirriff-house. We're the First Eastfarthing Troop now. There's hundreds of Shirriffs all told, and they want more, with all these new rules. Most of them are in it against their will, but not all. Even in the Shire there are some as like minding other folk's business and talking big. And there's worse than that: there's a few as do spy-work for the Chief and his Men.'

'Ah! So that's how you had news of us, is it?'

'That's right. We aren't allowed to send by it now, but they use the old Quick Post service, and keep special runners at different points. One came in from Whitfurrows last night with a "secret message", and another took it on from here. And a message came back this afternoon saying you was to be arrested and taken to Bywater, not direct to the Lockholes. The Chief wants to see you at once, evidently.'

'He won't be so eager when Mr. Frodo has finished with him,' said Sam.

The Shirriff-house at Frogmorton was as bad as the Bridge-house. It had only one storey, but it had the same narrow windows, and it was built of ugly pale bricks, badly laid. Inside it was damp and cheerless, and supper was served on a long bare table that had not been scrubbed for weeks. The food deserved no better setting. The travellers were glad to leave the place. It was about eighteen miles to Bywater, and they set off at ten o'clock in the morning. They would have started earlier, only the delay so plainly annoyed the Shirriff-leader. The west wind had shifted northward and it was turning colder, but the rain was gone.

It was rather a comic cavalcade that left the village, though the few folk that came out to stare at the 'get-up' of the travellers did not seem quite sure whether laughing was allowed. A dozen Shirriffs had been told off as escort to the 'prisoners'; but Merry made them march in front, while Frodo and his friends rode behind. Merry, Pippin, and Sam sat at their ease laughing and talking and singing, while the Shirriffs stumped along trying to look stern and important. Frodo, however, was silent and looked rather sad and thoughtful.

The last person they passed was a sturdy old gaffer clipping a hedge. 'Hullo, hullo!' he jeered. 'Now who's arrested who?'

Two of the Shirriffs immediately left the party and went towards him. 'Leader!' said Merry. 'Order your fellows back to their places at once, if you don't want me to deal with them!'

The two hobbits at a sharp word from the leader came back sulkily. 'Now get on!' said Merry, and after that the travellers saw to it that their ponies' pace was quick enough to push the Shirriffs along as fast as they could go. The sun came out, and in spite of the chilly wind they were soon puffing and sweating.

At the Three-Farthing Stone they gave it up. They had done nearly fourteen miles with only one rest at noon. It was now three o'clock. They were hungry and very footsore and they could not stand the pace.

'Well, come along in your own time!' said Merry. 'We are going on.'

'Good-bye, Cock-robin!' said Sam. 'I'll wait for you outside *The Green Dragon*, if you haven't forgotten where that is. Don't dawdle on the way!'

'You're breaking arrest, that's what you're doing,' said the leader ruefully, 'and I can't be answerable.'

'We shall break a good many things yet, and not ask you to answer,' said Pippin. 'Good luck to you!'

The travellers trotted on, and as the sun began to sink towards the White Downs far away on the western horizon they came to Bywater by its wide pool; and there they had their first really painful shock. This was Frodo and Sam's own country, and they found out now that they cared about it more than any other place in the world. Many of the houses that they had known were missing. Some seemed to have been burned down. The pleasant row of old hobbit-holes in the bank on the north side of the Pool were deserted, and their little gardens that used to run down bright to the water's edge were rank with weeds. Worse, there was a whole line of the ugly new houses all along Pool Side, where the Hobbiton Road ran close to the bank. An avenue of trees had stood there. They were all gone. And looking with dismay up the road towards Bag End they saw a tall chimney of brick in the distance. It was pouring out black smoke into the evening air.

Sam was beside himself. 'I'm going right on, Mr. Frodo!' he cried. 'I'm going to see what's up. I want to find my gaffer.'

'We ought to find out first what we're in for, Sam,' said Merry. 'I guess that the "Chief" will have a gang of ruffians handy. We had better find someone who will tell us how things are round here.'

But in the village of Bywater all the houses and holes were shut, and no one greeted them. They wondered at this, but they soon discovered the reason of it. When they reached *The Green Dragon*, the last house on the Hobbiton side, now lifeless and with broken windows, they were disturbed to see half a dozen large ill-favoured Men lounging against the inn-wall; they were squint-eyed and sallow-faced.

'Like that friend of Bill Ferny's at Bree,' said Sam.

'Like many that I saw at Isengard,' muttered Merry.

The ruffians had clubs in their hands and horns by their belts, but they had no other weapons, as far as could be seen. As the travellers rode up they left the wall and walked into the road, blocking the way.

'Where d'you think you're going?' said one, the largest and most evil-looking of the crew. 'There's no road for you any further. And where are those precious Shirriffs?'

'Coming along nicely,' said Merry. 'A little footsore, perhaps. We promised to wait for them here.'

'Garn, what did I say?' said the ruffian to his mates. 'I told Sharkey it was no good trusting those little fools. Some of our chaps ought to have been sent.'

'And what difference would that have made, pray?' said Merry. 'We are not used to footpads in this country, but we know how to deal with them.'

'Footpads, eh?' said the man. 'So that's your tone, is it? Change it, or we'll change it for you. You little folk are getting too uppish. Don't you trust too much in the Boss's kind heart. Sharkey's come now, and he'll do what Sharkey says.'

'And what may that be?' said Frodo quietly.

'This country wants waking up and setting to rights,' said the ruffian, 'and Sharkey's going to do it; and make it hard, if you drive him to it. You need a bigger Boss. And you'll get one before the year is out, if there's any more trouble. Then you'll learn a thing or two, you little rat-folk.'

'Indeed. I am glad to hear of your plans,' said Frodo. 'I am on my way to call on Mr. Lotho, and he may be interested to hear of them too.'

The ruffian laughed. 'Lotho! He knows all right. Don't you worry. He'll do what Sharkey says. Because if a Boss gives trouble, we can change him. See? And if little folks try to push in where they're not wanted, we can put them out of mischief. See?'

'Yes, I see,' said Frodo. 'For one thing, I see that you're behind the times and the news here. Much has happened since you left the South. Your day is over, and all other ruffians'. The Dark Tower has fallen, and there is a King in Gondor. And Isengard has been destroyed, and your precious master is a beggar in the wilderness. I passed him on the road. The King's messengers will ride up the Greenway now, not bullies from Isengard.'

The man stared at him and smiled. 'A beggar in the wilderness!' he mocked. 'Oh, is he indeed? Swagger it, swagger it, my little cock-a-whoop. But that won't stop us living in this fat little country where you have lazed long enough. And' – he snapped his fingers in Frodo's face – 'King's messengers! That for them! When I see one, I'll take notice, perhaps.'

This was too much for Pippin. His thoughts went back to the Field of Cormallen, and here was a squint-eyed rascal calling the Ring-bearer 'little cock-a-whoop'. He cast back his cloak, flashed out his sword, and the silver and sable of Gondor gleamed on him as he rode forward.

'I am a messenger of the King,' he said. 'You are speaking to the King's friend, and one of the most renowned in all the lands of the West. You are a ruffian and a fool. Down on your knees in the road and ask pardon, or I will set this troll's bane in you!'

The sword glinted in the westering sun. Merry and Sam drew their swords also and rode up to support Pippin; but Frodo did not move. The ruffians gave back. Scaring Breeland peasants, and bullying bewildered hobbits, had been their work. Fearless hobbits with bright swords and grim faces were a great surprise. And there was a note in the voices of these newcomers that they had not heard before. It chilled them with fear.

'Go!' said Merry. 'If you trouble this village again, you will regret it.' The three hobbits came on, and then the ruffians turned and fled, running away up the Hobbiton Road; but they blew their horns as they ran.

'Well, we've come back none too soon,' said Merry.

'Not a day too soon. Perhaps too late, at any rate to save Lotho,' said Frodo. 'Miserable fool, but I am sorry for him.'

'Save Lotho? Whatever do you mean?' said Pippin. 'Destroy him, I should say.'

'I don't think you quite understand things, Pippin,' said Frodo. 'Lotho never meant things to come to this pass. He has been a wicked fool, but he's caught now. The ruffians are on top, gathering, robbing and bullying, and running or ruining things as they like, in his name. And not in his name even for much longer. He's a prisoner in Bag End now, I expect, and very frightened. We ought to try and rescue him.'

'Well I am staggered!' said Pippin. 'Of all the ends to our journey that is the very last I should have thought of: to have to fight half-orcs and ruffians in the Shire itself – to rescue Lotho Pimple!'

'Fight?' said Frodo. 'Well, I suppose it may come to that. But remember: there is to be no slaying of hobbits, not even if they have gone over to the other side. Really gone over, I mean; not just obeying ruffians' orders because they are frightened. No hobbit has ever killed another on purpose in the Shire, and it is not to begin now. And nobody is to be killed at all, if it can be helped. Keep your tempers and hold your hands to the last possible moment!'

'But if there are many of these ruffians,' said Merry, 'it will certainly mean fighting. You won't rescue Lotho, or the Shire, just by being shocked and sad, my dear Frodo.'

'No,' said Pippin. 'It won't be so easy scaring them a second time. They were taken by surprise. You heard that horn-blowing? Evidently there are other ruffians near at hand. They'll be much bolder when there's more of them together. We ought to think of taking cover somewhere for the night. After all we're only four, even if we are armed.'

'I've an idea,' said Sam. 'Let's go to old Tom Cotton's down South Lane! He always was a stout fellow. And he has a lot of lads that were all friends of mine.'

'No!' said Merry. 'It's no good "getting under cover". That is just what people have been doing, and just what these ruffians like. They will simply come down on us in force, corner us, and then drive us out, or burn us in. No, we have got to do something at once.'

'Do what?' said Pippin.

'Raise the Shire!' said Merry. 'Now! Wake all our people! They hate all this, you can see: all of them except perhaps one or two rascals, and a few fools that want to be important, but don't at all understand what is really going on. But Shire-folk have been so comfortable so long they don't know what to do. They just want a match, though, and they'll go up in fire. The

Chief's Men must know that. They'll try to stamp on us and put us out quick. We've only got a very short time.

'Sam, you can make a dash for Cotton's farm, if you like. He's the chief person round here, and the sturdiest. Come on! I am going to blow the horn of Rohan, and give them all some music they have never heard before.'

They rode back to the middle of the village. There Sam turned aside and galloped off down the lane that led south to Cotton's. He had not gone far when he heard a sudden clear horn-call go up ringing into the sky. Far over hill and field it echoed; and so compelling was that call that Sam himself almost turned and dashed back. His pony reared and neighed.

'On, lad! On!' he cried. 'We'll be going back soon.'

Then he heard Merry change the note, and up went the Horn-cry of Buckland, shaking the air.

Awake! Awake! Fear, Fire, Foes! Awake!
Fire, Foes! Awake!

Behind him Sam heard a hubbub of voices and a great din and slamming of doors. In front of him lights sprang out in the gloaming; dogs barked; feet came running. Before he got to the lane's end there was Farmer Cotton with three of his lads, Young Tom, Jolly, and Nick, hurrying towards him. They had axes in their hands, and barred the way.

'Nay! It's not one of them ruffians,' Sam heard the farmer say. 'It's a hobbit by the size of it, but all dressed up queer. Hey!' he cried. 'Who are you, and what's all this to-do?'

'It's Sam, Sam Gamgee. I've come back.'

Farmer Cotton came up close and stared at him in the twilight. 'Well!' he exclaimed. 'The voice is right, and your face is no worse than it was, Sam. But I should a' passed you in the street in that gear. You've been in foreign parts, seemingly. We feared you were dead.'

'That I ain't!' said Sam. 'Nor Mr. Frodo. He's here and his friends. And that's the to-do. They're raising the Shire. We're going to clear out these ruffians, and their Chief too. We're starting now.'

'Good, good!' cried Farmer Cotton. 'So it's begun at last! I've been itching for trouble all this year, but folks wouldn't help. And I've had the wife and Rosie to think of. These ruffians don't stick at nothing. But come on now, lads! Bywater is up! We must be in it!'

'What about Mrs. Cotton and Rosie?' said Sam. 'It isn't safe yet for them to be left all alone.'

'My Nibs is with them. But you can go and help him, if you have a mind,' said Farmer Cotton with a grin. Then he and his sons ran off towards the village.

Sam hurried to the house. By the large round door at the top of the steps from the wide yard stood Mrs. Cotton and Rosie, and Nibs in front of them grasping a hay-fork.

'It's me!' shouted Sam as he trotted up. 'Sam Gamgee! So don't try prodding me, Nibs. Anyway, I've a mail-shirt on me.'

He jumped down from his pony and went up the steps. They stared at him in silence. 'Good evening, Mrs. Cotton!' he said. 'Hullo, Rosie!'

'Hullo, Sam!' said Rosie. 'Where've you been? They said you were dead; but I've been expecting you since the Spring. You haven't hurried, have you?'

'Perhaps not,' said Sam abashed. 'But I'm hurrying now. We're setting about the ruffians, and I've got to get back to Mr. Frodo. But I thought I'd have a look and see how Mrs. Cotton was keeping, and you, Rosie.'

'We're keeping nicely, thank you,' said Mrs. Cotton. 'Or should be, if it weren't for these thieving ruffians.'

'Well, be off with you!' said Rosie. 'If you've been looking after Mr. Frodo all this while, what d'you want to leave him for, as soon as things look dangerous?'

This was too much for Sam. It needed a week's answer, or none. He turned away and mounted his pony. But as he started off, Rosie ran down the steps.

'I think you look fine, Sam,' she said. 'Go on now! But take care of yourself, and come straight back as soon as you have settled the ruffians!'

When Sam got back he found the whole village roused. Already, apart from many younger lads, more than a hundred sturdy hobbits were assembled with axes, and heavy hammers, and long knives, and stout staves; and a few had hunting-bows. More were still coming in from outlying farms.

Some of the village-folk had lit a large fire, just to enliven things, and also because it was one of the things forbidden by the Chief. It burned bright as night came on. Others at Merry's orders were setting up barriers across the road at each end of the village. When the Shirriffs came up to the lower one they were dumbfounded; but as soon as they saw how things were, most of them took off their feathers and joined in the revolt. The others slunk away.

Sam found Frodo and his friends by the fire talking to old Tom Cotton, while an admiring crowd of Bywater folk stood round and stared.

'Well, what's the next move?' said Farmer Cotton.

'I can't say,' said Frodo, 'until I know more. How many of these ruffians are there?'

'That's hard to tell,' said Cotton. 'They moves about and comes and goes. There's sometimes fifty of them in their sheds up Hobbiton way; but they go out from there roving round, thieving or "gathering" as they call it. Still there's seldom less than a score round the Boss, as they names him. He's at Bag End, or was; but he don't go outside the grounds now. No one's seen him at all, in fact, for a week or two; but the Men don't let no one go near.'

'Hobbiton's not their only place, is it?' said Pippin.

'No, more's the pity,' said Cotton. 'There's a good few down south in Longbottom and by Sarn Ford, I hear; and some more lurking in the Woody End; and they've sheds at Waymeet. And then there's the Lockholes, as they call 'em: the old storage-tunnels at Michel Delving that they've made into prisons for those as stand up to them. Still I reckon there's not above three hundred of them in the Shire all told, and maybe less. We can master them, if we stick together.'

'Have they got any weapons?' asked Merry.

'Whips, knives, and clubs, enough for their dirty work: that's all they've showed so far,' said Cotton. 'But I dare say they've got other gear, if it comes to fighting. Some have bows, anyway. They've shot one or two of our folk.'

'There you are, Frodo!' said Merry. 'I knew we should have to fight. Well, they started the killing.'

'Not exactly,' said Cotton. 'Leastways not the shooting. Tooks started that. You see, your dad, Mr. Peregrin, he's never had no truck with this Lotho, not from the beginning: said that if anyone was going to play the chief at this time of day, it would be the right Thain of the Shire and no upstart. And when Lotho sent his Men they got no change out of him. Tooks are lucky, they've got those deep holes in the Green Hills, the Great Smials and all, and the ruffians can't come at 'em; and they won't let the ruffians come on their land. If they do, Tooks hunt 'em. Tooks shot three for prowling and robbing. After that the ruffians turned nastier. And they keep a pretty close watch on Tookland. No one gets in nor out of it now.'

'Good for the Tooks!' cried Pippin. 'But someone is going to get in again, now. I am off to the Smials. Anyone coming with me to Tuckborough?'

Pippin rode off with half a dozen lads on ponies. 'See you soon!' he cried. 'It's only fourteen miles or so over the fields. I'll bring you back an army of Tooks in the morning.' Merry blew a horn-call after them as they rode off into the gathering night. The people cheered.

'All the same,' said Frodo to all those who stood near, 'I wish for no killing; not even of the ruffians, unless it must be done, to prevent them from hurting hobbits.'

'All right!' said Merry. 'But we shall be having a visit from the Hobbiton gang any time now, I think. They won't come just to talk things over. We'll try to deal with them neatly, but we must be prepared for the worst. Now I've got a plan.'

'Very good,' said Frodo. 'You make the arrangements.'

Just then some hobbits, who had been sent out towards Hobbiton, came running in. 'They're coming!' they said. 'A score or more. But two have gone off west across country.'

'To Waymeet, that'll be,' said Cotton, 'to fetch more of the gang. Well, it's fifteen mile each way. We needn't trouble about them just yet.'

Merry hurried off to give orders. Farmer Cotton cleared the street, sending everyone indoors, except the older hobbits who had weapons of some sort. They had not long to wait. Soon they could hear loud voices, and then the tramping of heavy feet. Presently a whole squad of the ruffians came down the road. They saw the barrier and laughed. They did not imagine that there was anything in this little land that would stand up to twenty of their kind together.

The hobbits opened the barrier and stood aside. 'Thank you!' the Men jeered. 'Now run home to bed before you're whipped.' Then they marched along the street shouting: 'Put those lights out! Get indoors and stay there! Or we'll take fifty of you to the Lockholes for a year. Get in! The Boss is losing his temper.'

No one paid any heed to their orders; but as the ruffians passed, they closed in quietly behind and followed them. When the Men reached the fire there was Farmer Cotton standing all alone warming his hands.

'Who are you, and what d'you think you're doing?' said the ruffian-leader.

Farmer Cotton looked at him slowly. 'I was just going to ask you that,' he said. 'This isn't your country, and you're not wanted.'

'Well, you're wanted anyhow,' said the leader. 'We want you. Take him lads! Lockholes for him, and give him something to keep him quiet!'

The Men took one step forward and stopped short. There rose a roar of voices all round them, and suddenly they were aware that Farmer Cotton was not all alone. They were surrounded. In the dark on the edge of the firelight stood a ring of hobbits that had crept up out of the shadows. There was nearly two hundred of them, all holding some weapon.

Merry stepped forward. 'We have met before,' he said to the leader, 'and I warned you not to come back here. I warn you again: you are standing in the light and you are covered by archers. If you lay a finger on this farmer, or on anyone else, you will be shot at once. Lay down any weapons that you have!'

The leader looked round. He was trapped. But he was not scared, not now with a score of his fellows to back him. He knew too little of hobbits to understand his peril. Foolishly he decided to fight. It would be easy to break out.

'At 'em, lads!' he cried. 'Let 'em have it!'

With a long knife in his left hand and a club in the other he made a rush at the ring, trying to burst out back towards Hobbiton. He aimed a savage blow at Merry who stood in his way. He fell dead with four arrows in him.

That was enough for the others. They gave in. Their weapons were taken from them, and they were roped together, and marched off to an empty hut that they had built themselves, and there they were tied hand and foot, and locked up under guard. The dead leader was dragged off and buried.

'Seems almost too easy after all, don't it?' said Cotton. 'I said we could master them. But we needed a call. You came back in the nick o' time, Mr. Merry.'

'There's more to be done still,' said Merry. 'If you're right in your reckoning, we haven't dealt with a tithe of them yet. But it's dark now. I think the next stroke must wait until morning. Then we must call on the Chief.'

'Why not now?' said Sam. 'It's not much more than six o'clock. And I want to see my gaffer. D'you know what's come of him, Mr. Cotton?'

'He's not too well, and not too bad, Sam,' said the farmer. 'They dug up Bagshot Row, and that was a sad blow to him. He's in one of them new houses that the Chief's Men used to build while they still did any work other than burning and thieving: not above a mile from the end of Bywater. But he comes around to me, when he gets a chance, and I see he's better fed than some of the poor bodies. All against *The Rules*, of course. I'd have had him with me, but that wasn't allowed.'

'Thank'ee indeed, Mr. Cotton, and I'll never forget it,' said Sam. 'But I want to see him. That Boss and that Sharkey, as they spoke of, they might do a mischief up there before the morning.'

'All right, Sam,' said Cotton. 'Choose a lad or two, and go and fetch him to my house. You'll not have need to go near the old Hobbiton village over Water. My Jolly here will show you.'

Sam went off. Merry arranged for look-outs round the village and guards at the barriers during the night. Then he and Frodo went off with Farmer Cotton. They sat with the family in the warm kitchen, and the Cottons asked a few polite questions about their travels, but hardly listened to the answers: they were far more concerned with events in the Shire.

'It all began with Pimple, as we call him,' said Farmer Cotton; 'and it began as soon as you'd gone off, Mr. Frodo. He'd funny ideas, had Pimple. Seems he wanted to own everything himself, and then order other folk about. It soon came out that he already did own a sight more than was good for him; and he was always grabbing more, though where he got the money was a mystery: mills and malt-houses and inns, and farms, and leaf-plantations. He'd already bought Sandyman's mill before he came to Bag End, seemingly.

'Of course he started with a lot of property in the Southfarthing which he had from his dad; and it seems he'd been selling a lot o' the best leaf, and sending it away quietly for a year or two. But at the end o' last year he began sending away loads of stuff, not only leaf. Things began to get short, and winter coming on, too. Folk got angry, but he had his answer. A lot of Men, ruffians mostly, came with great waggons, some to carry off the goods south-away, and others to stay. And more came. And before we knew where we were they were planted here and there all over the Shire, and were felling trees and digging and building themselves sheds and houses just as they liked. At first goods and damage was paid for by Pimple; but soon they began lording it around and taking what they wanted.

'Then there was a bit of trouble, but not enough. Old Will the Mayor set off for Bag End to protest, but he never got there. Ruffians laid hands on him and took and locked him up in a hole in Michel Delving, and there he is now. And after that, it would be soon after New Year, there wasn't no more Mayor, and Pimple called himself Chief Shirriff, or just Chief, and did as he liked; and if anyone got "uppish" as they called it, they followed Will. So things went from bad to worse. There wasn't no smoke left, save for the Men; and the Chief didn't hold with beer, save for his Men, and closed all the inns; and everything except Rules got shorter and shorter, unless one could hide a bit of one's own when the ruffians went round gathering stuff up "for fair distribution": which meant they got it and we didn't, except for the leavings which you could have at the Shirriff-houses, if you could stomach them. All very bad. But since Sharkey came it's been plain ruination.'

'Who is this Sharkey?' said Merry. 'I heard one of the ruffians speak of him.'

'The biggest ruffian o' the lot, seemingly,' answered Cotton. 'It was about last harvest, end o' September maybe, that we first heard of him. We've never seen him, but he's up at Bag End; and he's the real Chief now, I guess. All the ruffians do what he says; and what he says is mostly: hack, burn, and ruin; and now it's come to killing. There's no longer even any bad sense in it. They cut down trees and let 'em lie, they burn houses and build no more.

'Take Sandyman's mill now. Pimple knocked it down almost as soon as he came to Bag End. Then he brought in a lot o' dirty-looking Men to build a bigger one and fill it full o' wheels and outlandish contraptions. Only that fool Ted was pleased by that, and he works there cleaning wheels for the Men, where his dad was the Miller and his own master. Pimple's idea was to grind more and faster, or so he said. He's got other mills like it. But you've got to have grist before you can grind; and there was no more for the new mill to do than for the old. But since Sharkey came they don't grind no more corn at all. They're always a-hammering and a-letting out a smoke and a stench, and there isn't no peace even at night in Hobbiton. And they pour out filth a purpose; they've fouled all the lower Water, and it's getting down into Brandywine. If they want to make the Shire into a desert, they're going the right way about it. I don't believe that fool of a Pimple's behind all this. It's Sharkey, I say.'

'That's right!' put in Young Tom. 'Why, they even took Pimple's old ma, that Lobelia, and he was fond of her, if no one else was. Some of the Hobbiton folk, they saw it. She comes down the lane with her old umberella. Some of the ruffians were going up with a big cart.

' "Where be you a-going?" says she.

' "To Bag End," says they.

' "What for?" says she.

' "To put up some sheds for Sharkey," says they.

' "Who said you could?" says she.

' "Sharkey," says they. "So get out o' the road, old hagling!"

' "I'll give you Sharkey, you dirty thieving ruffians!" says she, and ups with her umberella and goes for the leader, near twice her size. So they took her. Dragged her off to the Lockholes, at her age too. They've took others we miss more, but there's no denying she showed more spirit than most.'

Into the middle of this talk came Sam, bursting in with his gaffer. Old Gamgee did not look much older, but he was a little deafer.

'Good evening, Mr. Baggins!' he said. 'Glad indeed I am to see you safe back. But I've a bone to pick with you, in a manner o' speaking, if I may make so bold. You didn't never ought to have a' sold Bag End, as I always said. That's what started all the mischief. And while you've been trapessing in foreign parts, chasing Black Men up mountains from what my Sam says, though what for he don't make clear, they've been and dug up Bagshot Row and ruined my taters!'

'I am very sorry, Mr. Gamgee,' said Frodo. 'But now I've come back, I'll do my best to make amends.'

'Well, you can't say fairer than that,' said the gaffer. 'Mr. *Frodo* Baggins is a real gentlehobbit, I always have said, whatever you may think of some others of the name, begging your pardon. And I hope my Sam's behaved hisself and given satisfaction?'

'Perfect satisfaction, Mr. Gamgee,' said Frodo. 'Indeed, if you will believe it, he's now one of the most famous people in all the lands, and they are making songs about his deeds from here to the Sea and beyond the Great River.' Sam blushed, but he looked gratefully at Frodo, for Rosie's eyes were shining and she was smiling at him.

'It takes a lot o' believing,' said the gaffer, 'though I can see he's been mixing in strange company. What's come of his weskit? I don't hold with wearing ironmongery, whether it wears well or no.'

Farmer Cotton's household and all his guests were up early next morning. Nothing had been heard in the night, but more trouble would certainly come before the day was old. 'Seems as if none o' the ruffians were left up at Bag End,' said Cotton; 'but the gang from Waymeet will be along any time now.'

After breakfast a messenger from the Tookland rode in. He was in high spirits. 'The Thain has raised all our country,' he said, 'and the news is going like fire all ways. The ruffians that were watching our land have fled off south, those that escaped alive. The Thain has gone after them, to hold off the big gang down that way; but he's sent Mr. Peregrin back with all the other folk he can spare.'

The next news was less good. Merry, who had been out all night, came riding in about ten o'clock. 'There's a big band about four miles away,' he said. 'They're coming along the road from Waymeet, but a good many stray ruffians have joined up with them. There must be close on a hundred of them; and they're fire-raising as they come. Curse them!'

'Ah! This lot won't stay to talk, they'll kill, if they can,' said Farmer Cotton. 'If Tooks don't come sooner, we'd best get behind cover and shoot without arguing. There's got to be some fighting before this is settled, Mr. Frodo.'

The Tooks did come sooner. Before long they marched in, a hundred strong, from Tuckborough and the Green Hills with Pippin at their head. Merry now had enough sturdy hobbitry to deal with the ruffians. Scouts reported that they were keeping close together. They knew that the countryside had risen against them, and plainly meant to deal with the rebellion ruthlessly, at its centre in Bywater. But however grim they might be, they seemed to have no leader among them who understood warfare. They came on without any precautions. Merry laid his plans quickly.

The ruffians came tramping along the East Road, and without halting turned up the Bywater Road, which ran for some way sloping up between high banks with low hedges on top. Round a bend, about a furlong from the main road, they met a stout barrier of old farm-carts upturned. That halted them. At the same moment they became aware that the hedges on both sides, just above their heads, were all lined with hobbits. Behind them other hobbits now pushed out some more waggons that had been hidden in a field, and so blocked the way back. A voice spoke to them from above.

'Well, you have walked into a trap,' said Merry. 'Your fellows from Hobbiton did the same, and one is dead and the rest are prisoners. Lay down your weapons! Then go back twenty paces and sit down. Any who try to break out will be shot.'

But the ruffians could not now be cowed so easily. A few of them obeyed, but were immediately set on by their fellows. A score or more broke back and charged the waggons. Six were shot, but the remainder burst out, killing two hobbits, and then scattering across country in the direction of the Woody End. Two more fell as they ran. Merry blew a loud horn-call, and there were answering calls from a distance.

'They won't get far,' said Pippin. 'All that country is alive with our hunters now.'

Behind, the trapped Men in the lane, still about four score, tried to climb the barrier and the banks, and the hobbits were obliged to shoot many of them or hew them with axes. But many of the strongest and most desperate got out on the west side, and attacked their enemies fiercely, being now more bent on killing than escaping. Several hobbits fell, and the rest were wavering, when Merry and Pippin, who were on the east side, came across and charged the ruffians. Merry himself slew the leader, a great squint-eyed brute like a huge orc. Then he drew his forces off, encircling the last remnant of the Men in a wide ring of archers.

At last all was over. Nearly seventy of the ruffians lay dead on the field, and a dozen were prisoners. Nineteen hobbits were killed, and some thirty were wounded. The dead ruffians were laden on waggons and hauled off to an old sand-pit nearby and there buried: in the Battle Pit, as it was afterwards called. The fallen hobbits were laid together in a grave on the hill-side, where later a great stone was set up with a garden about it. So ended the Battle of Bywater, 1419, the last battle fought in the Shire, and the only battle since the Greenfields, 1147, away up in the Northfarthing. In consequence, though it happily cost very few lives, it has a chapter to itself in the Red Book, and the names of all those who took part were made into a Roll, and learned by heart by Shire-historians. The very considerable rise in the fame and fortune of the Cottons dates from this time; but at the top of the Roll in all accounts stand the names of Captains Meriadoc and Peregrin.

Frodo had been in the battle, but he had not drawn sword, and his chief part had been to prevent the hobbits in their wrath at their losses, from slaying those of their enemies who threw down their weapons. When the fighting was over, and the later labours were ordered, Merry, Pippin, and Sam joined him, and they rode back with the Cottons. They ate a late midday meal, and then Frodo said with a sigh: 'Well, I suppose it is time now that we dealt with the "Chief".'

'Yes indeed; the sooner the better,' said Merry. 'And don't be too gentle! He's responsible for bringing in these ruffians, and for all the evil they have done.'

Farmer Cotton collected an escort of some two dozen sturdy hobbits. 'For it's only a guess that there is no ruffians left at Bag End,' he said. 'We don't know.' Then they set out on foot. Frodo, Sam, Merry, and Pippin led the way.

It was one of the saddest hours in their lives. The great chimney rose up before them; and as they drew near the old village across the Water, through rows of new mean houses along each side of the road, they saw the new mill in all its frowning and dirty ugliness: a great brick building straddling the stream, which it fouled with a steaming and stinking outflow. All along the Bywater Road every tree had been felled.

As they crossed the bridge and looked up the Hill they gasped. Even Sam's vision in the Mirror had not prepared him for what they saw. The Old Grange on the west side had been knocked down, and its place taken by rows of tarred sheds. All the chestnuts were gone. The banks and hedgerows were broken. Great waggons were standing in disorder in a field beaten bare of grass. Bagshot Row was a yawning sand and gravel quarry. Bag End up beyond could not be seen for a clutter of large huts.

'They've cut it down!' cried Sam. 'They've cut down the Party Tree!' He pointed to where the tree had stood under which Bilbo had made his Farewell Speech. It was lying lopped and dead in the field. As if this was the last straw Sam burst into tears.

A laugh put an end to them. There was a surly hobbit lounging over the low wall of the mill-yard. He was grimy-faced and black-handed. 'Don't 'ee like it, Sam?' he sneered. 'But you always was soft. I thought you'd gone off in one o' them ships you used to prattle about, sailing, sailing. What d'you want to come back for? We've work to do in the Shire now.'

'So I see,' said Sam. 'No time for washing, but time for wall-propping. But see here, Master Sandyman, I've a score to pay in this village, and don't you make it any longer with your jeering, or you'll foot a bill too big for your purse.'

Ted Sandyman spat over the wall. 'Garn!' he said. 'You can't touch me.

I'm a friend o' the Boss's. But he'll touch you all right, if I have any more of your mouth.'

'Don't waste any more words on the fool, Sam!' said Frodo. 'I hope there are not many more hobbits that have become like this. It would be a worse trouble than all the damage the Men have done.'

'You are dirty and insolent, Sandyman,' said Merry. 'And also very much out of your reckoning. We are just going up the Hill to remove your precious Boss. We have dealt with his Men.'

Ted gaped, for at that moment he first caught sight of the escort that at a sign from Merry now marched over the bridge. Dashing back into the mill he ran out with a horn and blew it loudly.

'Save your breath!' laughed Merry. 'I've a better.' Then lifting up his silver horn he winded it, and its clear call rang over the Hill; and out of the holes and sheds and shabby houses of Hobbiton the hobbits answered, and came pouring out, and with cheers and loud cries they followed the company up the road to Bag End.

At the top of the lane the party halted, and Frodo and his friends went on; and they came at last to the once beloved place. The garden was full of huts and sheds, some so near the old westward windows that they cut off all their light. There were piles of refuse everywhere. The door was scarred; the bell-chain was dangling loose, and the bell would not ring. Knocking brought no answer. At length they pushed and the door yielded. They went in. The place stank and was full of filth and disorder: it did not appear to have been used for some time.

'Where is that miserable Lotho hiding?' said Merry. They had searched every room and found no living thing save rats and mice. 'Shall we turn on the others to search the sheds?'

'This is worse than Mordor!' said Sam. 'Much worse in a way. It comes home to you, as they say; because it is home, and you remember it before it was all ruined.'

'Yes, this is Mordor,' said Frodo. 'Just one of its works. Saruman was doing its work all the time, even when he thought he was working for himself. And the same with those that Saruman tricked, like Lotho.'

Merry looked round in dismay and disgust. 'Let's get out!' he said. 'If I had known all the mischief he had caused, I should have stuffed my pouch down Saruman's throat.'

'No doubt, no doubt! But you did not, and so I am able to welcome you home.' There standing at the door was Saruman himself, looking well-fed and well-pleased; his eyes gleamed with malice and amusement.

A sudden light broke on Frodo. 'Sharkey!' he cried.

Saruman laughed. 'So you have heard the name, have you? All my people used to call me that in Isengard, I believe. A sign of affection, possibly.* But evidently you did not expect to see me here.'

'I did not,' said Frodo. 'But I might have guessed. A little mischief in a mean way: Gandalf warned me that you were still capable of it.'

'Quite capable,' said Saruman, 'and more than a little. You made me laugh, you hobbit-lordlings, riding along with all those great people, so secure and so pleased with your little selves. You thought you had done very well out of it all, and could now just amble back and have a nice quiet time in the country. Saruman's home could be all wrecked, and he could be turned out, but no one could touch yours. Oh no! Gandalf would look after your affairs.'

Saruman laughed again. 'Not he! When his tools have done their task he drops them. But you must go dangling after him, dawdling and talking, and riding round twice as far as you needed. "Well," thought I, "if they're such fools, I will get ahead of them and teach them a lesson. One ill turn deserves another." It would have been a sharper lesson, if only you had given me a little more time and more Men. Still I have already done much that you will find it hard to mend or undo in your lives. And it will be pleasant to think of that and set it against my injuries.'

'Well, if that is what you find pleasure in,' said Frodo, 'I pity you. It will be a pleasure of memory only, I fear. Go at once and never return!'

The hobbits of the villages had seen Saruman come out of one of the huts, and at once they came crowding up to the door of Bag End. When they heard Frodo's command, they murmured angrily:

'Don't let him go! Kill him! He's a villain and a murderer. Kill him!'

Saruman looked round at their hostile faces and smiled. 'Kill him!' he mocked. 'Kill him, if you think there are enough of you, my brave hobbits!' He drew himself up and stared at them darkly with his black eyes. 'But do not think that when I lost all my goods I lost all my power! Whoever strikes me shall be accursed. And if my blood stains the Shire, it shall wither and never again be healed.'

The hobbits recoiled. But Frodo said: 'Do not believe him! He has lost all power, save his voice that can still daunt you and deceive you, if you let it. But I will not have him slain. It is useless to meet revenge with revenge: it will heal nothing. Go, Saruman, by the speediest way!'

'Worm! Worm!' Saruman called; and out of a nearby hut came Wormtongue, crawling, almost like a dog. 'To the road again, Worm!' said Saruman. 'These fine fellows and lordlings are turning us adrift again. Come along!'

Saruman turned to go, and Wormtongue shuffled after him. But even

* It was probably Orkish in origin: *sharkû*, 'old man'.

as Saruman passed close to Frodo a knife flashed in his hand, and he stabbed swiftly. The blade turned on the hidden mail-coat and snapped. A dozen hobbits, led by Sam, leaped forward with a cry and flung the villain to the ground. Sam drew his sword.

'No, Sam!' said Frodo. 'Do not kill him even now. For he has not hurt me. And in any case I do not wish him to be slain in this evil mood. He was great once, of a noble kind that we should not dare to raise our hands against. He is fallen, and his cure is beyond us; but I would still spare him, in the hope that he may find it.'

Saruman rose to his feet, and stared at Frodo. There was a strange look in his eyes of mingled wonder and respect and hatred. 'You have grown, Halfling,' he said. 'Yes, you have grown very much. You are wise, and cruel. You have robbed my revenge of sweetness, and now I must go hence in bitterness, in debt to your mercy. I hate it and you! Well, I go and I will trouble you no more. But do not expect me to wish you health and long life. You will have neither. But that is not my doing. I merely foretell.'

He walked away, and the hobbits made a lane for him to pass; but their knuckles whitened as they gripped on their weapons. Wormtongue hesitated, and then followed his master.

'Wormtongue!' called Frodo. 'You need not follow him. I know of no evil you have done to me. You can have rest and food here for a while, until you are stronger and can go your own ways.'

Wormtongue halted and looked back at him, half prepared to stay. Saruman turned. 'No evil?' he cackled. 'Oh no! Even when he sneaks out at night it is only to look at the stars. But did I hear someone ask where poor Lotho is hiding? You know, don't you, Worm? Will you tell them?'

Wormtongue cowered down and whimpered: 'No, no!'

'Then I will,' said Saruman. 'Worm killed your Chief, poor little fellow, your nice little Boss. Didn't you, Worm? Stabbed him in his sleep, I believe. Buried him, I hope; though Worm has been very hungry lately. No, Worm is not really nice. You had better leave him to me.'

A look of wild hatred came into Wormtongue's red eyes. 'You told me to; you made me do it,' he hissed.

Saruman laughed. 'You do what Sharkey says, always, don't you, Worm? Well, now he says: follow!' He kicked Wormtongue in the face as he grovelled, and turned and made off. But at that something snapped: suddenly Wormtongue rose up, drawing a hidden knife, and then with a snarl like a dog he sprang on Saruman's back, jerked his head back, cut his throat, and with a yell ran off down the lane. Before Frodo could recover or speak a word, three hobbit-bows twanged and Wormtongue fell dead.

To the dismay of those that stood by, about the body of Saruman a grey mist gathered, and rising slowly to a great height like smoke from a fire, as a pale shrouded figure it loomed over the Hill. For a moment it wavered, looking to the West; but out of the West came a cold wind, and it bent away, and with a sigh dissolved into nothing.

Frodo looked down at the body with pity and horror, for as he looked it seemed that long years of death were suddenly revealed in it, and it shrank, and the shrivelled face became rags of skin upon a hideous skull. Lifting up the skirt of the dirty cloak that sprawled beside it, he covered it over, and turned away.

'And that's the end of that,' said Sam. 'A nasty end, and I wish I needn't have seen it; but it's a good riddance.'

'And the very last end of the War, I hope,' said Merry.

'I hope so,' said Frodo and sighed. 'The very last stroke. But to think that it should fall here, at the very door of Bag End! Among all my hopes and fears at least I never expected that.'

'I shan't call it the end, till we've cleared up the mess,' said Sam gloomily. 'And that'll take a lot of time and work.'

CHAPTER IX

THE GREY HAVENS

The clearing up certainly needed a lot of work, but it took less time than Sam had feared. The day after the battle Frodo rode to Michel Delving and released the prisoners from the Lockholes. One of the first that they found was poor Fredegar Bolger, Fatty no longer. He had been taken when the ruffians smoked out a band of rebels that he led from their hidings up in the Brockenbores by the hills of Scary.

'You would have done better to come with us after all, poor old Fredegar!' said Pippin, as they carried him out too weak to walk.

He opened an eye and tried gallantly to smile. 'Who's this young giant with the loud voice?' he whispered. 'Not little Pippin! What's your size in hats now?'

Then there was Lobelia. Poor thing, she looked very old and thin when they rescued her from a dark and narrow cell. She insisted on hobbling out on her own feet; and she had such a welcome, and there was such clapping and cheering when she appeared, leaning on Frodo's arm but still clutching her umbrella, that she was quite touched, and drove away in tears. She had never in her life been popular before. But she was crushed by the news of Lotho's murder, and she would not return to Bag End. She gave it back to Frodo, and went to her own people, the Bracegirdles of Hardbottle.

When the poor creature died next Spring – she was after all more than a hundred years old – Frodo was surprised and much moved: she had left all that remained of her money and of Lotho's for him to use in helping hobbits made homeless by the troubles. So that feud was ended.

Old Will Whitfoot had been in the Lockholes longer than any, and though he had perhaps been treated less harshly than some, he needed a lot of feeding up before he could look the part of Mayor; so Frodo agreed to act as his Deputy, until Mr. Whitfoot was in shape again. The only thing that he did as Deputy Mayor was to reduce the Shirriffs to their proper functions and numbers. The task of hunting out the last remnant of the ruffians was left to Merry and Pippin, and it was soon done. The southern gangs, after hearing the news of the Battle of Bywater, fled out of the land and offered little resistance to the Thain. Before the Year's End the few survivors were rounded up in the woods, and those that surrendered were shown to the borders.

Meanwhile the labour of repair went on apace, and Sam was kept very busy. Hobbits can work like bees when the mood and the need comes on them. Now there were thousands of willing hands of all ages, from the small but nimble ones of the hobbit lads and lasses to the well-worn and horny ones of the gaffers and gammers. Before Yule not a brick was left standing of the new Shirriff-houses or of anything that had been built by 'Sharkey's Men'; but the bricks were used to repair many an old hole, to make it snugger and drier. Great stores of goods and food, and beer, were found that had been hidden away by the ruffians in sheds and barns and deserted holes, and especially in the tunnels at Michel Delving and in the old quarries at Scary; so that there was a great deal better cheer that Yule than anyone had hoped for.

One of the first things done in Hobbiton, before even the removal of the new mill, was the clearing of the Hill and Bag End, and the restoration of Bagshot Row. The front of the new sand-pit was all levelled and made into a large sheltered garden, and new holes were dug in the southward face, back into the Hill, and they were lined with brick. The Gaffer was restored to Number Three; and he said often and did not care who heard it:

'It's an ill wind as blows nobody no good, as I always say. And All's well as ends Better!'

There was some discussion of the name that the new row should be given. *Battle Gardens* was thought of, or *Better Smials*. But after a while in sensible hobbit-fashion it was just called *New Row*. It was a purely Bywater joke to refer to it as Sharkey's End.

The trees were the worst loss and damage, for at Sharkey's bidding they had been cut down recklessly far and wide over the Shire; and Sam grieved over this more than anything else. For one thing, this hurt would take long to heal, and only his great-grandchildren, he thought, would see the Shire as it ought to be.

Then suddenly one day, for he had been too busy for weeks to give a thought to his adventures, he remembered the gift of Galadriel. He brought the box out and showed it to the other Travellers (for so they were now called by everyone), and asked their advice.

'I wondered when you would think of it,' said Frodo. 'Open it!'

Inside it was filled with a grey dust, soft and fine, in the middle of which was a seed, like a small nut with a silver shale. 'What can I do with this?' said Sam.

'Throw it in the air on a breezy day and let it do its work!' said Pippin.

'On what?' said Sam.

'Choose one spot as a nursery, and see what happens to the plants there,' said Merry.

'But I'm sure the Lady would not like me to keep it all for my own garden, now so many folk have suffered,' said Sam.

'Use all the wits and knowledge you have of your own, Sam,' said Frodo, 'and then use the gift to help your work and better it. And use it sparingly. There is not much here, and I expect every grain has a value.'

So Sam planted saplings in all the places where specially beautiful or beloved trees had been destroyed, and he put a grain of the precious dust in the soil at the root of each. He went up and down the Shire in this labour; but if he paid special attention to Hobbiton and Bywater no one blamed him. And at the end he found that he still had a little of the dust left; so he went to the Three-Farthing Stone, which is as near the centre of the Shire as no matter, and cast it in the air with his blessing. The little silver nut he planted in the Party Field where the tree had once been; and he wondered what would come of it. All through the winter he remained as patient as he could, and tried to restrain himself from going round constantly to see if anything was happening.

Spring surpassed his wildest hopes. His trees began to sprout and grow, as if time was in a hurry and wished to make one year do for twenty. In the Party Field a beautiful young sapling leaped up: it had silver bark and long leaves and burst into golden flowers in April. It was indeed a *mallorn*, and it was the wonder of the neighbourhood. In after years, as it grew in grace and beauty, it was known far and wide and people would come long journeys to see it: the only *mallorn* west of the Mountains and east of the Sea, and one of the finest in the world.

Altogether 1420 in the Shire was a marvellous year. Not only was there wonderful sunshine and delicious rain, in due times and perfect measure, but there seemed something more: an air of richness and growth, and a gleam of a beauty beyond that of mortal summers that flicker and pass upon this Middle-earth. All the children born or begotten in that year, and there were many, were fair to see and strong, and most of them had a rich golden hair that had before been rare among hobbits. The fruit was so plentiful that young hobbits very nearly bathed in strawberries and cream; and later they sat on the lawns under the plum-trees and ate, until they had made piles of stones like small pyramids or the heaped skulls of a conqueror, and then they moved on. And no one was ill, and everyone was pleased, except those who had to mow the grass.

In the Southfarthing the vines were laden, and the yield of 'leaf' was astonishing; and everywhere there was so much corn that at Harvest every barn was stuffed. The Northfarthing barley was so fine that the beer of

1420 malt was long remembered and became a byword. Indeed a generation later one might hear an old gaffer in an inn, after a good pint of well-earned ale, put down his mug with a sigh: 'Ah! that was proper fourteen-twenty, that was!'

Sam stayed at first at the Cottons' with Frodo; but when the New Row was ready he went with the Gaffer. In addition to all his other labours he was busy directing the cleaning up and restoring of Bag End; but he was often away in the Shire on his forestry work. So he was not at home in early March and did not know that Frodo had been ill. On the thirteenth of that month Farmer Cotton found Frodo lying on his bed; he was clutching a white gem that hung on a chain about his neck and he seemed half in a dream.

'It is gone for ever,' he said, 'and now all is dark and empty.'

But the fit passed, and when Sam got back on the twenty-fifth, Frodo had recovered, and he said nothing about himself. In the meanwhile Bag End had been set in order, and Merry and Pippin came over from Crickhollow bringing back all the old furniture and gear, so that the old hole soon looked very much as it always had done.

When all was at last ready Frodo said: 'When are you going to move in and join me, Sam?'

Sam looked a bit awkward.

'There is no need to come yet, if you don't want to,' said Frodo. 'But you know the Gaffer is close at hand, and he will be very well looked after by Widow Rumble.'

'It's not that, Mr. Frodo,' said Sam, and he went very red.

'Well, what is it?'

'It's Rosie, Rose Cotton,' said Sam. 'It seems she didn't like my going abroad at all, poor lass; but as I hadn't spoken, she couldn't say so. And I didn't speak, because I had a job to do first. But now I have spoken, and she says: "Well, you've wasted a year, so why wait longer?" "Wasted?" I says. "I wouldn't call it that." Still I see what she means. I feel torn in two, as you might say.'

'I see,' said Frodo: 'you want to get married, and yet you want to live with me in Bag End too? But my dear Sam, how easy! Get married as soon as you can, and then move in with Rosie. There's room enough in Bag End for as big a family as you could wish for.'

And so it was settled. Sam Gamgee married Rose Cotton in the Spring of 1420 (which was also famous for its weddings), and they came and lived at Bag End. And if Sam thought himself lucky, Frodo knew that he was more lucky himself; for there was not a hobbit in the Shire that was looked after with such care. When the labours of repair had all been planned and set going he took to a quiet life, writing a great deal and going through all his notes. He resigned the office of Deputy Mayor at the Free Fair that mid-summer, and dear old Will Whitfoot had another seven years of presiding at Banquets.

Merry and Pippin lived together for some time at Crickhollow, and there was much coming and going between Buckland and Bag End. The two young Travellers cut a great dash in the Shire with their songs and their tales and their finery, and their wonderful parties. 'Lordly' folk called them, meaning nothing but good; for it warmed all hearts to see them go riding by with their mail-shirts so bright and their shields so splendid, laughing and singing songs of far away; and if they were now large and magnificent, they were unchanged otherwise, unless they were indeed more fairspoken and more jovial and full of merriment than ever before.

Frodo and Sam, however, went back to ordinary attire, except that when there was need they both wore long grey cloaks, finely woven and clasped at the throat with beautiful brooches; and Mr. Frodo wore always a white jewel on a chain that he often would finger.

All things now went well, with hope always of becoming still better; and Sam was as busy and as full of delight as even a hobbit could wish. Nothing for him marred that whole year, except for some vague anxiety about his master. Frodo dropped quietly out of all the doings of the Shire, and Sam was pained to notice how little honour he had in his own country. Few people knew or wanted to know about his deeds and adventures; their admiration and respect were given mostly to Mr. Meriadoc and Mr. Peregrin and (if Sam had known it) to himself. Also in the autumn there appeared a shadow of old troubles.

One evening Sam came into the study and found his master looking very strange. He was very pale and his eyes seemed to see things far away.

'What's the matter, Mr. Frodo?' said Sam.

'I am wounded,' he answered, 'wounded; it will never really heal.'

But then he got up, and the turn seemed to pass, and he was quite himself the next day. It was not until afterwards that Sam recalled that the date was October the sixth. Two years before on that day it was dark in the dell under Weathertop.

Time went on, and 1421 came in. Frodo was ill again in March, but with a great effort he concealed it, for Sam had other things to think about. The first of Sam and Rosie's children was born on the twenty-fifth of March, a date that Sam noted.

'Well, Mr. Frodo,' he said. 'I'm in a bit of a fix. Rose and me had settled to call him Frodo, with your leave; but it's not *him*, it's *her*. Though as pretty a maidchild as any one could hope for, taking after Rose more than me, luckily. So we don't know what to do.'

'Well, Sam,' said Frodo, 'what's wrong with the old customs? Choose a flower name like Rose. Half the maidchildren in the Shire are called by such names, and what could be better?'

'I suppose you're right, Mr. Frodo,' said Sam. 'I've heard some beautiful names on my travels, but I suppose they're a bit too grand for daily wear and tear, as you might say. The Gaffer, he says: "Make it short, and then you won't have to cut it short before you can use it." But if it's to be a flower-name, then I don't trouble about the length: it must be a beautiful flower, because, you see, I think she is very beautiful, and is going to be beautifuller still.'

Frodo thought for a moment. 'Well, Sam, what about *elanor*, the sun-star, you remember the little golden flower in the grass of Lothlórien?'

'You're right again, Mr. Frodo!' said Sam delighted. 'That's what I wanted.'

Little Elanor was nearly six months old, and 1421 had passed to its autumn, when Frodo called Sam into the study.

'It will be Bilbo's Birthday on Thursday, Sam,' he said. 'And he will pass the Old Took. He will be a hundred and thirty-one!'

'So he will!' said Sam. 'He's a marvel!'

'Well, Sam,' said Frodo, 'I want you to see Rose and find out if she can spare you, so that you and I can go off together. You can't go far or for a long time now, of course,' he said a little wistfully.

'Well, not very well, Mr. Frodo.'

'Of course not. But never mind. You can see me on my way. Tell Rose that you won't be away very long, not more than a fortnight; and you'll come back quite safe.'

'I wish I could go all the way with you to Rivendell, Mr. Frodo, and see Mr. Bilbo,' said Sam. 'And yet the only place I really want to be in is here. I am that torn in two.'

'Poor Sam! It will feel like that, I am afraid,' said Frodo. 'But you will be healed. You were meant to be solid and whole, and you will be.'

In the next day or two Frodo went through his papers and his writings with Sam, and he handed over his keys. There was a big book with plain red leather covers; its tall pages were now almost filled. At the beginning there were many leaves covered with Bilbo's thin wandering hand; but most of it was written in Frodo's firm flowing script. It was divided into chapters but Chapter 80 was unfinished, and after that were some blank leaves. The title page had many titles on it, crossed out one after another, so:

My Diary. My Unexpected Journey. There and Back Again. And What Happened After.

Adventures of Five Hobbits. The Tale of the Great Ring, compiled by Bilbo Baggins from his own observations and the accounts of his friends. What we did in the War of the Ring.

Here Bilbo's hand ended and Frodo had written:

THE DOWNFALL
OF THE
LORD OF THE RINGS
AND THE
RETURN OF THE KING

(as seen by the Little People; being the memoirs of Bilbo and Frodo of the Shire, supplemented by the accounts of their friends and the learning of the Wise.)

Together with extracts from Books of Lore translated by Bilbo in Rivendell.

'Why, you have nearly finished it, Mr. Frodo!' Sam exclaimed. 'Well, you have kept at it, I must say.'

'I have quite finished, Sam,' said Frodo. 'The last pages are for you.'

On September the twenty-first they set out together, Frodo on the pony that had borne him all the way from Minas Tirith, and was now called Strider; and Sam on his beloved Bill. It was a fair golden morning, and Sam did not ask where they were going: he thought he could guess.

They took the Stock Road over the hills and went towards the Woody End, and they let their ponies walk at their leisure. They camped in the Green Hills, and on September the twenty-second they rode gently down into the beginning of the trees as afternoon was wearing away.

'If that isn't the very tree you hid behind when the Black Rider first showed up, Mr. Frodo!' said Sam pointing to the left. 'It seems like a dream now.'

It was evening, and the stars were glimmering in the eastern sky as they passed the ruined oak and turned and went on down the hill between the hazel-thickets. Sam was silent, deep in his memories. Presently he became aware that Frodo was singing softly to himself, singing the old walking-song, but the words were not quite the same.

Still round the corner there may wait
A new road or a secret gate;
And though I oft have passed them by,
A day will come at last when I
Shall take the hidden paths that run
West of the Moon, East of the Sun.

And as if in answer, from down below, coming up the road out of the valley, voices sang:

A! Elbereth Gilthoniel!
silivren penna míriel
o menel aglar elenath,
Gilthoniel, A! Elbereth!
We still remember, we who dwell
In this far land beneath the trees
The starlight on the Western Seas.

Frodo and Sam halted and sat silent in the soft shadows, until they saw a shimmer as the travellers came towards them.

There was Gildor and many fair Elven folk; and there to Sam's wonder rode Elrond and Galadriel. Elrond wore a mantle of grey and had a star upon his forehead, and a silver harp was in his hand, and upon his finger was a ring of gold with a great blue stone, Vilya, mightiest of the Three. But Galadriel sat upon a white palfrey and was robed all in glimmering white, like clouds about the Moon; for she herself seemed to shine with a soft light. On her finger was Nenya, the ring wrought of *mithril*, that bore a single white stone flickering like a frosty star. Riding slowly behind on a small grey pony, and seeming to nod in his sleep, was Bilbo himself.

Elrond greeted them gravely and graciously, and Galadriel smiled upon them. 'Well, Master Samwise,' she said. 'I hear and see that you have used my gift well. The Shire shall now be more than ever blessed and beloved.' Sam bowed, but found nothing to say. He had forgotten how beautiful the Lady was.

Then Bilbo woke up and opened his eyes. 'Hullo, Frodo!' he said. 'Well,

I have passed the Old Took today! So that's settled. And now I think I am quite ready to go on another journey. Are you coming?'

'Yes, I am coming,' said Frodo. 'The Ring-bearers should go together.'

'Where are you going, Master?' cried Sam, though at last he understood what was happening.

'To the Havens, Sam,' said Frodo.

'And I can't come.'

'No, Sam. Not yet anyway, not further than the Havens. Though you too were a Ring-bearer, if only for a little while. Your time may come. Do not be too sad, Sam. You cannot be always torn in two. You will have to be one and whole, for many years. You have so much to enjoy and to be, and to do.'

'But,' said Sam, and tears started in his eyes, 'I thought you were going to enjoy the Shire, too, for years and years, after all you have done.'

'So I thought too, once. But I have been too deeply hurt, Sam. I tried to save the Shire, and it has been saved, but not for me. It must often be so, Sam, when things are in danger: some one has to give them up, lose them, so that others may keep them. But you are my heir: all that I had and might have had I leave to you. And also you have Rose, and Elanor; and Frodo-lad will come, and Rosie-lass, and Merry, and Goldilocks, and Pippin; and perhaps more that I cannot see. Your hands and your wits will be needed everywhere. You will be the Mayor, of course, as long as you want to be, and the most famous gardener in history; and you will read things out of the Red Book, and keep alive the memory of the age that is gone, so that people will remember the Great Danger and so love their beloved land all the more. And that will keep you as busy and as happy as anyone can be, as long as your part of the Story goes on.

'Come now, ride with me!'

Then Elrond and Galadriel rode on; for the Third Age was over, and the Days of the Rings were passed, and an end was come of the story and song of those times. With them went many Elves of the High Kindred who would no longer stay in Middle-earth; and among them, filled with a sadness that was yet blessed and without bitterness, rode Sam, and Frodo, and Bilbo, and the Elves delighted to honour them.

Though they rode through the midst of the Shire all the evening and all the night, none saw them pass, save the wild creatures; or here and there some wanderer in the dark who saw a swift shimmer under the trees, or a light and shadow flowing through the grass as the Moon went westward. And when they had passed from the Shire, going about the south skirts of the White Downs, they came to the Far Downs, and to the Towers, and looked on the distant Sea; and so they rode down at last to Mithlond, to the Grey Havens in the long firth of Lune.

As they came to the gates Círdan the Shipwright came forth to greet them. Very tall he was, and his beard was long, and he was grey and old, save that his eyes were keen as stars; and he looked at them and bowed, and said: 'All is now ready.'

Then Círdan led them to the Havens, and there was a white ship lying, and upon the quay beside a great grey horse stood a figure robed all in white awaiting them. As he turned and came towards them Frodo saw that Gandalf now wore openly on his hand the Third Ring, Narya the Great, and the stone upon it was red as fire. Then those who were to go were glad, for they knew that Gandalf also would take ship with them.

But Sam was now sorrowful at heart, and it seemed to him that if the parting would be bitter, more grievous still would be the long road home alone. But even as they stood there, and the Elves were going aboard, and all was being made ready to depart, up rode Merry and Pippin in great haste. And amid his tears Pippin laughed.

'You tried to give us the slip once before and failed, Frodo,' he said. 'This time you have nearly succeeded, but you have failed again. It was not Sam, though, that gave you away this time, but Gandalf himself!'

'Yes,' said Gandalf; 'for it will be better to ride back three together than one alone. Well, here at last, dear friends, on the shores of the Sea comes the end of our fellowship in Middle-earth. Go in peace! I will not say: do not weep; for not all tears are an evil.'

Then Frodo kissed Merry and Pippin, and last of all Sam, and went aboard; and the sails were drawn up, and the wind blew, and slowly the ship slipped away down the long grey firth; and the light of the glass of Galadriel that Frodo bore glimmered and was lost. And the ship went out into the High Sea and passed on into the West, until at last on a night of rain Frodo smelled a sweet fragrance on the air and heard the sound of singing that came over the water. And then it seemed to him that as in his dream in the house of Bombadil, the grey rain-curtain turned all to silver glass and was rolled back, and he beheld white shores and beyond them a far green country under a swift sunrise.

But to Sam the evening deepened to darkness as he stood at the Haven; and as he looked at the grey sea he saw only a shadow on the waters that was soon lost in the West. There still he stood far into the night, hearing only the sigh and murmur of the waves on the shores of Middle-earth, and the sound of them sank deep into his heart. Beside him stood Merry and Pippin, and they were silent.

At last the three companions turned away, and never again looking back they rode slowly homewards; and they spoke no word to one another until they came back to the Shire, but each had great comfort in his friends on the long grey road.

At last they rode over the downs and took the East Road, and then Merry and Pippin rode on to Buckland; and already they were singing again as they went. But Sam turned to Bywater, and so came back up the Hill, as day was ending once more. And he went on, and there was yellow light, and fire within; and the evening meal was ready, and he was expected. And Rose drew him in, and set him in his chair, and put little Elanor upon his lap.

He drew a deep breath. 'Well, I'm back,' he said.

APPENDIX A

ANNALS OF THE KINGS AND RULERS

Concerning the sources for most of the matter contained in the following Appendices, especially A to D, see the note at the end of the Prologue. The section A III, *Durin's Folk*, was probably derived from Gimli the Dwarf, who maintained his friendship with Peregrin and Meriadoc and met them again many times in Gondor and Rohan.

The legends, histories, and lore to be found in the sources are very extensive. Only selections from them, in most places much abridged, are here presented. Their principal purpose is to illustrate the War of the Ring and its origins, and to fill up some of the gaps in the main story. The ancient legends of the First Age, in which Bilbo's chief interest lay, are very briefly referred to, since they concern the ancestry of Elrond and the Númenorean kings and chieftains. Actual extracts from longer annals and tales are placed within quotation marks. Insertions of later date are enclosed in brackets. Notes within quotation marks are found in the sources. Others are editorial.[1]

The dates given are those of the Third Age, unless they are marked S.A. (Second Age) or F.A. (Fourth Age). The Third Age was held to have ended when the Three Rings passed away in September 3021, but for the purposes of records in Gondor F.A.1 began on March 25, 3021. On the equation of the dating of Gondor and Shire Reckoning see pp. 4 and 1136. In lists the dates following the names of kings and rulers are the dates of their deaths, if only one date is given. The sign † indicates a premature death, in battle or otherwise, though an annal of the event is not always included.

I
THE NÚMENOREAN KINGS

(i)
NÚMENOR

Fëanor was the greatest of the Eldar in arts and lore, but also the proudest and most selfwilled. He wrought the Three Jewels, the *Silmarilli*, and filled them with the radiance of the Two Trees, Telperion and Laurelin,[2] that gave light to the land of the Valar. The Jewels were coveted by Morgoth the Enemy, who stole them and, after destroying the Trees, took them to Middle-earth, and guarded them in his

[1] A few references are given by page to this edition of *The Lord of the Rings*, and to the hardback 3rd edition of *The Hobbit*.

[2] Cf. pp. 238, 584, 950: no likeness remained in Middle-earth of Laurelin the Golden.

great fortress of Thangorodrim.[1] Against the will of the Valar Fëanor forsook the Blessed Realm and went in exile to Middle-earth, leading with him a great part of his people; for in his pride he purposed to recover the Jewels from Morgoth by force. Thereafter followed the hopeless war of the Eldar and the Edain against Thangorodrim, in which they were at last utterly defeated. The Edain (*Atani*) were three peoples of Men who, coming first to the West of Middle-earth and the shores of the Great Sea, became allies of the Eldar against the Enemy.

There were three unions of the Eldar and the Edain: Lúthien and Beren; Idril and Tuor; Arwen and Aragorn. By the last the long-sundered branches of the Half-elven were reunited and their line was restored.

Lúthien Tinúviel was the daughter of King Thingol Grey-cloak of Doriath in the First Age, but her mother was Melian of the people of the Valar. Beren was the son of Barahir of the First House of the Edain. Together they wrested a *silmaril* from the Iron Crown of Morgoth.[2] Lúthien became mortal and was lost to Elven-kind. Dior was her son. Elwing was his daughter and had in her keeping the *silmaril*.

Idril Celebrindal was the daughter of Turgon, king of the hidden city of Gondolin.[3] Tuor was the son of Huor of the House of Hador, the Third House of the Edain and the most renowned in the wars with Morgoth. Eärendil the Mariner was their son.

Eärendil wedded Elwing, and with the power of the *silmaril* passed the Shadows[4] and came to the Uttermost West, and speaking as ambassador of both Elves and Men obtained the help by which Morgoth was overthrown. Eärendil was not permitted to return to mortal lands, and his ship bearing the *silmaril* was set to sail in the heavens as a star, and a sign of hope to the dwellers in Middle-earth oppressed by the Great Enemy or his servants.[5] The *silmarilli* alone preserved the ancient light of the Two Trees of Valinor before Morgoth poisoned them; but the other two were lost at the end of the First Age. Of these things the full tale, and much else concerning Elves and Men, is told in *The Silmarillion*.

The sons of Eärendil were Elros and Elrond, the *Peredhil* or Half-elven. In them alone the line of the heroic chieftains of the Edain in the First Age was preserved; and after the fall of Gil-galad[6] the lineage of the High-elven Kings was also in Middle-earth only represented by their descendants.

At the end of the First Age the Valar gave to the Half-elven an irrevocable choice to which kindred they would belong. Elrond chose to be of Elven-kind, and became a master of wisdom. To him therefore was granted the same grace as to those of the High Elves that still lingered in Middle-earth: that when weary at last of the mortal lands they could take ship from the Grey Havens and pass into the Uttermost West; and this grace continued after the change of the world. But to the children

[1] pp. 236–7, 696.
[2] p. 189, 696.
[3] *The Hobbit*, p. 51; *The Lord of the Rings*, pp. 308–9.
[4] pp. 227–30.
[5] p. 352–6, 696, 704, 894, 901.
[6] pp. 51, 181.

of Elrond a choice was also appointed: to pass with him from the circles of the world; or if they remained to become mortal and die in Middle-earth. For Elrond, therefore, all chances of the War of the Ring were fraught with sorrow.[1]

Elros chose to be of Man-kind and remain with the Edain; but a great life-span was granted to him many times that of lesser men.

As a reward for their sufferings in the cause against Morgoth, the Valar, the Guardians of the World, granted to the Edain a land to dwell in, removed from the dangers of Middle-earth. Most of them, therefore, set sail over Sea, and guided by the Star of Eärendil came to the great Isle of Elenna, westernmost of all Mortal lands. There they founded the realm of Númenor.

There was a tall mountain in the midst of the land, the Meneltarma, and from its summit the farsighted could descry the white tower of the Haven of the Eldar in Eressëa. Thence the Eldar came to the Edain and enriched them with knowledge and many gifts; but one command had been laid upon the Númenoreans, the 'Ban of the Valar': they were forbidden to sail west out of sight of their own shores or to attempt to set foot on the Undying Lands. For though a long span of life had been granted to them, in the beginning thrice that of lesser Men, they must remain mortal, since the Valar were not permitted to take from them the Gift of Men (or the Doom of Men, as it was afterwards called).

Elros was the first King of Númenor, and was afterwards known by the High-elven name Tar-Minyatur. His descendants were long-lived but mortal. Later when they became powerful they begrudged the choice of their forefather, desiring the immortality within the life of the world that was the fate of the Eldar, and murmuring against the Ban. In this way began their rebellion which, under the evil teaching of Sauron, brought about the Downfall of Númenor and the ruin of the ancient world, as is told in the *Akallabêth*.

These are the names of the Kings and Queens of Númenor: Elros-Tar-Minyatur, Vardamir, Tar-Amandil, Tar-Elendil, Tar-Meneldur, Tar-Aldarion, Tar-Ancalimë (the first Ruling Queen), Tar-Anárion, Tar-Súrion, Tar-Telperiën (the second Queen), Tar-Minastir, Tar-Ciryatan, Tar-Atanamir the Great, Tar-Ancalimon, Tar-Telemmaitë, Tar-Vanimeldë (the third Queen), Tar-Alcarin, Tar-Calmacil.

After Calmacil the Kings took the sceptre in names of the Númenorean (or Adûnaic) tongue: Ar-Adûnakhôr, Ar-Zimrathôn, Ar-Sakalthôr, Ar-Gimilzôr, Ar-Inziladûn. Inziladûn repented of the ways of the Kings and changed his name to Tar-Palantir 'The Farsighted'. His daughter should have been the fourth Queen, Tar-Míriel, but the King's nephew usurped the sceptre and became Ar-Pharazôn the Golden, last King of the Númenoreans.

In the days of Tar-Elendil the first ships of the Númenoreans came back to Middle-earth. His elder child was a daughter, Silmariën. Her son was Valandil, first of the Lords of Andúnië in the west of the land, renowned for their friendship with the Eldar. From him were descended Amandil, the last lord, and his son Elendil the Tall.

[1] See pp. 952, 956.

The sixth King left only one child, a daughter. She became the first Queen; for it was then made a law of the royal house that the eldest child of the King, whether man or woman, should receive the sceptre.

The realm of Númenor endured to the end of the Second Age and increased ever in power and splendour; and until half the Age had passed the Númenoreans grew also in wisdom and joy. The first sign of the shadow that was to fall upon them appeared in the days of Tar-Minastir, eleventh King. He it was that sent a great force to the aid of Gil-galad. He loved the Eldar but envied them. The Númenoreans had now become great mariners, exploring all the seas eastward, and they began to yearn for the West and the forbidden waters; and the more joyful was their life, the more they began to long for the immortality of the Eldar.

Moreover, after Minastir the Kings became greedy of wealth and power. At first the Númenoreans had come to Middle-earth as teachers and friends of lesser Men afflicted by Sauron; but now their havens became fortresses, holding wide coastlands in subjection. Atanamir and his successors levied heavy tribute, and the ships of the Númenoreans returned laden with spoil.

It was Tar-Atanamir who first spoke openly against the Ban and declared that the life of the Eldar was his by right. Thus the shadow deepened, and the thought of death darkened the hearts of the people. Then the Númenoreans became divided: on the one hand were the Kings and those who followed them, and were estranged from the Eldar and the Valar; on the other were the few who called themselves the Faithful. They lived mostly in the west of the land.

The Kings and their followers little by little abandoned the use of the Eldarin tongues; and at last the twentieth King took his royal name, in Númenorean form, calling himself Ar-Adûnakhôr, 'Lord of the West'. This seemed ill-omened to the Faithful, for hitherto they had given that title only to one of the Valar, or to the Elder King himself.[1] And indeed Ar-Adûnakhôr began to persecute the Faithful and punished those who used the Elven-tongues openly; and the Eldar came no more to Númenor.

The power and wealth of the Númenoreans nonetheless continued to increase; but their years lessened as their fear of death grew, and their joy departed. Tar-Palantir attempted to amend the evil; but it was too late, and there was rebellion and strife in Númenor. When he died, his nephew, leader of the rebellion, seized the sceptre, and became King Ar-Pharazôn. Ar-Pharazôn the Golden was the proudest and most powerful of all the Kings, and no less than the kingship of the world was his desire.

He resolved to challenge Sauron the Great for the supremacy in Middle-earth, and at length he himself set sail with a great navy, and he landed at Umbar. So great was the might and splendour of the Númenoreans that Sauron's own servants deserted him; and Sauron humbled himself, doing homage, and craving pardon. Then Ar-Pharazôn in the folly of his pride carried him back as a prisoner to Númenor. It was not long before he had bewitched the King and was master of his

[1] p. 229.

counsel; and soon he had turned the hearts of all the Númenoreans, except the remnant of the Faithful, back towards the darkness.

And Sauron lied to the King, declaring that everlasting life would be his who possessed the Undying Lands, and that the Ban was imposed only to prevent the Kings of Men from surpassing the Valar. 'But great Kings take what is their right,' he said.

At length Ar-Pharazôn listened to this counsel, for he felt the waning of his days and was besotted by the fear of Death. He prepared then the greatest armament that the world had seen, and when all was ready he sounded his trumpets and set sail; and he broke the Ban of the Valar, going up with war to wrest everlasting life from the Lords of the West. But when Ar-Pharazôn set foot upon the shores of Aman the Blessed, the Valar laid down their Guardianship and called upon the One, and the world was changed. Númenor was thrown down and swallowed in the Sea, and the Undying Lands were removed for ever from the circles of the world. So ended the glory of Númenor.

The last leaders of the Faithful, Elendil and his sons, escaped from the Downfall with nine ships, bearing a seedling of Nimloth, and the Seven Seeing-stones (gifts of the Eldar to their House);[1] and they were borne on the wind of a great storm and cast upon the shores of Middle-earth. There they established in the North-west the Númenorean realms in exile, Arnor and Gondor.[2] Elendil was the High King and dwelt in the North at Annúminas; and the rule in the South was committed to his sons, Isildur and Anárion. They founded there Osgiliath, between Minas Ithil and Minas Anor,[3] not far from the confines of Mordor. For this good at least they believed had come out of ruin, that Sauron also had perished.

But it was not so. Sauron was indeed caught in the wreck of Númenor, so that the bodily form in which he long had walked perished; but he fled back to Middle-earth, a spirit of hatred borne upon a dark wind. He was unable ever again to assume a form that seemed fair to men, but became black and hideous, and his power thereafter was through terror alone. He re-entered Mordor, and hid there for a time in silence. But his anger was great when he learned that Elendil, whom he most hated, had escaped him, and was now ordering a realm upon his borders.

Therefore, after a time he made war upon the Exiles, before they should take root. Orodruin burst once more into flame, and was named anew in Gondor *Amon Amarth*, Mount Doom. But Sauron struck too soon, before his own power was rebuilt, whereas the power of Gil-galad had increased in his absence; and in the Last Alliance that was made against him Sauron was overthrown and the One Ring was taken from him.[4] So ended the Second Age.

[1] pp. 583, 950.
[2] p. 236.
[3] p. 238.
[4] p. 237.

(ii)
THE REALMS IN EXILE

The Northern Line
Heirs of Isildur

Arnor. Elendil †S.A. 3441, Isildur †2, Valandil 249,[1] Eldacar 339, Arantar 435, Tarcil 515, Tarondor 602, Valandur †652, Elendur 777, Eärendur 861.

Arthedain. Amlaith of Fornost[2] (eldest son of Eärendur) 946, Beleg 1029, Mallor 1110, Celepharn 1191, Celebrindor 1272, Malvegil 1349,[3] Argeleb I †1356, Arveleg I 1409, Araphor 1589, Argeleb II 1670, Arvegil 1743, Arveleg II 1813, Araval 1891, Araphant 1964, Arvedui Last-king †1975. End of the North-kingdom.

Chieftains. Aranarth (elder son of Arvedui) 2106, Arahael 2177, Aranuir 2247, Aravir 2319, Aragorn I †2327. Araglas 2455, Arahad I 2523, Aragost 2588, Aravorn 2654, Arahad II 2719, Arassuil 2784, Arathorn I †2848, Argonui 2912, Arador †2930, Arathorn II †2933, Aragorn II F.A. 120.

The Southern Line
Heirs of Anárion

Kings of Gondor. Elendil (Isildur and) Anárion †S.A. 3440, Meneldil son of Anárion 158, Cemendur 238, Eärendil 324, Anardil 411, Ostoher 492, Rómendacil I (Tarostar) †541, Turambar 667, Atanatar I 748, Siriondil 830. Here followed the four 'Ship-kings':

Tarannon Falastur 913. He was the first childless king, and was succeeded by the son of his brother Tarciryan. Eärnil I †936, Ciryandil †1015, Hyarmendacil I (Ciryaher) 1149. Gondor now reached the height of its power.

Atanatar II Alcarin 'the Glorious' 1226, Narmacil I 1294. He was the second childless king and was succeeded by his younger brother. Calmacil 1304, Minalcar (regent 1240–1304), crowned as Rómendacil II 1304, died 1366, Valacar. In his time the first disaster of Gondor began, the Kin-strife.

Eldacar son of Valacar (at first called Vinitharya) deposed 1437. Castamir the Usurper †1447. Eldacar restored, died 1490.

Aldamir (second son of Eldacar) †1540. Hyarmendacil II (Vinyarion) 1621, Minardil †1634, Telemnar †1636. Telemnar and all his children perished in the plague; he was succeeded by his nephew, the son of Minastan, second son of Minardil. Tarondor 1798, Telumehtar Umbardacil 1850, Narmacil II †1856, Calimehtar 1936, Ondoher †1944. Ondoher and his two sons were slain in battle. After a year in 1945 the crown was given to the victorious general Eärnil, a descendant of Telumehtar Umbardacil, Eärnil II 2043, Eärnur †2050. Here the line of the Kings came to an end, until it was restored by Elessar Telcontar in 3019. The realm was then ruled by the Stewards.

[1] He was the fourth son of Isildur, born in Imladris. His brothers were slain in the Gladden Fields.

[2] After Eärendur the Kings no longer took names in High-elven form.

[3] After Malvegil, the Kings at Fornost again claimed lordship over the whole of Arnor, and took names with the prefix *ar(a)* in token of this.

Stewards of Gondor. The House of Húrin: Pelendur 1998. He ruled for a year after the fall of Ondoher, and advised Gondor to reject Arvedui's claim to the crown. Vorondil the Hunter 2029.[1] Mardil Voronwë 'the Steadfast', the first of the Ruling Stewards. His successors ceased to use High-elven names.

Ruling Stewards. Mardil 2080, Eradan 2116, Herion 2148, Belegorn 2204, Húrin I 2244, Túrin I 2278, Hador 2395, Barahir 2412, Dior 2435, Denethor I 2477, Boromir 2489, Cirion 2567. In his time the Rohirrim came to Calenardhon.

Hallas 2605, Húrin II 2628, Belecthor I 2655, Orodreth 2685, Ecthelion I 2698, Egalmoth 2743, Beren 2763, Beregond 2811, Belecthor II 2872, Thorondir 2882, Túrin II 2914, Turgon 2953, Ecthelion II 2984, Denethor II. He was the last of the Ruling Stewards, and was followed by his second son Faramir, Lord of Emyn Arnen, Steward to King Elessar, F.A. 82.

(iii)

ERIADOR, ARNOR, AND THE HEIRS OF ISILDUR

'Eriador was of old the name of all the lands between the Misty Mountains and the Blue; in the South it was bounded by the Greyflood and the Glanduin that flows into it above Tharbad.

'At its greatest Arnor included all Eriador, except the regions beyond the Lune, and the lands east of Greyflood and Loudwater, in which lay Rivendell and Hollin. Beyond the Lune was Elvish country, green and quiet, where no Men went; but Dwarves dwelt, and still dwell, in the east side of the Blue Mountains, especially in those parts south of the Gulf of Lune, where they have mines that are still in use. For this reason they were accustomed to pass east along the Great Road, as they had done for long years before we came to the Shire. At the Grey Havens dwelt Círdan the Shipwright, and some say he dwells there still, until the Last Ship sets sail into the West. In the days of the Kings most of the High Elves that still lingered in Middle-earth dwelt with Círdan or in the seaward lands of Lindon. If any now remain they are few.'

The North-kingdom and the Dúnedain

After Elendil and Isildur there were eight High Kings of Arnor. After Eärendur, owing to dissensions among his sons their realm was divided into three: Arthedain, Rhudaur, and Cardolan. Arthedain was in the North-west and included the land between Brandywine and Lune, and also the land north of the Great Road as far as the Weather Hills. Rhudaur was in the North-east and lay between the Ettenmoors, the Weather Hills, and the Misty Mountains, but included also the Angle between the Hoarwell and the Loudwater. Cardolan was in the South, its bounds being the Brandywine, the Greyflood, and the Great Road.

[1] See p. 738. The wild kine that were still to be found near the Sea of Rhûn were said in legend to be descended from the Kine of Araw, the huntsman of the Valar, who alone of the Valar came often to Middle-earth in the Elder Days. *Oromë* is the High-elven form of his name (p. 820).

In Arthedain the line of Isildur was maintained and endured, but the line soon perished in Cardolan and Rhudaur. There was often strife between the kingdoms, which hastened the waning of the Dúnedain. The chief matter of debate was the possession of the Weather Hills and the land westward towards Bree. Both Rhudaur and Cardolan desired to possess Amon Sûl (Weathertop), which stood on the borders of their realms; for the Tower of Amon Sûl held the chief *Palantír* of the North, and the other two were both in the keeping of Arthedain.

'It was in the beginning of the reign of Malvegil of Arthedain that evil came to Arnor. For at that time the realm of Angmar arose in the North beyond the Ettenmoors. Its lands lay on both sides of the Mountains, and there were gathered many evil men, and Orcs, and other fell creatures. [The lord of that land was known as the Witch-king, but it was not known until later that he was indeed the chief of the Ringwraiths, who came north with the purpose of destroying the Dúnedain in Arnor, seeing hope in their disunion, while Gondor was strong.]'

In the days of Argeleb son of Malvegil, since no descendants of Isildur remained in the other kingdoms, the kings of Arthedain again claimed the lordship of all Arnor. The claim was resisted by Rhudaur. There the Dúnedain were few, and power had been seized by an evil lord of the Hillmen, who was in secret league with Angmar. Argeleb therefore fortified the Weather Hills;[1] but he was slain in battle with Rhudaur and Angmar.

Arveleg son of Argeleb, with the help of Cardolan and Lindon, drove back his enemies from the Hills; and for many years Arthedain and Cardolan held in force a frontier along the Weather Hills, the Great Road, and the lower Hoarwell. It is said that at this time Rivendell was besieged.

A great host came out of Angmar in 1409, and crossing the river entered Cardolan and surrounded Weathertop. The Dúnedain were defeated and Arveleg was slain. The Tower of Amon Sûl was burned and razed; but the *palantír* was saved and carried back in retreat to Fornost, Rhudaur was occupied by evil Men subject to Angmar,[2] and the Dúnedain that remained there were slain or fled west. Cardolan was ravaged. Araphor son of Arveleg was not yet full-grown, but he was valiant, and with aid from Círdan he repelled the enemy from Fornost and the North Downs. A remnant of the faithful among the Dúnedain of Cardolan also held out in Tyrn Gorthad (the Barrowdowns), or took refuge in the Forest behind.

It is said that Angmar was for a time subdued by the Elvenfolk coming from Lindon; and from Rivendell, for Elrond brought help over the Mountains out of Lórien. It was at this time that the Stoors that had dwelt in the Angle (between Hoarwell and Loudwater) fled west and south, because of the wars, and the dread of Angmar, and because the land and clime of Eriador, especially in the east, worsened and became unfriendly. Some returned to Wilderland, and dwelt beside the Gladden, becoming a riverside people of fishers.

[1] p. 181.
[2] p. 196.

In the days of Argeleb II the plague came into Eriador from the South-east, and most of the people of Cardolan perished, especially in Minhiriath. The Hobbits and all other peoples suffered greatly, but the plague lessened as it passed northwards, and the northern parts of Arthedain were little affected. It was at this time that an end came of the Dúnedain of Cardolan, and evil spirits out of Angmar and Rhudaur entered into the deserted mounds and dwelt there.

'It is said that the mounds of Tyrn Gorthad, as the Barrowdowns were called of old, are very ancient, and that many were built in the days of the old world of the First Age by the forefathers of the Edain, before they crossed the Blue Mountains into Beleriand, of which Lindon is all that now remains. Those hills were therefore revered by the Dúnedain after their return; and there many of their lords and kings were buried. [Some say that the mound in which the Ring-bearer was imprisoned had been the grave of the last prince of Cardolan, who fell in the war of 1409.]'

'In 1974 the power of Angmar arose again, and the Witch-king came down upon Arthedain before winter was ended. He captured Fornost, and drove most of the remaining Dúnedain over the Lune; among them were the sons of the king. But King Arvedui held out upon the North Downs until the last, and then fled north with some of his guard; and they escaped by the swiftness of their horses.

'For a while Arvedui hid in the tunnels of the old dwarf-mines near the far end of the Mountains, but he was driven at last by hunger to seek the help of the Lossoth, the Snowmen of Forochel.[1] Some of these he found in camp by the seashore; but they did not help the king willingly, for he had nothing to offer them, save a few jewels which they did not value; and they were afraid of the Witch-king, who (they said) could make frost or thaw at his will. But partly out of pity for the gaunt king and his men, and partly out of fear of their weapons, they gave them a little food and built for them snow-huts. There Arvedui was forced to wait, hoping for help from the south; for his horses had perished.

'When Círdan heard from Aranarth son of Arvedui of the king's flight to the north, he at once sent a ship to Forochel to seek for him. The ship came there at last after many days, because of contrary winds, and the mariners saw from afar the little fire of drift-wood which the lost men contrived to keep alight. But the winter was long in loosing its grip that year; and though it was then March, the ice was only beginning to break, and lay far out from the shore.

'When the Snowmen saw the ship they were amazed and afraid, for they had seen no such ship on the sea within their memories; but they had become now more friendly, and they drew the king and those that survived of his company out over the ice in their sliding carts, as far as they dared. In this way a boat from the ship was able to reach them.

[1] These are a strange, unfriendly people, remnant of the Forodwaith, Men of far-off days, accustomed to the bitter colds of the realm of Morgoth. Indeed those colds linger still in that region, though they lie hardly more than a hundred leagues north of the Shire. The Lossoth house in the snow, and it is said that they can run on the ice with bones on their feet, and have carts without wheels. They live mostly, inaccessible to their enemies, on the great Cape of Forochel that shuts off to the north-west the immense bay of that name; but they often camp on the south shores of the bay at the feet of the Mountains.

'But the Snowmen were uneasy: for they said that they smelled danger in the wind. And the chief of the Lossoth said to Arvedui: "Do not mount on this sea-monster! If they have them, let the seamen bring us food and other things that we need, and you may stay here till the Witch-king goes home. For in summer his power wanes; but now his breath is deadly, and his cold arm is long."

'But Arvedui did not take his counsel. He thanked him, and at parting gave him his ring, saying: "This is a thing of worth beyond your reckoning. For its ancientry alone. It has no power, save the esteem in which those hold it who love my house. It will not help you, but if ever you are in need, my kin will ransom it with great store of all that you desire."[1]

'Yet the counsel of the Lossoth was good, by chance or by foresight; for the ship had not reached the open sea when a great storm of wind arose, and came with blinding snow out of the North; and it drove the ship back upon the ice and piled ice up against it. Even the mariners of Círdan were helpless, and in the night the ice crushed the hull, and the ship foundered. So perished Arvedui Last-king, and with him the *palantíri* were buried in the sea.[2] It was long afterwards that news of the shipwreck of Forochel was learned from the Snowmen.'

The Shire-folk survived, though war swept over them and most of them fled into hiding. To the help of the king they sent some archers who never returned; and others went also to the battle in which Angmar was overthrown (of which more is said in the annals of the South). Afterwards in the peace that followed the Shire-folk ruled themselves and prospered. They chose a Thain to take the place of the King, and were content; though for a long time many still looked for the return of the King. But at last that hope was forgotten, and remained only in the saying *When the King comes back*, used of some good that could not be achieved, or of some evil that could not be amended. The first Shire-thain was one Bucca of the Marish, from whom the Oldbucks claimed descent. He became Thain in 379 of our reckoning (1979).

After Arvedui the North-kingdom ended, for the Dúnedain were now few and all the peoples of Eriador diminished. Yet the line of the kings was continued by the Chieftains of the Dúnedain, of whom Aranarth son of Arvedui was the first. Arahael his son was fostered in tbRivendell, and so were all the sons of the chieftains after him; and there also were kept the heirlooms of their house: the ring of Barahir, the shards of Narsil, the star of Elendil, and the sceptre of Annúminas.[3]

[1] In this way the ring of the House of Isildur was saved; for it was afterwards ransomed by the Dúnedain. It is said that it was none other than the ring which Felagund of Nargothrond gave to Barahir, and Beren recovered at great peril.

[2] These were the Stones of Annúminas and Amon Sûl. The only Stone left in the North was the one in the Tower on Emyn Beraid that looks towards the Gulf of Lune. That was guarded by the Elves, and though we never knew it, it remained there, until Círdan put it aboard Elrond's ship when he left (pp. 44, 106). But we are told that is was unlike the others and not in accord with them; it looked only to the Sea. Elendil set it there so that he could look back with 'straight sight' and see Eressëa in the vanished West; but the bent seas below covered Númenor for ever.

[3] The sceptre was the chief mark of royalty in Númenor, the King tells us; and that was also so in Arnor, whose kings wore no crown, but bore a single white gem, the Elendilmir,

'When the kingdom ended the Dúnedain passed into the shadows and became a secret and wandering people, and their deeds and labours were seldom sung or recorded. Little now is remembered of them since Elrond departed. Although even before the Watchful Peace ended evil things again began to attack Eriador or to invade it secretly, the Chieftains for the most part lived out their long lives. Aragorn I, it is said, was slain by wolves, which ever after remained a peril in Eriador, and are not yet ended. In the days of Arahad I the Orcs, who had, as later appeared, long been secretly occupying strongholds in the Misty Mountains, so as to bar all the passes into Eriador, suddenly revealed themselves. In 2509 Celebrían wife of Elrond was journeying to Lórien when she was waylaid in the Redhorn Pass, and her escort being scattered by the sudden assault of the Orcs, she was seized and carried off. She was pursued and rescued by Elladan and Elrohir, but not before she had suffered torment and had received a poisoned wound.[1] She was brought back to Imladris, and though healed in body by Elrond, lost all delight in Middle-earth, and the next year went to the Havens and passed over Sea. And later in the days of Arassuil, Orcs, multiplying again in the Misty Mountains, began to ravage the lands, and the Dúnedain and the sons of Elrond fought with them. It was at this time that a large band came so far west as to enter the Shire, and were driven off by Bandobras Took.[2]

There were fifteen Chieftains, before the sixteenth and last was born, Aragorn II, who became again King of both Gondor and Arnor. 'Our King, we call him; and when he comes north to his house in Annúminas restored and stays for a while by Lake Evendim, then everyone in the Shire is glad. But he does not enter this land and binds himself by the law that he has made, that none of the Big People shall pass its borders. But he rides often with many fair people to the Great Bridge, and there he welcomes his friends, and any others who wish to see him; and some ride away with him and stay in his house as long as they have a mind. Thain Peregrin has been there many times; and so has Master Samwise the Mayor. His daughter Elanor the Fair is one of the maids of Queen Evenstar.'

It was the pride and wonder of the Northern Line that, though their power departed and their people dwindled, through all the many generations the succession was unbroken from father to son. Also, though the length of lives of the Dúnedain grew ever less in Middle-earth, after the ending of their kings the waning was swifter in Gondor; and many of the Chieftains of the North still lived to twice the age of

Star of Elendil, bound on their brows with a silver fillet (pp. 142, 829, 843, 946). In speaking of a crown (pp. 167, 241) Bilbo no doubt referred to Gondor; he seems to have become well acquainted with matters concerning Aragorn's line. The sceptre of Númenor is said to have perished with Ar-Pharazôn. That of Annúminas was the silver rod of the Lords of Andúnië, and is now perhaps the most ancient work of Men's hands preserved in Middle-earth. It was already more than five thousand years old when Elrond surrendered it to Aragorn (p. 951). The crown of Gondor was derived from the form of a Númenorean war-helm. In the beginning it was indeed a plain helm; and it is said to have been the one that Isildur wore in the Battle of Dagorlad (for the helm of Anárion was crushed by the stone-cast from Barad-dûr that slew him). But in the days of Atanatar Alcarin this was replaced by the jewelled helm that was used in the crowning of Aragorn.

[1] p. 221.

[2] p. 5, 992.

Men, and far beyond the days of even the oldest amongst us. Aragorn indeed lived to be two hundred and ten years old, longer than any of his line since King Arvegil; but in Aragorn Elessar the dignity of the kings of old was renewed.

(iv)
GONDOR AND THE HEIRS OF ANÁRION

There were thirty-one kings in Gondor after Anárion who was slain before the Barad-dûr. Though war never ceased on their borders, for more than a thousand years the Dúnedain of the South grew in wealth and power by land and sea, until the reign of Atanatar II, who was called Alcarin, the Glorious. Yet the signs of decay had then already appeared; for the high men of the South married late, and their children were few. The first childless king was Falastur, and the second Narmacil I, the son of Atanatar Alcarin.

It was Ostoher the seventh king who rebuilt Minas Anor, where afterwards the kings dwelt in summer rather than in Osgiliath. In his time Gondor was first attacked by wild men out of the East. But Tarostar, his son, defeated them and drove them out, and took the name of Rómendacil 'East-victor'. He was, however, later slain in battle with fresh hordes of Easterlings. Turambar his son avenged him, and won much territory eastwards.

With Tarannon, the twelfth king, began the line of the Ship-kings, who built navies and extended the sway of Gondor along the coasts west and south of the Mouths of Anduin. To commemorate his victories as Captain of the Hosts, Tarannon took the crown in the name of Falastur 'Lord of the Coasts'.

Eärnil I, his nephew, who succeeded him, repaired the ancient haven of Pelargir, and built a great navy. He laid siege by sea and land to Umbar, and took it, and it became a great harbour and fortress of the power of Gondor.[1] But Eärnil did not long survive his triumph. He was lost with many ships and men in a great storm off Umbar. Ciryandil his son continued the building of ships; but the Men of the Harad, led by the lords that had been driven from Umbar, came up with great power against that stronghold, and Ciryandil fell in battle in Haradwaith.

For many years Umbar was invested, but could not be taken because of the sea-power of Gondor. Ciryaher son of Ciryandil bided his time, and at last when he had gathered strength he came down from the north by sea and by land, and crossing the River Harnen his armies utterly defeated the Men of the Harad, and their kings were compelled to acknowledge the overlordship of Gondor (1050). Ciryaher then took the name of Hyarmendacil 'South-victor'.

The might of Hyarmendacil no enemy dared to contest during the remainder of his long reign. He was king for one hundred and thirty-four years, the longest reign

[1] The great cape and land-locked firth of Umbar had been Númenorean land since days of old; but it was a stronghold of the King's Men, who were afterwards called the Black Númenoreans, corrupted by Sauron, and who hated above all the followers of Elendil. After the fall of Sauron their race swiftly dwindled or became merged with the Men of Middle-earth, but they inherited without lessening their hatred of Gondor. Umbar, therefore, was only taken at great cost.

but one of all the Line of Anárion. In his day Gondor reached the summit of its power. The realm then extended north to Celebrant and the southern eaves of Mirkwood; west to the Greyflood; east to the inland Sea of Rhûn; south to the River Harnen, and thence along the coast to the peninsula and haven of Umbar. The Men of the Vales of Anduin acknowledged its authority; and the kings of the Harad did homage to Gondor, and their sons lived as hostages in the court of its King. Mordor was desolate, but was watched over by great fortresses that guarded the passes.

So ended the line of the Ship-kings. Atanatar Alcarin son of Hyarmendacil lived in great splendour, so that men said *precious stones are pebbles in Gondor for children to play with*. But Atanatar loved ease and did nothing to maintain the power that he had inherited, and his two sons were of like temper. The waning of Gondor had already begun before he died, and was doubtless observed by its enemies. The watch upon Mordor was neglected. Nonetheless it was not until the days of Valacar that the first great evil came upon Gondor: the civil war of the Kin-strife, in which great loss and ruin was caused and never fully repaired.

Minalcar, son of Calmacil, was a man of great vigour, and in 1240 Narmacil, to rid himself of all cares, made him Regent of the realm. From that time onwards he governed Gondor in the name of the kings until he succeeded his father. His chief concern was with the Northmen.

These had increased greatly in the peace brought by the power of Gondor. The kings showed them favour, since they were the nearest in kin of lesser Men to the Dúnedain (being for the most part descendants of those peoples from whom the Edain of old had come); and they gave them wide lands beyond Anduin south of Greenwood the Great, to be a defence against men of the East. For in the past the attacks of the Easterlings had come mostly over the plain between the Inland Sea and the Ash Mountains.

In the days of Narmacil I their attacks began again, though at first with little force; but it was learned by the regent that the Northmen did not always remain true to Gondor, and some would join forces with the Easterlings, either out of greed for spoil, or in the furtherance of feuds among their princes. Minalcar therefore in 1248 led out a great force, and between Rhovanion and the Inland Sea he defeated a large army of the Easterlings and destroyed all their camps and settlements east of the Sea. He then took the name of Rómendacil.

On his return Rómendacil fortified the west shore of Anduin as far as the inflow of the Limlight, and forbade any stranger to pass down the River beyond the Emyn Muil. He it was that built the pillars of the Argonath at the entrance to Nen Hithoel. But since he needed men, and desired to strengthen the bond between Gondor and the Northmen, he took many of them into his service and gave to some high rank in his armies.

Rómendacil showed especial favour to Vidugavia, who had aided him in the war. He called himself King of Rhovanion, and was indeed the most powerful of the Northern princes, though his own realm lay between Greenwood and the River Celduin.[1] In 1250 Rómendacil sent his son Valacar as an ambassador to dwell for

[1] The River Running.

a while with Vidugavia and make himself acquainted with the language, manners, and policies of the Northmen. But Valacar far exceeded his father's designs. He grew to love the Northern lands and people, and he married Vidumavi, daughter of Vidugavia. It was some years before he returned. From this marriage came later the war of the Kin-strife.

'For the high men of Gondor already looked askance at the Northmen among them; and it was a thing unheard of before that the heir of the crown, or any son of the King, should wed one of lesser and alien race. There was already rebellion in the southern provinces when King Valacar grew old. His queen had been a fair and noble lady, but short-lived according to the fate of lesser Men, and the Dúnedain feared that her descendants would prove the same and fall from the majesty of the Kings of Men. Also they were unwilling to accept as lord her son, who though he was now called Eldacar, had been born in an alien country and was named in his youth Vinitharya, a name of his mother's people.

'Therefore when Eldacar succeeded his father there was war in Gondor. But Eldacar did not prove easy to thrust from his heritage. To the lineage of Gondor he added the fearless spirit of the Northmen. He was handsome and valiant, and showed no sign of ageing more swiftly than his father. When the confederates led by descendants of the kings rose against him, he opposed them to the end of his strength. At last he was besieged in Osgiliath, and held it long, until hunger and the greater forces of the rebels drove him out, leaving the city in flames. In that siege and burning the Dome of Osgiliath was destroyed, and the *palantír* was lost in the waters.

'But Eldacar eluded his enemies, and came to the North, to his kinsfolk in Rhovanion. Many gathered to him there, both of the Northmen in the service of Gondor, and of the Dúnedain of the northern parts of the realm. For many of the latter had learned to esteem him, and many more came to hate his usurper. This was Castamir, grandson of Calimehtar, younger brother of Rómendacil II. He was not only one of those nearest by blood to the crown, but he had the greatest following of all the rebels; for he was the Captain of Ships, and was supported by the people of the coasts and of the great havens of Pelargir and Umbar.

'Castamir had not long sat upon the throne before he proved himself haughty and ungenerous. He was a cruel man, as he had first shown in the taking of Osgiliath. He caused Ornendil son of Eldacar, who was captured, to be put to death; and the slaughter and destruction done in the city at his bidding far exceeded the needs of war. This was remembered in Minas Anor and in Ithilien; and there love for Castamir was further lessened when it became seen that he cared little for the land, and thought only of the fleets, and purposed to remove the king's seat to Pelargir.

'Thus he had been king only ten years, when Eldacar, seeing his time, came with a great army out of the north, and folk flocked to him from Calenardhon and Anórien and Ithilien. There was a great battle in Lebennin at the Crossings of Erui, in which much of the best blood in Gondor was shed. Eldacar himself slew Castamir in combat, and so was avenged for Ornendil; but Castamir's sons escaped, and with others of their kin and many people of the fleets they held out long at Pelargir.

'When they had gathered there all the force that they could (for Eldacar had no ships to beset them by sea) they sailed away, and established themselves at Umbar.

There they made a refuge for all the enemies of the king, and a lordship independent of his crown. Umbar remained at war with Gondor for many lives of men, a threat to its coastlands and to all traffic on the sea. It was never again completely subdued until the days of Elessar; and the region of South Gondor became a debatable land between the Corsairs and the Kings.'

'The loss of Umbar was grievous to Gondor, not only because the realm was diminished in the south and its hold upon the Men of the Harad was loosened, but because it was there that Ar-Pharazôn the Golden, last King of Númenor, had landed and humbled the might of Sauron. Though great evil had come after, even the followers of Elendil remembered with pride the coming of the great host of Ar-Pharazôn out of the deeps of the Sea; and on the highest hill of the headland above the Haven they had set a great white pillar as a monument. It was crowned with a globe of crystal that took the rays of the Sun and of the Moon and shone like a bright star that could be seen in clear weather even on the coasts of Gondor or far out upon the western sea. So it stood, until after the second arising of Sauron, which now approached, Umbar fell under the domination of his servants, and the memorial of his humiliation was thrown down.'

After the return of Eldacar the blood of the kingly house and other houses of the Dúnedain became more mingled with that of lesser Men. For many of the great had been slain in the Kin-strife; while Eldacar showed favour to the Northmen, by whose help he had regained the crown, and the people of Gondor were replenished by great numbers that came from Rhovanion.

This mingling did not at first hasten the waning of the Dúnedain, as had been feared; but the waning still proceeded, little by little, as it had before. For no doubt it was due above all to Middle-earth itself, and to the slow withdrawing of the gifts of the Númenoreans after the downfall of the Land of the Star. Eldacar lived to his two hundred and thirty-fifth year, and was king for fifty-eight years, of which ten were spent in exile.

The second and greatest evil came upon Gondor in the reign of Telemnar, the twenty-six king, whose father Minardil, son of Eldacar, was slain at Pelargir by the Corsairs of Umbar. (They were led by Angamaitë and Sangahyando, the great-grandsons of Castamir.) Soon after a deadly plague came with dark winds out of the East. The King and all his children died, and great numbers of the people of Gondor, especially those that lived in Osgiliath. Then for weariness and fewness of men the watch on the borders of Mordor ceased and the fortresses that guarded the passes were unmanned.

Later it was noted that these things happened even as the Shadow grew deep in Greenwood, and many evil things reappeared, signs of the arising of Sauron. It is true that the enemies of Gondor also suffered, or they might have overwhelmed it in its weakness; but Sauron could wait, and it may well be that the opening of Mordor was what he chiefly desired.

When King Telemnar died the White Tree of Minas Anor also withered and died. But Tarondor, his nephew, who succeeded him, replanted a seedling in the citadel. He it was who removed the King's house permanently to Minas Anor, for Osgiliath was now partly deserted, and began to fall into ruin. Few of those who had fled from the plague into Ithilien or to the western dales were willing to return.

Tarondor, coming young to the throne, had the longest reign of all the Kings of Gondor; but he could achieve little more than the reordering of his realm within, and the slow nursing of its strength. But Telumehtar his son, remembering the death of Minardil, and being troubled by the insolence of the Corsairs, who raided his coasts even as far as the Anfalas, gathered his forces and in 1810 took Umbar by storm. In that war the last descendants of Castamir perished, and Umbar was again held for a while by the kings. Telumehtar added to his name the title Umbardacil. But in the new evils that soon befell Gondor Umbar was again lost, and fell into the hands of the Men of the Harad.

The third evil was the invasion of the Wainriders, which sapped the waning strength of Gondor in wars that lasted for almost a hundred years. The Wainriders were a people, or a confederacy of many peoples, that came from the East; but they were stronger and better armed than any that had appeared before. They journeyed in great wains, and their chieftains fought in chariots. Stirred up, as was afterwards seen, by the emissaries of Sauron, they made a sudden assault upon Gondor, and King Narmacil II was slain in battle with them beyond Anduin in 1856. The people of eastern and southern Rhovanion were enslaved; and the frontiers of Gondor were for that time withdrawn to the Anduin and the Emyn Muil. [At this time it is thought that the Ringwraiths re-entered Mordor.]

Calimehtar, son of Narmacil II, helped by a revolt in Rhovanion, avenged his father with a great victory over the Easterlings upon Dagorlad in 1899, and for a while the peril was averted. It was in the reign of Araphant in the North and of Ondoher son of Calimehtar in the South that the two kingdoms again took counsel together after long silence and estrangement. For at last they perceived that some single power and will was directing the assault from many quarters upon the survivors of Númenor. It was at that time that Arvedui heir of Araphant wedded Fíriel daughter of Ondoher (1940). But neither kingdom was able to send help to the other; for Angmar renewed its attack upon Arthedain at the same time as the Wainriders reappeared in great force.

Many of the Wainriders now passed south of Mordor and made alliance with men of Khand and of Near Harad; and in this great assault from north and south, Gondor came near to destruction. In 1944 King Ondoher and both his sons, Artamir and Faramir, fell in battle north of the Morannon, and the enemy poured into Ithilien. But Eärnil, Captain of the Southern Army, won a great victory in South Ithilien and destroyed the army of Harad that had crossed the River Poros. Hastening north, he gathered to him all that he could of the retreating Northern Army and came up against the main camp of the Wainriders, while they were feasting and revelling, believing that Gondor was overthrown and that nothing remained but to take the spoil. Eärnil stormed the camp and set fire to the wains, and drove the enemy in a great rout out of Ithilien. A great part of those who fled before him perished in the Dead Marshes.

'On the death of Ondoher and his sons, Arvedui of the North-kingdom claimed the crown of Gondor, as the direct descendant of Isildur, and as the husband of Fíriel, only surviving child of Ondoher. The claim was rejected. In this Pelendur, the Steward of King Ondoher, played the chief part.

'The Council of Gondor answered: "The crown and royalty of Gondor belongs solely to the heirs of Meneldil, son of Anárion, to whom Isildur relinquished this realm. In Gondor this heritage is reckoned through the sons only; and we have not heard that the law is otherwise in Arnor."

'To this Arvedui replied: "Elendil had two sons, of whom Isildur was the elder and the heir of his father. We have heard that the name of Elendil stands to this day at the head of the line of the Kings of Gondor, since he was accounted the high king of all lands of the Dúnedain. While Elendil still lived, the conjoint rule in the South was committed to his sons; but when Elendil fell, Isildur departed to take up the high kingship of his father, and committed the rule in the South in like manner to the son of his brother. He did not relinquish his royalty in Gondor, nor intend that the realm of Elendil should be divided for ever.

' "Moreover, in Númenor of old the sceptre descended to the eldest child of the king, whether man or woman. It is true that the law has not been observed in the lands of exile ever troubled by war; but such was the law of our people, to which we now refer, seeing that the sons of Ondoher died childless."[1]

'To this Gondor made no answer. The crown was claimed by Eärnil, the victorious captain; and it was granted to him with the approval of all the Dúnedain in Gondor, since he was of the royal house. He was the son of Siriondil, son of Calimmacil, son of Arciryas brother of Narmacil II. Arvedui did not press his claim; for he had neither the power nor the will to oppose the choice of the Dúnedain of Gondor; yet the claim was never forgotten by his descendants even when their kingship had passed away. For the time was now drawing near when the North-kingdom would come to an end.

'Arvedui was indeed the last king, as his name signifies. It is said that this name was given to him at his birth by Malbeth the Seer, who said to his father: "*Arvedui* you shall call him, for he will be the last in Arthedain. Though a choice will come to the Dúnedain, and if they take the one that seems less hopeful, then your son will change his name and become king of a great realm. If not, then much sorrow and many lives of men shall pass, until the Dúnedain arise and are united again."

'In Gondor also one king only followed Eärnil. It may be that if the crown and the sceptre had been united, then the kingship would have been maintained and much evil averted. But Eärnil was a wise man, and not arrogant, even if, as to most men in Gondor, the realm in Arthedain seemed a small thing, for all the lineage of its lords.

'He sent messages to Arvedui announcing that he received the crown of Gondor,

[1] That law was made in Númenor (as we have learned from the King) when Tar-Aldarion, the sixth king, left only one child, a daughter. She became the first Ruling Queen, Tar-Ancalimë. But the law was otherwise before her time. Tar-Elendil, the fourth king, was succeeded by his son Tar-Meneldur, though his daughter Silmariën was the elder. It was, however, from Silmariën that Elendil was descended.

according to the laws and the needs of the South-kingdom, "but I do not forget the royalty of Arnor, nor deny our kinship, nor wish that the realms of Elendil should be estranged. I will send to your aid when you have need, so far as I am able."

'It was, however, long before Eärnil felt himself sufficiently secure to do as he promised. King Araphant continued with dwindling strength to hold off the assaults of Angmar, and Arvedui when he succeeded did likewise; but at last in the autumn of 1973 messages came to Gondor that Arthedain was in great straits, and that the Witch-king was preparing a last stroke against it. Then Eärnil sent his son Eärnur north with a fleet, as swiftly as he could, and with as great strength as he could spare. Too late. Before Eärnur reached the havens of Lindon, the Witch-king had conquered Arthedain and Arvedui had perished.

'But when Eärnur came to the Grey Havens there was joy and great wonder among both Elves and Men. So great in draught and so many were his ships that they could scarcely find harbourage, though both the Harlond and the Forlond also were filled; and from them descended an army of power, with munition and provision for a war of great kings. Or so it seemed to the people of the North, though this was but a small sending-force of the whole might of Gondor. Most of all, the horses were praised, for many of them came from the Vales of Anduin and with them were riders tall and fair, and proud princes of Rhovanion.

'Then Círdan summoned all who would come to him, from Lindon or Arnor, and when all was ready the host crossed the Lune and marched north to challenge the Witch-king of Angmar. He was now dwelling, it is said, in Fornost, which he had filled with evil folk, usurping the house and rule of the kings. In his pride he did not await the onset of his enemies in his stronghold, but went out to meet them, thinking to sweep them, as others before, into the Lune.

'But the Host of the West came down on him out of the Hills of Evendim, and there was a great battle on the plain between Nenuial and the North Downs. The forces of Angmar were already giving way and retreating towards Fornost when the main body of the horsemen that had passed round the hills came down from the north and scattered them in a great rout. Then the Witch-king, with all that he could gather from the wreck, fled northwards, seeking his own land of Angmar. Before he could gain the shelter of Carn Dûm the cavalry of Gondor overtook him with Eärnur riding at their head. At the same time a force under Glorfindel the Elf-lord came up out of Rivendell. Then so utterly was Angmar defeated that not a man nor an orc of that realm remained west of the Mountains.

'But it is said that when all was lost suddenly the Witch-king himself appeared, black-robed and black-masked upon a black horse. Fear fell upon all who beheld him; but he singled out the Captain of Gondor for the fullness of his hatred, and with a terrible cry he rode straight upon him. Eärnur would have withstood him; but his horse could not endure that onset, and it swerved and bore him far away before he could master it.

'Then the Witch-king laughed, and none that heard it ever forgot the horror of that cry. But Glorfindel rode up then on his white horse, and in the midst of his laughter the Witch-king turned to flight and passed into the shadows. For night came down on the battlefield, and he was lost, and none saw whither he went.

'Eärnur now rode back, but Glorfindel, looking into the gathering dark, said:

"Do not pursue him! He will not return to this land. Far off yet is his doom, and not by the hand of man will he fall." These words many remembered; but Eärnur was angry, desiring only to be avenged for his disgrace.

'So ended the evil realm of Angmar; and so did Eärnur, Captain of Gondor, earn the chief hatred of the Witch-king; but many years were still to pass before that was revealed.'

It was thus in the reign of King Eärnil, as later became clear, that the Witch-king escaping from the North came to Mordor, and there gathered the other Ringwraiths, of whom he was the chief. But it was not until 2000 that they issued from Mordor by the Pass of Cirith Ungol and laid siege to Minas Ithil. This they took in 2002, and captured the *palantír* of the tower. They were not expelled while the Third Age lasted; and Minas Ithil became a place of fear, and was renamed Minas Morgul. Many of the people that still remained in Ithilien deserted it.

'Eärnur was a man like his father in valour, but not in wisdom. He was a man of strong body and hot mood; but he would take no wife, for his only pleasure was in fighting, or in the exercise of arms. His prowess was such that none in Gondor could stand against him in those weapon-sports in which he delighted, seeming rather a champion than a captain or king, and retaining his vigour and skill to a later age than was then usual.'

When Eärnur received the crown in 2043 the King of Minas Morgul challenged him to single combat, taunting him that he had not dared to stand before him in battle in the North. For that time Mardil the Steward restrained the wrath of the king. Minas Anor, which had become the chief city of the realm since the days of King Telemnar, and the residence of the kings, was now renamed Minas Tirith, as the city ever on guard against the evil of Morgul.

Eärnur had held the crown only seven years when the Lord of Morgul repeated his challenge, taunting the king that to the faint heart of his youth he had now added the weakness of age. Then Mardil could no longer restrain him, and he rode with a small escort of knights to the gate of Minas Morgul. None of that riding were ever heard of again. It was believed in Gondor that the faithless enemy had trapped the king, and that he had died in torment in Minas Morgul; but since there were no witnesses of his death, Mardil the Good Steward ruled Gondor in his name for many years.

Now the descendants of the kings had become few. Their numbers had been greatly diminished in the Kin-strife; whereas since that time the kings had become jealous and watchful of those near akin. Often those on whom suspicion fell had fled to Umbar and there joined the rebels; while others had renounced their lineage and taken wives not of Númenorean blood.

So it was that no claimant to the crown could be found who was of pure blood, or whose claim all would allow; and all feared the memory of the Kin-strife, knowing that if any such dissension arose again, then Gondor would perish. Therefore, though the years lengthened, the Steward continued to rule Gondor, and the crown of Elendil lay in the lap of King Eärnil in the Houses of the Dead, where Eärnur had left it.

The Stewards

The House of the Stewards was called the House of Húrin, for they were descendants of the Steward of King Minardil (1621–34), Húrin of Emyn Arnen, a man of high Númenorean race. After his day the kings had always chosen their stewards from among his descendants; and after the days of Pelendur the Stewardship became hereditary as a kingship, from father to son or nearest kin.

Each new Steward indeed took office with the oath 'to hold rod and rule in the name of the king, until he shall return'. But these soon became words of ritual little heeded, for the Stewards exercised all the power of the kings. Yet many in Gondor still believed that a king would indeed return in some time to come; and some remembered the ancient line of the North, which it was rumoured still lived on in the shadows. But against such thoughts the Ruling Stewards hardened their hearts.

Nonetheless the Stewards never sat on the ancient throne; and they wore no crown, and held no sceptre. They bore a white rod only as the token of their office; and their banner was white without charge; but the royal banner had been sable, upon which was displayed a white tree in blossom beneath seven stars.

After Mardil Voronwë, who was reckoned the first of the line, there followed twenty-four Ruling Stewards of Gondor, until the time of Denethor II, the twenty-sixth and last. At first they had quiet, for those were the days of the Watchful Peace, during which Sauron withdrew before the power of the White Council and the Ringwraiths remained hidden in Morgul Vale. But from the time of Denethor I, there was never full peace again, and even when Gondor had no great or open war its borders were under constant threat.

In the last years of Denethor I the race of uruks, black orcs of great strength, first appeared out of Mordor, and in 2475 they swept across Ithilien and took Osgiliath. Boromir son of Denethor (after whom Boromir of the Nine Walkers was later named) defeated them and regained Ithilien; but Osgiliath was finally ruined, and its great stone-bridge was broken. No people dwelt there afterwards. Boromir was a great captain, and even the Witch-king feared him. He was noble and fair of face, a man strong in body and in will, but he received a Morgul-wound in that war which shortened his days, and he became shrunken with pain and died twelve years after his father.

After him began the long rule of Cirion. He was watchful and wary, but the reach of Gondor had grown short, and he could do little more than defend his borders, while his enemies (or the power that moved them) prepared strokes against him that he could not hinder. The Corsairs harried his coasts, but it was in the north that his chief peril lay. In the wide lands of Rhovanion, between Mirkwood and the River Running, a fierce people now dwelt, wholly under the shadow of Dol Guldur. Often they made raids through the forest, until the vale of Anduin south of the Gladden was largely deserted. These Balchoth were constantly increased by others of like kind that came in from the east, whereas the people of Calenardhon had dwindled. Cirion was hard put to it to hold the line of the Anduin.

'Foreseeing the storm, Cirion sent north for aid, but over-late; for in that year (2510) the Balchoth, having built many great boats and rafts on the east shores of

Anduin, swarmed over the River and swept away the defenders. An army marching up from the south was cut off and driven north over the Limlight, and there it was suddenly attacked by a horde of Orcs from the Mountains and pressed towards the Anduin. Then out of the North there came help beyond hope, and the horns of the Rohirrim were first heard in Gondor. Eorl the Young came with his riders and swept away the enemy, and pursued the Balchoth to the death over the fields of Calenardhon. Cirion granted to Eorl that land to dwell in, and he swore to Cirion the Oath of Eorl, of friendship at need or at call to the Lords of Gondor.'

In the days of Beren, the nineteenth Steward, an even greater peril came upon Gondor. Three great fleets, long prepared, came up from Umbar and the Harad, and assailed the coasts of Gondor in great force; and the enemy made many landings, even as far north as the mouth of the Isen. At the same time the Rohirrim were assailed from the west and the east, and their land was overrun, and they were driven into the dales of the White Mountains. In that year (2758) the Long Winter began with cold and great snows out of the North and the East which lasted for almost five months. Helm of Rohan and both his sons perished in that war; and there was misery and death in Eriador and in Rohan. But in Gondor south of the mountains things were less evil, and before spring came Beregond son of Beren had overcome the invaders. At once he sent aid to Rohan. He was the greatest captain that had arisen in Gondor since Boromir; and when he succeeded his father (2763) Gondor began to recover its strength. But Rohan was slower to be healed of the hurts that it had received. It was for this reason that Beren welcomed Saruman, and gave to him the keys of Orthanc; and from that year on (2759) Saruman dwelt in Isengard.

It was in the days of Beregond that the War of the Dwarves and Orcs was fought in the Misty Mountains (2793–9), of which only rumour came south, until the Orcs fleeing from Nanduhirion attempted to cross Rohan and establish themselves in the White Mountains. There was fighting for many years in the dales before that danger was ended.

When Belecthor II, the twenty-first Steward, died, the White Tree died also in Minas Tirith; but it was left standing 'until the King returns', for no seedling could be found.

In the days of Túrin II the enemies of Gondor began to move again; for Sauron was grown again to power and the day of his arising was drawing near. All but the hardiest of its people deserted Ithilien and removed west over Anduin, for the land was infested by Mordor-orcs. It was Túrin that built secret refuges for his soldiers in Ithilien, of which Henneth Annûn was the longest guarded and manned. He also fortified again the isle of Cair Andros[1] to defend Anórien. But his chief peril lay in the south, where the Haradrim had occupied South Gondor, and there was much fighting along the Poros. When Ithilien was invaded in great strength, King Folcwine of Rohan fulfilled the Oath of Eorl and repaid his debt for the aid brought

[1] This name means 'Ship of Long-foam'; for the isle was shaped like a great ship, with a high prow pointing north, against which the white foam of Anduin broke on sharp rocks.

by Beregond, sending many men to Gondor. With their aid Túrin won a victory at the crossing of the Poros; but the sons of Folcwine both fell in the battle. The Riders buried them after the fashion of their people, and they were laid in one mound, for they were twin brothers. Long it stood, *Haudh in Gwanur*, high upon the shore of the river, and the enemies of Gondor feared to pass it.

Turgon followed Túrin, but of his time it is chiefly remembered that two years ere his death, Sauron arose again, and declared himself openly; and he re-entered Mordor long prepared for him. Then the Barad-dûr was raised once more, and Mount Doom burst into flame, and the last of the folk of Ithilien fled far away. When Turgon died Saruman took Isengard for his own, and fortified it.

'Ecthelion II, son of Turgon, was a man of wisdom. With what power was left to him he began to strengthen his realm against the assault of Mordor. He encouraged all men of worth from near or far to enter his service, and to those who proved trustworthy he gave rank and reward. In much that he did he had the aid and advice of a great captain whom he loved above all. Thorongil men called him in Gondor, the Eagle of the Star, for he was swift and keen-eyed, and wore a silver star upon his cloak; but no one knew his true name nor in what land he was born. He came to Ecthelion from Rohan, where he had served the King Thengel, but he was not one of the Rohirrim. He was a great leader of men, by land or by sea, but he departed into the shadows whence he came, before the days of Ecthelion were ended.

'Thorongil often counselled Ecthelion that the strength of the rebels in Umbar was a great peril to Gondor, and a threat to the fiefs of the south that would prove deadly, if Sauron moved to open war. At last he got leave of the Steward and gathered a small fleet, and he came to Umbar unlooked for by night, and there burned a great part of the ships of the Corsairs. He himself overthrew the Captain of the Haven in battle upon the quays, and then he withdrew his fleet with small loss. But when they came back to Pelargir, to men's grief and wonder, he would not return to Minas Tirith, where great honour awaited him.

'He sent a message of farewell to Ecthelion, saying: "Other tasks now call me, lord, and much time and many perils must pass, ere I come again to Gondor, if that be my fate." Though none could guess what those tasks might be, nor what summons he had received, it was known whither he went. For he took boat and crossed over Anduin, and there he said farewell to his companions and went on alone; and when he was last seen his face was towards the Mountains of Shadow.

'There was dismay in the City at the departure of Thorongil, and to all men it seemed a great loss, unless it were to Denethor, the son of Ecthelion, a man now ripe for the Stewardship, to which after four years he succeeded on the death of his father.

'Denethor II was a proud man, tall, valiant, and more kingly than any man that had appeared in Gondor for many lives of men; and he was wise also, and far-sighted, and learned in lore. Indeed he was as like to Thorongil as to one of nearest kin, and yet was ever placed second to the stranger in the hearts of men and the esteem of his father. At the time many thought that Thorongil had departed before his rival became his master; though indeed Thorongil had never himself vied with Denethor, nor held himself higher than the servant of his father. And in one matter only were their counsels to the Steward at variance: Thorongil often warned Ecthelion not to put trust in Saruman the White in Isengard, but to welcome rather Gandalf the Grey. But there was little love between Denethor and Gandalf; and after the days of Ecthelion there was less welcome for the Grey Pilgrim in Minas Tirith. Therefore later, when all was made clear, many believed that Denethor, who was subtle in mind and looked further and deeper than other men of his day, had discovered who this stranger Thorongil in truth was, and suspected that he and Mithrandir designed to supplant him.

'When Denethor became Steward (2984) he proved a masterful lord, holding the rule of all things in his own hand. He said little. He listened to counsel, and then followed his own mind. He had married late (2976), taking as wife Finduilas, daughter of Adrahil of Dol Amroth. She was a lady of great beauty and gentle heart, but before twelve years had passed she died. Denethor loved her, in his fashion, more dearly than any other, unless it were the elder of the sons that she bore him. But it seemed to men that she withered in the guarded city, as a flower of the seaward vales set upon a barren rock. The shadow in the east filled her with horror, and she turned her eyes ever south to the sea that she missed.

'After her death Denethor became more grim and silent than before, and would sit long alone in his tower deep in thought, foreseeing that the assault of Mordor would come in his time. It was afterwards believed that needing knowledge, but being proud, and trusting in his own strength of will, he dared to look in the *palantír* of the White Tower. None of the Stewards had dared to do this, nor even the kings Eärnil and Eärnur, after the fall of Minas Ithil when the *palantír* of Isildur came into the hands of the Enemy; for the Stone of Minas Tirith was the *palantír* of Anárion, most close in accord with the one that Sauron possessed.

'In this way Denethor gained his great knowledge of things that passed in his realm, and far beyond his borders, at which men marvelled; but he bought the knowledge dearly, being aged before his time by his contest with the will of Sauron. Thus pride increased in Denethor together with despair, until he saw in all the deeds of that time only a single combat between the Lord of the White Tower and the Lord of the Barad-dûr, and mistrusted all others who resisted Sauron, unless they served himself alone.

'So time drew on to the War of the Ring, and the sons of Denethor grew to manhood. Boromir, five years the elder, beloved by his father, was like him in face and pride, but in little else. Rather he was a man after the sort of King Eärnur of old, taking no wife and delighting chiefly in arms; fearless and strong, but caring little for lore, save the tales of old battles. Faramir the younger was like him in looks but otherwise in mind. He read the hearts of men as shrewdly as his father, but what he read moved him sooner to pity than to scorn. He was gentle in bearing, and a lover of lore and of music, and therefore by many in those days his courage was judged less than his brother's. But it was not so, except that he did not seek glory in danger without a purpose. He welcomed Gandalf at such times as he came to the City, and he learned what he could from his wisdom; and in this as in many other matters he displeased his father.

'Yet between the brothers there was great love, and had been since childhood, when Boromir was the helper and protector of Faramir. No jealousy or rivalry had arisen between them since, for their father's favour or for the praise of men. It did not seem possible to Faramir that any one in Gondor could rival Boromir, heir of Denethor, Captain of the White Tower; and of like mind was Boromir. Yet it proved otherwise at the test. But of all that befell these three in the War of the Ring much is said elsewhere. And after the War the days of the Ruling Stewards came to an end; for the heir of Isildur and Anárion returned and the kingship was renewed, and the standard of the White Tree flew once more from the Tower of Ecthelion.'

(v)
HERE FOLLOWS A PART OF THE TALE OF ARAGORN AND ARWEN

'Arador was the grandfather of the King. His son Arathorn sought in marriage Gilraen the Fair, daughter of Dírhael, who was himself a descendant of Aranarth. To this marriage Dírhael was opposed; for Gilraen was young and had not reached the age at which the women of the Dúnedain were accustomed to marry.

'"Moreover," he said, "Arathorn is a stern man of full age, and will be chieftain sooner than men looked for; yet my heart forebodes that he will be short-lived."

'But Ivorwen, his wife, who was also foresighted, answered: "The more need of haste! The days are darkening before the storm, and great things are to come. If these two wed now, hope may be born for our people; but if they delay, it will not come while this age lasts."

'And it happened that when Arathorn and Gilraen had been married only one year, Arador was taken by hill-trolls in the Coldfells north of Rivendell and was slain; and Arathorn became Chieftain of the Dúnedain. The next year Gilraen bore him a son, and he was called Aragorn. But Aragorn was only two years old when Arathorn went riding against the Orcs with the sons of Elrond, and he was slain by an orc-arrow that pierced his eye; and so he proved indeed short-lived for one of his race, being but sixty years old when he fell.

'Then Aragorn, being now the Heir of Isildur, was taken with his mother to dwell in the house of Elrond; and Elrond took the place of his father and came to love him as a son of his own. But he was called Estel, that is "Hope", and his true name and lineage were kept secret at the bidding of Elrond; for the Wise then knew that the Enemy was seeking to discover the Heir of Isildur, if any remained upon earth.

'But when Estel was only twenty years of age, it chanced that he returned to Rivendell after great deeds in the company of the sons of Elrond; and Elrond looked at him and was pleased, for he saw that he was fair and noble and was early come to manhood, though he would yet become greater in body and in mind. That day therefore Elrond called him by his true name, and told him who he was and whose son; and he delivered to him the heirlooms of his house.

'"Here is the ring of Barahir," he said, "the token of our kinship from afar; and here also are the shards of Narsil. With these you may yet do great deeds; for I foretell that the span of your life shall be greater than the measure of Men, unless evil befalls you or you fail at the test. But the test will be hard and long. The Sceptre of Annúminas I withhold, for you have yet to earn it."

'The next day at the hour of sunset Aragorn walked alone in the woods, and his heart was high within him; and he sang, for he was full of hope and the world was fair. And suddenly even as he sang he saw a maiden walking on a greensward among the white stems of the birches; and he halted amazed, thinking that he had strayed into a dream, or else that he had received the gift of the Elf-minstrels, who can make the things of which they sing appear before the eyes of those that listen.

'For Aragorn had been singing a part of the Lay of Lúthien which tells of the meeting of Lúthien and Beren in the forest of Neldoreth. And behold! there Lúthien walked before his eyes in Rivendell, clad in a mantle of silver and blue, fair as the twilight in Elven-home; her dark hair strayed in a sudden wind, and her brows were bound with gems like stars.

'For a moment Aragorn gazed in silence, but fearing that she would pass away and never be seen again, he called to her crying, *Tinúviel, Tinúviel!* even as Beren had done in the Elder Days long ago.

'Then the maiden turned to him and smiled, and she said: "Who are you? And why do you call me by that name?"

'And he answered: "Because I believed you to be indeed Lúthien Tinúviel, of whom I was singing. But if you are not she, then you walk in her likeness."

' "So many have said," she answered gravely. "Yet her name is not mine. Though maybe my doom will be not unlike hers. But who are you?"

' "Estel I was called," he said; "but I am Aragorn, Arathorn's son, Isildur's Heir, Lord of the Dúnedain"; yet even in the saying he felt that this high lineage, in which his heart had rejoiced, was now of little worth, and as nothing compared to her dignity and loveliness.

'But she laughed merrily and said: "Then we are akin from afar. For I am Arwen Elrond's daughter, and am named also Undómiel."

' "Often is it seen," said Aragorn, "that in dangerous days men hide their chief treasure. Yet I marvel at Elrond and your brothers; for though I have dwelt in this house from childhood, I have heard no word of you. How comes it that we have never met before? Surely your father has not kept you locked in his hoard?"

' "No," she said, and looked up at the Mountains that rose in the east. "I have dwelt for a time in the land of my mother's kin, in far Lothlórien. I have but lately returned to visit my father again. It is many years since I walked in Imladris."

'Then Aragorn wondered, for she had seemed of no greater age than he, who had lived yet no more than a score of years in Middle-earth. But Arwen looked in his eyes and said: "Do not wonder! For the children of Elrond have the life of the Eldar."

'Then Aragorn was abashed, for he saw the elven-light in her eyes and the wisdom of many days; yet from that hour he loved Arwen Undómiel daughter of Elrond.

'In the days that followed Aragorn fell silent, and his mother perceived that some strange thing had befallen him; and at last he yielded to her questions and told her of the meeting in the twilight of the trees.

'"My son," said Gilraen, "your aim is high, even for the descendant of many kings. For this lady is the noblest and fairest that now walks the earth. And it is not fit that mortal should wed with the Elf-kin."

'"Yet we have some part in that kinship," said Aragorn, "if the tale of my forefathers is true that I have learned."

'"It is true," said Gilraen, "but that was long ago and in another age of this world, before our race was diminished. Therefore I am afraid; for without the good will of Master Elrond the Heirs of Isildur will soon come to an end. But I do not think that you will have the good will of Elrond in this matter."

'"Then bitter will my days be, and I will walk in the wild alone," said Aragorn.

'"That will indeed be your fate," said Gilraen; but though she had in a measure the foresight of her people, she said no more to him of her foreboding, nor did she speak to any one of what her son had told her.

'But Elrond saw many things and read many hearts. One day, therefore, before the fall of the year he called Aragorn to his chamber, and he said: "Aragorn, Arathorn's son, Lord of the Dúnedain, listen to me! A great doom awaits you, either to rise above the height of all your fathers since the days of Elendil, or to fall into darkness with all that is left of your kin. Many years of trial lie before you. You shall neither have wife, nor bind any woman to you in troth, until your time comes and you are found worthy of it."

'Then Aragorn was troubled, and he said: "Can it be that my mother has spoken of this?"

'"No indeed," said Elrond. "Your own eyes have betrayed you. But I do not speak of my daughter alone. You shall be betrothed to no man's child as yet. But as for Arwen the Fair, Lady of Imladris and of Lórien, Evenstar of her people, she is of lineage greater than yours, and she has lived in the world already so long that to her you are but as a yearling shoot beside a young birch of many summers. She is too far above you. And so, I think, it may well seem to her. But even if it were not so, and her heart turned towards you, I should still be grieved because of the doom that is laid on us."

'"What is that doom?" said Aragorn.

'"That so long as I abide here, she shall live with the youth of the Eldar," answered Elrond, "and when I depart, she shall go with me, if she so chooses."

'"I see," said Aragorn, "that I have turned my eyes to a treasure no less dear than the treasure of Thingol that Beren once desired. Such is my fate." Then suddenly the foresight of his kindred came to him, and he said: "But lo! Master Elrond, the years of your abiding run short at last, and the choice must soon be laid on your children, to part either with you or with Middle-earth."

'"Truly," said Elrond. "Soon, as we account it, though many years of Men must still pass. But there will be no choice before Arwen, my beloved, unless you, Aragorn Arathorn's son, come between us and bring one of us, you or me, to a bitter parting beyond the end of the world. You do not know yet what you desire of me." He sighed, and after a while, looking gravely upon the young man, he said again: "The years will bring what they will. We will speak no more of this until many have passed. The days darken, and much evil is to come."

'Then Aragorn took leave lovingly of Elrond; and the next day he said farewell to his mother, and to the house of Elrond, and to Arwen, and he went out into the wild. For nearly thirty years he laboured in the cause against Sauron; and he became a friend of Gandalf the Wise, from whom he gained much wisdom. With him he made many perilous journeys, but as the years wore on he went more often alone. His ways were hard and long, and he became somewhat grim to look upon, unless he chanced to smile; and yet he seemed to Men worthy of honour, as a king that is in exile, when he did not hide his true shape. For he went in many guises, and won renown under many names. He rode in the host of the Rohirrim, and fought for the Lord of Gondor by land and by sea; and then in the hour of victory he passed out of the knowledge of Men of the West, and went alone far into the East and deep into the South, exploring the hearts of Men, both evil and good, and uncovering the plots and devices of the servants of Sauron.

'Thus he became at last the most hardy of living Men, skilled in their crafts and lore, and was yet more than they; for he was elven-wise, and there was a light in his eyes that when they were kindled few could endure. His face was sad and stern because of the doom that was laid on him, and yet hope dwelt ever in the depths of his heart, from which mirth would arise at times like a spring from the rock.

'It came to pass that when Aragorn was nine and forty years of age he returned from perils on the dark confines of Mordor, where Sauron now dwelt again and was busy with evil. He was weary and he wished to go back to Rivendell and rest there for a while ere he journeyed into the far countries; and on his way he came to the borders of Lórien and was admitted to the hidden land by the Lady Galadriel.

'He did not know it, but Arwen Undómiel was also there, dwelling again for a time with the kin of her mother. She was little changed, for the mortal years had passed her by; yet her face was more grave, and her laughter now seldom was heard. But Aragorn was grown to full stature of body and mind, and Galadriel bade him cast aside his wayworn raiment, and she clothed him in silver and white, with a cloak of elven-grey and bright gem on his brow. Then more than any kind of Men he appeared, and seemed rather an Elf-lord from the Isles of the West. And thus it was that Arwen first beheld him again after their long parting; and as he came walking towards her under the trees of Caras Galadhon laden with flowers of gold, her choice was made and her doom appointed.

'Then for a season they wandered together in the glades of Lothlórien, until it was time for him to depart. And on the evening of Midsummer Aragorn Arathorn's son, and Arwen daughter of Elrond went to the fair hill, Cerin Amroth, in the midst of the land, and they walked unshod on the undying grass with elanor and niphredil about their feet. And there upon that hill they looked east to the Shadow and west to the Twilight, and they plighted their troth and were glad.

'And Arwen said: "Dark is the Shadow, and yet my heart rejoices; for you, Estel, shall be among the great whose valour will destroy it."

'But Aragorn answered: "Alas! I cannot foresee it, and how it may come to pass is hidden from me. Yet with your hope I will hope. And the Shadow I utterly reject. But neither, lady, is the Twilight for me; for I a mortal, and if you will cleave to me, Evenstar, then the Twilight you must also renounce."

'And she stood then as still as a white tree, looking into the West, and at last she said: "I will cleave to you, Dúnadan, and turn from the Twilight. Yet there lies the land of my people and the long home of all my kin." She loved her father dearly.

'When Elrond learned the choice of his daughter, he was silent, though his heart was grieved and found the doom long feared none the easier to endure. But when Aragorn came again to Rivendell he called him to him, and he said:

' "My son, years come when hope will fade, and beyond them little is clear to me. And now a shadow lies between us. Maybe, it has been appointed so, that by my loss the kingship of Men may be restored. Therefore, though I love you, I say to you: Arwen Undómiel shall not diminish her life's grace for less cause. She shall not be the bride of any Man less than the King of both Gondor and Arnor. To me then even our victory can bring only sorrow and parting – but to you hope of joy for a while. Alas, my son! I fear that to Arwen the Doom of Men may seem hard at the ending."

'So it stood afterwards between Elrond and Aragorn, and they spoke no more of this matter; but Aragorn went forth again to danger and toil. And while the world darkened and fear fell on Middle-earth, as the power of Sauron grew and the Barad-dûr rose ever taller and stronger, Arwen remained in Rivendell, and when Aragorn was abroad, from afar she watched over him in thought; and in hope she made for him a great and kingly standard, such as only one might display who claimed the lordship of the Númenoreans and the inheritance of Elendil.

'After a few years Gilraen took leave of Elrond and returned to her own people in Eriador, and lived alone; and she seldom saw her son again, for he spent many years in far countries. But on a time, when Aragorn had returned to the North, he came to her, and she said to him before he went:

' "This is our last parting, Estel, my son. I am aged by care, even as one of lesser Men; and now that it draws near I cannot face the darkness of our time that gathers upon Middle-earth. I shall leave it soon."

'Aragorn tried to comfort her, saying: "Yet there may be a light beyond the darkness; and if so, I would have you see it and be glad."

'But she answered only with this *linnod*:

Onen i-Estel Edain, ú-chebin estel anim,[1]

and Aragorn went away heavy of heart. Gilraen died before the next spring.

'Thus the years drew on to the War of the Ring; of which more is told elsewhere: how the means unforeseen was revealed whereby Sauron might be overthrown, and how hope beyond hope was fulfilled. And it came to pass that in the hour of defeat Aragorn came up from the sea and unfurled the standard of Arwen in the battle of the Fields of Pelennor, and in that day he was first hailed as king. And at last when all was done he entered into the inheritance of his fathers and received the crown of Gondor and sceptre of Arnor; and at Midsummer in the year of the Fall of Sauron

[1] 'I gave Hope to the Dúnedain, I have kept no hope for myself.'

he took the hand of Arwen Undómiel, and they were wedded in the city of the Kings.

'The Third Age ended thus in victory and hope; and yet grievous among the sorrows of that Age was the parting of Elrond and Arwen, for they were sundered by the Sea and by a doom beyond the end of the world. When the Great Ring was unmade and the Three were shorn of their power, then Elrond grew weary at last and forsook Middle-earth, never to return. But Arwen became as a mortal woman, and yet it was not her lot to die until all that she had gained was lost.

'As Queen of Elves and Men she dwelt with Aragorn for six-score years in great glory and bliss; yet at last he felt the approach of old age and knew that the span of his life-days was drawing to an end, long though it had been. Then Aragorn said to Arwen:

'"At last, Lady Evenstar, fairest in this world, and most beloved, my world is fading. Lo! we have gathered, and we have spent, and now the time of payment draws near."

'Arwen knew well what he intended, and long had foreseen it; nonetheless she was overborne by her grief. "Would you then, lord, before your time leave your people that live by your word?" she said.

'"Not before my time," he answered. "For if I will not go now, then I must soon go perforce. And Eldarion our son is a man full-ripe for kingship."

'Then going to the House of the Kings in the Silent Street, Aragorn laid him down on the long bed that had been prepared for him. There he said farewell to Eldarion, and gave into his hands the winged crown of Gondor and the sceptre of Arnor; and then all left him save Arwen, and she stood alone by his bed. And for all her wisdom and lineage she could not forbear to plead with him to stay yet for a while. She was not yet weary of her days, and thus she tasted the bitterness of the mortality that she had taken upon her.

'"Lady Undómiel," said Aragorn, "the hour is indeed hard, yet it was made even in that day when we met under the white birches in the garden of Elrond where none now walk. And on the hill of Cerin Amroth when we forsook both the Shadow and the Twilight this doom we accepted. Take counsel with yourself, beloved, and ask whether you would indeed have me wait until I wither and fall from my high seat unmanned and witless. Nay, lady, I am the last of the Númenoreans and the latest King of the Elder Days; and to me has been given not only a span thrice that of Men of Middle-earth, but also the grace to go at my will, and give back the gift. Now, therefore, I will sleep.

'"I speak no comfort to you, for there is no comfort for such pain within the circles of the world. The uttermost choice is before you: to repent and go to the Havens and bear away into the West the memory of our days together that shall there be evergreen but never more than memory; or else to abide the Doom of Men."

'"Nay, dear lord," she said, "that choice is long over. There is now no ship that would bear me hence, and I must indeed abide the Doom of Men, whether I will or I nill: the loss and the silence. But I say to you, King of the Númenoreans, not till now have I understood the tale of your people and their fall. As wicked fools I scorned them, but I pity them at last. For if this is indeed, as the Eldar say, the gift of the One to Men, it is bitter to receive."

'"So it seems," he said. "But let us not be overthrown at the final test, who of old renounced the Shadow and the Ring. In sorrow we must go, but not in despair. Behold! we are not bound for ever to the circles of the world, and beyond them is more than memory. Farewell!"

'"Estel, Estel!" she cried, and with that even as he took her hand and kissed it, he fell into sleep. Then a great beauty was revealed in him, so that all who after came there looked on him in wonder; for they saw that the grace of his youth, and the valour of his manhood, and the wisdom and majesty of his age were blended together. And long there he lay, an image of the splendour of the Kings of Men in glory undimmed before the breaking of the world.

'But Arwen went forth from the House, and the light of her eyes was quenched, and it seemed to her people that she had become cold and grey as nightfall in winter that comes without a star. Then she said farewell to Eldarion, and to her daughters, and to all whom she had loved; and she went out from the city of Minas Tirith and passed away to the land of Lórien, and dwelt there alone under the fading trees until winter came. Galadriel had passed away and Celeborn also was gone, and the land was silent.

'There at last when the mallorn-leaves were falling, but spring had not yet come,[1] she laid herself to rest upon Cerin Amroth; and there is her green grave, until the world is changed, and all the days of her life are utterly forgotten by men that come after, and elanor and niphredil bloom no more east of the Sea.

'Here ends this tale, as it has come to us from the South; and with the passing of Evenstar no more is said in this book of the days of old.'

II
THE HOUSE OF EORL

'Eorl the Young was lord of the Men of Éothéod. That land lay near the sources of Anduin, between the furthest ranges of the Misty Mountains and the northernmost parts of Mirkwood. The Éothéod had moved to those regions in the days of King Eärnil II from lands in the vales of Anduin between the Carrock and the Gladden, and they were in origin close akin to the Beornings and the men of the west-eaves of the forest. The forefathers of Eorl claimed descent from kings of Rhovanion, whose realm lay beyond Mirkwood before the invasions of the Wainriders, and thus they accounted themselves kinsmen of the kings of Gondor descended from Eldacar. They loved best the plains, and delighted in horses and in all feats of horsemanship, but there were many men in the middle vales of Anduin in those days, and moreover the shadow of Dol Guldur was lengthening; when therefore they heard of the overthrow of the Witch-king, they sought more room in the North, and drove away the remnants of the people of Angmar on the east side of the Mountains. But in the days of Léod, father of Eorl, they had grown to be a numerous people and were again somewhat straitened in the land of their home.

[1] p. 326.

'In the two thousand five hundred and tenth year of the Third Age a new peril threatened Gondor. A great host of wild men from the North-east swept over Rhovanion and coming down out of the Brown-lands crossed the Anduin on rafts. At the same time by chance or design the Orcs (who at that time before their war with the Dwarves were in great strength) made a descent from the Mountains. The invaders overran Calenardhon, and Cirion, Steward of Gondor, sent north for help; for there had been long friendship between the Men of Anduin's Vale and the people of Gondor. But in the valley of the River men were now few and scattered, and slow to render such aid as they could. At last tidings came to Eorl of the need of Gondor, and late though it seemed, he set out with a great host of riders.

'Thus he came to the battle of the Field of Celebrant, for that was the name of the green land that lay between Silverlode and Limlight. There the northern army of Gondor was in peril. Defeated in the Wold and cut off from the south, it had been driven across the Limlight, and was then suddenly assailed by the Orc-host that pressed it towards the Anduin. All hope was lost when, unlooked for, the Riders came out of the North and broke upon the rear of the enemy. Then the fortunes of battle were reversed, and the enemy was driven with slaughter over Limlight. Eorl led his men in pursuit, and so great was the fear that went before horsemen of the North that the invaders of the Wold were also thrown into panic, and the Riders hunted them over the plains of Calenardhon.'

The people of that region had become few since the Plague, and most of those that remained had been slaughtered by the savage Easterlings. Cirion, therefore, in reward for his aid, gave Calenardhon between Anduin and Isen to Eorl and his people; and they sent north for their wives and children and their goods and settled in that land. They named it anew the Mark of the Riders, and they called themselves the Eorlingas; but in Gondor their land was called Rohan, and its people the Rohirrim (that is, the Horse-lords). Thus Eorl became the first King of the Mark, and he chose for his dwelling a green hill before the feet of the White Mountains that were the south-wall of his land. There the Rohirrim lived afterwards as free men under their own kings and laws, but in perpetual alliance with Gondor.

'Many lords and warriors, and many fair and valiant women, are named in the songs of Rohan that still remember the North. Frumgar, they say, was the name of the chieftain who led his people to Éothéod. Of his son, Fram, they tell that he slew Scatha, the great dragon of Ered Mithrin, and the land had peace from the long-worms afterwards. Thus Fram won great wealth, but was at feud with the Dwarves, who claimed the hoard of Scatha. Fram would not yield them a penny, and sent to them instead the teeth of Scatha made into a necklace, saying: "Jewels such as these you will not match in your treasuries, for they are hard to come by." Some say that the Dwarves slew Fram for this insult. There was no great love between Éothéod and the Dwarves.

'Léod was the name of Eorl's father. He was a tamer of wild horses; for there were many at that time in the land. He captured a white foal and it grew quickly to a horse strong, and fair, and proud. No man could tame it. When Léod dared to mount it, it bore him away, and at last threw him, and Léod's head struck a rock, and so he died. He was then only two and forty years old, and his son a youth of sixteen.

'Eorl vowed that he would avenge his father. He hunted long for the horse, and at last he caught sight of him; and his companions expected that he would try to come within bowshot and kill him. But when they drew near, Eorl stood up and called in a loud voice: "Come hither, Mansbane, and get a new name!" To their wonder the horse looked towards Eorl, and came and stood before him, and Eorl said: "Felaróf I name you. You loved your freedom, and I do not blame you for that. But now you owe me a great weregild, and you shall surrender your freedom to me until your life's end."

'Then Eorl mounted him, and Felaróf submitted; and Eorl rode him home without bit or bridle; and he rode him in like fashion ever after. The horse understood all that men said, though he would allow no man but Eorl to mount him. It was upon Felaróf that Eorl rode to the Field of Celebrant; for that horse proved as long lived as Men, and so were his descendants. These were the *mearas*, who would bear no one but the King of the Mark or his sons, until the time of Shadowfax. Men said of them that Béma (whom the Eldar call Oromë) must have brought their sire from West over Sea.

'Of the Kings of the Mark between Eorl and Théoden most is said of Helm Hammerhand. He was a grim man of great strength. There was at that time a man named Freca, who claimed descent from King Fréawine, though he had, men said, much Dunlendish blood, and was dark-haired. He grew rich and powerful, having wide lands on either side of the Adorn.[1] Near its source he made himself a stronghold and paid little heed to the king. Helm mistrusted him, but called him to his councils; and he came when it pleased him.

'To one of these councils Freca rode with many men, and he asked the hand of Helm's daughter for his son Wulf. But Helm said: "You have grown big since you were last here; but it is mostly fat, I guess"; and men laughed at that, for Freca was wide in the belt.

'Then Freca fell in a rage and reviled the king, and said this at the last: "Old kings that refuse a proffered staff may fall on their knees." Helm answered: "Come! The marriage of your son is a trifle. Let Helm and Freca deal with it later. Meanwhile the king and his council have matters of moment to consider."

'When the council was over, Helm stood up and laid his great hand on Freca's shoulder, saying: "The king does not permit brawls in his house, but men are freer outside"; and he forced Freca to walk before him out from Edoras into the field. To Freca's men that came up he said: "Be off! We need no hearers. We are going to speak of a private matter alone. Go and talk to my men!" And they looked and saw that the king's men and his friends far outnumbered them, and they drew back.

'"Now, Dunlending," said the king, "you have only Helm to deal with, alone and unarmed. But you have said much already, and it is my turn to speak. Freca, your folly has grown with your belly. You talk of a staff! If Helm dislikes a crooked staff that is thrust on him, he breaks it. So!" With that he smote Freca such a blow with his fist that he fell back stunned, and died soon after.

[1] It flows into Isen from the west of Ered Nimrais.

'Helm then proclaimed Freca's son and near kin the king's enemies; and they fled, for at once Helm sent many men riding to the west marches.'

Four years later (2758) great troubles came to Rohan, and no help could be sent from Gondor, for three fleets of the Corsairs attacked it and there was war on all its coasts. At the same time Rohan was again invaded from the East, and the Dunlendings seeing their chance came over the Isen and down from Isengard. It was soon known that Wulf was their leader. The were in great force, for they were joined by enemies of Gondor that landed in the mouths of Lefnui and Isen.

The Rohirrim were defeated and their land was overrun; and those who were not slain or enslaved fled to the dales of the mountains. Helm was driven back with great loss from the Crossings of Isen and took refuge in the Hornburg and the ravine behind (which was after known as Helm's Deep). There he was besieged. Wulf took Edoras and sat in Meduseld and called himself king. There Haleth Helm's son fell, last of all, defending the doors.

'Soon afterwards the Long Winter began, and Rohan lay under snow for nearly five months (November to March, 2758–9). Both the Rohirrim and their foes suffered grievously in the cold, and in the dearth that lasted longer. In Helm's Deep there was a great hunger after Yule; and being in despair, against the king's counsel, Háma his younger son led men out on a sortie and foray, but they were lost in the snow. Helm grew fierce and gaunt for famine and grief; and the dread of him alone was worth many men in the defence of the Burg. He would go out by himself, clad in white, and stalk like a snow-troll into the camps of his enemies, and slay many men with his hands. It was believed that if he bore no weapon no weapon would bite on him. The Dunlendings said that if he could find no food he ate men. That tale lasted long in Dunland. Helm had a great horn, and soon it was marked that before he sallied forth he would blow a blast upon it that echoed in the Deep; and then so great a fear fell on his enemies that instead of gathering to take him or kill him they fled away down the Coomb.

'One night men heard the horn blowing, but Helm did not return. In the morning there came a sun-gleam, the first for long days, and they saw a white figure standing still on the Dike, alone, for none of the Dunlendings dared come near. There stood Helm, dead as a stone, but his knees were unbent. Yet men said that the horn was still heard at times in the Deep and the wraith of Helm would walk among the foes of Rohan and kill men with fear.

'Soon after the winter broke. Then Fréaláf, son of Hild, Helm's sister, came down out of Dunharrow, to which many had fled; and with a small company of desperate men he surprised Wulf in Meduseld and slew him, and regained Edoras. There were great floods after the snows, and the vale of Entwash became a vast fen. The Eastern invaders perished or withdrew; and there came help at last from Gondor, by the roads both east and west of the mountains. Before the year (2759) was ended the Dunlendings were driven out, even from Isengard; and then Fréaláf became king.

'Helm was brought from the Hornburg and laid in the ninth mound. Ever after the white *simbelmynë* grew there most thickly, so that the mound seemed to be snow-clad. When Fréaláf died a new line of mounds was begun.'

The Rohirrim were grievously reduced by war and dearth and loss of cattle and horses; and it was well that no great danger threatened them again for many years, for it was not until the time of King Folcwine that they recovered their former strength.

It was at the crowning of Fréaláf that Saruman appeared, bringing gifts, and speaking great praise of the valour of the Rohirrim. All thought him a welcome guest. Soon after he took up his abode in Isengard. For this, Beren, Steward of Gondor, gave him leave, for Gondor still claimed Isengard as a fortress of its realm, and not part of Rohan. Beren also gave into Saruman's keeping the keys of Orthanc. That tower no enemy had been able to harm or to enter.

In this way Saruman began to behave as a lord of Men; for at first he held Isengard as a lieutenant of the Steward and warden of the tower. But Fréaláf was as glad as Beren to have this so, and to know that Isengard was in the hands of a strong friend. A friend he long seemed, and maybe in the beginning he was one in truth. Though afterwards there was little doubt in men's minds that Saruman went to Isengard in hope to find the Stone still there, and with the purpose of building up a power of his own. Certainly after the last White Council (2953) his designs towards Rohan, though he hid them, were evil. He then took Isengard for his own and began to make it a place of guarded strength and fear, as though to rival the Barad-dûr. His friends and servants he drew then from all who hated Gondor and Rohan, whether Men or other creatures more evil.

THE KINGS OF THE MARK

Year[1]	*First Line*
2485–2545	1. *Eorl the Young*. He was so named because he succeeded his father in youth and remained yellow-haired and ruddy to the end of his days. These were shortened by a renewed attack of the Easterlings. Eorl fell in battle in the Wold, and the first mound was raised. Felaróf was laid there also.
2512–70	2. *Brego*. He drove the enemy out of the Wold, and Rohan was not attacked again for many years. In 2569 he completed the great hall of Meduseld. At the feast his son Baldor vowed that he would tread 'the Paths of the Dead' and did not return.[2] Brego died of grief the next year.
2544–2645	3. *Aldor the Old*. He was Brego's second son. He became known as the Old, since he lived to a great age, and was king for 75 years. In his time the Rohirrim increased, and drove out or subdued the last of the Dunlendish people that lingered east of Isen. Harrowdale and other mountain-valleys were settled. Of the next three kings little is said, for Rohan had peace and prospered in their time.

[1] The dates are given according to the reckoning of Gondor (Third Age). Those in the margin are of birth and death.

[2] pp. 770, 780.

2570–2659 4. *Fréa.* Eldest son, but fourth child of Aldor; he was already old when he became king.

2594–2680 5. *Frëawine.*

2619–99 6. *Goldwine.*

2644–2718 7. *Déor.* In his time the Dunlendings raided often over the Isen. In 2710 they occupied the deserted ring of Isengard, and could not be dislodged.

2668–2741 8. *Gram.*

2691–2759 9. *Helm Hammerhand.* At the end of his reign Rohan suffered great loss, by invasion and the Long Winter. Helm and his sons Haleth and Háma perished. Fréaláf, Helm's sister's son, became king.

Year *Second Line*

2726–2798 10. *Fréaláf Hildeson.* In his time Saruman came to Isengard, from which the Dunlendings had been driven. The Rohirrim at first profited by his friendship in the days of dearth and weakness that followed.

2752–2842 11. *Brytta.* He was called by his people *Léofa*, for he was loved by all; he was openhanded and a help to all the needy. In his time there was war with Orcs that, driven from the North, sought refuges in the White Mountains.[1] When he died it was thought that they had all been hunted out; but it was not so.

2780–2851 12. *Walda.* He was king only nine years. He was slain with all his companions when they were trapped by Orcs, as they rode by mountain-paths from Dunharrow.

2804–64 13. *Folca.* He was a great hunter, but he vowed to chase no wild beast while there was an Orc left in Rohan. When the last orc-hold was found and destroyed, he went to hunt the great boar of Everholt in the Firien Wood. He slew the boar but died of the tusk-wounds that it gave him.

2830–2903 14. *Folcwine.* When he became king the Rohirrim had recovered their strength. He reconquered the west-march (between Adorn and Isen) that Dunlendings had occupied. Rohan had received great help from Gondor in the evil days. When, therefore, he heard that the Haradrim were assailing Gondor with great strength, he sent many men to the help of the Steward. He wished to lead them himself, but was dissuaded, and his twin sons Folcred and Fastred (born 2858) went in his stead. They fell side by side in battle in Ithilien (2885). Túrin II of Gondor sent to Folcwine a rich weregild of gold.

2870–2953 15. *Fengel.* He was the third son and fourth child of Folcwine. He is not remembered with praise. He was greedy of food and of gold, and at strife with his marshals, and with his children. Thengel, his third child and only son, left Rohan when he came to manhood and lived long in Gondor, and won honour in the service of Turgon.

[1] p. 1029.

2905–80 16. *Thengel*. He took no wife until late, but in 2943 he wedded Morwen of Lossarnach in Gondor, though she was seventeen years the younger. She bore him three children in Gondor, of whom Théoden, the second, was his only son. When Fengel died the Rohirrim recalled him, and he returned unwillingly. But he proved a good and wise king; though the speech of Gondor was used in his house, and not all men thought that good. Morwen bore him two more daughters in Rohan; and the last, Théodwyn, was the fairest, though she came late (2963), the child of his age. Her brother loved her dearly.

It was soon after Thengel's return that Saruman declared himself Lord of Isengard and began to give trouble to Rohan, encroaching on its borders and supporting its enemies.

2948–3019 17. *Théoden*. He is called Théoden Ednew in the lore of Rohan, for he fell into a decline under the spells of Saruman, but was healed by Gandalf, and in the last year of his life arose and led his men to victory at the Hornburg, and soon after to the Fields of Pelennor, the greatest battle of the Age. He fell before the gates of Mundburg. For a while he rested in the land of his birth, among the dead Kings of Gondor, but was brought back and laid in the eighth mound of his line at Edoras. Then a new line was begun.

Third Line

In 2989 Théodwyn married Éomund of Eastfold, the chief Marshal of the Mark. Her son Éomer was born in 2991, and her daughter Éowyn in 2995. At that time Sauron had arisen again, and the shadow of Mordor reached out to Rohan. Orcs began to raid in the eastern regions and slay or steal horses. Others also came down from the Misty Mountains, many being great uruks in the service of Saruman, though it was long before that was suspected. Éomund's chief charge lay in the east marches; and he was a great lover of horses and hater of Orcs. If news came of a raid he would often ride against them in hot anger, unwarily and with few men. Thus it came about that he was slain in 3002; for he pursued a small band to the borders of the Emyn Muil, and was there surprised by a strong force that lay in wait in the rocks.

Not long after Théodwyn took sick and died to the great grief of the king. Her children he took into his house, calling them son and daughter. He had only one child of his own, Théodred his son, then twenty-four years old; for the queen Elfhild had died in childbirth, and Théoden did not wed again. Éomer and Éowyn grew up at Edoras and saw the dark shadow fall on the halls of Théoden. Éomer was like his fathers before him; but Éowyn was slender and tall, with a grace and pride that came her out of the South from Morwen of Lossarnach, whom the Rohirrim had called Steelsheen.

2991–F.A. 63 (3084) *Éomer Éadig*. When still young he became a Marshal of the Mark (3017) and was given his father's charge in the east marches. In the War of the Ring Théodred fell in battle with Saruman at the

Crossings of Isen. Therefore before he died on the Fields of the Pelennor Théoden named Éomer his heir and called him king. In that day Éowyn also won renown, for she fought in that battle, riding in disguise; and was known after in the Mark as the Lady of the Shield-arm.[1]

Éomer became a great king, and being young when he succeeded Théoden he reigned for sixty-five years, longer than all their kings before him save Aldor the Old. In the War of the Ring he made the friendship of King Elessar, and of Imrahil of Dol Amroth; and he rode often to Gondor. In the last year of the Third Age he wedded Lothíriel, daughter of Imrahil. Their son Elfwine the Fair ruled after him.

In Éomer's day in the Mark men had peace who wished for it, and the people increased both in the dales and the plains, and their horses multiplied. In Gondor the King Elessar now ruled, and in Arnor also. In all the lands of those realms of old he was king, save in Rohan only; for he renewed to Éomer the gift of Cirion, and Éomer took again the Oath of Eorl. Often he fulfilled it. For though Sauron had passed, the hatreds and evils that he bred had not died, and the King of the West had many enemies to subdue before the White Tree could grow in peace. And wherever King Elessar went with war King Éomer went with him; and beyond the Sea of Rhûn and on the far fields of the South the thunder of the cavalry of the Mark was heard, and the White Horse upon Green flew in many winds until Éomer grew old.

III
DURIN'S FOLK

Concerning the beginning of the Dwarves strange tales are told both by the Eldar and by the Dwarves themselves; but since these things lie far back beyond our days little is said of them here. Durin is the name that the Dwarves used for the eldest of the Seven Fathers of their race, and the ancestor of all the kings of the Longbeards.[2] He slept alone, until in the deeps of time and the awakening of that people he came to Azanulbizar, and in the caves above Kheled-zâram in the east of the Misty Mountains he made his dwelling, where afterwards were the Mines of Moria renowned in song.

There he lived so long that he was known far and wide as Durin the Deathless. Yet in the end he died before the Elder Days had passed, and his tomb was in

[1] For her shield-arm was broken by the mace of the Witch-king; but he was brought to nothing, and thus the words of Glorfindel long before to King Eärnur were fulfilled, that the Witch-king would not fall by the hand of man. For it is said in the songs of the Mark that in this deed Éowyn had the aid of Théoden's esquire, and that he also was not a Man but a Halfling out of a far country, though Éomer gave him honour in the Mark and the name of Holdwine.

[This Holdwine was none other than Meriadoc the Magnificent who was Master of Buckland.]

[2] *The Hobbit*, p. 52.

Khazad-dûm; but his line never failed, and five times an heir was born in his House so like to his Forefather that he received the name of Durin. He was indeed held by the Dwarves to be the Deathless that returned; for they have many strange tales and beliefs concerning themselves and their fate in the world.

After the end of the First Age the power and wealth of Khazad-dûm was much increased; for it was enriched by many people and much lore and craft when the ancient cities of Nogrod and Belegost in the Blue Mountains were ruined at the breaking of Thangorodrim. The power of Moria endured throughout the Dark Years and the dominion of Sauron, for though Eregion was destroyed and the gates of Moria were shut, the halls of Khazad-dûm were too deep and strong and filled with a people too numerous and valiant for Sauron to conquer from without. Thus its wealth remained long unravished, though its people began to dwindle.

It came to pass that in the middle of the Third Age Durin was again its king, being the sixth of that name. The power of Sauron, servant of Morgoth, was then again growing in the world, though the Shadow in the Forest that looked towards Moria was not yet known for what it was. All evil things were stirring. The Dwarves delved deep at that time, seeking beneath Barazinbar for *mithril*, the metal beyond price that was becoming yearly ever harder to win.[1] Thus they roused from sleep[2] a thing of terror that, flying from Thangorodrim, had lain hidden at the foundations of the earth since the coming of the Host of the West: a Balrog of Morgoth. Durin was slain by it, and the year after Náin I, his son; and then the glory of Moria passed, and its people were destroyed or fled far away.

Most of these that escaped made their way into the North, and Thráin I, Náin's son, came to Erebor, the Lonely Mountain, near the eastern eaves of Mirkwood, and there he began new works, and became King under the Mountain. In Erebor he found the great jewel, the Arkenstone, Heart of the Mountain.[3] But Thorin I his son removed and went into the far North to the Grey Mountains, where most of Durin's folk were now gathering; for those mountains were rich and little explored. But there were dragons in the wastes beyond; and after many years they became strong again and multiplied, and they made war on the Dwarves, and plundered their works. At last Dáin I, together with Frór his second son, was slain at the door of his hall by a great cold-drake.

Not long after most of Durin's Folk abandoned the Grey Mountains. Grór, Dáin's son, went away with many followers to the Iron Hills; but Thrór, Dáin's heir, with Borin his father's brother and the remainder of the people returned to Erebor. To the Great Hall of Thráin, Thrór brought back the Arkenstone, and he and his folk prospered and became rich, and they had the friendship of all Men that dwelt near. For they made not only things of wonder and beauty but weapons and armour of great worth; and there was great traffic of ore between them and their kin in the Iron Hills. Thus the Northmen who lived between Celduin (River Running) and

[1] p. 309.
[2] Or released from prison; it may well be that it had already been awakened by the malice of Sauron.
[3] *The Hobbit*, p. 229.

Carnen (Redwater) became strong and drove back all enemies from the East; and the Dwarves lived in plenty, and there was feasting and song in the Halls of Erebor.[1]

So the rumour of the wealth of Erebor spread abroad and reached the ears of the dragons, and at last Smaug the Golden, greatest of the dragons of his day, arose and without warning came against King Thrór and descended on the Mountain in flames. It was not long before all that realm was destroyed, and the town of Dale near by was ruined and deserted; but Smaug entered into the Great Hall and lay there upon a bed of gold.

From the sack and the burning many of Thrór's kin escaped; and last of all from the halls by a secret door came Thrór himself and his son Thráin II. They went away south with their family[2] into long and homeless wandering. With them went also a small company of their kinsmen and faithful followers.

Years afterwards Thrór, now old, poor, and desperate, gave to his son Thráin the one great treasure he still possessed, the last of the Seven Rings, and then he went away with one old companion only, called Nár. Of the Ring he said to Thráin at their parting:

'This may prove the foundation of new fortune for you yet, though that seems unlikely. But it needs gold to breed gold.'

'Surely you do not think of returning to Erebor?' said Thráin.

'Not at my age,' said Thrór. 'Our vengeance on Smaug I bequeath to you and your sons. But I am tired of poverty and the scorn of Men. I go to see what I can find.' He did not say where.

He was a little crazed perhaps with age and misfortune and long brooding on the splendour of Moria in his forefathers' days; or the Ring, it may be, was turning to evil now that its master was awake, driving him to folly and destruction. From Dunland, where he was then dwelling, he went north with Nár, and they crossed the Redhorn Pass and came down into Azanulbizar.

When Thrór came to Moria the Gate was open. Nár begged him to beware, but he took no heed of him, and walked proudly in as an heir that returns. But he did not come back. Nár stayed near by for many days in hiding. One day he heard a loud shout and the blare of a horn, and a body was flung out on the steps. Fearing that it was Thrór, he began to creep near, but there came a voice from within the gate:

'Come on, beardling! We can see you. But there is no need to be afraid today. We need you as a messenger.'

Then Nár came up, and found that it was indeed the body of Thrór, but the head was severed and lay face downwards. As he knelt there, he heard orc-laughter in the shadows, and the voice said:

'If beggars will not wait at the door, but sneak in to try thieving, that is what we

[1] *The Hobbit*, p. 28.

[2] Among whom were the children of Thráin II: Thorin (Oakenshield), Frerin, and Dís. Thorin was then a youngster in the reckoning of the Dwarves. It was afterwards learned that more of the Folk under the Mountain had escaped than was at first hoped; but most of these went to the Iron Hills.

do to them. If any of your people poke their foul beards in here again, they will fare the same. Go and tell them so! But if his family wish to know who is now king here, the name is written on his face. I wrote it! I killed him! I am the master!'

Then Nár turned the head and saw branded on the brow in Dwarfrunes so that he could read it the name AZOG. That name was branded in his heart and in the hearts of all the Dwarves afterwards. Nár stooped to take the head, but the voice of Azog[1] said:

'Drop it! Be off! Here's your fee, beggar-beard.' A small bag struck him. It held a few coins of little worth.

Weeping, Nár fled down the Silverlode; but he looked back once and saw that Orcs had come from the gate and were hacking up the body and flinging the pieces to the black crows.

Such was the tale that Nár brought back to Thráin; and when he had wept and torn his beard he fell silent. Seven days he sat and said no word. Then he stood up and said: 'This cannot be borne!' That was the beginning of the War of the Dwarves and the Orcs, which was long and deadly, and fought for the most part in deep places beneath the earth.

Thráin at once sent messengers bearing the tale, north, east, and west; but it was three years before the Dwarves had mustered their strength. Durin's Folk gathered all their host, and they were joined by great forces sent from the Houses of other Fathers; for this dishonour to the heir of the Eldest of their race filled them with wrath. When all was ready they assailed and sacked one by one all the strongholds of the Orcs that they could from Gundabad to the Gladden. Both sides were pitiless, and there was death and cruel deeds by dark and by light. But the Dwarves had the victory through their strength, and their matchless weapons, and the fire of their anger, as they hunted for Azog in every den under mountain.

At last all the Orcs that fled before them were gathered in Moria, and the Dwarf-host in pursuit came to Azanulbizar. That was a great vale that lay between the arms of the mountains about the lake of Kheled-zâram and had been of old part of the kingdom of Khazad-dûm. When the Dwarves saw the gate of their ancient mansions upon the hill-side they sent up a great shout like thunder in the valley. But a great host of foes was arrayed on the slopes above them, and out of the gates poured a multitude of Orcs that had been held back by Azog for the last need.

At first fortune was against the Dwarves; for it was a dark day of winter without sun, and the Orcs did not waver, and they outnumbered their enemies, and had the higher ground. So began the Battle of Azanulbizar (or Nanduhirion in the Elvish tongue), at the memory of which the Orcs still shudder and the Dwarves weep. The first assault of the vanguard led by Thráin was thrown back with loss, and Thráin was driven into a wood of great trees that then still grew not far from Kheled-zâram. There Frerin his son fell, and Fundin his kinsman, and many others, and both Thráin and Thorin were wounded.[2] Elsewhere the battle swayed to and fro with

[1] Azog was the father of Bolg; see *The Hobbit*, p. 30.

[2] It is said that Thorin's shield was cloven and he cast it away and he hewed off with his axe a branch of an oak and held it in his left hand to ward off the strokes of his foes, or to wield as a club. In this way he got his name.

great slaughter, until at last the people of the Iron Hills turned the day. Coming late and fresh to the field the mailed warriors of Náin, Grór's son, drove through the Orcs to the very threshold of Moria, crying 'Azog! Azog!' as they hewed down with their mattocks all who stood in their way.

Then Náin stood before the Gate and cried with a great voice: 'Azog! If you are in come out! Or is the play in the valley too rough?'

Thereupon Azog came forth, and he was a great Orc with a huge iron-clad head, and yet agile and strong. With him came many like him, the fighters of his guard, and as they engaged Náin's company he turned to Náin, and said:

'What? Yet another beggar at my doors? Must I brand you too?' With that he rushed at Náin and they fought. But Náin was half blind with rage, and also very weary with battle, whereas Azog was fresh and fell and full of guile. Soon Náin made a great stroke with all his strength that remained, but Azog darted aside and kicked Náin's leg, so that the mattock splintered on the stone where he had stood, but Náin stumbled forward. Then Azog with a swift swing hewed his neck. His mail-collar withstood the edge, but so heavy was the blow that Náin's neck was broken and he fell.

Then Azog laughed, and he lifted up his head to let forth a great yell of triumph; but the cry died in his throat. For he saw that all his host in the valley was in a rout, and the Dwarves went this way and that slaying as they would, and those that could escape from them were flying south, shrieking as they ran. And hard by all the soldiers of his guard lay dead. He turned and fled back towards the Gate.

Up the steps after him leaped a Dwarf with a red axe. It was Dáin Ironfoot, Náin's son. Right before the doors he caught Azog, and there he slew him, and hewed off his head. That was held a great feat, for Dáin was then only a stripling in the reckoning of the Dwarves. But long life and many battles lay before him, until old but unbowed he fell at last in the War of the Ring. Yet hardy and full of wrath as he was, it is said that when he came down from the Gate he looked grey in the face, as one who has felt great fear.

When at last the battle was won the Dwarves that were left gathered in Azanulbizar. They took the head of Azog and thrust into its mouth the purse of small money, and then they set it on a stake. But no feast nor song was there that night; for their dead were beyond the count of grief. Barely half of their number, it is said, could still stand or had hope of healing.

None the less in the morning Thráin stood before them. He had one eye blinded beyond cure, and he was halt with a leg-wound; but he said: 'Good! We have the victory. Khazad-dûm is ours!'

But they answered: 'Durin's Heir you may be, but even with one eye you should see clearer. We fought this war for vengeance, and vengeance we have taken. But it is not sweet. If this is victory, then our hands are too small to hold it.'

And those who were not of Durin's Folk said also: 'Khazad-dûm was not our Fathers' house. What is it to us, unless a hope of treasure? But now, if we must go without the rewards and the weregilds that are owed to us, the sooner we return to our own lands the better pleased we shall be.'

Then Thráin turned to Dáin, and said: 'But surely my own kin will not desert me?' 'No,' said Dáin. 'You are the father of our Folk, and we have bled for you, and will again. But we will not enter Khazad-dûm. You will not enter Khazad-dûm. Only I have looked through the shadow of the Gate. Beyond the shadow it waits for you still: Durin's Bane. The world must change and some other power than ours must come before Durin's Folk walk again in Moria.'

So it was that after Azanulbizar the Dwarves dispersed again. But first with great labour they stripped all their dead, so that Orcs should not come and win there a store of weapons and mail. It is said that every Dwarf that went from that battlefield was bowed under a heavy burden. Then they built many pyres and burned all the bodies of their kin. There was a great felling of trees in the valley, which remained bare ever after, and the reek of the burning was seen in Lórien.[1]

When the dreadful fires were in ashes the allies went away to their own countries, and Dáin Ironfoot led his father's people back to the Iron Hills. Then standing by the great stake, Thráin said to Thorin Oakenshield: 'Some would think this head dearly bought! At least we have given our kingdom for it. Will you come with me back to the anvil? Or will you beg your bread at proud doors?'

'To the anvil,' answered Thorin. 'The hammer will at least keep the arms strong, until they can wield sharper tools again.'

So Thráin and Thorin with what remained of their following (among whom were Balin and Glóin) returned to Dunland, and soon afterwards they removed and wandered in Eriador, until at last they made a home in exile in the east of the Ered Luin beyond the Lune. Of iron were most of the things that they forged in those days, but they prospered after a fashion, and their numbers slowly increased.[2] But, as Thrór had said, the Ring needed gold to breed gold, and of that or any other precious metal they had little or none.

Of this Ring something may be said here. It was believed by the Dwarves of Durin's Folk to be the first of the Seven that was forged; and they say that it was given to the King of Khazad-dûm, Durin III, by the Elven-smiths themselves and not by Sauron, though doubtless his evil power was on it, since he had aided in the forging of all the Seven. But the possessors of the Ring did not display it or speak of it, and they seldom surrendered it until near death, so that others did not know for certain where it was bestowed. Some thought that it had remained in Khazad-dûm, in the secret tombs of the kings, if they had not been discovered and plundered; but among the kindred of Durin's Heir it was believed (wrongly) that Thrór had worn it when he rashly returned there. What then had become of it they did not know. It was not found on the body of Azog.[3]

[1] Such dealings with their dead seemed grievous to the Dwarves, for it was against their use; but to make such tombs as they were accustomed to build (since they will lay their dead only in stone not in earth) would have taken many years. To fire therefore they turned, rather than leave their kin to beast or bird or carrion-orc. But those who fell in Azanulbizar were honoured in memory, and to this day a Dwarf will say proudly of one of his sires: 'he was a burned Dwarf', and that is enough.

[2] They had very few women-folk. Dís Thráin's daughter was there. She was the mother of Fíli and Kíli, who were born in the Ered Luin. Thorin had no wife.

[3] pp. 261–2.

None the less it may well be, as the Dwarves now believe, that Sauron by his arts had discovered who had this Ring, the last to remain free, and that the singular misfortunes of the heirs of Durin were largely due to his malice. For the Dwarves had proved untameable by this means. The only power over them that the Rings wielded was to inflame their hearts with a greed of gold and precious things, so that if they lacked them all other good things seemed profitless, and they were filled with wrath and desire for vengeance on all who deprived them. But they were made from their beginning of a kind to resist most steadfastly any domination. Though they could be slain or broken, they could not be reduced to shadows enslaved to another will; and for the same reason their lives were not affected by any Ring, to live either longer or shorter because of it. All the more did Sauron hate the possessors and desire to dispossess them.

It was therefore perhaps partly by the malice of the Ring that Thráin after some years became restless and discontented. The lust for gold was ever in his mind. At last, when he could endure it no longer, he turned his thoughts to Erebor, and resolved to go back there. He said nothing to Thorin of what was in his heart; but with Balin and Dwalin and a few others, he arose and said farewell and departed.

Little is known of what happened to him afterwards. It would now seem that as soon as he was abroad with few companions he was hunted by the emissaries of Sauron. Wolves pursued him, Orcs waylaid him, evil birds shadowed his path, and the more he strove to go north the more misfortunes opposed him. There came a dark night when he and his companions were wandering in the land beyond Anduin, and they were driven by a black rain to take shelter under the eaves of Mirkwood. In the morning he was gone from the camp, and his companions called him in vain. They searched for him many days, until at last giving up hope they departed and came at length back to Thorin. Only long after was it learned that Thráin had been taken alive and brought to the pits of Dol Guldur. There he was tormented and the Ring taken from him, and there at last he died.

So Thorin Oakenshield became the Heir of Durin, but an heir without hope. When Thráin was lost he was ninety-five, a great dwarf of proud bearing; but he seemed content to remain in Eriador. There he laboured long, and trafficked, and gained such wealth as he could; and his people were increased by many of the wandering Folk of Durin who heard of his dwelling in the west and came to him. Now they had fair halls in the mountains, and store of goods, and their days did not seem so hard, though in their songs they spoke ever of the Lonely Mountain far away.

The years lengthened. The embers in the heart of Thorin grew hot again, as he brooded on the wrongs of his House and the vengeance upon the Dragon that he had inherited. He thought of weapons and armies and alliances, as his great hammer rang in his forge; but the armies were dispersed and the alliances broken and the axes of his people were few; and a great anger without hope burned him as he smote the red iron on the anvil.

But at last there came about by chance a meeting between Gandalf and Thorin that changed all the fortunes of the House of Durin, and led to other and greater ends beside. On a time[1] Thorin, returning west from a journey, stayed at Bree for the night. There Gandalf was also. He was on his way to the Shire, which he had not visited for some twenty years. He was weary, and thought to rest there for a while.

Among many cares he was troubled in mind by the perilous state of the North; because he knew then already that Sauron was plotting war, and intended, as soon as he felt strong enough, to attack Rivendell. But to resist any attempt from the East to regain the lands of Angmar and the northern passes in the mountains there were now only the Dwarves of the Iron Hills. And beyond them lay the desolation of the Dragon. The Dragon Sauron might use with terrible effect. How then could the end of Smaug be achieved?

It was even as Gandalf sat and pondered this that Thorin stood before him, and said: 'Master Gandalf, I know you only by sight, but now I should be glad to speak with you. For you have often come into my thoughts of late, as if I were bidden to seek you. Indeed I should have done so, if I had known where to find you.'

Gandalf looked at him with wonder. 'That is strange, Thorin Oakenshield,' he said. 'For I have thought of you also; and though I am on my way to the Shire, it was in my mind that is the way also to your halls.'

'Call them so, if you will,' said Thorin. 'They are only poor lodgings in exile. But you would be welcome there, if you would come. For they say that you are wise and know more than any other of what goes on in the world; and I have much on my mind and would be glad of your counsel.'

'I will come,' said Gandalf; 'for I guess that we share one trouble at least. The Dragon of Erebor is on my mind, and I do not think that he will be forgotten by the grandson of Thrór.'

The story is told elsewhere of what came of that meeting: of the strange plan that Gandalf made for the help of Thorin, and how Thorin and his companions set out from the Shire on the quest of the Lonely Mountain that came to great ends unforeseen. Here only those things are recalled that directly concern Durin's Folk.

The Dragon was slain by Bard of Esgaroth, but there was battle in Dale. For the Orcs came down upon Erebor as soon as they heard of the return of the Dwarves; and they were led by Bolg, son of that Azog whom Dáin slew in his youth. In that first Battle of Dale, Thorin Oakenshield was mortally wounded; and he died and was laid in a tomb under the Mountain with the Arkenstone upon his breast. There fell also Fíli and Kíli, his sister-sons. But Dáin Ironfoot, his cousin, who came from the Iron Hills to his aid and was also his rightful heir, became then King Dáin II, and the Kingdom under the Mountain was restored, even as Gandalf had desired. Dáin proved a great and wise king, and the Dwarves prospered and grew strong again in his day.

In the late summer of that same year (2941) Gandalf had at last prevailed upon Saruman and the White Council to attack Dol Guldur, and Sauron retreated and went to Mordor, there to be secure, as he thought, from all his enemies. So it was that when the War came at last the main assault was turned southwards; yet even so with his far-stretched right hand Sauron might have done great evil in the North,

[1] March 15, 2941.

if King Dáin and King Brand had not stood in his path. Even as Gandalf said afterwards to Frodo and Gimli, when they dwelt together for a time in Minas Tirith. Not long before news had come to Gondor of events far away.

'I grieved at the fall of Thorin,' said Gandalf; 'and now we hear that Dáin has fallen, fighting in Dale again, even while we fought here. I should call that a heavy loss, if it was not a wonder rather that in his great age he could still wield his axe as mightily as they say that he did, standing over the body of King Brand before the Gate of Erebor until the darkness fell.

'Yet things might have gone far otherwise and far worse. When you think of the great Battle of the Pelennor, do not forget the battles in Dale and the valour of Durin's Folk. Think of what might have been. Dragon-fire and savage swords in Eriador, night in Rivendell. There might be no Queen in Gondor. We might now hope to return from the victory here only to ruin and ash. But that has been averted – because I met Thorin Oakenshield one evening on the edge of spring in Bree. A chance-meeting, as we say in Middle-earth.'

Dís was the daughter of Thráin II. She is the only dwarf-woman named in these histories. It was said by Gimli that there are few dwarf-women, probably no more than a third of the whole people. They seldom walk abroad except at great need. They are in voice and appearance, and in garb if they must go on a journey, so like to the dwarf-men that the eyes and ears of other peoples cannot tell them apart. This has given rise to the foolish opinion among Men that there are no dwarf-women, and that the Dwarves 'grow out of stone'.

It is because of the fewness of women among them that the kind of the Dwarves increases slowly, and is in peril when they have no secure dwellings. For Dwarves take only one wife or husband each in their lives, and are jealous, as in all matters of their rights. The number of dwarf-men that marry is actually less than one-third. For not all the women take husbands: some desire none; some desire one that they cannot get, and so will have no other. As for the men, very many also do not desire marriage, being engrossed in their crafts.

Gimli Glóin's son is renowned, for he was one of the Nine Walkers that set out with the Ring; and he remained in the company of King Elessar throughout the War. He was named Elf-friend because of the great love that grew between him and Legolas, son of King Thranduil, and because of his reverence for the Lady Galadriel.

After the fall of Sauron, Gimli brought south a part of the Dwarf-folk of Erebor, and he became Lord of the Glittering Caves. He and his people did great works in Gondor and Rohan. For Minas Tirith they forged gates of *mithril* and steel to replace those broken by the Witch-king. Legolas his friend also brought south Elves out of Greenwood, and they dwelt in Ithilien, and it became once again the fairest country in all the westlands.

But when King Elessar gave up his life Legolas followed at last the desire of his heart and sailed over Sea.

The Line of the Dwarves of Erebor as it was set out by Gimli Glóin's son for King Elessar.

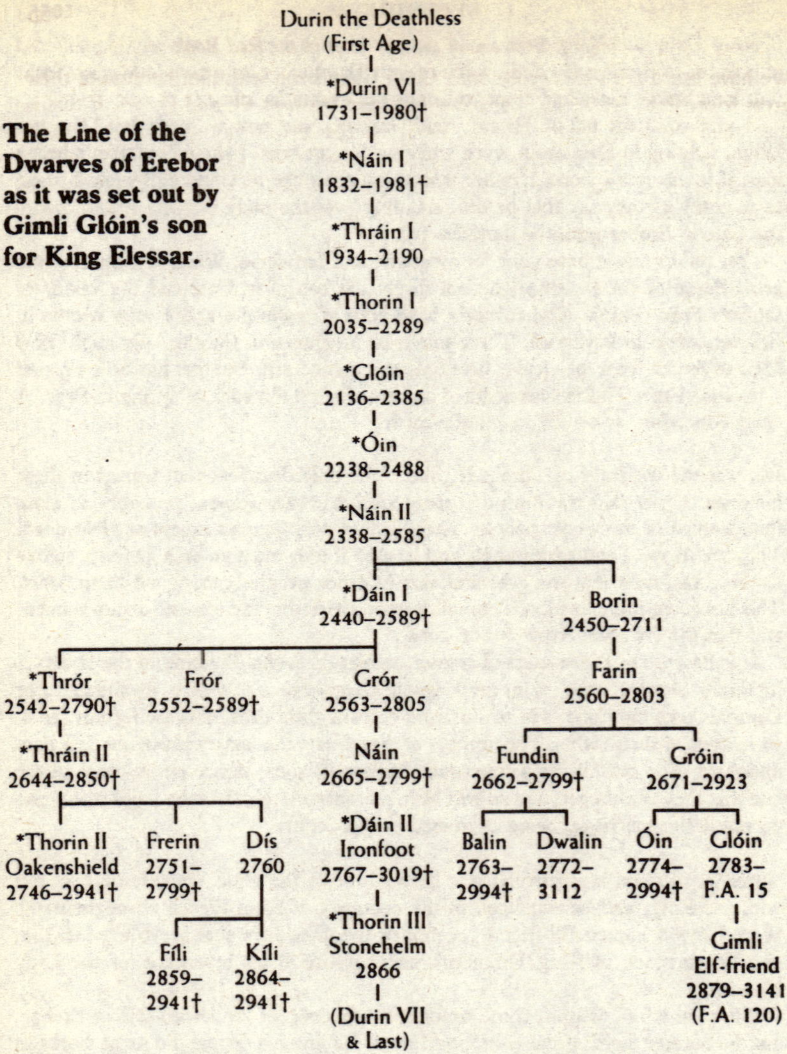

Foundation of Erebor, 1999.
Dáin I slain by a dragon, 2589
Return to Erebor, 2590.
Sack of Erebor, 2770.
Murder of Thrór, 2790.
Mustering of the Dwarves, 2790–3.
War of the Dwarves and Orcs, 2793–9.
Battle of Nanduhirion, 2799.
Thráin goes wandering, 2841.
Death of Thráin and loss of his Ring, 2850.
Battle of Five Armies and death of Thorin II, 2941.
Balin goes to Moria, 2989.

* The names of those who were held to be kings of Durin's Folk, whether in exile or not, are marked so. Of the other companions of Thorin Oakenshield in the journey to Erebor Ori, Nori, and Dori were also of the House of Durin, and more remote kinsmen of Thorin: Bifur, Bofur, and Bombur were descended from Dwarves of Moria but were not of Durin's line. For † see p. 1009.

Here follows one of the last notes in the Red Book

We have heard tell that Legolas took Gimli Glóin's son with him because of their great friendship, greater than any that has been between Elf and Dwarf. If this is true, then it is strange indeed: that a Dwarf should be willing to leave Middle-earth for any love, or that the Eldar should receive him, or that the Lords of the West should permit it. But it is said that Gimli went also out of desire to see again the beauty of Galadriel; and it may be that she, being mighty among the Eldar, obtained this grace for him. More cannot be said of this matter.

APPENDIX B

THE TALE OF YEARS

(CHRONOLOGY OF THE WESTLANDS)

The *First Age* ended with the Great Battle, in which the Host of Valinor broke Thangorodrim[1] and overthrew Morgoth. Then most of the Noldor returned into the Far West[2] and dwelt in Eressëa within sight of Valinor; and many of the Sindar went over Sea also.

The *Second Age* ended with the first overthrow of Sauron, servant of Morgoth, and the taking of the One Ring.

The *Third Age* came to its end in the War of the Ring; but the *Fourth Age* was not held to have begun until Master Elrond departed, and the time was come for the dominion of Men and the decline of all other 'speaking-peoples' in Middle-earth.[3]

In the Fourth Age the earlier ages were often called the *Elder Days*; but that name was properly given only to the days before the casting out of Morgoth. The histories of that time are not recorded here.

The Second Age

These were the dark years for Men of Middle-earth, but the years of the glory of Númenor. Of events in Middle-earth the records are few and brief, and their dates are often uncertain.

In the beginning of this age many of the High Elves still remained. Most of these dwelt in Lindon west of the Ered Luin; but before the building of the Barad-dûr many of the Sindar passed eastward, and some established realms in the forests far away, where their people were mostly Silvan Elves. Thranduil, king in the north of Greenwood the Great, was one of these. In Lindon north of the Lune dwelt Gil-galad, last heir of the kings of the Noldor in exile. He was acknowledged as High King of the Elves of the West. In Lindon south of the Lune dwelt for a time Celeborn, kinsman of Thingol; his wife was Galadriel, greatest of Elven women. She was sister of Finrod Felagund, Friend-of-Men, once king of Nargothrond, who gave his life to save Beren son of Barahir.

Later some of the Noldor went to Eregion, upon the west of the Misty Mountains, and near to the West-gate of Moria. This they did because they learned that *mithril* had been discovered in Moria.[4] The Noldor were great craftsmen and less unfriendly to the Dwarves than the Sindar; but the friendship that grew up between the people of Durin and the Elven-smiths of Eregion was the closest that there has ever been between the two races. Celebrimbor was Lord of Eregion and the greatest of their craftsmen; he was descended from Fëanor.

[1] p. 236–7.
[2] p. 583, *The Hobbit*, p. 144.
[3] p. 949–50.
[4] p. 309.

Year	
1	Foundation of the Grey Havens, and of Lindon.
32	The Edain reach Númenor.
c. 40	Many Dwarves leaving their old cities in Ered Luin go to Moria and swell its numbers.
442	Death of Elros Tar-Minyatur.
c. 500	Sauron begins to stir again in Middle-earth.
548	Birth in Númenor of Silmariën.
600	The first ships of the Númenoreans appear off the coasts.
750	Eregion founded by the Noldor.
c. 1000	Sauron, alarmed by the growing power of the Númenoreans, chooses Mordor as a land to make into a stronghold. He begins the building of Barad-dûr.
1075	Tar-Ancalimë becomes the first Ruling Queen of Númenor.
1200	Sauron endeavours to seduce the Eldar. Gil-galad refuses to treat with him; but the smiths of Eregion are won over. The Númenoreans begin to make permanent havens.
c. 1500	The Elven-smiths instructed by Sauron reach the height of their skill. They begin the forging of the Rings of Power.
c. 1590	The Three Rings are completed in Eregion.
c. 1600	Sauron forges the One Ring in Orodruin. He completes the Barad-dûr. Celebrimbor perceives the designs of Sauron.
1693	War of the Elves and Sauron begins. The Three Rings are hidden.
1695	Sauron's forces invade Eriador. Gil-galad sends Elrond to Eregion.
1697	Eregion laid waste. Death of Celebrimbor. The gates of Moria are shut. Elrond retreats with remnant of the Noldor and founds the refuge of Imladris.
1699	Sauron overruns Eriador.
1700	Tar-Minastir sends a great navy from Númenor to Lindon. Sauron is defeated.
1701	Sauron is driven out of Eriador. The Westlands have peace for a long while.
c. 1800	From about this time onward the Númenoreans begin to establish dominions on the coasts. Sauron extends his power eastwards. The shadow falls on Númenor.
2251	Tar-Atanamir takes the sceptre. Rebellion and division of the Númenoreans begins. About this time the Nazgûl or Ringwraiths, slaves of the Nine Rings, first appear.
2280	Umbar is made into a great fortress of Númenor.
2350	Pelargir is built. It becomes the chief haven of the Faithful Númenoreans.
2899	Ar-Adûnakhôr takes the sceptre.
3175	Repentance of Tar-Palantir. Civil war in Númenor.
3255	Ar-Pharazôn the Golden seizes the sceptre.
3261	Ar-Pharazôn sets sail and lands at Umbar.
3262	Sauron is taken as prisoner to Númenor; 3262–3310 Sauron seduces the King and corrupts the Númenoreans.

3310 Ar-Pharazôn begins the building of the Great Armament.

3319 Ar-Pharazôn assails Valinor. Downfall of Númenor. Elendil and his sons escape.

3320 Foundations of the Realms in Exile: Arnor and Gondor. The Stones are divided (p. 607). Sauron returns to Mordor.

3429 Sauron attacks Gondor, takes Minas Ithil and burns the White Tree. Isildur escapes down Anduin and goes to Elendil in the North. Anárion defends Minas Anor and Osgiliath.

3430 The Last Alliance of Elves and Men is formed.

3431 Gil-galad and Elendil march east to Imladris.

3434 The host of the Alliance crosses the Misty Mountains. Battle of Dagorlad and defeat of Sauron. Siege of Barad-dûr begins.

3440 Anárion slain.

3441 Sauron overthrown by Elendil and Gil-galad, who perish. Isildur takes the One Ring. Sauron passes away and the Ringwraiths go into the shadows. The Second Age ends.

The Third Age

These were the fading years of the Eldar. For long they were at peace, wielding the Three Rings while Sauron slept and the One Ring was lost; but they attempted nothing new, living in memory of the past. The Dwarves hid themselves in deep places, guarding their hoards; but when evil began to stir again and dragons reappeared, one by one their ancient treasures were plundered, and they became a wandering people. Moria for long remained secure, but its numbers dwindled until many of its vast mansions became dark and empty. The wisdom and the life-span of Númenoreans also waned as they became mingled with lesser Men.

When maybe a thousand years had passed, and the first shadow had fallen on Greenwood the Great, the *Istari* or Wizards appeared in Middle-earth. It was afterwards said that they came out of the Far West and were messengers sent to contest the power of Sauron, and to unite all those who had the will to resist him; but they were forbidden to match his power with power, or to seek to dominate Elves or Men by force and fear.

They came therefore in the shape of Men, though they were never young and aged only slowly, and they had many powers of mind and hand. They revealed their true names to few,[1] but used such names as were given to them. The two highest of this order (of whom it is said there were five) were called by the Eldar Curunír, 'the Man of Skill', and Mithrandir, 'the Grey Pilgrim', but by Men in the North Saruman and Gandalf. Curunír journeyed often into the East, but dwelt at last in Isengard. Mithrandir was closest in friendship with the Eldar, and wandered mostly in the West and never made for himself any lasting abode.

Throughout the Third Age the guardianship of the Three Rings was known only to those who possessed them. But at the end it became known that they had been held at first by the three greatest of the Eldar: Gil-galad, Galadriel and Círdan.

[1] p. 655.

Gil-galad before he died gave his ring to Elrond; Círdan later surrendered his to Mithrandir. For Círdan saw further and deeper than any other in Middle-earth, and he welcomed Mithrandir at the Grey Havens, knowing whence he came and whither he would return.

'Take this ring, Master,' he said, 'for your labours will be heavy; but it will support you in the weariness that you have taken upon yourself. For this is the Ring of Fire, and with it you may rekindle hearts in a world that grows chill. But as for me, my heart is with the Sea, and I will dwell by the grey shores until the last ship sails. I will await you.'

Year

2 Isildur plants a seedling of the White Tree in Minas Anor. He delivers the South-kingdom to Meneldil. Disaster of the Gladden Fields; Isildur and his three elder sons are slain.

3 Ohtar brings the shards of Narsil to Imladris.

10 Valandil becomes King of Arnor.

109 Elrond weds Celebrían, daughter of Celeborn.

130 Birth of Elladan and Elrohir, sons of Elrond.

241 Birth of Arwen Undómiel.

420 King Ostoher rebuilds Minas Anor.

490 First invasion of Easterlings.

500 Rómendacil I defeats the Easterlings.

541 Rómendacil slain in battle.

830 Falastur begins the line of the Ship-kings of Gondor.

861 Death of Eärendur, and division of Arnor.

933 King Eärnil I takes Umbar, which becomes a fortress of Gondor.

936 Eärnil lost at sea.

1015 King Ciryandil slain in the siege of Umbar.

1050 Hyarmendacil conquers the Harad. Gondor reaches the height of its power. About this time a shadow falls on Greenwood, and men begin to call it Mirkwood. The Periannath are first mentioned in records, with the coming of the Harfoots to Eriador.

c. 1100 The Wise (the Istari and the chief Eldar) discover that an evil power has made a stronghold at Dol Guldur. It is thought to be one of the Nazgûl.

1149 Reign of Atanatar Alcarin begins.

c. 1150 The Fallohides enter Eriador. The Stoors come over the Redhorn Pass and move to the Angle, or to Dunland.

c. 1300 Evil things begin to multiply again. Orcs increase in the Misty Mountains and attack the Dwarves. The Nazgûl reappear. The chief of these comes north to Angmar. The Periannath migrate westward; many settle at Bree.

1356 King Argeleb I slain in battle with Rhudaur. About this time the Stoors leave the Angle, and some return to Wilderland.

1409 The Witch-king of Angmar invades Arnor. King Arvaleg I slain. Fornost and Tyrn Gorthad are defended. The Tower of Amon Sûl destroyed.

1432 King Valacar of Gondor dies, and the civil war of the Kin-strife begins.

1437 Burning of Osgiliath and loss of the *palantír*. Eldacar flees to Rhovanion; his son Ornendil is murdered.
1447 Eldacar returns and drives out the usurper Castamir. Battle of the Crossings of Erui. Siege of Pelargir.
1448 Rebels escape and seize Umbar.
1540 King Aldamir slain in war with the Harad and Corsairs of Umbar.
1551 Hyarmendacil II defeats the Men of Harad.
1601 Many Periannath migrate from Bree, and are granted land beyond Baranduin by Argeleb II.
c. 1630 They are joined by Stoors coming up from Dunland.
1634 The Corsairs ravage Pelargir and slay King Minardil.
1636 The Great Plague devastates Gondor. Death of King Telemnar and his children. The White Tree dies in Minas Anor. The plague spreads north and west, and many parts of Eriador become desolate. Beyond the Baranduin the Periannath survive, but suffer great loss.
1640 King Tarondor removes the King's House to Minas Anor, plants a seedling of the White Tree. Osgiliath begins to fall into ruin. Mordor is left unguarded.
1810 King Telumehtar Umbardacil retakes Umbar and drives out the Corsairs.
1851 The attacks of the Wainriders upon Gondor begin.
1856 Gondor loses its eastern territories, and Narmacil II falls in battle.
1899 King Calimehtar defeats the Wainriders on Dagorlad.
1900 Calimehtar builds the White Tower in Minas Anor.
1940 Gondor and Arnor renew communications and form an alliance. Arvedui weds Fíriel daughter of Ondoher of Gondor.
1944 Ondoher falls in battle. Eärnil defeats the enemy in South Ithilien. He then wins the Battle of the Camp, and drives Wainriders into the Dead Marshes. Arvedui claims the crown of Gondor.
1945 Eärnil II receives the crown.
1974 End of the North-kingdom. The Witch-king overruns Arthedain and takes Fornost.
1975 Arvedui drowned in the Bay of Forochel. The *palantíri* of Annúminas and Amon Sûl are lost. Eärnur brings a fleet to Lindon. The Witch-king defeated at the Battle of Fornost, and pursued to the Ettenmoors. He vanishes from the North.
1976 Aranarth takes the title of Chieftain of the Dúnedain. The heirlooms of Arnor are given into the keeping of Elrond.
1977 Frumgar leads the Éothéod into the North.
1979 Bucca of the Marish becomes first Thain of the Shire.
1980 The Witch-king comes to Mordor and there gathers the Nazgûl. A Balrog appears in Moria, and slays Durin VI.
1981 Náin I slain. The Dwarves flee from Moria. Many of the Silvan Elves of Lórien flee south. Amroth and Nimrodel are lost.
1999 Thráin I comes to Erebor and founds a dwarf-kingdom 'under the Mountain'.

2000 The Nazgûl issue from Mordor and besiege Minas Ithil.

2002 Fall of Minas Ithil, afterwards known as Minas Morgul. The *palantír* is captured.

2043 Eärnur becomes King of Gondor. He is challenged by the Witch-king.

2050 The challenge is renewed. Eärnur rides to Minas Morgul and is lost. Mardil becomes the first Ruling Steward.

2060 The power of Dol Guldur grows. The Wise fear that it may be Sauron taking shape again.

2063 Gandalf goes to Dol Guldur. Sauron retreats and hides in the East. The Watchful Peace begins. The Nazgûl remain quiet in Minas Morgul.

2210 Thorin I leaves Erebor, and goes north to the Grey Mountains, where most of the remnants of Durin's Folk are now gathering.

2340 Isumbras I becomes thirteenth Thain, and first of the Took line. The Oldbucks occupy the Buckland.

2460 The Watchful Peace ends. Sauron returns with increased strength to Dol Guldur.

2463 The White Council is formed. About this time Déagol the Stoor finds the One Ring, and is murdered by Sméagol.

2470 About this time Sméagol-Gollum hides in the Misty Mountains.

2475 Attack on Gondor renewed. Osgiliath finally ruined, and its stone-bridge broken.

c. 2480 Orcs begin to make secret strongholds in the Misty Mountains so as to bar all the passes into Eriador. Sauron begins to people Moria with his creatures.

2509 Celebrían, journeying to Lórien, is waylaid in the Redhorn Pass, and receives a poisoned wound.

2510 Celebrían departs over Sea. Orcs and Easterlings overrun Calenardhon. Eorl the Young wins the victory of the Field of Celebrant. The Rohirrim settle in Calenardhon.

2545 Eorl falls in battle in the Wold.

2569 Brego son of Eorl completes the Golden Hall.

2570 Baldor son of Brego enters the Forbidden Door and is lost. About this time Dragons reappear in the far North and begin to afflict the Dwarves.

2589 Dáin I slain by a Dragon.

2590 Thrór returns to Erebor. Grór his brother goes to the Iron Hills.

c. 2670 Tobold plants 'pipe-weed' in the Southfarthing.

2683 Isengrim II becomes tenth Thain and begins the excavation of Great Smials.

2698 Ecthelion I rebuilds the White Tower in Minas Tirith.

2740 Orcs renew their invasions of Eriador.

2747 Bandobras Took defeats an Orc-band in the Northfarthing.

2758 Rohan attacked from west and east and overrun. Gondor attacked by fleets of the Corsairs. Helm of Rohan takes refuge in Helm's Deep. Wulf seizes Edoras. 2758–9: The Long Winter follows. Great suffering and loss of life in Eriador and Rohan. Gandalf comes to the aid of the Shire-folk.

2759 Death of Helm. Fréaláf drives out Wulf, and begins second line of Kings of the Mark. Saruman takes up his abode in Isengard.

2770 Smaug the Dragon descends on Erebor. Dale destroyed. Thrór escapes with Thráin II and Thorin II.

2790 Thrór slain by an Orc in Moria. The Dwarves gather for a war of vengeance. Birth of Gerontius, later known as the Old Took.

2793 The War of the Dwarves and Orcs begins.

2799 Battle of Nanduhirion before the East-gate of Moria. Dáin Ironfoot returns to the Iron Hills. Thráin II and his son Thorin wander westwards. They settle in the South of Ered Luin beyond the Shire (2802).

2800–64 Orcs from the North trouble Rohan. King Walda slain by them (2861).

2841 Thráin II sets out to revisit Erebor, but is pursued by the servants of Sauron.

2845 Thráin the Dwarf is imprisoned in Dol Guldur; the last of the Seven Rings is taken from him.

2850 Gandalf again enters Dol Guldur, and discovers that its master is indeed Sauron, who is gathering all the Rings and seeking for news of the One, and of Isildur's Heir. He finds Thráin and receives the key of Erebor. Thráin dies in Dol Guldur.

2851 The White Council meets. Gandalf urges an attack on Dol Guldur. Saruman overrules him.[1] Saruman begins to search near the Gladden Fields.

2852 Belecthor II of Gondor dies. The White Tree dies, and no seedling can be found. The Dead Tree is left standing.

2885 Stirred up by emissaries of Sauron the Haradrim cross the Poros and attack Gondor. The sons of Folcwine of Rohan are slain in the service of Gondor.

2890 Bilbo born in the Shire.

2901 Most of the remaining inhabitants of Ithilien desert it owing to the attacks of Uruks of Mordor. The secret refuge of Henneth Annûn is built.

2907 Birth of Gilraen mother of Aragorn II.

2911 The Fell Winter. The Baranduin and other rivers are frozen. White Wolves invade Eriador from the North.

2912 Great floods devastate Enedwaith and Minhiriath. Tharbad is ruined and deserted.

2920 Death of the Old Took.

2929 Arathorn son of Arador of the Dúnedain weds Gilraen.

2930 Arador slain by Trolls. Birth of Denethor II son of Ecthelion II in Minas Tirith.

2931 Aragorn son of Arathorn II born on March 1st.

2933 Arathorn II slain. Gilraen takes Aragorn to Imladris. Elrond receives

[1] It afterwards became clear that Saruman had then begun to desire to possess the One Ring himself, and he hoped that it might reveal itself, seeking its master, if Sauron were let be for a time.

him as foster-son and gives him the name Estel (Hope); his ancestry is concealed.

2939 Saruman discovers that Sauron's servants are searching the Anduin near Gladden Fields, and that Sauron therefore has learned of Isildur's end. He is alarmed, but says nothing to the Council.

2941 Thorin Oakenshield and Gandalf visit Bilbo in the Shire. Bilbo meets Sméagol-Gollum and finds the Ring. The White Council meets; Saruman agrees to an attack on Dol Guldur, since he now wishes to prevent Sauron from searching the River. Sauron having made his plans abandons Dol Guldur. The Battle of the Five Armies in Dale. Death of Thorin II. Bard of Esgaroth slays Smaug. Dáin of the Iron Hills becomes King under the Mountain (Dáin II).

2942 Bilbo returns to the Shire with the Ring. Sauron returns in secret to Mordor.

2944 Bard rebuilds Dale and becomes King. Gollum leaves the Mountains and begins his search for the 'thief' of the Ring.

2948 Théoden son of Thengel, King of Rohan, born.

2949 Gandalf and Balin visit Bilbo in the Shire.

2950 Finduilas, daughter of Adrahil of Dol Amroth, born.

2951 Sauron declares himself openly and gathers power in Mordor. He begins the rebuilding of Barad-dûr. Gollum turns towards Mordor. Sauron sends three of the Nazgûl to reoccupy Dol Guldur.

Elrond reveals to 'Estel' his true name and ancestry, and delivers to him the shards of Narsil. Arwen, newly returned from Lórien, meets Aragorn in the woods of Imladris. Aragorn goes out into the Wild.

2953 Last meeting of the White Council. They debate the Rings. Saruman feigns that he has discovered that the One Ring has passed down Anduin to the Sea. Saruman withdraws to Isengard, which he takes as his own, and fortifies it. Being jealous and afraid of Gandalf he sets spies to watch all his movements; and notes his interest in the Shire. He soon begins to keep agents in Bree and the Southfarthing.

2954 Mount Doom bursts into flame again. The last inhabitants of Ithilien flee over Anduin.

2956 Aragorn meets Gandalf and their friendship begins.

2957–80 Aragorn undertakes his great journeys and errantries. As Thorongil he serves in disguise both Thengel of Rohan and Ecthelion II of Gondor.

2968 Birth of Frodo.

2976 Denethor weds Finduilas of Dol Amroth.

2977 Bain son of Bard becomes King of Dale.

2978 Birth of Boromir son of Denethor II.

2980 Aragorn enters Lórien, and there meets again Arwen Undómiel. Aragorn gives her the ring of Barahir, and they plight their troth upon the hill of Cerin Amroth. About this time Gollum reaches the confines of Mordor and becomes acquainted with Shelob. Théoden becomes King of Rohan.

2983 Faramir son of Denethor born. Birth of Samwise.

2984 Death of Ecthelion II. Denethor II becomes Steward of Gondor.

2988 Finduilas dies young.
2989 Balin leaves Erebor and enters Moria.
2991 Éomer Éomund's son born in Rohan.
2994 Balin perishes, and the dwarf-colony is destroyed.
2995 Éowyn sister of Éomer born.
c. 3000 The shadow of Mordor lengthens. Saruman dares to use the *palantír* of Orthanc, but becomes ensnared by Sauron, who has the Ithil Stone. He becomes a traitor to the Council. His spies report that the Shire is being closely guarded by the Rangers.
3001 Bilbo's farewell feast. Gandalf suspects his ring to be the One Ring. The guard on the Shire is doubled. Gandalf seeks for news of Gollum and calls on the help of Aragorn.
3002 Bilbo becomes a guest of Elrond, and settles in Rivendell.
3004 Gandalf visits Frodo in the Shire, and does so at intervals during the next four years.
3007 Brand son of Bain becomes King in Dale. Death of Gilraen.
3008 In the autumn Gandalf pays his last visit to Frodo.
3009 Gandalf and Aragorn renew their hunt for Gollum at intervals during the next eight years, searching in the vales of Anduin, Mirkwood, and Rhovanion to the confines of Mordor. At some time during these years Gollum himself ventured into Mordor, and was captured by Sauron. Elrond sends for Arwen, and she returns to Imladris; the Mountains and all lands eastward are becoming dangerous.
3017 Gollum is released from Mordor. He is taken by Aragorn in the Dead Marshes, and brought to Thranduil in Mirkwood. Gandalf visits Minas Tirith and reads the scroll of Isildur.

THE GREAT YEARS
3018

April

12 Gandalf reaches Hobbiton.

June

20 Sauron attacks Osgiliath. About the same time Thranduil is attacked, and Gollum escapes.

July

4 Boromir sets out from Minas Tirith.
10 Gandalf imprisoned in Orthanc.

August

All trace of Gollum is lost. It is thought that at about this time, being hunted both by the Elves and Sauron's servants, he took refuge in Moria; but when he had at last discovered the way to the West-gate he could not get out.

September

18 Gandalf escapes from Orthanc in the early hours. The Black Riders cross the Fords of Isen.
19 Gandalf comes to Edoras as a beggar, and is refused admittance.
20 Gandalf gains entrance to Edoras. Théoden commands him to go: 'Take any horse, only be gone ere tomorrow is old!'
21 Gandalf meets Shadowfax, but the horse will not allow him to come near. He follows Shadowfax far over the fields.
22 The Black Riders reach Sarn Ford at evening; they drive off the guard of Rangers. Gandalf overtakes Shadowfax.
23 Four Riders enter the Shire before dawn. The others pursue the Rangers eastward, and then return to watch the Greenway. A Black Rider comes to Hobbiton at nightfall. Frodo leaves Bag End. Gandalf having tamed Shadowfax rides from Rohan.
24 Gandalf crosses the Isen.
26 The Old Forest. Frodo comes to Bombadil.
27 Gandalf crosses Greyflood. Second night with Bombadil.
28 The Hobbits captured by a Barrow-wight. Gandalf reaches Sarn Ford.
29 Frodo reaches Bree at night. Gandalf visits the Gaffer.
30 Crickhollow and the Inn at Bree are raided in the early hours. Frodo leaves Bree. Gandalf comes to Crickhollow, and reaches Bree at night.

October

1 Gandalf leaves Bree.
3 He is attacked at night on Weathertop.
6 The camp under Weathertop attacked at night. Frodo wounded.
9 Glorfindel leaves Rivendell.
11 He drives the Riders off the Bridge of Mitheithel.
13 Frodo crosses the Bridge.
18 Glorfindel finds Frodo at dusk. Gandalf reaches Rivendell.
20 Escape across the Ford of Bruinen.
24 Frodo recovers and wakes. Boromir arrives in Rivendell at night.
25 Council of Elrond.

December

25 The Company of the Ring leaves Rivendell at dusk.

3019

January

8 The Company reach Hollin.

11, 12 Snow on Caradhras.
13 Attack by Wolves in the early hours. The Company reaches West-gate of Moria at nightfall. Gollum begins to trail the Ringbearer.
14 Night in Hall Twenty-one.
15 The Bridge of Khazad-dûm, and fall of Gandalf. The Comp reaches Nimrodel late at night.
17 The Company comes to Caras Galadhon at evening.
23 Gandalf pursues the Balrog to the peak of Zirakzigil.
25 He casts down the Balrog, and passes away. His body lies on the peak.

February

14 The Mirror of Galadriel. Gandalf returns to life, and lies in a trance.
16 Farewell to Lórien. Gollum in hiding on the west bank observes the departure.
17 Gwaihir bears Gandalf to Lórien.
23 The boats are attacked at night near Sarn Gebir.
25 The Company pass the Argonath and camp at Parth Galen. First Battle of the Fords of Isen; Théodred son of Théoden slain.
26 Breaking of the Fellowship. Death of Boromir; his horn is heard in Minas Tirith. Meriadoc and Peregrin captured. Frodo and Samwise enter the eastern Emyn Muil. Aragorn sets out in pursuit of the Orcs at evening. Éomer hears of the descent of the Orc-band from Emyn Muil.
27 Aragorn reaches the west-cliff at sunrise. Éomer against Théoden's orders sets out from Eastfold about midnight to pursue the Orcs.
28 Éomer overtakes the Orcs just outside Fangorn Forest.
29 Meriadoc and Pippin escape and meet Treebeard. The Rohirrim attack at sunrise and destroy the Orcs. Frodo descends from the Emyn Muil and meets Gollum. Faramir sees the funeral boat of Boromir.
30 Entmoot begins. Éomer returning to Edoras meets Aragorn.

March

1 Frodo begins the passage of the Dead Marshes at dawn. Entmoot continues. Aragorn meets Gandalf the White. They set out for Edoras. Faramir leaves Minas Tirith on an errand to Ithilien.
2 Frodo comes to the end of the Marshes. Gandalf comes to Edoras and heals Théoden. The Rohirrim ride west against Saruman. Second Battle of Fords of Isen. Erkenbrand defeated. Entmoot ends in afternoon. The Ents march on Isengard and reach it at night.
3 Théoden retreats to Helm's Deep. Battle of the Hornburg begins. Ents complete the destruction of Isengard.
4 Théoden and Gandalf set out from Helm's Deep for Isengard. Frodo reaches the slag-mounds on the edge of the Desolation of the Morannon.
5 Théoden reaches Isengard at noon. Parley with Saruman in Orthanc. Winged Nazgûl passes over the camp at Dol Baran. Gandalf sets out with

Peregrin for Minas Tirith. Frodo hides in sight of the Morannon, and leaves at dusk.

6 Aragorn overtaken by the Dúnedain in the early hours. Théoden sets out from the Hornburg for Harrowdale. Aragorn sets out later.

7 Frodo taken by Faramir to Henneth Annûn. Aragorn comes to Dunharrow at nightfall.

8 Aragorn takes the 'Paths of the Dead' at daybreak; he reaches Erech at midnight. Frodo leaves Henneth Annûn.

9 Gandalf reaches Minas Tirith. Faramir leaves Henneth Annûn. Aragorn sets out from Erech and comes to Calembel. At dusk Frodo reaches the Morgul-road. Théoden comes to Dunharrow. Darkness begins to flow out of Mordor.

10 The Dawnless Day. The Muster of Rohan: the Rohirrim ride from Harrowdale. Faramir rescued by Gandalf outside the gates of the City. Aragorn crosses Ringló. An army from the Morannon takes Cair Andros and passes into Anórien. Frodo passes the Cross Roads, and sees the Morgul-host set forth.

11 Gollum visits Shelob, but seeing Frodo asleep nearly repents. Denethor sends Faramir to Osgiliath. Aragorn reaches Linhir and crosses into Lebennin. Eastern Rohan is invaded from the north. First assault on Lórien.

12 Gollum leads Frodo into Shelob's lair. Faramir retreats to the Causeway Forts. Théoden camps under Minrimmon. Aragorn drives the enemy towards Pelargir. The Ents defeat the invaders of Rohan.

13 Frodo captured by the Orcs of Cirith Ungol. The Pelennor is overrun. Faramir is wounded. Aragorn reaches Pelargir and captures the fleet. Théoden in Drúadan Forest.

14 Samwise finds Frodo in the Tower. Minas Tirith is besieged. The Rohirrim led by the Wild Men come to the Grey Wood.

15 In the early hours the Witch-king breaks the Gates of the City. Denethor burns himself on a pyre. The horns of the Rohirrim are heard at cockcrow. Battle of the Pelennor. Théoden is slain. Aragorn raises the standard of Arwen. Frodo and Samwise escape and begin their journey north along the Morgai. Battle under the trees in Mirkwood; Thranduil repels the forces of Dol Guldur. Second assault on Lórien.

16 Debate of the commanders. Frodo from the Morgai looks out over the camp to Mount Doom.

17 Battle of Dale. King Brand and King Dáin Ironfoot fall. Many Dwarves and Men take refuge in Erebor and are besieged. Shagrat brings Frodo's cloak, mail-shirt, and sword to Barad-dûr.

18 The Host of the West marches from Minas Tirith. Frodo comes in sight of the Isenmouthe; he is overtaken by Orcs on the road from Durthang to Udûn.

19 The Host comes to Morgul-vale. Frodo and Samwise escape and begin their journey along the road to the Barad-dûr.

22 The dreadful nightfall. Frodo and Samwise leave the road and turn south to Mount Doom. Third assault on Lórien.

23 The Host passes out of Ithilien. Aragorn dismisses the faint-hearted. Frodo and Samwise cast away their arms and gear.
24 Frodo and Samwise make their last journey to the feet of Mount Doom. The Host camps in the Desolation of the Morannon.
25 The Host is surrounded on the Slag-hills. Frodo and Samwise reach the Sammath Naur. Gollum seizes the Ring and falls in the Cracks of Doom. Downfall of Barad-dûr and passing of Sauron.

After the fall of the Dark Tower and the passing of Sauron the Shadow was lifted from the hearts of all who opposed him, but fear and despair fell upon his servants and allies. Three times Lórien had been assailed from Dol Guldur, but besides the valour of the elven people of that land, the power that dwelt there was too great for any to overcome, unless Sauron had come there himself. Though grievous harm was done to the fair woods on the borders, the assaults were driven back; and when the Shadow passed, Celeborn came forth and led the host of Lórien over Anduin in many boats. They took Dol Guldur, and Galadriel threw down its walls and laid bare its pits, and the forest was cleansed.

In the North also there had been war and evil. The realm of Thranduil was invaded, and there was long battle under the trees and great ruin of fire; but in the end Thranduil had the victory. And on the day of the New Year of the Elves, Celeborn and Thranduil met in the midst of the forest; and they renamed Mirkwood *Eryn Lasgalen*, The Wood of Greenleaves. Thranduil took all the northern region as far as the mountains that rise in the forest for his realm; and Celeborn took all the southern wood below the Narrows, and named it East Lórien; all the wide forest between was given to the Beornings and the Woodmen. But after the passing of Galadriel in a few years Celeborn grew weary of his realm and went to Imladris to dwell with the sons of Elrond. In the Greenwood the Silvan Elves remained untroubled, but in Lórien there lingered sadly only a few of its former people, and there was no longer light or song in Caras Galadhon.

At the same time as the great armies besieged Minas Tirith a host of the allies of Sauron that had long threatened the borders of King Brand crossed the River Carnen, and Brand was driven back to Dale. There he had the aid of the Dwarves of Erebor; and there was a great battle at the Mountain's feet. It lasted three days, but in the end both King Brand and King Dáin Ironfoot were slain, and the Easterlings had the victory. But they could not take the Gate, and many, both Dwarves and Men, took refuge in Erebor, and there withstood a siege.

When news came of the great victories in the South, then Sauron's northern army was filled with dismay; and the besieged came forth and routed them, and the remnant fled into the East and troubled Dale no more. Then Bard II, Brand's son, became King in Dale, and Thorin III Stonehelm, Dáin's son, became King under the Mountain. They sent their ambassadors to the crowning of King Elessar; and their realms remained ever after, as long as they lasted, in friendship with Gondor; and they were under the crown and protection of the King of the West.

THE CHIEF DAYS
FROM THE FALL OF BARAD-DÛR TO THE END OF THE THIRD AGE[1]

3019
S.R. 1419

March 27. Bard II and Thorin III Stonehelm drive the enemy from Dale.
28. Celeborn crosses Anduin; destruction of Dol Guldur begun.
April 6. Meeting of Celeborn and Thranduil.
8. The Ring-bearers are honoured on the Field of Cormallen.
May 1. Crowning of King Elessar; Elrond and Arwen set out from Rivendell.
8. Éomer and Éowyn depart from Rohan with the sons of Elrond.
20. Elrond and Arwen come to Lórien.
27. The escort of Arwen leaves Lórien.
June 14. The sons of Elrond meet the escort and bring Arwen to Edoras.
16. They set out for Gondor.
25. King Elessar finds the sapling of the White Tree.
1 Lithe. Arwen comes to the City.
Mid-year's Day. Wedding of Elessar and Arwen.
July 18. Éomer returns to Minas Tirith.
19. The funeral escort of King Théoden sets out.
August 7. The escort comes to Edoras.
10. Funeral of King Théoden.
14. The guests take leave of King Éomer.
18. They come to Helm's Deep.
22. They come to Isengard; they take leave of the King of the West at sunset.
28. They overtake Saruman; Saruman turns towards the Shire.
September 6. They halt in sight of the Mountains of Moria.
13. Celeborn and Galadriel depart, the others set out for Rivendell.
21. They return to Rivendell.
22. The hundred and twenty-ninth birthday of Bilbo. Saruman comes to the Shire.
October 5. Gandalf and the Hobbits leave Rivendell.
6. They cross the Ford of Bruinen; Frodo feels the first return of pain.
28. They reach Bree at nightfall.
30. They leave Bree. The 'Travellers' come to the Brandywine Bridge at dark.
November 1. They are arrested at Frogmorton.
2. They come to Bywater and rouse the Shire-folk.
3. Battle of Bywater, and Passing of Saruman. End of the War of the Ring.

[1] Months and days are given according to the Shire Calendar.

3020
S.R. 1420: The Great Year of Plenty

March 13. Frodo is taken ill (on the anniversary of his poisoning by Shelob).
April 6. The mallorn flowers in the Party Field.
May 1. Samwise marries Rose.
Mid-year's Day. Frodo resigns office of mayor, and Will Whitfoot is restored.
September 22. Bilbo's hundred and thirtieth birthday.
October 6. Frodo is again ill.

3021
S.R. 1421: The Last of the Third Age

March 13. Frodo is again ill.
25. Birth of Elanor the Fair,[1] daughter of Samwise. On this day the Fourth Age began in the reckoning of Gondor.
September 21. Frodo and Samwise set out from Hobbiton.
22. They meet the Last Riding of the Keepers of the Rings in Woody End.
29. They come to the Grey Havens. Frodo and Bilbo depart over Sea with the Three Keepers. The end of the Third Age.
October 6. Samwise returns to Bag End.

LATER EVENTS CONCERNING THE MEMBERS OF THE FELLOWSHIP OF THE RING

S.R.
1422 With the beginning of this year the Fourth Age began in the count of years in the Shire; but the numbers of the years of Shire Reckoning were continued.
1427 Will Whitfoot resigns. Samwise is elected Mayor of the Shire. Peregrin Took marries Diamond of Long Cleeve. King Elessar issues an edict that Men are not to enter the Shire, and he makes it a Free Land under the protection of the Northern Sceptre.
1430 Faramir, son of Peregrin, born.
1431 Goldilocks, daughter of Samwise, born.
1432 Meriadoc, called the Magnificent, becomes Master of Buckland. Great gifts are sent to him by King Éomer and the Lady Éowyn of Ithilien.
1434 Peregrin becomes the Took and Thain. King Elessar makes the Thain, the Master, and the Mayor Counsellors of the North-kingdom. Master Samwise is elected Mayor for the second time.
1436 King Elessar rides north, and dwells for a while by Lake Evendim. He

[1] She became known as 'the Fair' because of her beauty; many said that she looked more like an elf-maid than a hobbit. She had golden hair, which had been very rare in the Shire; but two others of Samwise's daughters were also golden-haired, and so were many of the children born at this time.

comes to the Brandywine Bridge, and there greets his friends. He gives the Star of the Dúnedain to Master Samwise, and Elanor is made a maid of honour to Queen Arwen.

1441 Master Samwise becomes Mayor for the third time.

1442 Master Samwise and his wife and Elanor ride to Gondor and stay there for a year. Master Tolman Cotton acts as deputy Mayor.

1448 Master Samwise becomes Mayor for the fourth time.

1451 Elanor the Fair marries Fastred of Greenholm on the Far Downs.

1452 The Westmarch, from the Far Downs to the Tower Hills (*Emyn Beraid*),[1] is added to the Shire by the gift of the King. Many hobbits remove to it.

1454 Elfstan Fairbairn, son of Fastred and Elanor, is born.

1455 Master Samwise becomes Mayor for the fifth time. At his request the Thain makes Fastred Warden of Westmarch. Fastred and Elanor make their dwelling at Undertowers on the Tower Hills, where their descendants, the Fairbairns of the Towers, dwelt for many generations.

1462 Master Samwise becomes Mayor for the sixth time.

1463 Faramir Took marries Goldilocks, daughter of Samwise.

1469 Master Samwise becomes Mayor for the seventh and last time, being in 1476, at the end of his office, ninety-six years old.

1482 Death of Mistress Rose, wife of Master Samwise, on Mid-year's Day. On September 22 Master Samwise rides out from Bag End. He comes to the Tower Hills, and is last seen by Elanor, to whom he gives the Red Book afterwards kept by the Fairbairns. Among them the tradition is handed down from Elanor that Samwise passed the Towers, and went to the Grey Havens, and passed over Sea, last of the Ring-bearers.

1484 In the spring of the year a message came from Rohan to Buckland that King Éomer wished to see Master Holdwine once again. Meriadoc was then old (102) but still hale. He took counsel with his friend the Thain, and soon after they handed over their goods and offices to their sons and rode away over the Sarn Ford, and they were not seen again in the Shire. It was heard after that Master Meriadoc came to Edoras and was with King Éomer before he died in that autumn. Then he and Thain Peregrin went to Gondor and passed what short years were left to them in that realm, until they died and were laid in Rath Dínen among the great of Gondor.

1541 In this year[2] on March 1st came at last the Passing of King Elessar. It is said that the beds of Meriadoc and Peregrin were set beside the bed of the great king. Then Legolas built a grey ship in Ithilien, and sailed down Anduin and so over Sea; and with him, it is said, went Gimli the Dwarf. And when that ship passed an end was come in Middle-earth of the Fellowship of the Ring.

[1] pp. 6–7, 1018, note 2.

[2] Fourth Age (Gondor) 120.

APPENDIX C

FAMILY TREES

The names given in these Trees are only a selection from many. Most of them are either guests at Bilbo's Farewell Party, or their direct ancestors. The guests at the Party are underlined. A few other names of persons concerned in the events recounted are also given. In addition some genealogical information is provided concerning Samwise the founder of the family of *Gardner*, later famous and influential.

The figures after the names are those of birth (and death where that is recorded). All dates are given according to the Shire-reckoning, calculated from the crossing of the Brandywine by the brothers Marcho and Blanco in the Year 1 of the Shire (Third Age 1601).

BAGGINS OF HOBBITON

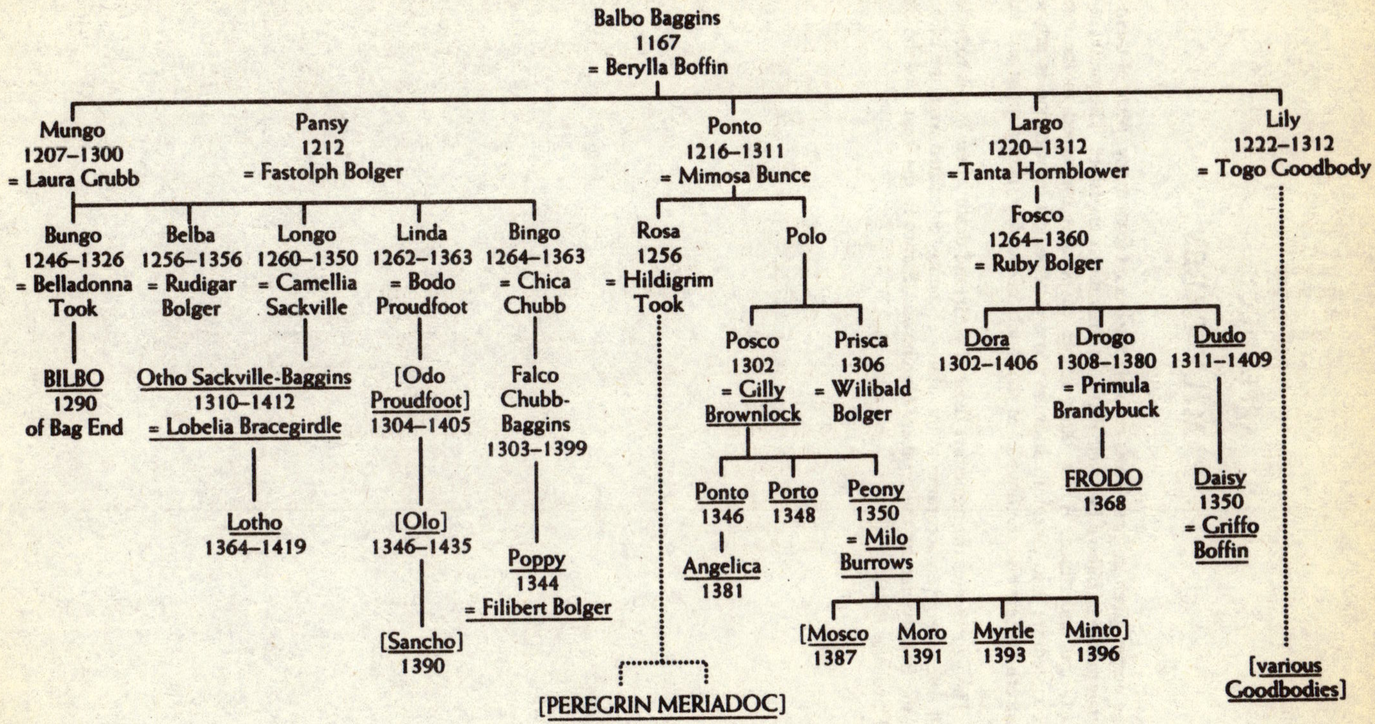

TOOK OF GREAT SMIALS

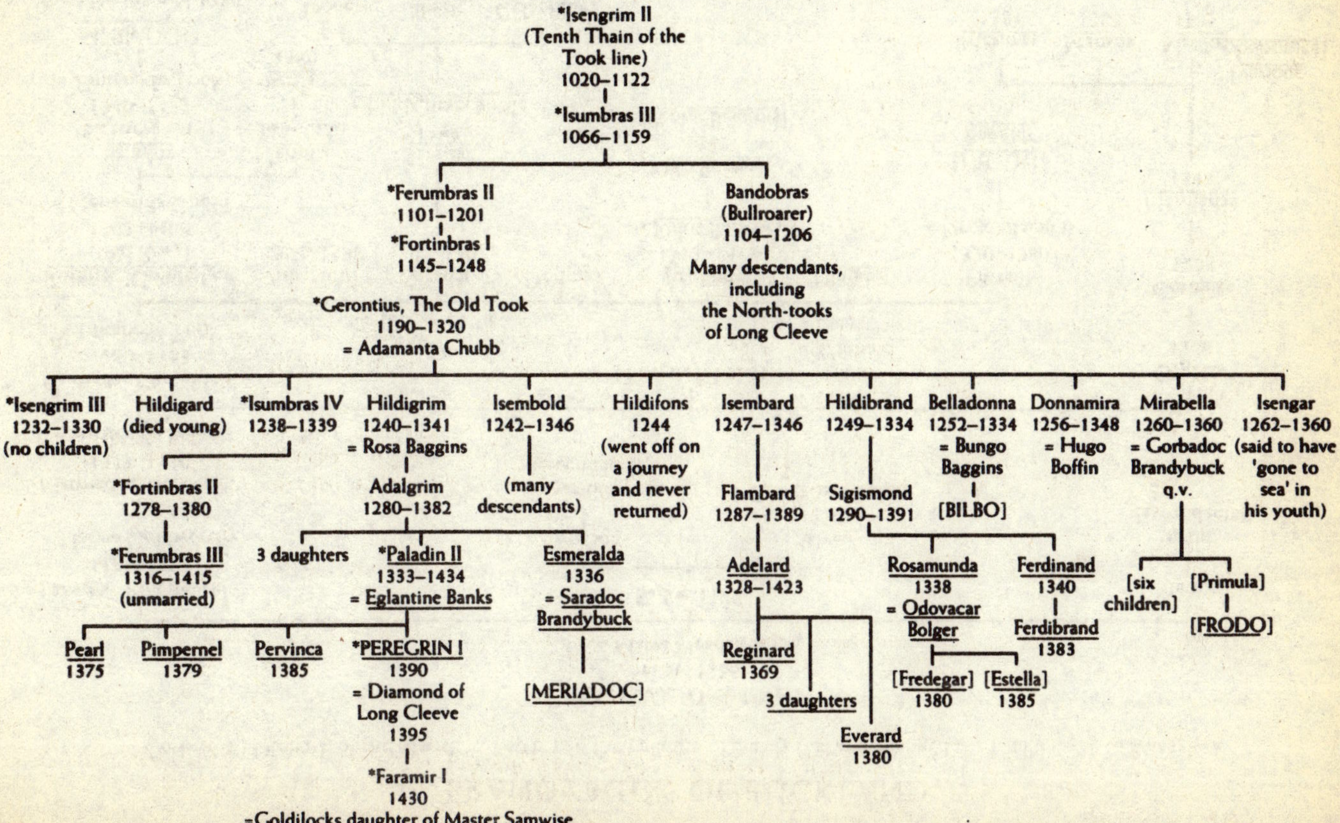

BRANDYBUCK OF BUCKLAND

Gorhendad Oldbuck of the Marish, c. 740 began the building of *Brandy Hall* and changed the family name to *Brandybuck*.

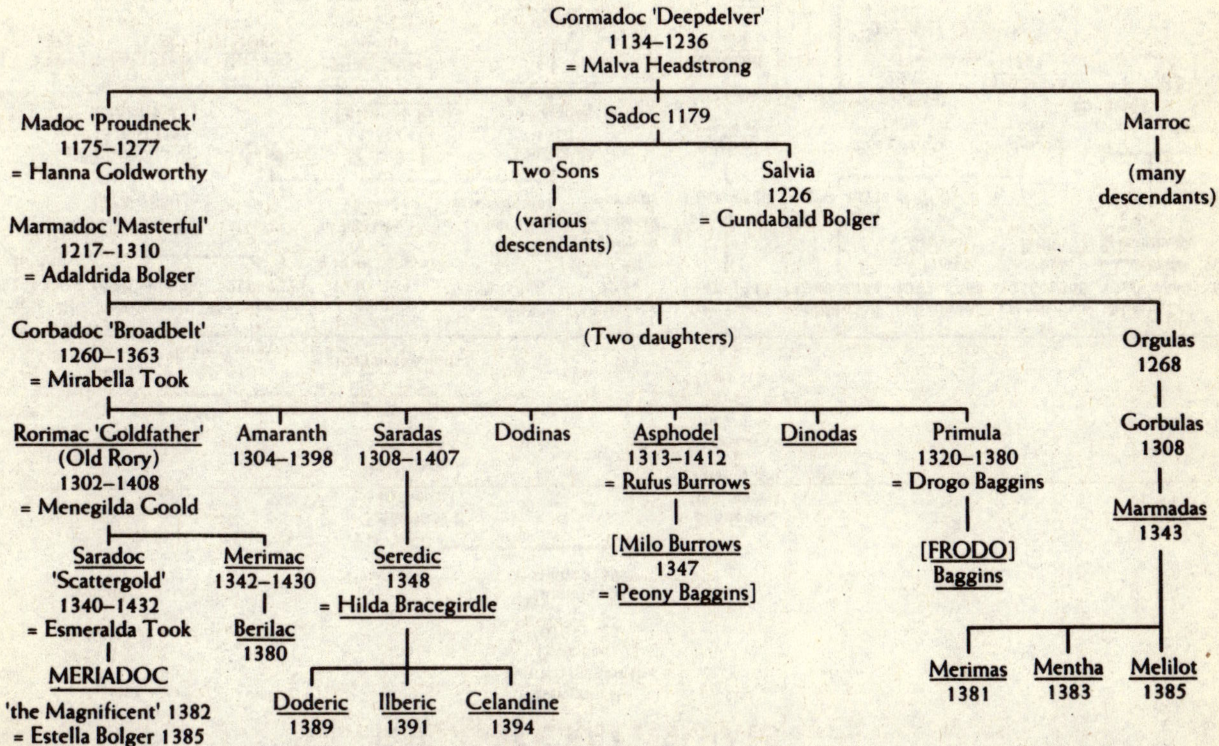

THE LONGFATHER-TREE OF MASTER SAMWISE

(showing also the rise of the families of Gardner of the Hill and of Fairbairn of the Towers.)

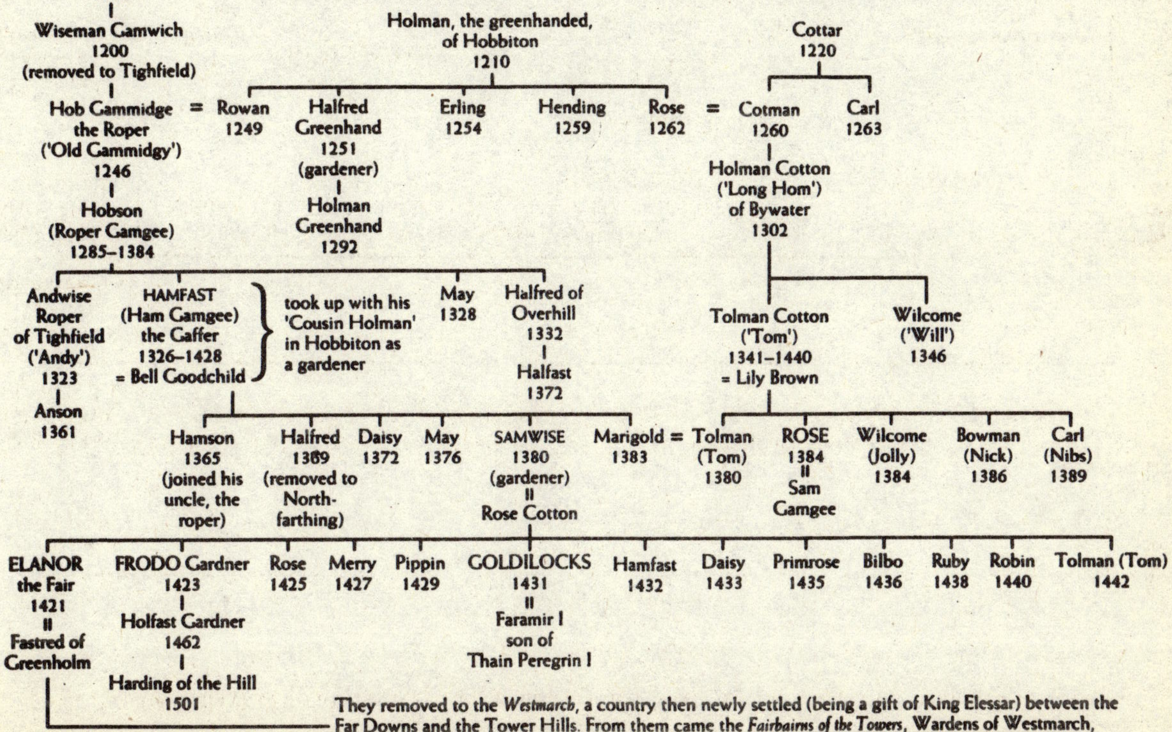

They removed to the *Westmarch*, a country then newly settled (being a gift of King Elessar) between the Far Downs and the Tower Hills. From them came the *Fairbairns of the Towers*, Wardens of Westmarch, who inherited the Red Book, and made several copies with various notes and later additions.

APPENDIX D

SHIRE CALENDAR

FOR USE IN ALL YEARS

(1) *Afteryule*	(4) *Astron*	(7) *Afterlithe*	(10) *Winterfilth*
YULE 7 14 21 28	1 8 15 22 29	LITHE 7 14 21 28	1 8 15 22 29
1 8 15 22 29	2 9 16 23 30	1 8 15 22 29	2 9 16 23 30
2 9 16 23 30	3 10 17 24 –	2 9 16 23 30	3 10 17 24 –
3 10 17 24 –	4 11 18 25 –	3 10 17 24 –	4 11 18 25 –
4 11 18 25 –	5 12 19 26 –	4 11 18 25 –	5 12 19 26 –
5 12 19 26 –	6 13 20 27 –	5 12 19 26 –	6 13 20 27 –
6 13 20 27 –	7 14 21 28 –	6 13 20 27 –	7 14 21 28 –
(2) *Solmath*	(5) *Thrimidge*	(8) *Wedmath*	(11) *Blotmath*
– 5 12 19 26	– 6 13 20 27	– 5 12 19 26	– 6 13 20 27
– 6 13 20 27	– 7 14 21 28	– 6 13 20 27	– 7 14 21 28
– 7 14 21 28	1 8 15 22 29	– 7 14 21 28	1 8 15 22 29
1 8 15 22 29	2 9 16 23 30	1 8 15 22 29	2 9 16 23 30
2 9 16 23 30	3 10 17 24 –	2 9 16 23 30	3 10 17 24 –
3 10 17 24 –	4 11 18 25 –	3 10 17 24 –	4 11 18 25 –
4 11 18 25 –	5 12 19 26 –	4 11 18 25 –	5 12 19 26 –
(3) *Rethe*	(6) *Forelithe*	(9) *Halimath*	(12) *Foreyule*
– 3 10 17 24	– 4 11 18 25	– 3 10 17 24	– 4 11 18 25
– 4 11 18 25	– 5 12 19 26	– 4 11 18 25	– 5 12 19 26
– 5 12 19 26	– 6 13 20 27	– 5 12 19 26	– 6 13 20 27
– 6 13 20 27	– 7 14 21 28	– 6 13 20 27	– 7 14 21 28
– 7 14 21 28	1 8 15 22 29	– 7 14 21 28	1 8 15 22 29
1 8 15 22 29	2 9 16 23 30	1 8 15 22 29	2 9 16 23 30
2 9 16 23 30	3 10 17 24 LITHE	2 9 16 23 30	3 10 17 24 YULE
	Midyear's Day (*Overlithe*)		

Every year began on the first day of the week, Saturday, and ended on the last day of the week, Friday. The Mid-year's Day, and in Leap-years the Overlithe, had no weekday name. The Lithe before Mid-year's Day was called 1 Lithe, and the one after was called 2 Lithe. The Yule at the end of the year was 1 Yule, and that at the beginning was 2 Yule. The Overlithe was a day of special holiday, but it did not occur in any of the years important to the history of the Great Ring. It occurred in 1420, the year of the famous harvest and wonderful summer, and the merrymaking in that year is said to have been the greatest in memory or record.

THE CALENDARS

The Calendar in the Shire differed in several features from ours. The year no doubt was of the same length,[1] for long ago as those times are now reckoned in years and lives of men, they were not very remote according to the memory of the Earth. It is recorded by the Hobbits that they had no 'week' when they were still a wandering people, and though they had 'months', governed more or less by the Moon, their keeping of dates and calculations of time were vague and inaccurate. In the westlands of Eriador, when they had begun to settle down, they adopted the King's reckoning of the Dúnedain, which was ultimately of Eldarin origin; but the Hobbits of the Shire introduced several minor alterations. This calendar, or 'Shire Reckoning' as it was called, was eventually adopted also in Bree, except for the Shire usage of counting as Year 1 the year of the colonization of the Shire.

It is often difficult to discover from old tales and traditions precise information about things which people knew well and took for granted in their own day (such as the names of letters, or of the days of the week, or the names and lengths of months). But owing to their general interest in genealogy, and to the interest in ancient history which the learned amongst them developed after the War of the Ring, the Shire-hobbits seem to have concerned themselves a good deal with dates; and they even drew up complicated tables showing the relations of their own system with others. I am not skilled in these matters, and may have made many errors; but at any rate the chronology of the crucial years S.R. 1418, 1419 is so carefully set out in the Red Book that there cannot be much doubt about days and times at that point.

It seems clear that the Eldar in Middle-earth, who had, as Samwise remarked, more time at their disposal, reckoned in long periods, and the Quenya word *yén*, often translated 'year' (p. 368), really means 144 of our years. The Eldar preferred to reckon in sixes and twelves as far as possible. A 'day' of the sun they called *ré* and reckoned from sunset to sunset. The *yén* contained 52,596 days. For ritual rather than practical purposes the Eldar observed a week or *enquië* of six days; and the *yén* contained 8,766 of these *enquier*, reckoned continuously throughout the period.

In Middle-earth the Eldar also observed a short period or solar year, called a *coranar* or 'sun-round' when considered more or less astronomically, but usually called *loa* 'growth' (especially in the north-western lands) when the seasonal changes in vegetation were primarily considered, as was usual with the Elves generally. The *loa* was broken up into periods that might be regarded either as long months or short seasons. These no doubt varied in different regions; but the Hobbits only provide information concerning the Calendar of Imladris. In that calendar there were six of these 'seasons', of which the Quenya names were *tuilë*, *lairë*, *yávië*, *quellë*, *hrívë*, *coirë*, which may be translated 'spring, summer, autumn, fading, winter, stirring'. The Sindarin names were *ethuil*, *laer*, *iavas*, *firith*, *rhîw*, *echuir*. 'Fading' was also called *lasse-lanta* 'leaf-fall', or in Sindarin *narbeleth* 'sun-waning'.

Lairë and *hrívë* each contained 72 days, and the remainder 54 each. The *loa* began

[1] 365 days, 5 hours, 48 minutes, 46 seconds.

with *yestarë*, the day immediately before *tuilë*, and ended with *mettarë*, the day immediately after *coirë*. Between *yávië* and *quellë* were inserted three *enderi* or 'middle-days'. This provided a year of 365 days which was supplemented by doubling the *enderi* (adding 3 days) in every twelfth year.

How any resulting inaccuracy was dealt with is uncertain. If the year was then of the same length as now, the *yén* would have been more than a day too long. That there was an inaccuracy is shown by a note in the Calendars of the Red Book to the effect that in the 'Reckoning of Rivendell' the last year of every third *yén* was shortened by three days: the doubling of the three *enderi* due in that year was omitted; 'but that has not happened in our time'. Of the adjustment of any remaining inaccuracy there is no record.

The Númenoreans altered these arrangements. They divided the *loa* into shorter periods of more regular length; and they adhered to the custom of beginning the year in mid-winter, which had been used by Men of the North-west from whom they were derived in the First Age. Later they also made their week one of 7 days, and they reckoned the day from sunrise (out of the eastern sea) to sunrise.

The Númenorean system, as used in Númenor, and in Arnor and Gondor until the end of the kings, was called King's Reckoning. The normal year had 365 days. It was divided into twelve *astar* or months, of which ten had 30 days and two had 31. The long *astar* were those on either side of the Mid-year, approximately our June and July. The first day of the year was called *yestarë*, the middle day (183rd) was called *loëndë*, and the last day *mettarë*; these 3 days belonged to no month. In every fourth year, except the last of a century (*haranyë*), two *enderi* or 'middle-days' were substituted for the *loëndë*.

In Númenor calculation started with S.A. 1. The *Deficit* caused by deducting 1 day from the last year of a century was not adjusted until the last year of a millennium, leaving a *millennial deficit* of 4 hours, 46 minutes, 40 seconds. This addition was made in Númenor in S.A. 1000, 2000, 3000. After the Downfall in S.A. 3319 the system was maintained by the exiles, but it was much dislocated by the beginning of the Third Age with a new numeration: S.A. 3442 became T.A. 1. By making T.A. 4 a leap year instead of T.A. 3 (S.A. 3444) 1 more short year of only 365 days was intruded causing a deficit of 5 hours, 48 minutes, 46 seconds. The millennial additions were made 441 years late: in T.A. 1000 (S.A. 4441) and 2000 (S.A. 5441). To reduce the errors so caused, and the accumulation of the millennial deficits, Mardil the Steward issued a revised calendar to take effect in T.A. 2060, after a special addition of 2 days to 2059 (S.A. 5500), which concluded 5½ millennia since the beginning of the Númenorean system. But this still left about 8 hours deficit. Hador to 2360 added 1 day though this deficiency had not quite reached that amount. After that no more adjustments were made. (In T.A. 3000 with the threat of imminent war such matters were neglected.) By the end of the Third Age, after 660 more years, the Deficit had not yet amounted to 1 day.

The Revised Calendar introduced by Mardil was called Stewards' Reckoning and was adopted eventually by most of the users of the Westron language, except the Hobbits. The months were all of 30 days, and 2 days outside the months were introduced: 1 between the third and four months (March, April), and 1 between the ninth and tenth (September, October). These 5 days outside the months, *yestarë*, *tuilérë*, *loëndë*, *yáviérë*, and *mettarë*, were holidays.

The Hobbits were conservative and continued to use a form of Kings' Reckoning adapted to fit their own customs. Their months were all equal and had 30 days each; but they had 3 Summerdays, called in the Shire the Lithe or the Lithedays, between June and July. The last day of the year and the first of the next year were called the Yuledays. The Yuledays and the Lithedays remained outside the months, so that January 1 was the second and not the first day of the year. Every fourth year, except in the last year of the century,[1] there were four Lithedays. The Lithedays and the Yuledays were the chief holidays and times of feasting. The additional Litheday was added after Mid-year's Day, and so the 184th day of the Leap-years was called Overlithe and was a day of special merrymaking. In full Yuletide was six days long, including the last three and first three days of each year.

The Shire-folk introduced one small innovation of their own (eventually also adopted in Bree), which they called Shire-reform. They found the shifting of the weekday names in relation to dates from year to year untidy and inconvenient. So in the time of Isengrim II they arranged that the odd day which put the succession out, should have no weekday name. After that Mid-year's Day (and the Overlithe) was known only by its name and belonged to no week (p. 174). In consequence of this reform the year always began on the First Day of the week and ended on the Last Day; and the same date in any one year had the same weekday name in all other years, so that Shire-folk no longer bothered to put the weekday in their letters or diaries.[2] They found this quite convenient at home, but not so convenient if they ever travelled further than Bree.

In the above notes, as in the narrative, I have used our modern names for both months and weekdays, though of course neither the Eldar nor the Dúnedain nor the Hobbits actually did so. Translation of the Westron names seemed to be essential to avoid confusion, while the seasonal implications of our names are more or less the same, at any rate in the Shire. It appears, however, that Mid-year's Day was intended to correspond as nearly as possible to the summer solstice. In that case the Shire dates were actually in advance of ours by some ten days, and our New Year's Day corresponded more or less to the Shire January 9.

In the Westron the Quenya names of the months were usually retained as the Latin names are now widely used in alien languages. They were: *Narvinyë*, *Nénimë*, *Súlimë*, *Víressë*, *Lótessë*, *Nárië*, *Cermië*, *Urimë*, *Yavannië*, *Narquelië*, *Hísimë*, *Ringarë*. The Sindarin names (used only by the Dúnedain) were: *Narwain*, *Nínui*, *Gwaeron*, *Gwirith*, *Lothron*, *Nórui*, *Cerveth*, *Urui*, *Ivanneth*, *Narbeleth*, *Hithui*, *Girithron*.

[1] In the Shire, in which Year 1 corresponded with T.A. 1601. In Bree in which Year 1 corresponded with T.A. 1300 it was the first year of the century.

[2] It will be noted if one glances at a Shire Calendar, that the only weekday on which no month began was Friday. It thus became a jesting idiom in the Shire to speak of 'on Friday the first' when referring to a day that did not exist, or to a day on which very unlikely events such as the flying of pigs or (in the Shire) the walking of trees might occur. In full the expression was 'on Friday the first of Summerfilth'.

In this nomenclature the Hobbits, however, both of the Shire and of Bree, diverged from the Westron usage, and adhered to old-fashioned local names of their own, which they seem to have picked up in antiquity from the Men of the vales of Anduin; at any rate similar names were found in Dale and Rohan (cf. the notes on the languages, pp. 1162–3). The meanings of these names, devised by Men, had as a rule long been forgotten by the Hobbits, even in cases where they had originally known what their significance was; and the forms of the names were much obscured in consequence: *math*, for instance, at the end of some of them is a reduction of *month*.

The Shire names are set out in the Calendar. It may be noted that *Solmath* was usually pronounced, and sometimes written, *Somath*; *Thrimidge* was often written *Thrimich* (archaically *Thrimilch*); and *Blotmath* was pronounced *Blodmath* or *Blommath*. In Bree the names differed, being *Frery*, *Solmath*, *Rethe*, *Chithing*, *Thrimidge*, *Lithe*, *The Summerdays*, *Mede*, *Wedmath*, *Harvestmath*, *Wintring*, *Blooting*, and *Yulemath*. *Frery*, *Chithing* and *Yulemath* were also used in the Eastfarthing.[1]

The Hobbit week was taken from the Dúnedain, and the names were translations of those given to the days in the old North-kingdom, which in their turn were derived from the Eldar. The six-day week of the Eldar had days dedicated to, or named after, the Stars, the Sun, the Moon, the Two Trees, the Heavens, and the Valar or Powers, in that order, the last day being the chief day of the week. Their names in Quenya were *Elenya*, *Anarya*, *Isilya*, *Aldúya*, *Menelya*, *Valanya* (or *Tárion*); the Sindarin names were *Orgilion*, *Oranor*, *Orithil*, *Orgaladhad*, *Ormenel*, *Orbelain* (or *Rodyn*).

The Númenoreans retained the dedications and order, but altered the fourth day to *Aldëa* (*Orgaladh*) with reference to the White Tree only, of which Nimloth that grew in the King's Court in Númenor was believed to be a descendant. Also desiring a seventh day, and being great mariners, they inserted a 'Sea-day', *Eärenya* (*Oraearon*), after the Heavens' Day.

The Hobbits took over this arrangement, but the meanings of their translated names were soon forgotten, or no longer attended to, and the forms were much reduced, especially in everyday pronunciation. The first translation of the Númenorean names was probably made two thousand years or more before the end of the Third Age, when the week of Dúnedain (the feature of their reckoning earliest adopted by alien peoples) was taken up by Men in the North. As with their names of months, the Hobbits adhered to these translations, although elsewhere in the Westron area the Quenya names were used.

Not many ancient documents were preserved in the Shire. At the end of the Third Age far the most notable survival was Yellowskin, or the Yearbook of Tuckborough.[2] Its earliest entries seem to have begun at least nine hundred years before

[1] It was a jest in Bree to speak of 'Winterfilth in the (muddy) Shire', but according to the Shire-folk Wintring was a Bree alteration of the older name, which had originally referred to the filling or completion of the year before Winter, and descended from times before the full adoption of Kings' Reckoning when their new year began after harvest.

[2] Recording births, marriages, and deaths in the Took families, as well as matters, such as land-sales, and various Shire events.

Frodo's time; and many are cited in the Red Book annals and genealogies. In these the weekday names appear in archaic forms, of which the following are the oldest: (1) *Sterrendei*, (2) *Sunnendei*, (3) *Monendei*, (4) *Trewesdei*, (5) *Hevenesdei*, (6) *Meresdei*, (7) *Highdei*. In the language of the time of the War of the Ring these had become *Sterday*, *Sunday*, *Monday*, *Trewsday*, *Hevensday* (or *Hensday*), *Mersday*, *Highday*.

I have translated these names also into our own names, naturally beginning with Sunday and Monday, which occur in the Shire week with the same names as ours, and re-naming the others in order. It must be noted, however, that the associations of the names were quite different in the Shire. The last day of the week, Friday (Highday), was the chief days, and one of holiday (after noon) and evening feasts. Saturday thus corresponds more nearly to our Monday, and Thursday to our Saturday.[1]

A few other names may be mentioned that have a reference to time, though not used in precise reckonings. The seasons usually named were *tuilë* spring, *lairë* summer, *yávië* autumn (or harvest), *hrívë* winter; but these had no exact definitions, and *quellë* (or *lasselanta*) was also used for the latter part of autumn and the beginning of winter.

The Eldar paid special attention to the 'twilight' (in the northerly regions), chiefly as the times of star-fading and star-opening. They had many names for these periods, of which the most usual were *tindómë* and *undómë*; the former most often referred to the time near dawn, and *undómë* to the evening. The Sindarin name was *uial*, which could be defined as *minuial* and *aduial*. These were often called in the Shire *morrowdim* and *evendim*. Cf. Lake Evendim as a translation of Nenuial.

The Shire Reckoning and dates are the only ones of importance for the narrative of the War of the Ring. All the days, months, and dates are in the Red Book translated into Shire terms, or equated with them in notes. The months and days, therefore, throughout *The Lord of the Rings* refer to the Shire Calendar. The only points in which the differences between this and our calendar are important to the story at the crucial period, the end of 3018 and the beginning of 3019 (S.R. 1418, 1419), are these: October 1418 has only 30 days, January 1 is the second day of 1419, and February has 30 days; so that March 25, the date of the downfall of the Barad-dûr, would correspond to our March 27, if our years began at the same seasonal point. The date was, however, March 25 in both Kings' and Stewards' Reckoning.

The New Reckoning was begun in the restored Kingdom in T.A. 3019. It represented a return to Kings' Reckoning adapted to fit a spring-beginning as in the Eldarin *loa*.[2]

In the New Reckoning the year began on March 25 old style, in commemoration of the fall of Sauron and the deeds of the Ring-bearers. The months retained their

[1] I have therefore in Bilbo's song (pp. 155–6) used Saturday and Sunday instead of Thursday and Friday.

[2] Though actually the *yestarë* of New Reckoning occurred earlier than in the Calendar of Imladris, in which it corresponded more or less with Shire April 6.

former names, beginning now with *Víressë* (April), but referred to periods beginning generally five days earlier than previously. All the months had 30 days. There were 3 *Enderi* or Middle-days (of which the second was called *Loëndë*), between *Yavannië* (September) and *Narquelië* (October), that corresponded with September 23, 24, 25 old style. But in honour of Frodo *Yavannië* 30, which corresponded with former September 22, his birthday, was made a festival, and the leap-year was provided for by doubling this feast, called *Cormarë* or Ringday.

The Fourth Age was held to have begun with the departure of Master Elrond, which took place in September 3021; but for purposes of record in the Kingdom Fourth Age 1 was the year that began according to the New Reckoning in March 25, 3021, old style.

This reckoning was in the course of the reign of King Elessar adopted in all his lands except the Shire, where the old calendar was retained and Shire Reckoning was continued. Fourth Age 1 was thus called 1422; and in so far as the Hobbits took any account of the change of Age, they maintained that it began with 2 Yule 1422, and not in the previous March.

There is no record of the Shire-folk commemorating either March 25 or September 22; but in the Westfarthing, especially in the country round Hobbiton Hill, there grew up a custom of making holiday and dancing in the Party Field, when weather permitted, on April 6. Some said that it was old Sam Gardner's birthday, some that it was the day on which the Golden Tree first flowered in 1420, and some that it was the Elves' New Year. In the Buckland the Horn of the Mark was blown at sundown every November 2 and bonfires and feastings followed.[1]

[1] Anniversary of its first blowing in the Shire in 3019.

APPENDIX E

WRITING AND SPELLING

I

PRONUNCIATION OF WORDS AND NAMES

The Westron or Common Speech has been entirely translated into English equivalents. All Hobbit names and special words are intended to be pronounced accordingly: for example, *Bolger* has *g* as in *bulge*, and *mathom* rhymes with *fathom*.

In transcribing the ancient scripts I have tried to represent the original sounds (so far as they can be determined) with fair accuracy, and at the same time to produce words and names that do not look uncouth in modern letters. The High-elven Quenya has been spelt as much like Latin as its sounds allowed. For this reason *c* has been preferred to *k* in both Eldarin languages.

The following points may be observed by those who are interested in such details.

CONSONANTS

C has always the value of *k* even before *e* and *i*: *celeb* 'silver' should be pronounced as *keleb*.

CH is only used to represent the sound heard in *bach* (in German or Welsh), not that in English *church*. Except at the end of words and before *t* this sound was weakened to *h* in the speech of Gondor, and that change has been recognized in a few names, such as *Rohan*, *Rohirrim*. (*Imrahil* is a Númenorean name.)

DH represents the voiced (soft) *th* of English *these clothes*. It is usually related to *d*, as in S. *galadh* 'tree' compared with Q. *alda*; but is sometimes derived from *n* + *r*, as in *Caradhras* 'Redhorn' from *caran-rass*.

F represents *f*, except at the end of words, where it is used to represent the sound of *v* (as in English *of*): *Nindalf*, *Fladrif*.

G has only the sound of *g* in *give*, *get*: *gil* 'star', in *Gildor*, *Gilraen*, *Osgiliath*, begins as in English *gild*.

H standing alone with no other consonant has the sound of *h* in *house*, *behold*. The Quenya combination *ht* has the sound of *cht*, as in German *echt*, *acht*: e.g. in the name *Telumehtar* 'Orion'.[1] See also CH, DH, L, R, TH, W, Y.

I initially before another vowel has the consonantal sound of *y* in *you*, *yore* in Sindarin only: as in *Ioreth*, *Iarwain*. See Y.

K is used in names drawn from other than Elvish languages, with the same value as *c*; *kh* thus represents the same sound as *ch* in Orkish *Grishnákh*, or Adûnaic (Númenorean) *Adunakhor*. On Dwarvish (Khuzdul) see note below.

[1] Usually called in Sindarin *Menelvagor* (p. 80), Q. *Menelmacar*.

L represents more or less the sound of English initial *l*, as in *let*. It was, however, to some degree 'palatalized' between *e*, *i* and a consonant, or finally after *e*, *i*. (The Eldar would probably have transcribed English *bell*, *fill* as *beol*, *fiol*.) LH represents this sound when voiceless (usually derived from initial *sl-*). In (archaic) Quenya this is written *hl*, but was in the Third Age usually pronounced as *l*.

NG represents *ng* in *finger*, except finally where it was sounded as in English *sing*. The latter sound also occurred initially in Quenya, but has been transcribed *n* (as in *Noldo*), according to the pronunciation of the Third Age.

PH has the same sound as *f*. It is used *(a)* where the *f*-sound occurs at the end of a word, as in *alph* 'swan'; *(b)* where the *f*-sound is related to or derived from a *p*, as in *i-Pheriannath* 'the Halflings' (*perian*); *(c)* in the middle of a few words where it represents a long *ff* (from *pp*) as in *Ephel* 'outer fence'; and *(d)* in Adûnaic and Westron, as in *Ar-Pharazôn* (*pharaz* 'gold').

QU has been used for *cw*, a combination very frequent in Quenya, though it did not occur in Sindarin.

R represents a trilled *r* in all positions; the sound was not lost before consonants (as in English *part*). The Orcs, and some Dwarves, are said to have used a back or uvular *r*, a sound which the Eldar found distasteful. RH represents a voiceless *r* (usually derived from older initial *sr-*). It was written *hr* in Quenya. Cf. L.

S is always voiceless, as in English *so*, *geese*; the *z*-sound did not occur in contemporary Quenya or Sindarin. SH, occurring in Westron, Dwarvish and Orkish, represents sounds similar to *sh* in English.

TH represents the voiceless *th* of English in *thin cloth*. This had become *s* in spoken Quenya, though still written with a different letter; as in Q. *Isil*, S. *Ithil*, 'Moon'.

TY represents a sound probably similar to the *t* in English *tune*. It was derived mainly from *c* or *t* + *y*. The sound of English *ch*, which was frequent in Westron, was usually substituted for it by speakers of that language. Cf. HY under Y.

V has the sound of English *v*, but is not used finally. See F.

W has the sound of English *w*. HW is a voiceless *w*, as in English *white* (in northern pronunciation). It was not an uncommon initial sound in Quenya, though examples seem not to occur in this book. Both *v* and *w* are used in the transcription of Quenya, in spite of the assimilation of its spelling to Latin, since the two sounds, distinct in origin, both occurred in the language.

Y is used in Quenya for the consonant *y*, as in English *you*. In Sindarin *y* is a vowel (see below). HY has the same relation to *y* as HW to *w*, and represents a sound like that often heard in English *hew*, *huge*; *h* in Quenya *eht*, *iht* had the same sound. The sound of English *sh*, which was common in Westron, was often substituted by speakers of that language. Cf. TY above. HY was usually derived from *sy-* and *khy-*; in both cases related Sindarin words show initial *h*, as in Q. *Hyarmen* 'south', S. *Harad*.

Note that consonants written twice, as *tt*, *ll*, *ss*, *nn*, represent long, 'double' consonants. At the end of words of more than one syllable these were usually shortened: as in *Rohan* from *Rochann* (archaic *Rochand*).

In Sindarin the combinations *ng*, *nd*, *mb*, which were specially favoured in the Eldarin languages at an earlier stage, suffered various changes. *mb* became *m* in all cases, but still counted as a long consonant for purposes of stress (see below), and is thus written *mm* in cases where otherwise the stress might be in doubt.[1] *ng* remained unchanged except initially and finally where it became the simple nasal (as in English *sing*). *nd* became *nn* usually, as *Ennor* 'Middle-earth', Q. *Endóre*; but remained *nd* at the end of fully accented monosyllables such as *thond* 'root' (cf. *Morthond* 'Blackroot'), and also before *r*, as *Andros* 'long-foam'. This *nd* is also seen in some ancient names derived from an older period, such as *Nargothrond*, *Gondolin*, *Beleriand*. In the Third Age final *nd* in long words had become *n* from *nn*, as in *Ithilien*, *Rohan*, *Anórien*.

VOWELS

For vowels the letters *i*, *e*, *a*, *o*, *u* are used, and (in Sindarin only) *y*. As far as can be determined the sounds represented by these letters (other than *y*) were of normal kind, though doubtless many local varieties escape detection. That is, the sounds were approximately those represented by *i*, *e*, *a*, *o*, *u* in English *machine*, *were*, *father*, *for*, *brute*, irrespective of quantity.

In Sindarin long *e*, *a*, *o* had the same quality as the short vowels, being derived in comparatively recent times from them (older *é*, *á*, *ó* had been changed). In Quenya long *é* and *ó* were, when correctly[2] pronounced, as by the Eldar, tenser and 'closer' than the short vowels.

Sindarin alone among contemporary languages possessed the 'modified' or fronted *u*, more or less as *u* in French *lune*. It was partly a modification of *o* and *u*, partly derived from older diphthongs *eu*, *iu*. For this sound *y* has been used (as in ancient English): as in *lyg* 'snake', Q. *leuca*, or *emyn* pl. of *amon* 'hill'. In Gondor this *y* was usually pronounced like *i*.

Long vowels are usually marked with the 'acute accent', as in some varieties of Fëanorian script. In Sindarin long vowels in stressed monosyllables are marked with the circumflex, since they tended in such cases to be specially prolonged;[3] so in *dûn* compared with *Dúnedan*. The use of the circumflex in other languages such as

[1] As in *galadhremmin ennorath* (p. 231) 'tree-woven lands of Middle-earth'. *Remmirath* (p. 80) contains *rem* 'mesh', Q. *rembe*, + *mîr* 'jewel'.

[2] A fairly widespread pronunciation of long *é* and *ó* as *ei* and *ou*, more or less as in English *say no*, both in Westron and in the renderings of Quenya names by Westron speakers, is shown by spellings such as *ei*, *ou* (or their equivalents in contemporary scripts). But such pronunciations were regarded as incorrect or rustic. They were naturally usual in the Shire. Those therefore who pronounce *yéni ûnótime* 'long-years innumerable', as is natural in English (*sc.* more or less as *yainy oonoatimy*) will err little more than Bilbo, Meriadoc, or Peregrin. Frodo said to have shown great 'skill with foreign sounds'.

[3] So also in *Annûn* 'sunset', *Amrûn* 'sunrise', under the influence of the related *dûn* 'west', and *rhûn* 'east'.

Adûnaic or Dwarvish has no special significance, and is used merely to mark these out as alien tongues (as with the use of *k*).

Final *e* is never mute or a mere sign of length as in English. To mark this final *e* it is often (but not consistently) written *ë*.

The groups *er*, *ir*, *ur* (finally or before a consonant) are not intended to be pronounced as in English *fern*, *fir*, *fur*, but rather as English *air*, *eer*, *oor*.

In Quenya *ui*, *oi*, *ai* and *iu*, *eu*, *au* are diphthongs (that is, pronounced in one syllable). All other pairs of vowels are dissyllabic. This is often dictated by writing *ëa* (*Eä*), *ëo*, *oë*.

In Sindarin the diphthongs are written *ae*, *ai*, *ei*, *oe*, *ui*, and *au*. Other combinations are not diphthongal. The writing of final *au* as *aw* is in accordance with English custom, but is actually not uncommon in Fëanorian spellings.

All these diphthongs[1] were 'falling' diphthongs, that is stressed on the first element, and composed of the simple vowels run together. Thus *ai*, *ei*, *oi*, *ui* are intended to be pronounced respectively as the vowels in English *rye* (not *ray*), *grey*, *boy*, *ruin*; and *au* (*aw*) as in *loud*, *how* and not as in *laud*, *haw*.

There is nothing in English closely corresponding to *ae*, *oe*, *eu*; *ae* and *oe* may be pronounced as *ai*, *oi*.

STRESS

The position of the 'accent' or stress is not marked, since in the Eldarin languages concerned its place is determined by the form of the word. In words of two syllables it falls in practically all cases on the first syllable. In longer words it falls on the last syllable but one, where that contains a long vowel, a diphthong, or a vowel followed by two (or more) consonants. Where the last syllable but one contains (as often) a short vowel followed by only one (or no) consonant, the stress falls on the syllable before it, the third from the end. Words of the last form are favoured in the Eldarin languages, especially Quenya.

In the following examples the stressed vowel is marked by a capital letter: *isIldur*, *Orome*, *erEssëa*, *fËanor*, *ancAlima*, *elentÁri*, *dEnethor*, *periAnnath*, *ecthElion*, *pelArgir*, *silIvren*. Words of the type *elentÁri* 'star-queen' seldom occur in Quenya where the vowel is *é*, *á*, *ó*, unless (as in this case) they are compounds; they are commoner with the vowels *í*, *ú*, as *andÚne* 'sunset, west'. They do not occur in Sindarin except in compounds. Note that Sindarin *dh*, *th*, *ch* are single consonants and represent single letters in the original scripts.

NOTE

In names drawn from other languages than Eldarin the same values for the letters are intended, where not specially described above, except in the case of Dwarvish.

[1] Originally. But *iu* in Quenya was in the Third Age usually pronounced as a rising dipthong as *yu* in English *yule*.

In Dwarvish, which did not possess the sounds represented above by *th* and *ch* (*kh*), *th* and *kh* are aspirates, that is *t* or *k* followed by an *h*, more or less as in *backhand*, *outhouse*.

Where *z* occurs the sound intended is that of English *z*. *gh* in the Black Speech and Orkish represents a 'back spirant' (related to *g* as *dh* to *d*): as in *ghâsh* and *agh*.

The 'outer' or Mannish names of the Dwarves have been given Northern forms, but the letter-values are those described. So also in the case of the personal and place-names of Rohan (where they have not been modernized), except that here *éa* and *éo* are diphthongs, which may be represented by the *ea* of English *bear*, and the *eo* of *Theobald*; *y* is the modified *u*. The modernized forms are easily recognized and are intended to be pronounced as in English. They are mostly place-names: as Dunharrow (for *Dúnharg*), except Shadowfax and Wormtongue.

II
WRITING

The scripts and letters used in the Third Age were all ultimately of Eldarin origin, and already at that time of great antiquity. They had reached the stage of full alphabetic development, but older modes in which only the consonants were denoted by full letters were still in use.

The alphabets were of two main, and in origin independent, kinds: the *Tengwar* or *Tîw*, here translated as 'letters'; and the *Certar* or *Cirth*, translated as 'runes'. The *Tengwar* were devised for writing with brush or pen, and the squared forms of inscriptions were in their case derivative from the written forms. The *Certar* were devised and mostly used only for scratched or incised inscriptions.

The *Tengwar* were the more ancient; for they had been developed by the Noldor, the kindred of the Eldar most skilled in such matters, long before their exile. The oldest Eldarin letters, the Tengwar of Rúmil, were not used in Middle-earth. The later letters, the Tengwar of Fëanor, were largely a new invention, though they owed something to the letters of Rúmil. They were brought to Middle-earth by the exiled Noldor, and so became known to the Edain and Númenoreans. In the Third Age their use had spread over much the same area as that in which the Common Speech was known.

The Cirth were devised first in Beleriand by the Sindar, and were long used only for inscribing names and brief memorials upon wood or stone. To that origin they owe their angular shapes, very similar to the runes of our times, though they differed from these in details and were wholly different in arrangement. The Cirth in their older and simpler form spread eastward in the Second Age, and became known to many peoples, to Men and Dwarves, and even to Orcs, all of whom altered them to suit their purposes and according to their skill or lack of it. One such simple form was still used by the Men of Dale, and a similar one by the Rohirrim.

But in Beleriand, before the end of the First Age, the Cirth, partly under the influence of the Tengwar of the Noldor, were rearranged and further developed. Their richest and most ordered form was known as the Alphabet of Daeron, since in Elvish tradition it was said to have been devised by Daeron, the minstrel and

THE TENGWAR

I
II
III
IV
1
2
3
4
5
6
7
8
9
10
11
12
13
14
15
16
17
18
19
20
21
22
23
24
25
26
27
28
29
30
31
32
33
34
35
36

loremaster of King Thingol of Doriath. Among the Eldar the Alphabet of Daeron did not develop true cursive forms, since for writing the Elves adopted the Fëanorian letters. The Elves of the West indeed for the most part gave up the use of runes altogether. In the country of Eregion, however, the Alphabet of Daeron was maintained in use and passed thence to Moria, where it became the alphabet most favoured by the Dwarves. It remained ever after in use among them and passed with them to the North. Hence in later times it was often called *Angerthas Moria* or the Long Rune-rows of Moria. As with their speech the Dwarves made use of such scripts as were current and many wrote the Fëanorian letters skilfully; but for their own tongue they adhered to the Cirth, and developed written pen-forms from them.

(i)
THE FËANORIAN LETTERS

The table shows, in formal book-hand shape, all the letters that were commonly used in the West-lands in the Third Age. The arrangement is the one most usual at the time, and the one in which the letters were then usually recited by name.

This script was not in origin an 'alphabet', that is, a haphazard series of letters, each with an independent value of its own, recited in a traditional order that has no reference either to their shapes or to their functions.[1] It was, rather, a system of consonantal signs, of similar shapes and style, which could be adapted at choice or convenience to represent the consonants of languages observed (or devised) by the Eldar. None of the letters had in itself a fixed value; but certain relations between them were gradually recognized.

The system contained twenty-four primary letters, 1–24, arranged in four *témar* (series), each of which had six *tyeller* (grades). There were also 'additional letters', of which 25–36 are examples. Of these 27 and 29 are the only strictly independent letters; the remainder are modifications of other letters. There was also a number of *tehtar* (signs) of varied uses. These do not appear in the table.[2]

The *primary letters* were each formed of a *telco* (stem) and a *lúva* (bow). The forms seen in 1–4 were regarded as normal. The stem could be raised, as in 9–16; or reduced, as in 17–24. The bow could be open, as in Series I and III; or closed, as in II and IV; and in either case it could be doubled, as e.g. in 5–8.

The theoretic freedom of application had in the Third Age been modified by custom to this extent that Series I was generally applied to the dental or *t*-series (*tincotéma*), and II to the labials or *p*-series (*parmatéma*). The application of Series III and IV varied according to the requirements of different languages.

[1] The only relation in our alphabet that would have appeared intelligible to the Eldar is that between P and B; and their separation from one another, and from F, M, V, would have seemed to them absurd.

[2] Many of them appear in the examples on the title-page, and in the inscription on p. 49, transcribed on p. 247. They were mainly used to express vowel-sounds, in Quenya usually regarded as modifications of the accompanying consonant; or to express more briefly some of the most frequent consonant combinations.

In languages like the Westron, which made much use of consonants[1] such as our *ch*, *j*, *sh*, Series III was usually applied to these; in which case Series IV was applied to the normal *k*-series (*calmatéma*). In Quenya, which possessed besides the *calmatéma* both a palatal series (*tyelpetéma*) and a labialized series (*quessetéma*), the palatals were represented by a Fëanorian diacritic denoting 'following *y*' (usually two underposed dots), while Series IV was a *kw*-series.

Within these general applications the following relations were also commonly observed. The normal letters, Grade 1, were applied to the 'voiceless stops': *t*, *p*, *k*, etc. The doubling of the bow indicated the addition of 'voice': thus if 1, 2, 3, 4=*t*, *p*, *ch*, *k* (or *t*, *p*, *k*, *kw*) then 5, 6, 7, 8 =*d*, *b*, *j*, *g* (or *d*, *b*, *g*, *gw*). The raising of the stem indicated the opening of the consonant to a 'spirant': thus assuming the above values for Grade 1, Grade 3 (9–12)=*th*, *f*, *sh*, *ch* (or *th*, *f*, *kh*, *khw*/*hw*), and Grade 4 (13–16)=*dh*, *v*, *zh*, *gh* (or *dh*, *v*, *gh*, *ghw*/*w*).

The original Fëanorian system also possessed a grade with extended stems, both above and below the line. These usually represented aspirated consonants (e.g. *t*+*h*, *p*+*h*, *k*+*h*), but might represent other consonantal variations required. They were not needed in the languages of the Third Age that used this script; but the extended forms were much used as variants (more clearly distinguished from Grade 1) of Grades 3 and 4.

Grade 5 (17–20) was usually applied to the nasal consonants: thus 17 and 18 were the most common signs for *n* and *m*. According to the principle observed above, Grade 6 should then have represented the voiceless nasals; but since such sounds (exemplified by Welsh *nh* or ancient English *hn*) were of very rare occurrence in the languages concerned, Grade 6 (21–24) was most often used for the weakest or 'semi-vocalic' consonants of each series. It consisted of the smallest and simplest shapes among the primary letters. Thus 21 was often used for a weak (untrilled) *r*, originally occurring in Quenya and regarded in the system of that language as the weakest consonant of the *tincotéma*; 22 was widely used for *w*; where Series III was used as a palatal series 23 was commonly used as consonantal *y*.[2]

Since some of the consonants of Grade 4 tended to become weaker in pronunciation, and to approach or to merge with those of Grade 6 (as described above), many of the latter ceased to have a clear function in the Eldarin languages; and it was from these letters that the letters expressing vowels were largely derived.

NOTE

The standard spelling of Quenya diverged from the applications of the letters above described. Grade 2 was used for *nd*, *mb*, *ng*, *ngw*, all of which were frequent, since

[1] The representation of the sounds here is the same as that employed in transcription and described above, except that here *ch* represents the *ch* in English *church*; *j* represents the sound of English *j*, and *zh* the sound heard in *azure* and *occasion*.

[2] The inscription on the West-gate of Moria gives an example of a mode, used for the spelling of Sindarin, in which Grade 6 represented the simple nasals, but Grade 5 represented the double or long nasals much used in Sindarin: 17=*nn*, but 21=*n*.

b, *g*, *gw* only appeared in these combinations, while for *rd*, *ld* the special letters 26, 28 were used. (For *lv*, not for *lw*, many speakers, especially Elves, used *lb*: this was written with 27+6, since *lmb* could not occur.) Similarly, Grade 4 was used for the extremely frequent combinations *nt*, *mp*, *nk*, *nqu*, since Quenya did not possess *dh*, *gh*, *ghw*, and for *v* used letter 22. See the Quenya letter-names pp. 1096 and 1097.

The additional letters. No. 27 was universally used for *l*. No. 25 (in origin a modification of 21) was used for 'full' trilled *r*. Nos. 26, 28 were modifications of these. They were frequently used for voiceless *r* (*rh*) and *l* (*lh*) respectively. But in Quenya they were used for *rd* and *ld*. 29 represented *s*, and 31 (with doubled curl) *z* in those languages that required it. The inverted forms, 30 and 32, though available for use as separate signs, were mostly used as mere variants of 29 and 31, according to the convenience of writing, e.g. they were much used when accompanied by superimposed *tehtar*.

No. 33 was in origin a variation representing some (weaker) variety of 11; its most frequent use in the Third Age was *h*. 34 was mostly used (if at all) for voiceless *w* (*hw*). 35 and 36 were, when used as consonants, mostly applied to *y* and *w* respectively.

The vowels were in many modes represented by *tehtar*, usually set above a consonantal letter. In languages such as Quenya, in which most words ended in a vowel, the *tehta* was placed above the preceding consonant; in those such as Sindarin, in which most words ended in a consonant, it was placed above the following consonant. When there was no consonant present in the required position, the *tehta* was placed above the 'short carrier', of which a common form was like an undotted ı. The actual *tehtar* used in different languages for vowel-signs were numerous. The commonest, usually applied to (varieties of) *e*, *i*, *a*, *o*, *u*, are exhibited in the examples given. The three dots, most usual in forming writing for *a*, were variously written in quicker styles, a form like a circumflex being often employed.[1] The single dot and the 'acute accent' were frequently used for *i* and *e* (but in some modes for *e* and *i*). The curls were used for *o* and *u*. In the Ring-inscription the curl open to the right is used for *u*; but on the title-page this stands for *o*, and the curl open to the left for *u*. The curl to the right was favoured, and the application depended on the language concerned: in the Black Speech *o* was rare.

Long vowels were usually represented by placing the *tehta* on the 'long carrier', of which a common form was like an undotted *ȷ*. But for the same purpose the *tehtar* could be doubled. This was, however, only frequently done with the curls, and sometimes with the 'accent'. Two dots was more often used as a sign for following *y*.

The West-gate inscription illustrates a mode of 'full writing' with the vowels

[1] In Quenya in which *a* was very frequent, its vowel sign was often omitted altogether. Thus for *calma* 'lamp' *clm* could be written. This would naturally read as *calma*, since *cl* was not in Quenya a possible initial combination, and *m* never occurred finally. A possible reading was *calama*, but no such word existed.

represented by separate letters. All the vocalic letters used in Sindarin are shown. The use of No. 30 as a sign for vocalic *y* may be noted; also the expression of diphthongs by placing the *tehta* for following *y* above the vowel-letter. The sign for following *w* (required for the expression of *au*, *aw*) was in this mode the *u*-curl or a modification of it ~. But the diphthongs were often written out in full, as in the transcription. In this mode length of vowel was usually indicated by the 'acute accent', called in that case *andaith* 'long mark'.

There were beside the *tehtar* already mentioned a number of others, chiefly used to abbreviate the writing, especially by expressing frequent consonant combinations without writing them out in full. Among these, a bar (or a sign like a Spanish *tilde*) placed above a consonant was often used to indicate that it was preceded by the nasal of the same series (as in *nt*, *mp*, or *nk*); a similar sign placed below was, however, mainly used to show that the consonant was long or doubled. A downward hook attached to the bow (as in *hobbits*, the last word on the title-page) was used to indicate a following *s*, especially in the combinations *ts*, *ps*, *ks* (*x*), that were favoured in Quenya.

There was of course no 'mode' for the representation of English. One adequate phonetically could be devised from the Fëanorian system. The brief example on the title-page does not attempt to exhibit this. It is rather an example of what a man of Gondor might have produced, hesitating between the values of the letters familiar in his 'mode' and the traditional spelling of English. It may be noted that a dot below (one of the uses of which was to represent weak obscured vowels) is here employed in the representation of unstressed *and*, but is also used in *here* for silent final *e*; *the*, *of*, and *of the* are expressed by abbreviations (extended *dh*, extended *v*, and the latter with an under-stroke).

The names of the letters. In all modes each letter and sign had a name; but these names were devised to fit or describe the phonetic uses in each particular mode. It was, however, often felt desirable, especially in describing the uses of the letters in other modes, to have a name for each letter in itself as a shape. For this purpose the Quenya 'full names' were commonly employed, even where they referred to uses peculiar to Quenya. Each 'full name' was an actual word in Quenya that contained the letter in question. Where possible it was the first sound of the word; but where the sound or the combination expressed did not occur initially it followed immediately after an initial vowel. The names of the letters in the table were (1) *tinco* metal, *parma* book, *calma* lamp, *quesse* feather; (2) *ando* gate, *umbar* fate, *anga* iron, *ungwe* spider's web; (3) *thúle* (*súle*) spirit, *formen* north, *harma* treasure (or *aha* rage), *hwesta* breeze; (4) *anto* mouth, *ampa* hook, *anca* jaws, *unque* a hollow; (5) *númen* west, *malta* gold, *noldo* (older *ngoldo*) one of the kindred of the Noldor, *nwalme* (older *ngwalme*) torment; (6) *óre* heart (inner mind), *vala* angelic power, *anna* gift, *vilya* air, sky (older *wilya*); *rómen* east, *arda* region, *lambe* tongue, *alda* tree; *silme* light, *silme nuquerna* (*s* reversed), *áre* sunlight (or *esse* name), *áre nuquerna*; *hyarmen* south, *hwesta sindarinwa*, *yanta* bridge, *úre* heat. Where there are variants this is due to the names being given before certain changes affected Quenya as spoken by the Exiles. Thus No. 11 was called *harma* when it represented the spirant *ch* in all positions, but when this sound became breath *h* initially[1] (though remaining medially) the name *aha* was devised. *áre* was originally *áze*, but when this *z* became merged with 21, the sign was in Quenya used for the very frequent *ss* of that language, and the name *esse* was given to it. *hwesta sindarinwa* or 'Grey-elven *hw*' was so called because in Quenya 12 had the sound of *hw*, and distinct signs for *chw* and *hw* were not required. The names of the letters most widely known and used were 17 *n*, 33 *hy*, 25 *r*, 9 *f*: *númen*, *hyarmen*, *rómen*, *formen*=west, south, east, north (cf. Sindarin *dûn* or *annûn*, *harad*, *rhûn* or *amrûn*, *forod*). These letters commonly indicated the points W, S, E, N even in languages that used quite different terms. They were, in the West-lands, named in this order, beginning with and facing west; *hyarmen* and *formen* indeed meant left-hand region and right-hand region (the opposite to the arrangement in many Mannish languages).

THE CIRTH

The *Certhas Daeron* was originally devised to represent the sounds of Sindarin only. The oldest *cirth* were Nos. 1, 2, 5, 6; 8, 9, 12; 18, 19, 22; 29, 31; 35, 36; 39, 42, 46, 50; and a *certh* varying between 13 and 15. The assignment of values was unsystematic. Nos. 39, 42, 46, 50 were vowels and remained so in all later developments. Nos. 13, 15 were used for *h* or *s*, according as 35 was used for *s* or *h*. This tendency to hesitate in the assignment of values for *s* and *h* continued in later arrangements. In those characters that consisted of a 'stem' and a 'branch', 1–31, the attachment of the branch was, if on one side only, usually made on the right side. The reverse was not infrequent, but had no phonetic significance.

The extension and elaboration of this *certhas* was called in its older form the *Angerthas Daeron*, since the additions to the old *cirth* and their reorganization was attributed to Daeron. The principal additions, however, the introductions of two new series, 13–17, and 23–28, were actually most probably inventions of the Noldor of Eregion, since they were used for the representation of sounds not found in Sindarin.

In the rearrangement of the *Angerthas* the following principles are observable (evidently inspired by the Fëanorian system): (1) adding a stroke to a branch added 'voice'; (2) reversing the *certh* indicated opening to a 'spirant'; (3) placing the branch on both sides of the stem added voice and nasality. These principles were regularly carried out, except in one point. For (archaic) Sindarin a sign for a spirant *m* (or nasal *v*) was required, and since this could best be provided by a reversal of the sign for *m*, the reversible No. 6 was given the value *m*, but No. 5 was given the value *hw*.

No. 36, the theoretic value of which was *z*, was used, in spelling Sindarin or Quenya, for *ss*: cf. Fëanorian 31. No. 39 was used for either *i* or *y* (consonant); 34, 35 were used indifferently for *s*; and 38 was used for the frequent sequence *nd*, though it was not clearly related in shape to the dentals.

[1] For breath *h* Quenya originally used a simple raised stem without bow, called *halla* 'tall'. This could be placed before a consonant to indicate that it was unvoiced and breathed; voiceless *r* and *l* were usually so expressed and are transcribed *hr*, *hl*. Later 33 was used for independent *h*, and the value of *hy* (its older value) was represented by adding the *tehta* for following *y*.

THE ANGERTHAS

THE ANGERTHAS

Values

1	p	16	zh	31	l	46	e
2	b	17	nj—z	32	lh	47	ē
3	f	18	k	33	ng—nd	48	a
4	v	19	g	34	s—h	49	ā
5	hw	20	kh	35	s—'	50	o
6	m	21	gh	36	z—ŋ	51	ō
7	(mh) mb	22	ŋ—n	37	ng*	52	ö
8	t	23	kw	38	nd—nj	53	n*
9	d	24	gw	39	i (y)	54	h—s
10	th	25	khw	40	y*	55	*
11	dh	26	ghw,w	41	hy*	56	*
12	n—r	27	ngw	42	u	57	ps*
13	ch	28	nw	43	ū	58	ts*
14	j	29	r—j	44	w		+h
15	sh	30	rh—zh	45	ü		&

In the Table of Values those on the left are, when separated by – , the values of the older *Angerthas*. Those on the right are the values of the Dwarvish *Angerthas Moria*.[1] The Dwarves of Moria, as can be seen, introduced a number of unsystematic changes in value, as well as certain new *cirth*: 37, 40, 41, 53, 55, 56. The dislocation in values was due mainly to two causes: (1) the alteration in the values of 34, 35, 54 respectively to *h*,' (the clear or glottal beginning of a word with an initial vowel that appeared in Khuzdul), and *s*; (2) the abandonment of the Nos. 14, 16 for which the Dwarves substituted 29, 30. The consequent use of 12 for *r*, the invention of 53 for *n* (and its confusion with 22); the use of 17 as *z*, to go with 54 in its value *s*, and the consequent use of 36 as *n* and the new *certh* 37 for *ng* may also be observed. The new 55, 56 were in origin a halved form of 46, and were used for vowels like those heard in English *butter*, which were frequent in Dwarvish and in the Westron. When weak or evanescent they were often reduced to a mere stroke without a stem. This *Angerthas Moria* is represented in the tomb-inscription.

The Dwarves of Erebor used a further modification of this system, known as the mode of Erebor, and exemplified in the Book of Mazarbul. Its chief characteristics were: the use of 43 as *z*; of 17 as *ks* (*x*); and the invention of two new *cirth*, 57, 58 for *ps* and *ts*. They also reintroduced 14, 16 for the values *j*, *zh*; but used 29, 30 for *g*, *gh*, or as mere variants of 19, 21. These peculiarities are not included in the table, except for the special Ereborian *cirth*, 57, 58.

[1] Those in ( ) are values only found in Elvish use; * marks *cirth* only used by Dwarves.

APPENDIX F

I

THE LANGUAGES AND PEOPLES OF THE THIRD AGE

The language represented in this history by English was the *Westron* or 'Common Speech' of the West-lands of Middle-earth in the Third Age. In the course of that age it had become the native language of nearly all the speaking-peoples (save the Elves) who dwelt within the bounds of the old kingdoms of Arnor and Gondor; that is along all the coasts from Umbar northward to the Bay of Forochel, and inland as far as the Misty Mountains and the Ephel Dúath. It had also spread north up the Anduin, occupying the lands west of the River and east of the mountains as far as the Gladden Fields.

At the time of the War of the Ring at the end of the age these were still its bounds as a native tongue, though large parts of Eriador were now deserted, and few Men dwelt on the shores of the Anduin between the Gladden and Rauros.

A few of the ancient Wild Men still lurked in the Drúadan Forest in Anórien; and in the hills of Dunland a remnant lingered of an old people, the former inhabitants of much of Gondor. These clung to their own languages; while in the plains of Rohan there dwelt now a Northern people, the Rohirrim, who had come into that land some five hundred years earlier. But the Westron was used as a second language of intercourse by all those who still retained a speech of their own, even by the Elves, not only in Arnor and Gondor but throughout the vales of Anduin, and eastward to the further eaves of Mirkwood. Even among the Wild Men and the Dunlendings who shunned other folk there were some that could speak it, though brokenly.

OF THE ELVES

The Elves far back in the Elder Days became divided into two main branches: the West-elves (the *Eldar*) and the East-elves. Of the latter kind were most of the elven-folk of Mirkwood and Lórien; but their languages do not appear in this history, in which all the Elvish names and words are of *Eldarin* form.[1]

Of the *Eldarin* tongues two are found in this book: the High-elven or *Quenya*, and the Grey-elven or *Sindarin*. The High-elven was an ancient tongue of Eldamar beyond the Sea, the first to be recorded in writing. It was no longer a birth-tongue, but had become, as it were, an 'Elven-latin', still used for ceremony, and for high matters of lore and song, by the High Elves, who had returned in exile to Middle-earth at the end of the First Age.

[1] In Lórien at this period Sindarin was spoken, though with an 'accent', since most of its folk were of Silvan origin. This 'accent' and his own limited acquaintance with Sindarin misled Frodo (as is pointed out in *The Thain's Book* by a commentator of Gondor). All the Elvish words cited in Book I, ii, chs 6, 7, 8 are in fact Sindarin, and so are most of the names of places and persons. But *Lórien*, *Caras Galadhon*, *Amroth*, *Nimrodel* are probably of Silvan origin, adapted to Sindarin.

The Grey-elven was in origin akin to *Quenya*; for it was the language of those Eldar who, coming to the shores of Middle-earth, had not passed over the Sea but had lingered on the coasts in the country of Beleriand. There Thingol Greycloak of Doriath was their king, and in the long twilight their tongue had changed with the changefulness of mortal lands and had become far estranged from the speech of the Eldar from beyond the Sea.

The Exiles, dwelling among the more numerous Grey-elves, had adopted the *Sindarin* for daily use; and hence it was the tongue of all those Elves and Elf-lords that appear in this history. For these were all of Eldarin race, even where the folk that they ruled were of the lesser kindreds. Noblest of all was the Lady Galadriel of the royal house of Finarfin and sister of Finrod Felagund, King of Nargothrond. In the hearts of the Exiles the yearning for the Sea was an unquiet never to be stilled; in the hearts of the Grey-elves it slumbered, but once awakened it could not be appeased.

OF MEN

The *Westron* was a Mannish speech, though enriched and softened under Elvish influence. It was in origin the language of those whom the Eldar called the *Atani* or *Edain*, 'Fathers of Men', being especially the people of the Three Houses of the Elf-friends who came west into Beleriand in the First Age, and aided the Eldar in the War of the Great Jewels against the Dark Power of the North.

After the overthrow of the Dark Power, in which Beleriand was for the most part drowned or broken, it was granted as a reward to the Elf-friends that they also, as the Eldar, might pass west over Sea. But since the Undying Realm was forbidden to them, a great isle was set apart for them, most westerly of all mortal lands. The name of that isle was *Númenor* (Westernesse). Most of the Elf-friends, therefore, departed and dwelt in Númenor, and there they became great and powerful, mariners of renown and lords of many ships. They were fair of face and tall, and the span of their lives was thrice that of the Men of Middle-earth. These were the Númenoreans, the Kings of Men, whom the Elves called the *Dúnedain*.

The *Dúnedain* alone of all races of Men knew and spoke an Elvish tongue; for their forefathers had learned the Sindarin tongue, and this they handed on to their children as a matter of lore, changing little with the passing of the years. And their men of wisdom learned also the High-elven Quenya and esteemed it above all other tongues, and in it they made names for many places of fame and reverence, and for many men of royalty and great renown.[1]

But the native speech of the Númenoreans remained for the most part their ancestral Mannish tongue, the Adûnaic, and to this in the latter days of their pride their kings and lords returned, abandoning the Elven-speech, save only those few that held still to their ancient friendship with the Eldar. In the years of their power

[1] Quenya, for example, are the names *Númenor* (or in full *Númenórë*), and *Elendil*, *Isildur*, and *Anárion*, and all the royal names of *Gondor*, including *Elessar* 'Elfstone'. Most of the names of the other men and women of the Dúnedain, such as *Aragorn*, *Denethor*, *Gilraen* are of Sindarin form, being often the names of Elves or Men remembered in the songs and histories of the First Age (as *Beren*, *Húrin*). Some few are of mixed forms, as *Boromir*.

the Númenoreans had maintained many forts and havens upon the western coasts of Middle-earth for the help of their ships; and one of the chief of these was at Pelargir near the Mouths of Anduin. There Adûnaic was spoken, and mingled with many words of the languages of lesser men it became a Common Speech that spread thence along the coasts among all that had dealings with Westernesse.

After the Downfall of Númenor, Elendil led the survivors of the Elf-friends back to the North-western shores of Middle-earth. There many already dwelt who were in whole or part of Númenorean blood; but few of them remembered the Elvish speech. All told the Dúnedain were thus from the beginning far fewer in number than the lesser men among whom they dwelt and whom they ruled, being lords of long life and great power and wisdom. They used therefore the Common Speech in their dealing with other folk and in the government of their wide realms; but they enlarged the language and enriched it with many words drawn from Elven-tongues.

In the days of the Númenorean kings this ennobled Westron speech spread far and wide, even among their enemies; and it became used more and more by the Dúnedain themselves, so that at the time of the War of the Ring the Elven-tongue was known to only a small part of the peoples of Gondor, and spoken daily by fewer. These dwelt mostly in Minas Tirith and the townlands adjacent, and in the land of the tributary princes of Dol Amroth. Yet the names of nearly all places and persons in the realm of Gondor were of Elvish form and meaning. A few were of forgotten origin, and descended doubtless from the days before the ships of the Númenoreans sailed the Sea; among these were *Umbar*, *Arnach* and *Erech*; and the mountain-names *Eilenach* and *Rimmon*. *Forlong* was also a name of the same sort.

Most of the Men of the northern regions of the West-lands were descended from the *Edain* of the First Age, or from their close kin. Their languages were, therefore, related to the Adûnaic, and some still preserved a likeness to the Common Speech. Of this kind were the peoples of the upper vales of Anduin: the Beornings, and the Woodmen of Western Mirkwood; and further north and east the Men of the Long Lake and of Dale. From the lands between the Gladden and the Carrock came the folk that were known in Gondor as the Rohirrim, Masters of Horses. They still spoke their ancestral tongue, and gave new names in it to nearly all the places in their new country; and they called themselves the Eorlings, or the Men of the Riddermark. But the lords of that people used the Common Speech freely, and spoke it nobly after the manner of their allies in Gondor; for in Gondor whence it came the Westron kept still a more gracious and antique style.

Wholly alien was the speech of the Wild Men of Drúadan Forest. Alien, too, or only remotely akin, was the language of the Dunlendings. These were a remnant of the peoples that had dwelt in the vales of the White Mountains in ages past. The Dead Men of Dunharrow were of their kin. But in the Dark Years others had removed to the southern dales of the Misty Mountains; and thence some had passed into the empty lands as far north as the Barrow-downs. From them came the Men of Bree; but long before these had become subjects of the North Kingdom of Arnor and had taken up the Westron tongue. Only in Dunland did Men of this race hold to their old speech and manners: a secret folk, unfriendly to the Dúnedain, hating the Rohirrim.

Of their language nothing appears in this book, save the name *Forgoil* which they gave to the Rohirrim (meaning Strawheads, it is said). *Dunland* and *Dunlending* are the names that the Rohirrim gave to them, because they were swarthy and dark-haired; there is thus no connexion between the word *dunn* in these names and the Grey-elven word *Dûn* 'west'.

OF HOBBITS

The Hobbits of the Shire and of Bree had at this time, for probably a thousand years, adopted the Common Speech. They used it in their own manner freely and carelessly; though the more learned among them had still at their command a more formal language when occasion required.

There is no record of any language peculiar to Hobbits. In ancient days they seem always to have used the languages of Men near whom, or among whom, they lived. Thus they quickly adopted the Common Speech after they entered Eriador, and by the time of their settlement at Bree they had already begun to forget their former tongue. This was evidently a Mannish language of the upper Anduin, akin to that of the Rohirrim; though the southern Stoors appear to have adopted a language related to Dunlendish before they came north to the Shire.[1]

Of these things in the time of Frodo there were still some traces left in local words and names, many of which closely resembled those found in Dale or in Rohan. Most notable were the names of days, months, and seasons; several other words of the same sort (such as *mathom* and *smial*) were also still in common use, while more were preserved in the place-names of Bree and the Shire. The personal names of the Hobbits were also peculiar and many had come down from ancient days.

Hobbit was the name usually applied by the Shire-folk to all their kind. Men called them *Halflings* and the Elves *Periannath*. The origin of the word *hobbit* was by most forgotten. It seems, however, to have been at first a name given to the Harfoots by the Fallohides and Stoors, and to be a worn-down form of a word preserved more fully in Rohan: *holbytla* 'hole-builder'.

OF OTHER RACES

Ents. The most ancient people surviving in the Third Age were the *Onodrim* or *Enyd. Ent* was the form of their name in the language of Rohan. They were known to the Eldar in ancient days, and to the Eldar indeed the Ents ascribed not their own language but the desire for speech. The language that they had made was unlike all others: slow, sonorous, agglomerated, repetitive, indeed long-winded; formed of a multiplicity of vowel-shades and distinctions of tone and quality which even the masters of the Eldar had not attempted to represent in writing. They used it only among themselves; but they had no need to keep it secret, for no others could learn it.

[1] The Stoors of the Angle, who returned to Wilderland, had already adopted the Common Speech; but *Déagol* and *Sméagol* are names in the Mannish language of the region near the Gladden.

Ents were, however, themselves skilled in tongues, learning them swiftly and never forgetting them. But they preferred the languages of the Eldar, and loved best the ancient High-elven tongue. The strange words and names that the Hobbits record as used by Treebeard and other Ents are thus Elvish, or fragments of Elf-speech strung together in Ent-fashion.[1] Some are Quenya: as *Taurelilómëa-tumbalemorna Tumbaletaurëa Lómëanor*, which may be rendered 'Forestmany-shadowed-deepvalleyblack Deepvalleyforested Gloomyland', and by which Treebeard meant, more or less: 'there is a black shadow in the deep dales of the forest'. Some are Sindarin: as *Fangorn* 'beard-(of)-tree', or *Fimbrethil* 'slender-beech'.

Orcs and the Black Speech. Orc is the form of the name that other races had for this foul people as it was in the language of Rohan. In Sindarin it was *orch*. Related, no doubt, was the word *uruk* of the Black Speech, though this was applied as a rule only to the great soldier-orcs that at this time issued from Mordor and Isengard. The lesser kinds were called, especially by the Uruk-hai, *snaga* 'slave'.

The Orcs were first bred by the Dark Power of the North in the Elder Days. It is said that they had no language of their own, but took what they could of other tongues and perverted it to their own liking; yet they made only brutal jargons, scarcely sufficient even for their own needs, unless it were for curses and abuse. And these creatures, being filled with malice, hating even their own kind, quickly developed as many barbarous dialects as there were groups or settlements of their race, so that their Orkish speech was of little use to them in intercourse between different tribes.

So it was that in the Third Age Orcs used for communication between breed and breed the Westron tongue; and many indeed of the older tribes, such as those that still lingered in the North and in the Misty Mountains, had long used the Westron as their native language, though in such a fashion as to make it hardly less unlovely than Orkish. In this jargon *tark*, 'man of Gondor', was a debased form of *tarkil*, a Quenya word used in Westron for one of Númenorean descent; see p. 885.

It is said that the Black Speech was devised by Sauron in the Dark Years, and that he had desired to make it the language of all those that served him, but he failed in that purpose. From the Black Speech, however, were derived many of the words that were in the Third Age wide-spread among the Orcs, such as *ghâsh* 'fire', but after the first overthrow of Sauron this language in its ancient form was forgotten by all but the Nazgûl. When Sauron arose again, it became once more the language of Barad-dûr and of the captains of Mordor. The inscription on the Ring was in the ancient Black Speech, while the curse of the Mordor-orc on p. 435 was in the more debased form used by the soldiers of the Dark Tower, of whom Grishnákh was the captain. Sharku in that tongue means *old man*.

Trolls. *Troll* has been used to translate the Sindarin *Torog*. In their beginning far back in the twilight of the Elder Days, these were creatures of dull and lumpish

[1] Except where the Hobbits seem to have made some attempts to represent shorter murmurs and calls made by the Ents; *a-lalla-lalla-rumba-kamanda-lindor-burúme* also is not Elvish, and is the only extant (probably very inaccurate) attempt to represent a fragment of actual Entish.

nature and had no more language than beasts. But Sauron had made use of them, teaching them what little they could learn and increasing their wits with wickedness. Trolls therefore took such language as they could master from the Orcs; and in the Westlands the Stone-trolls spoke a debased form of the Common Speech.

But at the end of the Third Age a troll-race not before seen appeared in southern Mirkwood and in the mountain borders of Mordor. Olog-hai they were called in the Black Speech. That Sauron bred them none doubted, though from what stock was not known. Some held that they were not Trolls but giant Orcs; but the Olog-hai were in fashion of body and mind quite unlike even the largest of Orc-kind, whom they far surpassed in size and power. Trolls they were, but filled with the evil will of their master: a fell race, strong, agile, fierce and cunning, but harder than stone. Unlike the older race of the Twilight they could endure the Sun, so long as the will of Sauron held sway over them. They spoke little, and the only tongue that they knew was the Black Speech of Barad-dûr.

Dwarves. The Dwarves are a race apart. Of their strange beginning, and why they are both like and unlike Elves and Men, the Silmarillion tells; but of this tale the lesser Elves of Middle-earth had no knowledge, while the tales of later Men are confused with memories of other races.

They are a tough, thrawn race for the most part, secretive, laborious, retentive of the memory of injuries (and of benefits), lovers of stone, of gems, of things that take shape under the hands of the craftsmen rather than things that live by their own life. But they are not evil by nature, and few ever served the Enemy of free will, whatever the tales of Men may have alleged. For Men of old lusted after their wealth and the work of their hands, and there has been enmity between the races.

But in the Third Age close friendship still was found in many places between Men and Dwarves; and it was according to the nature of the Dwarves that, travelling and labouring and trading about the lands, as they did after the destruction of their ancient mansions, they should use the languages of men among whom they dwelt. Yet in secret (a secret which unlike the Elves, they did not willingly unlock, even to their friends) they used their own strange tongue, changed little by the years; for it had become a tongue of lore rather than a cradle-speech, and they tended it and guarded it as a treasure of the past. Few of other race have succeeded in learning it. In this history it appears only in such place-names as Gimli revealed to his companions; and in the battle-cry which he uttered in the siege of the Hornburg. That at least was not secret, and had been heard on many a field since the world was young. *Baruk Khazâd! Khazâd ai-mênu!* 'Axes of the Dwarves! The Dwarves are upon you!'

Gimli's own name, however, and the names of all his kin, are of Northern (Mannish) origin. Their own secret and 'inner' names, their true names, the Dwarves have never revealed to any one of alien race. Not even on their tombs do they inscribe them.

II
ON TRANSLATION

In presenting the matter of the Red Book, as a history for people of today to read, the whole of the linguistic setting has been translated as far as possible into terms of our own times. Only the languages alien to the Common Speech have been left in their original form; but these appear mainly in the names of persons and places.

The Common Speech, as the language of the Hobbits and their narratives, has inevitably been turned into modern English. In the process the difference between the varieties observable in the use of the Westron has been lessened. Some attempt has been made to represent varieties by variations in the kind of English used; but the divergence between the pronunciation and idiom of the Shire and the Westron tongue in the mouths of the Elves or of the high men of Gondor was greater than has been shown in this book. Hobbits indeed spoke for the most part a rustic dialect, whereas in Gondor and Rohan a more antique language was used, more formal and more terse.

One point in the divergence may here be noted, since, though important, it has proved impossible to represent. The Westron tongue made in the pronouns of the second person (and often also in those of the third) a distinction, independent of number, between 'familiar' and 'deferential' forms. It was, however, one of the peculiarities of Shire-usage that the deferential forms had gone out of colloquial use. They lingered only among the villagers, especially of the Westfarthing, who used them as endearments. This was one of the things referred to when people of Gondor spoke of the strangeness of Hobbit-speech. Peregrin Took, for instance, in his first few days in Minas Tirith used the familiar for people of all ranks, including the Lord Denethor himself. This may have amused the aged Steward, but it must have astonished his servants. No doubt this free use of the familiar forms helped to spread the popular rumour that Peregrin was a person of very high rank in his own country.[1]

It will be noticed that Hobbits such as Frodo, and other persons such as Gandalf and Aragorn, do not always use the same style. This is intentional. The more learned and able among the Hobbits had some knowledge of 'book-language', as it was termed in the Shire; and they were quick to note and adopt the style of those whom they met. It was in any case natural for much-travelled folk to speak more or less after the manner of those among whom they found themselves, especially in the case of men who, like Aragorn, were often at pains to conceal their origin and their business. Yet in those days all the enemies of the Enemy revered what was ancient, in language no less than in other matters, and they took pleasure in it according to their knowledge. The Eldar, being above all skilled in words, had the command of many styles, though they spoke most naturally in a manner nearest to their own speech, one even more antique than that of Gondor. The Dwarves, too, spoke with

[1] In one or two places an attempt has been made to hint at these distinctions by an inconsistent use of *thou*. Since this pronoun is now unusual and archaic it is employed mainly to represent the use of ceremonious language; but a change from *you* to *thou*, *thee* is sometimes meant to show, there being no other means of doing this, a significant change from the deferential, or between men and women normal, forms to the familiar.

skill, readily adapting themselves to their company, though their utterance seemed to some rather harsh and guttural. But Orcs and Trolls spoke as they would, without love of words or things; and their language was actually more degraded and filthy than I have shown it. I do not suppose that any will wish for a closer rendering, though models are easy to find. Much the same sort of talk can still be heard among the orc-minded; dreary and repetitive with hatred and contempt, too long removed from good to retain even verbal vigour, save in the ears of those to whom only the squalid sounds strong.

Translation of this kind is, of course, usual because inevitable in any narrative dealing with the past. It seldom proceeds any further. But I have gone beyond it. I have also translated all Westron names according to their senses. When English names or titles appear in this book it is an indication that names in the Common Speech were current at the time, beside, or instead of, those in alien (usually Elvish) languages.

The Westron names were as a rule translations of older names: as Rivendell, Hoarwell, Silverlode, Langstrand, The Enemy, the Dark Tower. Some differed in meaning: as Mount Doom for *Orodruin* 'burning mountain', or Mirkwood for *Taur e-Ndaedelos* 'forest of the great fear'. A few were alterations of Elvish names: as Lune and Brandywine derived from *Lhûn* and *Baranduin*.

This procedure perhaps needs some defence. It seemed to me that to present all the names in their original forms would obscure an essential feature of the times as perceived by the Hobbits (whose point of view I was mainly concerned to preserve): the contrast between a wide-spread language, to them as ordinary and habitual as English is to us, and the living remains of far older and more reverend tongues. All names if merely transcribed would seem to modern readers equally remote: for instance, if the Elvish name *Imladris* and the Westron translation *Karningul* had both been left unchanged. But to refer to Rivendell as Imladris was as if one now was to speak of Winchester as Camelot, except that the identity was certain, while in Rivendell there still dwelt a lord of renown far older than Arthur would be, were he still king at Winchester today.

The name of the Shire (*Sûza*) and all other places of the Hobbits have thus been Englished. This was seldom difficult, since such names were commonly made up of elements similar to those used in our simpler English place-names; either words still current like *hill* or *field*; or a little worn down like *ton* beside *town*. But some were derived, as already noted, from old hobbit-words no longer in use, and these have been represent by similar English things, such as *wich*, or *bottle* 'dwelling', or *michel* 'great'.

In the case of persons, however, Hobbit-names in the Shire and in Bree were for those days peculiar, notably in the habit that had grown up, some centuries before this time, of having inherited names for families. Most of these surnames had obvious meanings (in the current language being derived from jesting nicknames, or from place-names, or – especially in Bree – from the names of plants and trees). Translation of these presented little difficulty; but there remained one or two older names of forgotten meaning, and these I have been content to anglicize in spelling: as Took for *Tûk*, or Boffin for *Bophîn*.

I have treated Hobbit first-names, as far as possible, in the same way. To their maid-children Hobbits commonly gave the names of flowers or jewels. To their man-children they usually gave names that had no meaning at all in their daily language; and some of their women's names were similar. Of this kind are Bilbo, Bungo, Polo, Lotho, Tanta, Nina, and so on. There are many inevitable but accidental resemblances to names we now have or know: for instance Otho, Odo, Drogo, Dora, Cora, and the like. These names I have retained, though I have usually anglicized them by altering their endings, since in Hobbit-names *a* was a masculine ending, and *o* and *e* were feminine.

In some old families, especially those of Fallohide origin such as the Tooks and the Bolgers, it was, however, the custom to give high-sounding first-names. Since most of these seem to have been drawn from legends of the past, of Men as well as of Hobbits, and many while now meaningless to Hobbits closely resembled the names of Men in the Vale of Anduin, or in Dale, or in the Mark, I have turned them into those old names, largely of Frankish and Gothic origin, that are still used by us or are met in our histories. I have thus at any rate preserved the often comic contrast between the first-names and surnames, of which the Hobbits themselves were well aware. Names of classical origin have rarely been used; for the nearest equivalents to Latin and Greek in Shire-lore were the Elvish tongues, and these the Hobbits seldom used in nomenclature. Few of them at any time knew the 'languages of the kings', as they called them.

The names of the Bucklanders were different from those of the rest of the Shire. The folk of the Marish and their offshoot across the Brandywine were in many ways peculiar, as has been told. It was from the former language of the southern Stoors, no doubt, that they inherited many of their very odd names. These I have usually left unaltered, for if queer now, they were queer in their own day. They had a style that we should perhaps feel vaguely to be 'Celtic'.

Since the survival of traces of the older language of the Stoors and the Bree-men resembled the survival of Celtic elements in England, I have sometimes imitated the latter in my translation. Thus Bree, Combe (Coomb), Archet, and Chetwood are modelled on relics of British nomenclature, chosen according to sense: *bree* 'hill' *chet* 'wood'. But only one personal name has been altered in this way. Meriadoc was chosen to fit the fact that this character's shortened name, Kali, meant in the Westron 'jolly, gay', though it was actually an abbreviation of the now unmeaning Buckland name Kalimac.

I have not used names of Hebraic or similar origin in my transpositions. Nothing in Hobbit-names corresponds to this element in our names. Short names such as Sam, Tom, Tim, Mat were common as abbreviations of actual Hobbit-names, such as Tomba, Tolma, Matta, and the like. But Sam and his father Ham were really called Ban and Ran. These were shortenings of *Banazîr* and *Ranugad*, originally nicknames, meaning 'halfwise, simple' and 'stay-at-home'; but being words that had fallen out of colloquial use they remained as traditional names in certain families. I have therefore tried to preserve these features by using Samwise and Hamfast, modernizations of ancient English *samwís* and *hámfoest* which corresponded closely in meaning.

Having gone so far in my attempt to modernize and make familiar the language and names of Hobbits, I found myself involved in a further process. The Mannish languages that were related to the Westron should, it seemed to me, be turned into forms related to English. The language of Rohan I have accordingly made to resemble ancient English, since it was related both (more distantly) to the Common Speech, and (very closely) to the former tongue of the northern Hobbits, and was in comparison with the Westron archaic. In the Red Book it is noted in several places that when Hobbits heard the speech of Rohan they recognized many words and felt the language to be akin to their own, so that it seemed absurd to leave the recorded names and words of the Rohirrim in a wholly alien style.

In several cases I have modernized the forms and spellings of place-names in Rohan: as in *Dunharrow* or *Snowbourn*; but I have not been consistent, for I have followed the Hobbits. They altered the names that they heard in the same way, if they were made of elements that they recognized, or if they resembled place-names in the Shire; but many they left alone, as I have done, for instance, in *Edoras* 'the courts'. For the same reasons a few personal names have also been modernized, as Shadowfax and Wormtongue.[1]

This assimilation also provided a convenient way of representing the peculiar local hobbit-words that were of northern origin. They have been given the forms that lost English words might well have had, if they had come down to our day. Thus *mathom is* meant to recall ancient English *máthm*, and so to represent the relationship of the actual Hobbit *kast* to R. *kastu*. Similarly *smial* (or *smile*) 'burrow' is a likely form for a descendant of *smygel*, and represents well the relationship of Hobbit *trân* to R. *trahan*. *Sméagol* and *Déagol* are equivalents made up in the same way for the names *Trahald* 'burrowing, worming in', and *Nahald* 'secret' in the Northern tongues.

The still more northerly language of Dale is in this book seen only in the names of the Dwarves that came from that region and so used the language of the Men there, taking their 'outer' names in that tongue. It may be observed that in this book as in *The Hobbit* the form *dwarves* is used, although the dictionaries tell us that the plural of *dwarf* is *dwarfs*. It should be *dwarrows* (or *dwerrows*), if singular and plural had each gone its own way down the years, as have *man* and *men*, or *goose* and *geese*. But we no longer speak of a dwarf as often as we do of a man, or even of a goose, and memories have not been fresh enough among Men to keep hold of a special plural for a race now abandoned to folk-tales, where at least a shadow of truth is preserved, or at last to nonsense-stories in which they have become mere figures of fun. But in the Third Age something of their old character and power is still glimpsed, if already a little dimmed; these are the descendants of the Naugrim of the Elder Days, in whose hearts still burns ancient fire of Aulë the Smith, and the embers smoulder of their long grudge against the Elves; and in whose hands still lives the skill in work of stone that none have surpassed.

It is to mark this that I have ventured to use the form *dwarves*, and remove them a little, perhaps, from the sillier tales of these latter days. *Dwarrows* would have

[1] This linguistic procedure does not imply that the Rohirrim closely resembled the ancient English otherwise, in culture or art, in weapons or modes of warfare, except in a general way due to their circumstances: a simpler and more primitive people living in contact with a higher and more venerable culture, and occupying lands that had once been part of its domain.

been better; but I have used that form only in the name *Dwarrowdelf*, to represent the name of Moria in the Common Speech: *Phurunargian*. For that meant 'Dwarf-delving' and yet was already a word of antique form. But Moria is an Elvish name, and given without love; for the Eldar, though they might at need, in their bitter wars with the Dark Power and his servants, contrive fortresses underground, were not dwellers in such places of choice. They were lovers of the green earth and the lights of heaven; and Moria in their tongue means the Black Chasm. But the Dwarves themselves, and this name at least was never kept secret, called it *Khazad-dûm*, the Mansion of the Khazâd; for such is their own name for their own race, and has been so, since Aulë gave it to them at their making in the deeps of time.

Elves has been used to translate both *Quendi*, 'the speakers', the High-elven name of all their kind, and *Eldar*, the name of the Three Kindreds that sought for the Undying Realm and came there at the beginning of Days (save the *Sindar* only). This old word was indeed the only one available, and was once fitted to apply to such memories of this people as Men preserved, or to the making of Men's minds not wholly dissimilar. But it has been diminished, and to many it may now suggest fancies either pretty or silly, as unlike to the Quendi of old as are butterflies to the falcon – not that any of the Quendi ever possessed wings of the body, as unnatural to them as to Men. They were a race high and beautiful, the older Children of the world, and among them the Eldar were as kings, who now are gone: the People of the Great Journey, the People of the Stars. They were tall, fair of skin and grey-eyed, though their locks were dark, save in the golden house of Finarfin; and their voices had more melodies than any mortal voice that now is heard. They were valiant, but the history of those that returned to Middle-earth in exile was grievous; and though it was in far-off days crossed by the fate of the Fathers, their fate is not that of Men. Their dominion passed long ago, and they dwell now beyond the circles of the world, and do not return.

Note on three names: *Hobbit*, *Gamgee*, and *Brandywine*.

Hobbit is an invention. In the Westron the word used, when this people was referred to at all, was *banakil* 'halfling'. But at this date the folk of the Shire and of Bree used the word *kuduk*, which was not found elsewhere. Meriadoc, however, actually records that the King of Rohan used the word *kûd-dûkan* 'hole-dweller'. Since, as has been noted, the Hobbits had once spoken a language closely related to that of the Rohirrim, it seems likely that *kuduk* was a worn-down form of *kûd-dûkan*. The latter I have translated, for reasons explained, by *holbytla*; and *hobbit* provides a word that might well be a worn-down form of *holbytla*, if that name had occurred in our own ancient language.

Gamgee. According to family tradition, set out in the Red Book, the surname *Galbasi*, or in reduced form *Galpsi*, came from the village of *Galabas*, popularly supposed to be derived from *galab-* 'game' and an old element *bas-*, more or less equivalent to our *wick*, *wich*. *Gamwich* (pronounced *Gammidge*) seemed therefore a very fair rendering. However, in reducing *Gammidgy* to *Gamgee*, to represent *Galpsi*, no reference was intended to the connexion of Samwise with the family of Cotton, though a jest of that kind would have been hobbit-like enough, had there been any warrant in their language.

Cotton, in fact, represents *Hlothran*, a fairly common village-name in the Shire, derived from *hloth*, 'a two-roomed dwelling or hole', and *ran*(*u*) a small group of such dwellings on a hill-side. As a surname it may be an alteration of *hlothram*(*a*) 'cottager'. *Hlothram*, which I have rendered Cotman, was the name of Farmer Cotton's grandfather.

Brandywine. The hobbit-names of this river were alterations of the Elvish *Baranduin* (accented on *and*), derived from *baran* 'golden brown' and *duin* '(large) river'. Of *Baranduin* Brandywine seemed a natural corruption in modern times. Actually the older hobbit-name was *Branda-nîn* 'border-water', which would have been more closely rendered by Marchbourn; but by a jest that had become habitual, referring again to its colour, at this time the river was usually called *Bralda-hîm* 'heady ale'.

It must be observed, however, that when the Oldbucks (*Zaragamba*) changed their name to Brandybuck (*Brandagamba*), the first element meant 'borderland', and Marchbuck would have been nearer. Only a very bold hobbit would have ventured to call the Master of Buckland *Braldagamba* in his hearing.

INDEX

I SONGS AND VERSES

(a)

(b) First Lines

II PERSONS BEASTS AND MONSTERS

references are selective

III PLACES

references are given to the first occurrence: for some names references are added to other occurrences of interest

IV THINGS

NOTE ON THE MAPS

Maps accompanying *The Lord of the Rings* were drawn by Christopher Tolkien for the original edition published in 1954–5. They consisted of a general map of the western regions of Middle-earth and a more detailed map of Rohan, Gondor, and Mordor; printed in red and black on large folded sheets pasted in at the end of each of the three books, *The Fellowship of the Ring* and *The Two Towers* carried the general map, while *The Return of the King* carried the other. In addition, there was a map of the Shire in red and black preceding Book I of *The Fellowship of the Ring*. Christopher Tolkien redrew the general map expressly for inclusion in *Unfinished Tales* (1980), but subsequently this replaced the original form in editions of *The Lord of the Rings*.

With paperback editions the arrangement was introduced whereby the general map was divided into four sections, in black only, fitting the size of the pages, while the whole map in greatly reduced form was also printed as a guide to the sections. The map of Rohan, Gondor, and Mordor was reduced to fit two facing pages. This arrangement is found in all current paperback and one-volume hardback editions.

The original maps, however, were not drawn and lettered in such a way as to make such reduction satisfactory. Mr Stephen Raw has therefore redrawn them all, very closely following the originals, and greatly increasing their clarity. As a guide to the four sections of the general map he has drawn a new outline map that provides all necessary indications in a simplified form.

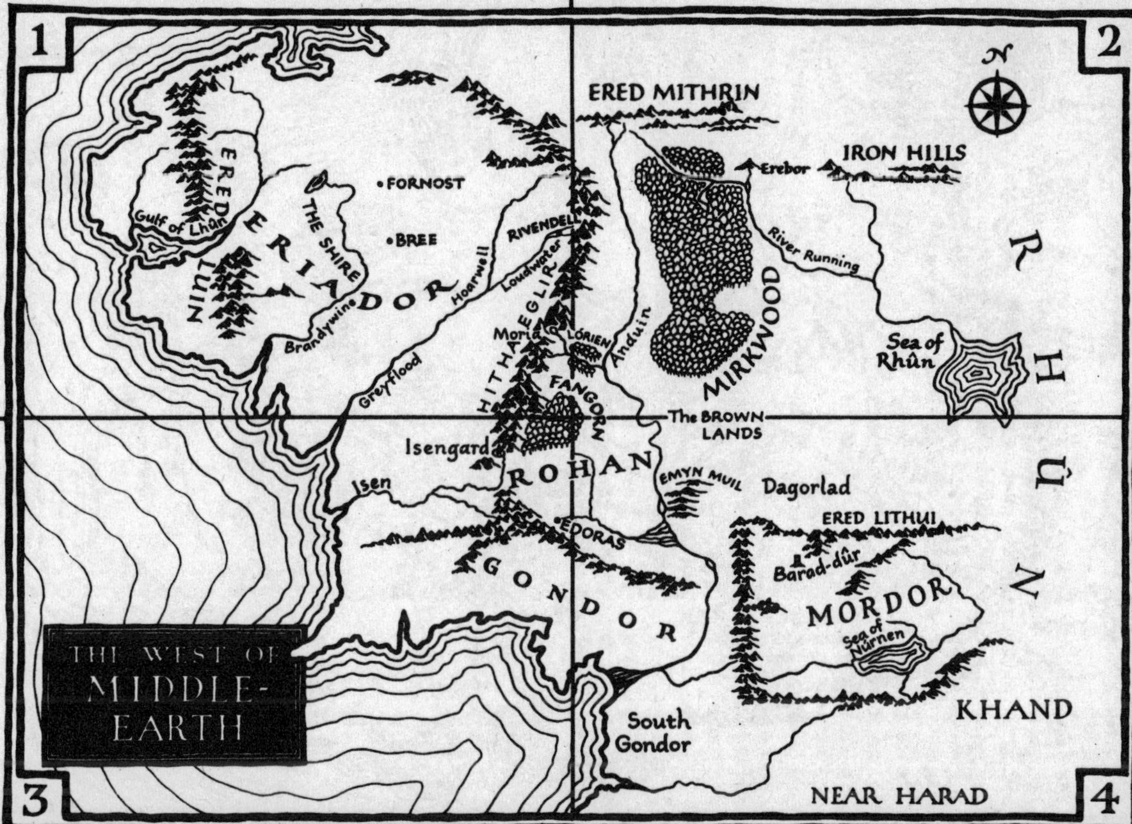
THE WEST OF
MIDDLE-
EARTH
1
2
3
4
N
ERED MITHRIN
IRON HILLS
Erebor
River Running
Sea of Rhûn
R H Û N
MIRKWOOD
Anduin
The BROWN LANDS
ERED LUIN
Gulf of Lhûn
ERIADOR
THE SHIRE
FORNOST
BREE
Brandywine
Hoarwell
Loudwater
RIVENDELL
Greyflood
Moria
LÓRIEN
HITHAEGLIR
FANGORN
Isengard
Isen
ROHAN
EMYN MUIL
Dagorlad
EDORAS
GONDOR
ERED LITHUI
Barad-dûr
MORDOR
Sea of Núrnen
KHAND
South Gondor
NEAR HARAD

1
FORODWAITH
Icebay of Forochel
Himling
ERED LUIN
Forlindon
Forlond
Gulf of Lhûn
Mithlond
(Grey Havens)
Harlond
Harlindon
Lhûn (Lune)
Tower Hills
Far Downs
White Downs
(Blue Mountains)
Eryn Vorn
Baranduin (Brandywine)
Sarn Ford
Hobbiton
THE SHIRE
Brandywine Bridge
Old Forest
Bree
EMYN UIAL
(Hills of Evendim)
Nenuial (Lake Evendim)
Annúminas
North Downs
Fornost
Chetwood
Midgewater
Weather Hills
Weathertop (Amon Sûl)
East-West Road
South Downs
Greenway
The Lost Realm of ARNOR
ARTHEDAIN
CARDOLAN
RHUDAUR
HITHAEGLIR
Carn Dûm
Here was of old the Witch-realm of Angmar
Angmar
Mtns of Angmar
Mount Gundabad
Ettenmoors
(Hoarwell)
Trollshaws
Last Bridge
Bruinen (Loudwater)
Rivendell
Ford
High Pass
Old Ford
Carrock
Langwell
Greylin
Mitheithel
(Misty Mtns.)
Eregion (Hollin)
Moria Gate
Sîr Ninglor (Gladden River)
Dimrill Dale
Nimrodel
LORIEN
Anduin (The Great River)
Field of Celebrant
Limlight
The Wold
Nîn-in-Eilph (Swanfleet)
Glanduin
Tharbad
Gwathló (Greyflood)
MINHIRIATH
ENEDWAITH
Lond Daer
Dunland
Isengard
N
Miles
50
100
150
200

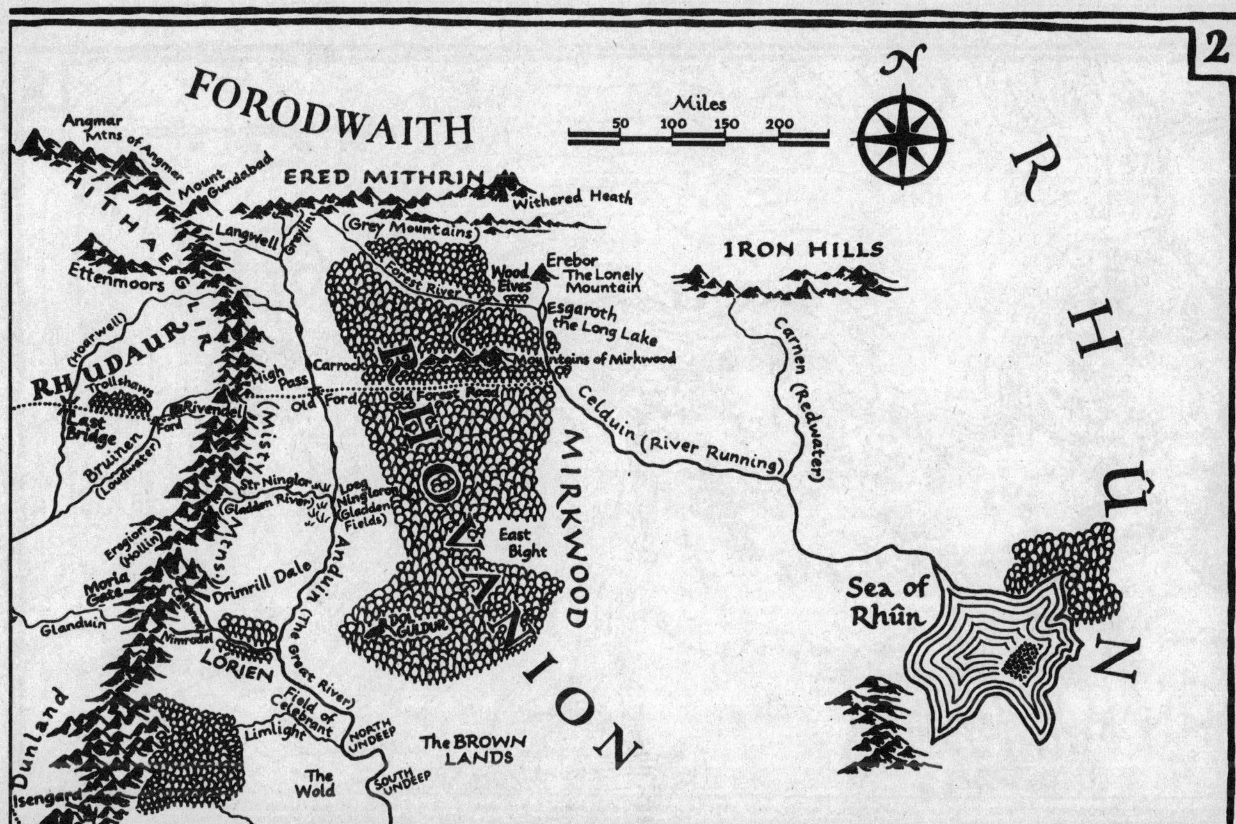
2
FORODWAITH
Miles
50
100
150
200
N
RHÛN
Angmar
Mtns of Angmar
HITHAEGLIR
Mount Gundabad
ERED MITHRIN
Withered Heath
(Grey Mountains)
Langwell
Greylin
IRON HILLS
Erebor
The Lonely Mountain
Wood Elves
Forest River
Ettenmoors
Esgaroth
the Long Lake
Mountains of Mirkwood
(Hoarwell)
RHUDAUR
Carrock
High Pass
Trollshaws
Old Forest Road
Old Ford
Rivendell
Ford
Last Bridge
Celduin (River Running)
Carnen (Redwater)
Bruinen
(Loudwater)
(Misty Mtns.)
RHOVANION
MIRKWOOD
Str Ninglor
(Gladden River)
Loeg Ningloron
(Gladden Fields)
East Bight
Eregion
(Hollin)
Moria Gate
Drimrill Dale
Anduin (The Great River)
Sea of Rhûn
Glanduin
Nimrodel
Dol Guldur
LÓRIEN
Field of Celebrant
Limlight
NORTH UNDEEP
SOUTH UNDEEP
The BROWN LANDS
Dunland
The Wold
Isengard

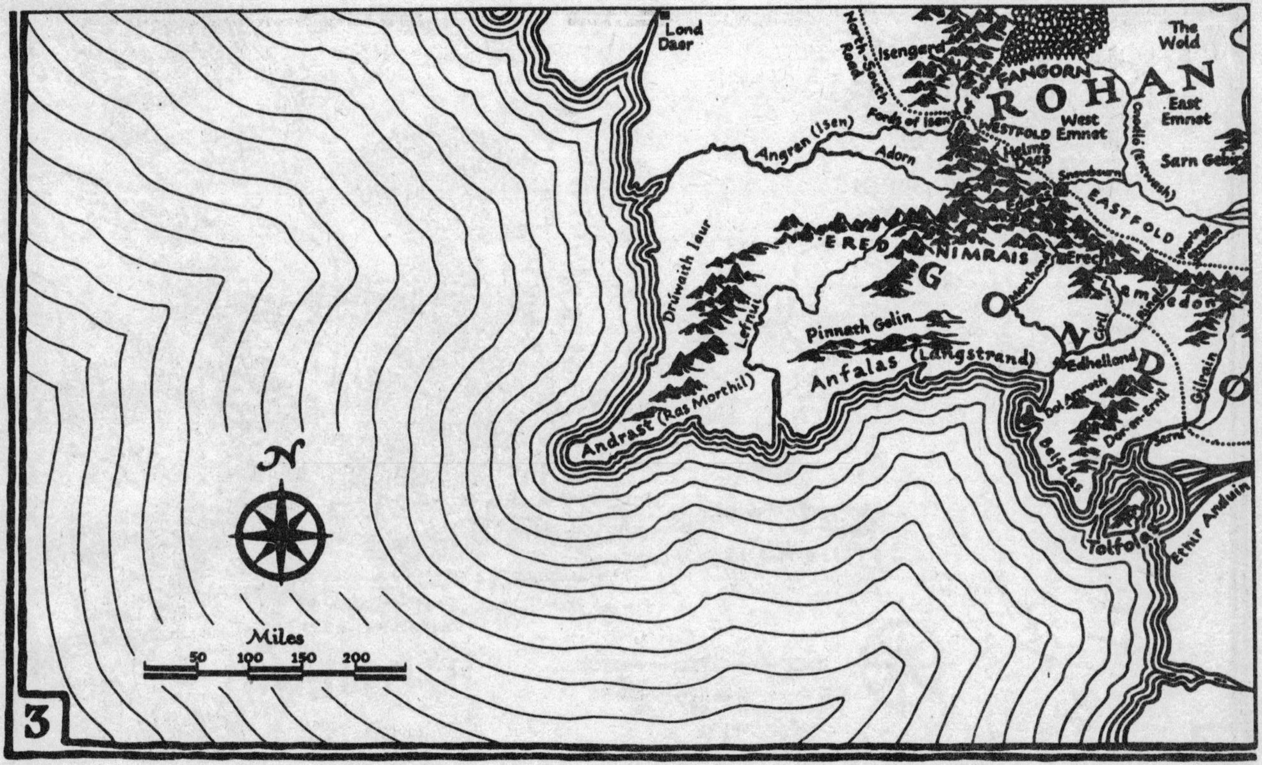

Lond Daer
North-South Road
Isengard
FANGORN
The Wold
ROHAN
East Emnet
West Emnet
WESTFOLD
Helm's Deep
Fords of Isen
Angren (Isen)
Adorn
Sarn Gebir
Onodló (Entwash)
Snowbourn
Edoras
EASTFOLD
EREDNIMRAIS
Erech
GONDOR
Drúwaith Iaur
Lefnui
Pinnath Gelin
Anfalas (Langstrand)
Andrast (Ras Morthil)
Morthond
Ringló
Lamedon
Gilrain
Serni
Edhellond
Dol Amroth
Dor-en-Ernil
Belfalas
Tolfalas
Ethir Anduin
N
Miles
50
100
150
200
3

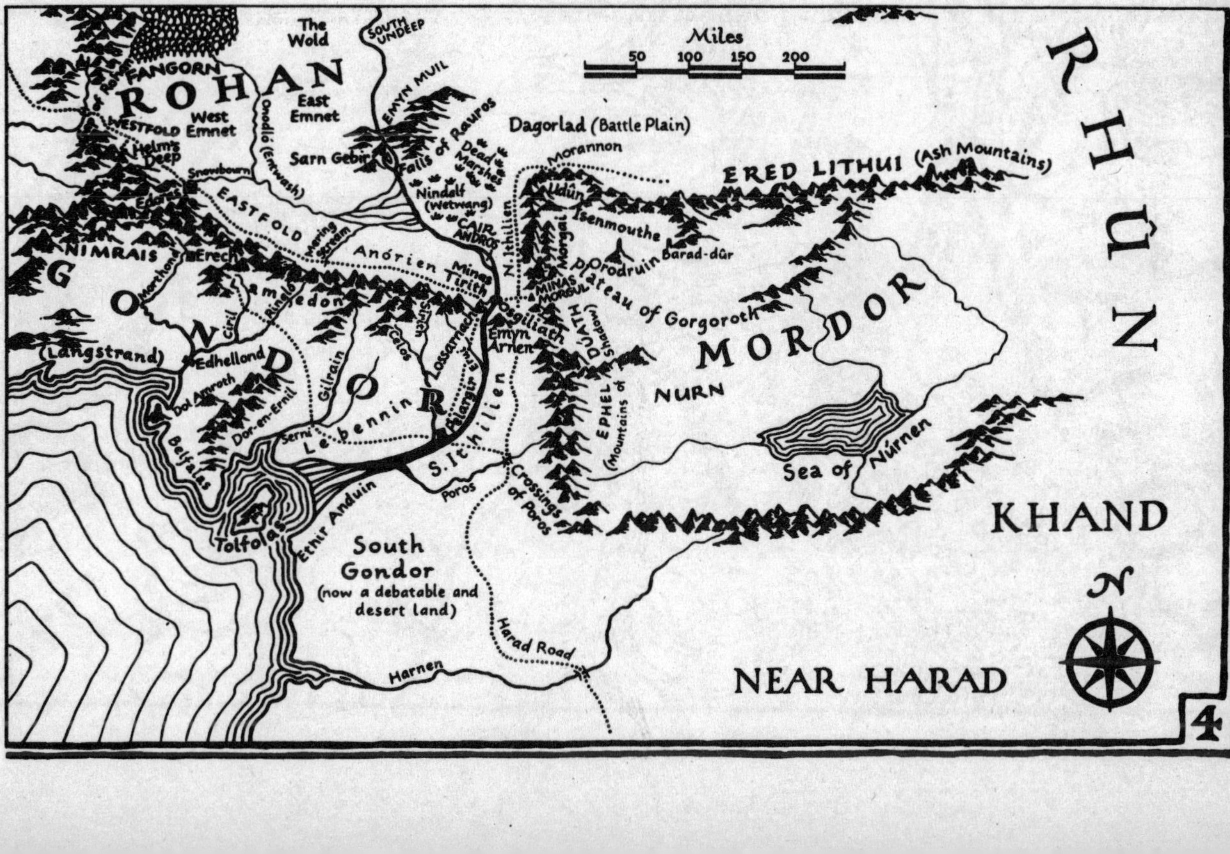

RHÛN
Miles
50
100
150
200
The Wold
SOUTH UNDEEP
FANGORN
ROHAN
East Emnet
West Emnet
WESTFOLD
Helm's Deep
Onodló (Entwash)
Sarn Gebir
EMYN MUIL
Falls of Rauros
Dagorlad (Battle Plain)
Dead Marshes
Morannon
Nindalf (Wetwang)
ERED LITHUI (Ash Mountains)
Udûn
Isenmouthe
Barad-dûr
Orodruin
Morgai
Snowbourn
Edoras
EASTFOLD
Mering Stream
CAIR ANDROS
N. Ithilien
NIMRAIS
Erech
Anórien
Minas Tirith
Morthond
Ringló
Ciril
Osgiliath
MINAS MORGUL
plateau of Gorgoroth
MORDOR
GONDOR
Emyn Arnen
DÚATH (Shadow)
EPHEL (Mountains of)
(Langstrand)
Edhellond
Celos
Sirith
Lossarnach
Erui
Gilrain
Lebennin
Dol Amroth
Dor-en-Ernil
Serni
NURN
Belfalas
S. Ithilien
Sea of Núrnen
Crossings of Poros
Poros
Tolfalas
Ethir Anduin
KHAND
South Gondor (now a debatable and desert land)
N
Harad Road
Harnen
NEAR HARAD
4

ROHAN
Entwade
EMYN
MUIL
Falls of Rauros
Dunharrow
Snowbourn
EDORAS
STARKHORN
FOLDE
EASTFOLD
River ENTWASH
Border of Rohan
Great West Road
EREd NIMRAIS
R. Morthond
Erech
MOUTHS of ENTWASH
FENMARCH
Mering Stream
Firien Wood
ANÓRIEN
Halifirien
Calenhad
Min-Rimmon
Erelas
Nardol
Tarlang's Neck
LAMEDON
River CIRIL
Calembel
GONDOR
River RINGLO
Ethring
River CELOS
LEBENNIN
River GILRAIN
River SIRITH
Dor-en-Ernil
River SERNI
Linhir
ETHIR ANDUIN
(Mouths of Anduin)
Belfalas

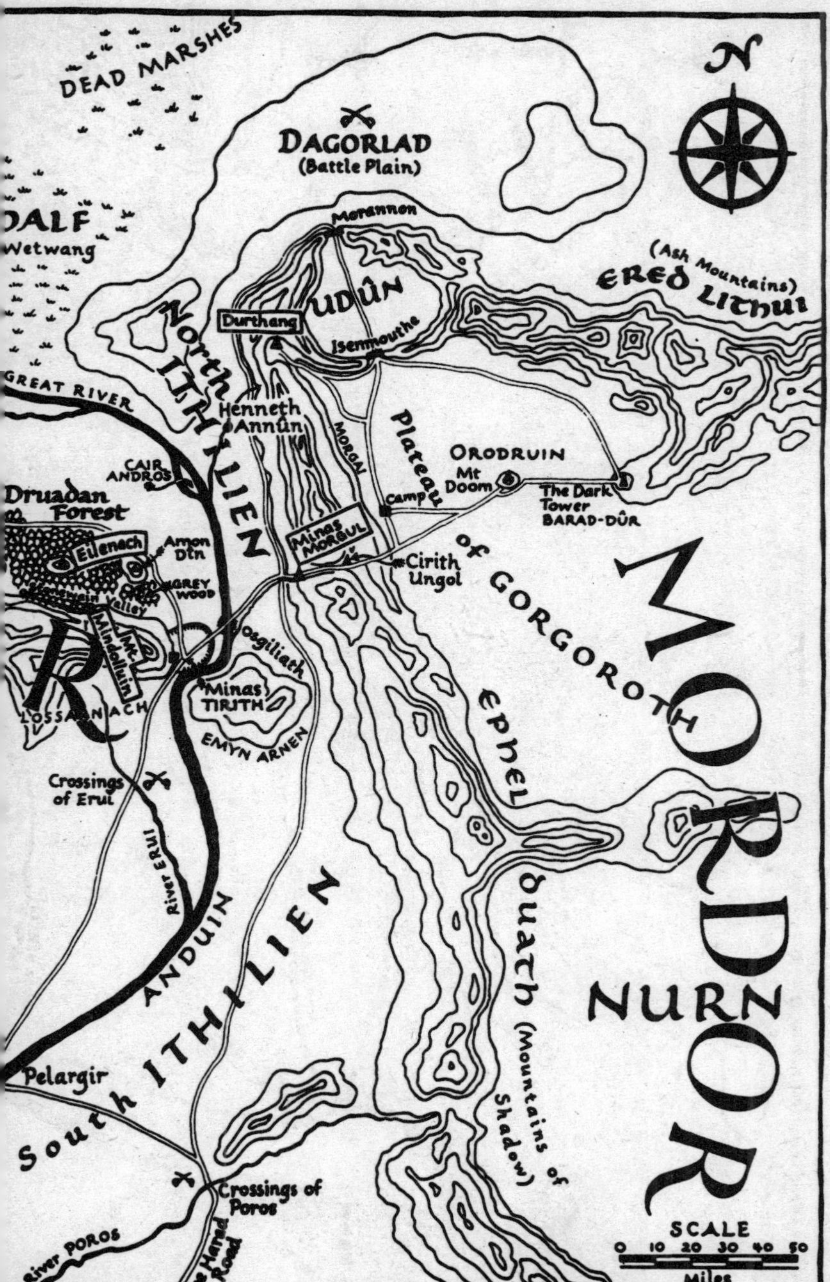

DEAD MARSHES
DAGORLAD
(Battle Plain)
DALF
Wetwang
Morannon
UDÛN
Durthang
Isenmouthe
(Ash Mountains)
ERED LITHUI
North ITHILIEN
GREAT RIVER
Henneth Annûn
MORGAI
Plateau of GORGOROTH
OROD RUIN
Mt Doom
The Dark Tower
BARAD-DÛR
CAIR ANDROS
Druadan Forest
Camp
Minas MORGUL
Eilenach
Amon Dîn
Cirith Ungol
GREY WOOD
Mindolluin
Osgiliath
Minas TIRITH
LOSSARNACH
EMYN ARNEN
EPHEL DUATH (Mountains of Shadow)
MORDOR
Crossings of Erui
River ERUI
ANDUIN
South ITHILIEN
NURN
Pelargir
Crossings of Poros
River POROS
The Harad Road
SCALE
0 10 20 30 40 50
Miles